The *Nagaro* Chronicle 7

Legacy of Loros

Carol Louise Wilde

Rivulus Books Trade Paperback Edition

Text, maps, and internal artwork by Carol Louise Wilde

Published in the United States of America by Rivulus Books, Arcadia, CA. The Rivulus Books name and Rivulus Books logo are trademarks of Rivulus Books.

ISBN: 978-1-944492-17-5

Cover art copyright by Cherie Foxley

Also by Carol Louise Wilde

Books of the Nagaro Chronicle

Gift of Chance (1)

Covenant of the Sword (2)

Return to Lankura (3)

Thief of Slaves (4)

Heir of Darion (5)

Brothers of the Blood (6)

Legacy of Loros (7)

To Kristie

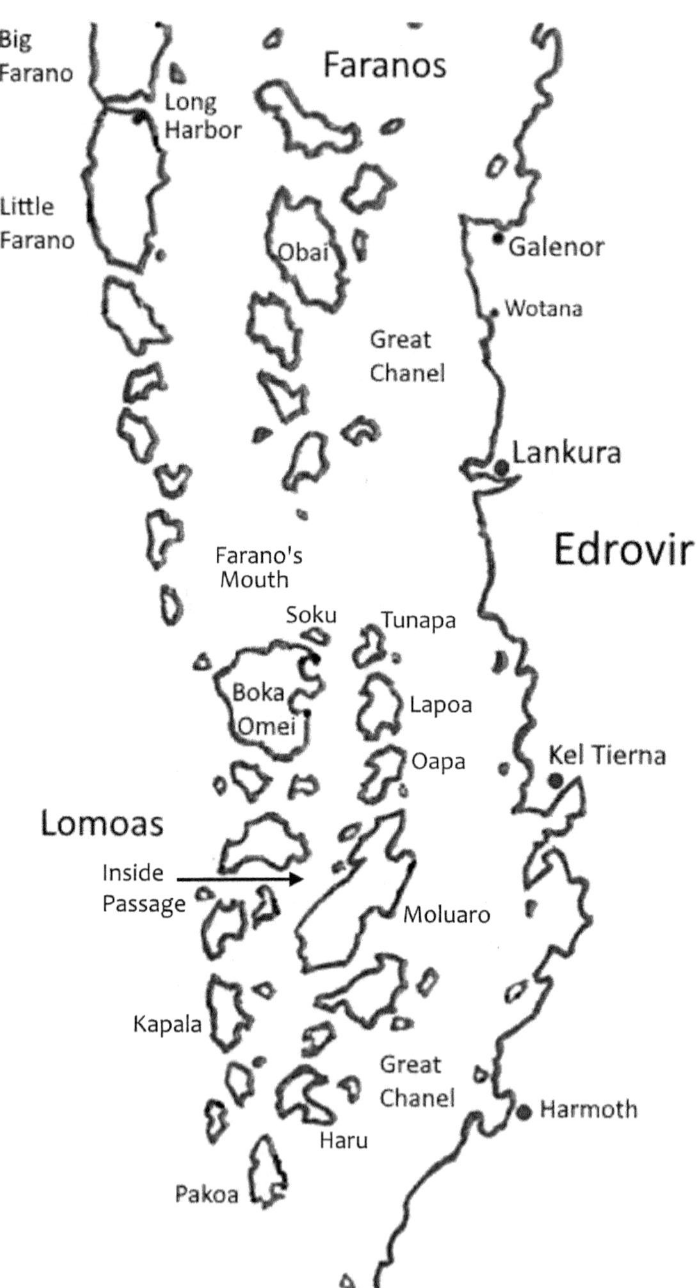

Big Farano
Faranos
Long Harbor
Little Farano
Obai
Galenor
Wotana
Great Chanel
Lankura
Edrovir
Farano's Mouth
Soku
Tunapa
Boka Omei
Lapoa
Oapa
Kel Tierna
Lomoas
Inside Passage
Moluaro
Kapala
Great Chanel
Harmoth
Haru
Pakoa

Pakoa
Harmoth
Edrovir
Chitaopa
Judaba
Tambali
Jinara
Janidi
Atadalba
Alam
Shufa
Mahuk
Baar
Osfaraad
Jaamra
Sar Tipaal
Paktaar

Furthing
Hurn
Galenor
Wotana
Lodge
Sobring
Fendred
Virden
Averwin
Kildoran
Kel
(Loros)
Lankura
Glenmark
Oranil
Gilforn
Sundorin
River
Road
Border
Town
Hall

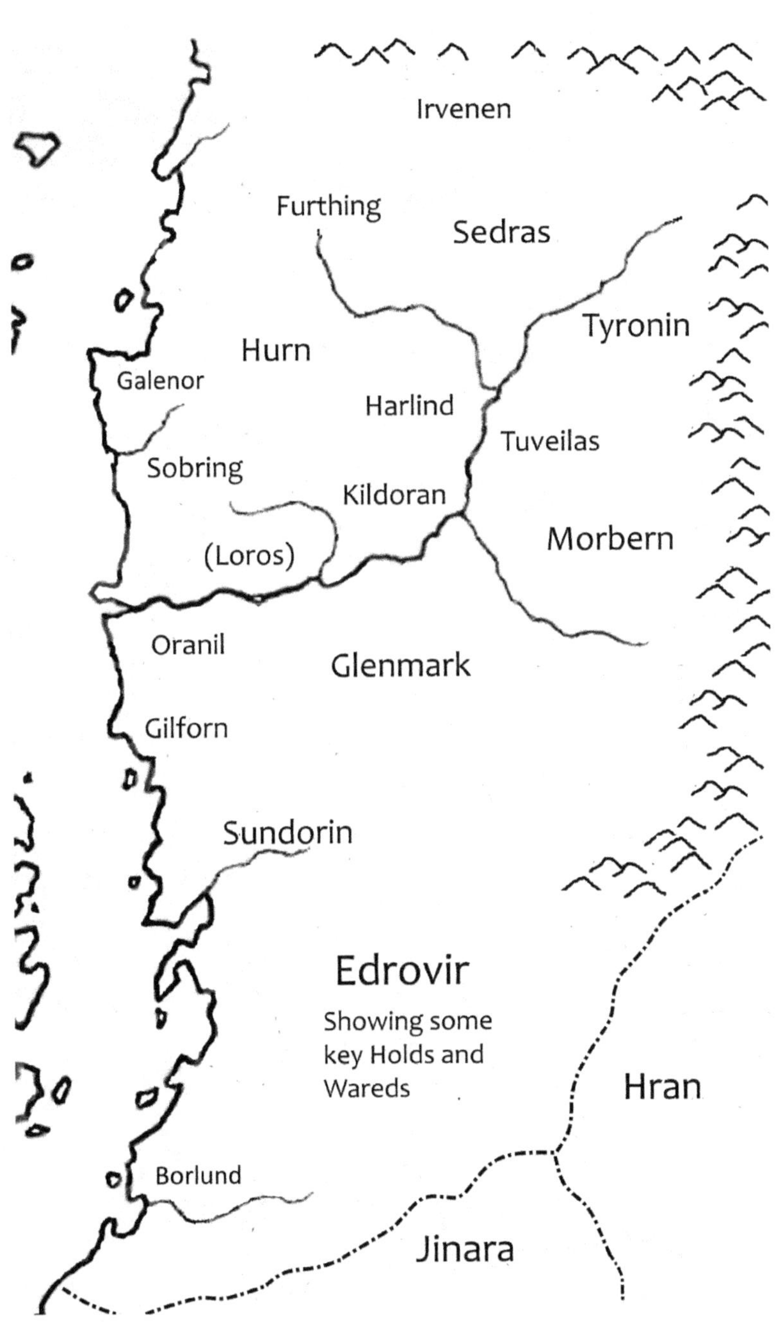

Irvenen
Furthing
Sedras
Tyronin
Hurn
Galenor
Harlind
Tuveilas
Sobring
Kildoran
Morbern
(Loros)
Oranil
Glenmark
Gilforn
Sundorin
Edrovir
Showing some
key Holds and
Wareds
Hran
Borlund
Jinara

CONTENTS

Chapter 1

Changing The Game

Nevien sat in the high-ceilinged Council Chamber in the Palace of Lankura in a chair placed at the right hand of her father, Elgurn Harlind, the King of Edrovir. The four members of the King's Council were also present, arrayed around the circular oak table that occupied the center of the room. Beginning at the Elgurn's left, there were the two Leithian lords, Odus Morbern and Pendrik Glenmark. Continuing around the table, there were seated the two Kelorin lords, Anduar Tyronin and Devral Sedras.

Nevien wore mourning gray, and all five men were dressed in similarly somber colors. It was the first official council meeting to be called since the untimely death of Ferenan Eiylas mere weeks after the announcement of the man's betrothal to the Princess Nevien.

Late morning shafts of sunlight slanted down from high windows to make glowing rectangles that splashed the wall and overflowed onto the floor, causing the room to appear incongruously bright and cheerful. Nevien was trying to pay attention to what the council members were saying, but she found herself distracted. This was partly due to the fact that she knew Nagaro was back in Lankura. Lord Kuran's small fleet had returned from its mission with a hundred freed galley slaves that very morning. The slaves, she understood, had been led on a triumphant— if somewhat subdued— circuit of the city and settled into temporary pavilions in the courtyard in front of the palace. Kuran and Nagaro were probably outside in the courtyard at that very moment.

The other reason for her distraction was Ferenan's fate. The last time she had seen her husband-to-be, in the Great Hall at festival time, he'd been very much alive. He had dutifully escorted her through a dance, being polite and pleasant, making small talk, and smiling with what she was sure had been his very best attempt at warmth. The Gods knew the man had tried, but he'd never managed to completely conceal the fact that he would rather have been somewhere else.

Well, he was somewhere else now.

He had met his death on a road a short distance from Lankura, and Ferenan's family had asked that his body be returned to his native soil so he could be laid to rest beside his beloved wife of nearly twenty years— whose early death had made it possible for Ferenan to be pressed into joining the courtship game. If the poor man hadn't yielded to the pressure to become one of her suitors, and eventually her betrothed, he would still be alive and looking forward to long peaceful years in the company of his children and grandchildren. That knowledge made Nevien feel deeply tainted.

The Council had already finished talking about poor Ferenan, barely touching on the enormity of his sacrifice. King Elgurn and his four councilors had then avidly reviewed the known facts surrounding the man's death. The two armed guards accompanying Ferenan had been unable to describe the assailants because they'd been jumped on from behind, had bags put over their heads, and had been beaten senseless. Ferenan, on the other hand, had received a single stab wound in the back, delivered with obvious skill by means of a narrow assassin's blade. The purses, weapons, and horses of all three victims had been taken, which was regarded as a transparent effort to conceal the true motive for the crime.

Having dispensed with the player who had just been permanently removed from the game, the discourse had moved on to the three remaining players. And the dominant emotion at that moment was not sorrow, but anger— directed against her most unwelcome suitor, Lothard Hurn.

"Can we at least be sure that Lothard was behind the murder?" The question came from Odus, the youngest man present. Roughly fifty, his bronze-gold hair and beard were just beginning to gray.

"Who else shows such callous disregard for honor and decency— that slinking, conniving, bloody-handed—" The aging lord Devral's abusive tirade was cut short by a fit of furious coughing that forced him to avail himself of the amber contents of his delicate stemmed glass.

Pendrik growled, "No one, of course!" Large, silver-blond, and florid, the older Leithian lord was in his sixties, and not in his usual jocular mood.

"But can we *prove* it?" Odus asked a more pointed question.

At Nevien's side, the king stirred. "Regrettably, no," he replied grimly. "The deed bears the same marks as the killing of young Fargil of Galenor, years ago. It's a style of political assassination that was common in Leith in times gone by, but beyond that, the attribution rests primarily on motive. Without actual witnesses, I'm afraid we have no grounds to bring a charge against Lothard or the House of Hurn."

"So the son-of-a-whore has left us no choice but to pick another match for the princess!" It was too early for wine, even had wine been allowed at a council meeting, and the lack of it wasn't helping Pendrik's temper. The older Leithian lord took a swig from his glass of sothiril and made a sour face. "And of course it must be young Nile."

"Nile, yes, obviously. And we mustn't waste time about it. Lothard must be shown that he cannot win by such means!" The color in Lord Odus' handsome face testified to his outrage.

"Yes, the sooner the better!" Pendrik's fist struck the table hard enough to make the sothiril slosh in those glasses that happened to be resting on it.

Nevien looked from one to the other of the Leithians in dismay. "Surely we should show more respect for Ferenan!" she protested.

"Ah, gentlemen, you stand corrected." Anduar spoke at last. The younger of the two Kelorin lords was of an age with Pendrik, but resembled him in no other way. Anduar lounged in his chair, the darkly saturnine lord contriving as always to exude a feline hauteur. Raising his glass of sothiril, he tipped it ever so slightly in Nevien's direction as if in salute, and took a delicate sip. "By all means, let us not appear callous. I would favor a delay in any case."

Pendrik steadied his vibrating glass. "A week or two then," he grumbled. "If we must."

Elgurn glanced at his daughter. "Perhaps a month would be more appropriate."

"Well, certainly no more than that!" Odus declared emphatically.

Nevien frowned. *Was she to gain only a month's respite?* "When Fargil was killed, my wedding to Gillard was delayed until after the turning of the year," she pointed out.

"The bride-to-be does not appear overly eager to wed again," observed Devral, eyeing her with an appraising look that made her blush to think how close he came to the mark. The scarred old Kelorin had been frowning even before she had raised her first objection. Now he added, "Perhaps she doesn't care for the proposed bridegroom? Nile is a callow youth, after all. Perhaps she prefers a man of more *maturity*." He gave her a wolfish wink.

"Maturity!" Pendrik snorted. "You're an old, lame war-horse, Devral. You can't expect a young woman to get her blood up about the prospect of marrying *you!*"

Devral, who was the oldest man present, drew himself up. "I admit that my youth is past," he said with dignity. "But I've a spark in me yet that will kindle a bit of fire. And when I am gone, she'll still have half her life before her. But why don't we hear what she has to say about it?" He turned his aging gray eyes to Nevien, and the other eyes followed.

Nevien lowered hers even as she felt her color rise. "I will do whatever the good of Edrovir requires," she said demurely. "But I confess that I am concerned about how you will prevent Lothard from doing the same thing again. If we're only debating the order in which Nile and Devral are to be buried, I would rather not be wed at all."

"I don't believe Lothard would touch Nile." Odus was leaning back in his chair now, his hands clasped behind his head. It was a pose of studied nonchalance, but to Nevien's eye the stocky Leithian still looked tense. "Madred will restrain him."

"You mean Madred will try!" Devral retorted. His mane of grizzled hair seemed to bristle, and the long scar running down his cheek beneath his right eye twitched. "I'm not at all sure he will succeed. But why must you insist it be Nile? Why do you dismiss my suit out of hand?"

"It must be Nile." Odus waved the old warrior's words aside. "I mean you no offense, My Lord Devral, but choosing you would change the entire nature of the game, and we aren't prepared to do that. Surely you must see that you can only be the choice of last resort—"

"I disagree," Devral growled. "It needn't be a complete change of the game, as you put it. It would only require a minor adjustment. One that will have to be made in any case— as Anduar has lately pointed out."

Nevien sat up at this. *What did Devral mean?* She had always assumed that a marriage to the aging Pact Signer would mean that she wouldn't be queen— at least as long as Devral lived. And that would certainly mean a change in the "game" of Edroviran politics. What was this "minor adjustment?" Had Anduar been consulting the other council members about things that concerned her future without bothering to tell *her?*

"Father," she murmured, leaning close to Elgurn's ear. "What is he talking about? Surely the Pact forbids any of the Signers from becoming king."

Elgurn shifted in his seat. Without glancing at her, he cleared his throat and spoke as if addressing the entire Council. "Apparently," he said acerbically, "the Pact of Lankura does *not* say that each man who signs it is forbidden to seek the crown for as long as he lives. It actually says, '*So long as these six men live and breathe, no one among them shall seek the crown.*' So while it doesn't specifically say that it only applies while *all six* men are alive, it allows that interpretation. Anduar wrote the document, of course, and he has only recently seen fit to point this out to the rest of us."

All six men? Nevien stared at him. "But that would mean that the Pact ceased to be in effect eight years ago— when Reith Hurn was killed in battle in the war with Jinara!"

"Nine years ago, actually." Anduar put in languidly.

"Preposterous isn't it?" Pendrik was now clearly enjoying Nevien's astonishment, his mood shifting predictably in the presence of a good joke. "I almost believe that Anduar must have done it on purpose!"

"Almost?" Anduar cocked a sardonic eyebrow at the Leithian lord. "Pendrik, you insult me. It would have been quite foolish to have tied our hands with something we couldn't wriggle out of in a pinch. Some of us didn't even covet the crown, after all— I for one, and you for another. And Devral and Odus were chiefly concerned with denying the crown to Reith and Berinar Sundorin. Because Reith very definitely *did* covet the crown out of lust for power. And Berinar— if he had won it— would have had Reith executed for the murders of Tevren and Lindra. The true function of the Pact was to secure the peace by thwarting Reith and Berinar."

Odus was glowering. "We thank you, Anduar, for favoring us with that charming explanation," he growled. "But if that's all there was to it, why in the name of all the Gods didn't you tell us as soon as both Reith and Berinar were out of the way?"

Anduar swirled his sothiril. "There was no immediate need at the time."

"And why, then, do you tell us *now?* Surely you don't favor the notion of giving the princess— *and* the crown— to Devral, just because he's the only one of us Pact Signers who hasn't got a wife!"

"Ha!" Devral struck the table with the flat of his hand. "Odus shows his true colors!"

"Gentlemen! *Please!*" Elgurn raised a stern restraining hand, then addressed himself to Anduar. "My Lord, would you care to explain your reasoning? No one here doubts your devotion to the good of Edrovir, but you can't blame us if we find your behavior in this matter somewhat *cavalier.*"

Anduar's eyes met the king's. And for once, the steel in them seemed blunted. He set down his glass and sat up straighter. The light from the windows touched his raven hair and found the strands of gray in it, making him seem older than his years.

Nevien leaned forward, her eyes fixed on the Kelorin lord's aquiline face.

Anduar cleared his throat. "At the time of the deaths of Reith and Berinar, the political situation was relatively stable," he began. "Edrovir had a king whose rule was well-accepted and who was content to continue to rule. While some bellicose words were exchanged following the deaths, there was a reluctance to put those words into action. There would therefore have been no advantage to shaking the tree at that time. But the situation is different now. Elgurn has grown weary of the burden of kingship. After twenty-five years, who can blame him? And we have men in Edrovir— Lothard and Grimbold, in particular, on the

Leithian side, but also Rathdar and Theren of the Kelorin Faction— who are prepared to put armies into the field. The recent skirmishes over the blacksmith, Kenthos, made that clear. The accord that was reached after that little *action* at Loros Hall has let some steam out of the kettle, but the kettle is still on the fire. The current circumstances demand maximum flexibility, which in turn requires a full awareness of our options."

Anduar ceased speaking.

Odus regarded him sourly. "I still think you should have told us sooner."

Anduar shrugged, and a trace of mockery flickered in his eyes. "The words have always been there in the Pact. It's remarkable what men don't trouble to read. But in all seriousness, My Lord Odus, secrets can be difficult to keep even with the best intentions, and keeping them from slipping out is only made harder when there are more mouths to utter them."

Nevien toyed with the stem of her glass. Unfortunately, Anduar's assessment made all too much sense. "So, what do you propose to do?" she asked. "Will you announce to the world that the Pact of Lankura no longer applies? That would mean that Devral could be chosen king, but—"

"I could indeed!" Devral interjected with a leer.

She turned toward the older lord. "But by *whom?*" she finished. "The Pact also decreed that the king be chosen by the Pact Signers. Or isn't that true either?" Her questioning eyes swung back to Anduar.

"It *is* true," he replied, vouchsafing her the barest nod of approval. "And therein lies the hitch in Devral's plan. However—" He held up a hand to forestall an indignant outburst from his fellow Kelorin. "That doesn't mean that Devral's idea has no merit. I share my esteemed colleague's concern for young Nile's safety if he were named as Nevien's betrothed. I would be concerned for the safety of any man so named." Here he had to silence Devral's indignation again with a raised hand. The old warrior obviously thought he could take care of himself.

"Lothard's ambition is exceeded only by his ruthlessness," Anduar continued. "He covets the crown every bit as much as his father did, and he has— if anything— fewer scruples. And less common sense."

"But he backed down at Loros Hall!" Odus objected. "He changed his tale under Madred's coaching. And the Leithian Faction will look favorably upon Nile as king because Nile is Madred's protégé. They will *not* look favorably upon Devral!"

Nevien frowned. Nile had indeed been tutored at Furthing Hall under Lord Madred and his ministers. Officially Nile and his sister had been orphaned in their late teens by the tragic deaths of their parents. That Kale Fendred was insane rather than dead was a secret her father held very close. In any case, Fendale, the Lord of Fendred Hold, had sent the two siblings to Lord Madred, presumably wishing to assure the sister a good marriage and to benefit young Nile's career. *Except that Nile was not ambitious. He would far rather marry Alisset, another of Madred's many wards...*

Abruptly she realized that Anduar was speaking again.

"I will grant you that Lothard has recently shown a limited capacity to see the advantage of restraining his public actions, my dear Odus." Anduar had refilled his glass with sothiril and resumed his lounging posture. He held the glass negligently in one hand, regarding the Leithian over the top of it. "He seems to show no such concern with respect to his *covert* actions, however. Or would you have us believe that Madred was in favor of Ferenan's assassination?"

"Surely not!"

"Well, then," rumbled Pendrik, "Let's assign young Nile a half a dozen bodyguards. If they keep watch over him day and night—"

"They might succeed in keeping the young man clear of the assassin's knife." Anduar spoke over the older Leithian. "But there are other ways to murder. We've had recent evidence that Lothard and Grimbold are in communication with *Dreigen*."

There was an audible intake of breaths around the table at the mention of the king's dreaded Lore Master, and Nevien shuddered involuntarily. She was aware of the lords shifting in their seats, of faces twitching. She saw her father's fingers tighten on the arm of his chair. Even the cool-headed Anduar had spoken the name with something decidedly stronger than distaste.

For several heartbeats no one spoke, until Pendrik inquired, with more resignation than hope, "Is there no way to be rid of that creature?"

Elgurn sighed. "Kale Fendred wanted to be rid of him, and it... cost him his life. I have also recently buried a servant who apparently chose to cross him in some relatively minor matter. And," he continued, "although we thought that the servant's death had made communication between Dreigen and his Leithian suppliers more difficult, it seems that he's already found a way around it. He has some way of slipping past our guards. The men report no memory of having seen him leave his room, when we know he must have done so. They describe a sense of having dozed briefly on their feet, only to find that an hour must have passed."

"All of which is beside the point." Anduar cut in. "Which is, that any man who Lothard sees as standing in his way is in danger. Such safety as the remaining suitors currently enjoy rests on the fact that we haven't yet named Ferenan's successor. Lothard may even be foolish enough to imagine that we've been cowed into giving him what he wants—"

"Well he'd be wrong!" Pendrik's beefy fist smote the table so hard this time that all of the dishes jumped.

"Indeed." Anduar inclined his head to the big Leithian. "Suffice it to say, My Lords, that there might be some advantage at this moment to *broadening* the field of candidates for the princess's hand, rather than narrowing it. Devral's candidacy has always been viewed with skepticism by many because he's a Pact Signer whom the people believed couldn't take the crown. Announcing that the Pact of Lankura has been abrogated would change that minor fact, and—"

This time Anduar had to raise both hands to restrain all three of his fellow council members. "—*and* we would *also* very soon be besieged by demands for reinstatement of the old Council of Lords," he finished smoothly. "Since it isn't a good idea to leave the selection of the king in the hands of a handful of men who could be king themselves. The restoration of the Council of Lords would, of course, change the established nature of the game completely."

The room erupted in argument as soon as Anduar ceased speaking.

"We *can't* reinstate the Council of Lords!" Pendrik sputtered, rising to his feet.

"*Why not?*" demanded Devral, leaning across the table.

"*Because It would mean chaos!*"

Odus was on his feet as well. "How could we possibly know who would be chosen if *all* of the lords were allowed to cast their *krits*?"

"*How indeed?*" Anduar had remained where he was, lounging languidly in his seat, but his two words were uttered with a sharpness that brought all eyes back to him.

Nevien drew a tense breath. The Council of Lords had been established by Darion the Great and had consisted of the lords of all the Holds and Wareds. She understood, in principle, that votes had once been cast by the members of the Council of Lords— by each member laying a carved wooden wand, his *krit*, on the table in front of the man he chose. But the ritual hadn't been performed in her lifetime.

Anduar sighed. "We would be reduced to polling the lords as to how each intended to cast his krit," he observed calmly, "— just as men did in Tevren's day, or Darion's." He surveyed their shocked faces. "Oh come now, gentlemen! You must have known we would return to this eventually."

Among the others, Devral recovered first. The idea of restoring the Council of Lords didn't seem to dismay him as much as it did the two Leithian Pact Signers. He briefly covered a cough with one hand while reaching for his sothiril with the other. "But seriously, Anduar," he said after moistening his throat with a swallow from his glass, "how do you think such a choosing would fall out?"

Odus and Pendrik immediately sank back into their seats, looking avidly to Anduar, acknowledging the shrewdness of the lean and saturnine lord.

Anduar received their attention as if it were his due. "As things stand, if the casting were done in a week?" He gestured ambiguously. "Pendrik isn't far wrong, I fear. The situation would be chaotic. The only constant that I see in our altered situation is the unparalleled popularity of the princess." Anduar accompanied this statement with a gracious, if languid, gesture in Nevien's direction. She took a hasty swallow of sothiril to cover her discomfort at being reminded of this fact.

"Since the late queen's passing," Anduar continued. "Nevien is arguably the most popular person in Edrovir, certainly in Lankura. Any man who wedded her would still have a great advantage in the competition for the crown. And the bestowing of her hand would be— as it always has been— in her father's hands." He paused for a sip of sothiril.

"Given those facts," he went on, "I can guess at the actions of the major players. The moderate members of the Leithian Faction would heavily favor Madred, or whomever he chose to put forward— though enthusiasm for Nile would be lukewarm at best if he weren't betrothed to the princess. Only the most extreme of the Brothers of the Blood would choose Lothard, and marriage to the Lady Nevien— if he were to contrive to force it in some way— would help *him* much less than he imagines. The most militant of the Kelorin Faction would come to some consensus among Soren, Theren, and Rathdar, making do without the princess by necessity, since all of those lords have wives. Then there are the lesser lords and those who are less partisan. They number enough to easily control the outcome, but as for how they would choose..." Anduar paused to lift his shoulders in an eloquent shrug.

Odus was the first to react. "So the field would be split too many ways," he said. "No one would have enough support to be assured of holding the crown if it fell to him. There would surely be war!"

Anduar swirled his sothiril with an air of speculation. "I fear so," he agreed. "The successful choosing of a king would require that two or more factions come together— which would be chancy. And the situation would be rendered more volatile by Lothard careening about, practicing his rather *pointed* version of politics. We, here in this room, would have a little hope of *influencing* some of the lords— since Elgurn has assured me that he sees no reason not to keep us on as his official Council even in the absence of the Pact."

Elgurn inclined his head in acquiescence, and the announcement was greeted by satisfied nods and grunts from the other three Pact Signers.

"Remember," Anduar continued, "that even if we made the announcement regarding the abrogation of the Pact tomorrow— dropping our bag of cats into the courtyard— the Council of Lords couldn't realistically be convened for some weeks. There would be time for jockeying, and deal-making— *and murder*. War might very well not wait for the casting of krits. The situation is not good, gentlemen." He paused, then added, "It would change very much for the better if Lothard were removed from the play."

"Well, *obviously*." Pendrik flicked a dismissive hand.

Devral glumly nodded agreement.

Odus frowned. "Friend though I am to Leithian folk and to their time-honored ways," he said soberly, "I confess that I can see no good in Lothard. His own actions dishonor him. He gives all of our folk a bad name."

Elgurn stirred. "Unfortunately," he said, "I fear that nothing short of that man's death would eliminate the threat he represents. And there is no way, within the law, to accomplish his demise."

Anduar let several gloomy seconds tick. Then he said, his words smooth as silk, "But suppose there were a way to use a time-honored tradition— one of the very traditions that Lothard favors— to his undoing?"

In the silence that followed *this*, Nevien could hear the soft wheeze of Lord Devral's labored breathing. "You mean a Challenge to Combat," the older Kelorin said at last. "You can only mean a Challenge to Combat."

"But who could stand against him?" wondered Pendrik.

"Aye, who indeed?" growled Devral. "I'd take him on myself— if he weren't the best swordsman in Edrovir!"

"But he may *not* be the best swordsman in Edrovir." Anduar fairly purred the words.

"Well... *who* then?"

Anduar gestured languidly. "I suggest... Captain Nagaro..."

Chapter 2

Looming Shadows

Nevien felt a cold, sick jolt in her stomach. She didn't like the glint in Anduar's eye, nor the slight upward twitching at the corners of his mouth.

A speculative gleam kindled in Devral's eyes. "He *is* very good, isn't he?" The old warrior smiled wolfishly. "We saw that at Loros Hall. He blocked Lothard's every stroke— wouldn't let the bloody bully get past him. Wouldn't let him get to Kenthos."

Pendrik let out a guffaw. "*Captain Nagaro!*" he exclaimed. "The noble pirate against the piratical noble! Ha, ha! What a good joke! But how do you mean to arrange it, Anduar?"

"Yes, Anduar, how?" Odus frowned. "The captain is a commoner. He can't challenge Lothard. And if Lothard were to challenge *him*, and the captain accepted and then killed Lothard— killed the lord of a Hold— he would stand for murder!"

For answer, Anduar shifted his narrow gaze to the king. "Has Kuran made his move yet, My Lord?" he inquired calmly.

Nevien saw her own bewilderment mirrored on the faces of Devral, Odus, and Pendrik.

Elgurn ran a hand through his short-cropped silver hair. "He hadn't yet when Captain Nagaro fell into Grimbold's clutches a few weeks ago. And there was no opportunity to inquire after the captain's escape, since both he and Kuran were immediately off about their mission to meet the Mautep Emperor at Chitaopa. But I'd be surprised if Kuran hasn't broached the subject by now. The captain's recent entanglement with Sobring Hold will have set the fire under his feet, I think."

Nevien's agitation was growing. She wanted desperately to ask her father what he was talking about, but dared not for fear of showing too much interest. Fortunately, Devral asked the question for her.

"What in the name of Lokundas' cat are you two talking about?" the old warrior demanded.

Elgurn explained. "Kuran has been eager for some time to bring Nagaro into the House of Kel— by adopting him as his heir. He's been nervous as a bridegroom, worrying that the captain wouldn't accept. The present circumstances, however— with the charges coming out of Sobring Hold— should provide a powerful incentive."

Nevien felt a little leap of hope at first. Adoption by Kuran would be good for Nagaro— would give him some protection. She liked Kuran and had grieved greatly for him when both his wife and young son, his only child, had been taken by the plague. Still, she was disturbed by the implications of what the men were saying. *And they were still talking...*

"Why in Hel's Pit wouldn't he accept?" Pendrik wondered aloud.

Elgurn shrugged. "It's hard to predict what Captain Nagaro will do."

"It isn't, if you understand his principles," Anduar observed sagely."

Odus' frown had eased only fractionally. "Kel isn't a very strong House," he objected. "Many Leithians don't consider it to be very... ah... *respectable.* Your captain would still be well-advised not to challenge Lothard directly—"

"That's true," agreed Devral. "It would be much better if Lothard were to challenge *him.*"

"Which shouldn't be difficult to achieve." Anduar pounced on the thought. "Lothard has already found the captain an annoyance on several occasions. He is being taunted by some, I understand, about what happened at Loros Hall and with the speculation that the captain could best him. All that is needed is to elevate Nagaro in Lothard's eyes from annoyance to rival— as would occur quite naturally if the captain were to join the ranks of the princess's suitors."

There was a ripple of movement around the table as everyone except Anduar sat up a little straighter, looking stunned. Nevien clutched her glass and raised it, trying to hide behind it, glad of the general dismay. Her heart had swooped at the thought of Nagaro as a suitor, then dropped like a stone as she realized the horrible risk involved. *This was far too dangerous! He would surely be killed...*

Devral made a growling noise in his throat. "*One of Nevien's suitors?* Anduar, you sly devil! After all those dances he's taken for me! How long have you been planning this?"

"You slander me, My Lord." Anduar spoke with wounded innocence. "Using him for a proxy was *your* idea. In fact, when I first heard of it, I tried to talk him out of it."

Pendrik's astonishment was dissolving into mirth. "So who will be whose proxy now, eh, Devral?" he chortled. "Ha, ha! I applaud you, Anduar. It's perfect! But of course we must be careful that your captain doesn't begin to think he could actually *have* the lady."

"Why shouldn't he?" Devral retorted. "If the man does your deed for you, why shouldn't he get the reward? In the old tales, doesn't the hero who slays the beast always win the hand of the princess?"

Nevien felt herself blushing scarlet as embarrassment was heaped on top of alarm. Beside her, her father stiffened. "My daughter is not a prize to be given out for favors rendered!" he snapped. "Any man may seek to court her— it *is* allowed. But just because it's allowed, doesn't guarantee him success!"

Anduar had been listening in silence, his eyes catching every nuance, while his own face betrayed nothing. "Of course the understanding would be that there is no *guarantee*," he said soothingly. "And if Lothard were truly a beast, there would be no need to concern ourselves with acting within the law."

Odus coughed. "You're overlooking the man's breeding— or lack of it. Many Leithians of the noble class don't consider adoption a substitute for nobility by birth— *by blood*. The issue bears upon both the courtship and the challenge. Captain Nagaro doesn't even know who his parents are—"

"Which means they could be almost anyone." Anduar spread his hands. "That's the beauty of unknown parentage. A... *useful rumor*... might be circulated, and who could say it wasn't true?"

Nevien could stand it no longer. "He won't do it!" she blurted. "He'll want no part of such a deception— of pretending to be something he's not! And if Nagaro were to fight Lothard at all, he would want it to be for honor— not for blood!" *And Lothard might kill him, rather than the other way around!* She came to a halt, feeling all their eyes on her.

Anduar didn't even blink. "I think we may depend on Lothard to make it a fight for blood," he observed calmly. "And the captain would then be forced to kill him in self defense. As for the matter of the deception... it wouldn't be necessary for Nagaro to be involved in that *himself*. In fact, it would be better if he weren't. The more vehemently something is denied, the more men believe it. Especially if they very much wish to. In fact, I've taken the liberty of essaying a little experiment in rumor-planting— just a small seed, and of a slightly different nature, placed among the men in the Fleet Compound. We can see how far this one goes, and whether the captain tries to deny it— as I expect he will— and proceed from there. "

And it seemed that the matter had been decided.

While Nevien sat in an agony of fear and frustration, the members of the Council bantered on about their plans. She scarcely heard any of it. She did hear mention of a charge of rape against Nagaro— coming from Lord Grimbold— and was briefly alarmed by it. But Anduar seemed to be saying that such a charge would be easily dealt with.

And then Vell Sobring arrived to give a report on some sort of mission he'd been sent on to Borlund Hold. It was about Leithians, and Jinara, and unlawful trade. Apparently the lord of Borlund Hold had been asked to put a stop to it and had responded with some facile assurances and cautious promises. Vell was apologetic, but the consensus seemed to be that he'd gotten about as much as could be expected.

Nevien wasn't really listening. Her mind was in turmoil. *They thought they were going to set a trap for Lothard... a trap in which Nagaro was to be both the deadly sting and the bait!* They seemed so sure it would work, too— unconcerned with the possibility that Lothard's sting would prove more deadly, and the bait would become the victim.

Lothard's death would undeniably be good for the country, but Anduar's plan was too risky. And she was actually far from certain that Nagaro would refuse. It depended too much on what they told him— and what they *didn't* tell him. If he thought he was to become a genuine suitor— without any reference to Lothard— he might accept, thinking he was doing her a kindness. If his friend Taru married the Turowan woman Hamani, he would then have little to lose. He might willingly embrace the danger to himself if he were convinced it was for the good of Edrovir.

Nevien didn't know whether or not Nagaro could best Lothard in a fair fight. She had never seen Nagaro wield a sword, though she'd heard people say he was very good. Kuran seemed to think that Nagaro's talent for the sword was something truly exceptional— but Kuran was so taken with his protégé that Nevien suspected the Lord of the Fleet might not be entirely objective. And she *had* seen Lothard fight. Years ago, when there had still been sword tourneys held at the palace every year, Lothard had taken the prize the last two times. His skill was legendary. *And Lothard's ruthlessness and treachery would give him an advantage over Nagaro's honor and restraint.*

As the talk ebbed and flowed, Nevien realized that she had to find a way to warn Nagaro before Anduar or one of his proxies could speak to him. She must tell Nagaro that she didn't want him to do this. But it could be days or weeks before she could arrange an opportunity to speak with him, while Anduar or any of the other members of the Council could easily manage a conversation with Nagaro any time they wished!

She needed a plan. And by the time the Council meeting adjourned, she had one.

She traversed the Audience Chamber and the central hallway in the company of her father and Pendrik, who were still discussing Vell's news. Parting with them at the foot of the main stair, she hurried up the two flights alone and paused at the top to ask the guard stationed there to call for one of the messenger boys.

To her surprise, the guard turned out to be Brandle. He must have only just been released to duty after his misadventure in Sobring Hold, and his face gave evidence of it in the form of fading bruises on his left cheek and several healing cuts. He received her request with his guardsman's deadpan.

"And please see that the messenger comes as soon as possible," she finished.

"As you wish, My Lady." He didn't even raise an eyebrow.

"I'm glad to see you back, Lieutenant," she added in parting. "I was very distressed to hear about how you had been set upon."

That at least earned her a smile. "You're very kind, My Lady," he said. "They say the best friend of a man is his dog, but at the moment I would argue for his horse— or for Captain Nagaro's horse, I should say." He saluted.

As Nevien hurried away, she realized that she could probably have told Brandle the entire story of her dilemma, and he would have been discreet. But it was better not to involve anyone else.

Once safely in her room, she sat down at her writing desk, got out paper, pen, and ink, and tried to compose her message. This required some thought. She was attempting to thwart the will of the Council. This fact did not concern her greatly under the circumstances, but she realized that the details of Anduar's plot, if they should become known, could be very damaging to the powers that ruled the country. She would have to avoid saying anything very specific in her note to Nagaro— and yet it must have the desired effect.

She stared at the paper in front of her and nibbled at the feathered tip of her quill. She tried to imagine what Anduar— or whoever they sent— would say to the captain. What exactly would they propose, and how would they put it to him? Soon she was imagining a discussion of his courtship of her. Then she was imagining the courtship itself— which brought a warm glow. And that, in turn, ignited the memory of a dream she'd had about him the night before.

Rianine's naughty little notion about lying with Nagaro under a tree had surely been the root of it. Only there'd been no tree in the dream, just grass— wonderful, warm, soft, billowing grass, arching over them and hiding them from view in a secret green bower. They'd been inexplicably naked, together, in the glade— or some place like it. And it had been utterly perfect. He'd been everything her three husbands had never been. Warm, and passionate, but gentle. Respectful of her every wish. It had been impossibly perfect, with warm sun and cool green light, birdsong, and the scent of clover—

Nevien jerked out of her reverie at the sound of a knock on the door. She sprang up guiltily, expecting it to be Brandle, or the messenger boy.

Instead it turned out to be Lady Merriel. The diminutive blond woman greeted her with a warm smile, seeming not to notice that Nevien was blushing.

"There's a man here to see you, dear," Merriel informed her. "A tailor. He says he used to do work for your family years ago, and I think I do remember him. I left him waiting in the library. He says he has something rather remarkable to show you. I suppose he hopes for some new business."

Nevien was trying to collect her thoughts, scattered by the interruption of her excursion into erotic fantasy. "I... I can see him in a minute, Merriel. As soon as I finish a letter."

"Good. I'll wait here then." Merriel began to putter about the room, absent-mindedly straightening things.

Nevien hastily sat down and bent over her paper. Re-dipping her quill, she penned her note as quickly as she could. She frowned a little over it. The wording was rather obscure, but she hoped it would have the desired effect. Really, she was afraid to be any more explicit. She blotted the note, folded the paper, and sealed it. Merriel trailed after her when she hurried down the hallway to the stairs where the messenger boy was waiting impatiently.

"You can slip it under his door," Nevien told the youth. "Just be sure that you push it all the way under— so it won't get lost."

"Aye, M' Lady. Ye can count on me." The lad gave her a jaunty salute and bounded away for the stairs. Brandle witnessed the exchange without comment.

Merriel, who had hung back as if not wishing to intrude, stepped forward to accompany her to the library. Once there, Nevien found that she actually recognized the tailor. He was a spare, bespectacled Kelorin, some years past forty, seated at the library table with a cloth-wrapped bundle in front of him. He had indeed worked for the royal family, but not since the time of her second husband. Delving into her memory as she approached the table, she greeted him by name.

"Good afternoon, Tor Einos. How good to see you again. If you have some new fabrics to show, I'd be interested in seeing them, but I'm afraid we currently have a palace tailor."

Tor Einos rose and bowed to her. His expression showed appreciation for having been remembered. Still he shook his head. "I know you have a tailor, My Lady," he said. "What I have to show you is something of a... different nature... though at one time it might have brought me some remuneration. After all these years, I'm not so sure. Still I thought that you, at least, would like to see it."

"Now whatever can this be?" Nevien was intrigued. She motioned for the tailor to sit down and seated herself in the chair opposite, while Merriel took the window seat. "Some remuneration, you say?"

"Reward, actually. There was a reward offered years ago, I believe, for information concerning the fate or whereabouts of Leyel Virden?"

"*Leyel Virden!*" Nevien was glad she was sitting down. "Surely you can't mean you have some news of him? That he is—" She caught herself.

Tor Einos blinked at her behind his spectacles. "Nothing so *direct*, My Lady, but yet *substantial*." He began to unwrap the bundle that lay on the table, exposing two garments, one purple, the other white. They had obviously long been folded, the creases crushed into the fabric. "These have but recently come to me," the tailor continued as he began to unfold the purple object, "by a series of fortunate chances. They are, I believe, the very shirt and britches that Prince Leyel was wearing on the day he disappeared. I would hardly remember such a detail for so long— or be so certain— were it not that I made them myself. See? Here, on the inside of the yoke, is stitched my mark. And the same is on the inner waist-band of the britches."

Leyel's shirt and britches...

The blood was pounding in Nevien's ears as she stared at the purple silk shirt, now unfolded on the table. She reached out to touch the cloth with a hand that trembled. "*Sweet Mother Solbrid...*" she murmured. "I believe you're right. But... but... *how?* Where did they come from? Where have they been all this time?"

"And however did they come into your hands, Zirda?" Merriel had risen and stepped nearer to examine the tailor's marks, clearly almost as interested as Nevien.

Tor Einos had just finished unfolding the britches as well, and laid them on the table beside the shirt. He glanced from one woman to the other, clearly gratified by their response.

"Where they have *been*," he said, addressing Nevien, "is at the bottom of a small wooden chest that was being used as a sewing box. And where the chest came from, apparently, is a village about twenty miles north of here, up the coast."

He turned to Merriel. "And well you may ask how the garments came to me, My Lady. It's a remarkable tale, and it goes like this: A woman living in a house in this village sold the chest to a trader bound for Lankura. She'd acquired the chest along with the house, it seems, but the chest was locked and the key was lost, and so it was of no use to her. The trader happened to sell the chest— still locked, mind you— to my brother-in-law, who owns a pawn shop in Wicket Street. My brother-in-law, in turn, took the chest to a locksmith to make a new key, and so was finally able to open it. You can imagine his surprise when he found *these*—" the tailor indicated the shirt and britches, "—in the bottom of the chest under some sewing implements and spools of thread. Since he is my brother-in-law, he immediately recognized my mark, and brought them to me, thinking it all a very curious mystery that I might find amusing. Now wouldn't you agree that it's a remarkable tale?"

"I certainly would." Merriel's blue eyes were wide. "Fancy it being your brother-in-law that the trader just happened to sell the box to!"

Nevien was bending over the purple shirt. "Look!" she cried. "Here's a place where it's been mended!"

A two-inch-long rent in one of the sleeves had been meticulously darned with course wool thread, dark gray rather than purple.

"Yes." Tor Einos bobbed his head. "The shirt has been mended in three places, and the britches in two. There are also scuffed places on both knees— though the garment was obviously washed before it was put away. I must say that whoever did the sewing used considerable care, too, and some skill— though of course she hadn't the right sort of thread to do the job properly. I say 'she', because, in a very small town where folk generally make their own clothes, it's the women who do the sewing."

Leyel's clothes... in a sewing box found twenty miles away. And mended... Relief flooded through Nevien as she gazed at the long-lost garments.

"It means he didn't drown," she said, speaking her thought aloud, and the others turned to look at her questioningly. "I mean," she said hastily, "that if he had drowned, and his body had... well... washed ashore somewhere, surely the folk who found him wouldn't have taken the clothes off of his body and washed and mended them."

Merriel looked shocked. "I certainly hope they would have given him a decent burial," she said. "*With* his clothes on."

"Yes, it's most likely that Prince Leyel arrived alive in that village," agreed the tailor. "I suppose he might have been parted from the clothes somewhere else, but then you'd have to imagine a reason why his clothes would have come there without him."

Nevien nodded. Her heart was beating faster. The clothes meant that Leyel had lived at least for a short time after disappearing from the palace and its environs on the fateful night of that Mautep attack. *Long enough for him to exchange his clothes, or for someone to consider it worthwhile to mend them for him.*

"But if he wasn't just drowned right away as everyone thought, why did we never hear anything?" wondered Merriel. "He *was* simple-minded, of course, but he had enough wit to remember his name and repeat it, hadn't he?"

And at that, Nevien's heart flinched within her. *Maybe not,* she thought. *The state he'd been in that night when the Mautep took him away... so strangely wild... almost like a different person altogether—*

Her mind veered violently away from things she didn't wish to think about. "I... I don't know," she said, studying her hands. "He'd been getting worse. The fits, I mean. Father always said if he wasn't drowned he would have died of a fit within a few days— without his medicine."

"Then it's possible that the folk he met just didn't know who he was." Lady Merriel finished the thought. "And that he died before anyone figured it out."

Tor Einos' brow was wrinkled in thought. "Well," he said. "That *is* wild country, up the coast to the north of here. I don't expect news would have traveled very fast." He sighed. "I'm sorry," he said. "I've spoiled your afternoon, ladies, with all of these unhappy memories. Especially since it's all for nothing, really. After all these years, he surely must be dead by now."

The tailor reached for the clothes as if to fold them up again, but Nevien stayed his hand. "Please leave them," she said. "And even though it's a sad thing to think about, I'm still glad that you brought them. Here," she added, reaching for her purse. "You should have something for your kind thoughts, and for your trouble."

The tailor protested at first, but in the end he accepted fifty rins when she insisted that she was, in effect, buying the garments from him. To her they were beyond price.

It was only as he was leaving that Nevien thought to ask him the name of the town where the sewing box had been found.

Tor Einos stopped in his tracks, at the library door, and stood for a long moment tapping his forehead with a forefinger. "The town..." he murmured. "My brother-in-law *did* say, but I can't quite recall..."

"Would it, by any chance, have been Wotana?" Nevien knew the large town of Galenor was not much more than twenty miles north of Lankura, and there weren't many small towns between the two.

The tailor brightened instantly. "Why yes., that was it! Wotana. The very name."

And then he was gone with another bow and a "Good afternoon My Lady Princess."

Merriel went to escort him out. Nevien could hear their voices receding down the hallway as she carefully refolded the two garments. She frowned over the task. She felt like a hypocrite for having resorted to the same argument her father had always used to dismiss the need to search further for Leyel— that he must have died of a fit. The truth was that she hadn't wanted either Merriel or Tor Einos to engage in further speculation. And she certainly wasn't going to tell her father about the tailor's discovery. The last thing she wanted was to risk re-opening the investigation.

She shook her head as she started to return to her room. She had never understood why her father had been so determined that there be an heir produced from her union with Leyel. For the better part of a year he had seemed almost obsessed with the idea— only to drop it like and old shoe as soon as the unfortunate prince had disappeared.

When she reached her room, she lost no time in finding a safe hiding place for the bundle of clothes in the bottom of her chest of drawers under a folded nightdress. She slid the drawer firmly closed, wishing she might consider the entire matter closed as securely. Unfortunately, it wasn't so easy to stop thinking about it.

If Leyel hadn't drowned, her greatest fear could be dismissed. But what, then, had been his end? Or was he possibly still alive somewhere? In what condition, then? Standing beside the chest of drawers, she bit her lip. Could anything ever completely absolve her of the burden of guilt that she carried? She'd only meant to help – or so she'd always told herself. But she knew it was, at best, only half the truth. She'd meant to help, yes, but who had she been more concerned with helping? Leyel Virden, or herself? She had made her confession to Solbrid in the temple of the Mother Goddess years ago, but it had never seemed enough.

She shook herself. "Take care of poor Leyel, Mother Solbrid," she murmured aloud, "Whether he is living or dead, wherever his spirit may dwell, keep him safe and bring him peace." She straightened her shoulders and turned away.

Crossing the room, her eye lit upon the writing materials left standing on her desktop. Seeing them made her think of Nagaro, and then of course she remembered that Nagaro had once lived in Wotana. It was an odd coincidence, especially considering how heated she had seen him become on the subject of Leyel Virden. Just for a moment it occurred to her to wonder whether the two young men's paths might have crossed. Upon reflection, however, she decided it wasn't likely. *Nagaro surely would have mentioned it.*

Chapter 3

A Cryptic Message

Nagaro had found the day emotionally exhausting. It should have been triumphal, with the four ships returning from their mission to Chitaopa baring a hundred newly freed galley slaves and the news of Emperor Baalkir's promise to free all the rest— to end forever the practice of using slaves to row the warships of the Mahuk Baar. This cause for joyous celebration had, of course, been completely overshadowed by the news of Ferenan's murder just a few days before. The city of Lankura was still in shock.

Nagaro felt the impact of the political assassination all the more acutely owing to his feelings for Princess Nevien. He could all too easily imagine the distress she was experiencing— the man wouldn't be dead, after all, if he hadn't been betrothed to her. And the weight of Ferenan's death also came on top of Nagaro's mental turmoil arising from the dilemma he faced over whether to agree to let Kuran to adopt him into the House of Kel. *There was just so much that Kuran didn't know about him... would surely want to know...*

And then there had come the rape charge.

After spending several hours getting the freed slaves settled into the tents that would temporarily house them, Nagaro and Kuran had returned to the Fleet Compound to find a reluctant Vell Sobring bearing papers, filed with the Crown by his uncle Grimbold, that formally charged Nagaro with the rape of Vell's sister Alliset. It was exactly the kind of legal jeopardy that Kuran had warned Nagaro he might face after escaping from Grimbold's clutches. As a commoner, without a family or Wared lord, Nagaro had no defense.

And *then*, it had become apparent that Grimbold was prepared to use heskial to compel Alisset to give false testimony against him! Nagaro had immediately felt that he had no choice but to accept Kuran's offer. He couldn't live with the idea of anyone doing such a terrible thing to an innocent young woman.

He had signed the necessary paper without even reading it.

He was now attempting to avoid thinking about the possible consequences of this action as he sat with his friends in the Fleet dining hall, trying to settle his nerves while eating his dinner. It would have been considerably easier if Taru and Pavo hadn't insisted on talking about what he'd just done.

"Kuran have show that he is good friend to you, Nagaro," Pavo was saying. "He will protect you from any other man like Grimbold. Now you are his heir, he will make everything better."

"Well, maybe not *everything*." Taru offered critically. "But he did all right *this* time, that's sure! With that letter he wrote saying that Nagaro would challenge Grimbold to combat. And if he tries to do anything that *isn't* all right, Nagaro can always just tear up the paper and make and end of it."

Nagaro frowned. "I don't think it would be quite that easy to back out of signing the paper," he said. "And you know what I think about the challenge to combat." He wiped his plate with a piece of bread, which he proceeded to eat, chewing resignedly.

They had originally arrived at the dining hall too early for dinner, but had waited over cups of sothiril rather than going to their quarters. The large, raftered room had gathered shadows as the light from the windows took on the golden hue of an autumn sunset. The oil lamps, suspended from the ceiling beams or placed in sconces around the walls, had by now been lit, and the three friends had filled up plates with buttered bread and savory lamb stew, and refilled their mugs with sothiril. The dining hall had filled up as well, with a background babble of voices that shielded their words from other ears. For that, at least, Nagaro was grateful.

"I'd still like to see that challenge bout." Taru grinned wickedly. "It'd teach Grimbold not to muck with ye, Nagaro— the lyin', sneakin', son-of-a-dog's-hind-leg! *Ha!*" He made a mock lunge across the table, pantomiming a sword thrust and nearly knocking over his sothiril cup.

"*I* hope that Kuran and Vell are right— that Grimbold won't accept the challenge," Nagaro said wearily. "I would much rather have him drop the charge."

Taru shook his head in obvious disappointment. "Why should ye let the coward creep away with his tail between his legs?"

"*Because I don't want a fight.*" Nagaro lowered his voice, which had risen with his annoyance. "And I never want to hear the word 'rape' again!"

"But ye'd win! Ye know ye would!"

Nagaro sighed. "Have you considered that if I bested Grimbold in a challenge, that might not be the end of it? I'd have made him look bad in public— because there would *have* to be witnesses. What makes you think he'd let that lie?"

"Nagaro is right, Taru." Pavo offered. "Always it is better to win without having to fight. And if Grimbold takes back his charge so he do not have to fight Nagaro, it means Nagaro *have* won. It means Grimbold knows his god will judge him for having told lie. It is victory for honor!"

Taru waved a hand and turned his attention back to his stew. "All right, all right," he said. "A victory for honor."

Nagaro heaved another sigh. He wasn't surprised that Pavo, with his abiding faith in the guiding hand of Sheptuum, would embrace the concept of a trial by combat. Personally, he doubted whether Grimbold thought along such lines. If the man dropped the rape charge it would be entirely out of fear of Nagaro's blade. "It's just not right," he muttered, "that I should only be able to get justice by being better at—

A voice interrupted him.

"Captain Nagaro, Zirda! I wonder if ye'd settle a little wager?"

Nagaro looked up, startled. He hadn't noticed the approach of the man who had just spoken, and who now stood on the other side of the table.

The speaker was a young Kelorin who had once sailed with him in their piratical forays against the Mautep. And he wasn't alone. There were half a dozen other men, crowding close, all with expectant expressions. Most were Kelorin, but there was one Turo, and even a Leithian, looking curious and a bit sheepish.

"That would depend on the wager," Nagaro observed mildly. He wasn't himself inclined to make wagers, but he considered the practice harmless as long as the stakes were low and the issue wasn't something that men were likely to come to blows over.

"Begging your pardon for disturbing ye, Captain," a second man put in, another Kelorin but older and sporting a beard that was pepper-and-salt. "We just wondered if ye'd mind telling us your birthday."

"My *birthday?*" Nagaro was nonplused. It seemed an unlikely subject for a wager considering the number of possible responses.

"Aye. The month and day."

Nagaro surveyed the eager faces. "I'm sorry to disappoint you," he said, "but I was a foundling— left on a doorstep as an infant. I don't know the day of my birth. Even the month isn't exactly certain."

There was obvious disappointment in the exchanged glances. The first man, the younger one, said, "Can ye tell us the most *likely* month?"

Taru had been listening with some impatience. "It's Madrel or Evrel," he said, obviously hoping get rid of the men. "Now will ye be off and leave us in peace?"

His words, however, were greeted with excited exclamations. The younger Kelorin leaned eagerly across the table, past Taru, and addressed Nagaro again.

"Captain, Zirda, d' ye mean it was at the *end* of Madrel?"

Nagaro frowned. "I was found on the third day of Evrel," he explained. "If one supposes that I wasn't more than two weeks old— as I've been told— then, yes, it would have been near the end of Madrel."

"*Hoo-ha!*" The young man slapped the table triumphantly and turned to the older one. "Just as I told ye! It could ha' been the day. The very same day!"

The older man stood with his mouth open, looking stunned. "*By the Eyes!*" he murmured. His gaze came back to focus on Nagaro, his face a picture of awestruck wonder.

"What is this about?" Nagaro looked from one to the other, feeling distinctly uncomfortable, the more so because the little crowd of listeners seemed to have grown, and several of its original members were excitedly explaining the situation to the newcomers.

The younger man shifted from foot to foot and cleared his throat as if to answer, but he seemed suddenly abashed. "It's... ah..." He cleared his throat again. "Ye see, Captain—"

The older man found his tongue. "King Darion was born on the twenty-seventh day of Madrel, Zirda," he said. "So ye could ha' been born on the same day."

Nagaro stared at the man. This was a complete surprise to him, since he'd never taken note of the date of Darion's birth. It wasn't a common topic of conversation. Still, he realized that older citizens of Edrovir— those who remembered the reign of King Darion— would likely have known it. His shock lasted only a few seconds. Then he shrugged. "So, it's a possible coincidence," he said. "What of it?'

But the younger man was talking excitedly to the crowd, not listening to Nagaro. "This as good as *proves* it," he was insisting. "For it to be *that close*, it must be true! The spirit of Darion is among us!"

The older man turned on the younger one. "It proves nothing, I tell ye! The birthday has nothing t' do with it. He could be Darion come back to us whether the birthday is the same or not!"

Darion come back to us?

Nagaro stood up in dismay. "Wait a minute!" he cried. "What are you talking about?"

The older man turned back to Nagaro, rubbing his bearded chin and looking apologetic. "There's some that are saying the spirit of Darion walks in ye, Captain," he explained. "Because of how good ye are with a sword— and because o' the way ye take your honor so seriously and ye make peace with your enemies..." His voice trailed into silence under

Nagaro's burning gaze. The rest of the little crowd that had gathered fell silent as well.

"I see." Nagaro swept the circle of faces with his eyes. How, he wondered, could men be so easily misled? "The *one* thing that anyone here has got right, is that the birthday makes no difference," he said, trying to maintain an even tone. "Do you suppose that each spirit, as it passes from life to life, is re-born always on the *same day?* How do you imagine that could work— when a birth comes according to the time of the begetting, and a returning spirit enters into a new-forming life only *after* the bud has begun to grow?" He stared around at their blank faces. "Hasn't anyone here read the Writings?"

There were sheepish shrugs and downcast gazes, and murmurs of, "Well... not *read*, as *such*—" and, "Not more 'n a little, Zirda—"

Nagaro passed a weary hand over his eyes. "Well, if you *had* read them, you would know," he said. "And as for the rest of it, it's the flesh that shapes the spirit, not the other way around. If I have talent for the sword, you should ask about my father's skill, or my grandfathers' to see how I came by it— not what other lives my spirit has lived. And as for my sense of honor, or making peace with enemies— *those* things come out of the Writings too! And if more men read more of the Writings, such ideas would be commonplace. Now I suggest that you all go back to your dinners and leave me to mine!"

"But ye're not saying ye *couldn't* have Darion's spirit, are ye?" The younger Kelorin still sounded hopeful.

Nagaro frowned. "Of course I can't say that," he said, "— since I was born two years after Darion's death. But if *I* could have Darion's spirit, so could any man, woman, or child who was born since Darion's passing. Whoever it is would never *know* it, either, because there's no way to *tell!* The attributes of the flesh are inherited through the flesh. *Do you understand?*"

The young man looked confused. Others in the crowd were exchanging whispered comments.

"Here, now!" Taru pushed back his chair and rounded the end of the table to confront the group of listeners. "Can't ye see that you're bothering the captain? Now be off about your own affairs, and leave him in peace!" He began trying to shoo the men away.

Pavo stood up also and began to move towards the end of the table as if he meant to join his friend's efforts. Pavo was a big man, and the prospect of having to contend with him was apparently too much for the men. The crowd abruptly broke up, its members turning tail and making off between the tables in little knots, talking to each other as they went.

Above the babble of the dining hall, the voice of the young Kelorin could be heard, saying, *"Did ye hear? He didn't deny it!"*

Frowning, Nagaro shook his head as he stared after the retreating figures. It was amazing what men would believe if they wanted to badly enough. Especially if they hadn't read enough to know how ridiculous it was. It sounded as if these men were responding to a rumor that someone else had started. He wondered whose idea it had originally been.

Taru wasn't inclined to be charitable. "What a pack o' fools," he muttered as he returned to his seat.

Pavo also sat back down. "Do Kelorin people really believe what you have said, Nagaro?" he asked. "That spirit of your King Darion could be in any man who have been born after Darion have died?"

Nagaro sank into his seat. "Any man, or any woman, Pavo."

"But man with spirit of Darion would not be *like* Darion? That does not make sense. Spirit of all man who die go to Chofir Naak. If spirit come back it is because Sheptuum have purpose to send it back. Surely that purpose is because of what dead man has done when he was alive!"

Nagaro gestured impatiently. "It's all in the Writings of Vothra, Pavo, and that means it's not just some theoretical notion. The Writings describe the knowledge and experience of the dozens of spirits that have joined together to form Vothra's spirit— the experiences of hundreds of lives."

"Oh." Pavo looked acutely uncomfortable, but then abruptly he brightened. "Maybe Sheptuum have special purpose for special spirit that are part of Vothra?"

"Maybe." Nagaro rubbed his forehead wearily. He wished he had spoken more carefully. He didn't really want to undermine his friend's beliefs. In point of fact, the Writings said that the same rules applied to all spirits. But he didn't have the heart to say this to Pavo.

He glanced from Pavo to Taru. "If you've both finished your dinners, let's take our dishes to the kitchen and gone to our quarters."

The other two men instantly agreed.

A few minutes later, outside in the mild autumn night, Taru turned to him. "Is it to be a night at your quarters, Nagaro? Shall I go fetch the game of King's Men?"

Nagaro shook his head. "I'm sorry, Taru," he said. "I'm afraid that I'm exhausted. If you two want to play, you'd best do it in your own quarters. Too many things have happened today. All I want to do is go to my bed."

Pavo nodded his shaggy head. "That is all right, Nagaro. We will play. You go sleep."

They parted at Nagaro's doorstep, wishing each other good night.

Nagaro yawned as he fished his key from his pocket. His seaman's bag was still on the *Sword*, but it didn't matter. He could fetch it in the morning. There was always a change of clothing in the sea chest that remained in his quarters. Talebra, the bright moon, was just rising above the peak of the barracks roof, with the pursuing dark moon, Naru, not yet visible. He found the keyhole by moonlight and unlocked the door.

As he swung it open, he noticed a small pale rectangle lying on the floor just inside the doorway. Frowning, he stepped over it and closed the door, then located firewood and a match by feel in the dark and kindled a fire on the small hearth in the sitting room. From the fire, he lit a candle, not bothering with the lamp since he meant to be in bed soon.

When he picked up the object by the door, he found that it was a folded, sealed piece of parchment paper. There was no writing on the outside and the sealing wax bore no impression. Still frowning, he broke the seal and unfolded the paper. His heart leaped when he recognized Nevien's flowing hand, but his frown quickly returned as he read the brief message:

To N. N.— It may be that a person in an official capacity, or some agent of such, will soon come to you with an unexpected proposition. Please understand that it is not any of my doing, or anything that I desire, and for the sake of our friendship I urge you to say no.— N. H.

Nagaro carried the note and the candlestick into his bedroom. There, he sat on the edge of the bed and stared at the note, which must have been slipped under his door. He re-read it, but it made no more sense the second time. What was he to make of this?

Clearly Nevien was deliberately being obscure— which suggested a need for secrecy. But she had succeeded too well! He could only guess at the meaning. He'd just been offered a proposition by Lord Kuran. Could this possibly be the thing she referred to? The note was undated. It could have been put under his door at any time during his absence on the mission to Chitaopa. It could have preceded Kuran's offer. *And he had already accepted that offer!* He had been trying all evening to convince himself that he'd done the right thing by signing Kuran's paper— by allowing Kuran to make him his heir and to issue a challenge to Grimbold on his behalf. *And now this.*

He shook his head disbelievingly. Nevien considered Kuran a friend. What could she possibly have against the idea of him taking shelter under Kuran's wing by pledging his allegiance to the House of Kel? Why would she object to that— and in such terms?

He frowned harder.

...for the sake of our friendship...

What possible connection could there be between his friendship with the princess and his acceptance of Kuran's offer? Surely there was none. But if the note had nothing to do with Kuran's proposal, then must he expect some *other* proposition? How would he be able to identify it? He ran a hand distractedly through his hair and massaged his temples. *If only he could go to Nevien and ask her. But of course he couldn't.*

He sighed wearily. He really needed to sleep. Surely time would show him the meaning of the message. He would just have to wait, and pay attention, and keep the matter to himself— not even tell Taru or Pavo about it. Nevien obviously meant it to be a secret, and his friends weren't likely to be able to shed light on it in any case.

So he folded the message and slipped it in among the small collection of correspondence in his sea chest. It was a collection that consisted largely of invitations from the princess— to celebrations at the palace or to outings at River House. Exhausted, he undressed, bathed quickly with a wet cloth, and toweled himself dry. Pulling on a nightshirt, he stretched on his bed, snuffed his candle, and closed his eyes.

Sleep came almost immediately.

Nagaro's dreams had left no memories for several days— not since that night on the ship when Vothra had breathed quieting words into his mind to ease the torment brought on by dreams of his painfully abortive sexual experiences years ago with the sixteen-year-old princess. Those words must have held some spirit magic. It might have been the note that caused a change, or perhaps it was being back in Lankura, or simply that his dreams couldn't be suppressed indefinitely. Whatever the case, for the first time in days, he dreamed— gloriously, passionately, and impossibly— of Nevien.

Chapter 4

Confessions

Nevien sighed as she carefully added her signature to the formal invitation on which she had just written Nagaro's name. She had wanted to add, "*I have to talk to you,*" but had only dared to write "*Please come*" below the engraved message requesting his attendance on an outing to River House at the end of the week.

The morning sun streamed through her bedroom windows. It was a bright, clear day. It seemed almost absurd to be worrying about the dark maneuverings of hidden powers.

"Aren't you finished with that yet?" Rianine was sitting cross-legged on Nevien's bed with her skirts tucked around her knees, idly playing with the tufted fringe of the embroidered bedspread.

Nevien folded the invitation. "I have to address this one and seal it," she said. "And then bundle them." She dipped her pen and began to write "Captain Nagaro, Number 14, Captain's Row, The Fleet Compound."

"Well, it's not as if there's any real hurry. I told the other's not to bother to wait. And with the new girl, Lissel, they'll have four for Oskampo even without Alisset. It's only a matter of appearances, really."

Nevien picked up her stick of sealing wax and carefully applied a lighted candle to the tip of it, waiting for it to drip. "I was hoping to get a chance to talk to Lissel," she said. "Since she's from Pakoa, I wondered if she had ever met Nagaro."

"Oh, she has. I already asked her, and it turns out they've been carrying on a correspondence."

Nevien's hand jerked and a large drop of sealing wax landed on the desk top. "They *have?* He never mentioned it."

Rianine unfolded her legs. "I can't tease you about it at all, can I?" Abandoning her seat on the bed, she crossed the floor to stand behind her friend.

"You mean it isn't true? Did you make it up?"

"Will you relax?" Rianine began massaging the princess's shoulders with strong, slender fingers. "I didn't make it up, I just exaggerated a little. It was only a few letters. Lissel is in love with a strange young man who grew up as a slave in the Mahuk Baar. She was trying to help him, on Pakoa, but he ran away to Lankura to try to join the Fleet, and he seems to have gotten himself lost. The captain has been trying to find him."

"Oh." Nevien sagged. "That sounds like Sindar. Nagaro did mention him, and it's very kind of him to try to help." She sighed, feeling the tension in her neck ease under Rianine's skillful kneading. She hastily re-melted the sealing wax and sealed the folded parchment, then opened her desk drawer to find a piece of string.

Rianine had been looking over her shoulder as she continued her massage. "You're planning it for the end of this week, and you're only sending the invitations today? That's rather short notice, isn't it? Suppose your dear captain can't come?"

"Then I shall have to postpone it."

"Postpone it! For lack of one guest? Aren't you afraid of how that will look? Why are you in such a hurry to see him, Nevien? Why not just schedule the outing for two or three weeks from now so he'll have more time to plan and to get permission?"

Nevien bit her lip. "Can you keep a secret, Rian?"

Rianine's fingers stopped their probing. She pulled up a stool and sat down beside Nevien. "You'd be surprised," she said archly, "at the secrets I keep."

"Oh. Good." Nevien chewed nervously on a fingernail. "Everything that's said in the Council is supposed to be confidential, but I think I'll burst if I don't tell someone—" She drew a breath. "They're going to try to persuade Nagaro to court me."

Rianine clapped her hands gleefully. "Oh, wonderful!"

"No it isn't!" Nevien wailed. "It's not as if they'd ever let him *marry* me! They're just hoping to maneuver him into a challenge bout with Lothard!"

"Not marry you? Well, that's a pity." Rianine emitted a sigh. "Still, if he could get rid of Lothard for you, that would be something. And since Kuran has adopted the captain, Lothard would have to take a challenge seriously. Grimbold certainly did. He dropped that rape charge so fast you'd think that it had stung him! It's only a shame he went and laid the blame on poor Alisset— saying she'd changed her tale. But he's a man, a lord, and a Leithian, so what can you expect?"

Nevien shook her head. "I'm afraid that Lothard will kill Nagaro! Kuran taking him into the House of Kel has played right into the Council's hands!"

Rianine considered her critically. "You haven't much confidence in the captain. He's reputed to be an exceptional swordsman."

"Do you have confidence that he's proof against a knife in the back, Rian? Have you forgotten what just happened to Ferenan?"

"Oh. You do have a point there." The other woman grimaced at her unintended play on words.

"I sent him a message the day he returned, but I had to word it *so* cautiously that he's probably been terribly confused for three days— not to mention worried. I need to talk to him!"

"All right then!" Rianine stood up. "Tie up that bundle and we can hand it to the guard on our way to the sitting room."

***

Nagaro stood in front of Kuran's desk, clutching the invitation.

"By the Eyes, Captain, you must have run to have gotten here so fast! The messenger boy just left and I've barely had time to read my own invitation." Kuran gestured at where his invitation lay on his desktop.

Nagaro frowned. He hadn't literally run, but he *had* walked as fast as he could. After three days of fretting over the meaning of the cryptic note, and three nights of passion-filled and guilt-riddled dreams of Nevien, he was at the point of distraction. "The message boy must have come to you last, My Lord," he said, trying to contain his impatience. "But, am I free to go to River House?"

Kuran considered him, noting the obvious tension in Nagaro's stance. He frowned. "The notice is short. You know I prefer to get this kind of request a full week in advance."

"Yes, but surely this once—"

Kuran waved him to silence. "Speaking solely as your commander," he said carefully. "I admit that your duties aren't so pressing as to prevent your attendance. Speaking as your *Wared Lord*, however, I would strongly advise you not to go."

Nagaro's shoulders jerked. "Why?" he asked sharply.

"Because I'm concerned for your safety. We may have dealt rather handily with Grimbold's trumped up charge, but there are other more serious threats. Grimbold and Lothard are like fist in glove, and have you forgotten that you've been in Lothard's way several times of late? I doubt very much that *he* has forgotten."

Nagaro's brows came together. He was desperate to see Nevien, and his chief fear had been that he would have duties on the day of the outing. He hadn't expected a lecture. "I don't see what any of that has to do with an outing in the country," he said, unable to keep the annoyance out of his voice. "Surely you don't expect Lothard to mount another false attack on the princess's carriage!"

"No, that's not very likely. But you would do well to distance yourself from the princess for a while, since Lothard has his sights on her—"

"She's not for him!"

Kuran blinked, taken aback by Nagaro's sudden vehemence. "Well, I certainly hope not, and there are others who intend to see that she isn't. But that's not your concern. The point is that by putting yourself close to Nevien, you risk being in Lothard's way again. As your Wared Lord, I strongly advise you to keep your distance from her until after she's wed."

"Until after she's *wed?*" Nagaro nearly choked. He knew he would have a much harder time getting close to Nevien after she was married, so in his mind, the time between now and then was to be taken advantage of. Besides, there was plainly something she wished to tell him.

He could feel Kuran's eyes, and he was very aware of his own rising agitation. He made an effort to master himself and tried to muster a logical argument that wouldn't give away any details he suspected were confidential.

"My Lord—" he began.

"Please, Nagaro, call me Kuran."

"Yes... Kuran. I can see that I shouldn't dance with her at the palace, but surely River House is safe. Lothard wouldn't even know I was there."

Kuran's frown didn't relent. "I'm by no means sure that River House is safe. We don't know how Grimbold learned of your intention to visit his Hold. He must have known exactly when and where to expect you or he couldn't have laid the trap with Alisset."

"Brandle said he could have been overheard talking about it to his commander in the guards' quarters," Nagaro protested. "He said the door was open and anyone passing in the hall could have stopped to listen!"

Kuran raised an eyebrow. "You don't think the princess's outings are discussed in the guards' quarters?"

"But surely no one would mention my name!"

Kuran sighed. "Nevien always tells her guards where she's going, and with whom," he said patiently. "It would take only a casual word spoken where the wrong ears could hear. I'm suggesting a sensible precaution, Nagaro. There will be other outings, in two or three months' time. After she's married Nile or Devral—"

Nagaro brandished his invitation. "She wrote '*please come!*' Should I disappoint her because someone *might* overhear something?"

"Of course she wants you to come, Nagaro. She's very fond of you. But I'm sure she'll understand—"

"*How* will she understand, if I don't explain it to her? And *how* can I explain it, if I'm not *there?*" Nagaro's voice had risen and the blood seemed to be pounding in his ears. He drew an unsteady breath. "In any case, you've said I have no pressing duties," he finished tightly. "So I'm free to go if I choose!"

Kuran had stiffened in his chair, his sharp black eyes intent upon Nagaro's face. "There's something here you're not telling me," he said quietly. "It isn't like you to be needlessly reckless. I can't help you if you aren't open with me. Now won't you tell me what this is really about?"

Keshaal! A cold stone landed in Nagaro's stomach. He turned away, his heart pounding as he moved towards the window that looked out onto the parade ground. The movement put his face to the light and his back to Kuran.

He was being an idiot. All the evidence suggested that Kuran only wished him well, and he owed the man some sort of explanation. But what could he possibly say? That he had received a cryptic message from the princess three days earlier? Did that remotely explain the way he'd just behaved? He might suspect that Nevien wanted to tell him something important, but he should be able to talk about it calmly without letting his emotions run away with him.

Only he couldn't— because the emotions were rooted in his feelings for Nevien. Honesty required him to acknowledge this. Kuran deserved honesty, but—

"Is it something concerning the princess?" Kuran spoke from behind him. The older man's voice was concerned, but kind. Gentle, really.

In that moment, something inside Nagaro gave way. He felt a sudden desire to show this man *some* openness. Hadn't Vothra advised him to find people he could talk to about the things that troubled him? That advice was quite impossible to follow when it came to his oldest and deepest secret, but there was one thing here that he might share with Kuran. A thing that Kuran's own personal history made him uniquely able to understand.

Nagaro turned around to face the Lord of Kel Wared, aware that the brightness of the window behind him would make it hard to read his face, and grateful for it. "I love her," he said. "And she's hopelessly beyond my reach."

Kuran's expression was as concerned and kind as his tone had been. "So that's it," he said quietly. "I had feared it might be so."

"Am I so transparent?" Chagrin made the words sound bitter.

"No, no." Kuran hastily reassured him. "At least not until very recently. But I think I know you better than most. And I've been watching you closely for some time. Are there others who know about this?"

"My friend Pavo. And Alisset, because of something I said when I was drugged. And I think Brandle Furthing has guessed it, but I trust him to be discreet... Oh, and the Lady Rianine—"

"You told *her?*"

Nagaro looked at the floor. "She... figured it out. I've sworn her to secrecy."

"Ah. Well, that's probably the best you could have done with *that* woman. Had you tried to pretend she was wrong, she would have stopped at nothing to prove she was right. But give her a secret to keep, and she'll sit on *that* egg until the end of the world. What about Nevien? Does she know?"

"No! And she mustn't. Ever!"

"She... ah... doesn't return your feelings, then?"

Nagaro shook his head. "She sees me as a friend— a dear friend, perhaps, but still just a friend."

"I see." Kuran sighed. "Please sit down, Nagaro."

Somewhat reluctantly Nagaro returned to his seat. "I... I said there were things you didn't know about me. Are you sure you still want me in your House?"

"Of course I do." Kuran's answer came without hesitation. "You've thrown in your lot with me, and we'll weather this— somehow. What kind of friend would I be— or family, for that matter— if I abandoned you at the first sign of trouble?"

The older man was leaning forward, elbows on his desk. There was genuine sympathy in his dark eyes. "This is a grave misfortune," he continued, "because the situation is so very hopeless. When I first sought the hand of my dear Indrid, I was still a commoner and she was of a noble house. But it was a minor House and her two older sisters had made good matches, so her father could afford to relax his standards a little for his youngest child. And then, Elgurn named me Lord of the Royal Fleet and made me lord of the newly-formed Kel Wared— both of which made me more acceptable as a son-in-law. But Nevien is a princess, with every expectation of being a queen. Having become my heir may alter your status, but not nearly enough, I'm afraid."

Nagaro nodded glumly. There was an even more intractable reason why he couldn't pursue Nevien's hand, which he dared not mention. Fortunately it appeared he wouldn't have to.

"I'm not sure I can stay in Lankura after she... after she marries," he said, voicing a fear that had been growing in him of late. "I'm not even sure I can continue to serve in the Fleet."

"Ah, don't be so hasty." Kuran straightened a little. "A period of absence from Lankura would indeed be wise— I would say an *extended* period. But that needn't mean leaving the service. Elgurn has wanted for some time to establish additional garrison posts in the islands besides the one at Long Harbor. He's been looking particularly at the southern isles— at Boka Omei, or even Pakoa. You would do well as a garrison commander.

And there's certainly no one better qualified for such a post, so we needn't fear it will be argued that I'm favoring my own. If you have no objection, I'll put your name forward at my next meeting with the king. In fact, I could add the suggestion to the report I'm writing and set the process in motion immediately."

"Immediately!" Nagaro felt a lurch of alarm. His fingers tightened involuntarily on the invitation he still held. The idea that there might be honorable work for him was reassuring, but the thought of leaving the city, and Nevien, still filled him with dismay.

"Relax, please, Nagaro." Kuran held up a placating hand. "The process will take time. Weeks, I would say, and I might begin by sending you to Boka Omei to discuss the matter with the Town Chief in Boka Bay, and to look into acquiring some temporary quarters there, pending new construction—" He broke off, studying Nagaro keenly. "What's the matter? You look so worried."

Nagaro swallowed. "I find that things don't get better... when I'm away from Lankura. I'm having trouble sleeping... I can't think."

Kuran sighed. "Ah yes, I remember that, from when I lost Indrid to the plague. Work helps, Nagaro. And time. There is no outright cure, I'm afraid— except perhaps to find a new love, and that can't be forced. But time, and distance, and straightforward work that needs doing— these things are palliative." He sighed again. "Of course, my own experience comes from having lost a love to death. It may be harder knowing that your love is still in the world. But I can tell you that the worst of it lasted no more than two years— because I threw myself into my work. And now, eight years after losing Indrid, I feel that I could love again. I'm not sure how reassuring all of that may be to you, but it's the best I can offer."

Numbly, Nagaro nodded. He hadn't expected there to be any real solution to his problem, and the prospect that it might take years to see improvement didn't therefore seem as bleak as it might have. "Then you should put the suggestion in your report," he said decisively. "And since it will take time for anything to come of it, there will be time for me to see Nevien and explain to her that—"

"No. No. *No!*" Kuran shook his head emphatically. "What you've just told me makes it even more imperative that you stay away from her!"

"But—" Nagaro held up the invitation.

"No! Your heart is leading your head, Nagaro. You're not thinking. Of *course* you want to see her— but can't you see that you only torment yourself that way? To be so *close*. To look, but not to touch. Not to speak. How long do you think you can hold yourself in check? And you risk giving yourself away through little things that you're not even aware of— to her, or to anyone else who may be present, I shudder to think what Lothard and his lot might do with this knowledge!"

Nagaro hung his head, fighting rising anger. *Kuran was right.* He knew it, though he wanted desperately to believe otherwise.

But there had been that other note.

He raised his eyes. "She... she sent me a message several days ago. I found it slipped under my door when I returned from Chitaopa. I couldn't understand it. And now this—" He gestured with the invitation. "I think she wants to explain something."

"What did the message say?"

"I... I don't remember exactly." He winced at his own evasiveness. "It seemed she was trying to be careful not to say too much. There was something about a proposition... coming from someone in an 'official capacity.' She said she wanted me to say no to it. Now you've made me two propositions in less than a week— and I've said yes to both!"

Kuran stiffened. "Surely you don't think I would propose anything that would harm you! Or the princess!"

"Of course not! At least not *intentionally...*"

Kuran's expression softened. "I see what you're getting at. I suppose there might be something afoot that I don't know about— some secret machination. But you can rest easy about the posting to the islands since I haven't spoken to anyone else about that. As for adopting you as my heir, well, I had to discuss that with the king because he had to give his approval, but I fail to see how there's any harm in it for you. I wouldn't have made you the offer otherwise."

"I know that. But don't you see why I need to talk to Nevien?"

But Kuran shook his head. "What I see is that one of us needs to. But that one had best be me. I've always been her friend, and I can talk to her frankly. Trust me in this, Nagaro. I'll explain about the danger of you getting in Lothard's way. I'll talk about my concern for your safety. I can honestly say that you would have gone to River House if I hadn't advised against it. That will make me the old hen, and you needn't look like a coward."

"I don't know..." Nagaro would have much rather have spoken to Nevien himself, but he could see, now, how suspect that desire was. His remaining concern was that Nevien might not be willing to speak freely to Kuran, but there was no one he would rather trust with the task.

"Come, now." Kuran began to get out paper, pen, and ink. "Let's both write our responses. I to say I'll come, and you to express your regrets. You can say you have some duty to attend to. And if it troubles you to speak falsely, I can easily think of something to make it true."

Nagaro let out a long sigh. "Oh, very well." He reluctantly reached for the pen.

Chapter 5

A Plot Unfolds

Four days later, Nagaro was back in the office of the Lord of the Fleet.

Kuran regarded him apologetically from behind an intimidating stack of paperwork, looking harried. "I'm sorry, Nagaro," he said. "I meant to tell you. The outing was cancelled for some reason, so I've had no chance to speak to Nevien."

Nagaro made an effort to contain his frustration. "Do you think it will be rescheduled?"

"I've no idea. We weren't told."

"You could just... make an appointment. Couldn't you?"

Kuran leaned back in his chair and rubbed his chin wearily. "Yes, I could. And if it comes to it, I will—if I ever have time." He cast a baleful eye over the papers that littered his desk. "But with the Festival of the Harvest Moon coming in just a few weeks, it might be easier simply to wait. I'll surely be able to speak to her then."

A few weeks! Nagaro bit back the words. "I'd rather it wasn't let go for so long."

Kuran arched a brow. "What, have there been mysterious strangers knocking at your door with unexpected propositions?"

"*No.*" Nagaro looked at the floor. "I've heard nothing at all."

"And it's been, what? All of four days—" Kuran had begun to sound exasperated, but he caught himself and sighed. "I'm sorry, Nagaro. You're worried to distraction, and it's understandable. I shouldn't be unkind." He paused, studying Nagaro with an earnest gaze. "I understand that Geldoran actually bested you at sword practice today," he said after a moment. "I'm afraid your state of mind is beginning to affect your work."

Nagaro laughed bitterly. "*That* has been true for some time."

"Well, if it's so, it hasn't been very apparent. But something like losing a bout... Well, if it's repeated, the men will begin to notice. There'll be talk. I may have to take you off of sword practice for a while."

Nagaro's shoulders sagged. "Whatever you think is best, My Lo—Kuran."

The Lord of the Fleet hunted among the disorder on his desktop, located a piece of blank paper, and made a note, then looked up. "Speaking of there being talk," he said with a hint of mirth in his eyes, "I also hear you're the walking incarnation of Darion the Great."

This time Nagaro stiffened and his brows came together in an angry frown. "It's utterly ridiculous!" he exclaimed in bitter annoyance. "They all should know better, and I've told them so. Several times!"

"And the more you say it's ridiculous, the more they believe it, isn't that right?"

"There is *no* reason to imagine that I was ever Darion!"

Kuran heaved a sigh. "No," he said, "You just think like him, talk like him, and act like him." He waved aside the angry retort he could see gathering behind Nagaro's thunderous look. "You should try laughing at this, Nagaro. Or, if you can't laugh, try saying nothing at all. The more seriously you appear to take it, the worse it will get. Anyway, that's my advice. Now, is there anything else we need to discuss?"

Dismally, Nagaro shook his head. He was in no mood for laughter, though he respected Kuran's good intentions. He took his leave, exiting Kuran's office to emerge into the gathering dusk. Since he and his friends had planned to make their dinner together in his quarters, he struck off across the compound for Captain's Row.

***

Nevien's hand shook with anger as she lit the elegant crystal and porcelain oil lamp that stood on her writing desk. She had gone in search of her father to inquire what else he wished her to read for her edification, and, after several inquiries, had finally found him— along with the members of the Council— just emerging from a meeting in the Council Chamber to which she obviously hadn't been invited. She hadn't even been told it was going to happen! *And to top it off, they hadn't had the grace to act even the least bit awkward about it when she'd caught them in the act!*

Nevien made an effort to compose herself. She'd caught a few snippets of conversation as the men had filed past her. They'd been talking about Captain Nagaro— and about Kuran. It seemed they were annoyed with Kuran, though that seemed unfair since he'd not only persuaded Nagaro to agree to being adopted, but had also dealt very neatly with the rape charge. He'd done exactly what the Council had hoped he would. Yet her father and the two Leithians, Pendrik and Odus, had looked decidedly displeased, and even Anduar had appeared to have his nose out of joint. Devral had actually been chuckling, amused by Anduar's discomfiture, but when she'd asked him what the joke was, the grizzled old Kelorin had immediately become dismissive, telling her it was nothing a young lady need be concerned with!

Nevien unclenched her hands and tried to re-focus. Obviously Kuran must have done something else that didn't fit into Anduar's plan. The only clue was that the two Leithians had been muttering something about being "overprotective." Well, if that was all it was, she was in favor. But her fear was that Kuran might do something to cause Anduar to alter the timing of his plan.

That plan's current timetable called for a month of mourning for Ferenan, followed by the announcement of the "discovery" of the voiding of the Pact, with the announcement of Nagaro's addition to the list of her suitors coming after that, coinciding roughly with the Festival of the Harvest Moon. She'd thought that she had at least a *little* time to find a chance to talk to Nagaro. Having to cancel her original date for the outing had been disappointing, though not unduly alarming. But now... *What if Anduar decided to approach Nagaro sooner?*

Nevien straightened decisively. Pulling open one of the desk drawers, she began to get out paper, pen, and ink.

Rianine found her in the act of meticulously hand-lettering an invitation. The young Kelorin woman didn't wait for a response to her knock before opening the bedchamber door, then crossing the room to stand behind the princess and look over her shoulder. "Not *again*," she said in response to what she saw.

"Well, what else am I to do? My father and the Council don't tell me things! How can I protect him when they won't tell me what's going on?"

Rianine sighed. "When is it to be this time? Not the end of this week, I hope."

"No. That's too close. It will have to be the end of next week."

"You're not going to have them engraved?"

"That would take too long."

"And this doesn't?"

Nevien shook her head, not missing a stroke of the pen. "No, I can finish this tonight and have them delivered first thing tomorrow morning. Are the other ladies playing Oskampo in the library?"

"Yes. They decided not to wait for you— again— since lately you always seem to have a book to read." Rianine paused, then added, "Shall I make some excuse for you?"

"Perhaps you should."

There was a pause during which the only sound was the scratching of the quill pen. Finally Rianine asked, "What if he can't come this time either?"

Nevien's brow creased in a frown and she bit her lip. "He had better be able to," she said. *He just had better.*

***

"I still can't believe ye let Geldoran get under your guard like that."

Taru was leaning back in his chair, nursing a mug of sothiril. He had addressed Nagaro across the kitchen table, which was littered with the remains of their repast. The latter had consisted of a chicken roasted on a little spit in Nagaro's kitchen fireplace, a loaf of bread, and the last of the carrots and potatoes harvested from a small plot of vegetables Nagaro had planted in his little back garden. The chicken had been basted with some fruity concoction supplied by Pavo, and the potatoes were baked to fluffy perfection among the embers. Altogether it had been a very satisfactory meal, harkening back to a time when the three young men had shared a house on Pakoa Island.

Nagaro sighed. That had been a simpler time. *Before he'd made the mistake of attempting to befriend a princess.* "It was bound to happen sooner or later, Taru," he said. "He's been trying to get the better of me for more than two years, after all. Today he did. I hope it gives him some satisfaction."

Pavo was leaning across the table, beginning to gather up the dishes. "I do not think so," he said. "Geldoran does not think his skill have beaten you. He says he think your mind is somewhere else. He will not believe it until it happen another time."

Nagaro took a sip of sothiril. "Part of the skill of swordsmanship is in maintaining your concentration. I lost my concentration today and he used his skill to take advantage of it. He deserved the win."

"And what have ye got t' be so distracted about?" Taru demanded. "Don't tell me ye're still upset about the way Grimbold set the blame on Lady Alisset for his having dropped that charge against ye!"

Nagaro frowned. "He had no right to say she changed her story," he said quickly, grateful that Taru had inadvertently provided him the excuse. "Especially since it wasn't *her* story in the first place! Alisset is one of the most honest people I know, and this lie is unfairly damaging to her reputation."

Taru rolled his eyes. "Aye, but everyone *knows* she's honest," he said exasperatedly. "Just like they know that Grimbold's a big fat liar! It's not as if ye have t' be very clever to figure out—" He stopped abruptly and cocked an ear. "Now who's that, knockin' on your door at this hour?"

"I don't know." Nagaro had heard the sound as well. He drained his cup and set it on top of the stack for Pavo to take to the wash basin. "I suppose I had better find out."

Rising, he left the kitchen and crossed the small sitting room to unbolt the front door, making a conscious effort to smooth his countenance. He was only a little concerned. It wasn't so very late, but it *was* after dark and after hours. Any ordinary sort of Fleet business that might arise at such a time would normally be left until morning.

As he swung the door open, a chilly gust of air swept in, causing the lamp on the sitting room table to flicker. The summer was truly past and the nights had been turning steadily colder. On top of that, this one was blustery. The lantern hanging from the eaves to the right of the front door swung gently in the wind, creaking a little on its chain and casting a wavering light on the cloaked and hooded figure standing on the bottom step of Nagaro's front porch.

Before Nagaro could speak, the man shook back his hood, revealing flaxen hair. Nagaro stared down at the young face that was turned up to him. The visitor was so unexpected that it took him a moment to identify Kendira's young beau, who was a member of the Palace Guard.

"Groft?" he asked. "What are you doing here?"

***

Nevien sighed as she put down the quill, then opened a drawer to get her sealing wax. The lettering was done, including the addresses. All that remained was to seal the invitations. Perhaps she could join her ladies in the library after all.

There came a sound of voices outside in the corridor, and she frowned because at least some of them were female. She hoped her ladies hadn't come looking for her. The voices grew louder and there came a staccato knock at her door.

"Nevien?" Rianine's voice was muffled by the solid oak. "Are you still dressed?"

"Yes, Rian," she called back. "What is it?"

The door opened a little way and Rianine put her head in. "I think you'd better hear this," she said, without any trace of her usual mockery.

The door was opened wider, then, to reveal Brandle, looking grim, and young Delvin, looking worried. Lady Merriel was there as well, and behind her were Kendira and the new girl, Lissel, both rather pale.

"What's going on? Nevien rose and crossed to the door.

Rianine and Merriel exchanged looks. Merriel cleared her throat. "It's rather irregular," she said, "But I think we had better all come in."

Baffled, Nevien turned inquiring eyes to Brandle. He nodded. "Yes," he said. "And we'd better close the door."

Nevien was now alarmed as well as baffled. She stood aside while the six of them all trooped in and arrayed themselves in a semicircle in front of her. They all looked worried. Once the door was closed, she asked, "Will someone now please tell me what this is about?"

Brandle took a breath. "It seems that Delvin may have discovered a plot against Nagaro."

"*Oh!*" Nevien's hand went to her throat.

"I didn't want to go to Commander Worling with this," Brandle continued. "The plotters didn't use the captain's name, and they didn't say *exactly* what they meant to do. Commander Worling would dither. I thought of going directly to your father, but I couldn't find him downstairs, or in his chamber. Then I thought of *you* and Aunt Merriel. You both at least will take this seriously."

"I certainly do!" Nevien turned to confront Delvin. "What have you found out?"

The young guardsman was shifting nervously from one foot to the other. "I'd... ah... just come back from visiting my mother, My Lady. I was in the stable, in one o' the stalls, tending to my horse— seeing as the stablemen were all gone for the night." He licked nervous lips. "I... I heard somebody walk in... and when I looked, it was that big red-haired fellow that the lieutenant transferred to the City Guard."

Nevien looked from Delvin to Brandle. "The man you were suspicious of after my carriage was attacked?"

Brandle's teeth flashed. "The very one. Murlak's his name. I had nothing solid against the man, so I told him there was no room for him to advance under my command and that I was transferring him with a recommendation that he be promoted to sergeant. Delvin was clever enough to wonder what a member of the City Guard was doing in the palace stables after hours."

"It wasn't just *that*," Delvin put in hurriedly. "He seemed to be *sneaking*. He hid in an empty stall, so I ducked down an' hid myself in another one, and waited. And after a minute or two, who comes in but Groft!"

At the mention of the name, Kendira emitted a small strangled whimper. Lissel patted her arm.

"And Groft says— speakin' low— 'The moons are rising.' And Murlak answers, 'Aye, the moons are high and the wind is in our favor'."

"Sign and counter-sign," muttered Brandle.

"Aye, Zirda." Delvin nodded eagerly. "That's what I thought—
especially 'cause the moons were already setting. And then Groft asks, 'Is
it to be tonight then?' And Murlak answers, 'Aye.' And then they started
talking about their plan."

"*Which was...?*" Nevien prompted urgently.

Brandle cut in with the answer. "It sounds as if they mean to lure the
captain into an ambush."

"To... to *kill* him?" Nevien's gaze flicked frantically from Brandle to
Delvin and back again.

"Well, they didn't say it in so many *words*." Brandle looked grim. "But
I don't think they mean to offer him another wife! If the Brothers of the
Blood can't control him, they mean to be rid of him. That's how I see it."

"They talked about 'doing the deed'," Delvin put in. "Groft didn't
want to be part o' that. He said he'd bring the captain to the place, and
then his part was done."

Nevien's heart had begun to hammer. *Oh Gods! Great Mother Solbrid!*
She had thought that Nagaro would be safe as long as she made sure he
didn't become her suitor... but these men— these horrible Leithian men!
They weren't even going to wait for that!

"Where?" she breathed. "Out on the road, somewhere?"

Brandle shook his head. "No. It's to be in Lankura. Somewhere on
Tanners' Row. Delvin got that much. Groft is to find the captain at the
Fleet Compound and deliver a message, then persuade him to come—
alone— and take him to the spot. I'm hoping he'll be suspicious— that
he'll see through it. That he won't come."

This had also occurred to Nevien. "What is the message?" she asked,
turning back to Delvin. "Do you know?"

"It's to be, '*The Princess has need of you.*' Murlak made Groft say it back
to him."

Nevien groaned as hope dropped out of her heart like the falling of
a dead sparrow. *They were using her name! And language so vague it could
mean almost anything...* He would surely think of her note. If only he'd been
able to go to River House! Or if only she'd never sent him that wretched
note!

"He'll come," she said hollowly. Then another thought struck her.
"Unless he doesn't believe the message came from me! I've always written
to him, before, and he knows my hand. But this—"

"They thought of that." Brandle cut in. "Groft has a ring to show him
as a token."

"What ring?" Nevien asked, with rising dread.

"I didn't get a look at it, My Lady," Delvin responded. "But it's
something of yours. Groft said the captain mentioned it at River House,

and that he'd tricked the 'little mouse' into borrowing it and giving it to him—"

With a jolt, Nevien remembered that she had recently lent Kendira her mother's opal ring! A glance at Kendira revealed that the young woman was hiding her face in her hands. "Kendira!" Nevien said severely. "Did you give him my ring?"

Kendira's hands flew up. "*I'm sorry! I'm sorry!*" she wailed in misery. "It was supposed to be only for a day or two— so a jeweler could make one like it and I could have one of my very own! He said it would be a present! *And all this time I thought he loved me!*" She burst into tears.

Lissel immediately put her arms around the sobbing young woman and began to murmur soothingly. Merriel gave Nevien a despairing look even as she patted Kendira's arm and said, "There, there, dear."

Rianine rolled her eyes and said, "I always say you can't trust a man."

Nevien let out her breath, feeling sick. "I'm sorry I snapped at you, Kendira," she said. "You couldn't possibly have known. He fooled us all." She chewed her lip, sweeping her eyes over the assembled group before her. "Does anyone else know about this? Besides the six of you?"

Brandle shook his head. "We've told no one else."

"Clarimel had a headache and went to bed before Brandle found us," Merriel explained. "Delasin was kind enough to walk with her."

"For now, let's keep it that way." Nevien turned to Brandle. "Can you get some men together and ride out there? Try to stop them?"

Brandle nodded agreement. "I was hoping to get your father's authorization, but there's no time for that now. Groft must have ridden out half an hour ago. He'll be at the Fleet Compound by now, though it'll take some time for the captain to get ready to ride. Without orders, I'll have to get men who are off duty—"

"That's all right," Nevien said hastily. "It's better that way— no uniforms— nothing to say who the rescuers are, or who sent them." She was by no means sure what her father would have done. *Would he have tried to take some sort of advantage of this?*

"I should be able to get six or seven men—" Brandle continued.

"Good," Nevien said decisively. "I'll meet you at the stable in a quarter hour. Saddle a horse for me. Not my white mare, a dark colored one—"

"Good heavens, child!" Merriel exclaimed, forgetting Kendira as she threw up her hands. "You don't mean to go *with* them!"

Nevien gave the older woman a determined look. "I have to," she said grimly. "Nagaro may not believe that the message didn't come from me unless I tell him so myself!"

Chapter 6

A Knife In The Dark

Groft blinked innocent blue eyes. "Captain Nagaro, I have a message for you."

Nagaro's surprise was scarcely diminished. It wasn't usual to use members of the Palace Guard as messenger boys. Never-the-less, he extended his hand. "All right then, let's have it."

"It's not written down. It's from the princess." Groft fumbled in his pocket. "I have a token here, so you'll know it's from her." He held out a small object that flashed sparks of orange and green fire.

Nagaro took the thing and carefully examined it by the light of the swinging lantern. It was unmistakably Nevien's opal ring— an excellent choice for a token. She often wore it, so he knew the setting. And besides that, no two opals are ever exactly alike in coloring and he recognized the pattern of rainbow-hued crystals in the polished cabochon. "All right," he said, with mounting trepidation. "This is her ring. Now tell me the message."

"I'm to say that she has need of you."

Nagaro's heart leaped, but this was an odd way to communicate. "Just that? What does she need me for?"

"I don't know, Zirda. But I'm to take you to a place where you can talk—"

"She wants to talk to me?" He couldn't disguise his eagerness.

Groft blinked his pale blue eyes. "Yes. That's right. She wants to talk to you."

He felt his pulse quicken. *Of course she wanted to talk to him! There was something important she needed to tell him, and he hadn't gone to River House— and Kuran hadn't spoken to her. Everything made sense.*

Everything except, perhaps, sending Groft. Nagaro frowned down at the blond youth who stood looking up at him, hugging his cloak about him against the chill in the wind, his face open, his expression expectant.

There were other members of the Palace Guard whom he would have trusted without question. Groft he scarcely knew. On the other hand, he had no specific reason *not* to trust Groft. The young man gave every appearance of being devoted to Kendira. Maybe Nevien hadn't had any other choice. Or maybe she'd chosen Groft exactly because he wasn't known to be Nagaro's friend— because others would be less likely to distrust him. Nagaro wavered. It was unfair to mistrust Groft simply because the man was a Leithian. Yet he couldn't deny that his most dangerous current enemies were Leithians.

But, if he turned the young man away— if he didn't go with Groft— and any harm came to Nevien as a result... There was really only one acceptable choice. But maybe he could improve things a little.

"My friends are here. Perhaps they could ride with us?"

But Groft immediately shook his head. "I'm sorry, Zirda. I was told to bring only you. She doesn't want to draw attention."

"Oh. I see." Nagaro frowned. "At least I should give them some explanation."

That got a flicker of uncertainty, but it vanished as quickly as it came. "Yes," Groft acknowledged. "Of course you should, Zirda."

A gust of wind chose that moment to whistle down the space between the adjacent barracks buildings, reminding Nagaro that he really shouldn't leave the young Leithian standing outside in the cold while he made his explanations. "You'd better come in then," he said. "You can wait in my sitting room while I talk to them. And I'll want a warmer tirka, and of course my cloak." He stood aside and ushered Groft in, then retreated to the kitchen where Taru and Pavo were in the process of doing the dishes. He closed the door behind him, hoping Groft wouldn't think it rude.

It took only a moment to describe the situation to his friends.

"I don't like it," Taru instantly declared. "I don't trust Leithians. It could be a trap. That ring may be hers, but they could ha' found some way t' get it from her."

"I know." Nagaro sighed. "But I don't see how I can take the chance. What if she really needs me?"

"I think you have to go, Nagaro," Pavo put in. "But I do not like it that you have to go alone."

"I know what you mean, Pavo, but it does make sense that she wouldn't want to attract attention."

"Then let us follow behind ye," Taru suggested. "We can keep back a ways, so that young whip doesn't see us, but still keep ye in sight so we can come t' the rescue if he leads ye into trouble."

Nagaro considered. "I like that, Taru. I like the idea of having you both nearby. And if you keep your hoods up and keep well back, I think it should be all right. On a night like this, no one will think twice about men going about cloaked and hooded."

"Right." Taru rubbed his hands together. "We'll just pretend t' be finishing with the dishes, here, 'til ye and that lad have gone out by the front door. Then we'll slip out by the back."

Nagaro nodded. "And I'll be sure we go straight across the parade ground to the stable, and straight back to the gate, so you can easily keep us in sight. Just try not to look like you're following us."

***

Nevien shivered and pulled her cloak tighter around her shoulders as they rode under the arch of the gate and into the city. She nervously clutched the reins of the black gelding they'd found for her. The beast lacked her mare's spirit, but went willingly in the midst of Brandle's company of un-uniformed guardsmen. This was a good thing since she had decided to wear her black veil under her hood to hide her face. In the dark of a moonless night, the thin fabric made it hard to see clearly where she was going.

A strong blast of wind pressed the hood of her cloak against the side of her face. It was a warm cloak, at least, heavily lined and of a dark blue-gray color. Rianine had leant it to her. The other young woman had also leant her a small dagger, which she now wore strapped at her waist. Remembering it, she fingered the hilt, but her mind slid away from the thought of actually using the thing.

Nevien was glad that Brandle and Merriel had readily accepted the reason she'd given for joining this expedition, despite its possible danger. There was truth in what she'd told them, of course, and they didn't need to know that she couldn't have borne being left behind in the palace to pace the floor, waiting for word of the outcome. Rianine had given her several arch looks while helping her change into her riding clothes, but had refrained from comment. In the end, she had given Nevien a quick, fierce hug and wished her luck.

Nevien was all too afraid she was going to need that luck. Her heart thudded against her ribs as she tried to make out the dim shapes of the other riders. The lighted windows of the buildings they passed were glowing rectangles and the occasional lamps that hung above doors looked like smoky stars through the fabric of her veil. She knew that Delvin was on her right, and the man looming on her left was Brandle. He had stopped long enough to exchange a few words with the guard in the gatehouse and had assured her that the knowledge of their passing would be handled with discretion. Now he was urging them forward at a moderate trot along Market Street. There were still a few townsfolk abroad, and he didn't want to go faster on such a main thoroughfare.

Nevien steered her mount to the left until their stirrups brushed. Leaning towards him, she asked breathlessly, "Is it far to Tanners' Row?"

"A few blocks. We'll be turning south soon and cutting three blocks across to strike the west end of it. Groft 'll be leading him in from the east end, so we can't miss them." He spoke staunchly, even as the wind threatened to carry away his words.

Unless we're too late, she thought, but she didn't want to give power to the words by speaking them aloud. Brandle knew the risk as well as she did. "Why would they pick Tanner's Row?" she asked ."Isn't it all shops selling leather goods?"

"I'll wager they picked it because it runs parallel to Damsel Street— and there's plenty of alleys connecting them."

"Damsel Street? I don't know it."

He laughed harshly. "There's no reason you should, My Lady. It's where the painted ladies ply their trade."

"Oh. You mean the women who sell their favors. But what has that to do with—"

"Isn't it obvious? If they kill him in Tanners' Row and drag the body into Damsel Street, they can take his life and his reputation with one stroke!" Brandle didn't wait for her response to this alarming speculation, but abruptly spurred his horse ahead and raised his voice. "To the right, lads, and pick up the pace! Three blocks to Tanner's Row!"

With a chorus of "Aye, Zirda's," the little company swept around the corner into a narrow side street and sprang into a rapid trot, hooves ringing on the cobblestones.

The wind caught Nevien's hood as she made the turn, flinging it back. She snatched her veil aside so she could see better, and peered tensely ahead into the darkness as she posted to the beat of her horse's hooves. *Three blocks to Tanners' Row!* Her heart was in her throat.

Please, Mother Solbrid, she prayed, *don't let us be too late!*

***

Nagaro caught himself starting to look over his shoulder for the third time and resisted the temptation. The nervous gesture could risk alerting Groft to his disobedience, or it might draw the kind of attention the young Leithian had warned against— though in fact there were few folk abroad in the streets. Those they had passed had all been bundled-up against the bite of the gusting wind, hurrying with their heads down, doubtless anxious to reach the comfort of home and hearth. Lamps burned behind curtained windows, shedding semi-circles of dim light at intervals along the street. The effect only served to emphasize the darkness of the night.

The wind whistled and moaned in the eaves, two stories overhead, or found its way between the closely-spaced walls of the adjacent buildings to blast the travelers with stinging force. High above the rooftops, stars like splinters of ice pricked the ink-black sky.

Groft had offered little information regarding their destination beyond asserting that they were bound in the general direction of the palace and that he'd been told to use back streets to avoid being seen. It was a plausible explanation, but unsettling as well. It seemed the farther they rode, the fewer folk they encountered. Nagaro told himself that this was to be expected considering the advancing hour, but he had an uncomfortable feeling that also had something to do with the district into which he was being led.

The streets had grown narrower, and there were fewer lighted windows. His previous glances behind had given him glimpses of the mounted figures of Taru and Pavo— the one short, hunching forward on a stocky steed, the other sitting tall on a larger beast. He hoped his friends hadn't missed the turning Groft had just made. For his part, he had to confess that he was lost. This part of the city was unfamiliar to him. He had no more than a general impression of the direction in which the palace lay.

At least Groft seemed confident. Nagaro was riding just behind the young Leithian when a sudden gust of wind drove a scattering of dry leaves and bits of refuse out of a side alley and directly across his path, causing Thunder-Heels to snort and shy.

"Easy there, lad." Nagaro patted the stallion's arched neck.

Groft turned about in the saddle and reined in his mount to allow Nagaro to catch up. "It's a strange night," he observed.

Nagaro couldn't read the young man's expression in the dark, but he thought Groft sounded nervous. "Yes, it is," he responded. Then, thinking that a little conversation might be reassuring to them both, he added, "But it's only the wind, and of course the moons have set early."

Groft laughed a little tensely, as he urged his horse forward again. "Yes, the moons have set. My sergeant would say that Naru and Talebra have gone to bed in each other's arms like a soldier and his whore."

"Your sergeant doesn't take the conjunction very seriously then?"

Groft laughed again, more easily this time. "That he doesn't. No more do I. What about you, Captain?"

"Vothra gives us no reason to think the turnings of stars have any influence on men's lives. But one shouldn't joke about things that other men sincerely believe. Such beliefs can be turned to good purposes sometimes. When Kuran asked the Emperor of the Mahuk Baar what *his* people thought of the conjunction, the Emperor said they think it heralds a time of change and that his people are more likely to accept a new idea— such as freeing all the galley slaves— because of it."

Groft shook his hooded head. "I marvel that you could sit and pass the time o' day with a man who had you nearly beaten to death," he said. "I'd have run the bastard through, given the chance!"

Nagaro shrugged and ducked his head against another gust of wind. "Vothra counsels against vengeance," he said. "Wisely in this case, since killing Emperor Baalkir would open the way for his chief rival— a man who prefers to see the galley slaves remain in their chains. Baalkir isn't, in my judgement, a bad man— or a bad ruler for that matter— and it's better to let a man make amends than to kill him."

"Make amends!" Groft snorted. "The Mahuk Emperor?"

"Actually, Baalkir apologized to me for the harsh punishment I received. And he offered me a woman of his house as a wife, to make it up to me."

"Kroneg's Blood!" Groft swore in frank astonishment. "A woman of his house! What did you say?"

"I turned him down— politely, of course. Because my heart lay elsewhere."

Groft turned his face away again, reaching to hold his hood as the wind tried to blow it back. "It must be a fine thing to able to do what you choose," he said with a note of bitterness, "instead of what your elders tell you."

Nagaro wondered whether Groft was expressing dissatisfaction with the Leithian tradition of filial obedience. "I think you always have a choice," he said after a moment. "Although you do have to accept the consequences."

To this Groft made no response. Instead, he glanced about as if trying to assure himself of his bearings, then urged his horse forward to take the lead once more.

Nagaro peered ahead along the dark street, past Groft's mounted figure. He could make out little of what lay before them. Remembering Taru and Pavo, he strained his ears for the sound of two riders somewhere behind in the night, but he could hear nothing above the sound of their own horses' hooves on the cobblestones and the rush of the wind. A surreptitious glance over his shoulder revealed that the street had angled slightly a hundred paces behind them so that his view in that direction would have been limited even without the darkness.

He turned back to face the way they were going and noticed that they were approaching a place where a pair of dark side-alleys opened, one on each side of the narrow street. As Groft's mount came abreast of the one on the left, the young Leithian suddenly emitted a cry and turned his horse sharply towards it. At the same time, the youth spurred the beast so that it leaped towards the alley's entrance.

After that, things happened very fast.

Thinking that Groft had nearly missed a turning, Nagaro reined Thunder-Heels sharply to the left, intending to follow his guide, only to find his way suddenly blocked by two horsemen who emerged from the alley, even as the rump of Groft's horse was disappearing into it. Their cloaks billowing, the two hooded figures brandished drawn swords that caught the lamplight from a curtained upstairs window.

Nagaro hauled on the reins, pulling Thunder-Heels to a plunging halt. "Groft!" he cried, desperately peering past the two riders, trying to make out the retreating form of the young man he'd been following. He caught a glimpse of a pale, round blur that might have been the young Leithian's face, looking back, but there was no answering cry and no evidence that Groft meant to come to his aid.

Nagaro's stomach tightened. His worst fears were proven real. Groft's message was false. *He was betrayed and Taru and Pavo were nowhere to be seen!*

The wind was whistling and the two horsemen were advancing. Nagaro wheeled his horse, intending to flee back along the street to find Taru and Pavo. To his dismay he found three more armed and hooded riders closing on him from behind. The full extent of the trap was now revealed. These men had been hidden in the alley on the other side of the street. The wind had prevented him from hearing their approach, and his own hood had kept him from glimpsing them from the corner of his eye.

With the swiftness of thought, his sword was in his hand. A quick shake of his head dropped his hood so he could see about him more clearly.

One of the men growled, "We're not afraid o' ye! We know who ye are, pirate, and ye'll die like any other man!"

Nagaro didn't waste breath on argument. Keenly aware of his danger, he drove his big gray straight at the speaker— the man who most directly blocked the direction in which he hoped to find his friends. "*Taru!*" he shouted. "*Pavo!*" But the wind whipped his words away. Steel rang as his sword connected with the other man's, but the rider backed and swivelled his mount, preventing full engagement, even as the other four horsemen maneuvered to hem in Thunder-Heels on all sides.

Harsh laughter sounded. "So the mighty captain cries for help? You'll die tonight, pirate— but a sword is too good for you!"

The voice came from behind him and to his left, and it sounded familiar, though he couldn't place it. Ignoring the taunt, Nagaro drove forward again, sword level, trying to push between two of the horses in front of him, to go back along the street in the direction from which he had come. The two horsemen promptly blocked him with their mounts even as they both moved to parry his stroke. Steel rang again. And again, as swords bit, then slid against each other.

"*Keshaal!*" Nagaro swore under his breath as his arm got tangled in his wind-blown cloak, causing an attempted thrust to come up short. Swordsmanship on horseback was always more difficult, and the weather was making it worse! His only consolation was that it was hampering everyone else as well.

It also seemed that the swordsmen in front of him were more intent on preventing his escape than doing him injury. *Well, he wasn't going to let that stop him from drawing their blood.* When the wind dropped momentarily, he made a quick cut that one of the men parried as he'd expected. Then he slipped inside the man's guard with a quick thrust. The man let out a yelp as Nagaro's sword pierced his upper arm just below the shoulder.

"Take him down, Master!" the man cried. "*Hurry!*"

Nagaro applied his heels to the gray stallion's flanks, trying yet again to press past the wounded rider, but he suddenly felt a jerk at his throat as someone grabbed his cloak from behind. Pulled off-balance, he was forced to rein in Thunder-Heels or risk losing his seat. He tried to twist about, swinging his sword wildly, only to realize that the man who had grabbed him must be to his left, not his right.

It was at that moment that there suddenly came shouts from some distance away, seemingly from the direction in which Groft had originally been leading him— though the wind made distance and direction uncertain. Nagaro struggled vainly against the grip on his cloak, twisting his neck to look over his shoulder, trying to turn his horse, trying to see where the shouts were coming from. *Could it be Taru and Pavo? Someone else who might aid him?*

A sudden light spilled into the street from above as a window curtain was drawn back. Some of Nagaro's assailants cried out in dismay, then pressed their horses even closer. There were shouts of, "*Do it! Do it now!*" And whoever it was that had the grip on his cloak gave a yank so vicious that it threatened to strangle him. Swiftly, Nagaro shifted his sword to his left hand and made a desperate slashing swing behind him with the weapon, trying to strike the unseen man who literally had him by the throat. He had the satisfaction of feeling the blade meet resistance and hearing the man swear violently. But the strangle-hold continued.

He was aware of more shouts, sounding closer this time. The horsemen around him were milling, jostling. He thought he heard his name being called by several voices. One was that of a woman. *Nevien, here, after all? No, he surely must be mistaken!*

Then he felt the blow. It struck him in the back, sending fiery pain lancing through him— piercing his chest and transfixing him where he felt sure his heart must be. *Was this how it felt to be run through?*

"*Die, farmer's bastard!*"

The words sounded almost in his ear, yet seemed to be half drowned out by the sudden roaring in his head. Too late, he realized whose voice it was. All around him was chaos and confusion. He felt himself tipping backwards, sideways... slipping from the saddle... *falling...*

The ground leaped up to meet him. There was a blinding flash as his head struck the pavement, followed by oblivion.

Chapter 7

A Hole In His Heart

Dim walls of rough-hewn stone hemmed him on either side. They were closing, closing... the ceiling descending, oppressive as the weight of the world... and the darkness was thick.

"Help me, Vothra!" His breath came with difficulty. There was something on fire in his chest. "Where is it? I can't find it! Vothra, why have you forgotten me?"

Spirit called Nagaro, I am here. What do you seek?

"The door! I have to find the door!"

There is no door here, Nagaro. Be still. Try to breathe slowly.

The corridor he was in ended in a blank wall! He put his hands against it, frantically searching for any chink. Nothing! No way out!

"Where is it? Vothra, help me!"

I am with you, Nagaro. I will not leave you.

"Where is the door!"

The door is not real. It is a construction of your mind. Try to be calm. Turn around now, and you will see me.

Calm? How could he be calm? But he turned... Behind him there was a figure... a shadow-outline, limned with light.

"Vothra? I don't understand. If the door isn't right, then show me the way! I have to find the void. I have to cross over! You promised to guide my spirit!"

You do not need to find the void. You are dreaming, Nagaro. You are not dead.

"But I must be! Or I will be! I've always tried to follow the path. Why won't you help me?" He tried to approach the figure, but it receded, always a few steps out of reach. "Please! Help me! I have to find it!"

Very well. You must be calm, and I will guide you. Let me lay my hand on you.

The figure moved towards him, stretching out a hand to touch his forehead. It was a caress, cool as satin on fevered skin.

Peace, Spirit called Nagaro. Peace.

His terror eased. The fire in his chest receded. He could breathe...

There, now. Is that better?

"Yes... yes... better..."

Come this way. I will show you a beautiful garden.

They moved together then, side by side, along a cool, cloistered walkway. A high, wide arch opened before them into dappled shade. Trellises with flowering vines arched overhead. The air was perfumed with rich, moist earth and growing things. Beyond the shadow of the trellis, where the sunlight fell, a bed of dark pink roses, nearly red as blood...

There. Is this not a fair place? Is it not peaceful here?

"Yes... peaceful..."

But it seemed he was looking for something. What was it? Or who? A name came to him. "Nevien! Where is Nevien? She was in the street— and she needs me. I have to go back to the street! I have to find her!"

Peace, spirit called Nagaro. You will not find her in the street. The message was false. Do you not remember? But perhaps we may find her here, if we look. Will you walk with me to see what we may find together?

"All right... If she's here..." He turned to look at the figure who had been guiding him— and found a woman at his side— a dark-haired woman, all in silver-gray, with an expression that was serene, and wise, and a little sad.

"Maramine?" He was puzzled. "Are you my mother?"

***

One room led to another, white-washed walls, and windows that looked out on different places. One gave a view of a city on a hill, in the distance across green fields. But that wasn't right... not a place he'd ever been, nor one he was going to. Another showed a moonlit forest. But the place he was looking for shouldn't have trees... or moonlight. The window in the next room yielded a view of a garden with sun and shade, as well as flowers. It was hard to walk away from that one because the place spoke of life and of peace. But the life he had left was too complicated, and the only way that led to a new life was through the void.

It must be peaceful in the void, he supposed, but it would be peace of different kind.

He crossed yet another threshold, into yet another room. Here also there was a window and when he drew close enough to look through it, he saw a dark, wind-swept street, lit only by the glow from a curtained second floor window. He drew a breath, stepping closer—

Spirit called Nagaro, what are you doing?

"Vothra?" He stopped, looked around. "Where are you?"

I am here with you. Abruptly the Sign of Vothra appeared in the air next to him, glowing, the circle-within-a-circle-joined. Advancing towards him, stepping through the glowing sign, came the familiar figure of the Benevolent Spirit. Shining with its own light, robed in a garment that could have been either black or silver, with hair, equally ambiguous, falling to its shoulders, the figure came to halt before him. The gentle, midnight eyes regarded him from a face that was neither male nor female and of indeterminate age. The lips moved and the voice that sounded in his mind was soft as a summer breeze, adamant as the stones of the earth. *Now tell me, please, what you are doing.*

"I..." He glanced at the window. The scene beyond it remained unchanged. "I'm looking for the way to cross over. Is this it? Must I return to the place where I was struck down? You... you told me the door was wrong..." He paused, frowning. "Didn't you?"

Not... exactly. And I am surprised that you remember. You have been wandering, Spirit called Nagaro. The healer gave you opa. It is all but impossible to have a meaningful conversation with someone in an opa dream.

"The healer?" He frowned. "What can a healer do for me?"

Very little, as it turns out. Except to try to ease the pain. The rest, it seems, is going to be up to you.

"Oh." He thought he understood. "Then I don't wish to linger— waiting in pain to die. I would rather just go now. You... will help me, won't you?"

This is unnecessary, Spirit called Nagaro. Your wound is not mortal.

"How can that be? Lothard stabbed me in the heart! I felt it! Surely a man can't live with a hole in his heart!"

Surely not. But the knife did not pierce your heart. It was a very narrow blade, passing in and out again at a peculiar angle— just exactly so that it missed everything vital. I could show you, if you like.

"No!" He recoiled. "Please don't!"

Very well. The Sprit seemed to sigh, then continued. *In any case, there was surprisingly little damage. The healing process will take time, of course, but not such a very great deal of time. You will never be exactly as you were before, either— but much more nearly so than one might expect. And there will be pain. Right now I am holding it back, but I cannot do that very much longer.*

"I'm really not going to die? Everything went black and—"

You cracked your head on the stones of the street when you fell. You have been unconscious, and you have been dreaming.

"Dreaming?" He glanced once more in the direction of the window, only to find that both the window and the image of the street beyond it had vanished. There was nothing there but formless, shifting fog.

You will have to rest for quite some time— the Spirit was saying— *and sleep a great deal, which may be difficult because of the pain. The healer will want to give you something, but you should try to be sure it is not opa. Do you understand?*

When he looked again at the figure of Vothra, the Spirit seemed to be studying him.

"Then I... I really must go back?

No, not back. Because you have not left. You are dreaming, even now, as I told you, and soon you will have to wake up. Do you not want to wake up, Spirit called Nagaro?

The dark eyes were studying his soul.

He faltered. "I... no... It's just that I thought I was dead— or at least dying. And I was thinking that perhaps it wasn't so bad..."

Not so bad, because...?

"Because there's nothing left for me to do in the world. The princess wants me to be her friend, but I can't be her friend. I can't court her. I can't even stay in Lankura. Kuran means to send me to Boka Omei, and my friends would have to decide whether to follow me or stay. It would be better for them, I think, to stay. And what is there for me to do in the islands? Baalkir has forbidden his warlords to take our gold or enslave our people. He means to free all the galley slaves in the Mahuk Baar. So the task I set for myself is done."

The Spirit regarded him with a thoughtful air. *Let us suppose, then, that your wound had weakened you enough that you would be able to let go of your life, with my help. Is that what you truly wish to do? Have you considered all sides of this? If you were to die as a result of Lothard's attack, it would be a victory for Lothard. Do you want Lothard to win?*

It seemed the question should have pricked him, but it only made him feel tired.

"I don't care about Lothard."

Really? There was a ripple of laughter, gentle and musical. *You are perhaps the least vengeful person I have ever encountered— or is it that I have breathed peace into you a few times too many? Have you considered the condition of the land of Edrovir? Does it not seem rather precarious?*

"Yes... yes it does... But what can I do about that?"

One never knows. Nothing, certainly, if you are dead. I have said that your life has possibilities. But here, really, is the crux of it: If you die, you will seriously disappoint a number of people who have been at great pains to prevent your death. Are you really prepared to cause so much pain to others?

Here at last was an arrow that struck the mark. He realized belatedly that he didn't know exactly how he had been rescued. Yet he must have been. Lothard would logically have dismounted and made sure of his kill if he'd been allowed to. And it seemed that there *had* been quite a number of people descending upon his attackers, there at the end.

"No," he said, and sighed. "No, I suppose not."

And there is your daughter. She is well cared for and she has a family. But she is very young to lose a father when that father need not be lost.

"Narei? Oh Vothra! I forgot about Narei!" The realization struck him like a blow. "How could I forget my daughter?"

You have been dreaming, Nagaro. You cannot be held responsible for the wayward wanderings of a dream. Your life has been very difficult and complicated of late, therefore the attraction of leaving it. But, what have you decided? Do you wish to try to leave it behind?

"No! I have to stay."

In that case, Spirit that calls itself Nagaro, there is really nothing to do but to open your eyes. Whenever you are ready.

Nagaro groaned. He opened his eyes, focused for a moment, and shut them again. He was lying face down, shirtless by the feel of it, on some sort of bed in a room that had worn wooden panels on the walls, a three-by-five-foot brown rug on the floor, with a pair of spotted cows woven into its design, and a somewhat dented end table of which he could see only a corner.

Of course it had to be face down. He always ended face down.

The pain Vothra had warned him about was a sharp throbbing ache in the center of his chest. By making a concerted effort to distract himself, it was just possible to avoid imagining that the throbbing corresponded to the beating of his heart, and thus avoid the creeping fear that his heart was going to burst.

Shutting his eyes didn't really help since it removed the main source of distractions, so he opened them again. From his position, he couldn't see any source of illumination, but the quality of the light suggested that it came from an oil lamp. Or possibly from a window with drawn curtains of a yellowish color? He attempted to raise himself a little so that he could turn his head to look around, and immediately let out a gasp as a much sharper pain lanced through him.

"Keshaal!" He swore, and discovered that the breath he drew to produce the word caused another stab of pain. He clamped his teeth tight shut, breathing fast and shallow.

"Nagaro?" The voice came from somewhere in the direction of his feet and was followed immediately by approaching footsteps. A moment later, Taru's anxious face was suddenly thrust into his view, held at an odd angle as the young Turo bent over him.

"Taru?" He managed the word painfully. "Where... is... this?" He had to breathe between each word, and it hurt.

"*Hamanei mata noa!*" Taru fervently invoked the World Spirits. "Ye're finally talking sense!" He sat down cross-legged on the floor, which brought them more or less eye to eye. "This is Tor Papano's house. They attacked ye right in front of it. He makes shoes and boots, and sells them in his shop at the front. Hats, too, I guess."

Nagaro rolled his eyes, ruefully wondering what this Tor Papano thought of seeing him fallen so low. He tried another question.

"What... hap...n'd..?"

"*Ai, Nagaro!*" Taru's eagerness instantly turned to mortification. "We lost ye in the wind and the dark, Pavo an' me! That slinkin' little Leithian took a turn we didn't see. We ended in Damsel Street— that's the next one over— and we couldn't tell if ye were somewhere up ahead of us or not! If one o' the bodjering bastards hadn't come shooting out o' the alley right in front of us, makin' his getaway, we'd never ha' found ye. And when I saw ye lying there in the street with Thunder-Heels standin' over ye like a bitch over her pup— I tell ye, Nagaro, I've never had a worse moment in my life! If I'd remembered that ye had the life stone, I'd ha' known better o' course, but I didn't *think* of it! I thought ye were dead for sure— that we'd gone and failed ye when ye were counting on us!"

Nagaro tried to shake his head. "My...fault. Shouldn't 've... gone..."

"No, no!" Taru waved his hands to indicate that Nagaro should lie still. "It was *me*— hangin' back too far! That, and the cursed wind! I couldn't hear a thing! It must ha' dropped just about the time ye went down, and that was some help, 'cause we could hear all the hollerin'. But when I saw ye lyin' there, I just froze up! It was Pavo, and the princess, that found ye were still breathing."

The princess! Oh Vothra... He hadn't imagined it!

"She... was... *there?*"

"Aye. She came with Brandle and his troop o' guardsmen— but o' course ye missed all o' that. I got the tale from Delvin— how he heard Groft plottin' with some red-haired fellow that Brandle didn't trust. Delvin told Brandle, and Brandle told the princess, and they all came out t' see if they could save ye. And since they chased the bloody bastards off, I guess ye could say they did."

"They... catch...?"

"Did they catch any o' them? No. Brandle an' his lot tried, but I didn't see any o' that 'cause the princess sent me for the healer. She lent me her horse for the healer to ride, and off I went with Tor Papano— on account of he knew the way— up behind me an' hangin' on for dear life!"

"Which... healer?" *It couldn't be Tred. Tred knew better than to use opa.*

"It's Master Ambras. The one they used for the queen, ye remember? The princess put her veil down when Tor Papano came out wi' the lantern. She was tryin' not to let on who she was, and Pavo and I played along— even with Master Ambras. She's seein' that ye get the very best doctoring there is, Nagaro. She's paid his fee in advance an' everything!"

"*Bishka!*" He swore aloud, and immediately regretted it as pain stabbed through him. He shut his eyes.

He had set out, thinking Nevien might be in trouble, and she'd had to rescue him! His folly had nearly gotten him killed— had caused her no end of worry— and she was paying the healer! Could things possibly get any worse?

"Nagaro? Are ye all right?" Taru sounded half-panicked.

He forced his eyes open again. "Hurts," he gasped. "That's... all." It was too complicated to try to explain. Too many words.

"I'll fetch the healer!"

Taru was gone before Nagaro could protest. He closed his eyes to wait... and in spite of the pain, he drifted.

***

Someone was holding his left arm. Fingers were probing along the skin just below the elbow.

"No!" He jerked his arm violently away, flexing it. Pain shot through his chest, but he didn't care. "*Not... the... thorn!*" His eyes snapped open to reveal Master Ambras, seated on a stool at his bedside.

The dapper, graying Kelorin looked taken aback. "You'll scarcely feel it, I assure you," he said. "I can see that you've had the bladder-thorn dozens of times, and compared with the other pain you're feeling, this will be quite minimal." He reached out to try to take Nagaro's arm once again.

Nagaro hugged the arm against his body. "No!" he said. "No... opa!"

"Are you sure, Captain? Vothra came to me last night and explained that I shouldn't give you opa— for a while, at least— because the Spirit wished to speak to you. But I can see that you're suffering."

Nagaro *was* suffering. His wound was throbbing violently and he seemed to be having trouble getting enough air. He drew a sharply painful breath, clenched his teeth, and spoke through them. "Some-thing... else..." he said. "Drink."

Master Ambras pursed his lips. "You'll have to be turned onto your side to drink. I'll have to get someone to help— and it will surely make the pain worse."

"*Drink!*"

"Oh, very well."

The healer stood up and moved out of Nagaro's field of view.

Nagaro focused on a knothole in the wood paneling of the wall opposite his bed and tried to control his breathing, tried to calm himself. He remembered the litany for pain: *All pain ends, if only in death... and death is not an end, but a new beginning.* The difficulty was that the litany was meant to go with long slow breaths, but long slow breaths hurt much worse than short fast ones.

...not an end... not an end... a new beginning...

After an agonizing time, Master Ambras came back with a cup— and with Taru at his heals. The young Turo helped roll Nagaro onto his side and steady him. There was some sort of plaster on his back that Taru was holding in place. It was all Nagaro could do not to cry out during the process of being moved. Once on his side, however, he was able, awkwardly, to drink the liquid from the cup. Master Ambras brought him water to drink, as well, before directing that he be laid prone once more. Then the healer went out again, leaving Taru to sit with his patient while waiting for the drug to take effect.

Nagaro found he could be calmer once he knew that relief was coming. As he lay there, breathing carefully and waiting for drugged oblivion, he recalled that the healer had said that Vothra had appeared to him "last night." Had that been the night of the attack? Or the night after it? He made the effort to ask Taru.

"How... long?"

"How long have ye been here?" Taru waited for him to nod. "It's been two days, Nagaro. That is, it's nearly the end o' the second one. The sun's just setting outside."

"You've... been... here?"

"The whole time? Aye. Well, me or Pavo."

"Kuran... let... you?"

Taru snorted. "Kuran was here himself— twice. Once each day. But the whole first day ye were as still as death, and today ye were... wandering. From the opa."

Inwardly Nagaro groaned. *It wasn't only Nevien. He was worrying Kuran, his commander... his Wared Lord. This just got worse and worse!* And now he was going to lose consciousness again. Already the drug was beginning to make his head swim. His eyelids were heavy. *At least he wouldn't have to think about any of it for a while. He could relax. The mattress pillowed his head... cradled him. He couldn't even feel his ring—*

His ring!

With a jerk of panic that brought his eyes fully open, he realized that he couldn't feel it *because it wasn't there!* It should have been dangling— getting in the way— when Taru rolled him onto his side!

"My... rinng..." The drug was making his tongue thick. Making him slow. "*Wh-where's...it..?*"

Taru's face, swimming in his vision, looked troubled. "I don't know, Nagaro." The words seemed to come from far away. "Now that ye mention it, I haven't seen it. But I'll be sure t' look—"

"Have t'...fin'... "

The room was turning around him in a slow, leisurely spin. He tried to get his hands on the mattress... to raise himself... but his body didn't seem to move properly. Everything was going from gray to black and he was falling...

***

He lay, dully staring at the rug with the cows woven into it.

He was having a little better luck with breathing carefully, treading a line between sharper pain on the one hand and panic on the other. Pain of one sort or another was a constant feature of his life whenever he was conscious. Consciousness came and went, of its own accord. And if he really needed to be unconscious, there was the dedrel.

Not that any of it mattered.

His ring was gone. He'd lost his precious keepsake that he'd kept safe through so many adventures. If only he had thought to tie it around his waist before leaving his quarters that night... an age and a half ago—

With a mental wrench, he dragged his attention away from pointless recrimination and back to the pair of cows. The rug's maker had executed them so that each one, viewed from its end of the rug, appeared to be walking from left to right, while the one at the farther end of the rug was upside-down and facing from right to left. They had exactly the same pattern of spots. Were they intended in some way to be the same cow?

It was Pavo who had told him about how they'd cut the tirka and shirt off of him while he was still lying in the street. Pavo and Nevien had been working together, frantic to discover where he was wounded. There hadn't been much light. And Pavo hadn't seen the ring. Neither had the healer who had arrived a little later to take over Nagaro's care.

He had everything that had been in his pockets— his purse, the Turowan life stone. Nevien's opal ring had been there, but she had reclaimed it, according to Pavo.

Taru and Pavo had searched the street by daylight, moving discreetly so as not to draw the attention of the gawkers and well-wishers who gathered outside the house on a daily basis ever since it had become known that Captain Nagaro was lying wounded inside. But their efforts had been to no avail, and Nagaro had been adamant that there must be no general announcement of his loss. Someone might well have found the ring and kept it, not knowing its origin, but to advertise for its return would mean providing a description of a thing that could be linked to Leyel Virden.

Nagaro's contemplation of the bovine-bedecked floor covering was interrupted by the sound of voices coming from outside his room, presumably from what he understood to be a hallway, or possibly from the sitting room where Master Ambras had set up shop and where Nagaro's friends retreated when they felt he needed to sleep. He made out the voice of Master Ambras, and— *Oh Vothra!* It was Kuran.

Nagaro considered pretending to be asleep, but he didn't have time to properly compose his features before the sound of booted footsteps told him that Kuran was already in the room.

The Lord of the Fleet presently entered his field of view, carrying the stool, which he sat down on directly in front of Nagaro. Kuran's small stature meant that the older man didn't have to bend over very far to look directly into Nagaro's face. The sharp black eyes studied him.

"Ah," he said at last. "You're awake." He leaned forward a little farther to place a hand on Nagaro's shoulder. "First I must tell you, Nagaro, how glad I am that those brigands didn't succeed in killing you." There was a pause, then, "You do understand that this was no chance encounter— no opportunistic attack? That this was a plot specifically to murder you?"

Nagaro nodded, saving his breath for a question that required a verbal answer.

Kuran considered him. "Why did you go, Nagaro? Why in Vothra's name did you take the risk of trusting yourself to a Leithian you scarcely knew? Even with Taru and Pavo following you, it was terribly dangerous. Did you really think it likely the princess would send for you in such a way if she were in some kind of trouble?"

Unable to avoid Kuran's gaze in any other way, Nagaro shut his eyes. He shook his head.

"Then *why?*"

Nagaro drew a painful breath. He could scarcely have felt more mortified by the question. *Wasn't it obvious that he'd ridden out with his heart on his sleeve?*

"Couldn't... take... chance..." he managed.

"That it was real?" There was a little pause, then, "No, of course you couldn't— even if it was unlikely. I'm sorry I asked."

The words were spoken gently and the hand on Nagaro's shoulder gave him an understanding squeeze. He felt a surge of gratitude and re-opened his eyes.

Kuran withdrew his hand and leaned closer. "Do you know who they were?" he asked. "Or who sent them?"

Nagaro drew a painful breath and answered with one word.

"Loth-ard."

The black eyes narrowed. "How do you know? Did one of them mention his name?"

Nagaro shook his head. "His... hand..."

"He stabbed you *himself?*" Kuran sounded astonished. "Did you *see* him?"

Again Nagaro shook his head. "Behind me. His...voice... Called... me... farmer's... bastard." The unprecedented number of words exhausted him, and he finished with a gasp and a wince of pain.

"*By the Eyes and Ears!*"

Kuran was on his feet in an explosion of fury that set the stool tottering. "By the Blessed Spirit's benevolent backside! That *bastard!* With all his talk of honor, and after I'd just taken you into my House to protect you! He stabs you in the back with his own bloody hand! That *bloody, bodjering, cowardly bastard!*"

The Lord of the Fleet went on for the better part of a minute before having vented enough of his ire to be able to master himself. He sat down again and passed a hand over his eyes. "Is there anything else you can tell me?" he asked wearily.

"Cut... him. I think..." Nagaro made a gesture with his left arm to show how he had struck the blow, and was rewarded with a stab of pain.

"Did you, lad?" Kuran's eyes glittered. "Striking blind? Behind you?"

Nagaro nodded. "Cut.. another. Right... arm." Weakly he flexed an elbow to illustrate, touching his own shoulder.

"Good for you!" Kuran reached out and gave Nagaro's arm another squeeze. "Don't you worry, now," he went on. "I have guards on this house— front and rear. Day and night. That vile toad won't get a second chance at you! And as soon as you can travel by coach, I'm moving you to my Hall in Kel Wared. Then, when you've got your strength back, I'll give you a safe posting in the islands." He frowned. "Elgurn is dragging his feet for some reason about the command at Boka Omei. He says he and the Council consider you too useful here—"

Kuran broke off as if a thought had struck him. He smote his thigh with his fist.

"I swear! If they think they can use you as a distraction to draw Lothard away from Nevien's suitors, I'll... I'll... Well, *I won't have it!* I'll post you to Long Harbor in Geldoran's place. I don't need anyone's bloody permission to do that!"

Nagaro winced at the older man's wrath. Was this what it was like to have a father? Someone who would go to any lengths to protect the life and reputation of his son? The depth of Kuran's concern did warm him, but at that moment recovery seemed an age away and the future entirely unimportant in any case. What did it matter where he went? Where he was posted? *He would see no more of Nevien... and he had lost his ring...*

Kuran was speaking again.

"—both of the known conspirators have disappeared. When Groft left you in the street, he must have just kept going. Murlak— the big red-haired fellow— stopped by his barracks to collect his things and gave some excuse about being called home unexpectedly." Kuran paused. "Now that I think of it, they told Brandle the man had a bulge— like a bandage— on one arm under his shirt. I'll wager that was your handiwork. I'll have to tell Brandle that you cut the man. He'll be glad of it. He's been hard on himself for not moving faster that night. He says if he hadn't stopped to tell Nevien about it—"

"Nevien!"

Nagaro had been only half listening. Kuran's voice seemed to be fading. Perhaps he was beginning to drift again, as he did sometimes due to the blow on his head. But the sound of the princess's name made him realize there was something he wanted to say.

Kuran stopped dead. "What about Nevien?" The older man bent over him. "What is it, lad?"

"Tell... her... I'm... sorry."

"Sorry?" Kuran sounded genuinely puzzled. "Sorry for what, Nagaro? Sorry you nearly got killed?"

Blearily, Nagaro managed to nod. "Sorry... to... worry... her."

"What, *that?*" Kuran shook his head in exasperation. "She doesn't need to hear that from you. Officially she was never here, and she can't show any special interest. But I'll tell her if I get the chance." A pause, then, "I'll leave you now. You need to rest."

***

The room was dim. It must be evening. Not that he could tell by the light. As he understood it, the room's only window— which he couldn't see from where he lay— was shuttered. Master Ambras believed bright light was bad for his patient. The light, therefore, came from a lamp, which the healer turned up when he needed to see, and down when he thought Nagaro should be sleeping. Right now it was turned down.

The real clue was that Pavo had just fed him soup and porridge. Porridge alone would have been breakfast. Soup alone was his midday meal. Soup and porridge together was dinner. He sighed. Such was the dreary rhythm of his days. At least it had been Pavo who had fed him. Being spoon-fed was an indignity made slightly more bearable by the Hashtep's sympathy and unfailing patience. Unlike Taru, Pavo never hurried him, never fussed over spills, and would never have dreamed of laughing at him no matter how ridiculous he looked.

He sighed again and tried to shift his position, groaning involuntarily at the pain. Immediately, he heard Pavo's step approaching. He could now tell his most frequent visitors apart by the sound of their tread. A moment later, Pavo was bending over him.

"Do you have pain, Nagaro?" the big man inquired solicitously. "Shall I tell Master Ambras to bring you cup?"

"No." Nagaro shook his head for emphasis. He was trying to do without the dedrel. He hated the groggy feeling that persisted for an hour after it wore off. Since Pavo was there, he added, "Help... me... move."

It was a familiar request. Pavo gently lifted him and helped him to swing his arms some, before resettling him on the mattress.

Pavo considered him with his narrow dark eyes. "Master Ambras say tomorrow he wants you to sit up for little while. He wants to get bandage whole way around your chest. But you must not lean your back on anything."

Nagaro rolled his eyes, but nodded. A different position would be welcome, but he knew the process would be painful.

Pavo stood up. "I must go back to Fleet Compound now." He moved away, but paused before leaving the room long enough to say, "Do not worry, Nagaro. This is not end of story."

Nagaro lay staring at the rug. *Not the end? No it was never the end... until you died. And even then, the story went on without you...*

***

Something had awakened him.

There were people moving in the other room. A mutter of voices— one he wasn't used to hearing, speaking too low for him to catch the words. Ambras' voice rising above it, sounded querulous.

"—so late, My Lord! Must you disturb him now?"

The answer must have been affirmative, because footsteps approached and entered the room. Unfamiliar footsteps.

The lamp was turned up, just a little, and a cloaked figure approached the bed.

"Captain? Are you awake? Can you hear me?"

Nagaro drew a painful breath. "Yes."

He was trying to place the voice, but a moment later the figure bent to take a seat on the stool and he caught a glimpse of the face. He sucked in his breath. *It was Lord Anduar!*

The tall Pact Signer appeared to reconsider his choice of seat. He rose, set the stool aside, and re-seated himself, this time cross-legged on the floor. Nagaro permitted himself a flicker of a smile. There was no way for the man to lounge in his habitual fashion while keeping Nagaro's face in view. Anduar, however, did not appear discomfitted.

"I must say, Captain, that your *durability* continues to amaze me," the Pact Signer said in a conversational tone. "According to Kuran's report, you have survived an assassination attempt by the hand of no less an assailant than Lothard Hurn. Master Ambras swears that Vothra has revealed to him how the blade pierced your chest nearly through-and-through, while contriving to miss heart, lungs, spine, and assorted other essential structures. He calls it a miracle. I prefer to think that Lokundas saw the opportunity for a better joke— one at Lothard's expense."

Anduar paused to shift his position, then continued.

"To top it off, your popularity among the common folk is completely undiminished. Did you know that the latest rumor has it that you were struck in the heart but didn't die— proving that you can't be slain by treachery? That's a trick I'd like to master."

Nagaro had heard nothing of the kind, and the unwelcome news elicited a heartfelt groan.

Anduar leaned towards him, perhaps misinterpreting. "Are you all right, Captain? I've neglected to ask how you're feeling."

Nagaro curbed his annoyance and answered with a single word. "Mor-tal."

"Ah." Anduar emitted a brief chuckle. "That's rather good. Are you in very much pain?"

"Hurts... to... breathe."

"And therefore to talk. I thought you were unusually reticent, and I do beg your pardon. I'll come to the point: I've a proposition for you."

Nagaro stiffened. He hadn't thought about Nevien's note in days, and he certainly hadn't expected to be approached *now...* in his current condition.

"It's a simple matter, really: How would you like to marry the princess?"

Whatever response Anduar might have anticipated, he clearly didn't expect the one that he got. Nagaro laughed. It was a brief, bitter sound, cut short by the series of stabbing pains that resulted from the jerking movements of his rib cage.

Anduar sat up straighter in his turn. "Will you explain what is amusing?"

"No." Nagaro managed a small shake of his head.

He had been struck by the irony of having this man ask the same question—in almost the same words—that Elgurn had asked him nearly ten years before. *The question that had been the beginning of all his troubles.*

"You think, perhaps, that I am jesting?" The Pact Signer's expression couldn't be read in the dim light, but his voice carried more than a trace of pique.

Again Nagaro shook his head. "*No,*" he gasped. He didn't imagine that Anduar would make so crass a joke, but he distrusted the Pact Signer's motives. And the man was not in possession of all of the facts. He drew another painful breath and tried to explain. "It's... impos-si...ble."

"Impossible? Not at all." Anduar's suaveness had returned. "Your adoption into the House of Kel makes it possible, in principle, for you to court her without actually needing permission. The marriage would require her father's consent, it's true, but that can be arranged." He paused. "I won't deceive you, Captain. I'm not officially offering you the crown. Life is uncertain. You understand."

Nagaro was mildly stunned to hear Anduar speak of the crown, though he wasn't unduly impressed. He didn't trust the cynical, manipulative lord. Regardless, this must be the proposition that Nevien had referred to in her note— the one she wanted no part of— and it was one he couldn't agree to for his own reasons. Fortunately, Kuran had explained to him why it wouldn't work. Once again he shook his head.

"Don't... know... my... parents."

"Who they were," Anduar conceded. "That may be an impediment in some quarters, but the beauty of not *knowing* who they were is that they *could* have been almost anyone. Now, wait!" The Pact Signer raised a hand in response to Nagaro's groan of protest. "I am aware of your aversion to untruths, Captain. But there is no need to invent lies where you are concerned. Folk seem to invent whatever tale suits them, and then persist in believing it regardless of all efforts to set them straight—"

Nagaro wanted none of this. "*Not... pos-si-ble!*" he croaked.

"You don't believe I could make you king?"

"*No!*"

"I assure you that there is little I cannot do when I put my mind to it."

Nagaro had meant the negative as a rejection, not a denial. He shook his head still more emphatically. "Don't... *want...* it!"

"But surely for the good of Edrovir—"

"*I... said... NO!*"

The combination of effort and agitation made Nagaro draw a deeper breath than he intended and something seemed to catch in his throat, triggering a spasm of coughing that wracked him with repeated lancing stabs of pain. The ensuing struggle for control left him spent and gasping. He lay with his eyes closed, trying to shut out everything but the deliberate in-and-out of his breath.

He heard Anduar's voice say, "I am sorry, Captain, I didn't mean—"

"Go. *Away.*" Nagaro hadn't even opened his eyes. The two words required concentration and control to avoid re-triggering the cough. After a moment's pause, he added, "Please," because it bothered him to appear impolite, even in such circumstances.

For the space of three heartbeats, Anduar was silent. Then he sighed, and Nagaro heard the rustle of his clothing as he stood up. "I see that I've erred by approaching you so soon," the Kelorin lord said easily. "I've caught you at a nadir of body and spirit. You've taken a grievous blow, and are suffering more than I realized, and this understandably casts a pall upon all prospects. We'll speak again when you're feeling better."

Nagaro didn't bother to respond. He couldn't, just then, imagine feeling better— nor that it would make any difference. But argument cost too much. It was enough that his guest was going to depart. He risked opening his eyes for the reassurance of watching the man leave.

Anduar was standing, looking down at him. He couldn't read the man's expression.

The Pact Signer stepped away from the bed. "It's a pity you're about to miss the celebration of the Festival of the Harvest Moon," he said conversationally. "And it is surely depressing to have to spend the holiday in this dismal place. I'll have the palace kitchens make up a basket of choice morsels and deliver it. Perhaps it will cheer you."

Without more ado, the man was gone, leaving Nagaro alone with the prancing cows on the carpet and the descending spiral of his thoughts.

What could it possibly matter if he missed what had been his favorite festival? He hadn't the slightest interest in cheese carved into the shapes of animals, or flowers made out of candied fruit.

He'd said no to Anduar's proposition. He'd done what Nevien wanted. Of course, he'd had no other choice. *You think you can do anything, Lord Anduar? But can you change the past? Can you wipe away the tracks of memory? Or cause a heart to love?*

In spite of knowing that he had no choice, it still hurt that Nevien wanted no part of marrying him. She liked him as a friend— assuming she still wanted to keep him as one after he'd made such a fool of himself— but she didn't fancy him as a husband.

His heart might have escaped the dagger's blade, but there was a hole in it all the same.

Chapter 8

A Discovery

"**N**agaro—!"

Nevien's eyes jerked open, and she felt an immediate flood of relief to find herself staring up at the wooden panels of her bed canopy. The designs carved into them gleamed softly in the reflected glow of the morning sunlight that was streaming through her bedroom windows.

It had been a dream—just a dream. About the night in Tanners' Row.

She gave silent thanks to Mother Solbrid. Then she threw off the tangled covers and pushed herself up into a sitting position, propping her back against the headboard and hitching the pillow up for padding. She drew up her knees and sat quietly inhaling the morning's peace and trying to shake off the memory of the dream.

It wasn't the first time that she had dreamed about that night in the weeks since Nagaro had been attacked. Nor had all of the dreams been bad. There was the one in which Nagaro had opened his eyes and sat up and taken her in his arms, and—

Stop it! She chastised herself. He wasn't for her. He could never be for her.

She knew that, but she would never forget the terrifying thrill of that mad gallop down Tanners' Row. The knot of mounted figures milling in the street ahead of her, revealed suddenly by light from a second floor window when its curtain was drawn back... The way the wind had suddenly dropped—as if the night had drawn its breath... The flash of the knife... that swift, cruel stabbing motion—

And then the hooded riders had scattered in all directions.

She had been swinging down from the saddle even as her horse's hooves were skidding to a halt on the cobblestones. And Nagaro's eyes had been closed, not open in the blind stare of death as in some of her dreams. But they had remained closed when she'd shaken him and called his name—and when she'd fumbled with his wrist, feeling desperately for a pulse that had eluded her. They had still been closed as she had leaned over him, her cheek held close to his parted lips, and felt— *Oh praise the Gods!* —the soft, warm puff of his breath.

He was going to be all right, she reminded herself. The most recent report from the healer had said that he was recovering as fast as might be expected.

She frowned. She had at first arranged with Master Ambras to send her daily reports, but the Council had found out and had preempted it. All messages now went directly to the king, which meant that she had to rely on the reports her father gave to the Council— unless she wanted to risk revealing the depth of her interest by probing her father for news in private. And if anything really important were to happen, she was likely to learn of it only *after* it had reached the ears of Lord Anduar— who, of course, would twist it to his own ends.

Nevien's frown deepened. Anduar's ends seemed to consist mainly of promoting the notion that Captain Nagaro shouldn't be considered "out of the game" —as Pendrik had succinctly put it on the morning after the assassination attempt.

There had been talk among the Council members regarding whether Nagaro would be crippled— unable to fight with the speed and skill he had formerly shown, or even whether he might be so broken in body or spirit that he would never wield a sword again.

All of this, Anduar had assured them, was mere speculation, even after the oddly cautious report he had given following his interview with the captain. The usually smooth and confident Kelorin lord had returned from his nocturnal visit to the wounded man to speak in carefully worded phrases. The captain was "experiencing significant pain." He was "understandably in a low mood", which made him "unnecessarily pessimistic." But there was no reason why the Council should be.

Nevien had been so troubled by Anduar's words that she had solicited a report directly from Kuran. After some delay, the Lord of the Fleet had responded to her written inquiry with a brief letter acknowledging that Nagaro had passed through a dark time that had been at its worst around the Festival of the Harvest Moon. But he was doing better, now that he could get up and move about a little. Nevien found this reassuring. Surely being confined to one's bed for weeks with a painful injury was enough to make anyone depressed.

And of course there was no telling what Anduar might have said to him...

That thought made Nevien squirm. She was beginning almost to hate Anduar— the cold-blooded schemer! Wasn't it enough that Nagaro had nearly been treacherously murdered by Lothard— that the poor man was wounded and would take months to recover? But no, Anduar was still plotting how to use his favorite pawn. Perhaps he would persuade

Nagaro to bring a charge against Lothard— a charge of attempted murder, which everyone agreed could not be proven. It would be Nagaro's word against Lothard's, after all. No, it couldn't be proven, but it would likely precipitate a challenge from Lothard, and *then*—

Sweet Lissafel!

Nevien's outraged energy bounced her out of bed and sent her marching across the floor to her dressing table. Once there, she found her hairbrush and began vigorously tugging tangles out of her hair while her thoughts continued to run.

Anduar was determined to find some way to get his challenge bout. He would not be satisfied unless he could pit these two consummate swordsmen against one another, like a pair of fighting cockerels! Fortunately, Kuran was planning to move Nagaro to Kel Wared. He had said so in his letter to her. In fact, the move was planned for the end of the week.

Nevien's hand wielding the hairbrush slowed as she smiled in grim satisfaction. That should put Nagaro out of Anduar's reach! She made a few final smoothing strokes with the brush and put it away. But then her smile faded. The letter had also said that Kuran meant to post Nagaro to some place in the islands as soon as he had recovered enough to resume his duties. Somewhere far away from Lankura... *Far away from her...*

She pushed the unworthy thought firmly aside as she rose and went to make the bed, laying the pillow flat again and pulling the covers smooth. *He would be going somewhere safe... and that was for the best.*

Having finished with the bed, she padded barefoot across the floor to one of her wardrobes, opened the door, and contemplated her assortment of gowns with supreme disinterest. She couldn't think of anything less important than what she was going to wear. The day promised to be extremely dull, containing nothing but routine interactions with her female companions. Nor was there anything to look forward to in the days ahead. She supposed she ought to schedule an outing to River House, but her heart wasn't in it. *Without Nagaro, it would be as bad as the Festival of the Harvest Moon...*

Well, no, she corrected herself. Not as bad as that.

The recent festival had been a nearly complete disaster. Nagaro hadn't been there, of course, and neither had Kuran— her best potential ally in the bid to keep Nagaro from coming to harm. The Lord of the Fleet had pleaded a pressing need to catch up on his paperwork. Rianine— that bastion of cynical good sense— hadn't been there either, having just left on an extended visit to her home in Irvenen Wared.

The match table had been quite decimated, in fact. Alisset was still being kept sequestered by her male relatives. Kendira had refused to attend, being still in the throws of grief and remorse over Groft's betrayal and her unwitting part in it. And the new girl, Lissel, had spent most of the evening upstairs comforting Kendira. These absences had left several young men un-partnered for the evening— including poor love-lorn Geivian whom Nevien had placed at the match table in hopes that he might provide Kendira some consolation.

Nevien shook her head as she distractedly pushed a dress hanger along the wardrobe's clothes rod. The Festival had also marked the resumption of her courtship by her remaining suitors. That hadn't gone well either.

Young Nile had danced one dance with her, during which he had been constantly looking over his shoulder and had managed to trip over his own feet as well as hers. At the end of it, he had fled when it appeared that Lothard was coming in their direction. Devral had intercepted her before Lothard could actually close the distance and had attempted to dance the Balandir with her despite his game leg. Nevien's efforts to avoid making the old warrior look too excessively ridiculous had taxed her skills to the utmost. By the time that dance was over, she had wanted nothing but to escape to the dubious refuge of the match table.

But Lothard had pounced, captured her arm in a vice-like grip, and insisted on being her escort for the judging of the Towers of Plenty. The big Leithian had proceeded to steer her from one towering vegetable construction to the next with excruciating slowness, pausing, ostensibly to admire each extravagant edifice, while keeping up a constant stream of self-aggrandizing banter that had nearly turned her stomach. It had taken her a while to realize that Lothard was favoring his right leg, and the reason why he'd been so slow in approaching her on the dance floor was suddenly blindingly obvious.

Nagaro had wounded his assailant and the man was trying to conceal the fact!

Nevien paused with her hand on a dress hanger to smile fleetingly at the memory of that realization. She'd been unable to resist inquiring innocently whether Lothard had suffered some injury, and had gotten the satisfaction of reading annoyance in his face, until he had laughed and dismissed his stiffness as due to a hunting accident.

She had then asked sweetly whether some beast had turned on him. It must have been a brave beast, she'd suggested, to attack a man so large and strong and skilled as Lothard. She had hoped to gall him, and perhaps she had— for a moment. Then he had laughed again, derisively. "Not brave, just desperate," he'd said. "Fear will make any beast turn when it sees its end is near." "Did you kill it, then?" she'd asked, and had been answered by a very nasty sneer and the words, "Let's just say that's one buck that won't be thinking he's master of the woods. I'll wager he knows who his real master is now!"

Nevien's hand jerked angrily at a hanger. She would have liked to have told Lothard what she thought of him, but of course she'd had to curb her tongue so Lothard wouldn't guess that her remarks were less innocent than they appeared.

Nevien's thoughts came to a guilty halt as she realized that she had come to the end of the array of gowns without having actually considered any of them.

Her hand was on the hanger of the last gown, the dark brown one at the end next to her riding clothes. She rarely wore it, not really caring for the somber color. Now she shrugged. It was as good a choice as any. She took the gown out of the wardrobe and laid it on the bed. It did have some rather nice green and gold embroidery on the bodice that contrasted prettily with the dark background.

With a sigh, she pulled off her nightdress and donned a clean shift, then pulled the brown dress over her head and wiggled into it. She found a pair of brown stockings and pulled them on, then turned back to the wardrobe to find the shoes that matched the gown. They were there— dark brown leather with green and gold stitching— pushed towards the back of the wardrobe because she wore them so infrequently.

In bending down to pick up the shoes, she noticed what looked like a piece of string sticking out of one of them. She reached down to pluck it away, and was surprised to find that it offered some resistance. She picked up the shoe and straightened, finally upending the shoe and shaking it.

The string fell into her hand— together with a heavy bronze ring that was threaded onto it.

Nevien stared. She remembered, now, that a small, hard object on a piece of string had fallen into her hand while she and the Hashtep, Pavo, had been frantically cutting their way through Nagaro's shirt. She'd been working with the little knife Rianine had lent her, and supposed that she must have accidentally cut the string. Being desperate to find out where the captain was hurt, and how badly, and thinking only to prevent the object from being lost, she had thrust it into the bodice of her shilka— and had completely forgotten about it until this very moment!

With a guilty pang, she turned towards the window to get a better look at the ring.

How the thing had come to be in one of her shoes wasn't hard to understand. She had returned to her chamber very late on that terrible night, physically exhausted and emotionally drained. Wanting nothing more than to fall into bed and surrender herself to slumber, she had undressed hurriedly by the light of a candle and numbly hung her riding clothes on a hanger without even considering whether they needed to be washed. The ring on its bit of severed string must have been caught inside the shilka as she had pulled it over her head and only fallen out after she'd hung the garment in the wardrobe.

More difficult to explain— and to excuse— was how she could have forgotten about it so completely for so long. *The poor man must imagine the thing was lost forever by now.* Nevien shook her head at herself as she turned the ring over in her hands, turning the cut face of it up to the light—

And she froze.

This ring! She had seen it somewhere before—

With a lurch, her perception of a portion of the world rearranged itself as she remembered *when* she had seen it, and *where.*

***

Kuran had been keeping his distance from the palace as a matter principle since Nagaro had told him of Lord Anduar's nocturnal visit. He didn't know exactly what Anduar was playing at, but the fact that he knew roughly what had passed between the two men that night made things a trifle awkward for Kuran as both Nagaro's wared lord and Lord of the Royal Fleet.

Nevertheless, he came as quickly as he could in response to the terse message he received from Nevien, delivered directly to his quarters. The wording— *"Come at once. I must speak with you"* —seemed too urgent an imperative to ignore. Since the matter of the mysterious "proposition" had presumably been dealt with, this must be something new.

The guard on duty at the top of the stairs directed him to the small blue-and-green sitting room not far from the royal chambers. In answer to his knock, Nevien ushered him in without a word and closed the door behind them.

"What is this all about, My Lady?" he inquired as he dropped unbidden onto a padded armchair. Such was his standing in the royal household that there was no need for formality, just as the guard had accepted that there was no need for a chaperon.

To his surprise, Nevien didn't seat herself on the small couch that faced his chair across the low table in the center of the floor. Instead, she continued to stand, facing him across the table. Her face wore a frown and her posture appeared unusually tense.

Her right hand was clenched into a fist around something she was holding. "It's about this," she said tightly, extending her clenched hand.

He leaned forward and put out his own hand to catch the thing that she dropped unceremoniously into his palm. What he found himself holding was a heavy bronze ring threaded onto a silver chain. He looked up at the princess, his glance questioning.

"Look at it," she said, in the same flat tone. "And tell me what you think of it. The ring, I mean. The chain is just something from my jewelry box."

Perplexed, he bent over the ring, examining it. Abruptly, he sucked in his breath, rose, and moved urgently towards the room's single window to get the full benefit of the light. After a moment's intense examination of the ring, he spun around, his face alight with a mixture of excitement and astonishment.

He gestured with the object that he held. "By the Eyes, Nevien!" he exclaimed. "This can only be the signet ring of the House of Loros that's been missing since the day of King Tevren's death!"

Her mouth twitched. "I thought it might be," she said. And now at last she took a seat on the little couch. There was a cloth-wrapped bundle on the cushion that she had to move aside as she did so.

"But where, in Vothra's name, did it come from?"

The princess was sitting, very erect and still. She lifted her chin and spoke with a measured care that made it clear that she fully understood the significance of her words. "It belonged to Leyel Virden," she said. "He wore it on a chain around his neck— under his shirt."

"*Leyel Virden?*"

The name was a ghost from the past and it took a second for Kuran to see beyond the non-sequitur, but then his face turned grave and he nodded. "Ah, I see," he said. He returned to his seat in the armchair and sat gazing somberly at the ring that he still held in his hand.

"Yes." Nevien spoke tightly. "It means, of course, that Leyel must have been the heir of Loros after all, as some people thought."

Kuran drew a long breath. "Yes, there were some who raised that possibility when your father first announced your betrothal to the lad. Why else choose an unknown youth— a child of a very minor house, and a bastard child, at that? Of course that speculation died as soon as everyone saw what he was. No one wanted to believe that the line of Loros could have come to such a sorry end." Kuran sighed heavily and raised his eyes to Nevien's face. "I suppose he must have left it behind when he disappeared, then? Have you only just found it? Or have you had it for some time and only recently looked at it again?"

Nevien's eyes were fixed on Kuran's face and they held a peculiar intensity that he was uncertain how to interpret.

"I have no reason to believe that the ring wasn't around his neck when Leyel was taken from my bedchamber," she said coolly.

Kuran frowned. "If that's the case, how on earth do you come to be in possession of it *now?*"

Nevien shifted in her seat, and for a moment she seemed to struggle for control. When the words came, they fell hard and sharp.

"Nagaro had it when he was attacked. It was around his neck on a piece of leather string that I must have cut when I was cutting his shirt. I put the thing away— for safekeeping— without getting a good look at it, and forgot all about it until I found it this morning at the bottom of my wardrobe."

This revelation was so unexpected that for a moment Kuran could only stare at her in shock. "*Nagaro* had it?" he managed at last. "But how could Nagaro have come by something that belonged to Leyel?"

At this, Nevien was suddenly on her feet. "Isn't it *obvious?*" she cried hotly. "*Their paths must have crossed!* Nagaro knows something about Leyel— I'm sure of it! That man may very well know what happened to him— *and he never told me!*"

Kuran stared, dismayed by her anger. He now realized that she must have been holding it in check ever since he'd entered the room. In fact, he now saw that she was furious— and her fury was directed at the young man whom Kuran had adopted as his heir. This was not an auspicious development, and Kuran immediately cast about for an alternative explanation to offer her.

"But think, Nevien," he countered, "Leyel was taken by the Mautep raiders, and he very likely perished among them. They'd have taken anything that he had as booty. And Nagaro took a great many Mautep ships during his pirate days. This ring could have come to him amongst the plunder from one of those ships— something he took a fancy to and kept without knowing what it was."

But Nevien was angrily shaking her head even before Kuran finished speaking. "Leyel did *not* die in the hands of the Mautep," she said flatly. "He went over the garden wall, and—"

"*Someone* went over the wall. It was never proven who—"

"It must have been Leyel! Do you want *proof?*" She snatched up the cloth bundle from beside her and pulled it open, flinging the contents onto the table in front of Kuran. "There's your proof! Those are the clothes that Leyel was wearing the night he disappeared! *And do you know where they turned up?*"

She paused, eyes flashing triumphantly.

Kuran looked from Nevien's face to the two garments and back again. "Ah, no," he said cautiously. "Where?"

"In Wotana! And you know as well as I do that Nagaro used to live in Wotana!"

Kuran put down the ring and bent over the clothes. His mind was racing, running through the implications of what he had just heard.

If Leyel had been the heir of Loros, Nevien's father must surely have known it. Yet the king had kept it a secret from the Council, it seemed, as well as from his own daughter. What had been Elgurn's plan? To reveal the truth only after the princess had borne a new heir of Loros? That seemed likely. But the plan had gone awry. Leyel had disappeared— run away, or gotten lost— and never been found.

And if Nagaro had somehow gotten mixed up in the disappearance of the idiot prince, the revelation of that involvement could put him in danger even now.

Kuran frowned. "Are you certain these were Leyel's?" he asked, indicating the clothes.

"Yes, I'm certain!" Nevien was vehement. "I *remember* them! And it was the very tailor who made them that brought them to me. He said they were in a little chest that came from Wotana— and why would he make up such a tale? It's too absurd not to be true!"

Kuran frowned harder, examining the shirt and britches more closely. The clothes certainly looked convincing. And as for the story, she was right. There was no imaginable reason for the tailor to make up such an outlandish tale. And Nagaro *had* lived in Wotana at about the right time... but still there could be other explanations.

He looked up to meet Nevien's smoldering gaze. "Even if they were in the same town, it doesn't mean they met face-to-face," he said carefully. "Leyel could have been parted from his ring, and Nagaro could have acquired it later."

Nevien's perfect brows came together sharply. "You've never talked to Nagaro about Leyel, have you?" she demanded.

"Well, no," he conceded. "It's never come up."

"Then you haven't seen how he acts when the subject *does* come up."

"How he... *acts?*"

Nevien gestured impatiently. "He gets *angry*— or goes silent. And he says outrageous things— that Leyel would have been better off dead... that my father should have left him alone..."

"Well he's not alone in *those* sentiments. I heard people say such things when Leyel was among us—"

"Yes, but *still?*" Nevien's tone was withering. "When was the last time you heard anyone say anything that showed they still cared about Leyel Virden? I tell you, *Nagaro still cares!* He cares far too much for someone who has no personal stake in it!" She shook her head. "I was such a fool that I had myself convinced it was just natural sympathy— fellow-feeling on the part of one young man for another of uncertain birth. I *thought* Nagaro was honest! And he never *once* admitted he had ever even known Leyel— not even after I made it clear how much I cared what had happened to him!"

By now Kuran was eyeing the princess with growing concern. She had become increasingly agitated, was breathing hard, and had punctuated her last point with a clenched fist.

"I *thought* I could trust Nagaro!" she continued, her voice spiraling upward. "I *thought* he was the most honest man in the world! *Why, I even allowed myself—*" She broke off, with something close to a sob, and stood with her chest heaving, a spot of bright pink color in each cheek. Finally, she collected herself with a visible effort, to finish, pleadingly. "Why couldn't he just have *told* me what he knew?"

Kuran drew a long breath and cleared his throat. "I am truly sorry, Nevien," he said. "I had no idea you felt so strongly about Leyel—"

"*He was my husband!*" she cried, shooting Kuran a reproachful look. "He was helpless! He was innocent! And I have a *right* to know what happened to him! Nagaro should have told me!"

Kuran ran a hand through his hair. Hoping to dampen her intensity, he said, "All right. I understand. And I agree that it's important to find out what happened to Leyel— if that is possible— for the sake of the country, if nothing else. And it's possible that Nagaro knows something. But if he does, and he hasn't told you, I'm sure he must have a reason. Perhaps he made a promise—"

Nevien had been listening with growing irritation, and now she pounced. "Well, if he *did*, it didn't stop him from telling Varsyl!"

"Varsyl Virden?"

"*Yes!*" She gestured impatiently. "Nagaro told Varsyl something, months ago. Some... *news*... they called it— and it has completely transformed Varsyl! The man actually smiles now. He goes about as if the weight of the world had been lifted from his shoulders! Do you realize it's possible that Leyel could still be *alive?*"

In fact Kuran had not thought of that, but as soon as Nevien said it, he saw the implications. There could be serious political repercussions if the princess's first husband suddenly turned up. *And if Nagaro was somehow involved...* "Have you told anyone else about this?" he asked urgently. "Have you shown these to anyone?" He indicated the ring and the garments on the table.

To his great relief, Nevien shook her head.

"Merriel was there when the tailor came with the clothes, and we talked about Leyel having been in Wotana, but we didn't make anything of it. And no one else knows about the ring. Who else but you can I trust anymore?" Her voice took on an edge of bitterness. "Not my father, that's plain. Rianine isn't here, and anyone else would want to *tell* my father. Besides," she added, "you've got Nagaro in your keeping, and I need to talk to him! I mean to make him tell me what he knows. I want you to have him stop at River House when you move him at the end of the week."

"Why don't you let me talk to him, Nevien—"

"*No!*"

Kuran's hand had been hovering over the ring, but Nevien leaned across the table and snatched it up. "I want to talk to him face to face!" she declared. "I want to hear what he says from his own mouth so he can't weasel his way around this!"

Kuran raised an eyebrow at the implication that Nevien thought she could get the truth from Nagaro better than he could. And it alarmed him to think how Nagaro might react to her anger, considering his feelings for her. Nagaro's mood was more precarious than Kuran had given Nevien to believe in his recent letter. He had meant to keep her from worrying about a dear friend, but now it seemed that "dear friend" was likely to find himself under attack!

And clearly Nevien was in no mood to be argued with. *I want to be present at this face-to-face meeting,* he thought. What he said was, "All right then, I'll let Nagaro know that you want to talk to him."

Nevien had risen and stood looking down at him. Her eyes narrowed. "I want you to tell him to stop at River House, Kuran, on the way to Kel Wared, and that is *all!* Anything else I wish him to know, I'll tell him *myself*— in a note I am going to write. Now promise me you won't give him any warning of what this is about!"

Kuran swore silently to himself. He had intended to give Nagaro a full advance briefing, but Nevien had just forbidden it! And he sensed that trying to negotiate the point would only get him into more trouble. He couldn't preempt the princess in this without the risk of losing her trust. And if this trail *did* lead to a living but simple-minded heir of Loros, it would be vitally important to have a cooler, wiser, and politically neutral head in a position to take charge of events. "Very well," he said, keeping his voice level. "I promise to do just as you've asked." He was *definitely* not going to bring up the issue of being present at her intended meeting, lest Nevien take it into her head to forbid that as well.

He stood up then, and changed the subject. "I'd like some additional evidence to confirm that Leyel Virden was Tevren's son," he said. "If I may, I'd like to borrow the portrait of Leyel that's hanging on the second floor landing of the back stairs. There's a portrait of Tevren and Lindra at Loros Hall. If I take the one of Leyel with me, I can stop there and compare the likenesses."

Nevien shrugged. "All right," she said. "But I don't see why. Knowing that Leyel was the heir of Loros explains why Father wanted me to marry him, and... *other things...*" A shadow crossed her face. "But it doesn't really matter... not *now.*"

"I think it does." Kuran made haste to set her straight. "If the heir of Loros is dead, then it's best that the Leithian Faction knows it— so we don't have another debacle like the one we had with Kenthos. And if he's *alive—*"

Nevien's eyes widened. "—then he needs to be protected." She finished the thought.

"That's right." Kuran held her gaze. "And if Nagaro has had anything to do with protecting Leyel Virden, or hiding him, he may well have thought it too much of a risk to tell you about it— since your father is the king—"

Nevien's thoughtful look vanished, and her eyes flashed anger again. "My father doesn't rule me!" she retorted. "Nagaro should know that!"

Kuran bit off a sharp rejoinder and strove for a neutral tone. "At least try not to judge him, Nevien, until he's had a chance to explain himself."

"He'll have his chance," Nevien said coldly. "And he had *better* explain himself!" She stooped and began to gather up the silk shirt and satin britches. "You may certainly take the portrait," she added after a moment, her voice tight. "I'll find you something to wrap it in."

Kuran shook his head at her. "He's a good man, Nevien. He has his secrets, but I would trust him with my life."

Nevien's hands stopped moving. "He's your protégé," she said bitterly, without looking at him. "So of course you will defend him." Her hands went back to angrily folding the purple shirt. "And I don't object to him keeping secrets about things that concern only him. He just shouldn't keep secrets about things that concern other people— or pretend to be so honest, when he's not!"

Kuran heaved a mental sigh and gave up. Today she would not relent. He could only hope that her mood would soften by the time she met with Nagaro at the end of the week— in a mere two day's time.

***

The lamp wasn't lit on the second floor landing, and the light was rather dim. Kuran glanced only fleetingly at the portrait of Leyel Virden as he lifted it from its hook. It was a familiar object— so familiar that he rarely looked at it any more. He wasted no time in wrapping up the portrait in the small tablecloth Nevien had lent him for the purpose. He had a number of pressing matters waiting for him at the Fleet Compound and he was in haste to get back to them.

On the ride back to the compound, he found that the bundled portrait, strapped to the back of his saddle, bounced alarmingly if he rode at any pace above a walk. Forced to go slowly, he had ample time to dwell on the morning's revelations.

It was vital to know whether Leyel Virden had truly been King Tevren's son. If he had been, then knowing the youth's fate became important as well. That much was clear, but Kuran wasn't sure that Nagaro could shed light on either question.

If Nagaro had acquired the ring ten years ago in Wotana, he must have somehow kept it safe during the year and a half that he'd been a galley slave— possible, though a bit hard to credit. And it was clear that Nagaro had no notion of the ring's significance. He had asked completely ingenuous questions about the House of Loros during the mission that had taken them to Loros Hall. So, if Nagaro *had* given aid to Leyel, it would have been without knowing he was helping the heir of Loros. Which was plausible since it was unlikely that Leyel himself had known who he truly was. It would have been safest, after all, to keep him ignorant while he was a child. And then the fever had come, damaging the lad's mind and leaving him simple— a perpetual child, as it were.

Kuran frowned as he reined his mount back down to a walking pace for the third time. The morning was brisk, and the horse was eager to return to its stable. He sighed. He had to accept Nevien's word that Nagaro had displayed an unnatural concern for the idiot prince. But such concern didn't surprise Kuran. Nagaro felt passionately about a great many things, and was inclined to speak his mind. Nagaro was also inclined to take action on matters that roused his passion. So it wasn't so very hard to imagine him helping Leyel find a safe haven somewhere to avoid going back to the palace— a place where the lad had been constantly ridiculed and paraded about in public.

Kuran's frown deepened as he turned into the street that led to the city's south gate. Nagaro would have been scarcely any older than Leyel at the time of the latter's disappearance. He could have been an idealistic youth with little knowledge of the world or appreciation of its risks. The simple-minded prince could have been lost for days, before wandering into Wotana at about the same time that Nagaro had arrived there. And Leyel might have given the ring to Nagaro— either before or after the time Nagaro had spent in the galleys. Or Leyel might have died during Nagaro's absence, and Nagaro might be carrying the ring in remembrance—

Abruptly, Kuran realized that he was passing the street that led most directly to Tor Papano's house in Tanners' Row. "*Bodjer!*" he muttered, reining his horse to a halt.

For a moment he sat, holding the impatient beast in check, while he engaged in a mental debate. He needed to tell Nagaro there would be a stop at River House, but perhaps this would best be done in a carefully worded note. He would rather have told Nagaro in person, of course, but the man would surely ask questions— questions that Kuran's promise to Nevien wouldn't allow him to answer. Kuran silently cursed that promise.

He was tempted to break it. Leaving Nagaro in the dark felt like a greater sin. Unfortunately, he knew better. While he could probably conceal his own breach of faith from Nevien, Nagaro probably couldn't conceal the fact that he knew more than he should. The man was too bloody honest for his own good!

Kuran shook his head as he rode on towards the South Gate. It was ironic that Nagaro should be in trouble with the princess over an issue of honesty. Nagaro came close to being the most honest man in the world. His chief disqualifier was the fact that he kept secrets. He was remarkably open about the fact that he kept them, of course— just not about what they *were*. He had actually told Kuran that there could be something dangerous about one or more of his secrets. Having gotten mixed up in the disappearance of the idiot prince would be exactly that.

The thing Kuran understood least was Nevien's reaction. Nevien had known that Nagaro kept secrets for as long as Kuran had. Why was she suddenly so outraged that he was hiding something? Was it really just because the thing he was hiding might have some connection to *her?* Kuran understood her feeling that an explanation was warranted, but why was she calling into question everything Nagaro had ever told her? It wasn't reasonable, and it wasn't like her.

Chapter 9

Revelations

Nagaro's mood was almost buoyant as he paced the floor of the little room. He was waiting for word that the coach had arrived to carry him away from his convalescent confinement. The hour was very early, but he'd been ready earlier still. He had bathed before dawn, combed his hair, and donned a fresh shirt and tirka— brought to him by Taru the day before— along with his familiar pants which had been freshly laundered. His skin was also freshly darkened with kuma stain, thanks to Pavo's patient assistance.

Physically, he'd been improving steadily for several weeks. The poultice and bandage were gone. He was able to breathe without pain and talk without pain, and he no longer faded in and out of consciousness. While there was still a persistent ache at the site of his wound, it had receded to such a low level that he could ignore it much of the time. Sharp stabs of pain came only when he moved abruptly in certain ways, or tried to exert himself. His mobility had greatly increased as well. Master Ambras had given him permission at first to sit up a little every day, then to lie on his back and sleep on his back if he chose, and finally to stand up and walk about whenever he wished— as he was doing now.

While his mood undeniably owed much to all of this, there was one other event that had done more than anything to lift his spirits in the last two days. *Nevien must have found his ring!*

At least he couldn't imagine anything else her message could refer to, cryptic as it was. For the third time that morning, he pulled the little piece of paper out of his tirka and reread the words.

Captain Nagaro, Something that was in your keeping is now in mine. It was misplaced for a time and only recently rediscovered, hence the delay in informing you. I will be at River House on Seventh Day. N. H.

Taru had been skeptical when Nagaro had read the note to him. "Why doesn't she just say she's got your ring an' she's had it since Lothard stabbed ye?" the young Turo had demanded. But Nagaro thought he understood. "She doesn't want to be too specific, in case the note were to fall into the wrong hands," he explained. "She doesn't want it known that she was here that night."

With a sigh, Nagaro returned the note to its place next to his heart. He had worried very briefly that Nevien might have seen the ring years before— during... *that time...* but had dismissed the idea. He couldn't remember any instance when the ring had not been safely concealed under his shirt or nightshirt.

No, he told himself, *there is nothing to fear.* He was going to get his treasure back. And he was going to be allowed to see Nevien one last time before going voluntarily into exile.

He had been mystified at first by Kuran's earlier message, telling him there would be a stop at River House. Though it lay in somewhat the same direction, River House was not on the way to Kel Wared. The mystery had been resolved, however, when the princess's note had arrived a few hours later. Obviously there had been some coordination there, and everyone was being careful to avoid saying so explicitly— which was just fine as far as Nagaro was concerned.

This morning he was grateful for everything. The world didn't seem so bleak as it had just a few weeks before. Life was a gift to be cherished, and the islands were not such a bad place. There would surely be useful work to be done there— schools to be built and water cisterns to be dug, if he could only persuade Elgurn to spare a little of the tax for such things. And, if he must learn to live without Nevien, at least he should be able to keep busy.

As he paced, he trod respectfully on the little rug with the twin cows that had kept him company all those weeks. The weaver who had made it had done an exemplary job of capturing the character of the animal. As he looked at it now, the cow that was right-side-up appeared to be smiling at him. It was a quintessential cow— a beatific bovine. He was almost going to miss it—

The sound of voices coming from somewhere in the hallway stopped his anxious movement. "Taru?" he called. "Is the coach here?"

His friend appeared in the doorway. "Aye, it's here. Are ye ready, Nagaro?"

"More than ready. Is my sea chest aboard it?"

"It's strapped on the back. I packed everything into it that ye told me to." Taru stood aside to usher him into the hallway.

Nagaro gave his friend a grateful glance. "Thank you, Taru. What about my horse? Were you able to bring Thunder?"

Taru laughed. "Aye, he's here— saddled and bridled so ye can ride a bit, later, if ye like."

"Are there any folk in the street?

Taru shrugged. "One or two. But we should be able t' get away without drawing a crowd if we're quick about it."

Together they passed into the parlor. There they were met by Master Ambras, who insisted upon giving Nagaro a final inspection. "You're looking remarkably fit, Captain," he declared at length. "You've healed more quickly than I expected, but don't think you can ignore my instructions. I want you to get two hours of bed rest every afternoon for the next month, and then taper it off over another month after that."

Nagaro grimaced and put a hand to his chest. "I'm not likely to forget, Master Ambras," he said ruefully, "with the pain to remind me."

The healer's brow furrowed. "I don't want you to be alarmed by the sharp pains," he said earnestly. "You will continue to have them when you move in certain ways for quite some time— years, most likely. You have a scar running through your chest, after all. But pain doesn't mean that you're in danger of reopening the wound— once it's completely healed. Still, I want you to avoid strenuous activity for at least another month, just to be safe. A little light exercise would probably do you good, though, right now."

Nagaro absorbed all of this advice, and nodded. "I understand," he said. "And thank you for everything, Tor Ambras— especially for being patient with my ill temper."

Tor Papano was standing at the door waiting to bid farewell to his houseguest. Nagaro extended a hand to the shoemaker and thanked him earnestly for his hospitality.

"Happy to be o' service to ye, Captain." Papano bobbed up and down as he shook the proffered hand. "I have something for ye, Zirda," he added, "with the compliments o' the house." He reached behind him and produced a black leather hat, which he thrust into Nagaro's hands.

"Is this a gift?" Nagaro took the hat awkwardly. "But you shouldn't do that, Tor Papano. It's I who should be giving *you* something, for all the trouble I've been to you and your wife."

"No, no!" Papano waived the protest aside. "No trouble at all!" Then he dropped his voice and spoke conspiratorially. "The truth is, Captain, ye've been good for business. I've had flocks o' folk in my shop wantin' t' be under the same roof with ye. And a good number o' them decided to buy something while they were here. Something to remember the occasion, as it were."

Nagaro stood for a moment, embarrassed and touched by this testament to his continued popularity. He looked at the hat. It had an oval crown, a broad brim, and a band woven of dark red-brown leather the color of old blood. Was it only coincidence, he wondered, that the shoemaker had chosen the colors of Nagaro the Pirate? He looked at Tor Papano. The man would obviously be crushed if he didn't accept the gift.

Nagaro drew a breath. "Well, in that case," he said. "I suppose I also ought to have something to remember my stay with you, Tor Papano. Thank you, Zirda, and I wish you continued prosperity." With that, he clapped the hat on his head and went out through the door that Taru was holding open.

After so long in his dim sickroom, the light dazzled his eyes when he emerged into the street— even though the morning was overcast and the hour so early that the sun's rays wouldn't have struck the pavement where he was standing in any case. He heard the people before he was able to focus on them.

"There he is!"

"Captain Nagaro! The Spirits bless ye!"

"Vothra keep ye, Captain!"

Squinting, he saw that Taru's "one or two people" had become more than twenty, including men and women and even a child or two. Pavo and a pair of Fleet warriors, mounted but out of uniform, were meant to serve as escort. They were holding the townspeople off at a little distance from the coach that stood directly in front of him. Pavo held Thunder-Heels on a lead rein. The big gray tossed his head at sight of Nagaro and whinnied a greeting.

Nagaro raised his hand to the onlookers. "Thank you, good people," he said, raising his voice so it would reach them clearly. "Thank you for your kind wishes and your prayers— you and all the others who've taken time to spare a thought for me." His heart was full.

As Taru moved to open the door of the coach, a Kelorin man amongst the gathered folk spoke up.

"Captain, is it true that ye died, and were brought back to us?"

Nagaro had been following Taru, but at this, he stopped, frowning. "Of course not," he said. "The knife missed my heart, that's all."

"What about the lady that was seen at your side, Captain?" This came from a woman holding a child by the hand. "Will ye tell us who she was?"

Nagaro was determined not to add grist to the rumor mill. "No, Zirdyn," he said firmly. "For her sake, I will not."

"*Nagaro!*" Taru hissed. "*Get in!*"

The young Turo was holding the coach's door open and gesturing urgently. Nagaro quickly crossed to the coach, mounted the single step, and ducked into the vehicle's interior. Taru immediately sprang in after him and pulled the door closed. Above the general cries of farewell, the woman's voice was heard:

"*When will ye be coming back to us?*"

Nagaro felt a pang at the words. It was a question to which he had no answer.

***

Nagaro sat with his eyes closed, leaning back in the cushioned seat and letting the swaying of the coach rock him gently. The hat lay on the seat beside him.

"We're well away from the city, Nagaro. Ye can open the curtain if ye like."

Nagaro sighed. He'd been mentally making his farewells to Lankura, to the Fleet Compound, to all the familiar scenes and faces. Knowing that his meeting with Nevien lay before him made it a little easier to think about leaving the city behind. It wouldn't be long, however, before he would be leaving Nevien behind as well.

He reached for the curtain and pulled it aside. The coach was rolling along the High Road, through the fields and pasture lands that lay to the east of the city. The sky was still gray, and the fields were bare. When they passed a copse of trees, the branches were bare as well, bearing not even a vestige of autumn leaves. During the time he had lain in the dark little room behind the shoemaker's shop, the winter had come.

The coach began to slow a little, then to turn and descend. He realized that they were turning off of the High Road onto the road that would ultimately take them to River House. In a moment, they would be passing the stand of trees that had concealed Lothard's hired men. With a frown, he twitched the curtain closed again.

"Where did you put my sword?" he asked.

Taru started and looked at him sharply. "Under the seat. But ye needn't worry, Nagaro. There'll not be anyone out there today. Lothard can't ha' known we were leaving."

"I know." Nagaro managed to shrug. He supposed he was safe. The coach was hired. It bore no Fleet insignia. And with the accompanying riders not in uniform, the only clues to its occupants were Pavo and Thunder-Heels, if anyone should happen to recognize them. That didn't seem likely. Pavo was cloaked and hooded against the chilly weather, and the gray stallion was less distinctive without his usual rider.

He studied his friend. Taru had the curtain open on the other side of the coach and had his face turned towards the window, but he didn't look as if his mind was on the scenery.

You've been very quiet, Taru."

Taru shot him a glance. "Ye didn't seem to want to talk," he said, sounding a little defensive. "I thought ye wanted t' rest."

"I guess I did. But I'm through resting. I'm surprised we haven't seen Kuran. Wasn't he supposed to rendezvous with us once we got out onto the High Road?"

Taru shrugged. "He said he had some errand. If he doesn't catch us on the road, he'll meet us at River House."

The coach rattled on over the rutted country road, creaking a little as it lurched over a bump. Taru was toying with a place where the leather upholstery of the seat had been torn and mended. Abruptly he shot Nagaro another glance and said, "I wish ye weren't going t' be posted to the Islands."

Nagaro frowned, aware that there were things he still hadn't told his oldest friend. *He knew he should remedy that, but it wasn't an easy subject to bring up.* "I wish it weren't necessary," he said. "But it is."

"Well, aye. I can see that— what with Lothard wantin' ye dead, an' all. But it's awfully bad luck that ye're not fit enough today t' ride on with Pavo and me to Wotana."

Nagaro sighed. "It's the healer's orders— and Kuran's. But there'll be other chances for us to ride to Wotana together while I'm staying at Kel Hall— before I get that posting."

Taru frowned and returned to his study of the torn upholstery. "It, ah, won't be the same as this time," he muttered.

"Why not? What do you mean?"

Taru squirmed and glanced at him uncomfortably. "There's, ah, something I've been meaning t' tell ye..." he began, and stopped.

"What?" Nagaro had been merely puzzled. Now he was beginning to be alarmed. "What is it, Taru?"

"It's just that, well... ye'll be missing my wedding, that's all." When the words finally came, they came out in a rush.

"*Your wedding?*" Nagaro couldn't keep the dismay from his voice. Here was something else that had happened while he'd been sequestered in Tor Papano's back bedroom. *He had thought that he had more time... that there would be more opportunities to influence his friend's choice.* "You're getting married? When?"

Taru looked even more uncomfortable. "Two days from now. I... ah... meant t' tell ye sooner, but it never seemed to be a good time."

"Never a good time? And now it's in *two days?*" Nagaro caught himself. He'd been ill for so long, and completely preoccupied with his own troubles. There was nothing he could do about the wedding now, obviously, and no advantage to making Taru feel bad about not having told him. "That's... ah... great news," he managed. "So Jitali's father must have decided that you were good enough to marry his daughter then?"

"Oh, aye... he did." Taru was watching him with a worried look. The young Turo paused, and Nagaro saw him swallow. "But ye see... It's... ah... it's not Jitali I'm going t' be marrying. It's Hamani."

For a moment Nagaro could do nothing but gape at his friend, completely dumbstruck, while Taru eyed him as if he were waiting for an explosion.

"You're going to marry *Hamani?*" he managed at last.

Taru winced and nodded.

"But, that's wonderful, Taru!"

And now it was Taru who looked nonplused. "It *is?*"

"Yes!"

"Ye don't mind then?"

"*Mind?* Why would I mind? Hamani's exactly the right woman for you, and she's loved you for years. I was just afraid you wouldn't figure it out in time."

Now Taru gaped. "But I thought ye had a notion t' court her yourself!"

Nagaro winced. He *had* raised that possibility— and done nothing to counter the idea. "I might have done that if you'd gone and broken her heart by marrying Jitali," he explained. "In *that* case, I thought Hamani and I might have consoled each other— since I can't marry the woman I love. But this is so much better! I'm very happy for both of you!"

Taru fairly sagged with relief. "An' here I've been afraid to tell ye," he said, shaking his head at himself. "Thinking I might be letting a woman come between us, when ye'd told me that was something ye'd never do. An' all this time—" He stopped. "Wait a minute," he said, sitting up straight. "What d' ye mean, ye can't marry the woman ye love? What woman is *that?*"

Nagaro winced again, but it was obviously time for a full disclosure. He picked up the hat. It gave him something to do with his hands. "I should have told you about that, Taru," he said. "It's Nevien, of course. I thought that she and I could be friends— that my heart was safe— but I was wrong. You warned me about it, too. I guess I haven't wanted to tell you partly because I knew you'd say, 'I told you so'." He looked up to find that his friend was regarding him with unexpected sympathy.

Taru shook his head ruefully. I won't say it," he said flatly. "It'd be like the mouse calling the rat vermin, when a year ago I'd ha' laughed at the idea that I'd ever be marrying Hamani. What I *will* say is, I'm sorry ye can't be happy. I suppose she doesn't know? The princess, I mean."

"Of course not! And she mustn't find out. Only a few people know. Pavo has known, since the mission to rescue Kenthos, and I've told Kuran—"

"*Pavo knows?*" Taru was instantly indignant. "And he knew all this time? The rotter! He could ha' set me straight about ye and Hamani! *And* ye told *Kuran?*"

Nagaro studied the hat in his hands. "I told him pretty soon after signing his paper. I... I needed advice. It was starting to make me act a little crazy."

"Oh. What advice did he give ye?"

"To stay away from her."

"Well, I *suppose* that's good sense... But ye're going to be seeing her today, aren't ye? Kuran must know that."

Nagaro frowned. "Yes he does. But it will be the last time. I suppose that's why he's allowing it."

"Oh. I'm sorry, Nagaro."

For a time they rode on in silence, not looking at each other. Finally Taru said, "So... I, ah, guess ye won't be comin' back to Lankura very soon then, will ye?"

Nagaro drew a long breath. "No, I don't suppose that I will," he said, looking up to meet Taru's anguished gaze. "Taking the posting in the Islands has at least as much to do with keeping me away from Nevien as it does with keeping me out of Lothard's reach. I'll have to stay away until my blood cools, or I find another woman— or until something else happens to change the way things are."

Taru shook his head in frustration. "It bloody well isn't fair, Nagaro— just when I'm looking forward to setting up housekeeping!"

Nagaro shrugged ruefully. "It is as it is. And there's no use cursing Lokundas. Will you be bringing Hamani to Lankura with you when you come back? I know you only have a three day furlough."

"We'll be going t' Galenor after the wedding. If we can hire a coach there, we'll come back together. Otherwise, she'll have to wait for a ship and meet me in Lankura.

Nagaro nodded his understanding. "How did you come to change your mind about Hamani?"

Taru looked sheepish. "It was on account o' talkin' to her. Ye were always the one for talkin' to a woman, Nagaro, an' I never took it seriously. But I started out talking to Hamani while I was waiting for Jitali— waiting for her to finish dressing, or finish her cooking, or doing her hair. Hamani was always there— always ready t' talk about this or that. After a while, I realized I liked spending time with Hamini better'n I liked spending it with Jitali. And then I got to thinking about how much *time* I'd be spending with the woman I married. And, well, it just made sense to marry the woman I liked spending time with, that's all."

Nagaro suppressed a smile. "I'd say that's very sound reasoning, Taru. How did Jitali take it?"

"Oh, well." Taru waved a hand. "I think she had a little cry, but she's over it. She's already got another young buck courtin' her. With her looks, she's got nothing to worry about— especially now that she can cook a little. 'Course, she can't hold a candle to Hamani when it comes t' cookery. There's not a woman in Wotana can do that."

A little farther on, they stopped the coach so Nagaro could try riding a little. Taru mounted the horse that had been brought for him, and Nagaro managed to mount Thunder-Heels, without more than a small jab of pain, by using a stone wall for a mounting block. He tried to ride at a walking pace. Unfortunately, he found that Thunder-Heels wanted to run, and the effort it took to hold the stallion back soon exhausted him. Chagrined, he was forced to dismount and return to the interior of the coach for the remainder of the journey. This time he rode alone because Taru expressed a desire to "have a few words with Pavo" on the matter of keeping secrets.

***

The Fleet Compound lay nearly deserted in the gray light. It was just past dawn, though the overcast concealed the exact position of the sun. Kuran stood beside his horse at the hitching rail in front of the building that housed his quarters, intent on easing the carefully-wrapped portrait into one of his saddlebags. He had just lowered the flap, when a voice called to him across the compound.

"Pardon, My Lord! Could I have a word with ye before ye ride out?"

Kuran turned to find the Fleet Swordmaster rapidly approaching across the parade ground. He frowned as the man came to a halt beside him. "I suppose I can spare you a minute, Fendar, if it's urgent."

"Well, ye might say it is." The grizzled Kelorin appeared agitated. "If only because it's the last chance I'll have before ye'll be gone for several days. The truth is, I first thought o' talking to ye when I heard ye'd taken Captain Nagaro on as your heir. I didn't, because I thought it wasn't my place, but then somebody tried t' murder him... and, well, it got me thinking again— that the captain may have enemies ye don't even know about."

Kuran's frown deepened. "So this is about Captain Nagaro?"

"Aye." Fendar looked uncomfortable. He lowered his voice. "I'm, ah, wondering what he's told ye about himself, My Lord— about his personal history."

This time Kuran kept his face neutral. He had not forgotten that Fendar had admitted to having privileged information on this subject. And, while Kuran had stopped prying into Nagaro's secrets some time ago out of respect for the young man's wishes, he had remained curious. In fact, he was now intensely curious because of his recent meeting with Nevien. He spoke carefully. "I believe I have a complete history beginning with his twentieth year."

"Nothing before that? He's not told ye anything of his early life since ye've taken him into your House?"

"Not yet."

Fendar looked at the ground. "I was afraid o' that," he said. "And I gave him my word not t' tell anyone what I know." The Swordmaster raised troubled eyes. "But the truth is, I believe it'd be safe to tell ye, My Lord. I think *he* should tell ye— but I'm afraid he won't. And I'd rest a lot easier if ye knew, since ye've made it clear that ye mean to protect him. Do ye think he'd forgive me if he knew why I spoke to ye, Zirda?"

Kuran put a hand on the man's shoulder. "There are times, my friend," he said seriously, "when it's better to follow the spirit of a promise than the letter of it. Come into my study. It's best not to discuss secrets under the open sky."

In the study, Kuran sat down at his desk.

Fendar sat on a chair, still looking worried and uncomfortable. He cleared his throat. "I imagine ye probably guessed that I was Nagaro's swordmaster," he began.

Kuran nodded. "I thought it likely."

Fendar grimaced. He had his hands clasped tensely in his lap and he kept rubbing one thumb with the other. "I worked with him for three years— from when he was fourteen 'til just before he turned seventeen. So ye can see that I'd ha' known him pretty well. He was a fine lad, just as ye'd expect him to be." Fendar paused nervously, then abruptly blurted, "And there was never anything wrong with his mind, I can tell ye that!"

"His *mind?*" Kuran was at a loss. "What does this have to do with his mind?"

The Swordmaster ducked his head and squirmed, then raised his eyes to meet Kuran's. "Were ye at the Royal Sword Tourney, My Lord?" he asked. "The last one they ever held?"

"You know I was, Fendar." Kuran frowned impatiently. "You and I were both in the lists."

"Then ye would ha' seen him, My Lord."

"What?" Kuran struggled to understand. "He couldn't have been in the lists. He'd have been little more than a boy— and I'd surely remember him besides!"

Fendar shook his head. "Not in the lists, My Lord. In the viewing stand."

"The *viewing stand?*"

"Pretty much front and center, My Lord. He was seventeen. And I don't know what they did to him, but whatever it was, it wasn't natural—"

"*Stop right there!*"

Kuran held up a restraining hand, because there had been only one seventeen-year-old youth in that viewing stand.

"You've said enough, Master Fendar, I think. And if you leave now, you can still hold on to some shred of your promise."

After the Swordmaster had gone, Kuran sat for perhaps half a minute at his desk staring at nothing. Then he got up and went outside to retrieve the portrait from his saddlebag. In his study again, he unwrapped the painting and propped it up on one of the straight-backed chairs. He studied it intently for several long seconds before calling for Simion.

The young clerk was living in one of the building's back rooms. He must have already been stirring, for he came at once. Stepping into the study, he immediately saw the portrait.

"By the Eyes!" he exclaimed. "That looks like Nagaro— when he was younger. Before the beard."

Kuran gave him a slightly sour look. "You knew him before he grew the beard?"

Simion shook his head. "No. But I can use my imagination. Who is it supposed to be?"

Kuran raised an eyebrow. "It's a portrait of Leyel Virden."

Simion's expression was suddenly studiously neutral. "How very remarkable," he said. "An amazing resemblance."

Kuran's eyes narrowed. "Yes, it is," he said. "And I'd rather you didn't mention it to anyone. Do you know where to find Tredhold Ferth?"

This time Simion raised an eyebrow. "Today? At this hour? He'll be at home in his new house with his wife and children, for the week's end."

"How long will it take you to fetch him?"

The eyebrow arched higher. "Not long. He found a place just inside the city gate. What's this about, My Lord?"

"Never mind. Just go as quickly as you can. It's important, and I can't afford to be too long about it. Take my horse, that's tied up in front, and send him back on it. I hope you don't mind walking back yourself."

Simion shrugged and made for the door. "Not really. But what should I tell Tred? He's off duty. He'll think someone's dying."

"Tell him I urgently need his professional opinion."

"Very good, My Lord." Simion saluted out of habit and went out the door.

Half an hour later, Tredhold came in by the same door, flushed and out of breath. "What's this about, My Lord—" He stopped dead. "*Kroneg's Blood!*" he murmured.

The portrait was still standing on the chair.

Kuran looked up from where he was seated at his desk, to all appearances doing some paperwork. "You look as if you think you might know that young man," he said, his tone casual.

Tredhold shifted his feet. "I thought for a moment that I might."

Kuran put his head a little on one side. "Would it be more likely... or less... if I told you that the portrait was painted about ten years ago?"

The healer looked more worried than surprised. "It would be more likely," he said quickly. "But I was told you needed my professional opinion, My Lord. And that it was urgent."

Kuran was suddenly brisk. "Yes," he said. "Please sit down, Tred."

Tredhold sank onto a chair, studiously not looking at the painting.

Kuran came right to the point. "Did you ever have occasion to observe Leyel Virden?"

Tredhold's mouth twitched and his glance flicked to the portrait and back again. "Just once, My Lord. I served as one o' the healers on duty for the last sword tourney at the palace. He was in the audience. I was standing not more than two dozen feet from him, so I got a pretty good look."

Kuran nodded. "What is your professional opinion concerning his condition?"

The healer looked acutely uncomfortable. "There was an official version—" he began.

"I know that, Tred. I want *your* opinion."

Tredhold ran a hand through his sandy hair and sat up straighter in his chair. He cleared his throat. "Then I'd have to say that his behavior didn't seem to me to be that of a simpleminded person— neither one so afflicted from birth, nor as the result of a fever or other accident."

Kuran tapped the desktop, frowning. "Could you...elaborate?"

The healer swallowed. "There's a range to simplemindedness, My Lord. The mildly affected act like children— they laugh too much, talk at the wrong times, can't sit still— that sort o' thing. And the severely affected may sit and stare, but that's *all* they do. I saw Leyel sit quietly for long periods and appear to be following the swordplay with his eyes. Yet he failed to applaud at the end of a bout until someone told him to— and then he had to be told to *stop* clapping. He also had to be told to stand up when it was time to leave, even after everyone else around him stood up. He did both too much, and too little. It didn't look like simple-mindedness."

Kuran's eyes had narrowed, and they bored into the healer. "So, if not simple-mindedness— then what? Again, I want *your* opinion, Tred."

"Well… of course I can't be sure…" Tredhold shifted nervously in his chair. "But I thought he acted more like he'd been drugged with some kind of hypnotic."

"I see." Kuran's eyes had narrowed further. "A potentially dangerous opinion, I would say. I don't suppose you've shared it with anyone?"

"You're the first, My Lord. And ye did ask."

"Leyel Virden was also reported to have suffered from fits. Did you happen to observe one of those?"

Tredhold shook his head. "No, My Lord." He frowned. "But at the time, I considered the possibility that the medicine he was being given to control the fits was responsible for the rest of his odd behavior."

"At the *time?*" Kuran raised an eyebrow. " So… you don't think so anymore?"

Tredhold swallowed visibly. "I have reason to think otherwise," he said carefully. "I suspect a drug may have caused *both* the fits and the odd behavior. But that's only speculation. Is that all, My Lord?"

Kuran leaned back in his chair. "There is one other matter," he said. "Do you have any reason to believe that Nagaro was ever drugged for an extended period?"

Tredhold stiffened. "Nagaro?" he asked guardedly. Then he managed a rather brittle smile. "Well, I've had to drug him myself, so—"

"I mean before you first met him as a galley slave."

"Oh." This time the healer sat gnawing his lip. "Before I'd answer that, My Lord," he said at last, "I'd want t' know why you're asking."

For several heartbeats, Kuran regarded the other man fixedly while Tredhold sat very still and pale under his gaze.

"I hope you don't think I mean him any harm—" Kuran began, then stopped. "Enough of this cat-and-mouse play," he said. "You're hiding something, Tred— and I'm pretty sure I know what it is. But I haven't the time to try to work it out of you. So I'm only going to ask you one more question. Then you can go if you like, or you can stay and we'll drop the pretenses."

He stood up and walked around his desk to stand behind the chair bearing the portrait. "You said you thought you knew who this might be. Who were you thinking of?"

Tredhold's eyes had followed him. There was resolution in them. "The first time, or the second time?" he asked quietly.

"Well, it's more than I asked for, but let's have them both."

"The first time it was Nagaro. The second it was Leyel." The healer sighed. "And it's not really a different answer, because I suspect they're the same person. From your questions, I think ye do, too. And if ye're thinking of confronting Nagaro with this, we had better talk."

Kuran looked slightly nonplused. "Why do you say that?" he asked, returning to his seat at the desk. "I wasn't planning on confronting him. But sooner or later it's going to happen. He can't hide this forever."

Tredhold rubbed his chin ruefully. "He won't talk about it, My Lord. At least I've never been able to get him to. He's been badly hurt, that much is clear. He keeps it all sealed up inside most o' the time— tighter 'n a clam. But I've seen him nearly come to pieces when something's touched on it."

Kuran frowned. "Are you saying I shouldn't press him? Just steer clear of the subject?"

Tredhold drew a long breath. "Not necessarily, My Lord. Talking about it would be good for him, I think. *If* he can manage to do it. All I can say is, go *very* gently, and don't judge him for *anything*— no matter how bad it looks. Neither ye nor I can ever truly know what he went through. How it felt to him then. Or how it feels to him now. We don't have the right to say that it shouldn't still trouble him after ten years' time."

Kuran's brows had knit sharply. He chewed a knuckle. "I don't like this, Tred. I wasn't planning to confront him about this myself. At least not right away. I only just learned about it this morning. But the princess is convinced that Nagaro knows something about Leyel, and *she's* planning to confront him— *today*. He should be on his way to meet her at River House right now, and he has no idea what she has in mind. I was supposed to meet his coach on the road, but this matter has delayed me." He gestured at the portrait.

Tredhold stood up, agitated. "Go, My Lord," he said urgently. "Don't delay any longer. Just go!"

Kuran rose, nodding. "You're right, Tred." He rounded the desk and began to re-wrap the portrait. "How sure are you that he was drugged? And that it had no legitimate purpose?"

"I'm as sure as I can be, without him telling me so himself. He has scars all up and down both arms from the bladder-thorn— and he can't abide the things. And as for a legitimate purpose... Well, there's no sign *now* of his having fits or needing medicine. I don't know what drug it would have been, though, to cause those fits and make him act the way he did."

Kuran paused to turn back at the door. "I think I could put a name to it, but there's no reason you should know it, Tred," he said grimly. "I don't think it has any medicinal use."

"Go, My Lord!" The healer made urgent shooing motions with his hands. "The Gods speed ye. And good luck!"

Chapter 10

Confrontation

It was perhaps an hour before noon when the coach rolled to a halt in the stable yard at River House. Nagaro climbed out and stood for a long moment, running his gaze over the modest two-story dwelling that had sheltered him from very near the time of his birth until he was seventeen. The day continued to be gloomy and cold, but the sight of Averwin couldn't fail to warm his heart.

Behind him, Taru, Pavo, and the other Fleet men began watering their horses while the coachman tended to his team. Presently, three members of the Princess's Guard emerged from the small guard building that had been added to his boyhood home. They spoke to Taru and Pavo, acknowledging the travelers' arrival.

One of the men approached Nagaro. "Good morning, Captain," he said, touching his forehead in an informal salute. "My Lady is in the house. I'm to say she'll receive ye in the parlor."

Nagaro nodded his understanding. "What of My Lord Kuran?" he asked. "Has he come before us? I don't see his horse," he added, surveying the hitching rails.

"No, we've not seen him. We expected him to be with you."

Taru and Pavo had come up behind the man, and Taru said, "Lord Kuran had an errand that must ha' kept him longer than he expected. I'm sure he'll be here soon."

"Good enough, Zirda," the guard responded. He touched his forehead to Taru and moved off towards the guard house.

Nagaro was relieved to see that Taru and Pavo appeared to be at ease with each other. Whatever clearing of the air there had been must have left them on good terms.

Taru gestured at the house. "So this is Avervin? Ye may say it's not fancy, but it seems pretty fine t' me!"

Nagaro swallowed past a lump in his throat. "Will you be stopping here for a while?" he inquired.

"Only as long as it takes to drink a hot cup o' sothiril in the guard house," Taru told him.

Pavo nodded his shaggy head. "Yes," he said, "Other guard have invited us to drink sothiril, and we should not be rude. But after that, Taru is in great hurry to see sweet Hamani!"

Taru took a mock swing at Pavo's ear, grinning. "It's just that we have such a long ride—"

"—and only a three day furlough." Nagaro finished for him, laughing. "I understand."

"And you must not be so sad, Nagaro," Pavo added, with perfect deadpan. "On our way back to Lankura we will come by road through Kel Wared and visit you."

"Yes, see that you do. I want to hear all about the wedding. And take care on the road, both of you."

"And *ye* be sure to get plenty o' rest!"

Nagaro watched them with a smile as they headed for the guard house— an oddly-matched pair, the one small and stocky, the other tall and massive. The coachman, he noted, had finished tending to his team and was moving in the same direction.

So there was nothing else for him to do but enter the house. He turned and walked towards the back door, the one that faced the stable yard. As he approached it, however, his feet slowed.

This encounter promised to be bittersweet. He wasn't in such good spirits as he had been when leaving Tor Papano's house. Learning that Taru was marrying Hamani had cheered him, but the journey had otherwise dampened his mood. He'd been reminded that he wouldn't likely set eyes on Nevien again for a very long time— if ever. Nor would there likely be anything that would bring him back to Averwin.

It wasn't until he touched the door handle, however, that it occurred to him to wonder who else might be inside besides the princess. Her carriage was conspicuously absent, so she must have arrived on horseback, escorted by her guards and undoubtedly accompanied by a female traveling companion— most likely Lady Merriel, or perhaps Rianine. Both of those ladies could ride. He assumed there must be at least one guard inside, as well as the woman who served as cook and housekeeper.

He had expected to have Kuran with him. Kuran would have been a sympathetic chaperon in some ways, but now, as he stood at the door, he realized that the older man's presence at a face-to-face encounter with Nevien would have made him nervous. *Kuran knew too much. It was probably just as well that the Lord of the Fleet had been delayed.* The guard he had spoken to had clearly been comfortable with having him enter the house without Kuran, so he supposed that it must be acceptable. Still, he decided he should at least knock.

After a long moment, the door opened, and it turned out to be Delvin who answered the knock. The young guardsman's face lit up at the sight of him. "Captain Nagaro!" he exclaimed. "Ye're looking well, and I'm glad t' see it! My Lady's in the parlor. Just down the hall there."

Nagaro thanked the young man, though he knew the way. As he moved down the hallway, Delvin disappeared into the kitchen and Nagaro heard him eagerly asking the cook for another bowl of soup.

The parlor door stood open, and Nagaro came to a stop outside. Seeing Delvin had cheered him, but he now found his unease returning. He couldn't help wondering why Nevien had chosen to meet him in *this* room. The parlor could also be entered from the front door of the house, but both the door and the parlor were rarely used. They were intended for formal occasions, which were rare at River House. Through the open doorway, he could see one end of the elegant Jinari carpet, resplendent in hues of wine-red, cream, and gold. The window draperies, he knew, were of a matching shade of red, the furniture was dark wood with cream-colored upholstery. The room's furnishings had been designed to impress. Nothing about it was the least bit homely or intimate.

It wasn't a place he would have chosen, but perhaps that was just as well. He would, after all, have to try to restrain himself, and the un-promising setting might make that easier. Wondering again who he might find in the room with the princess, he drew a deep breath and stepped through the doorway.

It took him but a moment to see that Nevien was alone.

The room contained an oval table that was usually placed under the window, but had been moved out closer to the center of the floor. Nevien sat in a chair at the far end of it, facing him. She was wearing riding clothes. He recognized the familiar gray shilka. At that moment, she was bent over something in her hands and the muted light of the wintry morning angled in to shine on her gold-brown hair.

His heart leaped at the sight, but he paused just inside the door. There was no one else visible, but there might be someone listening, perhaps in the hallway that led to the front door. The recent fiasco involving Alisset had made him wary of being alone with a young woman. He swallowed. "My Lady?"

Instantly she raised her head and a series of expressions chased each other across her face. The first was simple surprise, indicating that she hadn't heard him enter. This was followed by a kindling of light in her eyes that lasted only an instant before being replaced by an unaccustomed hardness that smote him like a blow.

It was as if something had changed since last he'd been in her presence. He could sense tension in the lines of her body and she seemed to be measuring him. There wasn't even any sign that she intended to offer him the common courtesy of a cup of sothiril!

His mind spun. *What had he done? Had Anduar failed to convey to the Council the forcefulness of his refusal of the infamous proposition? Or had Nevien somehow guessed at the feelings he harbored for her? Had his folly on that fateful night given him away?*

She didn't immediately address him, and he saw her gaze flick past him to the open doorway at his back, as if looking for someone else— perhaps Kuran. Or perhaps she was merely concerned about appearances.

"I... ah... expected to see Lady Merriel here," he ventured, backing up a step. "I don't wish to appear improper."

But she waved this aside. "Merriel is upstairs, nursing a headache," she said coolly. "I told her Kuran could serve as chaperon."

"He's not here. He was delayed. I... can wait outside until he comes."

She shook her head. "No," she said, and she almost sounded relieved. "That won't be necessary. Please sit down, Captain." The last was said rather briskly, and she indicated with a flick of her hand a second chair that had been placed at the end of the table closest to him.

Hesitantly, he approached the table and gingerly took a seat on the stiff-backed parlor chair. She was studying him, toying with something she held in her hands, and he thought he sensed ambivalence. Still thinking that he might be facing some disapproval stemming from his behavior on the night of the attack, he said, "I'm sorry to have given you cause for worry, My Lady, and to have caused you trouble and expense. I'm very grateful for all you've done for me."

This gracious speech caused her expression to soften fractionally. "You are welcome," she said, though the words lacked the warmth he would have expected. "And I'm pleased to see that the expense wasn't wasted. You look quite well. I could scarcely have done less in any case, considering that you thought you were responding to my summons— and also considering my earlier message, which may have confused you."

He frowned. "That earlier message—"

"It doesn't matter." She cut him off. "Kuran means to keep you well away from Lankura."

His frown deepened. *If Kuran had told her that, and she knew she needn't fear an unwelcome courtship... then what—?*

"That's not what this is about," she continued. She raised her hand and he saw that a silver chain dangled from her fingers. Swinging on the end of it, a familiar small bronze object caught the light from the window.

"You found my ring!" he exclaimed, rising in his eagerness, and stretching out his hand— before he froze.

A frown had flickered in Nevien's eyes and her brows briefly came together. But she smoothed her countenance as Nagaro hastily withdrew his hand and sat down again. "I have some questions for you," she said with studied evenness. "And I want you to answer truthfully."

"Of course," he answered, stung that she should feel the need to speak to him so. "I always try to tell the truth." He saw the frown flicker again and felt a rising unease as he belatedly remembered that the secrets he kept sometimes interfered with complete honesty.

Her frown was very brief this time, but she was watching him very closely as she said, "Will you tell me, please, how this ring came into your possession?"

For a moment, the wheels of his mind spun wildly. *Why would she ask him that? Did she know something about the ring that he didn't?* He supposed it might have some dark history that might explain the question— and her attitude as well. Still, he couldn't see why he shouldn't answer. He was confident of his own innocence as far as the ring was concerned, and he'd said he would answer truthfully.

He swallowed to moisten a dry throat. "My Lady Guardian gave it into my keeping when I was twelve," he said, "I've always believed it was a token left for me by the parents I never knew."

The princess had been leaning forward, but now she jerked upright as if drawing away from him, and her carefully controlled expression dissolved into outrage. "Is *this* how you answer me," she cried, "when I ask for the truth?"

He stiffened in shock. "It *is* the truth! I swear it in Vothra's name!"

"Must you make it worse by swearing?" Nevien brandished the ring and chain. "How can it be the truth when I know this ring belonged to Leyel Virden? I saw it in his possession not ten years ago!"

Vothra help me! Ice stabbed his chest, and for a moment the world seemed to fade. He clutched at the edge of the table. "You *saw* it?" he croaked. "*When? How?*"

She shook her head at him. "He was my *husband!*" she said scathingly. "Do you think I wouldn't know what he wore around his neck?"

For the space of several heartbeats he could only stare at her in horror. *She had seen it somehow! In the bedroom...? The harness shed...?* Panic gripped him until his frantic mind replayed her words and he realized she still hadn't guessed his secret! Rallying, he cast about wildly and snatched at the first thought that occurred to his desperate mind.

"Perhaps it wasn't the same ring you saw," he suggested. "Maybe there's more than one—" But as soon as he said it, he knew he had made a serious mistake.

Anger was now replaced by disappointment in Nevien's eyes. "*Oh Nagaro!*" she cried. "Now you have damned yourself for a liar! This is a signet ring." She held it up like an accusation. "There would only ever be one such as this!"

A signet ring? He gaped. In that moment, the wider implications of this revelation were lost on him. All he could think of was that he'd been caught in an unforgivable transgression. *He'd just tried to deceive Nevien after saying he would tell her the truth! And she'd caught him in it!*

"*Bishka!*" He bowed his head as rising guilt and shame threatened to drown him. But Nevien was still speaking.

"You can still redeem yourself," she was saying. "If you abandon these lies and tell me what you know! You must have some knowledge of Leyel. You get angry every time his name comes up, and the ring *proves* that your paths have crossed! I know he was in Wotana, because these clothes came from there—"

His head came up just in time to see her toss the purple silk shirt and white satin britches onto the table in front of her. He recognized them instantly.

"*Keshaal!*" He sprang from his chair, nearly upsetting it in his haste as he backed away from this new horror.

Nevien's eyes narrowed when she saw his reaction. She also rose, moving around the table to approach him. "You know them!" she exclaimed triumphantly. "They were Leyel's clothes that he was wearing the night he disappeared! They were found in a little wooden chest that came from Wotana and were identified by the tailor's marks sewn into them!"

"*Olomi's sewing box—*" he murmured, his voice scarcely above a whisper. "*Oh, Vothra!*" *Olomi had kept his clothes! He'd declined to wear them on the day he'd awakened in her house and had never thought to ask what she'd done with them. And dear, sensible, frugal Olomi must have tucked them away in the bottom of her sewing box. And he, himself, had suggested that Lanei try selling the box to trader Goran!* The irony was bitter beyond imagining.

Nevien had stopped a few paces away from from him. She still held the chain in her hand and the ring swung hypnotically. His eyes kept being drawn to it, even as his thoughts were spinning and he realized she was talking to him again.

"Just tell me the truth!" She pleaded, her voice strained with anguish. "I have to know whether he's alive or dead! And if he's dead, I have to know how he died. He was so *afflicted...* so *helpless*. Like a... a... child, that was in my keeping. *Please just tell me what you know!*"

And of course he knew that he *ought* to tell her. Guilt was now threatening to consume his soul. The memory of all his past deceptions, misdirections, and half-truths loomed over him like a thundercloud coming between him and the sun.

But if he told her, he would have to watch the look on her face— the look that would come as understanding dawned— when she realized that the helpless, hapless, child-man ...thing... she called a husband... had been him!

He swallowed past a throat that was so tight it hurt. "Don't do this, Nevien," he begged. "Please... Don't ask me to—"

"To do *what?*" she demanded. "To break a promise? Is that it? Did you promise him you wouldn't tell anyone? But if he's dead, what difference can it make? And if he's *alive*— you know I wouldn't hurt him! I don't want anything from him, ever! I just want to know what happened! I have a *right* to know! You told Varsyl Virden something. Surely you can tell *me!*"

She ceased speaking and stood, silently excoriating him with her gaze.

And he stood there, torn between the hold that gaze had upon him and an urge to turn and run— to escape from this terrible trap. His heart was thudding in his chest so hard that it hurt. His breath came with difficulty. Cold sweat slicked his palms. And at the same time, he understood her frustration. He was the source of all the answers she desired, if only he would speak! If only he could say the four little words...

I am Leyel Virden. Four words that would explain everything— the ring... the clothes...his anger... even his reticence... He owed it to her to tell her the truth!

He opened his mouth.

"*I*—"

That was as far as he got before his tongue seemed to freeze behind his teeth, and an unseen force seemed to stop the voice in his throat. He drew a gasping breath and tried again.

"*I*—"

It was no use. He couldn't get the words to come out. Not *those* words! And she was still looking at him. Those beautiful eyes... that beloved face... and such a look of reproach! He couldn't bear it. Desperately, he tried a different way, drawing on words he had already said and hoping she would guess the rest.

"I... spoke... the truth." The words came haltingly. "It is... my ring."

"How *can* it be?" she demanded, exasperated. "Do you mean he *gave* it to you? Did you help him escape and he gave it to you in gratitude? He might have had just wit enough to do that—"

*Just wit enough....*He groaned aloud.

"What is the matter with you?" she cried. "*Why won't you tell me?* It's not as if it matters what the truth is! I don't *care* what you did— even if you stole it! I just want to know what *happened.* Did he die, and you took it from his body for the sake of his memory? Or to keep it safe? Or just because you wanted it?"

He stood there in agony, knowing she was grasping at straws— trying to hit upon the true explanation and get him to say "yes." And in the process, she was offering him a litany of possible lies— any one of which she would believe if he seized upon it— but he couldn't lie to her. Not now. Not ever again.

The world was closing in around him. His vision seemed to narrow until he saw only her face. The blood was pounding in his ears and he could scarcely breathe. *She wanted the truth, and he couldn't tell her. It would be so much easier if he could get her to guess... he wouldn't have to speak the words...*

In one last desperate effort, he raised his hands to his chest. "*Look... at... me,*" he gasped. "*Can't you see?*"

But her eyes blazed back at him. "I see a man I trusted! A man I *thought* was honest! *Why won't you tell me the truth?*"

"*Aaii—!*"

He clutched at his head. It felt as is something inside was going to burst. He backed away. *She was never going to guess! Never! Because the truth was, for her, unthinkable. Even if he could tell her, she wouldn't believe it. Not without details... horrible details...*

"*I can't—*" he managed. The words came out sounding strangled.

Then he turned and fled.

Out of the room, he went... down the hall... where Delvin looked up, startled, to see him stagger past the kitchen door. Outside, under the looming gray sky, he found no one in the stable yard. His friends' horses were gone. *Just as well...* All he wanted was to get away... to be alone...

Thunder-Heels was standing at the hitching rail. The stallion whinnied a greeting. Nagaro fumbled to untie the loosely-knotted reins that secured the animal. He set a foot in the stirrup and flung himself into the saddle. Pain tore through his chest at the effort, but he didn't care.

What did it matter if his heart were to burst open and all his blood spill out onto the ground? He had truly lost her this time... lost her good will... lost her friendship... lost her respect. He had deceived her. Lied to her... failed to tell her what she needed to know... She would never want to look at him again!

"Master? I mean... Capt'n?"

Startled, Nagaro turned to find Chula, the gardener, watching him from the stable doorway.

The old man approached him with a shuffling step. The questioning look on his kindly face gave way to one of concern as he drew nearer. "Here now, Master, what ails ye?" he asked. "Ye don't look at all well."

Gazing down from astride the horse into the old Turo's familiar weather-beaten face, Nagaro suddenly saw a way. It was a coward's way, but a way nonetheless. "She needs to know the truth," he said, his voice tight with emotion. "I... I couldn't tell her. But *you* can, Chula. I release you from your promise. Tell her anything she wants to know."

***

Kuran swept the stable yard with his eyes as he swung down from his horse. He noted the presence of the rented coach and the absence of Thunder-Heels. He didn't wait to see if anyone would emerge from the guard house, but tied up his own horse, retrieving the wrapped portrait from his saddlebag. Tucking the precious bundle under one arm, he strode to the back door of the house, which he entered without knocking.

He found Nevien in the parlor and his heart immediately misgave him. She was sitting at the table, staring straight ahead with unseeing eyes— the picture of abject desolation. The white satin pants and purple shirt lay on the table. The ring on it's silver chain lay beside them.

Kuran strode across the floor and rapped sharply on the table top. "Where is Nagaro, My Lady?" he inquired, trying to keep the urgency out of his voice.

She returned him a look of devastation. "Gone." She waved her hand listlessly.

"What do you mean, 'gone'? Gone where?"

Abruptly she dissolved into tears. "Oh, Kuran!" she cried. "He is utterly false! He lied to me! He wouldn't answer my questions! *And then he ran away!*"

Kuran dropped the wrapped portrait unceremoniously onto the tabletop next to the purple shirt.

"Nevien," he said sternly. "Tell me exactly what happened."

Struggling to control her emotion, she told him, relating the most significant features of the disastrous encounter. Kuran listened patiently as her tale unfolded, trying not to wince visibly at the details. Based on what he'd learned earlier that morning, he could deduce with some confidence what must have been going through Nagaro's mind.

"This isn't as bad as it looks, Nevien," he told her when she'd finished. "Except that we've lost him. The only thing he can really be faulted for is suggesting that you might have seen a different ring, when he knew that wasn't true. He was obviously hoping you would accept that possibility and stop asking him all these difficult questions. For the rest of it, I believe he was telling the truth— or trying to. It's just that the truth is very painful for him, and—"

"Painful for *him!*" she cried indignantly, dashing tears away with the back of her hand. "Why should it be? *He* lied to *me!* He tried to pretend the ring was his!"

"That wasn't a lie, Nevien. The ring *is* his. He just doesn't know that he's the heir of Loros! Although he may have guessed it by now, after what you've told him."

Nevien was frowning, confused. "But you said *Leyel* must have been the heir of Loros!" she protested. "And I *know* it was Leyel's ring!"

Kuran drew a long breath, knowing that no matter how he said this, it was going to be a shock. It had certainly shocked *him*. He opted for logic. "That is also true," he said. "But the explanation is simple. Nagaro is Leyel Virden."

"*What?*" She shook her head. "*No!*"

"Nevien, it all makes *sense* once you realize that Nagaro Nareyo and Leyel Virden are one and the same."

"But they *can't* be! They're nothing like each other!" She stopped. "I mean... it's true they have the same color hair... and eyes... and there is some similarity of features, but..." Her voice trailed, and suddenly her eyes widened and she clapped a hand to her mouth. "*Oh Gods,*" she murmured, both tears and outrage forgotten. "If that's *true...*" She turned on Kuran. "What's your evidence? *Why* do you believe this?"

"Our Fleet Swordmaster knows him, Nevien. The man confessed to me this morning that he trained Leyel for three years." Remembering the portrait, he reached for it and hastily pulled off the string and the cloth wrapping. "Here is more evidence," he said. "Just think of Nagaro when you look at it, instead of Leyel. Once you know the truth, it's obvious. I know *I* felt like a fool for not seeing it sooner."

Nevien gazed at the image. "*Oh, sweet Lissafel!*" she breathed. It *is* him! The expression in the eyes... It was never right for Leyel, but it *is* right for Nagaro!" She turned an anguished face to Kuran. "And he *asked* me to look at him. He was *trying!* Great Mother Solbrid, what have I done to him?"

"Done to whom?"

Startled, they both turned to find Lady Merriel standing in the doorway.

Nevien sprang to her feet and held up the portrait. "Look at this, Merriel! It's Leyel Virden's portrait, but it's Nagaro! Can you see it?"

Merriel gazed at the painting in astonishment. "Well... *yes...*" she said. "Now that you say it, it *does* look like the captain... except for there being no beard, of course, and the color of his skin—"

"He uses kuma stain to darken his skin, Merriel. I've known that for years! Captain Nagaro is Leyel Virden! *That's* the secret he's been hiding all this time!"

"Oh, mercy!" Merriel sank onto one of the room's chairs. "No wonder he got angry when we started talking that way about Leyel in the carriage! We were talking about *him!* But I don't understand. What could have happened to him? He was so... *different!*"

Nevien looked troubled. "Yes, I know. It doesn't make sense. I mean... even if something had happened to cure his fits, he still had the mind of a child. Unless the effects of the fever he had were somehow *temporary*—"

Kuran cleared his throat. "I don't believe there ever was a fever," he said flatly. "The Swordmaster said there was nothing wrong with Leyel before he was brought to Lankura, and Tredhold Ferth believes he was drugged the entire time he was there."

"*Drugged?*" Merriel was shocked. "There's a *drug* that could turn someone like Captain Nagaro into... into... *that?*"

"Apparently so."

"But someone would have had to have done it *every day*," Nevien protested. "For *months!*"

"I know." Kuran's expression was grim. "It's monstrous. But we all know that Dreigen was dosing him with something. Is it really so surprising to discover that it wasn't medicine?"

Nevien's face had gone white. "What about the fits? Are you saying he didn't have fits before coming to Lankura *either?*"

"The Swordmaster made no mention of them. And Nagaro certainly doesn't have them *now*."

Nevien bit her lip and looked at the floor. "*Sweet Lissafel*," she murmured.

Kuran had picked up the ring on its chain from the table and now held it out for Merriel to see. "There's also this, Merriel," he observed. "It appears that Nagaro has been carrying the signet ring of Loros around with him ever since he was a boy."

Merriel examined the ring. "Gods above!" she exclaimed. "That surely is the crest of Loros!" She looked anxiously from one of them to the other. "But where *is* the captain?" she asked.

Nevien sagged. "I drove him away," she said in a small voice. "I was trying to get him to tell me what he knew about Leyel. And I... I... wasn't being very gentle. It must be very hard for him to talk about it. He was *very* upset when he left."

Kuran squared his shoulders. "We have to find him."

Merriel stood up. "Well, I should say so," she said. "Is there anything I can do, Kuran?"

He reached out to put a gentle hand on her arm. "Dear lady," he said. "The best thing you can do is to stay here and keep watch in case he comes back while Nevien and I are out looking for him. You're such a gentle, kind, soul that at least I don't think he would run away from *you*."

Merriel turned bright pink at the touch and the compliment. "Of course, My Lord," she murmured, casting her eyes down. "I can certainly do that."

Minutes later, Nevien and Kuran emerged into the deserted stable yard.

Nevien pulled her cloak closer and glanced at the lowering sky. "We should have brought Delvin to help," she said worriedly. "Should I go back for him?"

Kuran shook his head and made for the stable. "I don't want to take the time to explain everything to him," he said over his shoulder. "Nor do I want him blundering about looking for Nagaro without knowing what's going on. The same goes for your guards and my Fleet men. I'd rather not spread Nagaro's secret about any more widely, either. I'm afraid that if he saw we'd set up a man-hunt, it would only drive him further away."

Nevien was fighting a rising alarm as she struggled to keep up with Kuran's strides. "How will we ever find him, just you and me? It must be an hour since he left the house!"

Kuran paused in the stable doorway. "I hope he hasn't gone far, and there's reason to believe he hasn't. Everything the man owns is in that trunk strapped to the back of the coach." He gestured at it. "He's taken nothing but his horse and the clothes on his back. And the weather is threatening rain. He isn't fully recovered from his wound either, which means he'll tire easily. Even if he had some notion of just riding away, he may think better of it when he considers his situation."

Nevien nodded, biting her lip. She fervently hoped that Kuran was right. "If I could just guess where he's gone," she murmured, "He used to live here, after all, and he and I have ridden all over these grounds—"

"Beggin' yer pardon, M'Lady," said a quavering voice, speaking from the shadows of the stable, "but if it's my young master ye're lookin' for, I think I know where ye'll find him."

"Chula?" Nevien pushed past Kuran to confront the gardener. "We're looking for Captain Nagaro! Are you saying he's your 'young master'?"

"Aye, M'Lady. He told me I could tell ye whatever ye wish to know. And if I know him at all, he'll ha' gone where he always used to go when he wanted t' be alone. It's down the road where the river bends 'round the cliff an' the bridge crosses over. He'll be in his 'high seat.' It's a little bit of a ledge up on the side o' the cliff." The old Turo stood on the worn planking of the stable floor, blinking at her. He was holding her saddle in his arms. "And I expect ye'll be wantin' this, if ye mean to ride after him."

"The *ledge?*"

"Up on the *cliff?*"

Nevien and Kuran exchanged looks of alarm.

"Thank you, Chula. I'll take that." Kuran reached for the saddle. "You bring the mare out, Nevien. And hurry!"

Chapter 11

No More Secrets

Nagaro hugged his knees, shivering. He gazed out from his high seat over a landscape nearly devoid of color. The cloud-draped sky was as gray as lead. The familiar house was a pale shape seen through trees off to his right. Frost had nipped the color from the pastures that lay spread out between the house and the surrounding woods, and the woods themselves were a lacework of gray trunks and twigs where the oak and alder had shed their leaves. The distant stand of cedars that ringed the secret glade looked almost black. Twenty feet below where he sat, the river— swollen from recent rain— ran swift and streaked with foam. On the other side of the river, Thunder-Heels waited, contentedly cropping the dry grass under a spreading oak tree.

He wiped at his eyes. There had been tears but they had run out, leaving him feeling numb. The tears shamed him. He couldn't understand why he should need to weep over a thing like this, but for a time he'd been unable to stop. He drew a long breath and leaned back with his head against the cold stone. The bleakness of the scene was a perfect mirror for his thoughts.

Everything was lost. Gone. It was over.

He had spent the last ten years of his life hiding his past and trying to make a new life for himself. And he had succeeded too. He'd felt good about that success— until now, when he saw that it had all been built on deceit. *He had deceived almost everyone, including some very good people— people he cared about... people who had trusted him...*

But the die was cast. He had told Chula to tell Nevien, and Nevien would tell Kuran, and then they would both know how he had betrayed their trust. He didn't see how he could ever face either one of them again. Soon now, he would have to leave the ledge, descend, mount his horse and ride. *It wouldn't be easy, but he was going to have to start all over.*

Wearily he closed his eyes. Yes, he would go— as soon as he had gathered his strength... rested a little more... His chest hurt— more than it had in days.

Spirit that calls itself Nagaro!

He started violently at the sense of a voice inside his head and his eyes snapped open. "Vothra?" he asked aloud. "I... I didn't call you."

You have spoken my name aloud or in your thoughts several times in the last two hours— enough that I might claim to have been called. Though, truly, feeling your pain is enough for that. Besides, we have run out of time for you to call me. I must speak to you now to prepare you for what is to come.

"Why? What do you mean?" The Spirit's words sounded ominous.

The ones you call Kuran and Nevien will be here soon. The gardener has told them where to look for you and they are saddling the woman's horse—

"Oh no!" Nagaro sprang up in alarm. "I have to get out of here!"

Stay where you are! The command cut across his mind like a whip. It was an imperative of such power that it froze him where he stood.

Sit down, Spirit called Nagaro. This time it was a request, not a command.

"I can't let them find me! I have to go!" Yet still he stood frozen in his tracks. He was frantic to be away, but something held him.

Where would you go? The voice in his mind was gentle, probing.

"I'll ride to Wotana... I'll find Taru and Pavo..."

So you would run away to find those two people— friends who know your secret and do not reject you? Yet the ones you are running away from are also your friends. They also know your secret. And if they were going to reject you for it, they would surely not now be coming to find you. Think, Nagaro. If you run away now, when will you ever stop?

Nagaro groaned. He shifted his footing on the narrow ledge, torn by conflicting impulses.

Sit down, Nagaro. They will be alarmed if they see you standing on the brink, and they are worried enough about you already.

This was too much. How could he cause them more worry? He had deceived them, and they knew it, and yet they were coming because they were worried about him! With another painful groan, he sat down. Huddling at one end of the ledge, he hugged his knees and hung his head.

"I wish I hadn't let Chula answer her questions," he said bitterly.

It would have made little difference if you hadn't done so. The one called Kuran learned your secret before leaving Lankura. The Swordmaster hedged about his promise out of concern for you, and Kuran has also spoken to the one you call Tred. The healer has suspected the truth for some time, and he understands you pain—

"Keshaal!" Nagaro felt as if the world was crumbling around him. It seemed he could trust no one! In spite of the Spirit's command, he shifted as if gathering himself to stand. "What am I going to *do?*" he murmured.

Peace...

The word whispered through his brain, and he felt his agitation ebb. Some of the numbness came flowing back. *He was so tired...* Resignedly, he sank back against the stone.

Again the Spirit spoke to him. *Do not think of these events as betrayals. Think rather that the time has come for this. The wound you bear upon your soul has festered long enough. The time has come to open it with a clean knife and cleanse it so that it can begin to heal a little more.*

"But how can I face them— after deceiving them for so long?"

It will not be as difficult as you think, Spirit called Nagaro. In this you must trust me. A new chapter of your life is about to begin— one that will involve more openness and less pain. I have told you that your life has possibilities for good. One of them has already born fruit, but the path to more good lies through this meeting with these two people. They already know much of what you have feared to tell them. They will have questions, certainly, but they will not press you beyond your strength. And you need not fear that your secret will be revealed to the entire world. Your friends will respect your wishes.

Nagaro frowned. Some of what Vothra was telling him, he liked, but... "Are you sure?" he asked.

I am confident, yes. Are you ready now? Can you try?

"I... I don't know... I guess so."

That is well, because you will see that they are here, if you look.

With a whimper, Nagaro turned to look at the stretch of road that he could see, running along the other side of the river.

***

"That's his horse, under that tree by the bridge! The beast is loose, not tied!" Kuran spurred urgently forward as he and Nevien approached the edge of the trees and the open riverbank. "Where is Nagaro?"

"There!" Nevien pointed across the water. "He *is* on the ledge, up there on the side of the cliff. And— praise the Gods— he's sitting down!"

"Yes." Kuran had followed her gesture and he spoke with obvious relief. "And he sees us!"

Hurriedly the two dismounted, securing their own mounts to a low-hanging branch of the oak directly across the river from the rock face that Chula had called a cliff. It was formed where the river made a bend around the base of a massive outcropping of gray stone that thrust out from the side of one of the hills running along the farther bank of the river. The outcropping marked the river's closest approach to those hills. The ledge where Nagaro sat was formed by a kind of ragged notch in the stone about two-thirds of the way up the cliff face.

Kuran cupped his hands as he approached the riverbank and called across the water.

"Nagaro! I'm glad we've found you! Will you come down? Or should we cross the bridge and come up?"

After several heartbeats, they saw Nagaro beckon.

Nevien immediately started for the bridge with Kuran close behind her. The thirty-foot span was built of sturdy wooden planks set on stone piers and flanked by waist-high railings. It's main purpose was to allow access to a horse trail that started at the farther end of the bridge and ran away in the upstream direction between the hill slopes and the river. On the downstream side of the bridge's farther pier, the water swirled right against the base of the cliff and there was only a steep, narrow path, running up a crack in the rock, that led to the ledge.

Though she had often admired the cliff from the other side of the river, Nevien had never climbed the path before. It turned out to be less difficult than it appeared. The ledge was also less precarious than it looked. It was about six feet long and four feet wide for most of that length, with a surface that was fairly level.

Nagaro sat at the far end of it, leaning against the rock, his knees drawn up and his hands gripping them tensely. Nevien moved to sit beside him— close, because the ledge wasn't very spacious, but not too close. He cast her one brief glance and looked quickly away. It was enough for her to see that he had been weeping, and the sight smote her heart.

She waited until Kuran had seated himself at her other side, then reached for the silver chain around her neck and lifted it over her head, with the ring dangling. She held it out to Nagaro. "Here's your ring," she said. "I know now that it's always belonged to you. And I'm sorry— so *very* sorry— for all those things I said. I have wronged you terribly. I... I had no idea—"

Nagaro had taken the chain without meeting her eyes, then slipped the chain over his head and let the ring lie as it fell without bothering to tuck it inside his shirt. Now he interrupted her.

"Of *course* you didn't!" His voice came out husky, edged with bitterness. "Because I didn't *tell* you! I deceived you, when I should have told—"

"Nagaro, please! You don't need to explain anything—"

He shot her a look that silenced her. There was something he *did* have to say, and it was the more important because he had failed the first time. "I should have told you... that I am... that I was... Leyel Virden."

There. He had made the words come out. It was easier, knowing that she already knew. It was also easier putting it in the past tense. But there was more that he needed to say. "I was only thinking of myself," he said, keeping his gaze directed straight in front of him. "Protecting myself. I never thought of how you would have suffered from not knowing—"

"*Don't*, Nagaro!" She put an urgent hand on his arm. He flinched involuntarily at the touch, and she withdrew her hand. "You surely suffered more than I! And I never told you why I needed to know—"

"Nevien!" Kuran interrupted. "And Nagaro— both of you! We shouldn't be lamenting what might have been done differently. We should be thinking about how to go forward from where we now stand. And we should begin by resolving to be honest with each other."

Nagaro gloomily nodded agreement. "I will have no more secrets," he said dully. "Ask whatever you wish, and I will answer. At least," he added bitterly, "I will, if I can get the words to come out."

"That's good." Kuran gave him a nod of encouragement. "And *I* should begin by telling you that Fendar has told me much of what he knows."

"I know. And you talked to Tred. Vothra told me."

For a moment Kuran sat with his mouth open. "I... ah... keep forgetting that the Spirit talks to you," he said at last. "But I'm glad you know, because it makes this easier. To continue being honest, I should say that I should properly have told Fendar to keep his promise. Part of why I didn't is because he was worried that you had other enemies, and he believed I would protect you— which I will—"

Nagaro shook his head violently. "I should have told you before I let you take me into your House! I should have given you the chance to reconsider!"

"It would have made no difference, Nagaro! What I'm trying to say is that the other part of why I accepted Fendar's confidence is that I've wondered, ever since the day we first met on the deck of my flagship, what could possibly have happened to make so impressive a young man feel such a need to hide his past. I'm only more impressed, now that I know the truth. When I think of what you've endured—"

Nagaro emitted a sound that was so much like a sob and Kuran immediately stopped speaking to eye him solicitously. Nagaro had leaned his head back against the stone and closed his eyes, momentarily overcome by emotion.

Nevien, watching him, was aware of his pain even as she couldn't help admiring the way his lashes lay upon his cheek.

Kuran cleared his throat. "It's obvious that a crime was committed against you, Nagaro," he said carefully. "Realistically, we may have no recourse. But as your Wared lord, it's imperative that I understand the full nature of the crime— and the identities of those responsible."

Nagaro stirred and glanced at Nevien, catching her eyes on him. Both of them quickly looked away.

"Is it all right, Nagaro?" Kuran asked, concerned. "Can you talk about this now? Perhaps we should go back to the house."

"No." Nagaro shook his head. "This is *my* place." He felt safer on the ledge— where the Spirit had spoken to him— and stronger But he was thinking of how hard it might be for Nevien to hear some of the story he had to tell.

"Well, I can certainly see why you favor it," Kuran observed lightly. "The view is superb."

Nagaro frowned. "It... used to be better," he said. "Especially in *that* direction." He gestured with his head in the direction of the stable. "The trees have grown. And they built the guard house. Ten years ago— when I sat here— I could see the road where it runs up to the front door. I could see the stranger... who came riding, all alone. The man with the short blond hair and the red beard. That was... how it began..." his voice trailed.

He looked at Nevien. "Are you sure you want to hear this?"

She was sitting cross-legged, studying her hands, her face rigid. "No more secrets," she said in a low voice. "Remember?"

"I've already assumed that Elgurn must have known," Kuran put in. "But I can't judge the depth of his guilt until I've heard the facts. Let's begin, Nagaro, with the nature of the crime. I am guessing you were drugged, and I will further hazard the guess that the drug was *heskial*— the illicit drug from Jinara that Grimbold Sobring used to get information from Simion and that you feared he would use on the Lady Alisset. Am I right?"

Mutely Nagaro nodded.

"And what exactly does it do? Tell me again."

Nagaro found he could answer by not looking at either of them and speaking from the center of the numbness that still lay on him. "It enslaves the will... but spares conscious awareness— through spirit magic. Under its control, a person can do only what he is told to do. There is no choice. The command can be given in advance— hours, days— to do something whenever something else happens— to answer a question in a certain way..." His words ran out.

Nevien had sat rigidly still while he spoke. "How much do you remember?" she asked in a small voice.

He couldn't look at her. He knew what she was thinking. He kept his eyes on the gray landscape instead. "Dreigen commanded that I open my eyes if I was awake. So If my eyes were open, I was aware."

Nevien put her hand to her mouth. "*Sweet Lissafel!*"

"So it was Dreigen who gave you the commands?" Kuran inquired.

Nagaro swallowed. "Most of the advance commands, yes, but—" He stopped, then forced himself to continue. "If he had told me not to obey instructions from other people, it would have caused... *difficulties*. So I was at the mercy of... of anything that sounded like a command. Even if it was just a *suggestion*... or a *joke*..." He swallowed again, trying to re-center himself. "Sometimes I did things that... weren't even addressed to me..."

Kuran coughed. "I imagine that must have been rather *awkward*."

"It was *horrible!* And he couldn't cover everything that way. Which is why I... why I looked like a... like a—" He choked. "—*like an idiot!*" he finished fiercely.

"It's all right, Nagaro," Kuran put in hastily. "We all know that you aren't one. But could you tell me now about the fits? Did the drug cause them as well?"

"Yes... and *no*." Nagaro struggled for breath to make the words come out. "It was the drug's *absence*. When it began to wear off, I... I had a few minutes... when I could move— but not speak— a few minutes before... before the... the shaking started— and the pain! I always tried to get away. But I... but they—" His chest tightened and he drew a gasping breath.

"They caught you," Kuran put in quickly. "And fetched Dreigen to give you more heskial."

"*Yes!*" He forced the single syllable past the constriction in his throat. *Peace, Spirit called Nagaro.*

The Spirit's voice flowed over him, and with a shuddering sigh, he relaxed. *Vothra was still here. Vothra was watching over him.* He immediately felt calmer. But then he became aware that Nevien, sitting beside him, was wringing her hands.

"Oh, Nagaro!" she wailed. "That night in the harness shed— when you told me not to go, and I fetched Dreigen anyway. You could have gotten away if I hadn't done that!"

He wanted very much to look at her then, but he didn't dare. The sense of her distress, and the knowledge that it was on his account, were too much. "If you hadn't done that, I would have died," he said flatly.

"*Died?*" It was Kuran who spoke this time. "Why would you have died?"

So then Nagaro had to explain the full horror of chronic heskial administration. Being calmer, he did it with less difficulty than he had expected, though it was still easier if he didn't look at either of them. He wanted Nevien to understand that she had trruly saved his life that night.

"So of course I was trying to die," he finished, studying his hands. "As far as I knew, it was the only way out. But if I *had* died then, I wouldn't be here *now*."

For the space of several heartbeats, no one spoke. Then Kuran cleared his throat. "So, how is it that you're still alive? How did you manage to escape that night in the middle of a Mautep attack?"

Nagaro risked a glance at Kuran, and noticed before he looked away again that Nevien was staring at her hands in her lap, looking very pale. "I'm not sure," he said. "Although I have an idea."

Nevien made a small, miserable sound.

"Go on, Nagaro" Kuran prompted.

This was easier still, because it was something he had always wondered about. "There's another drug with spirit magic," he said, "—a benign one called *linjana*. I learned about it from a lore master named Fineas who keeps an apothecary shop in Lankura. Linjana has the power to restore a mind— from madness... and... other things. Fineas said it might be able to counter heskial— that if it were given to someone who was... enslaved that way... there would be a kind of war in the blood. He said it would burn the person's mind, but if it didn't kill him—"

"*Oh Gods!*" Nevien buried her face in her hands.

"Do you know something about this, Nevien?" Kuran asked sharply.

Nagaro turned his eyes fully upon her at last. "I've always wondered if there was something in the bottle of wine that night," he said. "I remember drinking the wine— because you... you told me to— and then a light exploded in my head. I think I stood up... knocked the chair over... But after that, I don't remember anything clearly until I woke up in Taru's house on Wotana Bay four days later. I had been in a fever, and my memory was... mostly gone— I didn't know who I was, or what had happened to me. It was nearly a year before it came back."

Nevien was pointedly not looking at him. "Great Mother Solbrid, be my witness," she murmured, her head down, starring at her lap. "We have said we would be honest with each other, and now it's my turn." She paused, as if to gather strength, then said, "Yes, there was something in the wine. I never knew the name of it, but I'm sure it must have been this *linjana* that you just described. And it was in your glass, only, Nagaro. Because I put it there."

"*You?*" Nagaro gaped at her. "But how did you *know*—?"

"That it would save you?" she asked bitterly. "I didn't. The most I thought it would do was cure the fits. And it *could* have killed you! You said so yourself, and so did the woman who sold it to me!"

"The *woman?*" Nagaro stared at her. "The woman who *sold* it to you?"

Kuran laid a hand gently on the princess's shoulder. "I think you had better tell us the whole tale, Nevien," he said.

She raised her hands and massaged her forehead with her fingertips. "Yes," she said with an air of resignation. "I always knew I would have to tell this to someone, someday— someone besides Solbrid, I mean." She lowered her hands and let out a long sigh. Her gaze was directed out over the dreary landscape, but she wasn't seeing the trees and fields.

"It was a few days after that night in the harness shed," she began. "I had slipped away to hide in the garden. It's something I used to do sometimes— say I was going for a walk, but really I would climb my favorite cedar tree and sit up there in my little nest among the branches—"

Nagaro shifted his position. "I think I know the tree," he said. "It was very near the wall on the east side of the garden. You showed it to me once. I wanted to say what a fine tree it was, but I—" He stopped, aware that Nevien had gone very tense. He swallowed. "I'm sorry," he said hastily. "Go on."

"Yes, it... it was near the wall," she said uncomfortably. "The far end of the wall that separates the palace grounds from the city. Some of the branches stuck out over the wall, and from up there I could see down into the street that ran along on the other side of it."

She drew a breath. "I was sitting up there that day, and two women came along the street and stopped to talk— almost underneath me, so I could hear every word. I really shouldn't have listened, and I think I would at least have *tried* not to, if it wasn't that they were talking about fits. One of the women said that her husband had fits. And the other one said she'd cured her son of fits with some medicine she'd bought."

Nevien swallowed visibly. "I... I listened because, of course, *I* had a husband who had fits." Here she risked a glance at Nagaro, from which he shied away.

She sat for a moment, twisting her fingers together, until she seemed to make a decision. When she continued, she kept speaking as if her husband were someone else entirely, not the man sitting beside her, and Nagaro was glad of it.

"I had been thinking a lot about my husband's fits," she said, "and about the medicine Dreigen was giving him. It seemed the fits were getting worse... and I... I thought the medicine might be making him dull— or *duller*, anyway. Because... well... just before each fit, he seemed *different*. There was something more alive in his eyes. There were emotions in there— fear... anger... hurt... I thought that maybe the emotions brought on the fits. But of course whenever he had a fit, Dreigen would give him more medicine to stop it. It seemed that my... my husband... didn't like the medicine either, since he kept running away. But they always caught him. And the medicine would make him fall unconscious, and the next time I'd see him, he would be dull again, and his eyes would be empty. It seemed as if the whole thing went in circles, and... and I thought that if the fits could just be *cured*, then maybe... other things... would be... better—"

She paused to gulp air, then plunged on.

"That's why I listened very carefully when the one woman told the other one how to find the Turowan woman who had sold her a medicine that cured her son. I thought Mother Solbrid must have sent these women to me. I fixed all the details in my mind— how to find the cave, just a little way outside the north city gate, where the old woman lived. I was sure that I was *meant* to find that old Turowan woman, and I decided I would go look for her the very next day."

"And you didn't tell anyone else about this?" Kuran inquired, frowning.

Nevien shook her head, "There was no one I *could* tell. My father obviously approved of what Dreigen was doing. My mother... well, I never told any of the bad things to her. Lady Merriel wasn't even one of my mother's ladies then, and I didn't yet have any ladies of my own. And besides, I'd been praying to Solbrid to help me... and this seemed to surely be the goddess' answer."

"It was probably a good thing you didn't tell anyone," Kuran observed. "Though it must have been very hard for you, having no one to confide in. But I confess I have difficulty believing that you got over that wall and all the way out through the north gate without anyone stopping you."

"I wouldn't be able to now," Nevien admitted. "This was before the first Mautep attack on the palace. In those days the wall wasn't patrolled in daylight and only the middle one of the three guard houses was manned. The one near my cedar tree wasn't. And the branches that used to stick out over the wall have since been cut back. But *then*, all I had to do was double a rope over the lowest branch to let myself down onto the top of the wall, and toss the rope back over the branch when I came back. I only had to creep a few steps along the wall to the empty guard house, go down the stairs, unbolt the door from the inside and leave it closed but unbolted behind me. I wore my riding clothes— for climbing— and a pair of old shoes. And I got an old, cloak from one of the kitchen maids to cover everything. Once in the street, I just kept my hood up and walked as if I knew where I was going. The guards at the north gate took no heed of a common woman going out and coming back in an hour later."

"Ha!" Kuran barked a laugh.

"And the Turowan woman?" Nagaro asked. He was impressed with Nevien's boldness and ingenuity, but he also wanted answers.

Nevien quickly resumed her narrative. "I had no trouble finding the old woman's cave, and she was sitting right at the mouth of it, tending her fire, surrounded by little bags, and baskets, and bundles of herbs. I told her how I had come to find her after hearing two women talking in the street— not saying who I was, of course. I was nervous at first about telling her my troubles, because I had to lie about some of it. I– I didn't dare give her any names, and I told her it was my brother who had fits. But she soon put me at ease with her kindly manner— offering me sothiril in a clay cup.

"She said she needed to know some things to be sure she had the right medicine to give— and that made sense, so I answered as truthfully as I dared. She seemed so wise, and so concerned for the welfare of my imaginary brother, that in the end I told her very nearly everything. I told her that my... *brother's*... fits had come from a fever, that his mind was simple... and that my father had found a healer who was giving him medicine that I didn't think was good for him. And that the fits were getting worse. She asked, and listened, and when she had it all, she began to tell me what I had to do. *That's* when it began to get more... frightening."

"What do you mean?" Kuran asked sharply.

Nagaro had been listening with his head down, but he now cast a quick glance at the princess and saw that she was worrying her lower lip with her teeth.

"She... she told me that my brother's condition was very serious," Nevien explained. "She said he could die of a fit, and he surely *would* die soon if something wasn't done. And what had to be done, she said, was to give him a dose of a very strong medicine. She told me that the healer my father was using wasn't a good healer. The medicine he were giving wasn't right for my... my brother. It was making things worse. She said I must trust to the good medicine that she would give me to overthrow the bad medicine in my brother's blood."

Nagaro, sitting beside her, had begun to frown, though she didn't see it because she wasn't looking at him. This woman seemed to be a Turowan medicine woman, and he wondered how she knew so much.

"She said that the struggle between the good medicine and the bad medicine would be like a... a battle... in his blood," Nevien continued, her words beginning to come more haltingly. "It...it would make him very sick. He might seem... a little mad... at first. Then burn with fever. And the battle could... could *kill* him... if he wasn't strong enough. She said that *I* would have to be strong— and brave. Because I would have to watch over him while he recovered, and keep the bad healer away."

Nevien paused, and her voice sank very low. "She asked me whether I could do that. And I said yes, I could. She... she made me *promise* I would do it. And... and then she undid the ribbon on one of her baskets and brought out a tiny bottle—"

"*Ribbon?*" Nagaro's mind had already been circling, and now it pounced. "Did she have all her baskets and things tied with ribbons? Different colored ribbons— mostly yellow and green?"

Nevien turned towards him, startled, to find that he was looking at her keenly. "Y-yes..." she stammered. "Yes, she did."

"And she was a very old woman? With hair quite gray, and a face all wrinkled and brown like a tried up apple, but with bright black eyes?"

Nevien's eyes had gone wide. "Yes!"

"You *know* this woman, Nagaro?" Kuran asked, leaning forward to see past Nevien.

Nagaro nodded excitedly. "It had to be Luka the medicine woman," he said. "As long as I can remember, she used to come here every autumn— to Averwin. She'd set up her little tent in the pasture over there near the house, stay for a week or two, selling her medicines, and then move on."

"So she knew you..." Kuran was thinking aloud. "And she would have guessed that something was wrong..."

Again Nagaro nodded. "She would have *known* something was wrong! She must have guessed what *kind* of thing too, and set out to find a remedy. I'm sure she planned it all— even the two women talking in the street! Here's the proof." He pulled the bit of folded leather— tied with a ribbon— from his pocket.

Kuran examined it. "There's a bit of dried plant inside," he observed.

"It's linjana. Master Fineas identified it. Luka gave that to me when I met her at the crossroads the first time I came on an outing to River House. She said it was 'for remembering'."

Nevien had been listening with growing agitation, and now she uttered a groan. "*This is terrible!*" she wailed. "The only excuse I ever had for what I did was that I thought it was an answer to my prayers— that I was doing Solbrid's will— when I was *really* just trying to make my own life more bearable!"

"You can hardly be blamed—" Kuran began.

"How can I *not* be blamed?" she cried. "I took a terrible risk with my husband's life! And I didn't *tell* him! I never asked whether he wanted it!"

Nagaro was resisting an urge to put his arms around her. "I wouldn't have been able to answer." he protested. "And if I *could* have answered, I would have said *yes!* I would have risked anything—"

"*But I didn't know that!*" she cried, rounding on him. "You were helpless! You were in my care! I had no right to do what I did! And I *promised* that I'd take care of you through whatever the medicine did to you, but instead I let the Mautep raiders take you away!

"How could you have stopped them?" he wondered aloud.

She shook her head at him in obvious misery. "When you wanted to hide me on top of the bed canopy, I should have refused! I should have stayed with you!"

He gaped at her. "*I* wanted to hide you on top of the bed canopy? I thought that was *your* hiding place—"

She shook her head again. "It was your idea! And I *let* you lift me up there! You were acting so strange— so wild— after you knocked over the chair. You grabbed my wrist so hard it hurt—"

"*Nevien, I'm sorry!*" Horrified, he reached out his hand, only to draw it back when she flinched away.

"*Don't apologize!*" she cried. "It wasn't your fault! You were out of your head from the medicine! But the truth is, I was afraid of you— after you got the sword off of the wall in the library—"

"I did *what?*"

"You got the old sword, from the library." She paused to wipe angrily at her eyes, where tears had sprung. "You said the palace was under attack! I thought you were mad— though it turned out you were right. You seemed to hear things before I could! You were so completely mad that you tried to fight the Mautep raiders!"

"Not so mad, perhaps," put in Kuran. "He was trained to the sword, even then."

"I may have been trained, but I had no experience!" Nagaro protested in dismay. "And I must have been mad to think of taking on seasoned warriors with *that* sword. It was clearly meant for show, not for use! Did I actually *fight* them?"

"Oh, yes!" Nevien nodded emphatically. "You seemed to feel invincible. There were a lot of them out in the hall, and two of them came into my bedchamber! I couldn't see very well from on top of the bed, because I was trying to keep my head down, but I heard the curses and the clashing of the blades. It was terribly dangerous! They could have killed you!"

Kuran leaned forward. "So what happened?"

She turned to the older man. "*He surrendered!* When a third and a fourth man came in, he just laughed and threw down the sword. So they took him... and the sword... and... and left—" She dropped her eyes. "I... I should have made sure that they took me too— but I was afraid. And I excused it by telling myself he was in Solbrid's hands."

"What good would it have done if you'd been taken?" Kuran wondered. "And getting captured was what got him out of the palace! It was the best thing that could have happened— as it turned out—"

"*But I didn't know that!*" Nevien cried. "All I knew was that he was out of his head, and I'd been told the medicine would make him very sick! I was *supposed* to look after him! *I should have gone with him!*"

"It wouldn't have made any difference." Nagaro was feeling her distress acutely, and he was desperate to staunch the flow of her self-blame. "I don't remember much about that night, but I *do* know that I went over the wall— at the back of the garden. And I had only one thought once I was on the other side. Which was to get as far away from the palace as I could! I went up the stream, because the Mautep were downstream and I did *not* want to be ransomed back to Elgurn. I was so determined to get away from the palace that I don't think I stopped running all the way to Wotana Bay— and *then* only because the fever came on and I couldn't run any more!"

"What if Taru hadn't found you? You would have died of the fever! Or what if you hadn't managed to get over the wall? Would those Mautep raiders have cared for you?" Nevien was beside herself. "*Nothing* changes the fact that I risked your life without permission! I put you in terrible danger! I didn't care about you enough to try to protect you! How can you ever forgive me for that?"

Hearing her pain, Nagaro felt that his heart would break. She was turned towards him, looking up into his face, her cheeks smudged where she had wiped tears away, her eyes brimming.

"Nevien," he said, his voice breaking. "I would forgive you anything!" And then, because he wanted so very badly to erase the suffering from her face, he yielded to an impulse borne on the rising tide of his own emotion. He bent to kiss her.

Startled by the gesture, she drew back.

Mortified in his turn, he began to apologize, but before he could get out one word, she suddenly reached up to throw her arms around his neck and pulled his head down until his lips met hers.

Nagaro responded with all the passion he held pent up inside.

Kuran swore under his breath and scrambled to his feet. Muttering something about "seeing to the horses," he bolted from the ledge, down the narrow path, and across the bridge.

On the ledge, Nagaro was careening into bliss, all trouble banished from his mind by the fact that he was holding Nevien, kissing Nevien. *He was tasting her lips... feeling her body, warm and alive in his arms. He was—*

—feeling her stiffening and trying to pull away, turning her head aside— pushing him back. He instantly let go, as if he'd been holding hot iron.

"*I'm sorry!*" he cried, in horrified dismay.

"It's... all right—" She sprang to her feet, not looking at him, then turned and started to pick her way down the path to the bridge.

And there was nothing he could do but stand up and slink after her.

Everything had gone wrong... again... Just as it had always done, all those years ago—

Chapter 12

The Awkward Dance

Kuran, waiting under the oak tree, was joined first by Nevien and then by Nagaro, trailing after. He noted how they avoided each other's eyes as they busied their hands unnecessarily with their saddle leathers. Mentally, he rolled his eyes. What was he to do with these two?

Nevien was the first to mount. From the saddle, she addressed Kuran. "I expect you will be staying for lunch," she said tersely. "I'll ride ahead and inform the cook."

Kuran cleared his throat. "Ah, yes," he said. "In fact, I think we should spend the night here. Nagaro needs to rest. All this... excitement... has surely taxed him."

Standing with his head down, Nagaro did not protest this. He mounted with a painful grimace. His eyes briefly followed Nevien as she cantered away, but after that he held Thunder-Heels to a walk, riding beside Kuran, his eyes fixed straight ahead.

The leather reins felt the same as always in his hands. The saddle beneath him felt solid and familiar. The motion of the stallion's stride was familiar too. The world around him was just as it had been... the gray light... the leafless trees... the cool air fanning his face... But he felt completely out of balance. His personal world had been turned upside down, splintered into shards, and scattered to the winds. His spirit was adrift— somewhere between floating away like a bubble, and sinking like a stone.

His thoughts kept circling, with two things at the center of the maelstrom. *The first was that Nevien had pushed him away when he'd tried to kiss her. The second was that he must be the long lost heir of Loros.*

The first was much too hard to think about, so he tried to focus on the second, which was scarcely any easier. Since first hearing the words *signet ring*, he had come to realize the implications— although his mind kept sliding sideways at the thought. But what else, really, could it be— his ring, with its image of a rising sun, wreathed with farusia blossoms opening to the dawn's first light? Nevrath had named his new House for that light, in honor of his bride, the Princess Minowei, whose name meant "dawn" in the Turowan tongue. A signet ring wouldn't be used as a love token. It was a thing to be passed from father to son— from a man to his heir. And what other noble House, besides Loros, was missing an heir?

So his secret was revealed. The box he had kept tightly locked for so many years— and guarded with such care— lay open, its contents spilled. And those contents were— inexplicably and most unfairly— not what they should have been! The secret that had been spilled was a *different* secret. It lay there, mocking him— not the secret he'd tried so hard to keep, and yet one that was still very much about *him.*

He was the missing heir of King Tevren of Loros... of Darion the Great... The motion of the stallion's strides made the ring on its chain bounce gently against his chest. He reached up with one hand to still it.

Beside him, Kuran noticed the gesture, and spoke. "Do you know what that is?" he asked.

Nagaro heaved a sigh. A hasty glance showed him that Nevien was out of sight ahead of them. "She said it was a signet ring," he ventured cautiously, uncomfortable with uttering the words aloud. "She didn't say of which House."

"Can't you guess?"

Nagaro frowned. He didn't like this game. He didn't want to be the first to say the word out loud. "I have a guess," he said. "But I hesitate to speak it, lest I aim too high."

"You couldn't possibly aim too high," Kuran told him. "There is no higher House in all of Edrovir than the House of Loros."

Nagaro nodded, his mouth dry as dust.

This answer to the riddle of his life was outside of anything he had ever imagined. Yet, at the same time, it explained so many things. And as he thought about those things, he felt resentment begin to rise, kindling to anger. *How many people had known this thing?*

"They never told me!" The words tasted bitter in his mouth and bitterness rang in his voice. "Elgurn must have known. Probably my... *keepers*... did. And Maramine..."

And how many more? He thought of Rastyl and Rastian... of Luka and Luka's daughter, Omei, looking at him with knowing eyes as she told him that she knew who the heir of Loros was, and that the man didn't know it himself. He clenched his teeth and his hands tightened on the reins. "A lot of people must have known! *And nobody ever told me!"*

"They would have been trying to keep you safe—"

"Safe!" He rounded on Kuran. "All those things I went through, and you call that *safe?"*

Kuran returned him a rueful glance. "Things don't always turn out as intended," he observed dryly. "But intentions do matter. And you must realize, Nagaro, that this changes everything with respect to you and Nevien. You could court her—"

Darkness welled in Nagaro's soul. "What good does that do?" he demanded. "If she doesn't want me?"

Kuran cast him a startled look. "It certainly looked to me as if she did."

"*She pushed me away!*" Anguish nearly choked him, but he struggled to explain. "I... I thought for a moment that she felt the same as I do. But then she started to *struggle*... and I— " He couldn't go on, couldn't look at Kuran. *She had said it was all right, but it hadn't felt all right.*

They had reached the stable yard, as he'd been speaking. Nagaro scanned the space in sudden panic, but there was no sign of Nevien. She must have already stabled her mare and gone into the house. He relaxed. *There was still time before he had to face her.* He reined Thunder-Heels in beside the hitching rail and Kuran drew to halt beside him.

The older man dismounted easily and spoke in a voice that was impossibly calm and matter-of-fact, picking up the thread of Nagaro's last utterance.

"So of course you let her go. Because you're a gentleman, and you didn't want to frighten her or hurt her. But you mustn't give up! You were probably just moving too fast for her, that's all."

Nagaro frowned, not looking at the older man. Without thinking, he swung his leg over the stallion's rump in a familiar motion and dropped to the ground. The jolt of pain that shot through his chest as he landed, made him gasp and stagger, clutching at the saddle bow.

Kuran was instantly at his elbow, steadying him. "Easy there, lad," he said solicitously. "You need to rest."

Nagaro shook off the other man's hand. "I... I don't think that's all it was, Kuran," he said, and he couldn't keep the bitterness out of his voice. "She knows *everything* now. And she *remembers*... The marriage we had was horrible!"

"How do you mean, *horrible?*" Kuran asked reasonably as he led his bay towards the stable entrance. "I understand that you were not in control. So what happened? Did you hurt her?"

"No!" Nagaro shook his head as he followed the older man, leading Thunder-Heels. He didn't want to talk about this. But it might help... a little— if he could just make Kuran understand. "She... she... only had to say '*stop*' and I had to stop—" He yanked his thoughts away from the excruciating memory.

They were in the stable now, amid the concealing dimness and the comforting smells of hay and horses and leather. Nagaro caught a glimpse of the white mare in her stall.

Kuran began to unsaddle his own horse. "Then, was your blood not hot?"

Nagaro swallowed, fumbling at the buckle on his saddle girth. He could feel the blood in his face. "It... was—" he began, struggling to find words to explain. It would have been so much easier not to try, but he needed another man's understanding, and if he couldn't trust Kuran, then who? "My blood was hot," he said again, at last. "But... because I wasn't in control... I just...kept... on..." He couldn't even finish the thought. "And I was..." he floundered for a way to say the thing that was, really, the most galling, and finally spat out the word, "— *incompetent*—"

"Ah." Kuran blew a sigh. He already had the saddle off of his bay and he now carried it to the row of saddle racks and slung it unceremoniously over one of them. "I begin to understand your trouble."

Nagaro's hands had come to a halt, the saddle girth unbuckled but nothing more. He could feel the blood pulsing in his ears. "She *always* had to tell me to stop! *She cried every night—*"

"Oh, this is cruel," Kuran murmured, "that you had this experience when you were so young! But," he glanced keenly at Nagaro. "All you need is confidence. We know you're not incompetent. You have a daughter to prove that."

Thunder-Heels impatiently stamped a foot and swung his head around to nudge Nagaro suggestively in the shoulder. Nagaro started to reach for the saddle. "I was very drunk when I fathered Narei," he said darkly. "And I didn't love her mother." He winced as the movement of raising his arms sent a new pain shooting through his chest.

"I... see. That doesn't really help then, does it?" Kuran had come up beside him. "Here, lad," he added, motioning Nagaro aside. "Let me handle the saddle. You take care of the bridle."

For a few moments they both worked at getting the remaining tack off of the horses and onto the appropriate hooks and racks. It was good familiar work, and Nagaro was able to use the time to get himself somewhat better in hand.

As they were getting the horses settled in their stalls, Kuran finally spoke again. "So, besides Narei's mother, have there been no *others?*"

Nagaro gave Thunder-Heels a parting slap on the rump and was rewarded with a low wuffling whinny. "No," he said. He was calmer, and this was safer territory in any case. "I couldn't lie with a woman unless I meant to marry her. And how could I marry a woman if I couldn't tell her the truth?"

Kuran arched a brow as he exited the bay's stall. "What you need," he declared, "is one night, with the *right* woman, in the right circumstances— when you *are* in control."

Nagaro shot him a look like a knife. "There can only ever be one woman for me," he said fiercely. "And now that she knows what I was, I'm afraid she'll never want me! I don't know what possessed me to do what I did on the ledge. All I've accomplished is that now, on top of everything else, she knows exactly how I feel about her!"

Kuran sighed. "She was begging for forgiveness! What better way to show how completely you forgive her? And as for not wanting you, Nagaro, trust me. A woman doesn't pull a man in like that if she finds him repulsive. And there was nothing the least bit incompetent about what you were doing on the ledge. Kiss her a few more times like *that*, and she'll come around to the wind!"

Nagaro was standing outside of Thunder-Heels' stall. He frowned. "She'll still remember that *other time*—" he began.

"As often as she does, kiss her again!" Kuran had started for the stable door, but he turned back, gesturing for emphasis. "For all that she's been married three times, she has yet to know a man's love. She's a starving woman. You can give her a feast, and when you do, you'll have her!"

"I don't want her to come to me because she's starving!" Nagaro's frown turned black as thunder. "I want her to love me the way I love her!"

"*Ai, Nagaro!*" Kuran threw up his hands. "Where is that famous boldness of yours?"

Nagaro jerked to halt, stung. "I'm bold when I can clearly see what is right— and what to do about it!" he retorted. "But here, nothing is clear to me! You seem to be saying that I should force my attentions on her because it's right for *me*, but it seems to me that I should be doing what's right for *her!*"

Kuran stepped closer and lowered his voice. They had both been speaking rather loudly. "But don't you see that *you* are what's right for her?" he said, fixing Nagaro with his sharp black eyes. "You are by far her best marital prospect. If you want her, you should go after her— and trust her to tell you if your attentions are unwelcome. The man makes a move, sees how the woman responds, and adjusts his actions accordingly. That's the dance. That's how it's done." Kuran stepped away and turned towards the stable door, tossing back over his shoulder as he went, "If I only had a worthy lass in sight, I'd show you the way!"

Nagaro trailed Kuran into the stable yard, still frowning. He wasn't convinced it would be as simple as Kuran seemed to think. *The man hadn't been there. He didn't know what it had been like.* Nor was Nagaro at all certain what Nevien wanted. *And yet...* The memory of how it had felt to hold her and kiss her was burning in his mind like a white-hot flame. What wouldn't he do to earn the right to experience that again?

As he followed Kuran across the stable yard, he remembered belatedly that marriage to the Princess Nevien came with certain strings attached, and his stomach clenched. *That was one more thing that Kuran had never had to deal with. If only Nevein weren't a princess...*

And, thinking about the obvious advantages of a less complicated courtship, something jogged his memory. He drew a breath, then hurried to catch up with the Lord of the Fleet, coming up beside him just as the older man had reached the steps leading up to the back door of the house.

"Are you really ready to consider marrying again?" he asked.

Kuran must have also been thinking about the last words he had spoken in the stable, for he came to a halt and gave Nagaro a rueful glance. "More than ready," he said with a sigh. "My bed has been empty far too long, but as I said, I have no prospects. At my age, it's not as if the field is large. The fathers of the younger women would prefer to find them younger husbands— besides which, they seem such children to me. And the ones closer to my age are already married."

"Would you consider Lady Merriel?"

Kuran's eyebrows shot up. "Merriel? I would indeed— if I had any reason to think she was interested. Why do you ask?"

Nagaro managed a shrug. "Because apparently she *is* interested."

"Interested in *me?* Merriel? The devil, you say!" Now Kuran's black eyes danced as they probed Nagaro's face. "What makes you say so? She's said nothing to *me.*"

"She's too proper a Leithian lady to do that, but she has talked to Nevien. And Nevien let it slip to me— and then tried to swear me to secrecy. I refused. I told her I wouldn't say anything to anyone but you, and only if the circumstances were right. What's the use of *not* telling the one person who might do something about it?"

"Ha!" Kuran barked a laugh. "What indeed?" He turned back toward the steps, and started up them. "Merriel," he murmured. "Fancy that."

***

Lunch was served in the sitting room, with its windows looking out onto the garden. The room had always served as both livingroom and diningroom when Nagaro had been growing up. He should have felt at ease in that place, but in fact he found the atmosphere during the meal almost unbearably tense.

He was seated next to Kuran, with Merrial directly across from him and Nevien across from Kuran. It was an arrangement that had seemed to be assumed by everyone without a word being spoken. He felt as if he were being watched even when no one was looking at him, and he was intensely grateful to Merriel because she bravely kept up a steady stream of small talk, to which Kuran and Nevien dutifully made contributions. Himself, he spoke minimally when specifically addressed. He forced himself to eat because he knew that he should. He was sick with the fear that he had lost all chance with Nevien— and very tired.

Nevien was clearly trying to act as if nothing had happened between them on the ledge, but she seemed tense and preoccupied. More than once Nagaro surprised her looking at him, which of course meant that she had also caught him looking at her.

When at last the meal was over, Kuran cleared his throat and said, "I know you've already been much taxed, Nagaro, but if you are able, I'd like to hear the rest of your story. This morning I learned how your ordeal ended, but I also need to know how it began, and who was involved. You've said that Elgurn paid a visit to this house?"

Nagaro studied the wall across the table from where he sat, looking past Merriel and avoiding Nevien's eyes. "We met in this room," he said. "He introduced himself as a lord of the House of Harlind. Maramine had told me only that the man had come to see me, that he had a proposition for me, and that the choice was mine. So when the man asked me if I wanted to go to Lankura and... marry the princess... I turned him down—"

"You said *no?*"

Nevien's voice startled him. In spite of himself, he turned to look at her and read the unspoken question in her eyes. *Why?*

He swallowed. "I was seventeen years old," he said in a low voice. "I... had other plans. And, of course, I didn't know you then."

"More to the point," Kuran put in. "You didn't know that you were the son of Tevren and Lindra of Loros."

Nagaro looked down at the table, uncomfortable under their eyes. It was going to take some time to get used to this. He shook his head. "No. I... I didn't. I thought surely there must be other young men who would serve this man's purpose just as well, and who would be glad of the offer. I had no idea that I'd just doomed my Lady Maramine to death. I thought that Elgurn had accepted my choice. But he... sent four men... to try using the drug. They started using it on Maramine... thinking to control me through her... She didn't die of a brain fever—"

He heard Merriel's sudden intake of breath and looked at her shocked face. "This isn't a pretty tale," he said. "There's no reason anyone but Kuran need stay to hear it."

"My dear lady." Kuran was out of his chair and around the table, bending solicitously over Merriel, who looked distinctly pale. "I think this isn't a subject for such a tender heart as yours."

"I fear you're right, Kuran." Merriel looked up at him with something more than gratitude. "Perhaps I shall find something to read— in the library." She started to rise, and Kuran immediately moved to help with her chair, then walked her to the foot of the stairs.

Nagaro glanced guiltily at Nevien. "You needn't stay, either... My Lady," he said, taking refuge in formality.

Nevien straightened and lifted her chin. "I know," she said, speaking with equal formality. "But this concerns my father, and it concerns me, so I think I must hear it. Besides," she added after Merriel was out of earshot and Kuran had returned to his seat, "I already know... some things... that I read in Dreigen's notebooks. Using the drug was Dreigen's plan. My father's sin was that he agreed to it."

Nagaro was relieved by how calmly Nevien made this assessment. "That was how it seemed to me," he said quickly. "And Dreigen didn't tell Elgurn everything at the outset. He kept some of the more... unpleasant properties... of heskial to himself. Also, Elgurn left Bron in charge, and Bron made some decisions on his own—"

Kuran raised a hand to stop him. "So Bron Sobring was part of the conspiracy? Who else?"

"Besides Dreigen and Bron, there were Kale Fendred, and Gillard Marchent."

Kuran frowned. "Those last two seem to me an unlikely pairing," he murmured.

Nagaro nodded. "Yes— Kale clearly hated what was being done. Gill, just as clearly...enjoyed it."

Kuran winced. "What you said concerning Maramine sounded like an accusation of murder. That's a serious charge."

Nagaro drew a long breath. "I don't know if you'd call it murder."

"Tell me what happened, and I'll be the judge."

So Nagaro began, painfully, to tell the tale of the death of Maramine Virden and the beginning of his own ordeal. Nevien remained silent throughout the telling, and he avoided looking at her directly. Kuran led him on with gently probing questions whenever he flagged. Though it was a little easier to speak of these things after having already said so much that was so difficult, he still nearly broke down while describing the final scene in the lady's bedchamber.

When he had finished, he risked looking at Nevien again. She was sitting, rigid, her face white, her gaze fixed straight before her.

"So Maramine died by Elgurn's hand?" Kuran prodded.

Nagaro couldn't take his eyes from Nevien's face. "I've always believed so, but it's hard to be certain. She was already close to death in any case. At the time, I thought that what he did was cowardice. I've since come to see that he acted to end her suffering. When he later asked me to help Queen Semorel die— by calling Vothra— I actually suggested that it should be easy for him to do the deed himself. He said he'd done that once and hadn't the strength to do it again."

Nevien looked at him then, and there was a glisten of tears in her eyes. "I have to thank you again, Nagaro, for what you did that night," she said, "—after what my father did to you... that you were willing to help us—"

Nagaro shook his head. "I did it for *her*. I could hear her suffering in the next room, and he said she had asked for me. Your father was... distraught. He said Semorel would go to Seralind, and he would go to Hel for the things he'd done. I wasn't gentle with him. But he ceased to be a murderer in my eyes that night and became just a man who had made some very bad mistakes."

The look she gave him then, through her tears, was equal parts relief and gratitude. He was grateful simply that she was talking to him.

"Well," Kuran observed. "I think you are perhaps being overgenerous, Nagaro, since you or I would never have made those kinds of mistakes. But then, we're not Leithians. We aren't accustomed to thinking that parents should arrange their children's marriages and that even grown children should still obey their parents without question. I do agree that what Elgurn did falls short of murder, however. Dreigen is clearly culpable for having so callously jeopardized the lives of both you and the Lady Maramine, even if he didn't actually kill anyone with his own hands. He and Bron, together, might have deserved a murder charge."

Nagaro frowned. "I don't think Bron knew that the 'demonstration' he had planned could kill Maramine. Bron didn't like me. He thought me disobedient and ungrateful, and he wanted to show me what would happen if I tried to escape— but I don't think causing the death of an innocent woman was part of his plan."

"Well, perhaps not. And in any case, he's dead. And so is Kale."

Nagaro shook his head. "Kale isn't—" he began, and caught himself, glancing apologetically at Nevien. He had promised to keep the secret that he'd just let slip.

Nevien only nodded. "Yes," she said, in reply to Kuran's questioning look. "Kale is alive, but he's quite mad. Father keeps him locked away in a room in the north tower. It isn't any natural madness, either— not any more than the madness that drove Gill Marchent to throw himself from a third floor balcony. Dreigen was responsible for both afflictions. I... I read it in his journals."

"Dreigen, again!" Kuran's face clouded. "But why did he do it? Or is he mad himself?"

Nevien bit her lip. "Dreigen's journals aren't always explicit, but I think that in both cases he feared exposure of his past actions. Gill was threatening to 'tell all he knew' about something— I suppose it may have been what was done to Maramine— and to... Leyel. And he suspected that Kale was secretly reading his journals with the intent of exposing his crimes— which included poisoning Darion, by the way, and the Pact Signer, Berinar Sundorin."

Kuran gave a low whistle. "Why is this man still alive under the sun? Why does your father keep him? I pray it isn't because he still makes use of this monster!"

"No!" Nevien was emphatic. "Father knows better now than to try to use Dreigen for anything. He's deathly afraid of the man. And after reading Dreigen's journals, *so am I*. Dreigen is utterly cold... capable of anything— of horrors we can't even imagine!"

Nagaro felt a chill that wracked him with an involuntary shudder.

Instantly he felt Kuran's hand on his arm. "This is enough, Nagaro. You need to rest."

"Yes." He nodded, pushing his chair back and getting unsteadily to his feet. "Yes, I am tired. I'll... I'll go to my room now and lie down." At the door he stopped, however, turning back for a moment, remembering something. "There is hope for Kale," he said. "In linjana. I have some in my seaman's chest. It's meant for him."

Then he turned again to cross the hallway and climb the stairs to the little room at the top that had been his so many years before. He lay down on what had been his boyhood bed. He probably couldn't have slept if he hadn't been so utterly drained. But he wasn't yet fully recovered from his wound, and the morning had sapped his strength.

***

He was awakened in the early evening by a light knock on the door that set his heart pounding until he discovered that it was only the cook, come to tell him that he'd missed dinner and asking whether she should bring some bread and stew up to his room. He accepted, shame-facedly grateful to be spared any further interactions with the other guests. He also asked to have his seaman's chest brought up from the coach.

He paced the floor while he waited, knowing there were things he should be trying to think about, but finding he couldn't focus on anything but those last moments with Nevien on his high stone seat above the river. Rather than easing with time, the trouble in his mind seemed to be growing— even as his feet began to stumble with weariness.

A pair of guardsmen eventually brought the chest. When the food came a little later, he forced himself to eat, although it wasn't food that he was hungry for. Kuran had said that Nevien was starved for love, but

Nagaro couldn't help feeling that he was the one who was starving— for *her*.

Finally, he lay down again and tried to empty his mind... to let the fog of weariness creep in. He must have drifted just enough, because Vothra came to him. The Benevolent Spirit was a shimmering silver figure, stepping out of sable shadow to stand beside his bed.

Are you angry with me, Spirit that calls itself Nagaro? I pushed you rather hard this day just past. Vothra's voice was gentle, as usual, but tinged with a note of regret.

"No," he told the spirit. "You were right. Running away wouldn't have helped. And Kuran is a very good man. I'm fortunate to have found him."

Yes he is. And you are.

There was a pause, and then the Spirit said, *You may as well put the other thought into words. I know it is there.*

He drew a breath. Of course the Spirit knew. "You could have told me who my parents were at any time," he said. "Because you knew everything that Maramine knew. Why, exactly, didn't you tell me? Was it because Maramine hadn't? Or because you deal in wisdom rather than knowledge?"

The spirit sighed, blinking starlit eyes. *I make rules for myself, and as often as not, I break them. Usually it is best to let the flower of the world unfold its petals as it will. But, when would have been the right time to tell you? Not while the Spirit of the White Flower was still working its healing upon you. And what would you have done with such knowledge while you were a galley slave? In truth, much of what you have done has been predicated on the belief that you were just an ordinary man—*

"I *am* just an ordinary man!"

Of course you are. But the name of Loros is potent in the minds of many, and your deeds have been, at times... uncommon. What will you do with this knowledge, now that you have it?

"I... don't know. I can't stop thinking about Nevien. Kuran thinks I can court her and win her. I'm not so sure of that."

The spirit appeared to consider him. *Kuran has experience with courtships, and some knowledge of the lady. His opinion therefore has merit. If the lady is so important to your future happiness, it would seem worthwhile to make the effort to pursue her.*

"But... can I possibly succeed? Now that she knows who I was? Kuran can never really understand what it was like..."

The silver figure blinked again. *I cannot say, because I do not know. Her mind is not very open to me. There is much conflict there, but I believe it has as much to do with her own past actions as with yours. Guilt is a bitter and corrosive thing.*

"I've told her I forgive her!"

Yes, you have. But the most difficult thing is often to forgive oneself.
"Well that's certainly true."

The spirit sighed. *And if you understand that, you have a hope of finding your way. I need really say no more. Fair well.* And with that, the Benevolent Spirit departed, fading into formlessness, leaving only the shimmering Sign of Vothra to float before Nagaro's eyes.

He lay there, trying to see how the things that the Spirit had told him could be of any use. So much depended on what Nevien was thinking, and he realized that he simply didn't know— *and he needed to.* He was going to have to stop avoiding her— try to talk to her. Having once decided that, he was finally able to relax. The sleep that claimed him, then, was deep and dreamless.

***

Nevien sat, trying unsuccessfully to read a book, turning pages to keep her hands busy as she did her best not to listen to the quiet conversation going on between Kuran and Lady Merriel. The sun had gone down outside the sitting room windows, and the lamps were lit.

The afternoon had been tedious and tense for her, with Nagaro's continuing absence and the hovering expectation that he might reappear at any moment. Nevien couldn't escape the nagging fear that her own actions were responsible for his absence, despite Kuran's repeated insistence that Nagaro had simply been overtaxed and needed to rest.

Nevien suspected that Kuran's lack of concern regarding Nagaro's behavior was related, in part, to the presence of Lady Merriel. Shortly after Nagaro's departure, a contingent of armed men that Kuran had ordered dispatched from Kel Wared had arrived, and Kuran had gone out to speak to their sergeant and to send the remaining Fleet men back to Lankura. He had no sooner returned to the sitting room than Merriel had reappeared and Kuran had immediately begun to catch her up on the parts of Nagaro's story that she had missed— omitting the most shocking details.

Nevien had tried not to listen to this reprise of the contorted scheme that she had unwittingly been part of. Her father was still her father, but he had fallen substantially in her estimation. She was going to have to deal with that eventually, she knew, but it wasn't at the center of her current difficulty.

No, her biggest problem right now was Nagaro.

She knew she had hurt him badly, there on the ledge. She had read it in his eyes in the instant before she'd turned and run away— *like a coward.* And how could she possibly explain to him what had happened?

That kissing him had felt extraordinary— right up to the moment when a memory of the awkward, wooden kiss that Leyel had given her on their wedding day had slithered into her mind, and she'd just needed to escape. How could she ever tell him that?

Dinnertime had come and gone without Nagaro coming down to rejoin them. The cook had eventually taken a tray up to his room, and later informed them that the captain had eaten. He had asked to have his seaman's chest brought up to him, then lain down to rest again. Kuran, still unconcerned, had returned to his animated discourse with Lady Merriel, which by this time had progressed to more private matters.

And that was how things now stood.

As glad as she was to see Kuran paying Merriel so much attention, Nevien was finding it hard not to fret. Trying to read the book was useless. The words refused to penetrate her preoccupation. She alternated between fearing that Nagaro had been so overtaxed that his wound had re-opened, and worrying that he was avoiding her because he'd had a change of heart as a result of her cruelties, past and present.

Her feelings towards him, which had undergone an undeserved reversal only days before, had been completely turned around once again. She hardly knew what to think. He both was, and wasn't, the man she had fallen in love with— the man she had believed could never be for her. He both wasn't— and was— the pathetic child-man she'd been married to... that awkward, simple-minded innocent whose clumsy attentions had made her weep. She found the idea that Leyel had been forced to marry her against his will quite appalling. It was no wonder he'd run away. And yet that runaway youth had somehow become Nagaro. He had come back. Incredibly, he'd become her friend, and now, against all sense and reason, it seemed that he loved her!

Unless of course she had ruined everything by pushing him away, up there on the ledge...

Nevien squirmed in her chair. *This was hopeless*. It was late enough by now that Nagaro was unlikely to come down before morning, and she wasn't sure what she would have said to him in any case. So she heaved a sigh, put down her book, and rose to tell the two chaparons that she was going to bed.

Kuran and Merriel, sitting at a discrete distance apart on the couch, bade her a distracted good night and promptly returned to their tete-a-tete.

Nevien took a candle and climbed the stairs. At the top, she noticed that the door of the room that had once been Leyel's was ajar. She peeked in cautiously, and saw Nagaro there— very obviously asleep. Like a sailor at sea, he lay sprawled on top of the bedclothes, fully dressed except for his boots. His face, in slumber, was untroubled.

Hastily she continued along the passage to the room where she slept— the room that had once been Maramine's. There she undressed and climbed trembling into bed, only to lie awake, struggling with her tangled emotions.

She couldn't understand how Nagaro could love her. It wasn't just that she had pushed him away on the ledge, or even the way she'd played dice with his life all those years ago. The memory of their conversation in the parlor also gnawed at her. *She should have known his behavior would have an explanation... should have trusted him...* If only she hadn't been so blinded by her need to know what had happened to the helpless youth she had dosed with an unknown medicine...

She was going to have to talk to him. But ever since that kiss, she had read pain and wariness in his eyes whenever he looked at her. *Like a child who has transgressed and been slapped for it by a beloved hand...*

She flinched at the image. Years ago, she had treated Leyel like a child, thinking he was no better than one. But Nagaro was certainly a man. The times when he'd held her, to comfort her, she had felt supported and protected by his embrace. Then, he had made her feel safe. On the ledge, she had felt something different— something that had a little unnerved her. The way he'd handled her had been... not ungentle, but *intense*. She'd felt both his strength and his restraint— the unspoken promise that he wouldn't hurt her, even as he'd held her as if he never meant to let her go.

Except of course he *had* let her go.

Because she'd pushed him away...

Just before she'd pushed him, she'd felt her own restraint beginning to slip— as if she was in danger of *losing herself...* And *then* the horrid thought had come worming into her mind that this was the same person who had kissed her like a marionette at the conclusion of their wedding vows... *and who had fumbled so clumsily with her nightdress—*

Abruptly, she heard voices in the hall.

It was Merriel and Kuran retiring for the night, quite modestly and properly to their own respective bedchambers by the sound of it. Nevien heard their muffled "good nights" and the closing of two separate doors. Merriel had her usual room, the one across the hall from Nevien's. Kuran would have the room next to Merriel's, across from the library— with the little corner room where Nagaro was sleeping on the farther side of it.

The sounds died away, leaving Nevien prey to her thoughts once again. The bright moon, Talebra, must have newly risen. Silver light penetrated the window curtain, picking out soft highlights on the polished wood of the dresser and the china bowl on the washstand. Nevien stared at the shadowed ceiling. Sleep was miles away.

Was it only the presence or absence of heskial that had made her experiences with Leyel and with Nagaro so different? Or could it also be because, now, he loved her? She could hear his voice in her mind, saying, "I would forgive you anything." That had to be love blinding him to her faults, because she'd surely never done anything to deserve such love from him...

And then, a terrible thought occurred to her.

"*Oh Gods!*" she murmured, sitting up in bed. She flung aside the covers, then hastily got up and located her dressing gown by moonlight, wrapping it hurriedly around her. Slipping out of the room, she crossed the hallway, barefoot, to knock urgently on Lady Merriel's door.

"Who is it?" Merriel's voice from within was eager, expectant.

"It's me, Nevien. I... have to talk to you..."

"Oh. Of course, dear. Do come in."

The words carried a tinge of disappointment and Nevien was pretty sure she knew why. Opening the door, she found Merriel seated at her dressing table, in her own dressing gown, with her hair down and a hairbrush in her hand.

The diminutive Leithian woman had twisted around on the stool to look at her guest. "I hope we didn't wake you, dear, Kuran and I. We tried to be quiet."

"You didn't wake me." Nevien closed the door and crossed the room.

Merriel must have caught her frown in the mirror and taken it for disapproval. "I know it was naughty of me to think it might be Kuran knocking," she confessed, applying the brush abstractedly to her hair. "But I'd just been thinking that he's never seen me with my hair down, and wondering if he'd like it this way. I'm being a silly girl, I know, but he seems *finally* to have noticed me, and when will I ever get another chance like this? With only the four of us here and no flock of young ladies and their beaus to look after?"

"Your hair is lovely, Merriel. And I'm sure Kuran will like it either way, up or down." Nevien's voice sounded distracted, even to her own ears.

"What's wrong, child?" Merriel repositioned herself on the little cushioned stool, to face her. "Couldn't you sleep?"

Nevien let out her breath in a shuddering sigh. Pulling up a chair, she sat down. "Do you remember the morning after Elyan died?" she asked. "When you came into my room and caught me reciting that rhyme— the one that ends, 'Send me a man who will love only me'?"

"Lissafel's rhyme? Yes, I do. I told you to be careful what you wished for."

"I know. And... and I should have. I never told you this, but... after you left, I went out onto the third floor balcony. And Nagaro was there. And I talked to him, and—"

"*Alone?*" Merriel's expression and tone both conveyed shocked disapproval.

Nevien shook her head impatiently. "It was perfectly innocent, Merriel! I went out for some air, and he was there with his spyglass looking for Kuran's fleet that should have been returning. We just talked. He was a perfect gentleman. But when I was leaving the balcony, I saw that Talebra was still in the sky— which means that the Lady was watching. And he was the first man I spoke to after saying the rhyme— except Brandle, of course, but Brandle doesn't count because he's crossed—" She stopped, because Merriel was staring at her in astonishment.

"But that was *years* ago, Nevien," the older woman protested. "Why are you upset about it now?"

"Because, it turns out, *now*, that he loves me, Merriel! What if the Goddess put her hand on him? What if he's been in love with me all this time because Lissafel has him under her spell?"

Merriel's brow furrowed. "How do you know he loves you, Nevien? Did he say so?"

"No-o..." Nevien frowned, abashed. "He... he kissed me today. Up on the ledge above the river."

Merriel's blue eyes went round. "Kuran *allowed* it?"

This time Nevien felt a surge of annoyance. "*I* allowed it. In fact, I'm rather afraid I encouraged it— once I understood what he wanted. Kuran was kind enough to allow us a little privacy, that's all."

"Oh." Merriel's brow puckered as she took this information under consideration. "Well," she said primly, "I suppose there's no *great* harm... in one little kiss."

"It wasn't so little, Merriel. He put his arms right around me, and he—"

"Oh my!" Merriel's hands fluttered. "But why did you encourage him if you're afraid the Lady has him under a spell?"

"I hadn't thought of that yet!" Nevien twisted her fingers together in her lap. "It just sort of happened. I find him so *very* attractive, and he was bending over me, and looking at me like— I don't know— And I... I thought I might never get another chance to see what it felt like. And it felt wonderful— like nothing I've ever felt before— and I suppose it must be because he loves me!"

Merriel seemed to be caught between curiosity and embarrassment. There was a spot of color in each of her dimpled cheeks. "I'm afraid it probably has more to do with how *you* feel about *him* than about how he feels about you, child," she said.

"Oh." Nevien studied her hands, feeling the blood in her own cheeks.

"Mind you," Merriel added, "I don't think the captain is the kind of man who would have kissed you if he didn't love you."

Nevien's head came up. "But he *shouldn't* love me! Not after how I've treated him! I don't deserve him, Merriel! I've done nothing to earn his love, and it would be horrible if the Lady was controlling him because I said that rhyme all those years ago. He's been controlled too much already— with the heskial... and then the linjana... I don't want to have him that way!"

Merriel frowned, her blue eyes full of concern. "But... you *do* want him?"

"I... yes..." Inwardly, Nevien writhed. "At least, I *did* want him before I knew who he really *was*. And I wish it could be like that again. But everything feels wrong now, because I know I don't deserve him—"

"Oh, dear child," Merriel rose and put her arms around Nevien's shoulders and gave her a squeeze. "I don't think love is something you have to earn. It's a gift. At least, if Kuran is finally coming around to loving me, *I'm* surely not going to ask why. I'm just going to be grateful for it."

"But *you* didn't say a silly selfish rhyme to make it happen!"

"Well, *no*," Merriel conceded. "But I did pray to the Goddess that Kuran would find someone who would make him happy, remember? It was your idea. And I *will* make him happy. That's what matters. And the way the captain feels about you probably has nothing to do with the rhyme—" She stopped, her eyes widening as an idea suddenly struck her. "I know what you should do!" she exclaimed. "You should say a prayer to Lissafel to set things straight. Then if he still loves you after *that*, you'll know it's real!"

"*Ye-es*... I could do that." Nevien felt relief wash through her. "That's a good idea, Merriel! The Lady will surely listen to a prayer that comes from my heart, won't she?"

"I've always believed so." Merriel patted her arm reassuringly. "Go on now, dear, and do it right away. You'll feel better, I'm sure."

Back in her own bedchamber, moments later, Nevien sat on the edge of her bed with her head bowed.

"*Sweet Lissafel, Lady of the Night and ruler of men's hearts, please hear my prayer,*" she began. "*All I want is for Nagaro to be happy. I want him to be free... to follow his own heart. I was very foolish and selfish to say your rhyme as I did that day without thinking what might come of it. And so, if it should chance that you're holding him for me... because of that... I pray you to let him go.*"

Chapter 13

Two Proposals

It was a little after dawn when Nevien awoke. Almost immediately, the memory of the previous day's events came flooding back, and a coil of tension re-wound itself around her stomach and began to squeeze. Yesterday had changed so many things, even the way she looked at this room that had once been Maramine Virden's. She had slept here many times over the years, but at that moment she was suddenly very glad that she had redecorated it. The altered furnishings made it harder to imagine that the horrific events Nagaro had described had actually happened here.

She shivered, then did her best to shake herself free of the dark thoughts as she climbed out of the bed and hurriedly straightened the bedclothes. Right now, the history of the bedchamber was the least of her worries. *She was going to have to find Nagaro, and when she did…*

She rose and exchanged her nightdress for her shift, then moved to the wash stand and poured water from the pitcher into the basin with a hand that trembled. Distractedly, she went through the motions of bathing with a washcloth. Standing in front of the mirror, she studied her reflection and noted that her eyes were a little puffy from her tears the day before, and that her face was rather pale. Frowning, she massaged a little color into her cheeks with her fingertips, then shook her head in dismay. She was primping for him, when she had no idea whether he would even want to look at her! Very deliberately, she finished dressing and brushed out her hair, leaving it loose on her shoulders. Then she left her bedroom and went out into the hallway.

The little room at the top of the stair was empty. The quilt on the bed had been smoothed. The only signs that the room was tenanted were the presence of the battered seaman's chest standing against one wall and the rumpled state of the towel hanging on the hook by the washstand.

Downstairs, she found Kuran alone in the sitting room, apparently busy with a book.

"Do you know where Nagaro is?" she asked, trying to keep her voice steady.

Kuran raised his eyes to regard her with an appraising glance. His voice when he answered, however, gave no hint that her question warranted any special concern. "He must have come down very early, and gone out. I got a glimpse of him in the garden a little while ago." He gestured toward the window with a tilt of his head.

"Oh. Good." Nevien allowed her relief to color her voice. "He must be feeling better." She paused, then added, "I... ah... I think I'll take a little air on the terrace."

Kuran didn't so much as twitch an eyebrow. "Good enough," he said easily. "The cook isn't planning breakfast for at least an hour. So you have time for a short walk if you like."

"I might do that."

She left him to his book, going out by the back door onto the terrace—where she lingered not at all. Instead, she made immediately for the garden, her only concession being to avoid the most direct route, in case Kuran was looking out the window.

It had rained during the night, although the clouds had blown over and the sky was clear. The winter sun's pale rays slanted through the naked branches of the trees that overarched the garden wall, casting a tracery of shadow across barren flower beds. Everything was still wet, the bare earth dark and water-soaked and richly musty-smelling. Droplets clung like jewels to the bare twigs.

Nagaro wasn't hard to find. He was standing on one of the paved paths, beside the single stone that marked Maramine's grave. His head was bowed as if in prayer or deep contemplation.

Nevien approached him warily. As desperate as she was for this encounter, she found herself trembling in fear of what she might discover. He was turned so that she saw his face in profile and he didn't immediately see her coming. His hair was unbound, and as she drew near she could see that it was wet from having bathed. The sleek black ringlets lay against the white fabric of his shirt collar in exactly the way they had on that fateful day when she'd found him with his spyglass on the third floor balcony of the palace in Lankura. She shivered, trying not to let it feel like an omen.

The morning was very quiet. A slight movement of air barely rustled the few remaining dry leaves. Nevien was aware of water dripping somewhere, and the muted gurgle of the little stream that wound its way over stones near the garden wall. Nagaro was so intent on his own thoughts, however, that she had come within a few paces of him before a soft scuff of her shoe on the paving stones alerted him to her presence.

He started when he heard her step, raising his head and turning towards her. His expression was somber, his gray eyes serious, but he met her glance this time and held it.

"Good morning, Nevien," he said, acknowledging her with a slight inclination of his head. "May I still call you that?'

"Yes... yes, of course." Her heart fluttered like a frightened bird. This didn't seem a very promising beginning. "I was walking," she ventured, "and not paying attention..." It was a lie, and she could carry it no further, but she couldn't bring herself to say that she had come looking for him. That would have begged the question of why, and she wasn't willing to explain her fears... the rhyme... the prayer...

He continued to regard her steadily, seeming much calmer than he'd been the previous day. In fact, he seemed as steady as she was flustered. Nor did he wait for her to explain herself further.

"I've been thinking about a lot of things," he said, placing the words carefully as if they were rehearsed, never taking his eyes from her face. "And I must apologize for my forwardness yesterday on the ledge. I acted on an impulse that I should have curbed."

Nevien's heart sank. "Are you saying that you're sorry you kissed me?" *It was rather blunt, but she had to know.*

He flinched a little at that, and his expression became, if anything, even more serious. "My heart doesn't regret it," he said, "but my head tells me it was unwise."

Her hope rose again, and she scarcely dared breathe. "Unwise?" she managed. "Why?"

"Because it changed something inside of me, and I can't undo it."

Now she trembled. "I... I don't understand."

He continued to regard her, his slim black brows knit together in a frown as he apparently sought for words. He looked down then, running a hand distractedly through his damp hair.

"I've had a taste of something," he said, and now the eyes that he raised to hers were full of longing. "And I want more of it. I know now that I love you too much to ever be able to stand by and watch you marry another man. If I can't win you, I'll have to take myself very far away indeed. I have to hope that Long Harbor or Boka Omei will be far enough."

I love you... There they were... the words she'd hoped for. Yet for a moment she could only stare at him. She had wanted to hear this, but now that he'd said it, she found herself stunned by his directness and the sheer extravagance of his confession.

"*Oh, Nagaro...*" she murmured. And this time it was she who dropped her eyes. This couldn't be Lissafel's doing, but it was too much, and her feelings of unworthiness came flooding back.

Apparently encouraged by the evidence of her emotion, he took a step nearer and reached tentatively for her hand, taking it gently in his "Do you love me, Nevien?" he asked huskily. "Or do you think you ever could?"

"I... I don't know..." she faltered, trying to think what to say and how to say it. Her heart was pounding and her hand trembled in his. "I surely did love the man I came to know as Nagaro—"

"Then you love *me!*" he cried, moving closer still in his eagerness. "Because I *am* Nagaro!"

She bit her lip. "I... I know you are. It just that... that's not *all* you are..." She risked looking into his eyes again. "And it's hard— knowing what I did to you... knowing that you were there all those years ago... inside... watching..."

Because she was looking into his eyes, she saw the hope in them, and she saw it die. He released her hand and spun away. "I *knew* it!" he cried bitterly, taking several strides along the path. "I *knew* it would ruin everything if you ever found out!"

"*No!*" She ran after him. "Nagaro! Wait!" She caught at his arm. "I didn't say it was hopeless!"

He stopped, turning back, emotions warring in his face. "*How*, then, Nevien? I can't erase the past!"

She halted, feeling his frustration. "I... I don't know. But if *you* can bear to love me, there must be hope! Only tell me how you do it! How do you keep your memories of that time from getting in the way?"

"*I don't know!*" he said bitterly. "By... by focusing on *now*, instead of *then*, I suppose. But, honestly, Nevien, I don't always succeed! When you were talking about me in the carriage, I couldn't help getting angry—"

"Who could blame you! When I treated you so horribly!"

"But you *didn't*, Nevien!' He raised his arms as if to embrace her, then let them drop again when she retreated a step. "*Other* people treated me horribly. Never you!"

"I treated you like a child—"

"For all you knew, I *was* a child!"

"I gambled with your life! And then I abandoned you—"

"Nevien! Stop! *Please!*" He closed the distance between them to capture her in his arms and press her against him. "*Please don't!*" he murmured, his face pressed against her hair, his voice catching. "I know it hurts, knowing you could have acted better. But you weren't even seventeen— and you were so alone! You were a pawn in your father's game, and Luka used you too! As grateful as I am to her, it wasn't fair to take advantage of your pain. She should have told you what she knew!"

"I... I wouldn't have believed her." Wrapped in his arms, Nevien this time felt no inclination to struggle free. "If Luka had accused my father, I wouldn't have trusted her, and I wouldn't have done what she wanted."

He shifted then, as if worried he was being too forward again. Dropping his arms, he drew away from her, and she felt a sharp pang at the separation.

"I suppose Luka may have acted wisely— from her point of view," he said. "But when it was all over, and I was safe, she could have tried to get a message to you. She could have told you I was alive and that you shouldn't worry about me anymore."

"She may have thought I'd tell my father. I might have, too."

"When you hadn't told him anything before?" He shook his head at her. "I don't know... *Maybe* Luka reasoned that way— But I think her only concern was to rescue me, with no thought for how you'd be hurt in the process. And I was no better— in the harness shed... when I told you not to go. Those were the only words of my own that I spoke the entire time... but if you had stayed, and I had died... you would have blamed yourself! And I didn't even think of that!

She reached for his arm. "It's all *right*, Nagaro! You were suffering—"

But he shook off her hand. "I never thought of it until *yesterday*, Nevien! How could I have missed it all those years? I kept telling myself you couldn't possibly have cared what became of me. I was *such* an embarrassment... *such* a burden. Doing that made it easier to be selfish. To protect myself—."

"I was protecting myself too!" Nevien couldn't bare to listen to his self-recrimination in the face of her own guilt. "If I'd only trusted you enough to tell you what I'd done— to... to Leyel— surely you would have told me everything!"

She searched his face for confirmation, but his eyes slid away.

"I don't think so, Nevien..." He kept his distance, not looking at her. "You would always have been the hardest one to tell— because of what you'd seen... what you knew. I told Varsyl because he needed to know that his sister had forgiven him. But Varsyl had never even *seen* Leyel." His eyes came back to her face, frowning, troubled. "I probably would have told you *something* to ease your mind, but I would have avoided telling you the whole truth— just as I did yesterday in the parlor—"

She felt a stab of pain. "*I'm* the one who behaved badly in the parlor! When I found the ring in the bottom of my wardrobe, it was as if I forgot everything I knew about you and—"

"It's all right, Nevien!" Suddenly he had his arms around her again. "You'd trusted me, and I deceived you. You felt betrayed—"

But that was too easy and she suddenly saw something clearly. "That's not it!" she said as she pushed herself out of his embrace. "I knew I had betrayed Leyel— years ago— I felt terribly guilty! I was angry at *myself*, and I turned my anger on *you!*"

He had let go instantly when she'd pushed against his chest, and he stood there, his face contorted. "How can I expect you to love me?" he asked, choking, "when I deceived you for *two and a half years*— because I was afraid! Yesterday on the ledge, I would have run away if the Spirit hadn't ordered me to stay! *I'm such a coward*—"

"*Then so am I!*" Nevien cried. "I kept my guilty secret for *ten years* because I was afraid to tell it! And don't say I shouldn't love you, because I *do!* When you were lying in the street— and I thought those Leithians had killed you— It felt as if I was going to die!"

And at last it seemed that her words struck home. He straightened his shoulders and there was a new look in his eyes.

"Look at us, Nevien," he said ruefully. "Each trying to prove we're the more guilty one! Vothra told me last night that forgiving yourself is the hardest part, and I'd already forgotten. Can't we just accept that we've both made mistakes, but that we love each other anyway?"

Nevien's heart lifted. He was standing there looking at her with the eyes of the young man in the portrait, eyes that held an earnest plea. "Merriel told me that love is a gift. Not something you have to earn...."

He smiled crookedly. "I think Merriel is a very wise woman. So... shall we try?" He held out a hand.

"Yes... yes, I want to." She reached for the offered hand.

He stepped right up to her then, taking her hand and looking down into her face "It's not going to be easy— because we can't erase the past. I'm going to need help from you, I know... to get through... certain things, even though I've had years of knowing about what passed between us...back then. You've only just found out. So I expect you'll find some things hard too."

Nevien drew a trembling breath. It seemed that her heart had made its choice long ago, and it was far too late to undo it. "Then you'll just have to help me," she said. "I... I think I'd like you to help me right now."

"How?" he asked. "What can I do?"

She dropped her eyes, feeling herself blush. "I think... maybe, if you kissed me..."

She didn't have to ask him twice.

***

Merriel came into the sitting room to find Kuran seated on the couch under the window that overlooked the garden. He was flipping idly through a book but looked up when she entered.

"Good morning, Merriel. You're looking very lovely this morning."

"Oh... why, thank you, Kuran" she said, blushing. Then she looked about, puzzled. "But where are Nevien and Nagaro?"

"They're outside. In the garden."

"What, *together?*"

"Oh, very much so."

"Shouldn't you be watching them?" Merriel approached the window.

Kuran coughed. "I tried watching for a while," he drawled. "But it was making my blood hot, so I thought I'd better give it up."

"*Mercy!*" Merriel was at the window. "What is he doing with her!"

Kuran was on his feet in one agile motion and at her side. "Just exactly what he should be doing, I'd say," he observed, peering at the couple in the garden. "It took him rather a long time to get around to it, but I expect he had to convince himself that there was no conceivable objection. I must say he seems to be making up for lost time."

"Sweet Lissafel!" Merriel clapped a guilty hand to her mouth.

Kuran gave a low whistle. "Come away from the window, Merriel," he said. "I'm beginning to get ideas."

"Kuran! You rogue!"

"Actually, dear Lady," he said, slipping an arm around her waste. "I don't need any other inspiration than your beauty to give me ideas. Come. Sit with me."

Her eyes went wide. "*Oh, Kuran...*" she said, breathlessly. She glanced again a guiltily at the window, yet offered no resistance as Kuran steered her gently to a seat on the couch.

"We should leave them to each other, Merriel," he continued as he sat down beside her at the barest minimum distance consistent with propriety. "They're not children, after all, any more than you and I. They've discovered that they love each other, and since we've learned that Nagaro is the heir of the House of Loros, it seems unnecessary to stand in his way. Don't you agree?"

"Well...*ye-es...*" she murmured, her blue eyes wide and riveted on his face. "I suppose we really needn't worry that anything *serious* will happen."

"Of course not. And besides..." Kuran leaned towards her with a wolfish gleam in his eye. "*Their* absence conveniently leaves us alone... *together...*"

***

"Would you consent to marry me, Nevien?" Nagaro asked.

It was during the third time they had come up for air.

"Oh, *yes!*" Nevien smiled blissfully. She was nestled in the crook of his arm as they sat together on one of the garden's stone benches, her head resting on his shoulder. "I would, and in fact, I do."

"Even if your father and the Council are against it?"

"Yes. Even then."

"Even if it means you would never be queen?"

At that, she stirred, moving so that she could look into his face. She regarded him seriously. "For myself, I really don't care if I'm ever queen," she said. "But I've always had to think of the good of Edrovir."

"Does that mean the answer is... no?"

Nevien felt his arm tighten ever so slightly about her shoulders. She saw the fear in his eyes. "You would make a good king," she said.

"I hardly think so!" He seemed to shrink.

"That's only because you can't see yourself, Nagaro, as I and others can. You *would* make a good king."

"I have no wish to be one!"

She sighed and raised a hand to caress his bearded cheek. "Then I would never ask it of you," she said. "Edrovir will just have to survive without me. And besides, I don't want to put you in danger. Lothard has already tried to kill you once just for being an inconvenience. If he saw you as a rival, he'd surely try again. It's not *me* that he wants— it's the crown. But if we were to wed quietly, in secret, and only make it known to the world *afterwards*—"

"I don't want to take you like a thief in night!" Nagaro stiffened and the storm clouds began to gather in his eyes. "Like a... *like a pirate!* That's what they'll say—"

"What do we care what they say?"

"If I make it clear that I have no interest in the crown, surely I should be able to court you openly—"

She put a finger to his lips to stop his words. "Lothard would never believe you! He'd think it was a ruse— because that's what it would be if he said it. It's much too dangerous to do it that way."

The storm receded, if only slightly. "Well, you would know that better than I," he conceded. "You've had more dealings with Lothard. But if your father and the Council objected to my suit, wouldn't that convince Lothard that I'd never be king?"

Nevien shook her head at him. "They *wouldn't* object— at least not to the courtship. They want you to fight Lothard for them. They want you to kill him!"

Nagaro stared at her, understanding dawning in his eyes. "Is *that* what Anduar wanted?"

"*Yes!* The council members were sure it would come to a fight between you and Lothard if you could be persuaded to court me."

"And... in your message... when you said you wanted no part of it—"

"It was because I was afraid Lothard would kill you! And I was *right* to be afraid. He didn't even wait for you to court me!"

Nagaro sat looking past her, frowning. "But... you're a princess," he said at last. "How would a secret marriage be regarded? Would anyone accept it?"

It was Nevien's turn to frown as she considered this objection. "I suppose we *would* need plenty of witnesses," she mused. "People who are well-respected—"

"But those are exactly the kind of people who would object!"

"Hush, Nagaro! Please!" She threw her arms around his neck. "Don't *worry* so much! We'll work it out somehow." She drew his head towards hers. "Kiss me again."

Lost for the moment in her eyes, he pushed his concerns aside and bent, obedient to her desire.

***

"That was lovely..." Merriel ran a shy finger over her lips as she leaned comfortably against Kuran's shoulder. His arm was draped across the back of the couch, encircling her possessively.

He gave her an indulgent smile. "We may not set the stars ablaze. Not like those two out there. But we still have some fire in us, I think."

"Oh, *yes.*" She blushed. "But it's been so *very* long..."

"Mmm." He grew somber. "Yes, it's been ten years since the plague carried off my dear wife— and your devoted husband. It *is* a long time to be alone, Merriel. I'd almost forgotten how good it is to feel a woman's arms around me."

"There was so much... *grief*... at first..." she murmured, remembering.

He nodded. "For the first year or two it seemed I could feel nothing else. I had to escape it somehow, so I threw myself into my work."

"And I devoted myself to my children." Merriel sighed with wistful sadness. "But they were nearly grown and didn't need me for long. So I gave myself to the service of Queen Semorel, and after that, to Nevien and her ladies."

"And so you found yourself thrown in with me, as a chaperon." Kuran chuckled. "Strange are the ways of Lokundas. If I hadn't forged a friendship with the princess, our paths would never have crossed."

"That... would have been very sad."

"Yes... Yes it would."

There was a pause, and then he added, "I can't imagine that my dear Indrid would have wished me to be lonely for the rest of my days, simply because she was forced to leave me so soon."

"Oh, surely not. And... I know Grovern would want me to be happy..."

There followed a slightly longer pause while neither of them looked at the other. At last Kuran shifted and looked down at her, his gaze warm with admiration and affection. "Then, if you will keep me company," he said, "I'd like to try to make you happy. Merriel, will you be my wife?"

She turned her face to his, her blue eyes open wide. "Oh, Kuran, I would be very glad to be your wife! But this is... rather sudden!"

"I would have courted you longer before asking, but at our age, frankly, there's no time to waste."

Merriel blushed crimson, and dropped her eyes. "I suppose no one needs to know how long we courted," she murmured. "If we say it was six months, who would be the wiser? We... we could wed as soon as you've asked permission—"

"*Permission?*" Kuran's brows came sharply together. "You're a grown woman! Of whom must I ask permission?"

"It's the tradition, Kuran!" All aflutter, Merriel raised her hands in a gesture of supplication. "You have to ask my closest male relative!"

"But your father is long dead, and you have no brothers!"

"It would be my son."

"Your *son!*" Kuran gaped at her. "How *old* is your son?"

"Twenty-four, last month."

"He's less than half my age!"

"But it's the *tradition!* You mustn't shame him by not asking! He's a man, after all, and men have their pride. It's not as if he'll say no!"

Kuran opened his mouth, and closed it again. "He won't say no?"

"Of course not!"

"Well, good enough, then." Kuran's ire abated. "For the sake of the young man's pride, I will ask him."

"With proper formality?" Her eyes pleaded. "And courtesy?"

He waved a hand. "Yes, yes."

"And... do you think you could manage maybe a little... *humility?*"

"Merriel," he said severely. "I am not known for being a humble man. But I *do* understand diplomacy. Now, do you trust me?"

"Yes, Kuran." She gave him a melting smile. "I trust you completely. And if I let you kiss me again, I know it will be our secret. But you had best be quick about it. They'll be coming back in soon for breakfast and they mustn't catch us."

"Mmm..." He leaned down to meet her upturned lips and collect the offered reward.

# Chapter 14

The Road Takes A Turn

Breakfast was much more convivial than the previous day's lunch had been, although the conversation was carefully superficial. The secret smiles and knowing glances exchanged across the table told the true story. As soon as the meal was done and the dishes cleared away, Nevien and Merriel rose simultaneously, as if by some agreement, and left the room on the pretext of needing to pack their things, since they all intended leave River House that morning.

Nagaro remained at the table, and his mood turned pensive. He'd come out of the encounter with Nevien in the garden riding on a tide of triumph, but his euphoria was subsiding as reality began to reassert itself.

Kuran pushed back his chair and turned an arch glance upon him. "I'll wager the women have gone to compare notes," he observed. "So this is our opportunity to do the same. And by the look of things, I'd say you had some success with the lady."

Nagaro sighed. "More than I expected," he admitted. "She loves me, and she's said that she'll marry me, even without the consent of her father or the Council."

Kuran's jaw dropped. "By the Eyes!" he exclaimed. "And here I was congratulating myself because Merriel has agreed to marry me if I get her son's consent first! It seems the novice has outstripped the master."

Nagaro shook his head. "Merriel is being a proper Leithian woman, that's all. Nevien doesn't feel bound by that tradition. But I should offer you congratulations," he added. "I'm very glad for you."

Kuran frowned. "And I for you," he said. "But I must say that you don't seem overly elated at your good fortune."

"I am thinking of the implications of marrying without that consent."

"Ah. I see."

"She says we should marry in secret— for my safety. But I don't see how that can possibly work. She's the princess. Everyone has expectations."

Kuran rubbed his chin speculatively. "Yes. And *you* are the heir of Loros. There are expectations connected with that as well."

Nagaro's frown deepened. "Those expectations nearly started a war a few months ago. Some of the Leithians were afraid that Kenthos was going to try to set himself up as king. I don't want to see that repeated!"

Kuran settled back in his chair. "Kenthos was an unknown, Nagaro," he said, assuming the air of one delivering an educational lecture. "There was serious concern regarding what kind of king he would be. He had limited support, at best— even among the Kelorin. The support for *you* would be much broader. You're generally loved by the common folk, widely respected among the nobility, and you're a proven leader— if on a modest scale."

Nagaro shifted in his chair. "What are you suggesting?"

"Only that I agree with you. A marriage made in secret, before you've established your claim to the name of Loros, would not work to your advantage. It would look as if the claim had been trumped up to justify the marriage— and by extension, your bid for the crown."

Nagaro went rigid as ice stabbed through him. "I don't intend to make a bid for the crown."

Kuran came to a halt in the act of reaching up to scratch his ear. "You... *don't?*" he said slowly, his black eyes sharply fixed on Nagaro's face.

"No. I don't."

"Ah." Kuran's hand sought his chin again as he worriedly fingered his beard. "I... see. Do you mind telling me, then, what exactly you were thinking when you proposed marriage to Nevien Harlind?"

Nagaro looked down at his hands, running his fingers along the edge of the tabletop, feeling the familiar smoothness of the polished wood. "I meant to ask it somewhat hypothetically," he admitted. "She took it rather less so. And, well, while kissing her a few times, as you suggested did stir her blood, it unfortunately had the same effect on mine."

"Well, there is that," Kuran conceded. "But however the proposal was intended, if it's been made and accepted, you can't go back on it."

"I know. And I don't intend to. I don't *want* to." He frowned. "I did a great deal of thinking, yesterday and this morning. I'd decided that I would throw all of my effort into winning Nevien's hand, if only she were agreeable to the idea."

"Ha! I'd say she is."

"Ye-es... but I had intended to court her openly. That's still the way I'd rather do it— after I've taken care of a few other things."

"What other things?" Kuran was studying him closely.

"Well, first I must formally establish my right to the name of Loros and reclaim any lands or property that my... father... left to me— so I have something to offer Nevien when we wed... besides being your adopted heir, I mean."

"That seems reasonable." Kuran's bright black eyes remained fixed on Nagaro's face. "And what of the lordship of Loros Wared?" he inquired with perfect deadpan.

Nagaro stared back at him, surprised. "Officially there *is* no Loros Wared right now," he pointed out. "Although I believe an effort is underway to gather the old Wared's scattered descendants. It will be up to them to choose a lord."

"Vothra's ass, man!" Kuran slapped the table. "Do you think for one minute that you wouldn't be their first choice— as soon as they learn that you're one of those descendants? Never mind being Tevren's son, they'd have you as Captain Nagaro in a minute!"

Nagaro blinked. "Well, I suppose they might. Though I also imagine there might be others they would consider. I suppose I wouldn't say no, either, if I were chosen. I believe I could do the work, and I wouldn't mind being a Wared lord."

Kuran shook his head. "You're willing to be lord of Loros Wared," he said weakly, "but you have no intention of being king."

"That's right."

"And you don't see that being the one will make it look as if you're positioning yourself for the other?"

Nagaro frowned. "If the people of the Wared truly want me for their lord—" he began, and stopped because at that moment Merriel appeared in the doorway with Nevien behind her.

"What, are you two still sitting here?" Merriel asked innocently.

"Yes, ladies." Kuran spoke lightly, but his eyes were serious. "Come, please. Sit and join us. There are matters to discuss."

Merriel and Nevien exchanged glances, but came obediently to the table. They arranged themselves with Merriel across from Kuran and Nevien across from Nagaro. Nevien carried a book, which she laid on the table, her hand resting lightly on the cover.

Kuran addressed the two women. "I think we all know that there have been two marriage proposals made and accepted this morning," he said. "And while my proposed marriage to Merriel is unlikely to encounter any serious obstacles, the same can't be said for Nagaro's proposed marriage to Nevien. You and I, Merriel, must be prepared to offer advice and support to our two young friends in their effort to achieve their desire."

Merriel immediately bobbed her head in agreement. "Yes," she said firmly. "We must help them in any way we can."

"Thank you, Merriel." Nevien gave the older woman a grateful smile.

Kuran acknowledged Merriel's words with a nod. "Unfortunately," he continued. "Nagaro doesn't wish to be king, and it follows that if he weds Nevien, she won't be queen. Since this violates the expectations of nearly every citizen of Edrovir, it means that his petition to court her on such terms is likely to meet some... *resistance*."

Nevien leaned forward, frowning. "That's why I think we should marry in secret," she interjected. "Once it's done, it can't be undone, and folk will have to accept it."

Nagaro had let Kuran speak, but he now felt the need to protest. "I'm sorry, Nevien," he said earnestly, "but I still don't like that idea. I've had rather too much of secrecy and deception."

"And I concur with Nagaro," Kuran put in quickly. "A kitchen maid and a groom might do as you suggest, Nevien. A princess really cannot. Nor can the heir of Loros. For your marriage to be widely accepted, it must be made openly."

Nevien's fingers tightened visibly on the book in front of her. "What of the danger, Kuran?" she asked sharply. "Did you know the Council is plotting to maneuver Nagaro into a challenge match with Lothard?"

Kuran frowned. "No, I didn't," he said. "But a man with a cool head may avoid a challenge."

At this, Nevien jumped to her feet. "But Lothard doesn't *need* a challenge!" she cried. "He can use treachery! He's tried it once already!"

For the space of three heartbeats, Kuran returned her blazing glance, his black eyes hard as two flints. "Lothard will have to come through me if he wants to try that again," he said at last. "Through me, or through my men. It's one thing to attack an unwary man alone in a dark street, and another to attack a man who's on his guard with armed men at his back. From now on, I intend to see that Nagaro is well guarded."

Nevien stood for a moment longer, impaling Kuran with her gaze, before she sank back into her seat. "Well," she said grudgingly, "there's some comfort in that."

Nagaro rose to give Kuran a small bow. "I will gladly accept your protection, My Lord," he said formally. He'd been alarmed by Nevien's reaction and was relieved that she seemed mollified. "I intend to make a formal claim to the Loros family name," he added, addressing the entire company as he returned to his seat. "And I mean to petition for the restoration of the House of Loros, with any lands that my father has bequeathed to me. But I don't intend to do it until I've decided how best to present my case— or before I've fully recovered my strength. For the present, I intend to keep my plans as quiet as possible."

"That would be wise." Kuran nodded his approval.

Nagaro sought Nevien's eyes across the table. "I won't seek your hand until I've gained formal recognition for myself," he told her. "When I've gotten that far, I hope I'll be able to see clearly how best to proceed. I've said that I prefer an open courtship and marriage, but it may be that secrecy is the only choice the world will give us."

Nevien returned his gaze warmly, and he read gratitude in her eyes for the acknowledgment of her concerns.

Kuran's sharp eyes had flicked back and forth between them. "That is fairly spoken, Nagaro," he observed. "It's too soon really to rule anything out. But make no mistake—" and here he fixed Nagaro with a level gaze. "The appearance of the true heir of Loros will change things in this land significantly."

"It needn't, if I don't press the issue!" Nagaro protested.

"Even if you don't press it," Kuran cut in, "it's inevitable that you'll be seen as a potential player in the power game. It will raise alarm among the Leithian Faction— and enthusiasm among the Kelorin. You'll have to make it *very* clear— from the outset— that your *only* ambition is to wed Nevien. If you can convince the opposing powers of *that*, it may be that the Council— and even the king— will be willing to set aside their expectations for Nevien's future in order to keep the peace."

There was silence when Kuran finished. Nagaro sat looking down at his hands. He would have preferred not to think there was so much riding on his actions, but he suspected Kuran's assessment was accurate.

"You're forgetting Lothard again," Nevien said, frowning. "The council members don't believe peace is possible as long as Lothard is in the world. They want to be rid of him, and they think Nagaro is the only man who can do it. What if they make the challenge a condition for our marriage?"

Kuran frowned. "If it comes to that," he said grimly. "We'll have to see what can be done."

Nagaro shifted uneasily. "I might not be able to give them what they want," he said in a low voice. "I'm not sure how much of my skill I'll recover. They'll have to understand that."

Merriel had been following the conversation attentively and now she spoke. "There's something I don't understand," she said, leaning forward, her blue eyes questioning. "Nagaro and Nevien were married once. Doesn't that give Nagaro some claim?"

Nagaro's revulsion was instantaneous. "*No!*" he cried. "I will *not* be Leyel Virden again! And that was no marriage!" He caught himself as his mind registered the reactions of the others seated at the table.

Nevien was staring at him in dismay. Kuran was eyeing him sharply. Merriel's hand had flown to her mouth even as her eyes went wide in alarm. "Oh mercy!" she squeaked. "I'm sorry!"

"No, *I'm* sorry, Merriel." Nagaro passed a hand over his eyes, embarrassed by his own outburst. The shocked expression on Nevien's face, in particular, smote his heart. He leaned across the table towards her as he tried to explain. "I'm sorry Nevien. I know it must have seemed a valid marriage to you, but the words weren't mine. I would never have abandoned you if I'd believed you were truly my wife."

Nevien reached out to cover his hand with hers, her shock melting into sympathy. "Of course," she said. "You weren't a willing party to it, so from your point of view, it wasn't binding."

Kuran coughed. "I don't know if it could be argued that it wasn't binding, under the law," he said carefully. "But to answer Merriel's question, Nagaro would likely have some difficulty staking a claim *now*, since he didn't come forward to contest either of Nevien's other marriages."

"Oh. I see." Merriel had recovered her aplomb.

Nagaro gave Nevien a grateful glance. "Leyel Virden must remain dead in the eyes of the world," he said firmly, "I have no wish to reclaim that name. *Ever!*"

Nevien and Kuran exchanged glances, but then Kuran cleared his throat. "I think that's enough of this talk for the time being," he said. "I confess I've been curious about that book you have, Nevien. Is there some reason why you brought it here?"

Nevien picked up the slim volume. "Not the book, actually, but what's inside it," she said and she opened the book to reveal a folded piece of paper. "It's that poem you found, Nagaro. Remember? The Lily and the Rose." She carefully unfolded the paper and looked up to meet Nagaro's eyes. "It was surely written by the Lady Maramine in memory of your mother. I'd like to read it aloud, if you don't mind."

Nagaro felt his throat tighten. "All right," he said, and Nevien proceeded to read:

"Dear heart, true heart, none truer that I know,
The rose is fallen. All her petals blow
Before the wind of memory, beneath the rain of tears
I shed for her, dear confidant and friend across the years.
Two flowers from a single stem were sprung,
To intertwine, one song together sung.
Across the miles between, our words have flown
To find each other's hearts with comfort sown.
The mother lost, the sister never born
Could not be more to me than her I mourn.
A wiser head the world may never see,
A hand more gentle, or a soul more free.
Together we had breasted hope and pain,
Now she is gone, and lonely I remain.
Poor poet, I, I struggle to compose
These lines for our memorial, the Lily and the Rose."

Nagaro sat silent as Nevien ceased speaking, his head bowed, fighting emotion.

Kuran shook himself. "How remarkable," he said. "It suggests a long-enduring friendship between Maramine and Queen Lindra— if you're right about the identities of the two people in the poem."

"Oh, I am sure of it, Kuran." Nevien spoke eagerly. "The hand is Maramine's, and she is obviously the Lily. She always loved lilies. And the Rose had to be someone she knew, who died. But I couldn't guess who it was until we learned that Leyel was Lindra's son. Even then it was only a guess until I showed the poem to Merriel this morning. She immediately understood the one line that had puzzled me."

"That's right." Merriel nodded brightly. "The part about 'two flowers from a single stem' means they were related. Maramine and Lindra were blood cousins, you see. Their mothers were sisters."

Kuran slapped his thigh. "And *you* just happen to know that, Merriel? When no one else has noticed?"

Merriel sat up primly in her chair. "You mean the *men* haven't noticed," she said. "Men never think the female line is important, but women notice. And we remember."

Nagaro stirred and raised his head. "I have, here, another piece of evidence," he said, reaching into his shirt to produce the little note he'd found in Maramine's desk. He had retrieved it from his sea chest earlier that morning, thinking to show it to Kuran.

Kuran took the note and read it aloud.

"*Look for him at dawn on the third day, and all my love and gratitude go with you always.*" He whistled. "And in place of a signature, it bears a drawing of a rose!" He passed the note across the table for Merriel and Nevien to examine. "The meaning is a bit cryptic, but when we find a sample of Lindra's writing, I'll wager it will match."

Nagaro swallowed. "Maramine told me I was found at her door around dawn on the third day of Evrel. When I first found that note, I hoped it had been written by my mother. Now I feel sure of it."

"Where did you find it?" Nevien asked. "I searched all over this house for any of Maramine's letters that could have identified the Rose in the poem."

"It was in a secret compartment in her desk upstairs." Nagaro ducked his head guiltily. "I saw her open it once, so I knew where to look for the catch. I can show you. There are other letters and some records, but there's nothing else in that hand— nothing else signed like that."

"That's odd." Nevien frowned.

"No, it isn't," Kuran said. "When Maramine undertook to raise the child of Tevren and Lindra, I'm sure the intention was to keep the child's identity strictly secret. Anything that could have identified him would have potentially endangered him. Maramine may well have destroyed all the other correspondence she ever received from Lindra. It's what I would have done in her place."

"How sad," Merriel murmured. "That these two writings should be the only things remaining to mark the friendship that they shared."

"Sad perhaps, but a necessary sacrifice..."

The conversation ran on as the others at the table continued discussing the actions of the two highborn cousins, but Nagaro wasn't listening. His thoughts were dwelling on the debt that he owed to these two women. The one, his mother, had given him life. She had surely loved him, yet she'd found the strength to give him into the keeping of another woman for his safety. And that other woman, his Lady Guardian, had bravely taken up the burden. She had given him seventeen years of care, guidance, and protection. She'd provided him an education and the opportunity to train in swordsmanship. He wished he could learn more about these two people and what had passed between them.

He wanted to know more about his mother, and also what part that his father had played in making the arrangement. But, sitting there under the roof that had sheltered Maramine for so many years, he realized that if there were anything more to be learned, it would not be found in this place. He stirred, coming out of his reverie, and spoke into a momentary lull in the flow of talk.

"I have to go to Loros Hall."

They all turned to stare at him, startled. He turned to Kuran. "I'm sorry, My Lord," he said. "I know you meant to offer me the protection and hospitality of Kell Hall, but there's nothing for me there. I *need* to go to Loros Wared— to Loros Hall."

To his surprise, Kuran's smile included his bright black eyes. "If you hadn't said it, I would have suggested it myself," he said. "Your road has taken a turn, Nagaro, and Loros Hall is clearly where it leads. I'll be pleased to offer you my company for the journey, and the escort of my men-at-arms."

Nagaro looked at Nevien, knowing what he wanted to ask but uncertain if he should.

Her eyes were very bright, glistening a little with the hint of tears, but she smiled also. "If that's where you're going, Nagaro, then I'm going there with you," she said, answering his unspoken wish.

Merriel threw up her hands. "Oh, *well*," she said. "In that case, I suppose I must go there as well!"

Chapter 15

Loros Hall

The coach lurched along a rutted road between stands of leafless trees. It was escorted by ten armed, cloaked horsemen, leading four riderless mounts. Among those four horses were a tall gray stallion and a dainty white mare, and the cloaks of the riders concealed that fact that half of them wore the livery of Kel Wared and half of the Palace Guard.

Inside the coach, Kuran and Nagaro sat on the forward-facing seat and Nevien and Merriel on the rearward-facing one. After some discussion, they had decided that the best hope for secrecy lay in them all sharing the unmarked coach in which Nagaro had arrived, the two women having come to River House on horseback, without a carriage of their own.

Kuran had dispatched one of his men to Kel Hall, carrying word of his change of plans and explaining it by saying he had business at Loros Hall. Nevien had sent one of her guards back to Lankura with a message to the effect that she and the Lady Merriel had decided to take a week's holiday in the country. The fact that both parties were in fact traveling together to Loros Hall had only been revealed to the remaining men-at-arms after the two messengers were well away.

Merriel had her curtain open and was looking out. "We've finally left the woods," she said, "and come into some open fields. How much farther is it to Loros Hall?"

Kuran answered. "Not far. When we pass through the village of Fenerwel, we'll know we're nearly there."

Nagaro cautiously twitched aside the curtain on his side of the coach. "The fields look as if they've been planted and harvested," he observed as he let the curtain fall closed again. "There's much more evidence of habitation than I remember from last spring when we were tracking Kenthos."

Kuran nodded. "It seems the effort to resettle the scattered folk of Loros Wared has been proceeding quite well in this area. I wish I knew what we'll find at the Hall."

A short time later, the coach slowed and the driver called down that they were entering Fenerwel. Nevien had been scanning the sky to assess the weather, but she hastily closed her curtain. Nagaro refrained from opening his. "You look," he said to Kuran. "Tell me what you see."

The Lord of the Fleet had his curtain open just enough to get a view of what lay immediately outside the carriage. "We're making a bit of stir," he said, grimly. "I wish there'd been some other choice than coming through the town, but we could never have taken this coach in by the back way we used last spring."

The sounds of excited voices could indeed be heard over the rattle of the coach.

Kuran craned to look around more widely. "I'd swear that smithy was abandoned six months ago," he muttered. Then abruptly he gave a cry, and rapped on the side of the coach, calling for the driver to stop. "I just saw Kenthos!" he said in response to the astonished questions of his fellow passengers. "I mean to have a word with him, and appearances be damned! He'll know how the wind is blowing."

In a moment, Kuran was out the door, opening it and closing it quickly behind him. A minute after that, the door opened again just long enough to admit Kenthos and Kuran together.

The young blacksmith blinked uncertainly at the occupants of the coach before his eye lit on Nagaro and his face brightened. "Good afternoon to ye, Captain," he said, taking a seat between Nagaro and Kuran. "I'm glad to see it's true they couldn't kill ye! And good afternoon to ye, too... Ladies..." he added, inclining his head respectfully to Nevien and Merriel. He seemed to be waiting for Kuran to introduce the two women and his expression grew worried as his gaze lingered on Merriel's blond hair and Leithian features.

Kuran coughed. "The fair lady sitting across from me is Lady Merriel, who is very soon to be my betrothed," he offered. "You may speak as freely in her presence as you would to me. She is a traveling companion to the other lady, who is Nevien Harlind, as dear a friend as any I have."

The second introduction made Kenthos start visibly. "Your... your pardon, My Lady Princess," he stammered. "I... I'm honored t' be in your presence."

Nevien returned him a warm smile. "And I'm pleased to make your acquaintance, Tor Kenthos," she said. "Your actions have gained you some fame in this land. And I have it from my friends, here, that you're a good-hearted man who never meant to do harm, in spite of anything that was said of you."

Kenthos went scarlet and murmured something unintelligible, then turned to Kuran. "I'm glad to get a ride in your coach," he ventured, "since I've a meeting at the Hall. It will spare me the walk. But what did ye want with me, My Lord?"

Kuran cleared his throat. "As I told you, I have some business at Loros Hall. I was wondering what I'll find when I get there. I can see there've been changes hereabouts."

Kenthos' blush was fading, and his handsome features now relaxed. "Well if that's all ye're wanting," he said, "we have nothing to fear, since we've gotten Lord Endemar's blessing for what we're doing."

"And what exactly is that?"

"Why, bringing the children of Loros home," Kenthos explained proudly. "—just to *this* part o' the old Wared, of course," he added quickly, reading Kuran's face. "The Kildoran part. We're not trying t' take back the part that went to Sobring Hold, or *your* part, My Lord. The folk in Kel Wared are happy as things are..." His voice trailed and he licked his lips worriedly.

Kuran sat looking stern for a moment, but then he laughed. "Well, I certainly hope they are," he said. "I've tried to be a good lord to them. So... you've settled here yourself, I assume?"

"Aye." Kenthos looked relieved. "I brought my wife here two months ago, and she and I have taken over the old blacksmith's place in the village, as ye saw. We've got a Citizen's Committee now, to see to the fair and orderly settling o' folk. We've found our 'twenty good men' that we needed t' make Loros a Wared again— found them, and a good many more besides. And our Seneschal is making the old Hall fit to be lived in—"

"Lived in!" Kuran exclaimed sharply. "You don't mean to say that you've chosen a lord?"

"Oh, well, no..." Kenthos' eagerness turned to chagrin. "We mean t' have everything ready for a Choosing by spring, but we're a long way from being ready to choose."

"Why is that?" Nagaro asked. "Six months ago you needed reining in— to give things a chance to calm down after the trouble that was stirred up."

"Oh, I know," Kenthos told him earnestly. "Ye told me so yourself, Captain. Give it year, ye said. But the truth o' the matter is, we've no clear man to put forward— none who has all the people's support, and that wants the task, that is."

"You've no one at all?" Nevien asked.

"Well I wouldn't say *no one*— My Lady." Kenthos rubbed his chin. "There's Venerev, that Lord Endemar chose for Seneschal. He says he'd do it for want of a better, but most folk don't know him. And there's me." The blacksmith looked down uncomfortably. "My name is widely known, as ye can guess, but I have no wish t' be lord of a Wared. I was all afire to see Loros Wared rise again, and I'm proud t' be part o' making that happen. But I've had my fill o' trying to tell other men what t' do. Just being on the Citizen's Committee is enough for me. In fact, I'll be glad when *that* task is done, and I can get back to just being a blacksmith. Shoeing horses and forging plowshares is what I'm best at."

There was momentary silence following this confession, broken by the rattle of the coach as it bounced over a stone in the road. After several seconds, Kuran spoke into it.

"Well now, friend Kenthos," he drawled, "Lokundas surely must have put us in each other's path, because I think I may have just the man you're looking for."

Kenthos' honest face lit up at this, then was darkened afresh by a frown. "Now who can ye mean, My Lord?" he asked. "Because, ye see, he'd have to be one o' the sons of Loros Wared."

"Ah, but he *is*." Kuran's eyes sparkled. "One that has wandered farther than most, I'll warrant. But he's willing and able and on his way home at this very moment."

Nagaro uttered a low groan and attempted to shrink into his corner of the coach.

Merriel put a hand to her mouth to cover a smile, and Nevien said, "Oh, Kuran, stop being such a tease!"

"Why? What is it? Are ye jesting with me?" Kenthos looked from on to another of them in confusion.

Kuran sobered. "I certainly am not. I tell you, I have your man. He's sitting right beside you." Kuran gestured towards Nagaro.

Kenthos spun about on the seat. "*You?*" he cried. "Captain Nagaro? Ye're one of us? Oh, this is wonderful!"

Nagaro could only nod weakly. He found the other man's enthusiasm a bit overwhelming.

"But this must mean that ye've found out who your father was!" Kenthos went on excitedly. "Ye must tell me all about it! I know ye haven't been to Irvenen Wared. I'd have heard."

Nagaro shot Kuran an ungrateful glance across Kenthos' chest. The older man affected an air of studied innocence.

Nagaro sighed. "I had no need to go so far to find a clue," he said, trying to think how best to present his story in a way that would satisfy Kenthos' curiosity without revealing too much. "It seems that I was carrying one around my neck." Reaching into his shirt, he brought out the bronze ring on its chain and held it out to the other man.

Kenthos bent over the ring. "What is it?" he asked.

Kuran made a small choking sound. "It's the signet ring of the House of Loros," he said dryly.

"A... signet ring...?"

Nagaro grimaced and explained. "It would have been used to stamp an impression into hot wax, to seal letters or put an official mark on a document. The rising sun surrounded by ferusia flowers represents the House of Loros. Nevrath must have had it made, and it must have passed to Darion, and to Tevren—"

"*Oh no!*" Kenthos suddenly clutched his head, and turned white as a sheet. "*Vothra's Eyes and Ears!*" he murmured, staring at Nagaro in consternation. "Ye're the heir of Loros! It's *ye* that I tried to impersonate. Oh, My Lord, forgive me!"

Nagaro stared at the other man. "Don't be silly," he began, but the look on Kenthos' face stopped him. He hastily returned the ring to its hiding place and put a hand on the blacksmith's shoulder. "You weren't trying to impersonate me or anyone else, Kenthos," he said gently. "And I'm not anyone's lord. You didn't know, and I didn't know, and there's nothing that needs to be forgiven."

"But I thought I was the heir!" Kenthos rocked back and forth in an agony. "And you saved my *life!*"

"I prevented a man who wasn't trying to defend himself from being murdered right in front of me. What else could I have done? Now, please. I don't want to hear any more about it!"

"Ye don't?"

"No."

"*Truly?*"

"Yes!"

"Well all right, then..." Kenthos was at last beginning to recover his equilibrium. "But... what am I to call ye, Zirda?" he faltered.

"'Captain Nagaro' will do very well. I'm still a captain in the Royal Fleet, and there's no other title I can claim."

"No other *title?*" Kenthos looked worried. "But ye *will* be our Wared lord, won't ye... Captain?"

Nagaro raised a hand to massage his forehead, acutely aware of the pregnant silence and the fact that Nevien, in particular, appeared to be awaiting his answer with bated breath. "If the people choose me, I'll do it," he said. "But it must be a proper Choosing. A count must be taken. I don't want you telling folk that this is how it will be just because of who my father was— or because I said I was willing."

"Of course, of course!" Kenthos nodded eagerly. "We'll do it however ye want, Captain."

"Why don't you put up the captain's name along with yours and the Senechal's," Kuran suggested. "That way it will be very clear that the people have a choice."

Kenthos looked questioningly to Nagaro. "Do ye like that idea? Does it please ye, Captain?"

Nagaro heaved a sigh. "I think that would be very appropriate."

"Well, it shall be so, then." Kenthos sounded greatly relieved. "And I suppose it'll look good t' the king and the Council when they hear it was done proper, won't it? But they *will* choose ye, Captain. I know they will."

Nagaro drew a long breath and let it out again. "We'll have to wait and see," he said. He glanced at Nevien and saw that her eyes were shining. He turned back to Kenthos. "I don't want any word of what we've told you getting about for a month or two. You'll have to try to keep it quiet," he said wearily. "I'll have to go to Lankura eventually, to officially make my claim to the name of Loros. But I'm not ready yet."

Kenthos started to say something in response, but Kuran signed him to silence. Nagaro gave the Lord of the Fleet a grateful glance, then closed his eyes and leaned against the back of the seat. So much was happening so fast that it made his head hurt. And his chest had begun to ache as well.

Outside, the sun was well past its zenith. Inside, the passengers rode in silence as the coach rattled on, carrying them closer to Loros Hall.

***

Nagaro was shaken out of a doze when the coach slowed and began to swing into a turn. Muzzily he opened his eyes.

Kuran was looking out of the window. "We've arrived," he informed his fellow passengers. "We just turned into the drive that leads to the front door of the Hall, but there's some construction underway. Is that a wall they're building?"

"Aye," Kenthos responded. "We call it Tevren's Wall."

"Tevren's Wall?" Nagaro shook himself and pulled his curtain aside to look. He couldn't see the Hall from the coach window because it lay directly in front of the vehicle, but he could clearly see the rising wall, built of gray stone, that stood out in sharp relief under the angled rays of a westering sun. The structure cast a lengthening purple shadow over its footing of mounded, grass-covered earth. Several men could be seen working on it.

The closest section of the wall was some twenty yards away and had reached a height of about five feet. It began at the formal drive that the coach was still rolling along, and swept away in a long arc that would ultimately encircle the Hall.

Nagaro frowned as he considered it. "Well, it *was* Tevren's idea to have a wall," he muttered. "Darion never wanted one. But the last time I was here, there was nothing but the earthwork. When was the stonework started? And by whose decision?"

"It was Venerev, the Seneschal," Kenthos answered promptly. "He's charged with the upkeep and defense o' the Hall, ye see. And Lord Endemar gave it his blessing. But... don't ye like it, Captain?" The blacksmith sounded worried. "I mean, ye're Darion's grandson, and ye just said he never wanted a wall."

Nagaro sighed. "Darion didn't like the idea of the Hall *needing* a wall," he explained. "He hoped there wouldn't be wars between the lords of Edrovir. And in his time, very few of the other halls had defenses."

"Almost all of them do now," Kuran put in. "When Tevren put up the earthwork, he was just bringing Loros Hall into alignment with what some of the other lords had done in *his* time— but he was slain before he could finish it."

By this time, the coach and its accompanying horsemen had come to a halt, abreast of the end of the unfinished wall. Kenthos turned to Kuran. "Ye'll have to state your business before they'll let ye pass, My Lord," he said. "There's to be a gate here, ye see, and anyone wanting t' pass through needs to clear it with the guard on duty."

Kuran sucked his teeth. "My business really is Nagaro's business. He wanted to return to his ancestral home, but we hoped to do it as quietly as possible."

Kenthos nodded sympathetically. "Well, if he's a returning son o' Loros Wared, ye'd best just say so," he advised. "That'll get ye into the Hall. It's where we put up newcomers 'til the Citizen's Committee can decide where t' place them."

They could hear that someone outside the coach was questioning Kuran's sergeant, and presently there came a sharp rapping on the coach's door.

"My Lord, ye'd best come out and speak to their Seneschal," came the sergeant's voice, low and urgent. "I've told him what ye said it was safe t' tell, but he's not satisfied."

Kuran frowned. "A moment, Sergeant," he said, speaking through the door. Then he arched a brow at Kenthos and lowered his voice. "What sort of man is this Seneschal of yours?"

"Venerev is a good man, My Lord.," Kenthos replied instantly. "I know him very well, since he... ah... rode with me. Ye met him once. Outside the palace in Lankura when we all had t' go an' see the king."

Nagaro sat up at that. "Was he that fellow with the sword cut on his chin?"

"Aye! That's him, Captain."

There came another knock on the coach door, followed by a different voice saying, "My Lord Kuran, will ye please open."

Kuran raised his voice. "Aye, Zirda, we will." Then he lowered it again. "I'll make sure there's no crowd about, and then I think it best if both Nagaro and Kenthos come out as well. But Nevien and Merriel should stay out of sight."

He stood up and opened the door, and glanced about. Then he descended the single step, beckoning for the other two men to follow.

Nagaro stepped down to the ground behind Kenthos and stood squinting against the waning afternoon light as his gaze took in the Seneschal, the front of Loros Hall, and the nearby stonework under construction. The last, in particular, drew his interest. The workmen were still some distance off, but from where he stood he had a clear view of the end of the half-finished wall and of the foundations of a gatehouse.

Venerev greeted Kuran with great respect, and Kenthos with some surprise. When he finally turned to Nagaro, his manner showed more than a little of both.

"I didn't expect to see ye here, Captain," he said. "But ye're always welcome. "Ye may not take easily to the title 'Defender of Loros,' but that's what ye'll always be to us. I was hiding in the cedar grove that day when ye crossed swords with Lothard Hurn. And if Lord Anduar gave ye an order t' do it, I'll eat my hat!"

Nagaro had taken Venerev's measure at a glance. The man was much as he remembered him, a keen eyed, clean-shaven Kelorin a little older than Kenthos, though not so big. The cut on his chin had left a neat but distinctive scar. He carried a broad-brimmed hat, which he had doffed to Kuran, and wore a dark blue tirka with brass buttons and a little gold braid on the shoulders. Though the garment was clearly intended to give him an air of importance, he wore it like a man accustomed to a uniform and with no inclination to strut.

Nagaro inclined his head respectfully to the man, though he frowned as he did so, having no wish to be drawn into a discussion of the events at the garden gate. "I've been studying your stonework, Tor Venerev," he said, changing the subject. "And I'd like to ask a few questions, if I may."

The Seneschal shrugged. "I'm overseeing the building o' the thing, according to the plan we found, and I'll answer if I can. But I'm no expert on stonework."

"I assume there are other guard towers planned besides this one here at the gate?"

Venerev nodded. "There's to be six others."

"Spaced so there's no part of the outer face of the wall that isn't in view of the two towers that flank it?"

Venerev frowned a little as he reviewed the features of the plan in his mind. "Yes, I'd say so."

"And I assume you mean to have a walkway along the top?

Venerev brightened. "Oh, aye. A walkway with a stone parapet on the outside. Though there'll be just a wooden railing on the inside," he added apologetically.

"That should be fine." Nagaro dismissed the apology. "Will the parapet have crenelations?"

The Seneschal's brow furrowed. "Ye mean those slots for archers t' shoot through?

Nagaro nodded. "Yes, you will want them, and if they're not in the plan yet, you'll need to add them..."

Kenthos and Kuran had been listening to all of this, Kenthos in wide-eyes astonishment and Kuran with a growing gleam in his eye. At this point, the Lord of the Fleet elbowed the blacksmith in the ribs and said, "Willing *and* able, didn't I say? This is the man who designed the defenses at Pakoa Harbor."

Nagaro caught the words. "I only advised the Town Council," he objected.

"Yes, and they took your advice. To their credit."

Venerev was rubbing his chin with a calculating expression. "We'd be very glad t' have your advice here as well, Captain—" he began.

"Oh, we'll have much better than that!" Kenthos burst out. "He'll be our Wared lord, Venerev! He's one of us..." The blacksmith's words trailed as he caught Kuran's look.

"One of us? He's born of the Wared?" Venerev looked from Kenthos, to Kuran, to Nagaro.

Nagaro ran an awkward hand through his hair. "It seems so, yes. I only found out yesterday."

Kuran coughed significantly. "This information must go no further, Tor Venerev, at least for the present," he said, lowering his voice. "But your long lost heir has come home. It seems our Captain, here, has had the missing signet ring of the House of Loros in his possession since he was a boy. His history is consistent with what little we know. The evidence is clear."

Venerev blinked. He looked hard at Nagaro, and there was just a slight twitch of his facial muscles. "Do ye know?" he said. "Now that ye say it, My Lord, I'm not surprised."

Nagaro frowned uncomfortably.

"And he's willing to be lord!" Kenthos seemed determined that the point not be missed.

"I'm willing to have my name put in," Nagaro added quickly. "But I've no wish to displace you or Kenthos from the Choosing."

Venerev instantly brushed the protest aside. "If ye want the lordship, ye can have it, Captain. I've been a soldier in the border war, and I was raised t' sergeant for showing some skill at ordering men about and getting things done, but I've no wish to rise higher than the post I've got now. Kenthos and I have been at our wits' end over this. I know I speak for both of us when I say we couldn't be more pleased at your coming. It seems Lokundas has finally done us a good turn."

Nagaro didn't know what to say to that. He stood uncomfortably under the gazes of the two young citizens of the future Loros Wared.

Fortunately Kuran rescued him. "Nagaro has come here seeking knowledge of his parents," he explained. "He had hoped to stay at the Hall for at least the remainder of his convalescence, which should be two months. He may look well, but he's still recovering from a very serious wound. I expect to stay for a briefer time, since my duties will require my return to Lankura. As his adoptive kinsman, I'm concerned for his safety and I hope you won't be offended if I leave some men-at-arms here for his protection."

Venerev considered this gravely. "We have no defensive force," he said. "So I won't object. We haven't wanted to alarm any travelers passing through, ye see, by training soldiers."

"But the people will defend the heir of Loros!" Kenthos put in staunchly.

"Aye," Venerev agreed. "They will. *If* they know he's here—"

"Which should be kept quiet for as long as possible," Kuran immediately interjected. "The safest thing to say is that Captain Nagaro is here as a rightful citizen of the Wared. The rest should be kept close until he's ready to declare himself openly."

Venerev nodded grimly. "We'll do our best, My Lord."

"There's still a bit more you should know," Kuran continued. "Princess Nevien and her traveling companion, the Lady Merriel, are with us as well. They're good friends of ours who we met along our way, and they accepted the comfort of our coach since they were going in the same direction. I expect they will stay a few days before riding on, but their presence should be kept secret from any who don't need to know."

Venerev started in astonishment at this final revelation. "Secrets and more secrets!" he exclaimed. "Ye ask for a deal o' concealment, My Lord. It's a good thing we're used t' that around here. We've made a lot o' changes inside of the old Wared without arousing the suspicions of anyone outside of it, I think. But if ye've no more surprises to add, My Lord," he continued. "I'll send ye on up to the Hall. If ye go 'round to the left, ye'll find the carriage house and the stable, where they'll see t' your coach and horses. Ye can go into the Hall by the side door, there. It's more private. Mundabo, the Steward will take the Captain's name to the sisters. Once they've seen that he is truly in the lists, they'll see t' your needs."

Kuran thanked the Senechal, and the man went back to overseeing the building.

"Who are the 'sisters' he spoke of?" Kuran inquired as they re-seated themselves inside the coach.

"That'll be Boka and Omei," Kenthos explained. "Ye remember Tira Omei, don't ye, Captain? Ye gave me her name and told me where t' find her."

"Yes, I remember." Nagaro frowned. Something was tugging at his memory. *Was it just that the sisters' names, taken together, were the name of one of the islands in the Lomoas?* "Tira Omei told me she was one of several Turowan women, called *Ku Taihana*, or Keepers, who had the histories of all the folk descended from the people of Loros Wared committed to memory. I never knew she had a sister, though. Are they sisters by blood?"

"Aye. In fact, they're sisters o' one birthing and as like as two peas. Ye'd never know which one ye were talking to if Boka didn't wear a ring in her ear. They reign like queens in this house, but ye'll see when ye meet them.

***

The side door Venerev had spoken of was solid oak, but otherwise modest and unremarkable. It reminded Nagaro of the side door at the palace in Lankura that led out to the stable yard, and indeed it seemed to have a similar function. After the second time he rapped on it, the door was opened by a fresh-faced young Kelorin wearing a dark blue tirka with a black and gold sash slung rakishly across it diagonally from shoulder to hip. The young man's eyes grew round as two eggs when he saw the company that was waiting outside under the shallow portico.

Kenthos had left them at the Hall's front door— that being the most convenient approach to the room where the Citizen's Committee met. Most of the accompanying guardsmen had remained with the coach and horses to make sure they were properly tended to, but Kuran and Nevien had each chosen two of their respective guards to attend them when they entered the building. Accordingly, the young doorman found himself confronted by a party of eight consisting of two gentlemen with swords at their hips, two elegant ladies, and four armed guards in two different liveries.

Nagaro had decided to take the lead, since it was his desire that had brought them there. He introduced himself, then Kuran, Nevien, and finally Merriel. If the doorman was astonished by the mere appearance of the group of travelers he was rendered nearly speechless by learning their identities. He gulped air, found his voice, and managed to convey that he would fetch the Steward, before hurrying away, leaving them still standing on the doorstep.

The Steward, when he appeared, turned out to be scarcely older than the doorman, though rather more self-possessed. He was Turowan, clean-shaven and with hair cut short in the Kelorin fashion. His blue tirka was crisscrossed by a pair of black and gold diagonal sashes.

"Good afternoon and welcome t' ye, Captain, and My Lord Kuran," he said, bowing a bit awkwardly as he stood aside for them to enter. "And welcome also, noble ladies. I'm Tor Mundabo, the Steward o' Loros Hall. Ye'll have to forgive Gilrin. He hadn't heard ye were here— which I had, from Tor Kenthos, just a minute ago. We're trying t' do things proper here, but we don't often get such fine folk as yourselves comin' to our door." He smiled ingratiatingly, then added, "Please follow me."

He proceeded to usher them down a short hall, lit by a pair of oil lamps, and into a spacious chamber illuminated both by lamps and by several high windows. It was paneled in blond wood, with a polished floor to match. Several high-backed, padded chairs and a pair of matching couches, all upholstered in blue and gold brocade, were arranged in front of a large fireplace in the middle of the wall to their left as they entered.

"Please sit down and rest yourselves." Tor Mundabo indicated the seats with a wave of his hand. "I'll just be fetching one o' the sisters and ye can tell her what brings ye here."

"That won't be necessary, Mundabo."

It was a woman's voice that had spoken, and they all started at the sound, then turned to find themselves being regarded by two Turowan women who had apparently just entered by a door at the farther end of the room.

Nagaro knew at once that one of them must be Omei, though they were so alike that he couldn't tell which. Both were past fifty years, with braided black hair shot with gray, and bright, dark eyes in creased brown faces. They were dressed very simply in gray wool skirts, and blouses of unbleached cotton. Each had a knitted shawl draped about her shoulders, one blue-gray, the other a dusty green. Other than the shawls, there was no way to choose between them. Except... yes... when the blue-shawled woman turned her head, the firelight picked out a golden highlight at her left earlobe. Nagaro deduced from this that she must be Boka and the other woman Omei. Something about the sight of the Turowan woman with her earring tugged at him again, and he frowned, trying to remember.

The two women advanced towards the group of travelers, moving side by side across the polished floor in soft leather shoes. They took no heed of the four guards who had begun to fan out, flanking their charges. Nor did they show any interest in Kuran, Nevien, or Merriel.

Their eyes were locked on Nagaro, their expressions enigmatic, their gazes unwavering, as they came to a halt directly in front of him.

The woman with the earing cocked her head at him, and he had a sudden flash of recognition— an image from years before of a woman stepping out of the forest beside Wotana Bay with a basket of mushrooms on her arm. Before he could react, however, the woman raised her hands with the palms turned towards him and spoke aloud.

"Welcome and hail, Lord of Loros!"

The other woman, Omei, then raised her hands in a similar gesture and spoke as if completing a ritual.

"Welcome and hail, Clan Chief of the People of Minowei!"

Both women lowered their hands and inclined their heads and bodies stiffly in a kind of bow.

The dramatic pronouncements drew surprised murmurs from the other members of Nagaro's party, but he scarcely noticed. He had focused on the words, and a frown was gathering on his brow.

As the two women straightened, Omei gave him one of her sly smiles. "Ye've been a long time in coming to us," she said.

He stiffened. "You could have had me a good deal sooner, I think," he said. "If either of you had seen fit to tell me what you've obviously known all along!"

"Here, now," Omei chided him, shaking her head. "Is that the way t' talk to those that have looked out for ye all these years?"

"Nay, sister." Boka put a hand on Omei's shoulder. "Ye shouldn't disapprove. He's a man, after all, and he carries the blood of kings. And he's been left a long time not knowing."

Nagaro's frown only grew darker as he shifted his gaze to Boka. "My blood has nothing to do with it!" he said angrily. "What's a king, after all, but a man with a crown on his head? I had a right to know, that's all."

The two Turowa exchanged glances. It was Boka who answered him. "Aye, Lord, I suppose ye did," she conceded. "We beg your forgiveness." The words were respectful, though her glance was not particularly repentant.

Nagaro's anger ran out like water through a sieve. He was simply too tired to sustain it. He decided, for the moment, to let the word 'Lord' pass. "Will you at least tell me *why* you never told me?"

"But ye know why," Omei answered archly. "I had it from your own mouth in the house of Tira Animara, on the island of Pakoa. Ye said that if the Ku Taihana were to reveal the name of the heir of Loros, it'd land him a kettle o' stew. Ye said ye thought he'd not be glad of it."

Nagaro stared at the woman. Now that she reminded him of it, he remembered the incident quite clearly. "I didn't know we were talking about *me!*" he protested plaintively.

"O' course ye didn't. And ye spoke the more wisely for not knowing." Omei was infuriatingly unperturbed.

"And I don't see how I can be your Clan Chief," he added. "When you told me on Pakoa that you already had one!"

"We did, and we do. Though I'll admit that having a Clan Chief what doesn't know he's a Clan Chief can be a bit awkward."

This was too much. Nagaro flung up his hands in exasperation, only to feel a stab of pain that made him flinch and put a hand to his chest.

Instantly he felt a hand under his elbow, and Kuran spoke into his ear. "That's enough, lad. They only meant to protect you, I'm sure."

"Nagaro, you should rest." It was Nevien, speaking from behind him.

In front of him, Boka and Omei had exchanged glances that at last seemed to contain some element of concern.

Nagaro shook off Kuran's hand and tried to ignore the dull ache that lingered where the sharp stab had struck. "I beg your pardon, Zirdyn," he said carefully. "I don't mean to be ungrateful. I believe I owe my life to the efforts of Luka, your mother."

"Indeed ye do," Omei informed him tartly. "And it was her brother, Takelei, who carried ye from this house to the safe place your parents chose for ye when ye were a brand-new babe!"

"The third man!" Kuran exclaimed. "He was a Turo then? And your uncle?"

"Aye." Boka affirmed. "Our family has had the honor— and the burden— of watching over Tevren's heir ever since."

"And I am grateful for it, as I said." Nagaro passed a hand across his eyes. "I want to hear all about it— *tomorrow*. But I... I came here chiefly to learn what I could about my parents, who used to dwell under this roof... and now everyone has all these... *expectations*..." He stopped, exhausted. "Your pardon," he murmured again. "I need to sit down..." He turned and started unsteadily towards the fireplace and the couches. As he passed the guards and saw the astonished expressions on their faces, he realized that they were finding the encounter extremely enlightening.

At that moment, however, he didn't care. He reached the nearest of the couches and sank onto it, closing his eyes. Leaning against the cushioned back, he tried to ease the ache in his chest by taking slow, even breaths.

When at last he felt a little better, he opened his eyes to find that Boka had followed him.

"My Lord—"she began, but he gave her a look that stopped her.

"Please don't call me that," he said. "I'm not a lord of anything— at least not yet. *If* I am chosen, I suppose I'll have to put up with it. But until then, captain or zirda will do."

She looked down at him and shook her head. "Ye're the heir o' the House of Loros," she told him firmly. "Ye are so by birth, I'm afraid, whether ye like it or not."

Nagaro scowled. "Well, if that's so, then I should at least be able to request that you find lodging for my friends in Loros Hall— and for their men-at-arms," he said sullenly.

"That we can, Zirda. There are suitable chambers for all o' them. And for yourself, there's the room your father slept in—"

"*No!*" Nagaro sat up and shook his head emphatically. "I'll want to *see* it— later— but I don't want to *sleep* in it! I thought maybe I could stay in the... the other house. The small one, that I saw in the garden when I was here last spring."

"Ye mean Minowei's house? That Nevrath built for her?" Omei had approached to stand beside her sister, and her manner had become noticeably more gentle. "Aye, Zirda, that would be a fine place for ye. Ye're father left ye that house, and there's a tract o' land that goes with it. Between the Hall and the river."

Boka nodded agreement. "We'll have a room made ready for ye there," she said. "Just rest a little in the meantime, here by the fire."

Kuran spoke from behind the couch. "There must be a guard on the house, Zirdyn. I hope you won't object if I set my men at the doors. He's my heir also, if only by adoption, and I take the matter of his safety very seriously."

Omei turned her attention to the Lord of the Fleet. "Of course, My Lord. If ye'll come with us, we can discuss the arrangements."

As the sisters moved away, with Kuran following, Nagaro felt a hand laid gently on his shoulder. Turning to look over the couch back, he met Nevien's eyes. She gave him a reassuring smile. "Peace, my love," she whispered, leaning down to his ear. "All will be well here. You'll see."

With a heartfelt sigh, he turned back to face the fireplace. "Dear Nevien," he murmured, covering her hand with his. He leaned his head against her arm, heedless of who might be watching. He seemed to draw strength from her touch.

Chapter 16

Questions And Answers

He awoke the next morning to a knock on the door. Opening his eyes, it took him a moment to remember what room he was in and how he'd come to be there. The winter sun was turning the plain white curtains on the window to a snowy blaze of light. The quilt on the bed was pieced out of squares of green, white, and brown fabric. The walls were white-washed plaster; the ceiling beams varnished to a dark luster. It was a place of unsophisticated comfort, very much like the house at Averwin where he'd grown up. He stretched under the covers and sighed contentedly.

The knock came again, and this time a woman's voice followed it.

"Breakfast is ready, Zirda, if ye're hungry. There's porridge and fresh scones."

He raised his voice to answer. "That sounds good. Thank you, Zirdyn. I'll come as soon as I've dressed."

Since he truly was hungry, and now quite wide awake, he rose and availed himself of the earthenware pitcher and basin on the wash stand. He found fresh clothes in his seaman's chest, which had been placed at the foot of the bed. He had no idea when it had been brought in.

He barely remembered entering the house the night before. He must have been extremely tired. He knew the building wasn't large, but he discovered that it had four bedrooms when he left his room and found his way along a short hall past their open doors. He located the modest dining room by following the aroma of fresh-baked scones and the sounds of crockery being laid on a wooden table.

Entering the dining room from the hallway, he found the Kelorin woman he'd been briefly introduced to the previous evening. She was setting the table with places for two. Somewhat older than the sisters, Boka and Omei, she was dressed in a similar fashion in cotton blouse and dark wool skirt. Her dark brown hair was liberally laced with silver, and she wore it braided and wound around her head in a way that reminded him of the Lady Maramine.

The woman raised her head to smile at him when he appeared in the doorway. It was a warm, motherly sort of smile. "Good morning, Zirda," she said.

"Good morning, Tira... Theseline." It took him a second to dredge the name from his hazy memory.

"Ah! Ye remember me, then. I wasn't sure ye would. Ye seemed more than half asleep when they brought ye in."

He laughed. "I think I was. But I remember the rabbit stew, and that it was you who served it to me. Did you cook it as well? It was excellent."

"Trust a man to remember the food." She laughed in her turn. "But I'm glad ye liked it, since it's my cooking that ye'll be getting if ye stay under this roof."

He sat down at the table on one of the four chairs, noting that it had a little decorative carving on the back, just enough to enhance the practical lines of its design.

"Do ye mind if I sit and eat with ye?" she asked, pausing on her way through a door that led to what was obviously the kitchen.

"Of course not."

She came back bearing a tray with two steaming bowls of porridge, a pot of honey, and a plate of scones. After transferring these to the table, she sat down at the place she'd set across from him. The pot of sothiril was already on the table, steeping.

Nagaro helped himself to two scones, some honey for them, and more for his porridge. When Theseline reached for the sothiril pot, he waved her hand away, picked up the pot, and poured for both of them. This she allowed without comment.

"I hope you are at least paid a good wage— if you're going to have to cook for me, I mean," he ventured, spreading honey on a scone and biting into it.

"I have my room and board and a stipend for my other needs," she said. "Thank you for asking. But I wouldn't want to work anywhere else."

"Oh."

For half a minute, they ate in silence, but then he asked, "How do you come to be working here then? Keeping this house?"

She smiled over her porridge. "I'm one o' the ones Lord Endemar kept on to see to the upkeep of the Hall, and my duties have mostly been there, in the big house— until your coming. But anything to do with *this* house has always fallen to me, since my mother and father had the keeping of it in their time. Not that keeping it since then has amounted to much. Just a bit o' dusting, and airing the linens from time to time."

"You've been airing the linens, for twenty-seven years?" Nagaro was astonished. "Why ever did you go to so much trouble?"

"So the sheets wouldn't be musty-smelling whenever ye came home," she returned with a twinkle in her gray eyes. "And it's a good thing I aired them just last week, because here ye are."

Nagaro had come to a halt with a scone poised for the next bite. "Please don't tell me you've known who I was all along!"

She laughed. "Not *all along*. Boka and Omei kept their secret better than that. Though it was obvious they knew that Tevren's heir was still alive. No, I've only known since the first time I met ye out there in the garden." She nodded her head towards the window, outside of which there was a general presence of trees.

Nagaro set the scone down. "In... the *garden?*" He stared at her, struggling to comprehend. He was sure they'd been introduced inside the house the previous evening. *Something was tugging at him but he couldn't quite grasp the thread.*

There was laughter in her eyes, though it was a gentle laughter. "It *was* rather dark that night," she said helpfully. "And there were quite a lot of other folk about."

And then he knew. *It had been after he'd faced Lothard at the garden gate.* "You're the woman who came to get the teacups," he said, gesturing at the cups on the table. "The one who was looking for the Heir of Loros!"

She nodded as she took a spoonful of porridge. "That's right, Zirda. And I found him, too— or I thought I had. I was afraid to say so, because it didn't seem that ye knew— and it would ha' been quite awful if I'd been wrong. After they'd spilled blood over the wrong man."

Nagaro swallowed past a dry throat. "But... how could you possibly have known?"

She smiled again, so very gently. "Because I knew your parents, Zirda. Your voice is very like your father's. And ye have your mother's high brow, and nose. Her eyes, too, now that I see ye in the light. But your coloring is darker even than your father's, which is strange."

Nagaro sat frozen, hearing his pulse in his ears. He still found it hard to believe who his parents had been. It didn't seem quite real to be talking to someone who had actually known them. "It's the kuma stain," he murmured, his voice sounding strange in his ears, somehow far away. "I suppose I'll have to stop using it now, but it will take several weeks to fade. Am I... am I really so like my mother?"

"Oh, yes." The housekeeper nodded, her gray eyes fixed on his face, her expression solicitous. "And not just to look at," she added. "Ye have that same kind o' seriousness about ye that I remember. But you're not *all* serious, either, any more than she was. The way ye laughed when ye first came in— Lady Lindra used to laugh like that."

Belatedly, Nagaro remembered his scone. He picked it up, took a bite, chewed mechanically, and swallowed. "What about my father?" he asked. "Is there anything? Besides my... voice?"

"Ah, you're a man, so ye'd want to know that, wouldn't ye?" Theseline considered him critically. "Ye don't favor him as much as your mother," she said at length. Your hair is black, like his, instead o' brown. But your beard hides so much... You're not very like him in manner, either. Tevren was a bit of a firebrand, ye know. Ye're more calm. I'm sorry I can't tell ye more."

"It's all right." Nagaro swallowed his disappointment. He forced himself to return his attention to his breakfast, though both his mind and his stomach were now in a turmoil.

When they had both finished eating, Theseline began clearing away the dishes. Nagaro sat for a moment, admiring again the pleasant simplicity of the room's furnishings. "Did Tevren ever live here?" he asked, suddenly curious.

She stopped in the act of putting the dishes onto the tray. "No, not Tevren," she said. "But Darion did. He was born in this house." She paused. "So were ye, for that matter."

"*I was?*" He looked around him again with a jolt of dismay. "How did that happen? If... if Tevren didn't live here, I mean."

"Lindra chose it for her lying in, because she liked it especially. So ye were born under this roof."

Her eyes were shining now as she looked at him.

"You remember it? You were here?"

"Aye." And now her expression turned somber. She sat down again in her chair, the laden tray forgotten. "A dark day it was when Tevren and Lindra rode out of here for the last time. And darker days followed. It was in that time that I lost my husband—"

"Oh, Tira Theseline! I'm sorry!"

But she shook her head at him. "It was many years ago. And I was hardly alone in grieving. So many were lost. Still, I'd rather remember the day ye were born." The housekeeper's eyes turned misty as her gaze seemed to look past him, past the room, to another time. "And I remember it so clearly. How ye hollered while the midwife was bathing ye. But when she wrapped ye in the blanket and put ye in my arms to hold, ye were quiet as a lamb. Ah, ye were a fine, strong babe."

Nagaro felt the blood in his face. "Do you remember what day it was?" he asked huskily.

Her gaze came back to rest on his face. "I'm not likely to forget," she said. "It was the twenty-seventh day o' Madrel." She saw his expression change. "Aye," she said. "Ye were born on your grandfather's birthday— besides being born in the same house. There were some that saw it as a portent. Of course, most o' them didn't live to see the end of Evrel. As I said, it was a dark time."

He swallowed hard. "Do you... do you know my birth name?" he faltered. "The name my mother gave me?"

"Oh yes. She named ye Alorin."

"*Alorin...*" he murmured. "*Alorin Loros.*" He shook his head. Then he frowned. "But 'Alorin' means 'one who brings light.' That's a bit too much, don't you think?"

She sighed and rose, picking up the tray. "It was a hopeful name, surely. Your mother always dared to hope."

***

He found Kuran, Nevien, and Merriel on the second-floor of the big house, in the main hallway, examining a row of portraits on one of the long walls.

Nevien gave him a beaming smile as he approached. "Come, Nagaro," she cried, beckoning. "Look at these. They're pictures of your ancestors."

She stepped away from the wall so that he could look.

Nagaro approached the portraits gingerly. *These were his ancestors?* They were, many of them, people he'd been hearing about all his life without imagining they had anything to do with him.

The portraits had names underneath, inscribed on little cards. He began at the left, with the oldest pictures. The first two were of Nevrath and Minowei, depicted in early middle age, mounted in separate frames. Nevrath, the founder of the House of Loros, was gray-eyed and stern, with a face cut in classic Kelorin lines and short, dark brown hair. Minowei looked out of her frame with an air of quiet dignity, but there was a hint of a secret smile in her eyes that reminded Nagaro of Boka and Omei. Her coloring and features were typically Turowan— black hair worn loose rather than braided, brown skin, and dark brown eyes. Though past the blush of youth, she was still beautiful.

There followed three small portraits in matching frames showing three children in their teens, a boy and two girls, with coloring that bespoke mixed blood. The youth was identified as Darion, and he was perhaps seventeen or eighteen, with an expression that was serious but open and unconflicted. The names of the two girls, Silvyr and Ilmorin, Nagaro didn't recognize. "Who are these?" he asked without turning around.

Kuran answered from behind him. "Darion's younger sisters."

"I didn't know he had sisters!"

Merriel gave a little cough. "Men tend to forget to mention these things," she said.

"But... are they still alive?" Nagaro turned to look questioningly from Merriel to Kuran and back again. "Did they marry? Do they have... descendants?" He was mentally trying to calculate what relation such descendants would be to him.

Merriel sniffed. "Yes, they married," she said primly. "Silvyr married into the House of Irvenen, and Ilmorin married the son of the Turowan Wared lords who lives way up on the north coast. Both are still alive. And both of them have children."

Nagaro stood for a moment in silence, digesting this. *Family! Rather distant family, but family nonetheless...* He filed the information for future reference and turned back to the remaining portraits.

The next frame held a family portrait showing an older Darion seated with his wife Selfira beside him and a boy of about six standing at his mother's knee. Nagaro knew the boy must be his father, but it was Darion's face that drew and held his attention. The square, brown face with it's blunt features was not particularly handsome, but the image had such gravity that it was impossible not to be struck by it. This was the man known as "Darion the Great." If you believed the tales, he had almost single-handedly forged the nation of Edrovir. A solidly-built, broad-shouldered man, he gazed out of the portrait, directly into the viewer's soul. The dark brown eyes were earnest with a hint of melancholy, as if he felt the weight of the world. Nagaro studied that face for a long moment before tearing his eyes away from it to consider the image of the woman who had been his grandmother.

Selfira was a beauty, with clear gray eyes graced by dark lashes, and cascading waves of raven hair. In marked contrast to her husband, she looked out of the portrait with eyes that mocked and danced, and a smile on her lips, as if she were laughing at the world. That world knew much less of her than it knew of Darion.

Nagaro frowned. "Selfira must have died not long after this was painted," he murmured aloud.

"Yes, she must have," Kuran said. "She died shortly before Darion was chosen king, and so was never queen. She tried to make her horse jump over a stone wall, as I recall. The beast refused and threw her, and she died of her injuries. There were many who wanted Darion to marry again, but during twenty years of kingship, he never did."

Nevien nodded. "Twenty years that ended when Dreigen poisoned him," she put in.

Nagaro's eyes had been drawn back to Darion's face, and he frowned afresh, surprised that Darion already looked so serious when he hadn't yet assumed the burden of the crown. The trait must have been integral to the man's character.

Leaving Edrovir's first king behind, Nagaro found there was only one portrait left. He felt emotion rise as he stopped in front of it. Here were his parents, painted together as they must have appeared during the two years of their marriage, two years that had ended with their untimely deaths on the road to Lankura only days after his birth. The image showed only their heads and shoulders. Lindra was placed slightly in front and to one side of her husband, and the top of her head came only to the level of his chin. As the taller of the two, Tevren should have dominated the picture, but it was Lindra who stole Nagaro's attention.

His breath caught in his throat as he gazed at her, and the world seemed to stand still. How much he truly resembled her he couldn't have said. There was no particular feature of her face that struck him. He was aware of intelligent, wide-set eyes that were gray as a storm-tossed sea with hints of blue and green in their depths, of the high brow, the finely-molded aquiline nose, and the gentle waves of dark brown hair. But it was none of these that held him. It was rather the way she seemed to be gazing at *him*, and him alone. And in that gaze he felt a warmth and a gentleness, and yes, he seemed to feel her love. His spirit answered with a single word... *Mother*...

It was the span of a dozen heartbeats before he could tear his eyes away from that loving face and raise them a little to examine the image of Tevren. The young king had straight black hair, cut short, and gray eyes a shade lighter than Lindra's. He held his head erect, his clean-shaven chin thrust out belligerently. His left arm encircled his wife, the fingers of his left hand just visible, curling possessively around her left shoulder. The challenge in his eyes seemed to say, "I'll marry whom I please!"

Nagaro frowned. *This was his father?* He sensed no personal message from the man— a man no older than he was now. A man who didn't look as if he'd ever been afraid of anything. *Had he been afraid that day in the glade, when the Leithians had pressed around him, challenging him one after another, each challenge taking its toll... until...*

"Vothra!" Nagaro backed away. Suddenly all he could think of was that his birth had contributed to the grim events that had cost these two people their lives.

He caught a movement as Kuran stepped forward, and turned to see that the Lord of the Fleet was holding a picture frame up to the empty wall just beyond the picture of Tevren and Lindra. It was the portrait Maramine had painted all those years ago of her young ward. Nagaro realized that Kuran must have been holding it all along and he'd been too focused on the other portraits to notice.

"This should be hung *here*." Kuran spoke conversationally.

"*No!*" Nagaro shook his head, utterly dismayed at the idea of having Leyel Virden's image displayed in that place.

"But it's surely where it belongs," Merriel protested.

"Why, yes," Nevien agreed. "It's an excellent likeness and equal in quality to any of the others."

"I don't want it here!" Nagaro stepped forward, reaching for the painting. "I don't want it hung anywhere! If people see it, they'll recognize me. *They'll know!*"

"Nagaro!" Nevien suddenly had her arms around him. "Please don't talk that way!" She was gazing up into his face, pleadingly. "That was so many years ago. No one will remember what you looked like then, so far away in Lankura. We won't put *that* name on it. We'll put your true name. Your birth name."

Nagaro pulled free of Nevien's embrace. "You mean *Alorin Loros?*" he asked. "That's never been my name— not that I ever knew anyway."

"But you've heard it?" Kuran was holding the portrait protectively.

"The woman who keeps Nevrath's house— Tira Theseline— told me." Nagaro drew a breath. "She said I was born in that house— that Lindra chose it for her birthing. She said I'd 'come home,' and I suppose it must seem so to *her*. But I don't know this place! I don't know the people here. And I've already had two names in my life! I don't know if I can get used to a third!"

"There's no reason you should," Kuran said seriously. "There's no reason to abandon the name Nagaro, since there's no law that says a man must have only one given name."

"What are you suggesting?"

"*Nagaro Alorin Loros.*" It was Nevien who said it.

Nagaro spun around to face her, frowning as he realized that the other three had been discussing this before his arrival. His annoyance evaporated, however, in the light of Nevien's shining eyes. "Do you like that name?" he asked.

"Yes, I do, Nagaro. It has a fine ring to it."

"Nagaro Alorin Loros." He said it aloud. "Well... *maybe—*"

They were interrupted by a polite cough from Mundabo, the Steward, who must have entered the hallway while they were speaking. Once he had their attention, he addressed Nagaro.

"If it please ye, My Lord, the two sisters wish to speak to ye."

Nagaro cringed at being called 'My Lord' and gave his friends a look of pleading protest. They only returned looks of encouragement.

"Oh, very well," he muttered. "I suppose I must get used to this."

The Steward took this for acquiescence, and beckoned for Nagaro to follow him.

***

The Turowan sisters were holding court in a room on the first floor that had been made up as a kind of office. It was dominated by a long table in the middle, with a number of chairs arrayed on both sides of it and a large map spread out on its worn, dented surface.

When Nagaro and Mundabo entered, Boka and Omei were seated on one side of the table, while a lean, bearded Kelorin man of about forty years sat in one of the chairs on the other side. As Nagaro approached, the man stood up and leaned over the table, stabbing the map with a calloused finger.

"So it's this bit o' land, here?" he asked, seeking confirmation. "Between the woods and the road, and running south o' the stream?"

"Aye," Boka answered him. "It's fair land for grazing, and there's a bit more of it than what your father held."

"And the house?"

Omei reached out to tap the map. "Here by the edge o' the woods. It's small for a family the size o' yours, but the chimney's clear, and the roof is sound. We asked the lads t' fill the woodshed for ye. Ye should fare well enough through the winter, and come spring, there'll be help in adding another room for the older children." She looked the man keenly in the face. "Are ye satisfied, Tor Andar?"

The man nodded gravely. "I'll want t' see it as soon as I can, but if it's all as ye say, it's good enough."

Tor Andar shook Omei's hand, then, and left the room. Even before the man was out the door, Omei was beckoning for Nagaro to come to the table. Both sisters rose as he did so and made small, stiff bows. Boka said, "Please sit down, Lord."

Nagaro frowned, but he sat. "Will you send someone around in two weeks or a month to see how that man and his family are faring?" he asked, being curious about the resettling of the land.

Omei inclined her head to him. "Aye, Zirda. That's how we do it."

"Does he have cattle, or sheep, since it's pasture land you've given him?"

Boka and Omei exchanged glances. "Well," Boka began carefully. "He'll have t' buy sheep. He sold his flock in Irvenen Wared rather than drive them so far. He has money t' buy with, but there's not so many sheep to be had, all at once, in these parts. So building a flock may take a few years."

"But if sheep are his livelihood, how will he manage in the meantime? And if he spends his money on other things, he won't have it to buy sheep when there are sheep to be had."

Again the glances were exchanged. Boka pursed her lips. "We've not got an answer t' that as yet."

"Aye, Lord" Omei added. "What would ye have us do?"

"Me?" Nagaro stared at her.

Boka gave her sister a little nudge with her elbow and cleared her throat. "Have ye anything to suggest, Zirda?"

"Other than going farther afield to find more sheep?" Nagaro cast about. "You might set up a charity fund, I suppose— to help with the needs of those who suffer as a result of their relocation. I don't know how you've been handling the work that was already done on the man's behalf— work on the house for example."

Omei considered this shrewdly. "Our Citizens' Committee has some money from Lord Endemar," she said. "But we also ask for a bit o' work from the neighbors. That's charity of a sort, so the idea's not so new. Yes, I'd say a charity fund is a fair idea. We'll see to it, Zirda."

Boka coughed. "That is," she said. "We'll put it to the full committee."

Nagaro's eyes narrowed. "You're determined to make me lord of this place, aren't you? Even if you have to manipulate me into it?"

Boka's glance flickered a little, but Omei's held steady. "Ye'll not begrudge us the benefit o' your wisdom, Captain, will ye?"

Nagaro was indignant. "You only had to ask! Though if you mean to make a habit of it, I might as well sit with the committee. I could also help you make a written list of the names you keep in your heads. You'll need it if there's to be a Choosing in the spring."

Omei nodded gravely. "Your offer is accepted, Captain. Shall we start tomorrow?"

He blinked. "We might. But is this why you called me here? I thought perhaps you were going to ask whether I was satisfied with where I slept last night and with Tira Theseline's service."

"Are ye?" Omei didn't so much as bat an eye.

Nagaro frowned. "As it happens, yes. But it hardly seems right that I should have the service of a housekeeper paid out of Lord Endemar's tax revenue when others in the same situation must depend on charity."

At this, both sisters sat up straighter, their faces registering dismay. "Ye'd not refuse Theseline's service, surely!" Boka exclaimed. "Ye'd cause her no end o' hurt!"

"That I can believe," Nagaro observed dryly. "I was thinking, rather, that I ought to pay for it. I'm still drawing a captain's wage, after all."

This precipitated an exchange of glances that seemed to contain an entire dialog. When the sisters turned back to face Nagaro, it was Omei who answered.

"Your suggestion will be put to the committee," she said almost primly. "And we thank ye, Zirda, for your generous offer. And now," she added. "There's another thing needs asking." She fixed Nagaro with her dark eyes. "Is the child Narei to bear the name o' Loros? And is she your heir? She's your first-born child, but she was gotten outside the marriage bed."

The change of subject took Nagaro by surprise, but he answered without hesitation. "If my name is Loros, then her name is Loros. She's my daughter, and she'll inherit from me equally with any other children I may have."

Omei didn't blink. "Then she's to be all there is o' the House of Loros if ye have no other child?"

He frowned. "She would be, yes, but I hope to have other children."

"But ye have no wife," Boka put in. Her tone was gentle but her eyes held a subtle challenge.

Nagaro straightened. He'd meant to keep his marriage plans secret, but these two women were the guardians of what was left of the House of Loros and they'd find out sooner or later. Nevertheless, the look he gave the sisters held a challenge as well. "I intend to marry Nevien Harlind," he said stiffly. "I've asked her, and she has agreed."

Boka and Omei shot each other a glance that said, "*I knew it!*" —after which Omei fixed him with a hard stare. "Ye choose the daughter o' the man that hurt ye?"

Nagaro grew, if anything, a little stiffer. "My heart has chosen. Who her father is need not concern you."

"She's Leithian."

"*Half* Leithian. Her mother was Kelorin— not that it matters."

"Some say she's barren."

The last came from Boka, and Nagaro gave her a look of suppressed anger. "I have reason to believe she is not. And it's none of your affair how I know it!"

Another smug look passed between the two sisters, but then Omei settled back in her chair. "Well," she said, to no one in particular. "He's Tevren's son and no mistake."

"Aye," Boka affirmed. "He is that, surely." Then she addressed Nagaro. "Are ye sure it's what ye want, Lord? There's the crown of Edrovir comes tied t' that lady's skirts."

"Not if I tell them I don't want it!" Nagaro couldn't keep the annoyance out of his voice. He was tired of hearing about the crown.

The sisters' faces registered surprise and Omei made a small gesture with her hand. "I'd like t' see how *that* goes," she said.

"Are you quite finished with this interrogation?" Nagaro was on his feet, pushing his chair back.

"Nay, Captain, please. Sit down." Omei was instantly conciliatory. "We didn't call ye here t' be asking ye questions. The truth is, we're more used t' asking than answering."

Nagaro remained standing. "What do you want of me?" he demanded in exasperation.

"Only that ye let us serve ye as our mother served your father."

"Aye," Boka put in. "We've been serving Loros— the House or the Wared— since we've been grown, like our parents before us. 'Twas your father that charged our mother with keepin' watch over ye, and after he was gone, she just kept doin' it, and taught us t' do the same. So here we are." She spread her hands in a gesture that included not only the room but all of what had once been Loros Wared.

Nagaro looked from one to the other of them. Two pairs of dark brown eyes looked back, serious, questioning. At last he sighed and grudgingly sat down again. "I have to respect the arrangements my father made," he said, wearily. "But they weren't *my* arrangements. I can see that you're giving good service to the people of Loros Wared. I expected Tira Omei to do that when I told Kenthos to seek her. He needed the names of the folk of the old Wared, and Omei had told me she kept them in her head. I thought it a good cause, and a natural match, but I didn't think it had anything to do with *me*. Now you're acting as if I gave you an order, and I never meant to!"

"We know that," Omei said gently. "And we would ha' done it anyway. But the question now is, do ye want us t' keep on doing it?"

"Of course." Nagaro gestured resignedly. "It needs to be done, and I can see that you're doing it well, as I said."

"And do ye accept our service? To ye personally? This was from Boka.

Again he searched their eyes, reading their sincerity. He drew a long breath. "Yes," he said. "In principle, I do. But I don't imagine your mother served my father without some sort of pay, and I wouldn't expect you to serve me without payment, either."

"There was a sum o' money set aside," Omei conceded. "For Luka and her brother. It was all spent years ago, and we've made our own way since."

"The service has been a thing that needed doing," Boka added. "And we were best placed t' do it—"

"—but we're pleased to accept your offer." Omei had given her sister a sidelong look and finished the sentence for her. "Let's say, for now, a hundred rins a month. That's fifty rins for each of us."

"A hundred rins?" Nagaro was relieved. "Yes, I can afford that. And fifty rins for Tira Theseline, as well. And shall we begin with the month of Nondorin, that started yesterday? I could never possibly repay you for all the years between."

The sisters nodded gravely, and accepted the coins that he proceeded to count out onto the table. After this was done, Omei asked, "What are your commands, then, Captain?"

Nagaro sighed, massaging his forehead with his fingers. "I wish to see the room my parents used— and anything they left behind. And I'd like you to do your best to see that no more is made of my presence here than is appropriate. I've come, as have so many others, to the place where I was sired. I'm living in Nevrath's house just as many others are living in or near the places of their origins. I've agreed to let my name be entered for the Choosing of the Wared lord that will be done in the spring. And that is *all*. That's only for the ears of the folk within this Wared too, mind you. I'd rather that none of it went beyond its borders, if that's possible."

"Aye, Zirda." Omei smiled her knowing smile.

"Oh, and I'd also like you to keep up the search for the man named Sindar. If you haven't found him yet."

Omei pursed her lips. "He's no child of this Wared."

"I know. But I accepted responsibility for him when I took him from Jinara. And since you're in my service—"

"Ye need say no more." Omei waved a hand. "He'd not been found the last I heard, and the search had gone cold. But I'll see to it."

Nagaro had risen again in anticipation of the conversation's end. "Thank you, Zirdyn" he said."

"And I thank ye too, Captain." Omei's eyes twinkled even as she inclined her head in formal acknowledgment.

Both women rose, and Boka smiled at him. "If ye'd like to see that room now, Zirda," she said, "I can show ye."

***

Nagaro cast Boka a sideways look as she escorted him along a first floor corridor in the direction of the main stairs. "I couldn't help noticing," he ventured, "that you and your sister have the same names as the twin harbors of the island of Boka Omei. You're not named after them, surely?"

She cocked an eyebrow at him. "We are named *Courage* and *Hope*, like those harbors," she replied. "They say that's what fishermen need. Courage to keep going out t' sea, and hope that the fish will be there."

"Not hope that they'll come safely home again?"

"Well, aye, that too."

"He laughed. "Those are good names. But tell me, did you happen to live near Wotana Bay years ago, or did you move there because I was there?"

Boka had reached the foot of the stairs and started up them. "I stayed close by with my uncle while ye were there. Do ye remember the wagon?"

"You slept in that wagon for an entire year?" Nagaro was coming up the stairs behind her.

"Aye— well, not during the worst o' the winter. But I don't begrudge it. Those wagons are more comfortable than ye might think. Someone had t' do it, and the task fell to Uncle Takelei and me."

"How did your people know where I'd gone?"

She cast him a smug smile over her shoulder. "We've always had some of our folk about the palace. So we knew ye'd gone over the wall in the night, and Uncle Takelei and I went out tracking ye as soon as 'twas light enough t' see. We would ha' taken ye to a safe place, but your friend Taru and his father found ye first and carried ye away."

"Were you worried about that? Taru's family must belong to a different clan."

"Well, they weren't Minowei's People, but they were Turo. And Turo don't do harm to strangers in need, 'cause they know the Spirits 'll send them ill fortune if they do. So we figured ye were safe enough." Boka had reached the top of the stairs and now started along the second floor hallway. "O' course," she added, "It turned out ye weren't as safe as we thought."

"You didn't anticipate the Mautep sea raiders, I guess."

"No, we didn't. And it was a black day when they took ye. I thought all our trouble had been for naught. But Mother Luka refused t' give up hope. The Spirits would send ye the luck ye needed, she said. And she was right."

Nagaro didn't believe in the Turowan World Spirits, but luck had indeed come to him in the form of a Mahuk sword, so he didn't argue. Instead, he asked, "Did Omei tell the medicine woman on Pakoa who I was when she visited the island?"

Boka gave him an arch look. "She didn't have to. It was Zomora that told *us* that ye'd washed up on her shore."

"*What?*" Nagaro bridled. "How did she know?"

"We'd put the word out all up an' down the coast when the raiders took ye," Boka responded placidly. "With a description, and a polite request t' send us word if there was any news."

Nagaro's memory had leaped back to the day he'd first met Tira Zomora. The way she'd questioned him... *almost as if she'd guessed...* That was what he had thought at the time. *"Bloody hel!"* he muttered. *"She* could have told me too!"

"Well, aye." Boka shrugged. "Except we'd told everyone not to."

"Bishka!" Nagaro cringed inside. "She was probably laughing! She never did seem to like me very much."

Boka shrugged again, but she gave him a sympathetic glance. "Ye weren't one o' her clan," she said. "I expect she just saw ye as trouble a-waitin', as it were. And ye hadn't been there but a few weeks when ye went an' tangled your bloodline with an island woman's. That probably didn't help."

Boka came to a halt in front of a closed door as she stopped speaking. "This is the room ye wanted," she said. "The Lord's Chamber. The folk o' this Wared chose Tevren t' be their lord after Darion passed. They both slept here when they stayed here, but that wasn't often because o' bein' king at the same time. After Tevren married Lindra, they both slept here when they came t' the Hall, but most o' the time they lived at the palace in Lankura."

Nagaro nodded soberly, worry over Zomora's opinion of him quite forgotten.

"Was this where they spent their last night?" he asked.

"Aye, it was. But when they left, they were bound for Lankura. They didn't mean t' be coming back here— at least not soon. So I don't know what ye'll find." Boka placed her hand on the door handle and turned it. The door creaked softly as she swung it open.

Nagaro winced. "Needs oil," he muttered as he stepped past her into the room.

"I'll see to it, Zirda." Boka's response was brisk.

The room was somberly impressive. The walls and floor were polished wood of a rich, deep, red-brown, with furniture to match. A deep blue carpet, edged in gold, graced the floor beside the bed. The draperies at the two tall windows were of the same deep blue, as were the cushions on the chairs that accompanied a dressing table and a pair of desks. The bed lacked a canopy, but the high head- and footboards were carved with elegant scroll-work. The counterpane was of snow-white satin, bordered in blue and gold and bearing a four-foot-diameter rendition of the seal of Loros. The golden sunburst and white farusia blossoms on their green-leafed sprigs were worked in embroidered applique on a field of royal blue. A number of paintings adorned the walls, depicting scenes of rolling fields and woodlands. A table stood against one wall with some objects spread out on it.

Nagaro advanced into the room, moving almost reverently. He was trying to imagine what it said about his parents that they could have been comfortable in such surroundings. The room was a rival to any he'd seen in the royal palace in Lankura. He supposed that Tevren, having been raised as a prince from the age of six, might have taken such things for granted. Lindra, however, had come from a more modest background. She hadn't been the daughter of a Wared lord. He could imagine Tevren dismissing the grandness with a gesture or a word, trying to put his young bride at ease.

Nagaro frowned. This wasn't why he'd come. He wanted something more concrete than imaginings. "Has anything been taken from this room?" he asked. "I suppose someone must have gone through it."

Boka was still standing in the doorway. She answered from behind him. "Those that've kept the Hall say that nothing's been taken. And no one's been in here for years— save t' do the cleaning. There were folk that came in the beginning, o' course— Lord Endemar, and Lord Rastyl from Irvenen. He's been here more than once, I'm told."

"What are these things on this table? Do you know?" Nagaro had approached the table and was examining the objects spread out on it. Most appeared to be folded articles of clothing.

"It's what was found in their saddlebags. They were traveling light, so there isn't much. It was all brought in here an' laid out like that."

"These clothes have lain here for twenty-seven years?" Nagaro shook his head. "They should be washed and pressed and put to use if they're still serviceable— and if anyone can be found who's willing to wear things with such a history." He frowned, suddenly realizing that the things were part of his own inheritance and it was unlikely that anyone else would want them.

"Very good, My Lord. I'll see to it when ye're finished with them. Shall I leave ye, then?"

"Yes. Thank you, Tira Boka," he said, deciding to ignore being called "Lord", yet again.

Chapter 17

The Legacy Of Loros

It didn't take long to go through the items on the table, since he was chiefly looking for any paper with writing on it. Besides the clothing, which was dusty and in some cases noticeably faded, there were two combs— a man's and a woman's— a straight razor in a leather case, and a hairbrush and small hand-mirror that matched the woman's comb.

The only significant find was a small leather-bound book. It was hand-written, in small, neat writing that matched the little note with the rose signature that he carried tucked inside his tirka. The first page bore the simple inscription, '*Musings*,' and his mother's name. About two thirds of the book's pages had been filled.

Nagaro carried the book with him as he moved on to investigate the dressing table, where he found very little. The drawer contained only a few hairpins in a little wooden dish and some sewing things. A small jewelry box held nothing but a broken silver locket and chain, quite black from lack of polish, and two miss-matched earrings. There was also a wooden shaker of musty-smelling powder on the dressing table's top, and a small crystal perfume bottle. Even through the cut glass, he could tell that the liquid in the bottle had evaporated. On a whim, he un-stoppered it and held it to his nose— and discovered that the yellowish residue inside still gave off a surprising pungent scent of... *roses...*

With a gasp, he put the bottle down. He'd been quite unacquainted with roses while growing up, and when he had occasionally encountered them as an adult, he'd found their scent pleasant and calming. But here, out of the context of a flower garden, he found the scent's effect far more powerful. A potent wave of warmth and security enveloped him.

Was it possible, he wondered, *that he still retained the memory of his mother's perfume from the few days he'd spent with her in early infancy?* He took an almost guilty second whiff of blissful serenity before hastily re-stoppering the bottle and returning it to its place.

From the dressing table, he moved to the first of the two desks. It was the smaller of the two and appeared not much used, being in perfect condition. The delicate carving of the legs had a distinctly feminine quality. A pair of raised compartments at the back of the desk, with little doors, contained the expected writing materials— on one side, a number of sheets of paper that were yellowed with age; on the other, a bottle of ink as dry as the perfume and several quills that had grown ragged and fragile with the years.

One of the three drawers that formed the desk's single pedestal, to the right of the chair, yielded something of much more interest. It was a trove of folded letters, most of them tied into bundles with ribbons. They were addressed to Lindra, and the majority were from her relatives in Irvenen Wared. Each bundle represented letters from a different person. Nagaro frowned as he went through them. Lindra's relatives were also his, and he knew he would have to return later and make a note of the names so he could determine whether the senders were still alive. Now, however, he was looking for letters from Maramine.

At first it seemed he was going to be disappointed. He'd started with the thicker bundles, working his way down to the thinner ones, and it wasn't until he got to the un-bundled, single letters that he at last found one whose familiar writing instantly leaped out at him. Eagerly, he unfolded it and spread it on the desktop, noting that in place of a signature it bore only a small drawing of a lily. Leaning over it, he read with a growing tightness in his throat.

Dear Gentle Spirit, comfort me if you can, for I am desolate. My child is dead. That which I carried within me all these months was delivered yester-eve, a boy-child, and perfect, save that he came into the world lifeless and without breath. So my hope, my life, my future, is stillborn, and the last thing that I had of my dear, sweet, murdered Love is gone.

The midwife helped me to bury him. We went out at first light and dug a little grave at the base of a white camellia bush that the gardener had planted the day before. I wrapped my poor babe in the embroidered blanket I had made for him. He was so small that no one will notice the grave, not even the gardener, since the ground had already been disturbed. The flowers of that camellia must be my child's memorial, for he will have no other. If only I had not promised my father I would cover his birth with a lie, saying he was no child of my flesh! Then at least I could show my grief openly to the world instead of holding it inside, where it chokes me.

I would have named him Leyendar, that means 'Gift of Love', but all the labor of my love is lost, and all that I have done, and sought to do, is in vain. From this day, I see before me only pain and sorrow. And when the pain ends, only emptiness. Tell me, tell me, Dear Heart, what is there left to me now in this world, and how shall I go on?'

Nagaro stared numbly at the paper. The ink was blurred in several places where drops of liquid had fallen. In all his life, he couldn't remember having ever seen Maramine shed tears. But she had wept once. Oh yes, she had wept. The strength and courage of the woman astounded him—to have lost her child, and then, within a matter of days, to have lost her closest friend, and yet to have gone on to become the steady, strong, and caring person he had known.

Maramine's letter explained some things that he'd wondered about, or guessed at. And he didn't need to see the rest of the correspondence between these two friends to guess how Maramine had been persuaded to find a reason for her continued existence. It was a poetic solution. The mother who had lost a child had found her reason to live in the child whose mother had been compelled to give him up. The argument had only been rendered more compelling by his mother's death. Maramine's unfortunate history had provided grist to the rumor mill, offering the additional camouflage of a presumed illegitimate child, and the lie she had promised her father she would tell had been transformed into the truth— the truth masquerading as a lie.

He wondered whose idea it had been to foster him with Maramine. Had the two women formed the plan, and his father merely agreed to it?

Since the first desk yielded nothing further, he turned to the second, hoping he might yet find a clue to what his father's thoughts had been. The second desk was large and heavy, and heavily used. It bore numerous scratches and ink stains on the writing surface. A panel, eight inches by fourteen and set with a small bronze medallion bearing the seal of Loros, dominated the raised portion at the back of it. Compartments on either side of the panel housed writing materials in a similar condition to those he'd already seen. Besides pens, ink, and paper, there was a stick of sealing wax and a stub of candle in a small brass candlestick. The candle clearly hadn't been lit for a very long time. The wax was caked with dust.

The desk had two pedestals with drawers, one on each side, but the contents of these proved disappointing. There was a small and very untidy cache of letters in one drawer that seemed to consist entirely of notices of needed repairs to various structures in and around Loros Hall. There was also a bound ledger with entries concerning the completion of those repairs. Besides these, there was a ball of string, a small scissors, three rusty pen knives, two glass paperweights, a china bowl full of empty walnut shells, and a pot of something that smelled like saddle soap but had achieved the consistency of limestone.

None of it conveyed anything about Tevren Loros— except perhaps that he'd been in the habit of disposing of unwanted objects by hiding them in drawers. Nagaro frowned in frustration. Was he destined to learn nothing about the man who had fathered him? Since the morning wasn't yet spent and it would be some time before he could expect lunch, he settled himself at Tevren's desk to peruse the contents Lindra's little book.

It didn't take him long to discover that the book wasn't a journal. The entries in it, none of them more than a page or two in length, provided scant insight into the events of Lindra's life. Rather, they presented a series of glimpses of the way she had viewed the world. They revealed the clarity of her vision, and the deep gratitude she'd apparently felt for everything the world contained, whether natural or made by the labor of human hands.

How fresh the air is after the rain, she wrote in the first entry. *When I stepped out into the wet garden and inhaled, I felt as if I were being made new from the inside. It was so wonderful a feeling that I stood there for a full minute, breathing in and out, with my eyes closed so I might fix the memory of the sensation in my mind and carry it with me the rest of the day. For truly every moment of every day is new, and we should never forget it.*

A little further on, she wrote of finding that someone had attached a cup to the post supporting the pump outside the kitchen door.

It was a modest tin cup, hung by its handle on a stout iron nail driven deep into the wooden post, and at the same time tied to that nail by a two-foot length of string. The string was hempen, smoothly twisted, and secured at either end by a sound square knot. And when I unhooked the cup and held it in my hand, I saw the beauty of the arrangement. I saw how one might hold the cup under the spigot with one hand while working the pump handle with the other, and so catch the water in the cup without wasting a precious drop. And if by ill chance one's cold-stiffened fingers were to slip and drop the cup, the string would catch it before it could land in the mud and be soiled. What simple wisdom was here displayed! So I did what some clever and thoughtful person had intended. I pumped a cupful of water, drank it, and wiped the cup and rehung it upon its nail for the next thirsty soul, giving thanks in equal measure for human ingenuity and for the sweet refreshment.

Reading his mother's words, Nagaro felt as if he were looking over her shoulder as she moved through each carefully recorded moment. The entries were undated, but as he flipped through the pages and sampled them, he found enough references to the passing seasons to conclude that the book represented Lindra's private reflections over a period of only a year and a half. Since the book had been in her saddlebag, and since it still contained blank pages, he supposed it had been in progress at the time of her death. So it must correspond roughly to the period of her marriage to Tevren, yet it seemed to contain no evidence of the gathering political storm that had cast its shadow over the entire brief period of their lives together.

Yet Lindra couldn't have been unaware of that storm. Her musings revealed an acute intelligence, a deep awareness and keen powers of observation. Frowning, Nagaro turned over the last few pages and began to read the final entry. Immediately he drew a startled breath.

Until I held my own infant child, I had not realized how perfectly designed we are to do this. My son's body is just the length of my forearm. His head is just the right size to fit into the cup of my hand. And holding him so, his sweet face is presented to my eyes at the perfect distance for admiring the feathering of his tiny lashes as he sleeps. Gazing upon him so, I find my heart fills up with such a joy and love that I would have the moment last forever. Alas that it cannot! Nothing lasts forever, of course, and this least of all—

The next words were scratched out, obliterated. There was a short line drawn on the page to make a break and then the very last entry was offered without preamble or explanation.

Be strong, be true, be forgiving. Go with open eyes, that you may see all that needs to be seen. Go with open ears, that you may hear what people truly are saying, and an open mind that you may understand them. And go with an open heart that you may love and be loved, and have compassion. This is my prayer for you, my Alorin. Fare well.

That was all there was, but it was enough.

Nagaro closed the book and held it against his heart, closing his eyes as he murmured his own prayer of gratitude for the preservation of this message and the confirmation of his mother's love. He would keep this book and treasure it. He would read every entry—

"Nagaro? Is something wrong?"

He started at the sound of Nevien's voice and opened his eyes to find her standing in the open doorway with a laden tray in her hands. His heart leaped at the sight of her face. Boka's face was visible over the princess's shoulder.

"No, I'm all right," he said quickly. "But see what I've found! My... my mother wrote this."

Nevien crossed the room and placed the tray on the desk in front of him. It bore bread, two kinds of cheese, a quartered apple, and a steaming mug of sothiril. "You didn't answer the bell," she said. "So I brought you your lunch."

"I'm sorry. I didn't hear the bell. And thank you."

She smiled her acknowledgment and bent to kiss him. It was a kiss that lingered, for Nagaro felt a surge of longing as their lips met, and he drew her down to a seat on his knee.

Boka, who had entered behind Nevien, carrying a laundry basket, discreetly looked the other way while busying herself with the folded garments on the table, until at last she resorted to coughing rather pointedly.

Nevien rose, as Nagaro reluctantly released her, and found a second chair for herself, which she placed beside his. She examined the final page of Lindra's little book while Nagaro gave his attention to the food. "It's lovely," she said after reading it. "I like the prayer, of course, but my favorite is the bit about filling up with joy and love."

"It's probably the last thing she ever wrote. And she wrote it for me." Nagaro blew on his sothiril and took a swallow to cover his emotion. "I'm very glad to have it, but I wish I could find something my father left for me— anything, really. I've searched this desk and there's nothing in it but odds and ends."

Nevien had pulled open a desk drawer and wrinkled her nose at the contents. "Well, he left you his ring, surely."

Nagaro frowned. "I'm afraid he couldn't have." He set down the cup and pulled the ring from its place under his shirt, to gaze at it. "As long as he lived he would have needed it, and he couldn't have known he was going to die the day he... sent me away. The ring must have come to me later, somehow."

"Aye, that it did." It was Boka who spoke. She'd been picking up the old garments one by one and transferring them to the laundry basket after first shaking them out at the open window to let the air carry the dust away. Now she paused in her work to answer his questioning look. "Uncle Takelei took it from Tevren's body while it was being made ready for burying, and I carried it t' Averwin. But your father did mean ye to have it. He gave my uncle the order himself. If he died, Takelei was t' see that the ring got to the place where his son was hidden. The lady there would see that the child had it when he was ready. Tevren told my uncle that he mustn't fail. That ring was the key t' the child's history."

Nagaro studied the ring. "I could easily have gone my whole life without knowing what it was," he murmured. Still holding it, he pushed the tray aside, having finished his lunch. As he did so, his eye fell on the bronze seal set into the wood of the desk. It looked identical to the design on the ring, except that its rising sun and farusia blossoms were raised instead of being cut in. It was exactly the same diameter. There were the same number of flowers in the same arrangement...

Abruptly he frowned. The flowers were *not* in the same arrangement. There were seven flowers in each design, but the ring had four on the left and three on the right while the design on the desk was the other way around. One design was a mirror image of the other...

The key to the child's history...

On a moment's inspiration, he pulled the chain over his head and pressed the face of the ring against the matching face of the medallion on the desk panel. The two meshed perfectly. And there was clearly room for a hidden compartment behind the panel, similar to the one in Maramine's desk at Averwin. In this case, just pressing didn't seem to be enough, but...

He gave the ring a clockwise twist and felt, as much as heard, the click of a mechanism as the panel sprang open, hinging on the left.

Nevien, who had been watching curiously, gave a little cry of surprise. "What have you done, Nagaro?"

He laughed. "I've turned the key in the lock, that's all. But let's see if there's anything inside." Carefully, he swung the panel wide, revealing a compartment with the height and breadth defined by the panel and about nine inches deep. It contained a single object— a leather-bound book, seven inches by nine, and three quarters of an inch thick.

"Oh!" Nevien breathed. "What is it?"

She leaned over to look as Nagaro opened the volume. A single-word title was written on the first page in a bold, strong hand that he hadn't seen before. It said: *Journal*. And under that, in the same hand, was the name *Tevren of Loros*. Nagaro turned over the first leaf, and read aloud:

"*I confess I hardly know what to do with this. My darling wife has presented it to me and encourages me to write in it 'to ease my mind' when I am troubled. She says she finds her journal a 'refuge from the world.' I don't see how writing can be any such thing, but I must try to write something here to please her.*"

"Oh dear!" Nevien bit her lip. "Did he manage to write anything else?"

Nagaro flipped through the pages. "Half the book is filled, so I'd say that he did."

Boka coughed again significantly. "I beg your pardon, Captain, but I've finished here. I'll be needing t' take this basket down to the laundry now, and My Lady Princess should be taking the tray back t' the kitchen."

"Oh. Yes." Nevien hastily picked up the tray. "And after I've done that, I really should spend some time with Merriel— for appearances— since we're supposed to be traveling together and only chanced to fall in with you and Kuran."

"Where is Kuran, by the way?" he asked.

"Gone to confer with Lord Endemar. He left right after lunch."

"Well, that's all right, I suppose." Nagaro frowned, wondering what Kuran meant to tell the old lord. After a moment's thought, he decided to trust Kuran's judgement.

The two women went out, but Nevien paused at the door to call over her shoulder, "Remember to take some rest this afternoon, Nagaro."

"I will when I've finished with this." He flourished Tevren's journal.

"Good. And I'll want to know what you discover."

Half an hour later, Nagaro had discovered a number of things. The first was that, while the signet ring might metaphorically be the key to his history, and while it had literally unlocked the compartment containing the journal, the journal itself presented an erratic history at best and not one that had been intended specifically for *him*.

The first two journal entries sounded forced, dealing with innocuous details of everyday life at court. Then, beginning with the third entry, Tevren struck off in a new direction, plunging into a torrent of frustrated expostulation on the shortcomings of Leithian philosophy. It began: *If I can't say what I truly think, I'm going to burst! These Leithian lords are surely the most arrogant and presumptuous fools on the face of the Earth, with their notion that everything of any importance must always be inherited.* It went on at some length and ended with a scrawled note: *Must make sure no one sees this. Especially Lindra.*

From that point on, the entries were all similarly candid— and often highly critical. Apparently Tevren had found a kind of release through the journal after all, though not as his wife had intended.

The entries were very irregular. Most were undated, and the few dates were separated by anything from days to months. The handwriting varied anywhere from firmly upright to dashing madly across the page as if driven by haste or strong emotion. However, as Nagaro alternately read and skipped through what was often a sea of invective, much of it unabashedly political, he began to find occasional passages that were of personal interest.

At one point, for example, he read: *I do not trust Bron Sobring. I don't think he had anything to do with my father's death directly, and I don't believe he covets the crown, unlike Reith Hurn and some others, but I can read his dislike for me in his eyes. I believe he holds it against me that my father slew his father, and I fear what that hatred might someday move him to do.*

And at another point: *I am more and more convinced that Dreigen killed my father by some dark art. The man has the very look of a serpent and my father was far too trusting, so that I am quite sure it would have been an easy thing to do. Unfortunately I have no proof of Dreigen's guilt, much less that it was for such a purpose that the Leithian Faction made my father a present of this creature— who formerly served Harl Sobring. If I thought there were any feeling in the man, I might imagine he did the deed for revenge, but that credits him with too much humanity. More likely those Leithians paid him to do it. It gives me no comfort to think that they might pay him to do me a similar turn if they grow too displeased with me.*

The writing broke off at that point, but the matter must have preyed on Tevren's mind because the next entry took up where the previous had left off: *I would be rid of Dreigen if I could, and set in his place a lore master from the Hatherin Lofts School. But it would look ill to dismiss such a man without giving just cause, and I doubt such cause can be found. Dreigen has spread the tale among the servants that it is death to enter his chambers, and they believe it. The more so since one of the kitchen staff— an elderly woman— fell dead on his very threshold some weeks ago. The healer who investigated says that she had a weak heart and may have died of fright, but the other servants are sure it was some spell of Dreigen's, and I confess I am wary of entering his rooms to search for clues. I would simply send him back to Bron Sobring, but Bron would surely take offense. The lore master came to us with high recommendations from Harl Sobring, after all. The rest of the Leithian Faction would do their best to be insulted as well, I am sure. So the matter is at an impasse.*

Nagaro winced as he read the last words. Nothing of what Tevren described had changed, except that Elgurn had perhaps even more reason to fear Dreigen.

From other entries, Nagaro began to piece together a picture of the political controversies of the time, and Tevren's personal view of them. One comment in particular seemed to sum up the situation: *They must understand that the country needs to have one law,* Tevren wrote in forceful pen strokes. *We cannot have the lord of each Hold or Wared doing as he pleases. For small things, they can perhaps have their discretion, but for the important things, no. There must be one law!* (The last sentence was underscored for emphasis.) At another place, Tevren wrote: *It is not a question of Kelorin law or Leithian law, but of what is good, just, and right. Yet they claim their fathers did it so, and their fathers' fathers, so it must always be done so. This is how they argue. One cannot call it reasoning since there is no reason in it! They would keep these practices even when it is plainly hurtful to the people they govern, which I cannot countenance.*

Reading on, Nagaro found that the method of determining how taxes were assessed had been a major bone of contention. Tevren discussed it at length, saying:

These Leithians insist upon assessing the tax at, say, five hundred rins per year per household. This, rather than as half of that part of a household's income that is over and above what is needed to support the household, as is the Kelorin custom. They claim their method is fair because it collects the same amount from each household, but it plainly is not fair because all households are not the same! A prosperous merchant will laugh at paying five hundred rins, while a poor farmer may scarcely produce enough to provide for his family in a bad year. Yet when I presented this argument to Tevus Morbern and Reith Hurn, their answer was that such a farmer should sell part of his land to raise the amount of the tax! But if the man does this, I countered, will he not find it that much harder to produce the tax in the following year, having less land to plough? May he not have to sell land again to meet the tax? And if this continues, in a few years he will have no land left, and you will get no tax from him at all! Still they would not concede my point. Being concerned only about the tax, they told me that if the man is such a bad farmer, then he must go to work for the man who bought the land and pay the tax out of his wages! When I asked if a man's loss of his independence were of no consequence, Reith actually laughed. Why, he wondered, should he be concerned about the doings of mere common folk? It is insufferable!

There was something blotted out, and then:

Since Lindra says I should not speak ill of anyone aloud, lest folk may hear, I must write it in this book, or choke! These high-born Leithians, who inherit their positions, have no idea how a farmer actually lives. They have never troubled to go out into the fields to talk to these men as I have done. Old Tevus Morbern is a prime example of this ignorance. I would consider it a blessing that the man is so old and frail that he must soon relinquish the lordship to his son, were it not that young Odus is so desperate to counter the doubts about his paternity that he can think of nothing but to mimic every word that comes out of Tevus' mouth. Reith Hurn is shockingly ignorant as well, and the worst man for arrogance that I have ever met.

There followed more scathing remarks about the Morberns, father and son, and an extremely uncomplimentary assessment of Reith Hurn's moral character, all ending with: *If the Leithian gods have chosen such men to rule over their people— as these men assert— then I think those gods must have exceedingly poor judgement!*

Nagaro could feel Tevren's righteous indignation fairly vibrating on the page. The young king must have had to bite his tongue almost daily to have maintained any sort of diplomatic relations with some of the Leithian lords. A few pages further on, there was more on the subject of the tax:

We have had instances of hard-pressed herdsmen, from the Holds of Furthing, Hurn, Morbern and Glenmark, driving what is left of their flocks into neighboring Wareds to avoid having to sell more animals in order to pay their own lord's tax. This is more than mere embarrassment, for the Kelorin lords of those Wareds are refusing to allow the Leithian lords to send soldiers across the border to fetch back their fleeing subjects. The Leithian lords insist they have a right to force their citizens to return, for they say it is unjust that their Holds should lose the wealth represented by the herdsmen's animals. The Kelorin Lords, meanwhile, maintain that everyone should be free to choose where he will live, and that these poor men can scarcely be blamed for seeking a place where they have a reasonable chance to prosper. Of course the Kelorin Wareds stand to be enriched by the flocks of the migrating Leithians, provided only that there is enough grazing land for them to settle, so these protests may be disingenuous. The loudest among the Kelorin lords are Devral Sedras, Berinar Sundorin, and Soren Tuveilas, but I have heard Anduar make similar arguments, although one can never be certain of that man's purpose in anything he does.

Nagaro was intrigued by all of this, since it seemed to be the root of the conflict that had nearly torn the country apart and had ended with the signing of the Pact of Lankura, but when he turned the page, curious to learn more about the disputed herdsmen and their flocks, he found instead the first reference to his own anticipated arrival. It said simply: *Lindra informed me last night that she may be with child. I hope for both our sakes that she is mistaken. I am beset on all sides by men so displeased with my leadership that they daily express the hope that my tenure will be short and my successor a Leithian— one who shares their views, of course. The possibility that I may soon have an heir will not sit well with these.*

Nagaro sat for a moment after reading the words. They struck him as both cold and ominous. He had to respect Tevren's fears, but he was stung by this dismissal of the entire idea of potential fatherhood. He was both relieved and disappointed to find that the next entry returned to the matter of the herdsmen:

The position I have taken on the Leithian herdsmen is making me unpopular on both sides, Tevren wrote. *The Leithians, of course, do not like my suggestion that they should conform their tax laws to the Kelorin model, and the Kelorin object to my insistence that the herdsmen be encouraged to return to the Hold of their origin once the tax laws have been brought into uniformity. Nor has Anduar Tyronin helped the matter by pointing out that it is only a matter of time before some merchant with less loyalty to his Wared than lust for wealth shall decide he would rather live under a Leithian lord who will tax him more lightly. Devral accuses Anduar of stirring up trouble by putting ideas into men's heads, reiterating that men should be able to live wherever they like. I agree with both men, and I don't see any contradiction in that. Our tax laws must be uniform as well as being designed to allow all men to prosper. As long as we have men in similar circumstances being taxed differently depending on where they live, we will have dissatisfaction. If they cannot understand this...*

There followed several pages of scathing criticism, this time directed at lords of the Kelorin Faction. Nagaro skipped through these to find another entry concerning his advent which was hardly more encouraging than the first:

My dear wife tells me there can no longer be any doubt of her pregnancy. A public announcement will have to be made, of course, though we may thankfully delay it yet a while. For Lindra's sake, I dare not pray for a miscarriage, and indeed I have never believed prayer to be of any avail. Lokundas will do what he will do.

The next relevant entry was made a month later and several pages further on. It made the source of Tevren's discomfort much more clear:

The announcement, made last week, of the Queen's condition is predictably eliciting joyous celebration among our Kelorin subjects and gnashing of teeth among the lords of the Leithian Faction. If only I were a Leithian, I could take a sack of gold to the Temple Compound, upend it upon the alter of whichever deity they hold responsible for such things, and pray for the birth of a girl child. Of course if I were a Leithian, I would not be in this predicament. There is nothing I can say that will please some of them, no matter how sensible and carefully reasoned! They claim that, being Kelorin, I cannot possibly understand their arguments— while in fact those arguments are quite transparent, being based on obvious self-interest and consisting of nothing but stubborn insistence on adhering to 'time-honored ways'. They say I naturally take the Kelorin side, being Kelorin, thus ignoring the balanced nature of my arguments, which fall sometimes on one side and sometimes on the other. If they would only listen to what I say instead of making these assumptions, they would have to see the sense of it! But they cannot permit themselves that possibility, and if Lindra gives me a son, they will imagine Kelorin kings ruling over them on into the future if they do not act to stop to it.

Nagaro read on with gathering distress, for the journal entries from this point dealt increasingly with the fatal events that had framed the end of Tevren's life, and these events were inextricably linked to his own birth. The next entry read:

There is now talk of a challenge to my kingship from Reith Hurn, and even the birth of a daughter rather than a son may not be sufficient to spare me this. If Reith challenges me and I best him, as I believe I can, I am very much afraid he and his supporters will not accept that defeat but will press their cause by force of arms.

And the next entry:

I have reluctantly agreed to my wife's request that we go to Loros Hall for her lying in. It worries me to be absent from Lankura when so many are speaking openly of taking my crown, and it is only my concern for Lindra that moves me to do this. She has never been fully comfortable in the palace my father built. She tries admirably to cover it, but I can read it all the same. For her sake we will go to Loros at week's end, and if ill shall come of it, so be it. It seems I can deny her nothing, she that is the Queen of my Heart.

Then, dated several days later:

Here I am, stuck in this place with nothing to do but wait and worry! Lindra says I should try to be calm— take walks in the garden, or what have you. That is all very well for her, being so heavy now with child that merely to walk must be an effort, but I have the stallion's need to run! Yet I dare not leave her long enough even to ride to Fenerwel for fear of what might happen while I am away. I have arranged for Rastyl to send me news from Lankura by courier but it is several hours ride in each direction, and much can happen in the city while the rider is on the road. Why did I let myself be persuaded to leave Lankura?"

The next several entries dealt with messages received by courier telling of the mustering and training of troops by various lords. All the same names were involved, with the addition of the lords of some minor Holds and Wareds who apparently feared to find themselves defenseless if the more powerful lords came to armed conflict. Tevren's distress at this news was evident and he repeatedly lamented the isolation of Loros Hall. When word came from Lord Endemar that he also was recruiting more men, Tevren wrote, *Much as I dislike becoming part of this escalation, it would be folly not to look to the defenses of Loros Wared.*

Then, the next entry abruptly returned to the subject of Tevren's domestic situation:

Lindra has taken up residence in the old house— what she calls Minowei's house— for these final days. And her women, being concerned that she not be over-tired, will only let me visit her once or twice a day, and for no more than half an hour at a time! So now I lack both the comfort of her company and the benefit of her wisdom.

This was followed by a passage that explained the absence of Rastyl Korvin during the crucial time that was to come:

Rastyl came today to the Hall on his way to Irvenen. He is being called to stand as a candidate in the Choosing for the lordship of the Wared, so of course he must go. He has arranged for Anduar to send me news in his absence, and he was very apologetic. Clearly it distresses him to abandon me at this time. Of course I told him he must answer to a higher duty and that Anduar will surely serve me well. Besides, I have Endemar close at hand, who has ever been my friend. I sent him on his way with these assurances, hiding my regret. If things turn ill, I fear I may miss him sorely, my oldest and staunchest friend. But what can be done?

And then more politics:

Anduar paid me a visit today. His intelligence confirms what I have feared, that Reith's real objective in bolstering his army is to support an effort to seize the crown— by challenge or by force. Anduar suggests that a challenge may be preempted by summoning the Council of Lords and calling for another Royal Choosing. As matters now stand, he says, I am not likely to take a majority of the krits in the first casting, but I should have more support than Reith Hurn, particularly if there is a Leithian who is more popular than Reith among those who are more friendly to us. For this purpose, he suggested we put forward young Elgurn Harlind. Elgurn's family was ever staunch in support of my father. He has distinguished himself in battle in the border wars, and he is too young yet to have given anyone offense— having but recently succeeded to the Lordship of Harlind Hold.

Anduar put all of this to me and then leaned back in his chair the way he does and said, "It would also be wise to have someone to put forward in the event that anything should happen to you." And all the while he was looking at me with that measuring way of his. By the Eyes, but the man unsettles me! Was he reminding me that I face the threat of assassination? Or did he mean to suggest I might be supplanted at the Choosing? I had not the heart in me to press him to explain himself.'

Politics and domestic concerns then came together:

I had today a letter from Berinar Sundorin in which he says that I must on no account risk losing the crown through a Choosing, which is opposite to Anduar's advice. Of course Berinar also hopes that Lindra will bear me a son to carry on the line of Darion. In this, at least, I must instead agree with Anduar that I should pray the child is a girl. That or stillborn, though I fear such an outcome would crush my poor Lindra. She herself has told me she believes she is carrying a boy— that she can feel it— and that I should prepare a plan for that event. But how can I possibly plan for such a catastrophe? I only pray she is mistaken.

And then at last:

Lindra's travail has finally begun. The woman Theseline came to the Hall to tell me just as I was preparing for bed, so now I cannot sleep. She says this time is not like the other two, when the midwife came and declared it to be false labor and went home again. I don't know how the old woman can tell, but I suppose she must know what she is about. I'm told she managed her first birthing when she was twenty and her age must stand now at three quarters of a century, by the look of her.

From this point, Nagaro read on without stopping, turning page after page, as Tevren's entries became increasingly frantic.

Let it be a girl. Please, Lokundas, send me a girl-child. Oh, but it must be too late for such prayers now, when it must have been decided nine months ago! I can wish for nothing now, if it is a boy, but for a stillbirth. Anything, oh anything, but not a living boy-child!

And the next entry:

I have said I wish for anything but a living boy-child, but I would not tempt Lokundas so. Only give me my wife, whole and well, and I will take whatever else the Turner of Worlds sees fit to give me.

And the next:

They will not let me in to see my wife! Already it is an hour after midnight and still the labor continues with no outcome. Theseline, who came to the door in answer to my knock, told me not to worry, that all is well. It is common, she said, for a first birthing to be long, and I should go to bed! But if all is well with my Lindra, why can I not see her? And how could I possibly sleep, not knowing if she is alive or dead?

And the next:

Two hours more have passed and still no word. When I went again to see if I might be allowed to see her, I was met by a wall of women, all adamant that a birthing is no place for a man and least of all the husband! Surely something must be wrong, or they would have let me in! What else am I to think?

And then:

From the window of my chamber I can look down and see the light in the window of the little house. I can see the back door of it. Now and again, someone comes out or goes in— women always— and each time one comes out I imagine it is to tell me something. To give me some news— wonderful or terrible— but no one comes, and so I am left to the mercy of my dire imaginings.

And again:

Another hour! Still they come and go, go and come. Why is this child so reluctant to come into the world? It is almost as if it knows how fraught with danger this world can be. Or is it reluctant to disappoint me? Is Lindra right, after all? Please be wrong, My Lindra. Please be wrong!

And then a single line, dashed across the page:

Oh when will they ever come? The night is nearly gone, and I am dying every moment!

And finally, just as it seemed to Nagaro that he could endure no more of this stew of anxiety and rejection, he turned over another page and read:

I have a son! Praise be to Lokundas! Lindra is sitting up, and smiling. And it is dawn and I have a son! They allowed me to hold him, and he is so small and helpless, and so beautiful and so very much alive. For this most precious gift, My Lindra, you will have my gratitude forever. I would shout it to the world! I have a son! I have a son! I have a son!'

The page began to blur and Nagaro had to put the book down, swallowing past the tightness in his throat. He had resigned himself to the fact that the last thing his father had wanted was a son, and now this! It was the most precious gift imaginable, this evidence of a change of heart that was so unmistakable in his father's words. His father, for whom there had been such good reason not to want a living son.

It took some moments for Nagaro to regain his composure, but at last he picked up the book again and read on. The last entry had been undated at its beginning, but after it Tevren had written: Madrel 27, 533, underscored as if to fix the date in his memory. The next entry was dated the following day.

My son has hair that is as black as mine, but his eyes, I think, will be dark gray like Lindra's. She insists upon calling him Alorin, because, she says, he came with the rising sun. I know I should regret his birth, but I cannot. Not now that I have seen him and held him in my arms. My son must live. Nothing else matters so much to me right now but that he should have a chance to live, and grow to manhood, and enjoy all that this fair world has to offer. But how is this to be?

The Leithians will probably try to kill me. They may well succeed. When we return to Lankura, I half expect that serpent, Dreigen, to be waiting for me with a poisoned tooth. Lindra, I do not think they would harm, but a male heir to the line of Loros is another matter. It is too much to expect they would leave him untouched if I were gone. How, then, can I protect him even beyond the end of my life? How can I ensure that the gift of life we have given him will not be snatched away?

The next entry detailed the genesis of the young parents' plan:

There is only one course I can see. If we love this child, we must part with him. We must foster him somewhere, in secret, pretending that he did not live. It happens sometimes, after all, that a newborn child is not strong, or sickens and dies. We must say that this has happened, and feign grief, and tell only those we most trust the entire truth. The only question is, where can we send him, where no one will suspect, but where he will be safe?

The next entry showed the plan beginning to take shape:

It seems that Lindra may have a solution to our need, if only her cousin can be persuaded to take the child. I am proud of my young wife. She did not weep or plead when I put the matter to her. She only looked at me gravely. "Yes," she said, as if she had already thought on the matter. "I know that to spare him, we must let him go." And when she got word of her kinswoman's misfortune, she came to me to tell me her plan straightaway, with the letter still in her hand and the tears of gentle sympathy still staining her cheeks.

And the next entry continued:

Praise Lokundas, our Lily will take him! We owe a debt of deep gratitude to this woman who has suffered so much yet is willing to take on a labor that must continue for many years. I have set two stipulations. The first is that the child must be kept in ignorance of his origin, for his own safety, until he reaches eighteen years. The second is that both women must destroy the letters they have had from one another, to obliterate the trail. Only one letter each may they keep, provided it makes no explicit mention of our arrangement. To this, both have agreed, though I know it costs them pain.

And then the final details:

All is made ready. I dug the little grave myself, despite the protests of the gardener. The paper for Endemar to find, I put into a small chest, which we carried out, wrapped in a blanket, and laid in the earth. We made a mock funeral and stood with our heads bowed, and Lindra's tears were quite convincing. She told me she only had to think about how much she loves little Alorin and how painful it will be to part with him. Word of the birth had already gotten out, of course, and I'm sure we did not fool all the servants with our ruse. In some cases we did not try. To Theseline, dearest of Lindra's maidservants, we told the truth. And Luka's folk, of necessity, must be trusted. This secret is as much theirs to keep as it is ours, after all, and the Turo know how to keep their secrets. It helps that few members of the other two races pay them much heed. Luka and her kin will look out for him; I have seen to that, and also sent an artfully-worded letter to Endemar so that he will know what to do. I would rather it had been Rastyl, but he is too far away and so must get this news second-hand. So we are ready for tomorrow. At least as ready as ever we will be.

And then came the final entry, one that went on for several paragraphs.

I cannot sleep, though I know I should do so now, while the child sleeps. To me it seems he scarcely does, though Theseline says he is a good baby because he sleeps two or three hours after feeding and does not cry much as long as he knows we are close. At least Lindra is sleeping soundly. Of course she knows she must nurse him again before we can set forth, so that he will be content and quiet for the journey. His little face and hers are both so peaceful in repose. But my stomach feels as if it were full of worms. If only we three might live together as a family. I would gladly forego the crown if it could be so— if only I could be sure that Edrovir would not suffer. Perhaps if I write a little more it will ease my mind.

I don't know why I feel such a sense of foreboding. We had late word today that Tevus Morbern has swung about, as Pendrik did earlier, on the matter of the tax assessment. This is unexpected and it gives reason for hope, though the message said also that Tevus still backs Reith Hurn in his bid to depose me. So Tevus is a wise man and a fool all at once! Or maybe not such a fool, since his shift on the tax has made Reith furious. Perhaps Tevus' continued endorsement is aimed at saving his own skin? Whatever the case, there are now so few holdouts that Reith may see the sense of conforming to our wishes on the tax, and the storm will all blow by. Then at least the people of Edrovir would live under a more equitable system, no matter what might become of me.

Maybe this is my trouble: I fear I may never see my son again when I bid farewell to him tomorrow. I keep thinking of him growing up without knowing me. If he survives to eighteen years, of course, he may be told who he is. But what will he do then? What manner of man will he have become, and what will the world ask of him? By doing what we are doing, I hope to spare him from feeling pressed to take the crown as I was. If he is no more suited to it than I, it is better that he not be so pressed, just for the sake of his name. Certainly my father never intended the rule of Edrovir to be hereditary. And even if my son is more suited than I, he should not be made king if there are too many who oppose it. I don't wish him to face what I am facing.

If I am still living when he comes of age, he may seek me out, and in that case I can advise him. But if I am not there... What would I wish him to know? Just this, I think. That he should not think he must be king for my sake. I only wish him to be happy, and to know the joy of love and companionship that I have known with Lindra, his mother. To have children of his own and to see them grow. Nor should he take it for his own sake, out of ambition. That is unworthy. Only for the sake of peace and the good of Edrovir should he take up the crown, and if it truly were for the good of Edrovir, I would not have him refuse.

But enough of this! I should lie down again beside my wife while there are still some few hours before sunrise. Tomorrow will bring what it will bring.

There was no more. Nagaro stared at the page while his father's words reverberated in his brain. Tevren's thoughts on the last night of his life had been as much for the safety and future of his son and his country as for himself. The man had lived to see the sunrise of which he had written, but not another sunset. As for his views on taking the crown... Nagaro frowned. Tevren hadn't explicitly written the words for him, though it had perhaps occurred to him that his son might one day read them. Had he thought of that in the morning, and locked the journal away for that reason? Or had he merely realized that the journal must be kept secret to preserve his son's safety?

Nagaro shook his head. He wasn't ready to try to analyze the full significance of the book and its contents. It was enough for that moment that his father had wanted him to live. For the second time that day he murmured a prayer of thanks.

He looked up then, realizing that it was past the middle of the afternoon, and suddenly felt enormously tired. Going to the bed, he turned down the gorgeous coverlet, fearful of doing it harm by lying on it. He pulled off his boots and lay down, cradling his father's journal against his chest, and abandoned himself to his weariness.

When they came to look for him, Nevien and Boka found him so, asleep in the Lord's Chamber, tumbled across the lord's bed with an expression of peace on his slumbering features and the fingers of his right hand still curled around the spine of the leather-bound journal.

Chapter 18

Days Of Idrin

K uran left for Lankura at the end of the week. Nevien and Meriel followed a week later, leaving Nagaro to try to settle into a place that seemed determined to make itself his whether he wished it or not.

It was mid winter before Taru and Pavo finally caught up with him, arriving just before Idrin on a long winter furlough. They told a tale of traveling from Wotana to Kel Hall with Hamani and her few possessions in a hired cart, only to find that Nagaro had mysteriously changed plans and wasn't there. They'd gotten the full history of events from Kuran in Lankura, and by the time they came to Loros Hall, Taru was over his astonishment regarding Nagaro's pedigree and ready to either tease his friend about it or try to take advantage of it. In contrast, Pavo acted as if Nagaro news was nothing more that what he'd always expected. Quite possibly it wasn't.

On their first afternoon together, the three men went hunting in a patch of woods not far from the Hall, creeping stealthily among the trees, snow crunching under their feet. The woods were a mixture of deciduous and evergreen trees, and the winter sunlight slanting through the branches made confusing patterns of light and shadow under the interlacing canopy, further complicated by the undergrowth of bushes and withered ferns, all decorated with snow.

Nagaro, who was in the lead, raised a silent hand, and Taru and Pavo came to a halt. A moment later, he nocked an arrow and drew the string back until his hand brushed his shaven cheek. Wincing a little at the effort, he held his stance to aim, then let fly. The bird that was his target fell to the ground in a flutter of feathers.

"When do you get so good at hunting with bow, Nagaro?" Pavo asked. He had never learned the art and was much in awe of it.

"He always was." Taru put in. "And I'm a fair hand myself. As ye'll see when he gives me the bow."

"Shhh!" Pavo suddenly stiffened, staring at a dense tangle of holly and hazelnut bushes about a dozen paces away in the gloom. "I think is somebody over there. Two times I have heard sound."

Nagaro had collected his prey and withdrawn the arrow. He slung the bird over his shoulder and straightened his hat as he scanned the area Pavo had indicated. Nothing stirred.

"It may just have been one of the local lads, he suggested. "Looking for the last of the hazelnuts."

Taru struck a belligerent stance. "As long as he's not hunting game in *your* forest!"

Nagaro sighed. "Nothing is 'mine' until I've proved my claim in Lankura. And even then, these woods wouldn't be. This forest has furnished winter meat, nuts, and firewood to all the folk around here for years."

Pavo was still watching the bushes. "Maybe it was animal I heard," he said.

Nagaro handed the bow and quiver to Taru. "Here, it's your turn. And remember that we're hunting for our dinner. If we don't come back with enough, the rest will be potato soup."

"We can't have that." Taru began creeping forward, scanning the branches of the trees ahead of them. "And I still say we shouldn't be out hunting our own dinner," he added. "What's the use o' being a lord if ye and your guests have t' hunt their own meat?"

"Taru, I'm not a lord!"

"Well ye're as good as one. The Choosing is just for show. Everybody knows it! Those folk up at the Hall could send out for some meat for our dinner if ye asked them.

Nagaro shook his head. "I rode with the men who went to see how the folk are faring, and what I saw was that there are too many newcomers and not enough harvest. I've advised the Seneschal to make no more claims against the tax until spring. We can see then how much or little everyone has left in store. In the meantime, the staff and I can manage with a little bit of hunting."

Taru came to a halt and leveled a finger at his friend. "That sounds like lord talk t' me... Alorin Loros!"

"It's just common sense, Taru. My Lady Guardian always took stock of the harvest and took as little as she could for the winter."

Taru gave Pavo a meaningful glance. "See what I mean? Lord-talk comes from his mouth like salt from the sea."

Pavo shook his shaggy head. "I think you should keep mind on hunting," he said. "I see bird. Over there." He pointed.

For the next several minutes the three held their peace while Taru stalked his quarry. The bird took to flight twice, each time landing again within sight so that it led them on a breathless chase before Taru finally brought it down. The end of the chase brought them to the southern border of the wood, and they paused there at the edge of the trees, gazing down the long snow-covered slope to the dark line that marked the course of the River Edro.

Abruptly, Pavo stiffened and turned back towards the forest. "I think somebody have followed us," he said.

Nagaro frowned, glancing back in the direction they had come, scanning the underbrush. "I don't see anyone, Pavo, but why don't you look around just in case?"

Pavo grunted and moved quietly back under the trees, fading into the intermittent shadows as he moved stealthily among the undergrowth, leaving Nagaro and Taru to enjoy the view.

Nagaro brushed snow from a fallen log that lay just under the eaves of the wood, and sat down to rest. Taru sat down beside him. It was past mid-afternoon and although the sun wasn't high, its rays reflecting off of the open expanse of snow seemed dazzlingly bright in contrast to the dim light under the trees.

Nagaro adjusted the tilt of his broad-brimmed black hat to shield his eyes. It was the hat the shoemaker had given him in Lankura. It's dark red band now sported a single black raven's quill.

Taru's attention was drawn by Nagaro's movement. Glancing at his friend, he shook his head. "I still can't get used to it," he said. "Ye don't look like yourself without the beard and the kuma stain and with your hair cut short. Why don't ye want t' look like a Turo anymore?"

Nagaro fingered his chin. He wasn't going to miss the kuma stain. He'd long been weary of always needing help with applying it. Wearing his hair shorter didn't bother him either, but his face felt naked without the beard. He meant to let it grow again when this was all over. "I told you," he said patiently. "I have to look the part so I can convince the folk in Lankura that I'm Alorin Loros. None of my male kin wore beards."

Taru waved a hand in a gesture of mock annoyance. "I understand *that*," he said. "I just don't see why ye had t' make the change so soon. Ye'll not be going to Lankura for two months."

"I wanted time to get used to it and—"

A sudden cry coming from the woods behind them made them both jump to their feet and turn around.

The sound was followed by scuffling, and then Pavo's massive form loomed into view with a much smaller man— a gray-haired Turowan— held by the collar.

"Look what I have found!" Pavo's usually impassive face was split by a triumphant grin. "I told you someone have been following us."

Nagaro stared at the grizzled Turo, who looked genuinely frightened. The man had a face like wrinkled leather and was dressed all in leather and dark wool, materials that blended well with dark trees and shadows. And the man looked familiar.

Nagaro felt a wash of apprehension as he realized that he'd met this man the previous spring, during the mission that had ended outside the garden wall of Loros Hall only a few hundred yards from where they were now standing. He hoped the man wouldn't recognize him.

He drew himself up. "Let him get his feet, Pavo," he directed, and once the man was standing he fixed the fellow with a cool stare and said sternly, "Who are you, and what are you doing here, Zirda?"

Pavo still held his prisoner by the collar, but the old man's alarm was diminishing and he was peering at Nagaro with disconcerting interest.

"My name's Jato, if ye don't remember, Zirda. And folk may be calling ye Alorin Loros, but now that I see ye up close, I know who ye are, Capt'n, even though ye've changed your looks since last I saw ye."

Nagaro winced. *So much for hope.*

Taru stepped between them. "He has every right t' change his looks. And this is *his* land, so ye'd best answer his questions! Now what were ye doing sneaking around here and spying on us?"

Jato bristled. "I saw no fence or wall— so this land is free for any man t' walk!"

Taru started to say something more, but Nagaro forestalled him with a gesture. He'd just remembered something, and an idea was forming in his mind. "He has a point, Taru," he said. "Let me talk to him. And let go of him, Pavo. I don't want him thinking we mean him harm."

Pavo released the man's collar.

"There, now." Nagaro addressed the old Turo. "Sit down, Zirda, so we can talk more comfortably." He reseated himself on the log and indicated a place beside him.

Jato rubbed at his neck and glanced warily at Pavo and Taru, but he took the offered seat.

Taru gave Nagaro a worried look and continued to stand in front of the log, eyeing Jato, while Pavo stood behind it, impassive once again.

Nagaro considered the old man. "Jato..." he said thoughtfully. "You work for Lord Anduar, don't you? As a scout?"

"Aye." Jato eyed him narrowly.

And your full name is Jato Mobaro?"

This time Jato looked surprised, as did Taru. "Now, how d' ye come t' know that, Zirda?"

"You're on the role of Loros." Nagaro explained, as much for Taru and Pavo's benefit as Jato's. "It's a list of all the people who originally came from inside the borders of Loros Wared."

Jato stuck out his chin. "I should be on it. I was born not three miles from here. I expect I know this part o' the country better'n ye do, Zirda."

"I'm sure you do, but I still want to know what you're doing here *right now*. Are you on your master's business, or were you thinking of coming back here to live?"

"It'd be the first one. I've no reason t' come back after more 'n twenty years. Anduar's a good master. Takes good care o' his people, he does."

Nagaro sighed. "So I've seen, and I respect him for it. But I'm not one of his people, Jato, and I don't want him to know where I am. I hope you'll keep my secret."

At this, Jato looked indignant. "Ye're askin' me not t' do my job! What'd I be if I served my master so badly?" he demanded.

Nagaro took off his hat, ran a hand through his hair, and settled the hat back on his head, using the action to give himself time to collect his thoughts. The argument he planned to make hinged on his father's words, and it meant revealing even more of himself in the hope of winning a share of the old man's loyalty. "This may not be your Wared anymore, Jato," he said carefully, "but your roots are here— your people. Haven't you as much duty to them as to your master? I've heard that the Turo know how to guard their secrets, and my secret belongs as much to Minowei's people as it does to me."

Jato's sharp eyes probed him. "Well, I suppose that we do keep our secrets," he conceded. "But what are ye t' Minowei's people? Beggin' yer pardon, Zirda."

Nagaro met the old man's challenging gaze unflinchingly. "Minowei was my great grandmother," he said quietly, and he heard Taru's intake of breath.

Jato gaped at him. "The *real* heir o' the House of Loros is *you?* How d' ye know it?"

"I have my father's ring." Nagaro reached into his tirka and brought his treasure out into the light.

Jato bent over it as if it were some holy talisman. "*Hamanei mata noa!*" he breathed. "Then it's *true!*" He raised his eyes as Nagaro slipped the ring back into its hiding place. "Ye should ha' said something from the first, Zirda. But what am I t' do, M' Lord? I can't go back to Anduar with nothin' to show!"

"I don't see why not," grumbled Taru. "Or why ye have to go back t' him at all."

"Ye'd have me throw away twenty years o' service?"

Taru moved a step closer to the old man, flexing his fingers. "We *could* just keep ye here..."

Nagaro immediately raised a restraining hand. "That would be unlawful imprisonment, Taru. I've had some experience with it, and I want no part of it." He turned back to Jato, frowning.

The old man shot Taru a disapproving glance. "It'd be no use anyway," he said darkly. "Lord Anduar would only send somebody else. His scouts are combin' the whole country for Capt'n Nagaro. And since there's been rumors of another heir o' Loros at Loros Hall, he's been very keen t' find out what he can about that too!"

Nagaro's frown deepened. He didn't like all this attention from the most clever and manipulative member of the King's Council. "And I suppose the same thing would happen if you went back and reported that you'd found nothing?" he ventured.

"Aye. Sure as tides an' taxes, Zirda. But ye needn't fear Lord Anduar. He's a good man. Always workin' for the good o' the country."

Nagaro sighed. "I'm sure he means to serve the good of Edrovir," he said carefully. "But he uses men hard sometimes in pursuit of his plans. He would have let Lothard kill Kenthos, last spring. He thought to use the killing— with all those witnesses— to rein Lothard in."

"I... I didn't know that." Jato frowned. "But if he did, I'd say it was 'cause he was angry, on account o' how Lothard killed poor Pedran."

"Yes. Pedran was one of Anduar's people. But Kenthos wasn't, so Anduar didn't care about Kenthos. That's my point. I'm afraid he means to use *me*— without regard for my wishes— and I'd rather make my own course without his interference."

Jato looked uncomfortable. "I can't blame ye for that, Zirda. And ye're a good man too. None better. But I have my duty..." His voice trailed.

Nagaro thought he saw a way. "What did you see and hear in the forest before Pavo caught you?" he asked. "And what did you make of it?"

Jato frowned. "I *heard* more 'n I *saw*. It was dark in there. I saw that ye were Kelorin, an' that ye wore a black hat and feather. An' I heard that talk about how ye owned the forest, and expectin' t' be chosen lord, and makin' a claim in Lankura. I thought I'd found the new man who's claimin' to be the heir o' Loros— not that I'd found Capt'n Nagaro."

Nagaro nodded. "And if Pavo hadn't collared you, that's what you would have told Anduar."

At this, Pavo moved and said, "I am sorry, Nagaro."

"It's all right, Pavo." Nagaro waved the apology away. "But... if he'd heard you looking for him, and decided he'd better not get caught..."

Understanding dawned in Jato's seamed face. "Aye, Zyrda," he said, beginning to brighten. "I'd ha' thought that I'd gotten all I could safely get— and without seein' yer face real clear, so I wouldn't ha' known."

"And we would never have had this conversation."

Jato's grin widened. "I can tell him everything I saw in the woods, Zirda, an' still keep yer secret. It'd be the truth as far as it went, and news for his ears."

"That's it, then." Nagaro nodded decisively. He glanced at Taru and at Pavo. "That's the tale we must tell if any of us is pressed on the matter. Is it agreed?"

It was duly agreed, and Jato departed, disappearing back into the forest like smoke on the wind. Nagaro and Taru picked up their kills and the three friends started to walk back to Loros Hall, this time keeping to open ground where they could be sure they weren't being followed.

Pavo shook his shaggy head as he crunched through snow that was up to a foot deep in places. "It is good thing I did not catch that man," he said, his expression betraying no hint of irony. "If I have catch him, he maybe would have recognized you."

"Hmpf!" Taru snorted. "I hope Nagaro's done the right thing. I don't like letting Anduar know even that much! And I wish this hadn't happened in Idrin."

Nagaro sighed. "I don't believe Idrin is unlucky," he said. "But I'll admit that I don't like there being a rumor about a new heir of Loros. Anduar won't rest until he thinks he knows the full tale. At least the description of my present appearance should put him off the scent. Still, I'd best keep out of sight as much as possible from now on. There could be other spies about— Anduar's, or someone else's."

The garden wall rose ahead of them, and beyond it the bulk of the Hall, both awash in the light of a winter sun that was descending as the afternoon waned. The sky overhead was a deepening cobalt, and just past the shoulder of the Hall, the two moons were rising nearly full, a pair of overlapping disks. Talebra seemed to be reaching down to wrap bright silver arms around Naru's dusky, leaden orb. In spite of himself, Nagaro felt a shiver as he gazed at the spectacle. He'd lost track of the movement of the moons for many weeks during his convalescence, but the conjunction had been moving all the while, ponderously, towards its climax. It now seemed that the climax would be reached in a month or two— at approximately the time when Loros Wared would be choosing a new lord.

It was also the time Nagaro had chosen for his journey to Lankura to claim his heritage...

War or love... love or war... Nagaro deliberately turned his gaze elsewhere. It was all coincidence, of course, but he was having to remind himself more and more often that he didn't believe in omens.

***

What were you *thinking*, My Lord?" demanded Pendrik. "Making the announcement that the Pact is dead in the month of Idrin!"

Nevien, seated beside her father in the Council Chamber, was paying close attention to every detail since she intended to send Kuran a full report. She flinched involuntarily at Pendrik's scathing tone. Her father, for his part, returned the Leithian lord a stony look across the table.

"I did it *two days* before the start of Idrin," Elgurn said testily. "And the notion that Idrin is inauspicious is nothing but nonsense!"

"*I* know that," Pendrik's ire was undiminished, "but the common folk take it seriously! And by the time the news trickled down to *them*, it was the first of Idrin! Now they're saying the Pact was voided in Idrin and that means there's sure to be war! And with the dance the moons are doing, half of them think it'll be the end of the world!"

Pendrik had arrived at the council meeting in an unusually belligerent mood. He was by now quite red in the face, and had uncharacteristically forgotten all about his glass of wine. He'd brought the bottle himself in defiance of the usual protocol of the Council Chamber, and no one had been inclined to deny him his favored vice. Now he apparently remembered it, for he seized the brimming goblet in front of him and tossed off half its contents before returning it to the table with a force that rattled the china sothiril pot and made the cups dance in their saucers.

"I've just come from my Hold," Odus put in cautiously. "And the common folk there are, I'm afraid, very *unsettled*, in part because the news came in Idrin. I hope the celebration of the Festival of Lights will lighten their mood—"

"Hah!" It was Devral who interrupted this time. "It might do so in Morbern Hold, but not in Lankura— nor in Hurn! Lothard's gone home to muster his men, I'll wager. It surely isn't lost on *him* how the announcement changes things. You may send him an invitation, My Lady—" This was directed to Nevien and spoken less stridently in consequence, "—but I doubt that he'll come to the feast." The old warrior shifted his gaze back to Elgurn. "If you hoped for a confrontation at the Festival between our man and Lothard, I'm afraid you won't get it!"

Elgurn frowned and glanced questioningly at Anduar, who had so far remained silent. The Kelorin lord was hunched forward, toying with the handle of his teacup. The man had always struck Nevien as feline, but just now she had the distinct impression that the cat was not purring.

"Won't you support me, My Lord?" Elgurn ventured. "I thought we'd decided that the announcement should come shortly before the Festival of Lights, and since *that* comes just three days after Idrin, I had very little latitude."

Anduar shifted his position, straightening and withdrawing his hand from the cup in what almost seemed a guilty movement. He placed his words precisely into the waiting silence. "We *had* so agreed," he said, "but events have conspired to make the perceived timing rather... *unfortunate.* Had I been here when you issued the statement, My Lord, rather than on the road, I would have advised delaying it until further notice."

"Then you're saying you've changed the plan?" Pendrik raised an eyebrow.

"*Why*, Anduar?" Elgurn asked.

Devral leaned forward. "Yes," he said darkly. "Why?"

Anduar picked up his teacup, took a delicate sip, and returned it to its saucer. The motion had much of his usual sleekness, but from the expression on his face one would have thought the cup contained lemon juice rather than sothiril. "I would of course prefer that Lothard were here in Lankura rather than at home, marshaling troops," he said at last. "But it will matter little whether we can lure him back, since a confrontation requires that there be someone to *confront.*"

"Ah-ha!" Pendrik slapped the table. "You've lost your man, that's it! You can't find the errant captain."

"Is this true?" Devral demanded.

Anduar returned the two lords a sour look. "It is unfortunately accurate."

It was all Nevien could do not to smile, even as the men at the table all registered dismay.

Elgurn scowled. "I thought you went to Kel Wared to speak to him."

Anduar rose from his seat with the lithe grace of a cat springing to a tabletop. "I did. I was returning from there when you issued your statement." The Kelorin lord began to pace the floor with the prowl of a stalking animal. His voice when he continued carried more than an edge of annoyance. "I was told at Kel Hall that he wasn't *there*— had never *been* there. I stayed at the Hall for two days— hence my delay— to assure myself that the people there were telling the truth as they understood it. During that time, my scouts began scouring the countryside for any sign of him. I can say confidently that although Captain Nagaro ostensibly left Lankura bound for Kel Wared, he never arrived at that destination. There is some evidence that he may have been diverted to River House."

Nevien covered her jolt of dismay at the last words by reaching for her cup. Over the rim of it her eyes darted to Anduar. She caught him looking at her, but his glance moved quickly on to sweep the other faces, and the question she feared he might ask didn't come.

The other men at the table were frowning and shaking their heads in perplexity.

"Could there have been foul play?" inquired Odus Morbern.

Anduar had ceased pacing, coming to a halt behind his chair with his hands gripping the chair-back. "If he had come to grief, Kuran would be openly grieving instead of evading my efforts to meet him face to face."

Elgurn's eyes narrowed. "Evading your efforts?"

Anduar flicked a wrist. "He responded to the summons I sent upon my return by claiming an intent to comply at his *earliest opportunity*. Apparently he has yet to find one. When I sought him at the Fleet Compound, he wasn't in his study. The clerk said he had been *called away*, and would be back *momentarily*. Then, after I'd waited for an hour, the other clerk— that baby-faced new fellow— came to say that Lord Kuran had been *detained* and he had no idea when the man would return."

"So," Devral turned upon Elgurn. "It seems your old friend is playing cat-and-mouse, My Lord."

Pendrik smote the table. "It's ridiculous! I wouldn't stand for it!"

Nevien stole a glance at her father and saw that the king was looking distinctly troubled.

"We have no actual recourse, Pendrik," Elgurn said wearily. "I could threaten him with some sanction for not appearing, but I really have no grounds to demand to know the whereabouts of his heir, since the captain isn't a criminal fugitive." The king paused, his frown darkening. "I've always considered Kuran completely reliable, but adopting Nagaro was *his* idea, if you'll recall. We only hoped to take advantage of it. I'm beginning to wonder if he might be hatching something."

"Let us hope not." Anduar reclaimed everyone's attention, speaking with something approaching his usual smoothness. "And I have no doubt the captain will reappear in due course. A man like that cannot long remain invisible. Our concern, therefore, should be how to manage matters in the meantime."

"That's easy," growled Devral. "If Lothard has gone home to muster his men, I'll go home and muster mine!"

Anduar fixed his fellow Kelorin with a level gaze. "It would be better if you remained here, for now," he said delicately. "Have you a deputy who can see to the muster in your absence?"

Devral scowled. "Yes..."

"We should all adopt the same plan." Anduar's steely eyes swept the men at the table. "Force should be available in case it proves necessary, but we should present the appearance of having hope for a peaceful outcome."

Pendrik scowled. "If Lothard marches on Lankura, we'd have little time to respond."

Anduar leaned forward. "He may perhaps find something to *occupy* him on the way."

All eyes locked on the Kelorin lord. "What do you mean, My Lord?" Odus inquired warily.

"There's an effort underway to reinstate the old Loros Wared. My scouts are looking into it." Anduar now seemed to be enjoying himself again. "The entire western half of Kildoran Wared is astir with rumors of the return of the heir of Loros. There's a man moving about among the common folk, taking an interest in their affairs. He appears to dwell at Loros Hall and is favored to be chosen lord of the new Wared."

Nevien had frozen with her teacup halfway to her lips at the first mention of an heir of Loros. She forced herself to complete the motion of taking a sip. Fortunately, no one seemed to be paying her any attention.

"What, *again?*" Pendrik gestured extravagantly with his wine goblet, nearly spilling its contents. "Don't tell me that man Kenthos is fool enough to break the oath he swore!"

"It isn't Kenthos this time." Anduar spoke decisively. "Kenthos has taken up residence in the village of Fenerwel, but I have recently gotten a good description of the new man. He's of smaller stature and slighter build than Kenthos, and he wears a black hat with a dark red band and a black feather. Apparently he is being styled Alorin Loros."

This time Nevien wasn't the only one to react to Anduar's words. Her father jerked involuntarily, and the action was mirrored around the table. Nevien's pulse began to pound as she saw the members of the council exchange meaningful glances.

Odus was the first to speak. "I... ah... didn't think that name was widely known."

"It isn't," Pendrik observed flatly, over his wine.

Devral's gaze remained locked on Anduar. "We've seen that the child wasn't buried in the garden at Loros Hall, My Lord, and therefore didn't die in infancy," he drawled. "And Rastyl claims to have set eyes on the man. Is it possible this heir of Loros could be genuine?"

"It's conceivable, of course."

At this, Elgurn stirred, and Nevien saw that his face had become drawn. "It's at least as likely that this man is an imposter," he put in quickly. "Another opportunist, taking advantage of the common people's desire to believe."

"That also may be true," Anduar affirmed calmly. "The name Alorin has surely never been forgotten by the folk at Loros Hall. And I'm not much impressed by a man who has either spent twenty-seven years hiding from the world, or else is so unremarkable that he's lived twenty-seven years without doing anything to merit attention."

"Perhaps he has benefitted from observing Kenthos' experience," Devral suggested.

"Well, he's certainly done *that*." Anduar smiled one of his less pleasant smiles. "The man is keeping his head down and going about his activities very quietly. But that is hardly the point."

"Which is?"

"That a newly-formed Loros Wared, ruled by a lord who claims to be the son of Tevren Loros, would surely interest Lothard Hurn, if he became aware of it..." It was Anduar's turn to let his sentence dangle as he lolled in his chair and reached negligently for his cup.

Odus took the bait. "If Lothard knew about it, he'd take his army to Loros Hall first, rather than to Lankura!"

"But he mustn't be allowed to!" Nevien had been listening with growing alarm and could no longer restrain herself.

Five pairs of eyes immediately turned to her.

"I mean," she said hastily, "that Lothard shouldn't be allowed to make war on Loros Hall— whether this man is the heir of Loros or not. The place has no defenses!" She turned to her father. "When Lothard's men pursued Kenthos all the way from Irvenen Wared, you sent a force to stop him— to prevent the spilling of innocent blood!"

She stopped, avoiding Anduar's gaze, well aware of how that mission had ended— of who had stepped between Lothard and his prey.

"My Lady is quite right, of course." Anduar's response was smooth as satin. "We couldn't do less the second time than the first— if this man should find himself in similar straights."

Odus looked nonplused. Devral and Pendrik exchanged glances.

Nevien risked meeting Anduar's steel-grey eyes and found that they were on her. "Forgive me, My Lord," she murmured, thinking she might have misjudged him. "For a moment I thought you were suggesting sacrificing the man."

"Banish that thought, dear Lady," he said gravely. "I raised the matter only because it represents a possible distraction for Lothard." Ignoring the questioning looks of the other Pact Signers, he transferred his gaze from her to her father and changed the subject. "My Lord, have there been any requests for reinstatement of the Council of Lords?"

Elgurn's expression suggested that his mind had been elsewhere. "Ah, no... not yet." he said, then added tartly, "Perhaps they're all waiting for the end of Idrin."

"It could be that." Anduar ignored the irony. "But I think most of them are waiting until they can see how to make it work to their advantage, rather than otherwise." He paused to reach for the pot of sothiril and poured himself another cup.

"The situation hasn't changed since we first discussed it before the Festival of the Harvest Moon," he continued as he swirled his cup and looked across it to let his gaze touch upon each of the other council members in turn. "As things stand, no group or faction can muster enough support for its favored candidate to take a majority of the krits. And no one will risk calling for a Choosing only to see the crown go to a rival."

"Then we have time—" Odus began.

Anduar impaled him with a look that silenced him. "Only while the peace holds," he said pointedly. "A formal Choosing holds little hope for Lothard's cause. He may well decide not to wait for someone to force his hand."

"Then what hope do we have?" Pendrik had been nursing his wine, a tonic that could normally be counted upon to mellow his mood, but in this case it seemed to be making him morose.

"We have a warrior's hope!" Devral responded grimly. "We've already said we must gird for war."

"Gird for war, even as we work to maintain peace," Anduar put in quickly. "War is not inevitable, and if it comes despite our efforts, Edrovir will still need a king when the war is over. Some man must still be found who commands broad enough respect and trust that a majority of the Lords will be willing to place the crown on his head. I suggest, My Lords, that we all give thought to who that man might be."

And that was really the end of it. There was a brief, desultory discussion, but in the end Elgurn adjourned the council meeting without anything further being decided.

Nevien immediately threaded her way out of the Council Chamber and struck off across the Audience Chamber, making for the room's back door and moving as quickly as she could without abandoning all semblance of a ladylike gate.

She didn't get far, however, before she became aware of Anduar at her side.

"The generosity of your spirit puts us all to shame, My Lady, he said, his voice devoid of any trace of irony. "I applaud the way you came to the defense of a man you've never met."

Nevien answered carefully. "I was also thinking of the people of Loros Wared," she said. "They've been waiting so long, and this must mean so much to them. If this man is taking an interest in their affairs and they're pleased with him, does it really matter whether he is genuine or not?"

She had slowed her steps so as not to appear to be running away from Anduar, and the result was that they were overtaken by Elgurn. The king was in a hurry and apparently headed in the same direction, but he must have overheard Nevien's reply because he slowed enough to comment vehemently.

"Of course it matters if the man is falsely claiming the blood of Loros! I have reason to believe the heir is dead. Rastyl is surely mistaken, and he's in Irvenen right now to the best of my knowledge, in any case."

"Rastyl is in Irvenen to the best of my knowledge, also." Anduar's response was spoken conversationally, though he'd matched his stride to Elgurn's, leaving Nevien to keep up as best she could. "But I wonder, My Lord, what evidence you have concerning the fate of the heir of Loros?"

It was an obvious question, but Elgurn turned sharply away, his shoulders hunching. "I haven't time for this," he muttered. "I have things to do." And with that he strode on.

Nevien came to a halt, aware of the implications of Anduar's question and Elgurn's evasive answer. She knew what her father's evidence must be. He must have known both *what* was being done to Leyel, and *why*. And it was knowledge he clearly hadn't shared with the members of his Council. *What would he do when he learned the truth? What would the council members do?*

Anduar had also stopped. He stood for a moment looking after the king, his eyes narrowed. Then he turned back to her. "Whoever is chosen as lord of Loros Wared," he observed as if picking up a piece of string, "will have to present himself here in this room to formally claim the title."

"Yes... I suppose so," Nevien answered uneasily.

"He would be wise to come well escorted."

"Escorted?"

"Yes, My lady." Anduar spoke patiently. "He should remember the fate of his predecessor and not try to come from Loros Hall to Lankura with only a handful of men to protect him."

This time Nevien felt a cold finger down her spine. Mutely, she nodded.

"And he shouldn't delay too long. It will be much safer for him if he doesn't wait until Lothard has an army in the field."

"I... I'm sure you're right, My Lord."

"Of course I am." Anduar smiled benignly. "But I expect the man has thought of these things— if he isn't altogether a fool. And now I'm afraid I must leave you. I also have things to do."

So saying, Anduar made her a bow and strode away, making this time for the main entrance of the Audience Chamber, as were the other members of the Council who by this time were well ahead of him.

Nevien stood staring after Anduar for several seconds before she recollected herself and started again for the Chamber's back door. Exiting through it, she hurried along the hall, only making sure not to go *too* fast, lest she overtake her father. She frowned as she mounted the main stairs. The concerns Anduar had raised were unsettling. She must include them in her report to Kuran. *He would know what to do.*

Chapter 19

The Gathering Storm

Loros Hall had a substantial library, with an eclectic assortment of books. In the weeks following their encounter with Jato, Nagaro spent much of his time there, reading and keeping out of sight. So the days slid by— until one afternoon when he was summoned by one of Omei's polite but peremptory requests for his attendance at the room she and Boka used as an office. Since he couldn't claim to be doing anything important, he went without protest.

He found the two sisters seated behind their long table with two Turowan men, dressed for winter travel, waiting in front of it. A chair had been placed for him to the sisters' right, and a sheaf of papers lay on the table in front of it. Everyone present was eyeing him expectantly.

As he took the indicated seat, Omei cleared her throat. "Ye once said ye'd be willing t' present a petition on behalf o' the soldiers that lost their houses, farms, or boats for want of a piece o' paper, Zirda," she said. "I hope ye've not changed your mind."

"I certainly haven't." Nagaro eyed the stack of papers. "I said I would need detailed examples." He glanced at the two men. "Is that what you have here?"

"Aye, Zirda." The older man bobbed him an awkward bow. "We've done our best."

"Well then, let me have a look."

There followed a period of silence while Nagaro sat frowning, turning pages as he deciphered the scratchy pen strokes on the papers in front of him. The two sisters waited with imperturbable patience. The two Turowan men shifted worriedly from foot to foot. They'd been provided a pair of chairs, but apparently chose to remain standing. Finally the older man spoke up hesitantly.

"I know it's not very important, Zirda. But it'd mean a lot t' us."

Nagaro looked up from his examination of the last paper. "Actually, I think it's too important not to do properly. When a man is called up by his lord to fight, and does his duty, he shouldn't come home to find that someone has appropriated his property and he can't get it back. I see that you've done a fair job of collecting the details for six people." Nagaro tapped the papers in front of him. "You've recorded what they lost, and where, and when, and to whom. And you have the names and testimony of witnesses to prove that they were wronged. But it's not enough to set things right for just these six. There must be others in similar circumstances, and I want to help them also— to make sure that this kind of thing doesn't happen to others in the future."

The two Turowans exchanged worried glances. "But what's to be done, then, M' Lord?" the older man asked.

"Aye," protested the younger one. "It was hard enough gettin' all o' *that*." He gestured at the stack of papers. "How can we hope t' do the same for every man that's been robbed while he was out soldiering?"

"No, no, that won't be necessary." Nagaro ignored the misplaced use of the title in his haste to reassure the men. "We only have to clearly state the general principle."

"Meanin' what, M' Lord?"

"Meaning that I will prepare a petition— on behalf of every citizen of Edrovir— for the right to present witnesses in support of ownership of property in lieu of a paper deed or a bill of sale in the event that such papers have been lost, destroyed, or never existed in the first place. Your nicely detailed six cases will become examples, demonstrating the need for such a new law and showing how it would work."

"We'd be askin' for a new *law?*" The older man was impressed.

"Yes. Exactly."

"An' ye think the king 'll do this? For *us?*"

"I don't see why not. The cause is just, and your examples are quite thorough."

"And ye'll be drawin' up this— *petishun*— for us *yourself*, Zirda?"

"Yes, of course. If you'll just leave the papers with me for reference, and come back tomorrow afternoon, I should be able to show you what I've written and make sure you approve of it."

"Oh, thank ye, M' Lord!"

"The Spirits bless ye, Zirda!"

The two men filed out, looking relieved and gratified.

Nagaro picked up the papers and stood up. "At least, I hope Elgurn will grant it. It would be better, of course, if they had one of the lords to present it."

"That they have." Omei spoke casually.

"What?" Nagaro was startled, but then he frowned. "You're being premature again, Omei. If they're willing to wait until after the Choosing, they *may* have one."

Omei's eyes twinkled. "No, they have one now." She rose and went to one of the cabinets, returning with a number of papers in her hands, which she spread on the table. "Here's the record o' the Choosing. Ye'll see that ye have three and a half pages full o' names. Tor Kenthos has seven names, and Tor Venerev has four. I'd say the choice is clear."

"*But—*" Nagaro stared at the pages. They were clearly in order, with the candidate's name and place of residence spelled out at the top of each, and the undersigned householder's names duly accompanied by place of residence and two sets of initials to indicate witnesses. In fact, he'd set up one page for each candidate himself. "*But—*" He legs seemed to fold, and he found himself sitting in his chair again. "*When...?*"

"We just finished last week."

"But it was supposed to be in the *spring!* It's not a month past Idrin. It's snowing outside!"

Boka spoke up. "Lord Kuran suggested we do it sooner. He said it'd be safer if it was done afore the armies begin t' march."

"*What armies?*"

"Every lord has an army, Zirda. And since they're sayin' the Pact has been broke, there's sure t' be war on the way."

Nagaro stared at the two sisters. He knew about the abrogation of the Pact of Lankura. Kuran had brought that news during his most recent visit, but Nagaro hadn't given it much thought. "Why didn't you at least *tell* me you were doing this?" he asked weakly.

"Lord Kuran didn't want t' trouble ye during your recovery." It was Omei who answered.

"Which is to say, he knew I wouldn't like it!"

Omei regarded him calmly. "Does it really make so much difference, Zirda? Ye'll not be saying ye didn't expect to be chosen."

"I...wasn't sure, no. And I...I thought I had more time."

He stood up again and rounded the end of the table, moving towards the window. Outside, the snow was falling. He felt the mantle of responsibility descending, settling its weight on his shoulders. "*I'm the lord of a Wared,*" he murmured. "One that hasn't yet been officially recognized." He turned around to face the two women. "Getting it recognized is the first thing I must do for the people. You have the papers for that too, I suppose? The petition for re-establishment of Loros Wared?"

Omei answered from her seat at the table. "Aye, M' Lord. They're in my cabinet."

Well, at least the sisters' thoroughness would make his first task easier. *Or maybe it wasn't the first task.* He ran a hand distractedly through his hair. "Are the lords really mustering their armies?" he asked.

Boka answered him. "Lord Endemar is drilling his soldiers. That we know. As for the others..." She shrugged.

"If Endemar is drilling troops, it must be for good reason, and we would do well to do the same." Nagaro frowned, hearing the echo of his father's logic in his own words. "But quietly," he added. "So as not to draw attention." *It was fortunate that he had experience in training men. But this was so sudden....* "I've had too little news," he muttered. "I've been reading... and thinking about myself, instead of... other things." Another thought occurred to him. "Is there some ceremony to mark a new lord's choosing?"

"In the old days, the new lord would ride a circuit of all the farms and villages," Omei told him. "To greet the people."

"I can do that." He glanced at the window. "As soon as it stops snowing. And while I'm about it, I can take a count of all the able-bodied men... and see how many might be willing to undertake military training..."

***

As it turned out, the snow didn't stop falling for three days, leaving the world so deep in drifts as to seriously hinder the passage of a horse. It was another three days after that before the weather turned, in a thaw that reduced the drifts to slush in a matter of hours. There was mud everywhere, but Nagaro— who had chafed and paced for six days— was not to be deterred.

He set out on his circuit accompanied by Venerev the Seneschal, by Kenthos, and by Mundabo the Steward, who had lived all his life in Fenerwel and knew the surrounding country and its Turowan inhabitants. With these three to make introductions, he traveled from village to village in a long zig-zag circuit through the former Loros Wared. Any concerns about the validity of his choosing were put to rest by the joyous responses of the people he encountered, both the long-established residents and the new arrivals. He had the other two candidates traveling with him, and yet everywhere he went he was welcomed gladly as Lord Alorin.

That name had been decided upon, after some discussion, for his formal presentation to his people. That the new "Lord Alorin" was also "Captain Nagaro" could hardly be concealed from folk, but he was anxious for everyone to understand that he didn't want that fact to get abroad. Besides, as strange as it felt to be called Alorin, he doubted he could ever get used to hearing the title "Lord" in front of the name Nagaro.

If he was to be called "Lord" anything, it would have to be Alorin. Both the title and the name became increasingly less strange as the circuit progressed and he heard them from every mouth.

It took five days to complete the circuit, including a diversion to Kildoran Hall to let Nagaro formally report the recent events to Endemar.

The old lord embraced him warmly, with tears in his eyes, saying, "I couldn't be more pleased to welcome the son of an old friend who was taken from this world much too soon. I've kept your Wared as best I knew how, even though I long believed there was no living heir to claim it. I have no words to say how glad I am that I was wrong. And I'm grateful that I've lived to see this day."

The weather turned bitter again before the end of their journey. Nagaro returned to Loros Hall, weary and chilled, as the sun was setting on the fifth day. For the last mile he'd been feeling a growing ache in his chest at the site of his wound. Kenthos parted from the company at Fenerwel, but the other three rode on to the half-finished gatehouse, through the gate, and at last into the stable yard.

Nagaro winced as he swung down from the saddle, his boots landing hard on the frozen mud. Thunder-Heels snorted steam in the frosty air and shook himself, eager for a warm stall. The blue of the sky was deepening in the east. Soon the first stars would be pricking through. To the west, amid the gloaming, the two moons were riding down the sky, a pair of overlapping crescents chasing the vanished sun.

Venorev called for the grooms at the stable door and they emerged from the haven of warmth just long enough to lead the horses inside.

"Will ye be coming into the Hall, M' Lord?" Mundabo asked as he stood blowing on his hands.

Nagaro shook his head. "No, I'll go directly to the little house."

Venerev eyed him in the gathering dusk. "Ye should be thinking about moving to the Hall, My Lord," he ventured. "It'll be expected."

"I know that, and I will. But not yet." All Nagaro wanted at that moment was a warm meal and a familiar bed.

"As ye wish, Zirda" Venerev saluted him, then turned and made for the side door of the large Hall with Mundabo at his heels.

Nagaro strode off along the path that skirted the garden wall, leading to the small side gate that gave access to the private yard of Nevrath's little house. The yard was a combined flower- and kitchen-garden and was surrounded by a wall of its own, one side of which was part of the larger wall that enclosed the Hall's much larger garden, making it a garden within a garden. Nagaro had just closed the gate behind him and turned towards the house when he stifled a cry as a shape suddenly emerged from the twilight shadow of a large lilac bush.

"Hail to ye, Lord Alorin!" exclaimed the shadow. Then, seeing Nagaro's flinch, the owner of the voice added, "No need t' fear, M' Lord. It's only me."

"Jato? You gave me a turn! How did you get in here?" Nagaro could scarcely make out the old Turo's face in the failing light, but the voice was unmistakable.

"The gate warn't locked, Zirda."

"But how did you know I was coming here tonight? And how did you get inside the defensive wall?"

"Oh, *that*." Jato was clearly pleased with himself. "I climbed over it on the west side." He gestured. "Where it needs the most work. And I figured ye'd be coming in this way after I spied ye an' the other lot makin' for the Hall. So I legged it 'round and got in here afore ye."

"So I see." Nagaro made a mental note to have the workmen give extra attention to raising the western wall as soon as the weather permitted. "But *should* you be here, Jato? Anduar hasn't sent you back to spy on me again, has he?"

"No, praise the Spirits, he hasn't." Jato spoke with evident relief. "I'm assigned to watch some o' the Lords t' the north o' here to see if they're musterin' troops. I was on my way back t' Lankura with my report when I chanced to see ye ridin' with those other two. I came lookin' for ye t' give ye some news I think ye ought to know."

Nagaro felt apprehension blossom. "What news?"

"It's this, Zirda. The word is out that the heir o' Loros has come at last."

"It... *has?*" Nagaro felt a cold clutch of fear. "But *how?* The folk here have been so careful."

"I don't think it's comin' from inside the Wared, Zirda. But it must be runnin' like fire afore the wind. It's gone all the way from Lankura t' Hurn Hold in the last two weeks."

"Are they... giving this heir a name?"

"The name he ought t' have, Zirda— Alorin Loros."

"*Vothra!*" Nagaro put a hand to his chest, feeling as if his heart had given him a painful jolt. *He'd just been riding around the Wared under that name!* Then he steadied. "*Not* Captain Nagaro, then?"

"No, M' Lord. An' here's the odd part. The rumors don't put the heir here in Loros Wared— which is why I don't think they're comin' from inside it. They're puttin' him in Irvenen, or Kel, or Sundorin Wared. Even in Glenmark Hold with Lord Pendrik. But not here."

"That *is* odd." *Odd but fortunate...*

"I thought ye might ha' started the rumors yourself— to put the Leithians off the scent. But I can see ye didn't."

Nagaro shook his head. "Does anyone believe these tales? After what happened last spring?"

"Oh, *well...*" Jato spread his hands. "It's how ye'd expect. None of 'em wants to say he believes it, but those that wants it t' be true are hopin'. An' those that don't want it t' be true are lookin' worried. But no one knows where the tales are comin' from."

Nagaro stood in the darkening garden and shivered. It wasn't the worst news he could have had, since it wouldn't draw anyone to Loros Hall. *At least not anyone who thought in simple ways.* "Has Anduar sent anyone else to spy on me?" he asked.

"Not that I've heard, M' Lord. He says there's no time t' waste chasin' shadows when war is brewing."

Well that was a relief. "And *is* war brewing? Are the Holds and Wareds you've been watching mustering their men?"

"Aye, Zirda. Every one o' them— which is Kel, Virden, Sobring, and Hurn. Grimbold has nearly four hundred men. Lothard has nearer eight hundred."

"Eight hundred men!" Nagaro exclaimed. "What does he mean to do with so many?"

March 'em to Lankura to try an' take the crown. That's what Lord Anduar thinks. And Grimbold 'll stand with Lothard."

Nagaro shook his head and shivered again. His chest hurt. "When? Are they ready now?"

"I'd say not yet, Zirda. Nobody likes marchin' in the middle o' winter, but I expect they will if something happens t' make the Lords feel pressed." Jato's teeth flashed in a cynical grin. "What about Loros Wared, if ye don't mind me askin'?"

"I haven't trained a single man. And I don't care if you repeat that to Anduar. Loros is no threat to anyone."

Jato stamped his feet, trying to warm them. "I should be going, Zirda. The night's fair on us, and I want to find a warm place t' spend it in."

"Yes, yes, by all means, Jato." Nagaro stepped aside to let the old man pass, then headed for the house. He turned one final time just as Jato was slipping out the gate and called after him. "Take care of yourself, friend." Then he let himself in by the back door.

He stopped in the little back hall to hang his cloak and hat on a peg. Hearing him, Theseline emerged from the door of the dining room to greet him. "Welcome back, Zirda," she said, smiling warmly. "I'll fetch ye some soup straight away, to warm ye, and there's some bread to go with it. If I'd known ye were coming tonight, I'd have had something more substantial waiting. But don't worry. That's soon mended."

"Thank you Zirdyn. Bread and soup will be very good right now, and I don't mind waiting for whatever you mean to cook."

He followed her back into the dining room and sank onto one of the plain wooden chairs as she went on into the kitchen. Sitting there, he closed his eyes and gave silent thanks for the roof over his head and the glorious warmth that flowed around him. Weariness receded and pain grew less. *It was good to be home.* He frowned a little at the thought. *Odd that this should feel like home after such a short time...* He shook off the thought and deliberately turned his mind to other things.

Jato's news was unsettling. Fortunately Kuran would come again soon. *He could talk it all over with Kuran.*

***

The peace of the winter garden was shattered by the clash of steel. Kuran's blade slid past a parry that came up fractionally short, and struck home on Nagaro's left side just below the ribs. "Another hit!" the older man gasped as he retreated beyond Nagaro's reach and circled, crouching. Nagaro acknowledged the hit with a tense nod and circled as well, keeping his opponent before him, his blade held low and ready.

Other sounds of metal on metal could be heard from the other end of the garden, closer to the Hall, where the first handful of recruits were finishing their training session under the watchful eyes of the Seneschal. Kuran had arrived to find the training in progress and had suggested that he and Nagaro should try a practice bout. Nagaro had accepted and the bout had begun well, with him quickly scoring two hits. He'd soon begun to flag, however, and now he was sweating despite the chill air.

He knew he was tiring, and the swift movement needed to parry Kuran's thrust had brought a sharp stab of pain through his chest—not for the first time. Any movement requiring swift or forceful exertion could trigger one, and they were coming more frequently as he grew more winded. The result was that he kept trying to limit his movements to spare himself the sudden jabs, and he'd twice let Kuran past his guard. He was dreading Kuran's next attack. The distraction of trying to avoid anticipated pain was taking its toll as much as the pain itself.

The attack, when it came, was hardly a surprise. Kuran had used similar ploys before, and had scored with one of them. Nagaro thought he was ready for it. He side-stepped and brought his arm up sharply for the counter measure, only to have pain lance through him again so that he hesitated and Kuran again came in past his guard. He felt the older man's dull-edged practice sword clip his right shoulder.

"Three! That's the bout." Kuran flung up his sword and stepped back, his black eyes boring into Nagaro. "What ails you, man? I shouldn't be able to best you like that."

Nagaro straightened, not meeting the older man's eyes. He didn't like to have Kuran worry about him. "How do you know?" he asked. "We've never crossed swords before."

"Because I've seen you fight! You're quicker than I am— or you should be. You outreach me. You've beaten Geldoran dozens of times. I've gone against him three times; twice he bested me outright and the third time I swear he was holding back to spare me embarrassment. If you're holding back on my account, I'd have you belay the tactic! You need practice, and I don't need codling!"

Nagaro winced at the tone. He wasn't going to be able to avoid the subject. Brushing his hair from his damp forehead, he took several steps to a nearby bench and sat down. "If I'm holding back, it's not for your sake," he said. "Some of the moves hurt, that's all."

Kuran was immediately at his side, standing over him solicitously. "Your wound? It's not getting worse, is it?"

"No. It only hurts when I make sudden moves. Or when I'm tired, it aches."

"Perhaps it's not healing properly." Kuran's voice was taut with concern. "I should fetch Tred out here to examine you."

Nagaro shook his head. "Ambras told me to expect there to be pain even after it healed. It doesn't mean there's anything wrong."

"You're sure?"

"Yes. But I don't think I'll ever be the sea warrior I was. Even without this, I was thinking I should probably resign my commission. There's so much work to be done here. The people of this Wared chose me for their lord, and I should give them my full attention— at least until the Wared is fully re-established and the defensive wall is complete."

Kuran stood for a moment, frowning. Then he sat down on the bench beside Nagaro. "I'm not surprised to hear you say that," he said. "I've seen it coming."

"I'm sorry to have given you only three years of service."

Kuran swept the apology away with a gesture. "You've done more good in those three years than I have in all my time as Lord of the Fleet. And I can see that you are... needed more elsewhere... right now. So don't give it another thought. But the pain you're feeling worries me in another way. I don't like the idea of your being unable to defend yourself if you're challenged or attacked. You have to work on this. We should have another bout or two— see if you can learn to ignore it."

Nagaro drew a long sigh. "I expect you're right. Just let me rest some more first."

A half hour later they were settled at the dining table in Nevrath's house, enjoying toast and hot sothiril provided by Tira Theseline. The last two sword bouts had offered some encouragement, and they planned to do more the following day.

"Why are you still living here?" Kuran inquired between bites of toast.

Nagaro ducked his head guiltily. "I just find it more comfortable. The lord's chamber in the Hall is too grand."

"I understand." Kuran sighed. "But as a Lord, you really should act the part. If I can get used to it, so can you." He paused, then said, "When were you planning to make the journey to Lankura?"

"I don't know." Nagaro frowned and gestured at several papers he'd left spread out on the table. "These are lists of the able-bodied men, the men skilled with the bow, and the men with some knowledge of sword or pike. A few have had military service, but the number that could be counted on to fight without training is very small, and we've barely begun training. There's no plan yet for defense. I don't like to think of going away and leaving the Wared so unprotected."

Kuran shook his head. "That's the wrong way to think, Nagaro. Lothard wants the crown, not your Wared. You'd be the chief prize to be taken, and I don't believe he knows you're here."

Nagaro took a gulp of sothiril, his frown deepening. "Jato told me there've been new rumors about the heir of Loros."

"He told you right. Did he also tell you that the rumors are saying *I* have the heir in Kel Wared? Or that he's with Rastyl in Irvenen?"

"Yes. And other places. Not here, at least not when he spoke to me."

"That's still true." Kuran put down his cup. "I don't know where the rumors are coming from, but they're surely worrying Lothard. And while he might be diverted from his intended march on Lankura if he knew were to find the heir, he isn't going to go riding about the country in the middle of winter chasing rumors. What he *is* likely to do is march on Lankura sooner than he'd intended, to head off what he sees as a potential threat."

Nagaro raised an eyebrow, studying Kuran over the rim of his cup. "Is this what Anduar believes?"

Kuran reached for the teapot. "Him and everyone else— me, the King, the Council— because it makes sense and it's consistent with the news we're getting out of Hurn Hold. That's why you should ride to Lankura as soon as you can, to secure your rights and the recognition of your Wared before Lothard makes his move. Because *his* move will precipitate others, and once there are armies in play, everything will get much more complicated."

"But you've said I should ride with some force of arms—"

"And there's no time to train your men? I know." Kuran gestured preemptively. "You must make do with whatever escort I and Endemar can give you. And trust Endemar to defend your Wared as he's always done, if it comes to it. Though I don't think it will. We should send word to Kel Wared and Kildoran Hall. And soon."

Nagaro had stopped, frozen with his cup in his hand. "So the time is at hand…" He felt a tightness about his heart. "I'll have to face them— Elgurn… the Council…" He didn't like to admit how much he wished he could avoid that confrontation.

"I'll be with you." Kuran spoke with sympathy. "And waiting won't make you more ready than you are right now."

Nagaro heaved a sigh. "I know. I suppose I should gather my *witnesses*…" Much as he hoped he could avoid revealing his secret to the members of the court, he knew he needed to be prepared to prove that he had once been Leyel Virden.

So Kuran sent a message the next morning to Kel Hall, requesting a score of men at arms. And Nagaro wrote to Endemar, asking for whatever support the aging lord could give him. He then penned letters to his swordmaster, Fendar, and to Master Fineas the apothecary, explaining in carefully elliptical terms that their services would be required when he came to Lankura. Men were sent to Averwin to fetch Chula the gardener. After some hesitation, Nagaro also wrote to Varsyl Virden. The letter read, in part:

I have recently learned the truth, which is that my mother was a cousin to you and your sister. I can show you the proofs. You and I are therefore kin, though not as close as you supposed. You once said that if you could be of any help to me, I had only to ask. Therefore I dare to ask of you the favor of your company when I go to Lankura to claim what is rightfully mine.

While awaiting the results of these dispatches, Nagaro and Kuran did sword practice— every day to build Nagaro's strength. He found that it helped. The pain came less frequently when he wasn't winded and with continuing practice he became winded less easily. Increasingly, he was able to win bouts. But the hardest thing was still to avoid a reflexive flinch whenever a sharp stab of pain caught him off guard.

So the time edged by, and the moons moved closer to their full conjunction. The weather was turning colder. A day came that was marred by freezing rain, but even so, the twenty armed men from Kel Wared arrived that afternoon. The morning of the next day revealed that a little snow had fallen overnight, and also brought a message that Nagaro hadn't expected. Omei brought the news to Nagaro and Kuran where they lingered over breakfast in the little house.

"I sent Boka's son Teyano to Uncle Takelei to see if he could ride with ye, but the lad's come back with word that Takelei is near t' death. If ye'd bid farewell to him that was the 'Third Man', ye'd best do it now. He'll not see the spring."

Nagaro put down his cup. "Of course I want to see him. We didn't stop there when riding the circuit only because his house was so far from the road."

"I wish to see him also." Kuran echoed the sentiment.

So the two men saddled their horses, and prepared a carriage so that Boka and Omei could make the journey. It was an old carriage, long unused, but it was sound, and Teyano was willing to drive it. The last mile along a narrow, rutted track was a sore test of the vehicle, but they managed to get through to arrive at a sturdy stone farmhouse.

They were met at the door of by a woman who introduced herself as Kani, Takelei's granddaughter. She ushered them into the sickroom. There, propped up on a simple pallet bed, was a very old Turowan man. His hair was almost completely white, his skin creased and mottled like old leather, his eyes sunken. His breathing was labored and he looked extremely frail, but he opened his eyes and turned his face to his guests.

Nagaro knelt beside the bed. "I am Nagaro Alorin Loros, Tor Takelei," he said, speaking loudly, since Kani had told him that her grandfather was a little deaf.

"Alorin Loros?" Takelei's voice quavered as he peered at Nagaro.

"Aye, Grandfather," Kani put in. "He's the one ye carried all those years ago. Come t' thank ye."

"O' course he is." The old man reached out shaking fingers to grasp Nagaro's arm. "I remember him from Wotana Bay. Our Clan Chief, an' he's Lord o' Loros, too?"

"Yes, Zirda." Nagaro answered. "The Choosing is just finished. I want to thank you for watching over me at Wotana Bay, and for carrying me to Averwin, years ago. It was a great service you did for my family."

"For Minowei's line, ye mean? 'Twas an honor t' do it, Zirda." A spasm of pain briefly twisted the old man's features, but he rallied when it passed to finish his thought. "An' it warn't no trouble. The yellow-hairs didn' bother an old Turo."

"Maybe not," Nagaro answered earnestly. "But they would have killed you if they'd caught you— to assure your silence. They would have killed us both."

Kuran leaned forward. "I'm Kuran Kel," he said. "Lord of the Royal Fleet. I came to witness this. And I'd like to hear how you did it."

"How 'twas done?" The old man was interrupted by a coughing fit, wincing with each heave of his chest. Then he had to pause to catch his breath. "Had a sling," he managed at last. "Strapped t' me chest." He gestured weakly to illustrate. "Luka made it." He paused to breathe some more, wheezing a little, then continued. "Left the Hall at dawn. All of us t'gether. Stopped at th' Stone Circle, an' the Lady put the sleepin' babe— that was ye, Zirda," he gripped Nagaro's arm again, "—in the sling, with her own hands. Kissed ye on yer forehead, she did. Then they rode west, an' I rode north."

The old man was seized with another painful fit of coughing.

"You had a horse?" Kuran prompted when Takelei at last lay still and quiet again.

"Aye. Me old... plough horse... it was." Takelei managed a toothless grin in spite of the apparent painfulness of drawing breath. "An I had me hands free... t' ride, ye see. 'Cause o' the sling. Went over the fields. Not by th' road." He paused to breathe some more. Then, "All the way t' Averwin. No one took any heed."

"Did you... Did you give me into the hands of the Lady Maramine?" Nagaro asked.

Takelei shook his head. "I laid ye down... very careful... on the doorstep. Knocked on the door... Hid in the bushes. 'Til she come out... an' took ye up."

Nagaro took the man's withered hand in his. "Thank you," he said, his heart too full to find more words. "Thank you." And he laid Takelei's hand gently on top of the blanket.

The old man closed his eyes. A look of peace suffused his ravaged features. "It was for Minoei's heir," he mumbled. "An' it warn't no trouble at all."

Nagaro and Kuran retreated to the house's kitchen, where they sat at the rough table while Boka and Omei joined Kani in the sickroom. About an hour later, the sisters came out to tell them that Takelei was asleep and might not wake again that day.

Nagaro shifted worriedly. "I hope we didn't tire him too much."

But Boka shook her head. "It's good ye both came," she said. "Ye, most especially, M' Lord," (this to Nagaro). "He may live a few weeks now, or only a few days, but nothing can change that. And though he made light o' what he did, it meant something to him t' see ye here, to thank him for his labor."

It was past mid afternoon by the time the party returned to Loros Hall, and an erratic wind was rising as the sun descended. Approaching the unfinished gatehouse, they discovered a crowd of uniformed men and horses, milling about a carriage drawn up in front of the gate. Nagaro was at first alarmed, but the Hall clearly wasn't under attack. Drawing rein while they were still some distance away, he signaled a halt. "Who are they, Kuran?" he asked. "Do you know the livery?"

Kuran squinted at the men. "Those are the colors of Irvenen Wared."

"Irvenen? That would mean Rastyl Korven. What is he doing here?"

Kuran cocked an eyebrow. "I suggest you ask him."

With some trepidation, Nagaro signaled for their coach to proceed and urged his horse forward again. He was wary of meeting the Lord of Irvenen. Rastyl had recognized him even as Leyel Virden, and had recognized him again when he'd returned to Lankura seven years later. Rastyl had been a friend of his father— had spent his life searching for Tevren's missing child. Unfortunately Nagaro, in his ignorance, had once told the man in no uncertain terms to leave him alone.

Among the letters he'd recently sent, there had been no message to the pale-eyed lord. Yet here he was.

As they approached the armed men, Rastyl detached himself from the group and advanced on foot to meet Nagaro. He halted, standing very erect, the gusting wind ruffling his mane of graying hair. His face was set in stern lines. The pale gray eyes, always so difficult to read, stared fixedly into Nagaro's face.

Nagaro dismounted and faced his visitor, aware that Kuran had also dismounted and was standing a pace behind him. He cleared his throat. "My Lord Rastyl, welcome. How may we serve you?"

Rastyl inclined his head ever so slightly in acknowledgment of the courtesy. "We've come seeking whatever hospitality this place may offer, but the Seneschal won't let us in without permission from the lord of the hall. Have I the honor of addressing him?" The words were polite, though spoken with a trace of irony.

Nagaro bowed. "Yes," he said. "I am the Lord of Loros Wared, newly chosen by the people." And then, because this evoked no flicker of reaction, and he still couldn't read those strange, pale eyes, he added, "You do know who I am, My Lord?" As an afterthought, he doffed his black leather hat.

"Oh, be assured that I do." Rastyl abruptly smiled wolfishly. "I would know you in the dead of night, at the dark of the moons. But I confess I'm not sure what name to call you by."

Nagaro winced. "I've decided to officially be Nagaro Alorin Loros," he said diffidently. "I prefer just 'Nagaro', but if folk are going to call me 'Lord', it will have be Alorin for that."

Rastyl bowed with a crooked smile and an exaggerated flourish. "In that case, *My Lord Alorin*, will you permit me and my company to enter your gate?"

"By all means. If you'll let me pass through first, I'll tell Venerev. But you spoke of hospitality. How many are you?" He swept his eyes over the very considerable body of men.

"Besides myself, there are the two ladies we've been escorting— they're in the carriage— and sixty men-at-arms."

"Sixty!" Kuran had held his peace up to this point, but now he spoke in frank astonishment. "Surely, Rastyl, you don't need that many just to escort two ladies, even in these uncertain times?"

"My Lord Kuran." Rastyl turned his pale eyes upon the Lord of the Fleet. "Well met. And I didn't say that was our only purpose." He turned back to Nagaro. "But you needn't fear. My men carry their own provisions and have tents they can pitch. They'd just rather pitch them inside the wall you're building, than outside. These are, as you say, uncertain times."

Nagaro allowed himself a smile. "In that case, there should be no difficulty." He remounted, the better to make his way through the press. From the saddle he added, "I'm glad your men have provisions. Last season's harvest was poor, and we haven't enough to spare for so many. They're welcome to hunt and forage in the adjoining woods, however. And we will of course expect you and the ladies to join us for dinner in the Hall, where we'll also find chambers for the three of you."

With that, he squeezed Thunder-Heels' sides with his knees and started forward. Rastyl fell in beside his stirrup, on foot. Kuran had remounted his horse and came behind, their own coach following as the armed throng parted before them.

As they passed the carriage from Irvenen, it occurred to Nagaro to ask the names of the two ladies.

"Ah. Your pardon." Rastyl was genuinely contrite. "I tend to forget my manners. One of them you know—that's the Lady Rianine. The other, her companion, is Lady Tamith. They intend to settle here."

Nagaro nearly choked. "*Rianine? Here?*" He shot a glance at the carriage and saw a familiar mocking face at one of the windows. As their gazes met, Rianine blew him a kiss. He hurriedly looked away. "I thought her family was from Irvenen. I never heard she had any connection with Loros Wared!"

"Her connection is through Tamith." Rastyl looked uncomfortable. "They are... how should I put it... a couple? The Lady Tamith was recently released from her marriage to a gentleman of my House."

"Oh." Nagaro thought he understood, and the implications were not lost on him. "*Thank goodness*," he murmured under his breath.

Rastyl looked up at him sharply and raised an eyebrow, but Nagaro didn't elaborate. He saw no need to explain the complexities of his relationship with Rianine to the Lord of Irvenen. There were other things he felt he should explain, but this wasn't the time or place.

A few words to Venerev saw the gate duly opened. Once inside, Rastyl's officers struck off to find a place to pitch their encampment, while the carriages pulled up at the Hall's front entrance and their passengers disembarked.

Rastyl gave his attention to his two charges, while Nagaro hastily informed Boka and Omei of their guests' needs, so they could alert the Hall's small staff. He had just handed Thunder-Heels to one of the stable grooms when he was approached by a rather harried-looking Venerev.

"There's more riders at the gate, M' Lord! They just got here.

"*More?*" Nagaro was nonplused. "Where did *these* come from?"

"They're not all together, M' Lord. They're wearing two different liveries. One's from Kildoran Wared. The other I don't know."

Nagaro sighed. "I'd best go see."

The second troop turned out to be Varsyl Virden's. They were thirty in number, with Varsyl himself at their head. The men from Kildoran Wared numbered twenty-five, under a young man, Commander Rodin, who explained that Lord Endemar was his great uncle. Nagaro greeted Varsyl with pleasure and the commander with appropriate respect. Once their horses were duly attended to, and their men sent to find campsites inside the half-finished wall, Nagaro escorted their leaders into the Hall's entrance passage where he told the steward to see about finding the two men suitable chambers.

He then took Varsyl aside long enough to thank him personally for coming, concluding with, "I'm sorry that I can't actually call you Uncle."

Varsyl smiled a little wistfully. "Yes, I've lost the possibility of a nephew," he said. "Still, I am no less pleased by the truth. And I'm more proud than I can say of the part my sister played in all of it."

Upon parting with Varsyl, Nagaro made his way upstairs to the lord's chamber. The last thing he'd done before leaving that morning had been to order his seaman's chest and other belongings transferred from Nevrath's small house to the chamber that had been his father's. Having delayed the move as long he could, he had finally relented in the face of Kuran's reminder that there would soon be outsiders coming to call. His action had come none too soon.

It didn't take long to unpack and distribute his modest assortment of clothing between the carved mahogany chest of drawers and the matching wardrobe. He then availed himself of the basin on the washstand and put on a clean shirt for dinner. By the time he had finished, the sun was set and the light was fading, so he lit a candle from the fire that had been started in the fireplace to warm the chamber for him.

He sat in the candle's glow for a time, on the edge of his father's bed, lost in thought. The bed had been fitted with a new mattress, fresh linens, and a plain coverlet of midnight blue in place of the spectacular embroidered counterpane. The simplicity of the new coverlet suited him better, but still he wondered if he would ever feel at home in the place. He had made the move, but didn't feel ready for it. More than that, external events were pressing on him, and he wasn't sure he could deal with them as everyone seemed to assume that he would. *If only there were some other choice than the impending journey to Lankura.*

He shook himself. *Best not to think about it.* Rising, he extinguished the candle as he prepared to leave the room, so it wouldn't be a hazard. He expected the oil lamps in the hall to be lit and was surprised to find they were not. A faint glow at the farther end of the hallway, where it joined the one containing the guest chambers, near the stairs, indicated that the lamps in the other wing were lit. Nagaro felt his way along the hall in the gloom rather than go back to relight his candle.

Halfway down the hall, he realized that someone else was moving in the dark near the top of the stairs. "Who is there?" he asked, raising his voice. "Be careful you don't fall. I'm surprised the lamps aren't lit."

A man's voice answered him. "Ah, it's Nagaro Alorin Loros. A moment, if you will. I've found a lamp."

There was a distinctive *scritch*, and a small flair of light, followed by the slower blossoming of a sustained glow that revealed the figure of Rastyl Korven in the act of adjusting the wick on the oil lamp mounted on the wall at the head of the stairs.

Nagaro cleared his throat. "Please call me Nagaro, My Lord Rastyl. Do you always carry matches in your pocket?"

Rastyl laughed shortly. "Not always, but often. I travel a good deal, and they're very useful for starting a campfire when there's a shortage of dry tinder." He had advanced towards Nagaro as he spoke and now stopped a few feet away. "I was looking for the library, but I'm glad to have found you. I'd like a word with you, if I may."

Nagaro tried to ignore the sinking feeling in his stomach. "Of course," he managed. "The library would be a good place to talk, and the door is just behind you." He reached past Rastyl to open the door in question. "No light here either," he observed.

"A moment." Rastyl moved past him and struck another match to light the oil lamp on the library's table, which was set in the middle of a polished wood floor and was surrounded by four comfortable chairs. Shadowy shelves full of books filled two of the room's walls from floor to ceiling.

Nagaro gestured for the man to take a seat in one of the chairs, seating himself in another. "Well," he said, speaking lightly. "It seems that you can indeed identify me in the dark, just as you said."

Rastyl's pale eyes bored into him, holding his gaze. "You have your father's voice," he said. "Three years ago, after you helped route the Mahuk raiders from the palace, when you stood up in the Great Hall to praise your men, I thought for a moment that Tevren had returned to walk among us. The words might have been his, but more than that, it was the voice. I wondered that no one else seemed to mark it, but then, I knew him better than most."

Nagaro dropped his eyes, uncomfortable as always under that stare. He recalled the incident, how Rastyl had crossed the room to speak to him, obviously expecting recognition and finding none.

"I owe you an apology, My Lord," he said. "I believe you have tried several times to offer me assistance, and I turned you away."

"Yes, I have. And you did."

It was a statement of fact. Nagaro could detect no rancor in it. When he looked up, the pale gray eyes were still unreadable. He sought to explain. "Please understand. I didn't know why you were doing it. The circumstances of my birth have only become known to me very recently."

"So I have surmised," was the curt response. "Therefore, I am not offended."

This was a relief, but Nagaro felt he should say more. "You... seemed to know me, and I didn't wish to be known—"

"As Leyel Virden?"

Nagaro reflexively looked away. "Yes. I still don't."

"I understand." This time there was audible sympathy in the older man's voice, but still he didn't drop the painful subject. "Kale wouldn't tell me what had been done to you— I suppose he'd sworn an oath of silence. But it was obvious you were under some sort of influence—"

This time Nagaro's chair scraped on the floor, teetering, as he abruptly stood up and spun away from the table. He checked himself, however, before going more than a few steps, and half turned back without meeting Rastyl's eyes.

"I was... drugged..." Briefly, haltingly, he described the effects of chronically administered heskial.

"You remember it all? You remember my speaking to you at a table in the palace?"

Nagaro nodded, still standing. "I... don't know what you said. I wasn't listening. I was waiting for the... the drug... to begin to wear off."

"Yes." Rastyl spoke blandly. "I saw your eyes go from vacant, to watchful, to angry and determined. And then, when I stopped speaking, you just stood up and bowed and struck off across the Hall. Of course I followed— until Kale stopped me. He said you couldn't be allowed to run away because you'd die without what he called 'the medicine,' and that nothing could be done."

"He... he believed that." Nagaro swallowed. He returned cautiously to his chair, sinking into it. "So did I. I wanted to die... It was better than..." He gestured vaguely, finding no words.

"Than going on like that." Rastyl finished for him. "But you were both wrong, clearly. What then was the solution?

Nagaro told him. It was easier to talk about linjana than heskial.

Rastyl listened until he understood fully how it had all been accomplished. Then he abruptly slapped the table. "Luka's people! I should have guessed they would have known where you were! I should have sought them out—" He seemed to catch himself. "Nagaro?" he ventured more gently.

Startled, Nagaro forced his eyes to meet the other man's. "My Lord?"

Rastyl was studying him keenly but with sympathy. "I can see that this is hard for you," he said. "But there is something more I have to say." And now it was Rastyl who averted his eyes, staring past Nagaro into the shadowed recesses of the room. "I failed your father," he said quietly.

Nagaro shook his head. "No. You had to go to Irvenen. He understood that. He meant you to know what his plan was for me. He meant you to learn of it from Endemar."

Rastyl's eyes came back to him, questioning. "You know this? How?"

"It's in his journal."

"That thing?" A bitter laugh. "You found it, did you?"

"It was locked in a hidden compartment of his desk. The signet ring was the key."

Rastyl put a hand over his eyes. "So much trouble that might have been avoided," he murmured. Then he removed his hand to meet Nagaro's gaze. "I always believed it must have been as you've just said, but I'm glad to hear it all the same. Thank you." He sighed. "Yes, I had to go to Irvenen. And I had to stay there, too, through the bloody time that followed. As a newly chosen lord, I was needed in my Wared, and Irvenen became a refuge for many of those who fled from Loros. Their protection was my charge. It was nearly two years before I was able to come here, and by then the trail was long cold. Still, I should have been clever enough to find you— if Elgurn did."

Nagaro frowned. He was moved by the bitterness in the older man's voice. "But we know that Endemar misunderstood my father's letter. He thought I'd died soon after my birth—"

"The nursemaid, Theseline, knew better," Rastyl retorted. "She knew the burial was a ruse, and she told me so! But she couldn't tell me more. I *should* have thought of Luka's people! They had all vanished, but I should have looked for them. Why do we always discount the Turowan folk?"

"I don't believe Elgurn paid them any heed either."

"No? Well, probably not. But he used his wits— and his eyes, I'm sure. *I* should have looked closer at the child Maramine was rearing, but I thought I knew all about her little indiscretion. Her lover was from Irvenen. His family was there, and I inherited that scandal along with the lordship. I knew she was carrying a child— that she could keep it as long as she claimed it wasn't hers. What became of it, by the way?"

Nagaro stirred. "Stillborn."

"Ah. Lokundas sent a convenient twist of fate." Rastyl spoke bitterly. "I *thought* I knew how things stood in Virden Wared. I was so sure of it that I never looked closely— until Elgurn married his daughter to this supposed child of Maramine! Then, of course, I knew that either he or I was a fool. I went to Lankura to find out which it was. And the moment I set eyes on you, *I knew…*"

The older man's voice trailed even as his gaze became avidly fixed on Nagaro's face.

Nagaro swallowed. "I… I'm… told I favor my mother," he faltered.

Rastyl snorted. "From here up." He indicated his own upper lip for reference. "You have more of your father about the mouth and chin and jaw—all the parts that a beard conceals. But you have your mother's nose, brow, and eyes, and it's the eyes folk look at first. So they didn't see—"

A bell sounded somewhere, distantly.

Relieved, Nagaro stood up. "That will be the bell for dinner."

"Ah. Good." Rastyl also rose. "I'm quite ravenous.

They moved out into the hallway, which by now was well illuminated by a second oil lamp at the opposite end of it. Rastyl spoke casually as they started down the stairs. "At least I hope you'll now accept the help I offer."

"Of course." Nagaro answered unguardedly, then paused. "What help do you mean?"

"Why, my sixty men, of course. You'll need protection. You do mean to ride to Lankura, don't you?"

Nagaro stopped dead. "You came for *that?* How did you know?"

Rastyl paused also, cocking his head. "Endemar. He sent me a letter almost a month ago. All about how the heir had returned, in Kuran's company. There were proofs. It was certain. No name given, of course, but I *knew* who it was."

"So you came. With sixty men."

"All I could spare, I'm afraid." Rastyl started down the stairs again, gesturing for Nagaro to follow. "I had to leave some force behind for defense. I'm sorry to have been so long about it. I came as soon as I could, and none too soon, it appears."

"What do you mean?" They had reached the bottom of the stairs, and Nagaro started to lead the way towards the dining hall. He was trying to think how to break it to this man that he already had an escort.

"Haven't you heard the news?" Rastyl gave him a searching look as they reached the doorway that opened into the dining room. "Lothard is marching in force. Heading south. We can assume he means to join his force with Grimbold's and continue to Lankura to make his bid for the crown. If you mean to get there before him, you'd best make haste."

Chapter 20

In A Dark Hour

The dining hall was the largest room in Loros Hall. Though smaller than the Great Hall of the palace in Lankura, it was impressive, with a high-beamed ceiling, a floor of polished marble, and long trestle tables with high-backed chairs. The furniture and the wall paneling were all in dark wood, but there was a warm glow on the two tables nearest to the kitchen, coming from two of the many oil lamps that were set at intervals around the walls. The other lamps were unlit since most of the room wasn't in use. The lamplight was supplemented by candles in handsome silver candlesticks on the two tables that were set for dining, but the farther recesses of the room were submerged in gloom, and shadows hung in the rafters.

The two lighted tables were already laden with bread and sothiril and steaming tureens of stewed chicken with herbs, carrots, and dumplings. The Hall's staff were seated at one table, while the other was for the lord and his guests. Nagaro noted that Chula, the gardener from River House, had apparently arrived while he and Kuran were out and was seated with the staff.

Rastyl naturally had to repeat his news for the benefit of Kuran, Varsyl, and Commander Rodin. Rianine and Tamith already knew it, since they'd been traveling with Irvenen's lord, but the news made a great stir among everyone else, at both tables. The instant consensus among Kuran, Rastyl and Varsyl was that Nagaro must set out for Lankura the following morning, as early as possible.

Rodin looked surprised. "Why can't we just wait for everything to blow over?" he asked ingenuously. "It might take a few months, but—"

Rastyl spoke quickly: "It's only a short ride, and Nagaro will actually be safer in Lankura, which is well-defended and defensible— than here, which is neither."

Nagaro shifted. "And the people of Loros shouldn't have to wait so long for their Wared," he pointed out. *As little as he was looking forward to the ordeal before him, he also didn't want the wait to drag on.*

Kuran immediately looked grim. "They might not get their Wared at all, if Lothard takes the crown," he growled.

"Which we must all try to make sure doesn't happen!" Varsyl put in, with some heat.

The conversation continued from there while Nagaro sat, unhappily picking at his dinner. He could easily have been to Lankura and back again by now if he hadn't been so afraid of facing Elgurn and the Council. That knowledge made him feel both guilty and resentful— guilty because the citizens of Loros Wared deserved decisive action from their lord, and resentful that circumstances were forcing him into a course that so unnerved him.

The conversation presently came around to the size of the escort that was needed. None of the men considered his own contribution superfluous. So, since Nagaro didn't wish to offend anyone, he found himself accepting everything that was offered, although it seemed to him an overabundance of support for the journey.

It wasn't as if armed men could help him in the Audience Chamber.

Kuran had just finished expressing general thanks to all on Nagaro's behalf when Omei suddenly stood up at the other table and raised her voice to say, "Welcome, My Lady Princess."

Nagaro sat up as everyone turned, startled, to follow Omei's gesture towards the doorway through which they had entered the hall.

Nevien was there, dressed in a simple gown of muted green silk, embroidered in darker green. Her hair was loose, simply brushed smooth, and she wore no jewelry. So simply dressed, she hardly looked the part of a princess, but the sight of her sent Nagaro's heart soaring.

"Nevien!" he exclaimed. Rising before anyone else could move or speak, he rounded the table and was striding to meet her.

"Nagaro!" She said breathlessly as she put out both hands to grasp the ones he extended.

Their gazes locked, and for a moment there might have been no one else in the room.

"I didn't know you were coming," he murmured. "When did you arrive?"

"Just before sunset." She smiled up at him. "My escort has joined the encampment outside for dinner. I'm sorry to be late to table, but I was talking with Rianine and when the bell rang, I realized I still needed to wash and change."

"It's quite all right—"

A cough sounded behind him, and Nagaro recollected himself. He hastily transferred Nevien's hand to his flexed arm and escorted her to a chair at the table, belatedly noticing that there was an unclaimed place setting. Regrettably, it was on the opposite side of the table and at the far end from his. He circled the table back to his own chair amid a murmur of greetings directed to the princess. It was clear from the expressions on the faces of the male diners that Rianine had neglected to mention that she'd already spoken to Nevien.

In fact, Rianine was looking distinctly amused and a trifle smug. She had so far been uncharacteristically silent, though her gaze had leapt from speaker to speaker. Her companion, Tamith, a shy young woman with mouse-brown hair and wide dark blue eyes, seemed quite overwhelmed by the whole situation.

Nagaro winced as he resumed his seat. The glances he was getting from Rastyl, Varsyl, and Rodin made it clear that the enthusiasm with which he had greeted the princess hadn't gone unnoticed.

Kuran's watchful eyes had been taking in all the nuances, and now he spoke, drawing attention away from Nagaro as he addressed Nevien.

"We were just discussing the need to depart in haste tomorrow, My Lady, since Lord Rastyl has brought word that Lothard is marching south. Had the news reached Lankura before you left?"

"It hadn't gotten to the ears of the people," Nevien said as she ladled stewed chicken onto her plate from the nearest tureen. "Anduar had heard, of course, through his scouts, and he'd informed the Council. Since it was obviously important for Nagaro to know about it as soon as possible, I came at once." She gave them a rueful look. "And now I find that you already know!"

"You are acting as a messenger, then, on behalf of the Council and your father?"

Nevien turned to Rastyl, who had spoken. "No, My Lord," she said carefully. "Neither my father nor the Council know that Nagaro is here. I came at my own discretion."

"Was that wise, My Lady?" Varsyl wondered aloud. "With Lothard's forces on the march? And it's likely that other armies will soon be on the move as well."

"Yes, I suppose they will." Nevien calmly picked up her cup of sothiril and took a sip. "Devral stormed out of the Council meeting, bent on riding home at once to marshal his troops to stop Lothard. But, as you can see, I arrived here quite safely."

At this, Kuran put down his fork so forcefully that it clattered on his plate. "Devral will be hard-pressed to get his troops to Lankura in time!"

Nevien nodded. "Yes, the other council members said he couldn't possibly. They think Lothard and Grimbold could reach the city as early as some time tomorrow."

Varsyl looked alarmed. "Then I offer respectfully that you shouldn't be here, My Lady," he said. "By tomorrow there could be a hostile army between you and your home. An army led by a man who would be very pleased to have you in his power."

"I'm inclined to agree with Varsyl." Rastyl put in gravely. "Do your father and the Council know where you are?"

Nevien looked uncomfortable. "I left word with Lady Merriel to tell them I had gone to River House."

"River House!" Rastyl was incredulous. "Lothard's army is within a day's march, and you told them you were riding out into the country? With only a handful of guards for escort? Your father is probably beside himself!"

The color rose in Nevien's cheeks. "He doesn't yet know I'm gone," she said. "I made a show of going to bed early, and Merriel is to deliver my message when asked, and not before. Besides, I mean to return in your company." She glanced around the table, searching their faces. "Surely Nagaro must ride tomorrow, and all those men camped out there must be for his escort?"

"Yes, they are." Nagaro spoke for the first time. "And you should be quite safe riding with so large a company." The idea of having Nevien at his side was the most heartening thing he had heard all evening.

Kuran was still frowning darkly, however. "I'm afraid that might be considered somewhat *provocative...*" he said cautiously.

"It certainly would!" Rastyl had been buttering a roll and he now gestured emphatically with the butter knife. "Even without his true parentage being known, Nagaro will look like a challenger to Lothard if he is escorting the princess under such circumstances."

"Oh dear." Nevien lowered her eyes. "I only wanted to ride with Nagaro when he came to Lankura. I... I didn't mean to increase the risk."

Kuran pinched the bridge of his nose. "Of course you didn't, Nevien, but these concerns are valid, and I really don't think—"

"Oh for goodness sake, Kuran!" Rianine burst out, drawing all eyes. "Why shouldn't they ride together. They're affianced!"

"*What?*"

The word came in a chorus as more than one fork clattered against a plate. Kuran looked ill. Varsyl and Rastyl stared. Rodin's mouth hung open.

"*Rian!*" Nevien stared at her friend in dismay.

Nagaro sat frozen, feeling as if the bottom had dropped out of his stomach.

"Oh dear! Was it a secret?" Rianine's surprise sounded genuine. "Honestly, Nevien, you should have *said!*" At her side, Lady Tamith had both hands clamped over her mouth and her face had gone nearly as white as the tablecloth.

Varsyl was the first of the gentlemen to recover. "They're... *affianced?*" he asked, looking from face to face. "Kuran, were you aware of this?"

The others stirred, turning also to Kuran. Commander Rodin at last recollected himself enough to close his mouth.

Kuran coughed. "Well, ah... they have an understanding— although 'affianced' is perhaps a *slight* overstatement—"

Rastyl didn't let him finish. He turned to fix his eyes on Nagaro. "Why didn't you say you meant to make a bid for the crown?" he asked sharply.

Nagaro was instantly on his feet. "*Because I don't!*"

Rastyl's words had jolted him out of his shock into a bristling fury that silenced everyone at the table. He glared first at Rastyl, then shot a look like a flaming dagger at Rianine, who for once in her life looked daunted. Beside her, Tamith, still ashen, seemed to shrink under the heat of his gaze. Nagaro was too distracted to notice the effect on Rianine's companion, however, because his searing glance had swept on to Nevien, and her anguished look brought him up short.

"I'm *terribly* sorry, Nagaro!" Nevien's voice was clearly audible because the room was otherwise as silent as a crypt. "I'm afraid I rushed off in such a hurry when the bell rang for dinner that I forgot to tell Rian not to speak of it!"

Nagaro shut his eyes, his anger collapsing. He drew a long breath, trying to regain his equilibrium. When he opened he eyes again he had recovered enough mastery to keep his voice from shaking. He surveyed the stunned faces around the table.

"Know this," he said, addressing them all. "What is between me and the Lady Nevien has nothing to do with politics or ambition. It is a matter of the heart. I don't know what will come of it, but it is for *me* to deal with— or for her and me, together— *not any of you!* Therefore, I ask that you all keep what you have just heard strictly to yourselves!"

Rastyl stirred. "Nagaro, I'm sorry—"

"*Accepted.*" Nagaro acknowledged the apology with a curt nod and the single word. He was in no mood to listen to anyone, and besides that, he wasn't finished. He drew a ragged breath. "I am truly grateful to all of you who have come to give me your support," he said stiffly, sweeping their faces again with his eyes. "And it appears that I am to ride to Lankura tomorrow with a hundred and eighty men at my back. Since that in itself might be perceived as *provocative,* I hardly see that it matters if Nevien rides with us. Therefore, she shall. She can ride hidden in the carriage if need be."

Kuran exchanged glances with Rastyl and Varsyl. "Leaving her *here* would require also leaving some force to protect her," he said carefully.

Varsyl nodded wearily. "Given that she *is* here, I suppose it would be the safest way to return her to the palace."

Rastyl said nothing. His pale gaze moved from Nagaro to Nevien and back again. He appeared to be thinking hard.

Nagaro had remained standing, his chin thrust out defiantly.

Nevien sat with her eyes down. "Thank you," she murmured, her voice scarcely audible.

"Well then, that's settled." Kuran spoke with evident relief. "Shall we all continue our dinner?"

Nagaro passed a hand over his eyes. He suddenly felt drained. "I'm afraid you will all have to excuse me," he murmured. "I... think I need to rest." And with that he turned away from the table and walked out of the room without looking back.

Since he didn't look back, he didn't see how their eyes followed him.

***

Nagaro lay stretched out on top of the coverlet on the bed in the lord's chamber, trying to lie very still. He had turned the lamp down low and closed his eyes. Lying that way, and breathing slowly, he'd hoped that the tension might begin to drain away, but it wasn't working.

When he heard a knock on the door and Kuran's voice asking if he might enter, he sighed resignedly and sat up, moved to the edge of the bed, and said, "Come in, Kuran."

The lord of the Fleet entered. "I wanted to be sure you were all right," he said as he appropriated one of the desk chairs, set it beside the bed, and sat down on it.

"Yes, I'm all right." Nagaro looked at his hands. "Was I terribly rude, Kuran?"

Kuran puffed out his cheeks. "Not... unduly, I think. I explained to them that you've been under some strain."

"What did they talk about after I left?"

Kuran sighed. "I'd be lying if I said they didn't talk about a possible bid for the crown. But I made sure they understood how you feel about it."

"I thought I did that!"

"You made it clear that you aren't pursuing Nevien for that purpose. I elaborated."

"Oh." Nagaro rubbed his forehead. "Well, thank you. Ah... how is Nevien?"

Kuran gave a little snort of laugher. "You needn't worry about her. She got what she wanted, after all, thanks to you. She said she was going to bed early when she left the table, which is wise. You should do the same."

Nagaro didn't immediately respond. He'd gotten what *he* wanted, as well, but he couldn't help worrying about the risk involved in having Nevien ride with him. It was one of the things that was making it so hard for him to calm his mind. *There were other things as well... things like Rastyl's reflexive question.* He shifted in annoyance. "Why does everyone assume I want the crown?" he asked fretfully.

Kuran didn't blink at the change of subject. "Because the crown is important. It matters who wears it. And, I suppose, because ambition is common among men." He paused, then added, "You must realize that the men you're planning to speak to tomorrow in Lankura will have similar concerns— even without knowing your intentions with respect to Nevien. They'll ask similar questions."

Nagaro shot the older man a sharp glance. "That thought has crossed my mind."

"Are you ready for tomorrow?"

"How can I possibly be? When I don't know how much I'll have to tell them?"

Kuran sighed. "You have nothing to be ashamed of, Nagaro. The fault was never yours. Just tell them what you must to achieve your ends."

Nagaro had to bite back an angry retort. Kuran meant well, but the man didn't understand the size of the gulf between what he *ought* to feel and what he actually felt. No one could understand it who hadn't experienced the hel of heskial.

Kuran's thoughts had been running in a different direction, because presently he said, "I wish there had been more time for sword practice."

Nagaro could only shrug. "That seems the least of my worries," he said. "But then I always hope I won't have to fight."

"So do I, if it comes to that. But still I'd feel better if we could have done another dozen bouts."

Since Nagaro had no answer, he merely shrugged again. He didn't disagree, but what difference did it make— when he faced the prospect of having his past laid bare before the King and Council?

Kuran sat for a time regarding him sympathetically, at last the older man sighed again and rose to go. "Try to get some sleep," he said gently. "Right now that's probably the best thing you can do."

Nagaro didn't disagree with that either, though he knew the advice wouldn't be easy to follow. Once Kuran had gone, he dutifully prepared for bed, stripping to bathe at the wash basin, and donning his nightshirt.

Then he put out the oil lamp, turned down the covers, and crawled between the sheets. He'd left the heavy curtains on the window open, and there was moonlight, but he tried not to think about how high the moons might stand in the sky or how deeply Naru now lay within Talebra's embrace.

He stretched again, and closed his eyes, trying to empty his mind. When thoughts of Lankura kept intruding, he tried to find something safer to think about. He pictured sitting with Nevien in the garden at River House, but that only led to the fact that they were pledged to one another— which in turn led to memories of the events at dinner, not to mention the knowledge that Nevien had left the safety of the city for his sake. Trying again to redirect his thoughts only brought him back to the way Rastyl had pounced on his presumed interest in the crown. And thinking about the crown led back to what he might have to face in Lankura...

He tried lying first on one side, then the other. He flung off the covers when they seemed too constricting, only to draw them up again a minute later when he realized he was shivering.

The sound of a soft knock on the door brought his thrashing to a halt. He lay still, frozen, straining his ears. At first he thought he might have imagined the knock. Apart from his own breathing, the room was perfectly silent. No sounds penetrated the closed door. There were no guests housed in this entire wing of the second floor. He realized that he had no idea how late it was, and he wondered whether Kuran had returned to check on him one more time.

Since he had no desire to talk further, he resolved not to answer and hope the Lord of the Fleet— or whoever it was— would assume he was asleep.

The knock was repeated, this time a little louder. *No such assumption, then...*

"Who is it?" He called, raising his voice to be heard through the door's solid wood.

The only answer was a third knock, still louder, and more urgent.

Nagaro swore to himself and sat up. Kuran would surely have answered him. It must be some member of the staff, perhaps with a matter considered so pressing that it couldn't wait until morning.

"A moment," he called as he quickly got up and went to the wardrobe for a dark blue robe he had noticed there earlier. As he wrapped it around himself, he tried not to think about whether it had belonged to his father. It smelled musty, but was otherwise serviceable. Crossing the room barefoot in the moonlight, he paused at the door just long enough to compose his face, then opened it, fully expecting to find one of the staff on the other side.

Instead, it was Nevien.

His heart gave a leap and a thud. She was standing with her back to the stairs and holding a lighted candle in one hand, shielding the flame with the other. The image of the flame danced in the mirror of her eyes as the wavering light caressed her features, awakening golden highlights in her unbound hair.

"May I come in?" she whispered urgently. "I need to talk to you."

"What's the matter?" Alarmed, Nagaro immediately stood aside to let her slip past him into the room, the implications of the action quite escaping him.

She shook her head as she turned to face him. "Nothing's wrong, really. But I couldn't sleep, and I didn't want anyone to catch me in the hall."

She crossed to the bed, the candle flame chasing the moonlight before it, pushing back the shadows. Once there, she set the candle on the night stand, then unceremoniously sat down on the edge of the mattress. He had left the covers in such disarray that she necessarily had to sit directly on the bare sheet.

"I've been lying there for what seems like *hours,*" she continued, "waiting for everyone else to go to bed."

Nagaro had begun by following her, but had stopped, suddenly uncertain. Now that she had moved a little distance from the source of light, her form was revealed more fully and he saw that, like him, she was wearing a dressing gown. It glowed a rich, dark rose in the candlelight. It was a very chaste garment, really, being of a heavy fabric with long sleeves and some modest ruffles at the neck and wrists. And it was tied securely with a sash. She wore a pair of matching slippers, but between those slippers and the hem of the dressing gown he could see three inches of ankle— conspicuously bare.

What had stopped Nagaro was an awareness of how instantly his eyes were drawn to that bare ankle. He could see how the lines of it flowed into the curve of her calf, and inevitably he found himself imagining how that curve continued— until he felt a sudden flush of warmth as desire stirred. Embarrassed, he dragged his eyes back to her face and sat down awkwardly on the chair that still stood where Kuran had left it. The only alternative would have been to sit beside her on the bed, which didn't seem like a good idea. *If he got that close to her, he'd want to kiss her ...and if he let himself do that...*

Belatedly he realized that Nevien was looking at him, expecting some response to her words and he had to cast about to recall what they had been. "I...ah... couldn't sleep either," he managed, and then the significance of the rest of what she'd said sank in. "Everyone is in bed? It's that late?"

She nodded, her sea-green eyes still fixed on his.

She was sitting quite demurely, with her hands clasped in her lap, but her proximity was enough to unsettle him even without the added realization that they were alone together at night in a bedchamber. Desire flared afresh, only to collide head-on with hideously unpleasant memories from all those earlier times he'd been alone with her in a bedchamber— *under the thrall of heskial...*

"Ah... Nevien..." he began. "Are you sure you should—?"

But she waved his words aside with a small, impatient gesture. "There's something I have to tell you, Nagaro. I don't mean to ride in the carriage tomorrow. I can ride my horse—"

"But you'll be seen!" Nagaro protested, instantly recalling his fears for her safety. "And there has to be a carriage, anyway, to carry Chula and Boka since neither of them can ride."

"I know, but then we'd have to keep the curtains closed, and a curtained carriage always draws attention because folk wonder *why* it's curtained. On a horse, I can pass for one of the men. I have a plain, dark cloak. I'll tie up my hair and keep the hood up to hide my face. Then, if I borrow Tamith's boots, there'll be nothing showing that will give me away."

Nagaro immediately pictured her riding at his side so attired. It was a very pleasing image. Her argument seemed entirely reasonable, although the last part of it puzzled him. "Tamith has *boots?*" he asked, frowning. "Whatever for?"

At this, Nevien squirmed and fiddled with the ruffle on one sleeve of her robe. "Tamith and Rian both have boots. Apparently they've passed as men before. But Tamith won't be joining us, so Rian can wear her own boots, and I can wear Tamith's."

Nagaro's frown deepened sharply. "Rianine means to come with us?" This he didn't like at all.

"Well... yes." Nevien appeared surprised by the heat of his response. "She says it's the least she can do... after the trouble at dinner."

"The *least!*" Nagaro was on his feet, fists clenched. "I don't trust Rianine! All she does is tease and criticize!"

"Nagaro!" Nevien sprang to her feet as well. "Rian is my friend! She feels terrible about spilling our secret, and want's to keep me company to make up for it!"

"Why can't you ride with *me?*"

"That won't work!" Nevien moved closer, reaching for his knotted fists. "If I ride beside you, everyone will wonder who I am— and they'll look at me. For the disguise to work, I have to ride with the men. Don't you see?"

And he did see. She was right, and he was acting like a fool. But it still *hurt.* He jerked away, evading her hands.

"I'm sorry! Do whatever you want..."

Nevien came after him, grabbing his arm. "Nagaro, what's the matter?"

She wasn't letting go, and she was much too close. He could smell the scent of her body. Afterward he wasn't sure exactly how it happened. Somehow he found he had gotten his arms around her— but then he could go no further.

He clung to her desperately, burying his face in her hair.

"Nevien, I'm afraid!"

"Come here." She was simultaneously pulling away from him and tugging at him, drawing him towards the bed. "Come sit. Talk to me."

They ended up side by side on the edge of the bed, Nevien with one arm around his shoulders as one might do with a frightened child. He didn't resist. He was too glad of the comfort.

"Now," she said gently. "What are you afraid of?"

He sat, staring at his hands clasped together awkwardly in his lap. It took him several long breaths before he could find the words, but when he at last began to speak, they all came tumbling out.

"I'm afraid I'm going to have to tell them everything, Nevien! I thought maybe your father wouldn't want the secret to come out... but the Council will want to know everything! They'll ask *questions!* And I'll have to *answer!* I can't just lie to them!"

"And you shouldn't have to, Nagaro. Someone hurt you. My... my father hurt you— years ago. It wasn't your fault!"

"What difference does that make?" He was clenching his fists and the knuckles showed white. He was still staring at his hands, not meeting her eyes. "They're going to *know,* Nevien! And if *they* know, soon *everyone* will know. *The whole country will know!"*

"Would that really be so bad?"

"*Yes!*" He beat his fists against his thighs and shot her hurt look. "Nevien, this is worse than when I thought the Emperor was going to kill me! If I died, my spirit would pass into the void and I'd leave everything behind. I wouldn't have to *worry* about any of it anymore. But whatever happens tomorrow isn't going to kill me— *which means I'll have to live with it for the rest of my life!"*

Nevien sat silent for several long seconds following this tirade. At last she said, "Well, I'm glad you don't expect it to kill you, at least. But listen, Nagaro. You've told *me,* and you've told *Kuran.* And it's been all right, hasn't it?"

"Nevien, you're my *friends.* And besides, you already knew, so I didn't really *tell* you—"

"But you didn't *want* us to know, remember?"

His thoughts jumped back to the agonizing moments on the ledge above the river. "That's true… When Vothra told me you were coming, I thought it would be the end of everything— that I'd have to run away. If Vothra hadn't ordered me to stay—"

"But it's all right, don't you see? She gave him a bright smile. "We *know* now, and everything is still all right. Isn't it?"

He studied his fingernails. "*Most* of the time."

"Then I don't see why it shouldn't be the same with the Council."

"You and Kuran both thought well of me. You had for a long time…"

"But *those* men think well of you too, Nagaro. I've sat in the Council Chamber and heard them speak of you. They're all impressed!"

"What, even Odus and Pendrik?"

"Yes! The Leithians may think less of a man because he's a commoner, but they're still impressed with things like courage, honor, and service to Edrovir. And besides that, they're about to learn that you're not a commoner—"

He shot her a dark look. "*That* shouldn't matter!"

"I know." She gave him a squeeze. "But it's not going to hurt."

Nagaro drew a breath. "What about Anduar? What will *he* do with this?"

Nevien frowned thoughtfully. "I don't know, but I know he won't think any the less of you for what you've been through." She took her arm from around his shoulders and turned a little more to face him. "And the common people love you for what you've done for them. They won't care about something that happened years ago— if they even believe it." She paused. "Does that help?"

He managed a wan smile. "A little, I guess. Thank you."

"Good." She beamed. "Because I have something I want to give you."

She slid off of the bed and turned her back to him. She seemed to be doing something with her hands.

"Something for me?" He was nonplused. "I'd swear that you brought nothing with you except the candle, unless you have a pocket somewhere in your— *Oh, Nevien!*"

She had turned around to face him again, and she must have been untying the sash of her dressing gown, because she was holding the gown open— *and she was wearing nothing underneath!* The candlelight fell full upon the tantalizing convexities of her naked form.

"Well?" she said, her head a little on one side and a sparkle in her eyes. "Do you like it?"

"*Nevien… I…*" He swallowed desperately. His throat was so tight he could hardly speak.

He had risen when she turned, surging to his feet in response to what he saw, the vision of her body kindling desire that coursed through him like wildfire. But in the next instant, he had come to a halt where he stood, rigid and immobile, caught in a knot of opposing forces that threatened to strangle him.

He ached to fling himself at her, but was frozen by an unreasoning fear of what would happen next. The memories were flooding— of thwarted lust, of incompetence... humiliation... Hot, eager blood pounded in his ears even as his terrified heart thudded against his ribs.

The sparkle faded from Nevien's eyes as she read his agony. She extended her arms to him. "Please, Nagaro," she begged. "I want you so!"

She took a step towards him.

And he actually took a step back. He saw the hurt in her eyes, but he couldn't help himself.

"*Nagaro!*" She dropped her arms, her shoulders sagging. "My Love! Don't you want me?"

"*I... yes...*" he gasped. "But... *I don't think... I... can!*"

"Nagaro, that's *all right!*" Her mouth trembled as she tried to smile encouragingly, her eyes imploring him. "You don't have to do anything... except hold me for a little while. Please! I need to feel your touch!"

He tried to move towards her— and couldn't. "*Oh Vothra...*" he murmured in agony, and closed his eyes.

He felt something, then. It was a touch on his mind, wordless and feather-light, as if a breath of air had moved through him, and with it something seemed to come unlocked. He swallowed past the easing constriction in his throat as his eyes sprang open.

"I... I don't know if I *should*, Nevien. If you... I mean... if I got you with child... And we couldn't marry..."

But she shook her head at him. "It's all right. It will be safe tonight."

"Oh." Still he hesitated in spite of his need. Whatever the Spirit had done was helping, but he had no relevant experience to draw on, and he wanted so badly to do this *right*.

She gave him an exasperated look. "Nagaro, when the woman you love offers herself to you, it's very bad manners to keep her waiting."

And somehow that did it.

"You're right," he said, shrugging off the blue robe and letting it fall to the floor. The reins that he always held so tightly were slipping through his fingers. He jerked the nightshirt over his head, flung it aside, and launched himself at the object of his desire.

Startled, Nevien gave a little squeak and drew back.

Instantly he came up short, inches from her, his hands frozen in the act of reaching to caress her. He started to apologize but she silenced him with a finger laid to his lips.

Then, letting her dressing gown slip from her shoulders, she flung her arms around his neck and drew him into a kiss, pressing her body against his. He gasped and wrapped his arms around her.

They fell together. Fortunately, the bed caught them.

***

Considerably later, when all the inconvenient inhibitions had finally been forced into submission and the flood of passion had run its course, he lay beside her amid the devastation of the bedclothes in dreamy lassitude.

Still, a little worrying thought nagged at him. "Was that the way it's supposed to be?" he asked. "The... the last bit of it, I mean."

She languidly traced the brand on his shoulder with her fingertip. "Until tonight I wouldn't have known how to answer that, but yes, I think that last bit was exactly the way it's supposed to be."

He sighed, then said, "I'm... sorry about all the..." he gestured vaguely. "Before that..."

"Nagaro, it will get easier! Don't apologize!"

"I'm sorry—"

"*Nagaro!*" She cuffed him. "Stop that!"

He bit his tongue. "I'll try to remember," he said meekly.

"That's all anyone can ask." She snuggled closer.

"Mmm. I think I want to just hold you now, for a while." He rolled over, found the sheets and pulled them up, then drew her close, cupping the curve of his body protectively around hers. They lay nestled together and he closed his eyes, allowing himself to drift on a lazy, warm sea of exhaustion.

So it was that he slept at last, the deep, restoring sleep of perfect peace.

Chapter 21

Forward To Lankura

Nagaro was awakened by Nevien wriggling as she attempted to disentangle herself from his embrace. Reflexively he tightened his grip. "Don't leave me, Nevien," he murmured drowsily. "Stay with me always."

"Soon, my love, but right now it's nearly dawn and I have to go back to my room before anyone else wakes up."

With a suppressed groan, he opened his eyes. The rectangle of sky visible through the window was a deep luminous blue, rather than black, attesting to the fact that dawn was indeed not far away. And of course it wouldn't do for Nevien to be found in the lord's chamber.

He heaved a sigh and reluctantly released her. Then he watched appreciatively in the pre-dawn glow from the window as she retrieved her dressing gown from the floor, nestled the naked curves of her body into it, tied it securely, and stepped into her slippers. When she found his nightshirt and tossed it to him, he sat up and shrugged it on while she went to light her candle from the embers of the fire.

She returned with the light cupped in her hand and stood for a long moment, gazing at him. Though she'd said she meant to go, she was clearly reluctant, and when he held out his hand she quickly set the candle on the night stand again and sat down beside him. He reached for her even as she reached for him, and they shared a kiss and a lingering embrace.

When at last they broke for air, she asked, "How do you feel this morning?"

"As if I could do anything."

"Good." She stood up again and reclaimed the candle. "Hold fast to that feeling."

Something in the way she said it made him frown. "Is *that* why you came to me last night?"

The candlelight played on her features, reflecting in her eyes. "I came because I wanted to," she said earnestly. "But if there's an added benefit,

I'm glad of it. Now try to sleep a little more. I'm sure breakfast won't be for at least an hour."

***

Three hours later, Nagaro stood at the bottom of the steps leading down from the Hall's front door. He held Thunder-Heels' bridle as he surveyed the marshaling of his rather motley escort. Since none of the men were directly under his command, he'd contented himself with telling their commanding officers how the groups should be ordered when the company rode out. Now he had nothing to do but watch.

He shivered as a gust of wind probed with icy fingers under his cloak. The hour was early, and the morning was clear and blustery, though not quite cold enough for snow— had there been any clouds to do the snowing. But there was more to his involuntary shudder than the weather. Waiting was wearing on him. *He wanted to get this over with.*

The feeling of power engendered by the night's activities had ebbed some, but hadn't completely left him. There was no denying that he felt more ready to get through this day than he ever had before, but he still didn't expect it to be easy. The sooner it was behind him, the happier he would be.

He shifted his cloak and self-consciously straightened the tirka of royal blue with gold trim that he wore over his usual plain white shirt. Omei had brought the garment to him that morning, with the explanation that Tira Theseline had made it for him. Under the circumstances, he could hardly have refused it, though it was too fancy for his taste. He also suspected that it contrasted awkwardly with the rest of his attire, which consisted of the plain shirt, comfortable black pants and boots, and a serviceable cloak of well-worn gray wool. He was bare-headed this morning. None of his male ancestors had been in the habit of wearing hats.

The morning's preparations were actually more or less on schedule. The muster of the men was proceeding with an expected amount of chaos in the open space between the facade of Loros Hall and the half-finished wall and gatehouse. From where Nagaro stood, it looked as if the preparations would soon be complete, although the carriage still stood empty and the grooms were waiting with the horses that would bear Nevien and Rianine.

Presently Kuran emerged from the general hurly-burly and came striding towards him. The Lord of the Fleet came to a halt in front of Nagaro and gave him a perfunctory salute. "My men are ready to mount at a moment's notice," he announced. "And Varsyl's are ready as well. Do you have all the documents?"

"Yes. They're in a satchel in my saddlebag." Nagaro had one other thing, as well, that he didn't mention. A tiny vial containing a thimble-full of pale-green liquid nestled in his pocket beside the familiar smooth, etched pebble that Luka had given him years before. *Appropriate that the vial of linjana should keep company with Luka's keepsake...*

There were voices behind Nagaro. Looking past him towards the top of the steps, Kuran said, "Ah, here come the women and the gardener at last."

Nagaro turned to see the missing members of their party emerging from the Hall's front door accompanied by some others who had come to see them off. Boka descended the steps with Omei, and Chula the gardener came, chatting with Tira Theseline. Nevien and Rianine were right behind them, and Tamith brought up the rear, so completely swathed in a heavy cloak that only her face peeked out. Theseline bore a large cloth-draped basket, presumably laden with refreshments for the journey. She and the sisters and Chula reached the bottom of the steps and made for the carriage, waiting a few yards away.

Nevien and Rianine, with Tamith trailing behind, descended to where Kuran and Nagaro stood. They both carried riding crops and wore hooded cloaks over their riding clothes— and, of course, the boots. Nagaro hadn't been sure what he would think of boots on a woman, but he found he quite liked the effect of gray silk shapas tucked into the tops of a sleek pair of calf-hugging leather boots— at least when Nevien was wearing them. Without stopping to consider, he took two strides to meet her, and once met, embraced her and planted a kiss that was perhaps not quite chaste enough for company.

"Here now, Captain! None of that!" Rianine swatted Nagaro with her riding crop. "How can I be expected to keep your secret if you won't keep it yourselves?"

Nagaro reluctantly stepped back, his eyes lingering on Nevien's face. The look she returned to him made it clear that she was as loath as he was to relinquish the moment.

Kuran coughed and looked sharply from one to the other of them.

Rianine caught the question in his glance. "I think Naru and Talebra were rather intimate last night," she observed archly.

"Ah?" Kuran raised an eyebrow.

Nagaro, for once, was beyond embarrassment. He turned to Kuran. "Didn't you say something about one night with the right woman?"

"Yes, I did. And that's enough said about that, I think."

"*Enough?*" Rianine was indignant. "When I have yet to release the captain?" Her eyes sparkled maliciously as she turned on Nagaro. "Or are you going to pretend that you've forgotten that we were discussing marriage?"

Nagaro bridled. "*You* were discussing it. *I* was trying to tell you it was a terrible idea!"

"It takes *two* to discuss anything, and you were—"

"Stop it, Rian!" Tamith had been standing unnoticed a little to one side, clutching her cloak. She had been listening, shyly silent, but with growing agitation. Now it appeared she could no longer contain herself. "You know you're only teasing!" she cried. "And you can see he doesn't like it!"

Rianine sniffed. "If he *liked* it, there wouldn't be much point."

"But it's *wrong*, Rian! It's... it's not *nice!*" Tamith's eyes flashed. "Promise me you won't do it anymore!" The mousy young woman was fairly bristling and all eyes were turned to her in astonishment.

Rianine started to say something, but then closed her mouth.

Nevien straightened her shoulders. "I have to agree with Tamith, Rian. I think you've teased Nagaro quite enough!"

From the fierceness in Rianine's eyes, Nagaro was afraid that she was contemplating some blistering retort, but instead she threw up her hands. "Oh very well, Tamith! I promise I will leave him alone. It was becoming rather tiresome, anyway. He's so *terribly* predictable!"

Tamith beamed at her lover. "That's better. Thank you, Rian."

Nagaro could scarcely believe his good fortune. "Thank *you* Tamith," he said fervently, and made her his very best bow. "I am forever in your debt."

This time Tamith blushed bright pink. "Y–you're welcome, Zirda," she stammered.

"Are you sure you won't join us?" he asked. "There's still room in the carriage."

"Oh, no... I..." Tamith looked at the ground, her blush unabated.

"I won't hear of it!" Rianine declared flatly. "Tamith will remain safely here until I return. She's had a hard enough time traveling all the way from Irvenen in her condition, and I can't bear to see her suffer another minute!"

"Oh, Rian!" Tamith turned even pinker, if that were possible. Letting go of her cloak, she threw her arms around the other woman and gave her a brief but fervent hug. "Vothra keep you!" she cried. "And come safe back to me!" Then she re-gathered her cloak, turned, and fled up the steps and into the Hall.

Nagaro and Kuran exchanged puzzled looks. "Her...ah... condition?" Kuran ventured.

Nevien glanced at Rianine for approval and then cleared her throat. "Tamith is carrying the child of her former husband," she explained.

"It's a child that she and Rianine intend to raise together. It will be her second child. The first one, a son, remains with her husband, and this arrangement has been accepted by all parties."

"Oh." Kuran rubbed his chin. "I suppose, then, that congratulations are in order?"

"Of course!" Rianine preened, looking every bit as pleased as if she'd begotten the child herself.

Nagaro made her an elegant bow. "Congratulations to you both, and I wish you joy. Though I'm sorry that Tamith must be separated from her firstborn."

Rianine dismissed this with a wave of her hand. "Oh, that's all right. She can visit him whenever she likes."

"Good morning, ladies! Are you ready to mount up?" Rastyl had approached and now addressed himself to Nevien and Rianine.

It was Nevien who answered. "Yes, My Lord, we're ready."

"Then may I suggest we be on our way?"

Nagaro squared his shoulders. He surveyed the field, noting the ordered ranks and the faces of Boka and Chula at the window of the carriage. There were no more excuses. Turning to Thunder-Heels, he set his foot in the stirrup and swung into the saddle, doing his best to ignore the small, sharp twinge of pain in his chest. Once astride, he took up the reins and raised his voice. "Mount up and prepare to ride!"

There was a ripple of motion among the assembled men. Nevien and Rianine swung onto their horses as Rastyl and Kuran made haste to return to their places at the heads of their waiting troops.

***

It was barely two hours after sunrise when they departed Loros Hall. Nagaro rode in the vanguard beside Kuran, whose small force led the cavalcade. Next came Commander Rodin with the men sent by Lord Endemar, then Rastyl with his force. Varsyl and his men brought up the rear. Since the carriage had arrived at Loros Hall with Rastyl's party, the logic of appearances dictated that it depart in the same company, although it carried different passengers.

Nagaro knew that Nevien and Rianine were also riding with Rastyl's company since it was the largest and offered the best chance of them going unnoticed. He tried not to think about how far Nevien was from the protection of his sword. There were armed men all around her, after all, including Brandle and others members of her own small escort.

The party struck out along the road to Fenerwel. They could have bypassed the town, but Kuran had decided it was a good thing to have as many citizens of the new Wared as possible see their lord set off to Lankura to lay their petition before the king.

Before the party had even reached the outskirts of the town, they encountered a group of about two dozen riders whose leader hailed them with a great shout. The man spurred his horse forward ahead of his fellows, and Nagaro saw that it was Kenthos.

"My Lord! Captain Nagaro!" the blacksmith cried. "We've come to join you!"

Nagaro cast Kuran a look of dismay. "What, *more?*" he muttered under his breath.

"I know," Kuran said out of the side of his mouth. "But you'd best accept them."

Nagaro had to agree. He couldn't possibly turn Kenthos away when the man had shown him so much loyalty. He greeted the blacksmith a show of enthusiasm. "Well met, Kenthos. You and your men are most welcome."

Kenthos beamed. "They're some o' the ones what followed me," he confided. "But they've all got their own swords— and their own horses too!"

Nagaro was none too sure of the skill of the men in handling those swords, and some of the horses looked like they were more accustomed to pulling a plough than carrying a rider, but he refrained from comment. "How many have you?" he asked.

"Twenty seven, counting myself."

"Excellent." Kuran interjected. "You can fall in just behind my men in the green and gray." As soon as Kenthos and his men were out of earshot, he muttered. "That puts our number at over two hundred."

By the time the cavalcade had passed out of Fenerwel, Nagaro estimated its number at between two hundred twenty and two hundred thirty, though most of the late additions were on foot and carried an assortment of sickles, hatchets, and, in one case, a pitchfork. He had tried to discourage the townspeople from tagging along by telling them that the company couldn't slow its pace if they fell behind, but his efforts had proved futile.

Kuran merely shrugged. "They come to witness history," he said. "We shouldn't deny them that."

"My concern is that they may come to harm."

Kuran sighed. "Some will fall behind. And as for the rest, they know the risk. If it comes to a fight they'll likely take to the hedgerows."

"I hope you're right," Nagaro muttered. "And I hope we don't pick up any more of them."

His hope turned out to be vain, though he wasn't immediately aware of it. He discovered it only when they halted at the place where his parents had been murdered. He would have rather ridden farther before stopping, but Kuran insisted that he make a quick pilgrimage to the little glade.

"But I've already seen it," Nagaro protested.

"Yes, but there were no witnesses when you did. You must go."

So Nagaro ordered a halt to water the horses and walked with Kuran to the little tree-encircled clearing. Spring wasn't yet come, and the place was barren and windswept, not the sunny green glade he remembered. He stood beside the moss-covered marker stone and bowed his head, reflecting on the fragility of life and hope— on how much effort might be put into the making of a thing, and how easily it could be destroyed by a single stroke.

It was when he returned to where the men were reassembling into an ordered file that he was astonished to find a rag-tag assemblage of common folk at the rear of the line that outnumbered Rastyl's uniformed men at arms.

"Where did all these people come from?" he exclaimed in dismay.

One of the men who stood closest to him, a herdsman by the look of him, turned at the sound of Nagaro's voice.

"Good day t' ye, M' Lord," he said, ducking his head respectfully. "We come from all along the way. From the farms an' fields. When we saw ye passing, and asked what was afoot, we had t' be part of it. Besides, I always wanted to see Lankura."

"Do you know that Lothard is on the march? I hope we won't meet him before we reach the city, but if we do, there could be trouble."

The man stuck out his chin. "I'm not afraid, M' Lord. I've me trusty stick!" He brandished a stout sheep-herder's staff. "And I've got sound legs, if that's what's needed."

Nagaro gave the man a stern look. "I'd rather you used the legs than the stick, Zirda. You and all of these. I'd rather see you alive at the end of the day than dead in a ditch."

The man grew sober under his gaze. "I hear ye, M' Lord," he said "And I'll pass the word."

Nagaro quickly returned to his position at the front of the cavalcade. Once there, he called Kenthos to him before giving the order to ride. "I've a task for you and your men," he told the blacksmith. "Could you scout ahead, and along the roads leading north? I'd like some warning if Lothard is in front of us, or if he's approaching on our flank."

Kenthos' face lit up and he saluted smartly. "Aye, M' Lord, that we can. The lads 'll be proud t' do it!"

So they rode along the high road, through what remained of the former Loros Wared and on into lands held directly by the Crown.

Though Nagaro knew they were still acquiring followers even outside the boundaries of Loros, he could only guess at their numbers. Nor could he bring himself to push for speed and risk outdistancing them, in spite of what he'd told the citizens of Fenerwel. Instead, he kept a modest pace and tried not to let worry get the better of him. He was becoming resigned to the fact that much of what happened on this day was likely to be beyond his control.

For a time, at least, their luck seemed to be holding. They saw no sign of Lothard's forces, and the first scouts returned with no word of any men on the march in front of them or behind them. They were only a few miles from Lankura, passing between fallow fields under clear skies, when the first warning finally came. One of Kenthos' men, a weedy Kelorin mounted on a massive plough horse, emerged from a side road at an ungainly canter and hailed them excitedly.

"Ho! M' Lords! Look what I have!"

What the man had, was Jato, mounted behind him on the horse's broad rump, clinging to the rider's belt.

The Kelorin scout swung in beside Nagaro, and the wiry little Turo was transferred to Thunder-Heels' back, behind the saddle.

Nagaro addressed him. "What news, Jato? Have we caught you on your way back to Anduar with a report?"

"That ye have—" Jato was out of breath. "But I don't mind tellin' it to ye first. I've seen Lothard's army!"

"*Where?*" Kuran demanded. "How far away? And are they moving?"

"They camped last night at Sobring Hall— where they joined forces wi' Grimbold. The whole lot was t' ride out this morning— bound for Lankura."

"*Keshaal!*" Thunder-Heels moved skittishly and Nagaro felt Jato's hand tighten on his belt. "Where are they now?"

"Headin' down the road that 'll bring 'em to the North Gate. They'll reach it by mid afternoon, I expect. But I came a different way, 'cause I was hopin' I'd find ye."

Nagaro winced, remembering his unpleasant adventure on the stretch of road Jato had just mentioned.

Kuran cut in. "You knew we'd be riding? How?"

Jato chuckled. "I've got me own ways o' learning things, M' Lord. An' now I have an escort!"

Kuran laughed grimly. "I'll let that go. So long as we get to Lankura first!"

"If ye keep a good pace, ye should. By an hour or two."

An hour or two! Nagaro pressed his heels to Thunder-heels' flanks, urging more speed. He addressed Kenthos' man, who still kept pace on his plough horse. "Pass the word back through the ranks, Zirda. We must make haste! Those who follow on foot must make better speed or turn back." *As little as an hour? He wished it might be a day.*

A little later, they met Kenthos himself, riding back along the High Road in haste to meet them.

"I've been within sight o' the walls of Lankura," he gasped as he swung in beside Nagaro. "And there's armed companies o' men— more 'n one o' them— camped outside the gate!"

Nagaro and Kuran exchanged glances of dismay. "Can it be Lothard and Grimbold?" Nagaro wondered aloud.

"No! It can't be!" Jato was emphatic. "They'd have never got there so fast!"

Kenthos also shook his head in denial. "They're small companies, not an army! And not all together. They're on both sides o' the road. A score or two on the right, I'd say, and three or four score on the left— in different liveries."

"What does this mean?" Nagaro wondered.

Kuran looked grim. "I don't know— except, perhaps, that there may be others here ahead of us with business to conduct with the king and Council. We'll find out soon enough."

Half an hour later, when they came in sight of Lankura, they found the situation just as Kenthos had described, with groups of armed men camped to either side of the road leading up to the main gate. Most of these were gathered around campfires for warmth, but many rose to stare at the newcomers across the ditches that flanked the High Road. Nagaro noted that those on the north side of the road, the smaller number, appeared to be Leithian, while those on the south were Kelorin. As Nagaro's company moved past these encampments, and approached the main East Gate of the city, they found the entry barred by a row of guardsmen with lowered pikes.

Nagaro gave the order to halt when his vanguard was still some fifty feet from the towering stone gate. Before them lay the crossroads where the High Road met the Circle Road that skirted the city wall. The pike-wielding guardsmen on the other side of the crossroads had by then taken stock of the size of the force bearing down on them and had called for their superior officer. The latter turned out to be Korenthos, the Commander of the City Guard, who came out to stand at the edge of the crossroads with his pikemen at his back.

Nagaro and Kuran swung down from their horses and stood at the head of their unwieldy entourage. The column behind them stretched back along the High Road for half a mile.

Jato took one look at the pikemen and let out a squeak before sliding down from Thunder-Heels' rump and scurrying out of the way.

Nagaro gave an order for the rest of the men to stand, and started forward, leading his horse and motioning for Kuran to accompany him. As they approached the Commander of the Guard, a gust of wind briefly lifted dust from the bare earth of the crossroads and a shadow fell across the scene as a wraith of cloud veiled the face of the late morning sun.

Kuran coolly ignored the vagaries of the weather. "What's this, now, Commander?" he inquired banteringly when he came to a halt before Korenthos. "Are you barring the gates against honest citizens?"

Kornenthos was a muscular, middle-aged Kelorin with a shaven chin and a brush of gray at each temple. He stood stolidly with arms folded across his broad chest, plainly trying to appear in control of the situation. Just as plainly, he wasn't happy about it. He looked Nagaro up and down suspiciously before addressing himself to Kuran. "There's a threat o' war, My Lord Kuran, as you may have heard," he said stiffly. "So no one's to enter without stating his business. Your army must stay outside, and they can't block the road. They'll have to wait, there, on the south side." He gestured to an open stretch of land between the High Road and the river where roughly three score men-at-arms were already encamped.

Kuran inclined his head respectfully. "As for our business, we have a number of petitions to put before the King," he said mildly. "And of course we understand that so large a company of men cannot *all* enter the city."

"It's not an army," Nagaro added. "It's my escort."

Korenthos turned on him challengingly "And who may *you* be, Zirda, to need an escort the likes o' *that?*"

Nagaro's hand strayed self-consciously to his shaven chin. "The number is greater than I intended—" he began.

Kuran interrupted. "What ails you, Korenthos?" he chided. "Don't you recognize the best captain in the Fleet, and my adopted heir?"

"Your *adopted heir?*" Korenthos peered more closely at Nagaro. "*By the Eyes and Ears,*" he murmured after a moment, unfolding his arms and relaxing visibly. "It *is* Captain Nagaro! Welcome back, Zirda! I'll confess I didn't recognize you— without the beard... and the..." He waved a hand helplessly at Nagaro's face.

"Kuma stain," Nagaro supplied, embarrassed. He could feel the blood in his face and hoped it didn't show.

"Is that what it was? But... but why have you changed your looks?"

"He's come to Lankura to claim his true heritage," Kuran interjected, sparing Nagaro the need to respond. "So it seemed appropriate he should look like his father's son."

"His *true heritage?* His *father's son?*" This time Korenthos was puzzled. He stared at Nagaro for several long seconds. Then his face lit up like a midsummer sunrise. "You mean the rumors we've been hearing all winter are *true?* And it's Captain Nagaro, here, that's—"

"The heir of the House of Loros? Yes." Kuran was matter-of-fact.

"But this is wonderful!" Korenthos cried. "Why it's... it's perfect!" He slapped his thigh. "And now that you've told me, I can't think of anyone more likely." He turned to Nagaro. "But why have you waited so long to come forward, Zirda,, if I may be so bold?"

Nagaro had been standing silent in gathering dismay. The reaction of the folk of Loros Wared to the revelation of his true identity had been understandable, but Korenthos wasn't one of the scattered men of Loros— and yet the man was ecstatic at the news! "I... ah... only found out a few months ago," he confessed. "I've been trying to work out what to do about it."

"What to *do* about it? I'll tell you what to do, Zirda! It's plain this land needs a new king. One who can stand up to—"

"*Commander!*" Kuran cut the man off. "Remember where your loyalty lies! The captain has no desire to be king, and the choosing of a king is no light matter in any case. We have petitions to lay before King Elgurn, and little time to waste. I assume there's no difficulty in the captain entering the city with the witnesses he's brought and such other supporters as he deems necessary?"

Korenthos had guiltily subsided under Kuran's remonstrance and he now looked uncomfortable. "Ah, well, that *depends*..." he began. "I'm afraid we have orders not to give entry to any party o' men that numbers more than five."

"*Five?*" It was Kuran's turn to be dismayed. "There are lords in our company who have ridden some distance to join us. Surely under the circumstances..."

Korenthos drew himself up stiffly. "The order was very clear, My Lord, and I've my loyalty to think of as you just pointed out. There can be no exceptions."

"*But—*" Kuran sputtered.

"Of course he can't make exceptions, Kuran," Nagaro put in quickly. "Fairness demands that all be treated alike. We'll just have to do the best we can." He turned to address Korenthos, who was looking distinctly relieved at this unexpected support. "But you did say five *men*, didn't you, Commander? I don't imagine that a *woman* need be counted?" He was thinking of Boka.

The Commander rubbed his chin, grinning. "Well now, I suppose that's so," he said speculatively. "No one has asked that before, and if any should ask *after* you, I can allow them the same privilege."

"To be sure you can." Kuran had a gleam in his eye. "And also you said five men in *any party*. We have here, in fact, *two* parties, traveling together merely for convenience. You'll allow each party to enter separately, I assume?"

Korenthos' grin widened. "I suppose I'd have to. Provided there's no more than five men in either one, o' course. And provided you leave time enough between the two to make it clear that they're separate."

"Well, that's fair enough then." Kuran dusted his hands together. "We'll do just as you say. And now, we have some news for you concerning the movements of Lothard and Grimbold, and perhaps in return you can tell us what you know about these men who've come here before us."

Korenthos was very glad to exchange information. He listened grimly to the news Jato had brought. "Lothard and Grimbold here this afternoon, you say?" He glanced at the sun, which was riding towards its zenith. "I'd hoped for more time."

"Isn't the city ready for a siege?" Kuran looked worried.

"We're as ready as we can be." Korenthos spoke stoutly, though he frowned all the same. "And these walls 'll keep 'em out a good while. I'm more afraid for your men that you leave outside— and for these others, here. I've no wish to see a pitched battle on my doorstep! You'd be outnumbered four to one, at least, if our information is right. I've done what I can, putting the Leithians on one side and the Kelorin on the other with the High Road and its ditches in between, but that won't stop anyone that's spoiling for a fight."

Nagaro frowned. "None of those who follow me will start one," he said earnestly. "I'll make that quite clear to them. I can't speak for the other Kelorin, though."

"Aye, that's the rub." Korenthos chewed a knuckle. "There's three companies of 'em. They came as escorts for Soren, Theren, and Rathdar."

Kuran's face clouded as soon as he heard the names. "The lords of the Kelorin Faction! What are *they* doing here?"

Korenthos' expression said plainly that he shared Kuran's concern. "They claimed to have come at the request of the Crown— to see the King and the Council."

"How long have they been here? Did they arrive together?"

Korenthos shook his head. "Theren got here yesterday morning and the other two about two hours apart yesterday afternoon. The three lords went in together, though." The Commander jerked his thumb at the gate behind him. "That was yesterday afternoon, and they've yet to come out again."

"What about the Leithians?"

"It seems they've brought business of their own. The men you see are escorts for Lord Madred and for a messenger from Sobring Hold. They arrived together, yesterday, near sunset."

Nagaro tensed at the name of Sobring. "Was the messenger from Grimbold?"

Korenthos grimaced. "I asked him, and he was quick to deny it. He said he was sent by the Elders of the Hold, with a message for the King and for Vell Sobring."

Kuran was frowning darkly. "And Madred was traveling with this man? Did they go in together?"

"Aye. He was, and they did."

"And when was that?"

"This morning. About two hours ago."

Kuran stood for a moment, stroking his chin and frowning in concentration, but then he shook himself. "I can't fathom it," he said. "So there's nothing to do but go in ourselves and perhaps all will become clear."

They left Korenthos at the gate and went to explain matters to the other leaders of their party. Nagaro had feared there might be some dispute over who would accompany him into the city, since he could choose only two more men after counting himself, Kuran, and the old gardener, Chula. Fortunately the commanders of his escort made things easy.

Rastyl listened grim-faced to what they had learned from Korenthos, and said, "I'll stay here. My reputation would likely do you more harm than good in the palace. Out here I may be of some use if there's trouble."

Rodin shrugged then, and said he would also stay outside the walls, which meant that, in addition to Varsyl, Kenthos could be included as he very much wished to be.

Nevien declared that she and Rianine would enter the city about a quarter hour after Nagaro's party, with three of the princess's guards. For Nevien's safety the two women chose to continue to go in the guise of men, though they didn't expect to fool Korenthos. Brandle, Nevien's fourth guard, took the task of riding around by the Circle Road to the Fleet Compound to carry the news of Nagaro's coming to his friends in the Fleet and to summon Tredhold and Fendar as potential witnesses. They would all simply enter the city by the South Gate as a separate party, with no one the wiser.

Under the circumstances, Nagaro and Nevien couldn't embrace in parting. "Will I see you in the palace?" he asked, stepping close to her and dropping his voice.

"I don't know." She frowned. "My father may be angry with me for going off on my own without telling him— or he may not even have heard of it. If you need me to bear witness, I hope he'll consent to summon me."

Nagaro's stomach tightened. "I hope you won't have to do that. If it becomes necessary to reveal his crimes to the Council, we don't know what he'll do."

Nevien lifted her chin. ""My father is in the wrong," she said, " and I'm done with making excuses for him. If he chooses to stand against you in this, I'll be on your side, not his, and I will bear the consequences of my choice."

With that, she touched his cheek with a fingertip and stepped away, giving him a brave smile.

He could only watch admiringly as she turned to go, reminding him of all that was at stake. After a moment, he turned to Kuran. "I'm ready," he said. "Let's be about it."

Chapter 22

The Audience

For the third time, Nagaro caught himself pacing and forced himself to stop. For what must have been the twentieth time, his hand strayed to the leather satchel in which he carried the papers he'd brought. He was in the Compass Room, waiting outside the big carved double doors that led into the Audience Chamber. A dozen of his witnesses and friends waited with him for his audience to be granted.

The Compass Room could be dauntingly impressive to anyone not accustomed to palaces, with its marble floor in a compass rose design, polished wood paneling, gilt-bronze lamps, and velvet hangings. Nagaro's nervousness, however, had nothing to do with his surroundings and everything to do with what might happen on the other side of the double doors.

Kenthos had been there before, though only once, and he didn't expect to be entering the Audience Chamber this time. Still he looked very nearly as nervous as when he'd presented himself for judgement as a man who'd mistakenly imagined himself to be the heir of Loros. He kept glancing at the two guards who flanked the doors, a Leithian on the left and a Kelorin on the right. Nagaro was grateful to the young blacksmith for coming, even if he was too nervous to offer any real support as Nagaro prepared to face the Council with his own claim to the heritage of Loros.

Others had also come that far and would go no farther. Taru, Pavo, and Landros had insisted on coming with Tredhold, although only Tred was a potential witness. Simion had also come, and was standing apart from the other Fleet men with Brandle beside him. As Kuran's personal secretary, Simion had an official connection to the Royal Fleet and a tenuous excuse for being present, but really he had simply invited himself. Brandle had no excuse for being there at all, except as "escort" for the two men he'd been sent to summon. Apparently he had yet to find a pressing reason to be elsewhere. It didn't appear that he was trying very hard to find one.

Among the men who would join the audience, Kuran and Varsyl represented the nobility. They stood a few paces away from Nagaro, eyeing him as they talked together in low tones. Nagaro could read worry in their glances and he knew they were concerned about his mental state— not without reason.

The Fleet Swordmaster, Fendar, was also there as a witness. The spry old Kelorin looked as if he felt undressed without his sword. He stood with the other Fleet men and kept glancing anxiously at Nagaro and at Kuran, plainly aware that the present situation was the result of events he'd set in motion by confiding in the Lord of the Fleet.

The last three witnesses had found seats on a bench placed against the wall across from the double doors. Boka, Chula, and Fineas the lore master, sat in row. Boka sat with her hands folded in her lap, calmly watching the other members of the assembled company. Chula sat huddled, fidgeting as he gazed wide-eyed around the Compass Room, obviously intimidated by the richness of the surroundings.

Nagaro appreciated Chula's courage in coming more than anyone's. He'd managed to speak once, briefly, to the loyal gardener since the man's arrival at Loros Hall, thanking the old Turo for coming and trying to reassure him. "I don't know if you'll have to speak," he had told the man. "I may not need to confess openly who I was. But if it comes to it, you've only to truthfully answer any question that's put to you." Chula had shaken his gray head. "I'd do anything for ye, Zirda, ye know that," he said. "But I'm just an old Turo. Why should these great folk listen t' the likes o' me?" Nagaro's response had been swift and firm: "You're a citizen of Edrovir, Chula. They had better listen!" Chula hadn't looked convinced.

Nagaro's attention was drawn to Master Fineas when the lore master removed his spectacles from his nose, for the third time, to polish them. Nagaro grimaced. At least the little Kelorin peered around the room through those glasses with interest rather than awe. Like Nagaro, the lore master's nervousness was in anticipation of what might happen in the Audience Chamber.

Nagaro had taken a detour while passing through the city, to Brass Bell Lane, to find Fineas. The Lore Master hadn't recognized him at first when Nagaro had entered the apothecary shop alone, leaving the rest of his party outside. Then, when he'd realized his error, the little man had apologized profusely, and finally said, "I expect you've come about that letter ye sent, Captain. And it was a *most* enigmatic letter, I must say. I will certainly help in any way I can, but I hope you don't mind telling me what this is all about."

Nagaro had taken a deep breath and explained that he needed Master Fineas as a potential witness when he made a formal claim to the heritage of Loros. Fineas had been remarkably unsurprised by the revelation, only asking what testimony of his could possibly be relevant. So Nagaro had explained, haltingly, why he might need an expert on the two herbs possessed of spirit magic, linjana and heskial. He had finished with, "Do you remember what you said about the two drugs warring in the blood of a single man and it burning the mind? Well, they did, and it wasn't pleasant, but I do believe that the linjana saved my life." Fineas' reaction to the explanation had included a succession of shocked expressions and astonished exclamations. Nagaro winced as the scene replayed itself in his mind. He supposed it was good practice for what lay ahead.

Kuran's voice, speaking close beside him, startled him from his thoughts.

"I still wish you hadn't left your sword at the door. You've a right to wear it here."

Nagaro cast the older man a look of mild annoyance. "You heard what Delvin said. The right isn't officially granted until my status is officially recognized. I don't wish to begin by being presumptuous." He also hadn't wanted to put poor Delvin in a difficult position. He had a vivid picture of the young guardsman's agonized face.

Abruptly, there was a commotion as one of the two double doors to the Audience chamber swung open a little way and Vell Sobring stuck out his handsome blond head to speak in a hurried whisper to the two guards. The two men shrugged and gestured to Nagaro who was standing a half dozen feet away. At that Vell turned to face him and stared for a moment before saying, as if to himself, "Why yes, that is Nagaro." Then, speaking to Nagaro, he added, "I must say you look much better that way." He then opened the door a little further and stepped out. Pulling it closed behind him, he added, "The Council has decided to let you in now."

Nagaro squared his shoulders. "They've finished with their other business?"

Vell gave him a wry look. "Not... exactly. But they're waiting for something, and they've just gotten word that Lothard and Grimbold will be here with their armies— maybe within the hour— so they mean to finish the picnic before the storm breaks, so to speak."

Kuran nodded grimly and spoke out of the side of his mouth to Nagaro. "That would be Jato's news. He must have gotten here ahead of us." To Vell, he said jestingly, "Is the Council now putting one of my captains to work as their errand boy?"

Vell toyed with his mustache. "Actually, I volunteered. Thought you might like to hear what's been going on in there. And I can't be one of your captains anymore, Kuran, in any case. The Sobring Elders have named me Lord of the Hold."

"Lord of Sobring Hold? But Grimbold is still alive, isn't he?"

"Alive and causing no end of trouble." Vell made a face. "And since he still thinks he's the lord, things could get ugly when he gets here."

"What led the Elders to this decision?" Nagaro wondered aloud.

Vell's blue gaze shifted to him. "I actually have you to thank."

"Me? Why?"

"It was that affair with you and my sister. Seems you made some... *allegations...* to Lord Madred, and he took it upon himself to investigate. He took what he learned to the Sobring Elders, and *they* declared my uncle unfit to rule. And, well," Vell spread his hands helplessly, "I'm next in line."

"Oh. Ah... congratulations, I guess. I've been chosen too, by the people of the old Loros Wared."

Vell's eyebrows shot up. "You're the Lord of Loros? Really? I say! Well done!" Then he rolled his eyes. "Personally I'd rather not take on the task, but one doesn't refuse the Elders. And it isn't just that my uncle is hazarding Sobring's men-at-arms in support of Lothard— against the Elders' counsel— he also did something *unlawful*. He was paying a band of thieves to steal horses for the army he was building! They were working out of my grandfather's hunting lodge!" Vell's face was a picture of moral outrage. "Can you believe it?"

Nagaro gave him a sour look. "Having met the man, I can. And I ran afoul of those very horse thieves— *twice*."

"This is all well and good," Kuran interjected. "But they're waiting for us, and I'd like to know how many council members are in there. We know Devral is away gathering his army. What of the others?"

"Ah." Vell shifted mental direction. "Pendrik is gone as well. Left about an hour ago to meet *his* army that's already on the march. He's also been charged with gathering whatever forces he can muster on the way that would include both Leithians and Kelorin. The Council's very keen to have a force made up of both, to face off against Lothard's lot."

Of course, Nagaro thought. *Balance.* What he said was, "So the only members of the Council who are here are Anduar and Odus?

"Well... yes and no." Vell grimaced. "There's two *new* members of the Council, you see, that they just named— the Lords Theren and Madred."

Kuran gave a low whistle. "Theren and Madred are both Council members now?"

Nagaro made a rueful face. *One each from the Leithian and Kelorin Factions. Balance, again...* "Well," he said, "at least we now know why the Council sent for Soren, Theren, and Rathdar."

Vell nodded. "Elgurn didn't dare slight any of them, even though there was only one chair to fill. He told *them* to decide who got it— which led to some discussion, I gather. In Madred's case, of course, there was no argument."

"Had they sent for Madred as well?" Kuran asked.

"Ah.. *yes*... but Madred was already on the way here— for other reasons."

"Such as escorting the messenger from Sobring Hold with the news of your advancement?"

"That was part of it. But there's this other matter— the one they're waiting on. They've been very close about it. Went into the Council Chamber to speak in private, and so on— leaving me standing about for nearly an hour with my business half finished!"

At this point, the door of the Audience Chamber opened again and the king's Sergeant-at-Arms thrust out his blond head. "My Lords? Zirda? Is there some difficulty? he inquired rather pointedly.

Vell looked guilty. "Just getting a few things sorted out," he muttered. "But I think they're ready now."

Nagaro's stomach tightened at the knowledge that he must now enter that room. He swallowed and raised his voice. "Friends, it's time."

There was a chorus of eager voices, and he was surrounded by a press of his supporters, wishing him luck.

"He doesn't need *luck*, he's Captain Nagaro!" cried Kenthos. "The Lord of Loros!"

Taru sidled in close. "Have ye got the life stone in your pocket?" he asked.

Nagaro managed to nod.

"Good." Taru grinned. "At least they can't kill ye." Then he sobered. "Oh, and Hamani said she'd pray to Hakura Kili."

Nagaro tried to smile. "Please thank her for me."

Pavo elbowed Taru in the ribs. "Do not make Nagaro worry," he said with his typical air of calm certainty. "Sheptuum will make sure story have good ending."

Nagaro could only manage another forced smile. He raised his voice over the babble. "Please! I need the witnesses to stand by the door!"

"Witnesses!" exclaimed the Sergeant-at-Arms. "All of these?" He gestured at the roomful of people. "I'm to let you in, Captain, and Lord Kuran, only. The king was very clear about that."

"But it's only six witnesses," Kuran put in smoothly. "Including Lord Varsyl."

"Lord Varsyl, you say?" The Sergeant looked worried. "And only six? Oh, well, that's all right, I suppose. They can sit in the gallery on the left side until they're called."

Kuran gave Nagaro a wink as their six witnesses gathered before the double doors. "Never hurts to throw a lord into the pot," he muttered under his breath.

***

The atmosphere when they entered the Audience Chamber was hushed and expectant. Nagaro took a deep breath as he surveyed the grand room. Light from arrays of windows high overhead provided a general diffuse illumination, punctuated by rays that shafted down through the dust motes to create rectangles on the polished marble floor. Lighted oil lamps glowed at intervals along the walls above the seating galleries on either side, making additional pools of yellow light. On the expanses of wall between the lamps were hung a series of huge tapestries illustrating the events leading up to the founding of the nation of Edrovir. Darion the Great featured prominently among their images, and Nevrath, his sire, was depicted several times as well. A number of people were seated at several tables arranged at the farther end of the room in front of the dais where King Elgurn presided in his heavy, high-backed chair.

There was whispered conversation from various quarters, but the room was large enough to swallow soft sounds almost completely. At the same time, it was also large enough that the sharp sounds of their boot heels echoed the entire length of the room as Nagaro advanced, flanked by Kuran and Vell. The six witnesses trailed after them in the company of a pair of guards. Knowing that all eyes were on him, Nagaro held his head up and tried to walk boldly, keeping his own eyes on the dais and the tables in front of it.

He easily identified the four attending council members, old and new, seated at a pair of tables a few feet apart just in front of the dais. Theren and Anduar were at the left-hand table, Odus and Madred on the right. *There it was again... balance...* A clerk sat at the third table, set aside on the left, with paper and writing implements before him as well as a small chest and several other objects that Nagaro was too distracted to note in detail. When his gaze wandered past the clerk's table, he saw that Soren and Rathdar were sitting in the bottom row of the left-hand gallery.

He could feel his heart beating as he approached the tables, and perspiration prickled along his sides. *You have a right to be here*, he reminded himself, *even if those weren't your ancestors on the walls, you're a born citizen of Edrovir.*

"This is where I leave you," Vell whispered as they came to a halt in front of the four council members, and with that he slipped quickly away to a seat in the bottom row of the right-hand gallery.

Following Vell's departing figure with his eyes, Nagaro noticed several other Leithians sitting in the same row, a few seats from the place Vell had chosen. One of them, he realized with a jolt, was Minister Torlung with his distinctive waxed mustache and pomaded hair that gleamed in the light of the oil lamps. Seated beside the minister was a figure whose bowed head was covered by a hood that hid his face in shadow. Beyond him, was a portly Leithian man with a little pointed beard, holding a large black satchel on his knees.

"How many people are in this room?" Nagaro muttered nervously, more to himself than to Kuran.

Kuran heard him, however, and must have been keeping a mental count, for he answered in a tone that was obviously meant to be reassuring. "Only about twenty, not counting our own folk behind us."

"Do you see Nevien?"

"No."

Twenty! And if each of those tells twenty others... Nagaro tried to suppress the thought and focus on gaging the moods of the king and council members.

He felt their collective stares and scanned them from left to right. Theren appeared on edge. Middle-aged and dapper with brown hair and gray eyes, the man's face registered puzzlement as his gaze came to rest on Nagaro. He exchanged glances with his two Kelorin colleagues in the nearby gallery. Next to him, Anduar lounged in his chair as languidly as a cat by the fire— at least to outward appearances. The Kelorin Lord's expression was a study in indifference except that his steel-gray eyes were subtly narrowed. Their gaze flitted here and there, missing nothing. When those eyes very briefly met Nagaro's, there was no change in them, no hint of any reaction.

Odus, in contrast, was sitting with his compact frame angled forward, his mouth set in a hard line in the midst of his close-trimmed bronze beard. His eyes bored into the two men who had come to a halt before him. Lastly, at the far right, The golden-haired Madred sat stiffly erect, his handsome aristocratic features cast in lines of studied hauteur. When his gaze fell on Nagaro, he frowned at first, then gave the barest nod of recognition.

The survey of the council members took only a moment, after which Nagaro turned his anxious attention to the king. He was relieved to see as yet no evidence in Elgurn's face of the recognition that he feared. The glance the king cast in his direction was cool and distant— and very brief, for Elgurn's attention was swiftly transferred to Kuran, at which point the glance became a glower. Though the king sat straight as a poker in his chair, he looked haggard. Age had by now leached all of the gold from his hair and the copper from his beard, leaving them more leaden than silver. New lines etched the man's forehead and the corners of his mouth.

The Sergeant-at-Arms spoke briefly to the king and the council members concerning the witnesses, who were directed to the bottom row of the left-hand gallery at a little distance from Lords Soren and Rathdar.

Poor Chula looked even more uncomfortable in the Audience Chamber than he had in the Compass Room, and Master Fineas' agitation seemed to double as soon as he set eyes on his former employer, Minister Torlung. Boka took her place as if it were no more than her due. Varsyl was very self-possessed, but Tredhold and Fendred looked tense.

Once the witnesses were seated, Elgurn broke the pregnant silence. It was to Kuran that he spoke, undisguised bitterness edging his voice.

"*So*, My Lord Kuran, you at last see fit to present yourself— not in answer to my summons, but at some whim of your own! What have you to say for yourself?"

"My Lord King." Kuran executed a sweeping bow. "I most humbly beg your pardon. I fear I have been much distracted by my concerns for the safety of my chosen heir— who so narrowly escaped death at the hands of a would-be assassin and has but recently recovered. Between that and the pressing needs of my command, I fear I've been guilty of neglecting my duties to my king. I only hope you can find it in your heart to forgive me."

It was a fair speech, delivered with every appearance of humility and sincerity.

Elgurn's glare didn't soften appreciably, however. "Your precious heir looks well enough to me," he growled. "Did you think I would be fooled because he's abandoned his kuma stain to accentuate his pallor? Or perhaps he thinks to look the part since he now expects to inherit your Wared? I've considered you a trusted friend, Kuran, but what am I to make of it when you turn me a deaf ear and ride off on business of your own at a time when Lankura needs you? And now you reappear on our doorstep with an army at your back—"

The king might have said more, but he made the mistake of drawing breath and Anduar inserted himself smoothly into the pause. "My Lord, your grievances are just, but I respectfully submit that time is short and war is threatening. We should gladly embrace all our friends and allies and put aside any lesser quarrels."

"Anduar is right, My Lord," Theren put in. "If Lord Kuran has brought an army, I am sure he doesn't mean to turn it on us." He gave Kuran an ingratiating smile.

Elgurn sat up even straighter as he looked from one speaker to the other. His eyes smoldered briefly, but then he sank back in his seat and dismissed the matter with a wave of his hand. "Very well," he said with ill grace. "We'll discuss it later."

Kuran bowed his acquiescence. "This was to be Nagaro's audience, My Lord, in any case," he ventured. "I'm only here to stand with him as kin and friend."

"Yes, yes." Elgurn brushed this aside as well and turned his frowning gaze upon Nagaro. "You have some petitions, I am told, Captain. Let's have them, and be quick about it. As we've been reminded, time is short."

Nagaro had relaxed a little when attention had shifted to Kuran, but he tensed again under the king's renewed stare. Reminding himself that others had put their faith in him and he mustn't let them down, he drew a breath, cleared his throat, and opened his satchel to draw out the first of three sheaves of paper. "I have three petitions, My Lord," he said, keeping his voice steady with an effort. "I'll begin with the one that personally concerns me the least. It's a request on behalf of a number of men who were called to military service in the border wars and returned to find themselves robbed of property they couldn't reclaim owing to the lack of a deed or bill of sale. They humbly request enactment of a new law that would allow the use of witnesses in lieu of documents to prove such claims."

Elgurn considered him narrowly. "How is it that these men come to lack the documents? Were they so careless as to lose them?"

"It could be so," Nagaro conceded, relaxing again as he spoke in defense of others. "But in most cases it's because the property has been passed down in the family for generations and no such documents ever existed. In some cases it's because the man built the thing— a boat or a house, for example— with his own hands, rather than having purchased it."

"I see." Elgurn rubbed his beard. "This would seem to have merit. What do you say, My Lords?" The last was addressed to the council members.

"How is it that *you* are presenting this petition on behalf of these men?" Theren asked.

"They came to me because I'm known to care about the people. They brought testimony they had collected, which I used to write the petition."

Lord Madred looked down his nose. "Were these men Turowan by any chance?"

Nagaro frowned at the implication that this should matter.

"Turowan folk are often unlettered and not accustomed to using papers, so they're very vulnerable to this kind of theft," he said carefully. "But it might happen to any man— or woman, for that matter, if she inherits property but lacks papers for any reason. I saw a general need and suggested petitioning for a new law."

Elgurn cut in. "That is very commendable, Captain, but surely these men could have presented the petition themselves."

Nagaro met the king's challenging gaze. "Some have tried, My Lord. They were told they must take up the matter with their own lords— only to have those lords tell them that the law recognizes only possession, or papers. Since they couldn't produce the papers, there was nothing to be done."

Elgurn scowled. "These lords aren't worthy of the name if they can't do better than that—" he began.

Anduar swung around to face the king. "It is a defect in the law that should be remedied, My Lord. It's well that the captain has brought it to our attention."

Elgurn checked himself at the interruption. "Yes, yes. So it would seem," he muttered, waving a hand. "Give the papers to my clerk, there, and I'll look at them. If no objection presents itself on closer inspection, you shall have your law."

"Thank you, My Lord." Nagaro bowed and crossed to the side table to deliver the papers into the hands of the clerk, a small middle-aged Kelorin who accepted them gravely.

Returning to the place in front of the dais, Nagaro pulled a second sheaf of papers from his satchel. "This is the second petition. It is a request for the Crown to recognize the newly-formed Loros Wared, to be encompassed by the boundaries of the part of the former Loros Wared that has been governed by Lord Endemar."

He had expected there to be a stronger reaction to the second petition, and there was. A ripple of voices ran through the Audience Chamber. The king sat up, frowning, and the members of the council leaned forward in their seats with exclamations of surprise— all except Lord Anduar whose only reaction was a fleeting smile.

Had the man expected this?

"How is it that *you* are representing this new Loros Wared?" Theren demanded.

Nagaro inclined his head in deference. "The people of the Wared have chosen me as their Lord."

Elgurn bridled. "Isn't it enough that you'll have Kel Wared in the future? You mean to have Loros Wared now?"

Nagaro turned to meet the king's blazing blue stare. "I didn't seek this, My Lord," he said evenly. "I told them I would accept the task if they chose me for it, and they have. All the papers are here. You will see that it was done according to Kelorin law as is the right of the people of a Wared."

"Here, let's see those." Odus thrust out his hand.

Nagaro took two steps and handed the papers to the Leithian lord, then waited, sweating, while the man subjected them to a frowning scrutiny. At last Odus put the papers down. "They do seem to be in order, My Lord," he conceded, addressing Elgurn. "The number of signed names is more than adequate. There is also a letter from Endemar giving his approval. I know the man's hand and the letter appears genuine."

"But isn't it odd to chose a man as lord if he isn't an inhabitant of the Wared?" Madred inquired. He turned an imperious gaze upon Nagaro. "Will you tell us that you've been living there all this time, Captain?"

Nagaro didn't care for the look, or for Madred's tone, but he kept his own carefully level. "I've been living there for several months— ever since learning that I was born there."

Not surprisingly, this evoked cries of astonishment. And then, suddenly, Odus, who had continued to examine the papers, smote the table, sputtering, *"By the Gods!* He's written his name here as Nagaro Alorin Loros!"

"What?" This time Anduar was on his feet, his coolness abandoned. He covered the distance to Odus' chair in a rapid prowl and reached for the papers. "Let me see those."

Elgurn had also risen to his feet and come down the steps of the dais to stand behind the two lords. After a moment's focused scrutiny of the document in Anduar's hands, he looked up, boring into Nagaro with his eyes. *"What is the meaning of this?"* he demanded, stabbing a finger at the paper.

Nagaro swallowed to moisten a mouth that had gone suddenly dry. "That is the heart of my third petition, My Lord," he said, and his words sounded loud in the silence of the great room. "I have come to formally claim the name of Loros— by right of birth."

For several heartbeats, the silence in the Audience Chamber was so complete that a paper dropped at one end of it would have been heard at the other. Then the room erupted in a clamor of surprise and disbelief. The three lords of the Kelorin Faction looked gleeful. Odus launched into a verbal protest. Lord Madred rose to his feet, his fine patrician features distorted with emotion as he loudly expressed his incredulity.

Elgurn flung up his arms in a commanding gesture.

"Silence!"

And there was silence, a somewhat stunned silence, as various people who had risen sat down again. For a moment it seemed that Elgurn had thrown off his weariness. He stood, stiff and tall, as he swept the assemblage with a baleful glare. Then he turned his ire upon Nagaro.

"This is no trifling matter, *Captain,*" he rasped. "You were ever a bold man, but in this I fear you've overstepped the mark, and it will go hard with you indeed if you have knowingly made a false claim." The burning blue gaze shifted to the Lord of the Fleet. "And it will go hard with *you,* Kuran, if it turns out that you've misled your heir in this."

Kuran met the king's stare without flinching. "There is compelling evidence, My Lord," he said levelly. "Will you allow us to present it?"

Confronted with such steadiness, Elgurn's ire receded. The fire died in his eyes. He gestured dismissively. "Present what you will," he said, then remounted the steps of the dais and resumed his seat in the big oak chair. There he sat like a man resigned to sitting through a boring stage performance.

Nagaro drew a breath and spoke into the waiting pause. "Will you first rule on the second petition, My Lord? What word can I take back to the people of Loros?"

Elgurn looked pained. "I have no objection to the re-institution of Loros Wared," he said stiffly. "It was dissolved years ago for want of enough grown men to till its fields, nothing more. If that situation is remedied, and the papers are in order as Odus says, the people of Loros shall have their Wared. But—"and here the king leveled a finger at Nagaro and pinned him with a cold stare. "If you have won the lordship through some deceit, I will insist that they choose again. Is that clear?"

"Perfectly, My Lord. I would expect nothing else, were it to turn out that I'm mistaken about my birth."

"Not that it would make any difference, if I'm any judge," Kuran muttered. "The people of Loros would be pleased to have Captain Nagaro for their lord, whatever his parentage."

The Fleet Lord's words were loud enough for the Council and the king to hear. Elgurn looked sour. "I dare say they would," he snapped. "But let's get to your evidence. Time presses."

Nagaro drew a long breath and reached into the neck of his shirt to draw out the ring on its silver chain, his one safe piece of evidence. "I will begin with this."

"And this *is...*?" Anduar rose and reached out to take what Nagaro offered. The Kelorin lord had completely regained his composure. The intensity of his interest was betrayed only by the avid gleam in his eyes.

It was Kuran who answered him. "It's the signet ring of the House of Loros."

At this, Odus immediately threw up his hands and exclaimed, "What, *another* one?"

"Ridiculous!" Madred was on his feet again. "We have already presented the ring to the Council. This one must be counterfeit!"

"Why must *this* one be counterfeit?" Theren objected. "Why not the other one?"

"What other one?" Nagaro looked worriedly from one face to another. Elgurn, he noted, hadn't said a word. The king had looked sharply from Nagaro to Madred and back again. Something had flickered in his eyes but his face remained rigid.

Anduar also hadn't spoken. Instead he pointedly examined Nagaro's ring, then walked deliberately to the clerk's table where he opened the wooden box that stood upon it and lifted out a loop of cord from which dangled another large bronze ring.

"Most interesting," he observed languidly. "We've been shown *two* signets of Loros in one morning. And with them come two claims— one of which, at least, must be false." His gaze stabbed, knife-like, at Nagaro and then at Kuran before passing on first to Madred and then to Minister Torlung sitting in the gallery. Madred met the look with regal confidence. Torlung smiled an unctuous smile that couldn't quite avoid resembling a sneer.

Kuran leaned close to Nagaro's ear. "Stand steady," he muttered. "We know our claim is true."

Dry mouthed, Nagaro nodded. This new development didn't really change his situation, but it was unexpected and unsettling. *Who was the other claimant? Was it the hooded man who so far hadn't moved a muscle?*

Anduar still stood by the clerk's table with a ring dangling from each hand. "*Two* signet rings and *two* claims," he drawled. Then he raised his voice a notch as if to be sure it would carry the full length of the chamber. "We were waiting for the goldsmith to come and examine the first ring. Is he here?"

The voice of the Sergeant-at-Arms answered from the far end of the room. "He came but a few minutes ago, My Lord."

Anduar turned a questioning glance to Elgurn.

Elgurn sat stiffly upright in his chair, but the weariness had returned to his eyes. He lifted his shoulders slightly and made a small gesture with one hand. "I yield the investigation to you, Anduar," he said. "Proceed."

Anduar bowed and turned back to address the Sergeant-at-Arms. "Bring the goldsmith in, Sergeant, and have him escorted to the king's study. The clerk, here, will show him the various... *objects*. And please clear all unnecessary people from the galleries. This is a matter of some delicacy."

The goldsmith turned out to be a portly, middle-aged Leithian with a set of lenses strung around his neck. He was no sooner brought in than he and the clerk were whisked away by a pair of guards to one of the smaller rooms that adjoined the Audience Chamber. Both rings, and the box with whatever it contained, went with them.

There followed some argument over who should be regarded as "unnecessary" and Nagaro could only wait with mounting anxiety while this was sorted out. Soren and Rathdar were allowed to stay, being lords, to bear witness to such a significant proceeding. Vell and Varsil, as lords, were also retained. The rest of Nagaro's witnesses were allowed to stay in case their testimony was needed, and there seemed to be an assumption that Torlung should remain, as well as the hooded man beside him and the Leithian with the satchel on his knees. All other personal retainers who had come with various noble folk were removed, however, and only a half dozen guards remained inside the Audience Chamber, one of them the Sergeant-at-Arms.

"Our goldsmith will require some time for his task," Anduar informed those who remained as he resumed his seat. "He must examine both rings and compare them with the seals on several documents— documents from the hand of Tevren or Darion." He paused to glance keenly at Nagaro, Kuran, Madred, and Torlung, in turn, as if to see whether any of them might blink. When none of them did, he continued.

"In the meantime, we will pursue our own investigation." He turned his penetrating gaze to Nagaro. "Have you perhaps heard, Captain, of the rumor that Leyel Virden was in fact the heir of Loros?"

Nagaro felt an icy hand grip his heart and begin to squeeze. *They knew!* His throat tightened, but before he could answer, the three members of the Kelorin Faction responded with outrage to Anduar's assertion, all insisting that it couldn't be true.

"You mean you don't wish it to be," Madred retorted. "Even when I've told you that Bron Sobring had certain knowledge of it— knowledge that Elgurn confirms. We've shown you Leyel Virden—" Here he gestured at the hooded figure in the gallery. "And produced the signet ring. And still you won't accept the truth!"

At this, Elgurn suddenly stood up, his face livid. "That is *not* Leyel Virden!" He stabbed a finger at the hooded man. "Leyel was Tevren's son, yes, that I believe. But he is surely dead!"

Madred turned in his seat to face the king. "So you have said, My Lord," he observed, with studied courtesy. "But you have declined to give us an explanation for your certainty. And of course one can hardly blame you if you aren't pleased that your daughter has a living husband, and therefore can't marry someone else—"

"She is certainly not married to *that!*"

"My Lord! Gentlemen!" Anduar didn't shout, but there was a sharp edge to his voice that brought silence. "We have already been through this." He turned back to Nagaro as Elgurn sank red-faced into his chair. "You see now, Captain," he said mildly, "what position you put yourself in by claiming to be the heir of Loros? Do you perhaps wish to amend your claim?"

Oh Vothra! Nagaro shut his eyes. The sounds in the room around him seemed to fade. *There was no way out —unless he were to say he was mistaken...*

He felt a hand grip his shoulder, and heard Kuran's voice in his ear. "You must speak, Nagaro! You are the true heir, and we can't have Nevien wedded to an imposter!"

Nagaro forced himself to steady his breathing and open his eyes. Kuran was right. If these Leithians were going to insist that Nevien was still married to Leyel, then Leyel he must be. But his heart was hammering against his ribs. Anduar was watching him, his steely gaze sharp and probing. Beyond the Kelorin Lord, the king leaned forward in his chair, staring at him hard. He could feel all the other eyes on him as well. Everyone was waiting for him to speak.

"Start with what you know," Kuran urged.

Nagaro swallowed hard. "Your information is correct, My Lord Anduar," he said. "I have Tevren's journal here." He drew the book from the satchel at his side. "In it he tells of how he came to foster his child with Lindra's cousin, called 'Lily', which must be Maramine Virden."

Voices broke out around him, demanding to see the proof that the journal contained.

Anduar, however, raised his hand to silence the onlookers. "We will examine this journal in due time," he said, accepting the small volume from Nagaro's hands. "But, since you concede the point, Captain, I must ask you again. Do you wish to withdraw your claim?"

Nagaro swallowed again. "No," he said huskily. "I believe I am the son of Tevren and Lindra of Loros." His words were greeted this time by a ripple of laughter.

"*You?*" Odus was frankly incredulous. "You would have us now believe that you are Leyel Virden, when you've always maintained that your parentage was unknown? This is very convenient— besides being utterly absurd!"

"Oh, Nagaro!" Vell forgot his place in the gallery. "If you'd ever *seen* him, you wouldn't suggest such a thing!"

Anduar gestured again for silence before turning again to Nagaro. "Captain," he said carefully. "You perhaps are not aware of how ridiculous your claim appears. Leyel Virden was called the Idiot Prince with good reason. He was, by all evidence, profoundly simple-minded. He sat and stared unless spoken to, said inappropriate things, could scarcely put a dozen words together. He showed no capacity for any sort of complex thought—"

Nagaro stood, cringing with embarrassment and feeling the blood suffusing his face, as Anduar unrolled his humiliating catalog of the attributes displayed by Leyel Virden. He dropped his eyes, unable to meet the man's gaze.

Anduar immediately stopped his recitation, doubtless misjudging the cause of Nagaro's embarrassment. "Captain...?" he probed.

Nagaro felt Kuran's hand on his arm, but the blood was pounding in his ears and he feared his knees might give way. *Vothra, I can't...*

Peace, Spirit that calls itself Nagaro.

He felt a touch upon his mind, and it steadied him. He drew a shuddering breath and found his voice, even as he raised his eyes. "No one knows those things better than I, My Lord," he said huskily. "I had sworn never to use that name again, but Leyel Virden was the name I bore for the first eighteen years of my life." He glanced past Anduar, to where the king sat in his high-backed chair, and what he saw made his heart miss a beat. Elgurn had gone white as sheet and was staring at him as if at some kind of apparition.

Seeing this, Nagaro spoke directly to the king. "Yes, I am alive, Elgurn. I stand before you in the flesh. And I know what I endured."

Elgurn made a small choking sound, and there instantly were movements and murmurs of alarm from several quarters.

"Are you unwell, My Lord?" Odus inquired urgently.

"I have a healer here." Madred gestured to the Leithian in the gallery with the satchel.

The king, however, shook his head, declining assistance. Instead he leaned back against the support of the chair-back, and closed his eyes.

Anduar had followed the exchange with narrowed eyes, and he now spoke to Nagaro. "Do you have evidence to support this extraordinary claim, Captain? Besides the ring on which we await a judgement?"

Nagaro drew a long breath. "Yes, My Lord. I have brought witnesses. I have the gardener from the Lady Maramine's estate, and the man who taught me swordsmanship. Both of them knew me by... *that name*. There is also the woman, Boka, whose family my father had set to keep watch over me."

"Ah." There was a glint now in Anduar's eye as he turned his attention to the left-hand gallery where Nagaro's witnesses were seated. Nagaro saw Fendar sit up straight under that gaze, while Boka leaned over to speak some word to the cowering Chula. Tredhold, Fineas, and Varsyl had been engaged in a whispered conversation, which they hurriedly broke off as attention turned in their direction. Fineas cast a look like a dagger at Torlung in the opposite gallery.

Anduar approached the six witnesses and addressed Chula in a respectful tone.

"You were the gardener at Averwin when the Lady Maramine Virden was mistress there?"

Chula stood up, wide eyed. He was plainly surprised to be treated so graciously by such a high-born personage. He bobbed a nervous bow and shot Nagaro a questioningly look. Nagaro nodded encouragement. Emboldened, Chula raised his voice. "Aye, Zirda," he said. "That I was."

"And were you at that time acquainted with her ward, Leyel Virden?"

Chula blinked. "Did I know him then, d' ye mean?"

"That's right." There was a hint of a smile about Anduar's lips, but he kept the amusement out of his voice.

The gardener drew himself up. "Aye, M' Lord, I did. I swear it by Hakura Kili an' all the Spirits. And he's standing right over there, t' save yer asking." He jabbed a finger at Nagaro.

This drew an amused murmur from several quarters, but Anduar's lips didn't even twitch this time. "Well answered, Zirda," he said and made the gardener a small bow before turning to Fendar. Chula was so astonished that Boka had to tug on his sleeve to remind him to sit down.

"And you, Zirda." Anduar addressed Fendar. "You were Leyel Virden's swordmaster?"

Fendar had stood up even as Chula sat down. "Aye, My Lord," he said stoutly. "The Lady Maramine hired me. I worked with him for three years."

"And based on your knowledge of him from that time, you are able to identify him now?"

"Yes, My Lord. That's him." Fendar indicated Nagaro with a nod of his head. "I swear it in Vothra's name. A man doesn't forget his best pupil."

"I would imagine not. Thank you, Zirda."

Boka didn't wait for Anduar to address her. As soon as he ceased speaking to Fendar, she rose with all the gravity of a queen. "I am Boka Anu," she announced to the assemblage. "My sister and I are Ku Taihanai of Minowei's People. We keep the names of all our folk, and their histories— *here*." She tapped her temple. "And I tell ye that this one—" she leveled a finger at Nagaro that made him feel like ducking, "—is the great grandson o' Princess Minowei and the lord Nevrath that was her husband. My family has followed him since the day of his birth."

"Oh, but this is ridiculous, Anduar!" Madred had risen and he spoke with the air of one who is belaboring the obvious. "Captain Nagaro simply cannot be Leyel Virden. He has neither the speech nor the manner, while the man Torlung has found displays both— you have seen it! These... *common people*," he gestured at the witnesses who had spoken, "...must be mistaken— if indeed they are not lying. Surely you must see that!"

Chula, Boka, and Fendar instantly burst into indignant protests and had to be warned into silence by the Sergeant-at-Arms.

"Why must they be mistaken?" Theren demanded. "Obviously there must have been some sort of... *substitution*." He looked imploringly at Nagaro and at Kuran. "Leyel must have been held prisoner somewhere, and that creature Torlung has found must have been put in his place."

"And who do you accuse of doing that?" Madred's blue eyes blazed.

Torlung's glance had darted from speaker to speaker. Beside him, the hooded man continued to sit unmoving. The man identified as a healer huddled in his seat, blinking worriedly.

"Gentlemen! Please!" Anduar raised both hands for silence. "Captain Nagaro, will you speak to this?"

Nagaro looked at the floor. *How could he counter such disbelief?* It would have been worse, of course, to be easily accepted as the idiot prince, but...

Once more Kuran's hand gripped his shoulder, but he didn't look up, and Kuran spoke instead, addressing the entire assemblage.

"I don't know who this man is that Torlung has found," Kuran began. "Perhaps some play-actor—"

"Play-actor? You insult me!"

That was Madred's voice, highly offended. The force of the words brought Nagaro's head up in time to see that Varsyl had risen and was standing in the gallery.

"My Lords! I can shed some light on this." Varsyl raised his voice to be heard over the murmurs that had arisen in the hall and all eyes were immediately turned to him. "I never had occasion to meet Leyel during the years before he came to Lankura, and I wasn't in the habit of spending time in the capital, as you know. But I tell you this: Nagaro convinced me more than a year ago that he was both the child my sister raised, and the youth who was brought to Lankura to wed the princess."

There were fresh protests from the three lords of the Kelorin Faction at this, but Varsyl waved them down. "Believe me," he said. "I, too, found it hard to credit, and I asked him to explain. He found it so painful he could scarcely speak of it, but he told me he had been drugged—"

"*Drugged?*"

The room echoed with a clamor of voices, among which, Soren cried, "What manner of drug could do this?"

Rathdar demanded, "Who would have done such a thing?"

Odus was on his feet. "I have all possible respect for Lord Varsyl, but this a ridiculous explanation—"

Madred remained in his seat, but made a gesture of frustration. "There surely is no such drug!"

Nagaro felt as much as heard the barrage of voices. They seemed to beat upon him, and he raised his hands to his head, vaguely aware that men were standing up, even in the galleries.

Drugged. Varsyl had spoken the word that explained everything, and still no one believed it! How could he possibly persuade them, except by providing the unspeakable details? And even then— after he had bared himself— they still might not believe it! There was only one man who could put a stop to this...

Nagaro's eyes sought Elgurn, too late to catch the man's initial reaction to Varsyl's words. The king was sitting very still, leaning against the back of his carved chair. His face was pale and drawn, but his eyes were open now, his gaze abstracted as if focused on some distant vision.

Ignoring the confusion around him, Nagaro began to move toward the dais. He was certain the king must know the truth. *If the man would only acknowledge his claim, the other lords might accept it.* From the corner of his eye, he saw Anduar start to move as if to stop him, then apparently check himself.

Abruptly Madred was blocking his path.

"Stand, a moment, Captain!" The Leithian lord pinned him with his patrician stare. "Let us put our man beside you and let all these folk compare—"

"Yes, yes. An excellent idea!" Odus had come around the table to stand with Madred. "Let's have them side by side. Torlung, bring your man over here!"

"But I don't want—" Nagaro began.

"Why not?" Odus demanded. "Because you know you'll get the worst of it?"

Nagaro mutely shook his head. He was curious about the false Leyel Virden, but he suspected the man was a genuine idiot— some simple-minded creature who had been manipulated into taking part in this pretense. He found the very idea of putting such a man on display offensive.

"My Lord Anduar!" Kuran raised his voice. "Is this how you wish the investigation to proceed?"

All eyes turned to Anduar who was leaning against the edge of a table and observing everything with keen interest. The Kelorin lord stroked his chin. "I think it might prove *instructive*... so, yes... But first I must ask you this, Captain. Do you affirm or deny Lord Varsyl's testimony?"

Nagaro swallowed. "What Varsyl said is true, My Lord. What I told him was true, as well."

Anduar raised a hand to silence protests from Madred and Odus. "Please, Gentlemen! There have been assertions and accusations made on both sides, and objections raised. There's no need to repeat it all again. Perhaps some of those who have spoken may be moved to change their claims when more is revealed. Will you proceed now, Minister Torlung?"

Torlung was standing in the opposite gallery looking insufferably smug. His well-oiled hair gleamed and his eyes glittered. At Anduar's directive, he smiled unctuously. "Certainly, My Lord. Whatever you wish." Turning to the hooded figure still seated beside him, he leaned down and spoke some words, low into the man's ear.

At last the hooded man moved. He rose to his feet and stepped out of the gallery, advancing a few steps and coming to a halt a dozen feet from where Nagaro, Odus, and Madred stood. His face was still shrouded by the heavy hood that he wore. His movements weren't stiff or jerky, but there was something wrong in the way he held his head too steadily facing forward, showing no apparent interest in anything or anyone in the room.

Torlung had followed his charge, and now issued an instruction that was plain for all to hear. "Put down your hood."

The man immediately raised both hands, grasped the hood on either side and pushed it back so that it fell to his shoulders. As he lowered his hands, his face was at last fully revealed to view.

For a moment Nagaro could only stare in astonishment at the handsome dark-haired man who stood before him. Then he started forward with a cry.

"Sindar!"

Chapter 23

To Prove A Point

It was unmistakably Sindar. Under the cloak he was wearing, which now hung open, he was dressed in clothing Nagaro didn't recognize. His face was freshly shaven. His hair had been allowed to grow until it hung nearly to his shoulders. He did not respond to Nagaro's cry, but remained as he had been, standing, gazing straight before him.

"Sindar?" Nagaro came to a halt in front of the statue-like figure. The face remained expressionless, the eyes focused at some indeterminate distance. "Please look at me!" Nagaro saw the head tilt slightly and the gray eyes come to a focus on his face, but that was all. "Don't you know me, Sindar? Why won't you speak?"

The lips moved then, producing speech that was fluent but flat, words spoken in monotone. "I do not understand."

For a moment Nagaro could only stand, frozen, while cold horror stole over him. Then the chill began to give way to the rising heat of anger. Through it, he was aware of Odus saying, "Captain? You claim to know this man?" And Madred saying, "He is surely mistaken."

"He is *not* mistaken," Kuran declared. "I know him also. He is Sindar Korinos, grandson of Burdal Korinos, a merchant who dwells in Vered Mahir. He disappeared some months ago while living in Lankura. We've been looking for him."

Tred spoke up from the gallery. "I know him too, My Lords— if ye'll pardon my speaking out of turn. And there has never been anything wrong with his mind before this."

Nagaro had been watching Torlung as Kuran spoke of Sindar's history. He had seen a hint of alarm in the Minister's eyes, before it was displaced by defiance, and the man's habitual unctuous smile returned.

Madred actually laughed, the easy, confident laugh of innocence. "Well there must be a close resemblance to another man," he said. "But you are all making a mistake nonetheless, as I will show you." The

Leithian lord gestured with an imperious flick of his wrist to Sindar. "Tell them who you are," he commanded.

"I am Leyel Virden." The words had the same flat inflection. There was scarcely a trace of Hashti accent in them. Sindar must have been schooled meticulously.

Torlung's oily smile broadened.

Nagaro clenched his fists.

"And tell us, did you marry the princess?" Madred continued his interrogation.

"Yes."

"And where did you live when you were married to her?"

"I lived in the palace."

"Why don't you live in the palace any more?"

"I ran away when bad men came. I got lost."

"There, you see?" Madred addressed the room in general "My Lords, surely it is time to end this—"

"*By the Eyes, it is not!*" Nagaro couldn't contain himself any longer. He could very well guess what agony Sindar must be feeling behind that drug-enforced facade, and he knew he couldn't rest until he'd put a stop to it. This imperative swept aside the issue of his own humiliation. *He knew how this was being done!* Furiously, he rounded on Torlung. "You crawling snake!" he raged. "I know exactly what you've done! This is heskial, isn't it? The same drug that was used on me! Of *course* he looks and acts as I did. *You've used the same damned, bloody drug!*"

He took a step towards the Minister and stopped, mastering himself by force of will before he actually did violence to the man. Instead he stood, seething with rage.

Torlung had blanched and backed away, but now he turned to Madred for support. "There's no truth to any of it, My Lord! It's a ruse— a desperate ploy! This man obviously wants the princess and the crown for himself and will stop at nothing to get them!"

Nagaro's jaw tightened. "I have no interest in the crown," he said through his teeth. "But I do wonder why *you* have gone to such lengths."

"Isn't it obvious?" Rathdar cried. "The Brothers of the Blood are desperate to keep Devral from winning the crown. They want to make sure he can't marry the princess!"

Nagaro turned urgently to Madred. "My Lord, I don't believe this is any of your doing. Minister Torlung has deceived you. But you can end this crime by ordering this man's release." He gestured at Sindar, who still stood woodenly where his feet had originally come to rest.

Madred was frowning. He looked from Nagaro to Torlung and back again. "But... the man is not a prisoner—"

"His will has been enslaved with heskial! Torlung has him in his power!"

"He is in Torlung's care— and the healer's. He needs medicine for his fits—"

"That *'medicine'* is heskial! The 'fits' are what happens when it starts to wear off! Nagaro drew a breath. He was shaking. Madred, as well as every other person in the room, was gaping at him, but there was more that needed to be said. He plunged on. "I tell you, this man is not an idiot! He understands every word we're saying. But he can't *move* of his own choosing! He can't *speak* for himself. He can do only what he is commanded to do, and say what he has been told to say. You can perhaps imagine what that's like, but *I know!* He is trapped! He is suffering! He will die a painful death if the heskial is withheld, but I may be able to save him if you'll let me try!"

Nagaro's voice had risen until it rang throughout the great room. In the stunned silence that followed, Anduar cleared his throat. "This is a serious charge," he said, addressing Lord Madred. "The use of heskial is forbidden in Jinara, where it is made, and it is not to be traded. Elgurn has approved a pact with the Jinari High Council to that effect, and this information was circulated to all the lords of Edrovir."

Madred ran a hand distractedly through his fastidious blond hair, leaving it rather less fastidious. "I do remember something about that," he muttered. He turned his eyes to the Leithian healer who still sat in the right-hand gallery with his bag on his lap. "What can you tell us of this, Master Nildred?"

The healer fidgeted nervously with the clasp of his bag. "My Lord, I was hired to administer the medicine, only. Minister Torlung gives it to me, and I apply the bladder-thorn. The medicine stops the fits. I have no reason to believe it does anything else."

Madred shifted his gaze to Minister Torlung. "What have you to say, Minister? Do you deny this charge?"

Torlung managed a light laugh. "Of course I deny it, My Lord. It's ridiculous. Why, I had never even heard of this... this *heskial*... until today—"

"*Liar! Liar!*" In the gallery Master Fineas had leaped to his feet and bounced up and down in his outrage. "My Lord Anduar, I tell you he lies! This man dismissed me a year ago because I refused to procure him a quantity of heskial!"

The Sergeant-at-Arms promptly insisted that Fineas sit down and hold his peace, but everyone had heard the man and there were murmurs and exchanged glances among the three lords of the Kelorin Faction.

Odus spoke over the voices. "My Lord Anduar, I must point out that we've heard claims and counter-claims, but we've yet to see any positive proof, or even any substantial evidence. Captain Nagaro speaks very eloquently, and with great passion, but can he prove his extraordinary assertions?"

Anduar had returned to his chair and was lounging with his usual exaggerated ease. The careful neutrality of his expression was belied, however, by the intensity of his gaze. "The point is well taken," he said with studied mildness. "If you will all be seated again, My Lords, we will hear what the captain has to say in response."

Nagaro waited in trepidation as the lords took their seats. He had to prove his claim in order to save Sindar. But how could he do it? His eyes swept the doubting faces around him and returned to Sindar, who was still standing with a frozen countenance, vacantly staring eyes, and rigid stance. *This must be exactly how he himself had looked all those years ago...*

Feeling heartsick, he turned back to face the council members. "Will you at least let this poor man sit down, My Lords?"

"But we're not done with him," Odus protested. "We want him here, not in the gallery."

"Then let him have a chair. Standing frozen like that is torment!"

"He can move if he wishes—"

"*No he cannot!* Please, My Lord Anduar? A chair for him?"

Anduar waved a hand. "Very well. A chair."

Nagaro didn't wait for the Kelorin lord to finish speaking, but strode immediately to one of the tables. Picking up an unused chair, he returned with it and set it down beside the unmoving Sindar "Sindar," he said, "please sit down." Then he hastily added, "on this chair," as the memory of a particularly embarrassing incident replayed itself in his mind.

Without a word, or any change in facial expression, Sindar sat down on the chair.

Nagaro stood looking down at the drug-bound man, cudgeling his brain. "The proof you ask for is difficult, My Lords," he said at length. "The heskial binds his will absolutely, and he will have been told what to say... when to answer... when to keep silent. I'm going to try working with Hashti, which he understands and speaks fluently because he was born a slave in the Mahuk Baar."

Anduar raised an eyebrow. "Interesting. Proceed."

Nagaro addressed the seated man. "Sindar, please count to ten in Hashti."

Sindar's lips moved, producing a flat and predictable response. "I do not understand."

Nagaro frowned. He tried repeating the instruction in Hashti, but this time the result was stony silence. He shook his head in frustration. "He must have been instructed not to speak in Hashti and not to respond to it."

From the tail of his eye, Nagaro caught the Minister's look of triumph, and he had to suppress an impulse to go and strike the man. He cast about again for something else to try. At last an idea came to him. Leaning close to Sindar, he spoke low and fast to him in Hashti.

"Sindar, there is hope. I believe it is true that you will die without heskial, but I have something here." He fished out the little vial and displayed it briefly in his open palm before returning it to his pocket. "It is called linjana. It saved me years ago. I hope it can save you too, if you are strong."

He straightened and stepped back. Sindar remained as unmoving as before.

"What did you say to him?" Odus demanded suspiciously. "What was that in your hand?"

Nagaro explained. "I said before that I may be able to save him. I've just explained this to him in Hashti, which he understands better than the Common Speech. If we wait until the heskial begins to wear off and watch what he does, he will show his understanding by his actions."

"But how will he be able to do so?" Anduar inquired sharply. "You have said that he'll have a fit when the drug wears off, and that he'll die if the drug is withheld."

"Yes, that's true." Nagaro approached the table where Anduar sat. "What's being called a 'fit' is nothing more than the beginning of the torment of the drug's withdrawal. There is shaking... pain..." He shuddered at the recollection, but continued. "Withdrawal is fatal if allowed to continue for as little as an hour. Another dose of heskial will stop it— at the cost of perpetuating the enslavement. But, at the beginning of withdrawal, there will be a little time— before the shaking and the pain begin— when he'll be able to move, but not to speak. I just showed him a vial containing another drug, called linjana, that counters the effects of heskial— completely and permanently. So, when he can move, he will surely come to me seeking the linjana. All we have to do is wait—"

"But we can't afford to wait!" Odus had sat listening to Nagaro's explanation with mounting impatience. "There's an army about to arrive at our gates, and this has taken too long already!"

Anduar rapped on the table for silence. He turned to Nagaro, his eyes narrowed shrewdly. "My Lord Odus is unfortunately correct. But think a moment, Captain. If you can't prove that this man is *not* Leiyel Virden, can you prove that you *are?*"

Nagaro swallowed. If they wouldn't believe his witnesses, he could only prove he had been Leyel by giving them details from the time of his enslavement. It would mean an agony of embarrassment... *and it might not even work.* But if it was the only way to save Sindar, he had to try. He glanced again at Sindar's face, reminding himself of what was at stake. Then he faced Anduar and the council members squarely and said, "Ask me anything from... *that time.* Anything Leyel Virden ought to know."

And then of course he had to stand and wait, with anxiety twisting his stomach, as the four members of the Council huddled around Anduar's table discussing in low voices what questions they might use. Judging by the frustrated tone of their voices they were having difficulty agreeing on what to ask. His eyes wandered to the king in his chair on the dais. Elgurn seemed to have shrunk into himself; his eyes were still open, but their gaze seemed to be turned inward and his face was gray.

Was the man aware at all of what was happening? Had he heard a single word of it?

"My Lords, I have it!" Vell suddenly sprang to his feet in the gallery. "A way to test them both! Give me leave and I'll explain."

The council members raised their heads. Anduar spoke, and it was clear from his expression how little progress the group had made. "You may as well, My Lord Vell," he said sourly, "since we're at an impasse here." He silenced protests from Theren and Madred with a perfunctory gesture, and beckoned Vell to join the group at the table.

The discussion then resumed, but apparently with better effect since Anduar presently rapped on the table for attention and stood up. "Gentlemen— and Zirdyn," he said with a slight bow that encompassed all those assembled. "We are reminded that Leyel Virden should bear a scar on the right side of his head, above the temple."

Nagaro felt an immediate flood of relief. This was so easy that he actually laughed. "Do you wish to see it?" He raised a hand to lift the hair from his right temple.

The council members came crowding around him, poking with their fingers and peering at his scalp When they'd finished with him, they subjected Sindar to the same scrutiny. During the whole process, Nagaro observed that Torlung was shifting from foot to foot, frowning, and glancing questioningly at Master Nildred. The healer returned only a blank look.

It was Odus who finally rendered the verdict.

"The evidence is inconclusive. Both men are marked. Torlung's man has two small scars on that side of his head, and our information isn't precise enough to rule either of them out. The captain, on the other hand, bears a single scar."

Nagaro sagged. *Sindar had scars as well?* He saw Torlung's frown transformed into a confident smirk. *Was no one else watching that man's face?* "My Lords, if I may speak— " he began, but Anduar cut him off.

"Indeed you may not, Captain. I wish to question the two healers who are present." Anduar turned to the left-hand gallery. "Tredhold Ferth, I believe you have been Captain Nagaro's personal physician?"

Tredhold rose and stood at attention. "Aye, My Lord. I've been ship's doctor under him since we first began the work of freeing galley slaves."

Anduar nodded an acknowledgment. "And have you taken note of the scar in question?"

"I have, My Lord."

"What can you tell us of it's origin?"

Treadhold shifted his feet. "My Lord, that injury dates from before the time I've had him in my care, so it must have occurred nine years ago or more."

"I see." Anduar's face was now carefully deadpan. "Now tell us, Zirda, in your professional opinion, what manner of injury would have produced it? Was it, for example, made by a blade?"

Tred immediately shook his head. "No, My Lord. It would have been a blow to the head by something only moderately sharp. It must have been a hard blow too. There's palpable scarring of the bone under the skin."

Anduar's eyes narrowed just perceptibly. "Could this blow have produced unconsciousness?"

"I would say it's likely, My Lord. Though I can't be certain."

"Thank you, Zirda. You may sit down." There was no hint of a smile as Anduar turned to the other healer in the room. "Master Nildred, have you had occasion to examine the two scars on the right side of your patient's head?"

Nildred rose to his feet. "I had noticed them, My Lord, but he has a great many scars."

"What can you say, professionally, about these two?"

Nildred glanced at Torlung, whose face was impassive except for a nervous twitch about the mouth. Nildred licked his lips and plunged on. "They're the result of cuts or deep scratches, My Lord. Something... er... broke the skin."

"Can you tell us how he received these injuries?"

"I... ah... no, My Lord. I questioned him, but he said that he didn't understand. Considering his... er... condition, I thought perhaps he didn't remember."

"I see." Anduar's voice and face remained, scrupulously neutral. "Could either of them have produced unconsciousness?"

Nildred consulted the ceiling. "With respect to the one on the right cheekbone, I doubt it, My Lord."

"And the other? The one under the hair on the right side of his forehead?"

Nildred glanced again at Torlung, who moved his shoulders in what might have been a shrug. "It's... ah... possible," the healer ventured. "I can't be sure."

"Very well." Anduar spoke coolly, as before, but there was a hint of frustration in his eyes. "Thank you, Zirda. You may sit down."

Master Nildred did so, looking relieved.

"So." Anduar lounged back in his chair. "We have the medical opinions, and the situation remains ambiguous. Therefore, I must ask the captain one more question." His steely gaze swung to Nagaro. "Will you please tell us, Zirda, how you came by your scar?"

Nagaro closed his eyes. *It had come down to details after all.*

He felt a hand grip his shoulder yet again, and Kuran spoke close to his ear. "Just tell them what happened, Nagaro. The truth can't harm you, and it may save Sindar."

Nagaro sighed. He had to do this. He opened his eyes, swallowed, and began to speak. He couldn't, however, bring himself to watch Anduar's face. Instead he focused on the wall above the dais— and tried to imagine that he was telling his story to the empty air.

"It happened on the day of the Festival of the Harvest Moon..."

Haltingly, he explained the effects of heskial, of the deep trance state, and the lighter trance that followed it. Of how Dreigen had brought him out at the very end of the deep trance that day, before his protective reflexes had returned...

"...so when someone in the crowd outside the Great Hall stuck out his foot to trip me, I... didn't automatically put my hands out to catch myself. I... I fell like a... a piece of wood... and struck my head on the edge of a little table that used to stand by the door. I was knocked unconscious. I suppose that they... they must have carried me away... since I woke up in the little room where they kept me on the third floor. They brought in a healer who said he thought I had cracked my skull—"

"Oh Nagaro, *I'm sorry!*" Vell had been sitting in a chair at the table where Odus and Madred sat, but he now sprang up, his features contorted in anguish. "It was my foot! *I* tripped you! An unworthy act— I don't play tricks like that anymore—"

Anduar rapped on the table. "Please restrain yourself, My Lord Vell. And thank you, Captain. You have accurately described the event. The weight of evidence increasingly favors your claim—"

"He might have heard an account of the incident," Odus pointed out. "It was much spoken of at the time."

Anduar looked dour. "That is true," he conceded."

"Am I allowed to ask a question?" Madred demanded. "Since the other claim— the one you seem bent on refuting— is the one I've put forward? — under assurances from a man I have trusted." The last words were accompanied by a piercing glance leveled at a stone-faced Minister Torlung.

"By all means, My Lord." Anduar was magnanimous.

Madred swung to face Nagaro. "I notice that you have avoided giving the names to those behind this alleged scheme, Captain," he said pointedly. "We know that it was Dreigen who administered the medicine you claim was a drug. Are we to believe that the Lore Master perpetrated this entire crime on his own?"

Nagaro hesitated, and his eyes leaped to the figure of the king seated on the dais. Elgurn's eyes were open and their gaze was riveted on him. There was a strange light in those eyes, though the king's face was still pale, and he still showed no inclination to speak.

Nagaro swallowed to moisten a throat that had gone very dry. He returned his gaze to Lord Madred. "No, My Lord," he began. "The original plan was to use the drug on the Lady Maramine... to control me through her. Dreigen conceived that plan— I believe— and proposed it to Elgurn— who approved it." He heard shocked murmurs in response to this revelation, and raised his own voice to be heard over them. "Elgurn chose three men to carry out the plan— they were Bron Sobring, Kale Fendred, and Gilard Marchent."

The murmur rose in volume and he could make out some of the words.

"*They're dead.*"

"*All dead.*"

"*How convenient...*"

He plunged on, though he spoke with increasing difficulty.

"That plan failed. It... it didn't convince me of anything— except that something very bad was being done to Maramine. Bron decided, then... to... to use the... heskial... on me. Elgurn approved that too— *after* he learned that it was already being done. But to be fair—"

At this point, he had to stop because his throat was tight, and the clamor of other voices had risen to such a level that he couldn't be heard in any case. He stood with his head bowed under that wash of sound.

He heard Anduar and Odus both call loudly for silence. The request was echoed repeatedly by the Sergeant-at-Arms until at last a degree of quiet was restored, by which time, Nagaro had collected himself enough to finish what he meant to say.

"To be fair," he continued. "I believe that both Bron and Elgurn intended the use of... of the drug... to be temporary. Dreigen didn't tell them about the... fatal dependence— until it was too late. And he never said anything about linjana— which is why Elgurn has long believed me to be dead."

He ceased speaking, and stood waiting. The stunned hush of the room settled like a weight on his shoulders.

Anduar rose to his feet. "Thank you, Captain," he said gravely. "I appreciate that you didn't find that easy." At last, he turned to face the dais, where the king sat pale and silent, staring fixedly before him. "My Lord Elgurn, will you speak regarding the truth or falsehood of this testimony?"

Elgurn didn't initially stir or flinch. His face registered deep pain, mingled with something else— was it dread?

It was a fateful moment. Nagaro realized that he was holding his breath. *What would the man say?* For a moment, he feared that the king wouldn't speak— that he might be beyond speech— that the shock had overthrown his mind. But then, finally, Elgurn's lips moved, producing words in a husky voice that was widely audible only because the room was so silent.

"It is the truth," he said, dropping the words like stones. "All of it."

Anduar raised his hands to still the outcry that followed this stunning admission. He had his eyes on Elgurn as if waiting to see if the king would offer some further explanation. But Elgurn remained silent. His gaze was turned in Nagaro's direction, but it seemed to be focused far away. The silence of the Audience Chamber was so nearly complete that Nagaro could hear his own heartbeat in his ears.

After what seemed an age, but was surely only seconds, Elgurn stirred, and rose unsteadily to his feet. He swayed a little, as if his legs would barely carry him, but then he began to move— slowly and purposefully— down the steps from the dais to the marble floor of the Audience Chamber, and across that floor towards the place where Nagaro stood. He moved like a sleepwalker.

"My Lord?" Anduar took a step as if to intercept the king, but then stopped, frowning, as if something in the king's demeanor gave him pause.

Elgurn didn't appear to have heard the Kelorin lord. He continued to walk, trance-like, his eyes fixed on Nagaro. He passed between the tables in front of the dais, passed the chair where Sindar's figure sat mute and motionless. The soft tap of the king's boots on the smooth marble was the only sound to be heard as everyone else in the room waited to see what Elgurn would do.

The king came to a halt, at last, two paces from where Nagaro stood. His right hand moved to his sword hilt.

"By the Eyes, what's this?" Kuran exclaimed. The Lord of the Fleet had moved to stand protectively at Nagaro's side. At the movement of the king's hand, he started to reach for his own blade.

"No." Nagaro gestured for Kuran to stay his hand. He'd been watching the king's advance with mingled wariness and hope. His own gaze was locked on Elgurn's, and while he couldn't decipher all that was written in the king's eyes, he didn't see murder there.

Elgurn gave no sign that he was aware of what had just passed. His hand closed on his sword hilt and he drew the blade, sweeping it out and holding it with the tip directed at the floor. Then, at last, he spoke again, directly to Nagaro, in a voice that was clear for all to hear in the silent room.

"I have wronged you, Alorin Loros, heir of Darion who was my king. The Gods know what harm I've done in my arrogance and folly. I, who should have protected you, brought you instead very nearly to your death. My life is now forfeit for my crimes— together with my sword, my lands, and all that is mine."

As he ceased speaking, Elgurn dropped to his knees on the marble floor. Bowing his head and taking his sword in both hands, he held it up, presenting the hilt to Nagaro with hands that shook.

Gasps of dismay were audible from every side.

Nagaro stared at the king in utter astonishment. He'd hoped for words of contrition, but nothing in his experience of the man had prepared him for *this*. He was aware of muttered voices around him: "*It's the Law... the Old Law... Leithian Law...*" but he couldn't grasp their meaning. All he knew was that the King of Edrovir was on his knees in front of him apparently asking to be slain with his own sword!

"Get up, Elgurn," he said. "Please. I don't want this."

The king raised eyes of agony. "You must!" he croaked. "The Gods demand the price be paid! Only I beg you to be merciful and swift."

Nagaro swallowed. "No. I won't do this."

Elgurn shut his eyes. "*I beg you! Please!*"

Nagaro backed up a step, shaking his head. "There was a time when I would gladly have put a knife in your belly, Elgurn, but that time is past. I think I know the depth and the limits of your guilt. I know you've suffered for what you did— these past ten years."

A look of utter despair had begun to contort the king's features, but at Nagaro's last words his eyes sprang open and there was a glimmer in them of something that hadn't been there during all the time since Nagaro had entered the Audience Chamber.

"Then, will you... can you possibly... *forgive?*" The king's voice shook with emotion.

Nagaro's frown lifted. "Is *that* what you want? Then, yes, I forgive you. Now will you please get up?"

For a moment it seemed as if Elgurn might collapse in a faint. His eyes rolled upward in his head as what little blood there was in his face drained away. He uttered a groan that was more than half a sob, and his sword dropped from his hands, ringing loudly as it struck the marble floor. For the space of several heartbeats he remained so, swaying a little, on his knees. Then he staggered to his feet. Turning away from Nagaro, he moved with his head down and a hand over his eyes as he blundered off in the direction of the dais.

Odus had risen, and he now moved quickly to take the king's elbow, guiding him to a seat on the edge of the raised platform. There Elgurn sank down, covering his face with his hands as his shoulders shook with silent sobs.

Chapter 24

Linjana

Nagaro looked after the king's departing figure in dismay, then down at the sword that lay at his feet. "What's the matter?" he wondered aloud. "What have I done now?"

Theren and Madred had also both risen, and it was Madred who approached Nagaro, bowing deferentially as he sought to answer him.

"You don't understand, My Lord, because you're not a Leithian. He'd prepared himself to pay the price of penance demanded by the Gods, but you refused to take his life. It seemed at first that you meant to punish him by leaving him alive to suffer with the curse of his guilt. But *then* you wiped the curse away when you forgave him. You have both spared his life *and* saved his soul from Hel. He doesn't weep for sorrow or pain, I assure you."

"Oh. Good." Nagaro was so relieved that he failed to notice the title Madred had bestowed upon him. "He doesn't still mean me to take that, does he?" He gestured at the fallen sword.

"Perhaps. But if you let it lie, he'll have the choice to take it up again. I know him a little, and I think he will. I must say that you've impressed me. They say it takes a great man to forgive a great wrong."

Nagaro shook his head. "It's only Vothrin teaching, to forgive. But I thought Leithians were more fond of vengeance."

Madred sighed. "That's only to say how few of us qualify as great men, I suppose. Revenge, after all, is sweet."

Before Nagaro could say anything to this, they were interrupted by one of the guards.

"My Lords, the goldsmith has finished with his study. Do ye wish to hear what he has to say?" The guard had apparently just returned to the Audience Chamber with the goldsmith and the clerk in tow.

Anduar had been deep in conversation with Theren and Odus, but he immediately waved the other two lords to their seats. "Yes, by all means, but please be brief," he said smoothly as he seated himself.

Madred respectfully inclined his head to Nagaro and sought his seat as well.

The goldsmith stood up straight. "To be *brief*," he said, "The ring on the silver chain is the original— the one that was used to make the wax seals on the documents dated from Darion's time. The one on the leather cord is a copy of the first."

"You're quite sure of this?" Anduar asked, his eyes steely.

"Yes, My Lord."

"And how could such a copy have been made?" inquired Odus. "Could it be done without having possession of the original?"

"Oh, easily, My Lord. It's a casting, you see, as is evident from fact that the design on the face of it is less crisply cut. It could have been made from a wax impression of the original, such as—"

"—such as would be found on any document to which Darion had set his seal." Anduar finished the explanation. "Thank you, Zirda, for your service. That will be all." He paused just long enough for the goldsmith to be escorted away, then said, "And I think it's time we obtained a more accurate account from Minister Torlung—"

Anduar turned in his chair, seeking the man he'd just named, only to find that Torlung was no longer where he had been left standing. The minister must have been quietly edging away, and at the mention of his name, he turned and bolted for the chamber's back door, in the corner of the room beyond the right-hand end of the dais.

"Stop that man!" Anduar was on his feet pointing at the fleeing figure. "Stop Minister Torlung! Don't let him escape!"

Several people started to move in response to the command, but the one who moved fastest was Sindar. The young Kelorin lunged out of his chair so violently that it fell with a clatter. He raced after Torlung, his cloak flying behind him, and overtook the man half a dozen feet short of the door. There, without the slightest hesitation, he tackled the minister, bearing him to the ground underneath him with a bone-jarring thud.

"Well done, Zirda!" cried the Sergeant-at-Arms, who was the first of the guards to reach the two fallen men. "Ye can let him up, now. We'll take charge of him."

Sindar made no response, but remained on top of his quarry, his hands griping the minister's shoulders like a pair of talons. Under him, Torlung was making feeble gasping sounds.

"Here, now," protested Odus, who had arrived, with Nagaro, Vell, and Theren close behind. "There's no need to crush the man! Didn't you hear the Sergeant?"

Nagaro knelt down beside the fallen pair, leaning over to get a look at Sindar's blankly staring face. "It's the heskial, My Lord, " he said, straightening. "He must be commanded clearly in words he can understand. He couldn't help responding to Anduar's command because no one had instructed him not to— though I'm sure he's rejoicing inside right now at the outcome."

Bending down again, he said, "Let go of the man's shoulders, Sindar."

Sindar's fingers immediately flew open.

"Now get off of him and stand up. And don't worry. The guards will take him."

Sindar obeyed, rolling off of Torlung, then gathering himself and rising to his feet.

The guards promptly closed in around the minister. Nagaro left them to their work. He stepped close to Sindar, searching the man's eyes in vain for the tiniest spark of self-awareness. *If only the drug would begin to wear off.* He didn't want to do as Nevien had done and take Sindar's life into his hands without some indication of agreement from the man himself.

"Come with me back to the gallery, and sit down, Sindar," he said. "I hope I will be able to help you soon." He then accompanied the drugged man and directed him to sit in the front row of the right-hand gallery, not as close to Nildred's seat as he'd been before.

Nagaro stood for a moment, then, torn between wishing to watch over Sindar and his desire to participate in the questioning of Torlung. His indecision was resolved when Vell returned to take his former seat in the gallery.

He turned to the Leithian. "Would you do a favor for me, Vell? Will you keep watch over Sindar and call me if he begins to move?"

Vell's face brightened. "Of course I will! Be glad to."

"Thank you."

Nagaro turned, brushing past Nildred.

The nervous healer reached out to tug at his sleeve. "Please believe me, Zirda!" he quavered. "I had no knowledge of this... this *infamy*. They told me it was medicine!"

Nagaro gave the man a stern look. "Just see that you tell the truth if you're asked any questions," he said, and left the man to take any comfort he could from those words.

The guards had escorted Torlung back to the area in front of the dais, where he'd been placed on the chair vacated by Sindar. He was flanked by two guards and was being interrogated by the council members from their seats at the tables. The minister had apparently bloodied his nose in the fall, besides having had the wind knocked out of him. He appeared visibly shaken as he sat, miserably pressing a bloody handkerchief to his face.

Nagaro returned to stand beside Kuran as Anduar was addressing the seated man.

"I suggest you tell us the truth now, Zirda. The Captain— or I should say Lord Alorin, since the king has so named him— has proven his identity to my satisfaction. The goldsmith's testimony further confirms the deception you've had a hand in perpetrating, and your attempt at flight bespeaks your guilt. What, if anything, can you say for yourself?"

Torlung emitted a groan. "It was Grimbold Sobring's doing, My Lord," he whined. "It was *his* plan! He had the false ring made. He secured the heskial. He bargained with Dreigen for instructions on how to use it!"

Nagaro spoke up. "And who kidnaped poor Sindar? Who held him and drugged him?"

"Kidnaped? Oh now, that's such a harsh word..." Some of Torlung's oiliness returned. "The man's a commoner. We found him working in a stable, shoveling manure for his board and a few rins. We offered him easier work... better pay—"

Nagaro exploded. "*Work!* You call it *work?* And *pay?* What use would money be to him when he has no will of his own? You tricked him! You enslaved him!" Nagaro started forward, but Kuran restrained him by grasping his arm and murmuring, "Easy, lad."

Nagaro remembered something else. "And don't try to claim you had no hand in drugging him! I saw you exchanging packets with Dreigen at festival time in the Great Hall."

Torlung cowered away from him. "Mercy, My Lords! Don't let him hurt me," he cried, rolling his eyes. "I was only the go-between! I tell you, it was Grimbold's plan!"

"And where is Grimbold then?" Odus demanded coldly. "I don't see him here. I see only you."

"He's out riding with Lothard Hurn— as you well know!" Torlung's anger flared, but an instant later he choked it down and assumed a deprecating tone. "It fell to me to make the presentation. But the plan was Grimbold's!"

"And what was the purpose of this plan?" Anduar had been following the exchange with narrowed eyes. "Was it, as Theren has suggested, to ensure that the princess couldn't be wedded to Devral?"

"Of course, My Lord!" Torlung dabbed at his nose and smiled ingratiatingly. "Not just to Devral, either, but to any of Lothard's rivals. Grimbold and Lothard planned it, together. They knew Elgurn would never give his daughter to Lothard."

"That makes sense—" Odus began.

"But why *you*, Torlung?" Madred spoke for the first time, genuine sorrow in his voice. He leaned forward in his chair, searching the minister's face. "Grimbold sees his best chance for power through Lothard, I understand that. And they hope together to force the old ways on everyone, Leithian and Kelorin alike. But surely you can see that this is folly? There isn't enough force in this land to effect so unpopular a change. Were you blinded by your love for the old ways? Or did you hope for more power than what you've had from me?"

"Oh, My Lord!" Torlung nearly dropped his handkerchief. "I did it for *you!* I let them believe I supported Lothard's ambitions, but seeing the princess married to a harmless idiot would clear the way for *you* as well— since you already have a wife. *I did it for you!* You should be king— not that swaggering fool from Hurn! You should wear the crown for the honor and glory of the House of Furthing!"

Madred's face had been growing redder as he listened, and now, as the man ceased speaking, he rose angrily from his seat and leveled an accusing finger at the minister. "How *dare* you speak of the honor of the House of Furthing!" he thundered. "When you've sullied it with these dishonorable deeds!"

Torlung cowered in his chair. "Oh, My Lord! Mercy! Mercy!"

"You dare to beg for mercy? When you've made me your unwitting accomplice?"

"*Oh, My Lord—*"

"Nagaro! He's moving!" Vell's sudden cry cut short the escalating confrontation.

All eyes turned to Sindar. The drugged man was on his feet, crossing the floor towards Nagaro with unsteady steps. His movements had a jerky quality, as if he were having to overcome some kind of resistance.

Nagaro ran to the man and gripped him by the shoulders, steadying him. "Sindar, do you want to try the linjana?"

Sindar nodded with a frantic jerking of his head. He clasped his hands together in a gesture of supplication. His jaw worked as if he were trying to speak, and there was a silent plea in his eyes.

Nagaro looked straight into those eyes. "The battle between the two drugs will make you very sick," he said earnestly. "There's a chance it could kill you. Do you still want to do this?"

There was more frantic nodding.

Nagaro's mind began to race. He had imagined, in general terms, what to do if Sindar's dose of heskial began to wear off, but now that it was happening, he realized he didn't know how the linjana would behave in the veins of someone already undergoing withdrawal. He'd been given the linjana by mouth, while in the light trance state. Would it work fast enough for Sindar if given that way? He knew it worked faster if administered by bladder-thorn than by mouth... and was more potent that way. But being more potent, would it be more likely to kill a man who was already in a weakened state?

He let go of Sindar and dug the vial out of his pocket. As soon as Sindar saw the vial, he tried to reach for it with trembling hands.

"No, Sindar! Wait!" Nagaro looked all around frantically for the Sergeant-at-Arms. "We should send to the kitchen for a cup of water to put it in. There's such a small amount in the vial. If you were to spill it—"

Sindar's hands continued to clutch at him. The young man's eyes continued their pleading. The Sergeant-at-Arms was nowhere in sight. Instead, Nagaro found Nildred in front of him, rummaging in his healer's satchel.

"I have a dose of the medi— That is, of the... the *drug*, here, Zirda," the plump Leithian ventured eagerly. "That would quiet him so you could have time to—"

Sindar rounded on the man and aimed a blow at him that failed to connect only because the normally agile young Kelorin didn't have complete control over his limbs.

Nildred paled and jumped back. "I... I guess not, then."

Nagaro moved to interpose himself between the two men and extended his free hand to Nildred. "Have you a bladder-thorn I could use?" he asked. The healer's suggestion would indeed buy them time, but Sindar clearly didn't want more helkial.

"Oh yes, Zirda!" Nildred appeared ecstatic at the chance to help in any way. He rummaged in his bag again and produced the requested object.

Nagaro managed to take the bladder-thorn without flinching. Once he held it in his hand, however, he felt a wave of something almost like nausea as memories flooded him.

Sindar's reaction was completely different. The former slave took one look at the bladder-thorn and flung himself down on the floor. Rolling onto his back, he looked up at Nagaro beseechingly as he tugged frantically at his left sleeve, clearly trying to bare his forearm for the thorn.

Nagaro stood looking down at the man, the vial in one hand, the bladder-thorn in the other. He realized he was sweating, and there was a weight like a stone in his stomach. He knew what needed to be done but he wasn't sure he could do it.

"Here, Nagaro, let me."

Nagaro started at the sound of Tredhold's voice by his ear. The small, sandy-haired ship's doctor was standing beside him, reaching for the bladder-thorn.

Nagaro was suddenly aware that almost everyone else in the room had gathered around them. Kuran was on one side of him, Anduar on the other. The nominal head of the Council appeared to have momentarily given up trying to restore order in the face of the drama that was unfolding. The other council members were arrayed on one side of Sindar's supine form, with Soren, Rathdar, and Vell on the other.

Chula, Fendar, and Varsil were behind the lords, craning their necks to see, completing the ring of faces staring down at the stricken man. Boka knelt at Sindar's head, gazing at him with silent sympathy.

"Let me do it, Nagaro." Tred reiterated, his hand still outstretched, reaching for the bladder-thorn.

"No." Nagaro tightened his fingers. "I should be the one. I've seen it done."

"You know that isn't the same, Nagaro." Tred withdrew his hand. He spoke calmly, focusing on persuasion. "It takes practice and steadiness. You've proven enough things for one day. You don't need to prove that you can do this."

"I know that!" Nagaro's stomach felt like lead. "But it should be my responsibility! If he should die, I don't want you to have that on your conscience—"

"Then order me to do it, and it *will* be your responsibility. You're still my captain." Tred had moved to stand directly in front of Nagaro and was gazing earnestly into his face. He extended his hands again, the palms held open.

Sindar at this point emitted a strangled moan and clutched Nagaro's booted ankle with his left hand. Boka reached out and took the suffering man's head in her hands. "Peace, friend," she crooned. "The linjana will save ye."

Nagaro looked down at the drugged man's contorted face. Sindar's legs were starting to twitch. He swallowed, knowing what the man was going through, and made two decisions.

"You're right, Tred," he said, pressing the vial and the bladder-thorn into the healer's open hands. He instantly felt the weight leave his stomach as he did so. He drew a shuddering breath. "I order you to administer a dose of linjana to Sindar. Use half the contents of the vial."

Tred nodded decisively. Motioning for the crowd to step back, he knelt by Sindar's left side. "Half the contents..." he murmured. Reaching with the hand holding the vial, he teased a folded handkerchief from his pocket and dropped it on the floor. He then laid down the bladder-thorn on the handkerchief and deftly broke the wax seal on the vial.

Nagaro knelt down as well, prying the fingers of Sindar's left hand as gently as he could from his ankle. He stretched the man's arm out and finished rolling up the sleeve before pinning Sindar's arm firmly against the floor. He could feel the spasms in the muscles under his fingers, and by this time, Sindar's legs were also jerking spasmodically.

"What can I do?" The voice belonged to Master Fineas.

Nagaro looked up and twisted around to find that the lore master was standing behind him, looking pale but determined. "Hold his other hand." Nagaro gestured with his head. "Let him grip you as hard as he needs to."

Fineas nodded and circled Sindar's body, the crowd moving back to allow his passage. Kneeling, the lore master took the man's twitching right hand in both of his.

"I'll hold his legs." Kuran shouldered his way towards Sindar's feet and dropped into position, grasping Sindar's ankles. He frowned up at the crowd. "Please, everyone, give us some air—"

Abruptly one of the guards who had been watching Torlung gave a shout. "Stop him! He's running away again!"

There was a clatter of running feet, and shouts rose from the gathered onlookers, some of whom broke away to join the pursuit. Nagaro glanced up long enough to get a glimpse of Minister Torlung dashing away down the length of the Audience Chamber towards double doors with several guards on his heels, as well as lords Varsil, Vell, and Rathdar. He fervently hoped they would catch the man, but that was all he could do. Sindar needed him. He gave his attention back to Tred, who had inserted the needle of the bladder-thorn into the vial and was preparing to draw up some of the liquid.

Anduar cleared his throat. "How fortunate that you happened to have that with you," he remarked. "You couldn't have known you would have a chance to make this demonstration."

Nagaro answered without looking up. "I had a different patient in mind. I meant it for Kale."

"Kale? Kale Fendred? Don't you know the man's dead?"

Before Nagaro could answer, another voice spoke. One that made him look up in astonishment.

"Kale is not dead."

Elgurn had approached unnoticed and the crowd now parted before him.

The king's recovery was remarkable. His face had regained its color and he carried himself with his accustomed self-assurance. There was a grimness in his tone as he continued, however, and a hungry gleam in his eyes. "Kale is alive and dwelling within these walls, but he's quite mad— a madness that is Dreigen's doing!"

"Kale lives?" Anduar looked frowningly from Elgurn to Nagaro. "And you *both* knew this?"

"I... ah... discovered it by accident—" Nagaro began, uncertainly glancing from Anduar to Elgurn.

The king's burning eyes had not left Nagaro's face, and he ignored Anduar's question as he asked, "This... *linjana*... is what saved you, Lord Alorin?"

"Ah... yes." Nagaro still found the title jarring, especially coming from Elgurn, but he knew he had better get used to it.

"And are you sure it can restore Kale's mind?"

Nagaro was struggling to hold Sindar's arm still, a task that was becoming more difficult as the man's shaking grew worse. "I've been told that it should," he answered through gritted teeth. "It was Master Fineas, here, who told me so." He indicated the lore master with a jerk of his head.

Elgurn's avid gaze immediately transferred to Fineas. "Is it true, Lore Master?"

Fineas was also grimacing, in his case from the strength of Sindar's grip on his hand. His glasses had slipped so far down his nose that they were in danger of sliding off. Nevertheless he answered with his usual verbosity. "It should, according to everything I have read on the subject, My Lord. There are no fewer than three reputable sources, all of which state that linjana is possessed of potent spirit magic and that its healing power is specific to afflictions of the mind— such as madness."

"These sources... are they *obscure?*" The heat of Elgurn's stare could have ignited parchment.

Fineas blinked owlishly over his spectacles. "Oh, hardly obscure, My Lord. Any lore master worth his wages should know at least one of the them."

"*That bastard!*"

This time Fineas flinched at the forcefulness of the utterance, but Elgurn wasn't speaking to him— wasn't even looking at him. His ire was aimed at someone who wasn't in the room.

"That lying *filth!* That treacherous, murdering snake!" Elgurn was all but spitting with rage. "He told me there was no cure for heskial! Why have I ever believed one word that came out of that man's mouth? The only truth he's ever spoken was when he promised to do harm. He's a murderer four times over! The evidence is in his journals— my daughter has read them! Now, by the Gods, I've had enough!" Elgurn brandished a clenched fist. "Today I am reborn, and I shall have justice!"

With that, the king turned and started away in the direction of the back door of the Audience Chamber.

"My Lord! Wait!" Odus hurried after him. "What do you mean to do?"

Elgurn paused to fling a response over his shoulder. "Roust the snake from his hole, arrest him, and throw him in the dungeon to be properly tried and hanged!"

Nagaro, still on his knees beside Sindar, cried out in dismay. "Elgurn! He's very dangerous!"

"That's true, My Lord!" Madred agreed. "He *is* very dangerous. You shouldn't face him alone."

Elgurn laughed. "Let anyone join me, then, who will." He took two steps to the side to scoop up his sword from the floor, straightened, and strode on.

Anduar instantly barked orders. "Odus, Therin, go after him! Madred, you stay here with me to see this through— this that you had a hand in. Sergeant, alert the guards!"

The crowd around Sindar was further diminished as Odus and Theren hurried after the king. Soren cried, "Wait for me!" and went after them at an old man's hobbling run.

Tredhold had by this time drawn the dose of linjana into the bladder-thorn and was in the act of bending over his patient's forearm, selecting his injection site. Nagaro tore his mind away from the harrowing mental image of Elgurn confronting Dreigen and leaned down to speak into Sindar's ear.

"There will be a bright light in your head, Sindar, and after that everything will be different. You may not remember much of it later. I expect you will be very sick for several days."

Sindar had squeezed his eyes tight shut. He was clenching his teeth and breathing in gasps as he clutched Fineas' hand with all his might. A whimper escaped him, but he managed to nod once.

Nagaro forced himself to watch as Tred's skillful fingers pushed the tip of the slender, hollow thorn through the skin and slipped the shaft of the thorn into a vein, then compressed the bladder to inject its contents.

There was no immediate sign that Sindar had felt the thorn-prick. In the full grip of the pain of heskial withdrawal, the young Kelorin was already twisting in the hands of those who held him and moaning behind gritted teeth. Sweat beaded his forehead.

Tred withdrew the bladder-thorn and stood up, stepping away from his patient. Nagaro shifted his grasp, taking Sindar's left hand in his and instantly finding his fingers crushed by the sufferer's desperate grip.

There passed the space of half a dozen heartbeats while the onlookers murmured questions that Nagaro made no effort to answer.

Then, without warning, Sindar screamed.

It was a heart-wrenching sound of mingled shock and pain. Nagaro found his hand released as the young man rolled onto his side and curled himself into a ball, clutching his head with both hands. Kuran released his hold and leaped away. Fineas nearly fell over backward. Several of those watching cried out in alarm and backed away.

Boka lost her hold on Sindar's head when he moved, but quickly reached out to place one of her strong, brown hands on his brow. Leaning low over him, she began murmuring words in the Turowan tongue, over and over.

Nagaro was on his knees, bending over the huddled man. All he could think of was that something had gone wrong. "Sindar!" he cried. "Are you all right?"

Even as he spoke, however, Sindar abruptly relaxed. The former slave took his hands from his head, uncurled his body, and rolled onto his back. For a moment he stared, wide-eyed and blinking. Then he laughed aloud and scrambled to his feet.

He caught the startled Nagaro, who had also risen, in a crushing embrace. "*Daashu!*" he cried. "*Daashu daashu daashu!*" He set Nagaro free and turned on Tred, who had failed to back away fast enough to avoid a similar embrace. Then he bounded away, gesticulating wildly, as a torrent of excited syllables spilled from his lips. The onlookers parted before him, murmuring their surprise and dismay.

"I assume that's Hashti that he's speaking?" It was Anduar who made the inquiry.

Nagaro turned to find the Kelorin lord standing beside him. "Yes, it is."

"What is he saying?" Master Fineas asked.

"I can't make out more than one word in seven, but it's safe to say that he's pleased. And we must go after him to make sure he doesn't do anything too daft."

"Too daft?" Tred cocked his head. "What do you mean?"

Nagaro winced. "This is a kind of... manic phase. I'm... ah... told that I tried to take on two seasoned sea-raiders with a ceremonial sword from the wall in the library."

Anduar raised an eyebrow. "I would have liked to have seen that."

Nagaro colored. "I... don't remember any of it." He turned back to Tred and Fineas. "The manic phase will pass into a fever in an hour or two. We should find him a room with a bed where he can spend the next several days—"

"Yes, by all means," Anduar interrupted. "Kuran, would you please see to it? You may inform the Chamberlain that you are acting on my authority."

Kuran bowed. "As you wish, My Lord," he said. He gave Nagaro a wink before beckoning to Tred and Fineas and striking off across the room towards where Sindar was spinning about with his arms outstretched, gazing at the ceiling.

Boka and Chula exchanged glances and hurried after Tred and Fineas, leaving Nagaro alone with Anduar and Madred.

Nagaro winced in vicarious embarrassment at the sight of Sindar's antics. He shook his head. "I should go with him," he murmured.

"I see no such necessity," Anduar observed calmly. "And we're not through with you."

Nagaro felt better than he'd expected he would— after having bared his secret— but he felt drained. He was ready to be gone from the Audience Chamber— to devote himself to anything that didn't concern his own past, present, or future. "But... Elgurn has acknowledged me as the heir of Loros," he protested. "That was my last petition—"

"There are still some questions..."

"For instance," Madred put in. "There's the matter of your marriage to the Lady Nevien ten years ago. Or had you forgotten it?"

Nagaro's brows came together sharply. "That was no marriage! How could I have been married when the words that came out of my mouth were put there by someone else?"

Anduar frowned. "An interesting perspective."

"Which I would be more ready to accept," Madred interjected, "if I were sure that the marriage wasn't consummated."

Nagaro looked at the ground, feeling the blood hot in his face. "It wasn't," he said bitterly. "She was... unwilling. I had Dreigen on one side... telling me to do the thing... and Nevien on the other side saying *stop!*" *He'd been a puppet— with whoever happened to be closest jerking the strings.*

"Then you have no intention of claiming her as your wife?" Madred was regarding him narrowly.

"Based on *that?* No! I intend to marry her properly."

"You do?" Anduar's frown had been deepening, but it evaporated in an instant at Nagaro's last words. And although the Kelorin lord's expression immediately returned to its accustomed deadpan, there was an avid gleam in his eye that Nagaro couldn't help noticing— and didn't like.

He suspected he had made a misstep by expressing his intention so openly, but it was too late to take it back. He straightened his shoulders. "I've asked her, and she has consented," he said guardedly.

"Has she indeed!" Madred sounded affronted. "Her father may have something to say about that! And if you expect to gain the crown so easily—"

Nagaro felt a wave of exasperation. "How many times must I say I have no interest in the crown?" He should, perhaps, have curbed his temper, but he was too tired to make the effort. Instead he plunged on. "I love Nevien, and she loves me! We intend to marry. Elgurn doesn't own her, and there's nothing in the law that says the crown of Edrovir must go with her hand in marriage!"

He thought he caught an eager movement from Anduar and rounded on the Kelorin Lord. "I will not be your puppet, Anduar!"

The gleam instantly vanished from the other man's eyes and Anduar's face fell into lines of benevolent innocence. "Perish the thought, My Lord." He bowed from the waist. "In fact, I was about to agree with you. The law, as set forth by your grandsire, is quite clear that the rule of Edrovir is not intended to descend by line of blood. Darion's intent was that the man deemed best suited should be chosen king. The difficulty we face is in the manner of that choosing. Since the Pact of Lankura has been dissolved, there is no clear mechanism."

For a moment Nagaro could only stare at Anduar's somber face, so astonished that he almost laughed. "If that's all that troubles you, My Lord," he said, "It's easily remedied by re-instituting the Council of Lords."

Madred sputtered. "*What?* Turn the matter over to the whole lot of them?"

Anduar raised a hand for Madred's silence. "If even a single lord of a Hold or Wared were to formally request it, we would have no choice."

Nagaro looked from one to the other of the two men. Anduar's expression appeared deeply serious. Madred radiated disapproval. Nagaro hadn't thought very much for days about the future of Edrovir, but now the course seemed clear to him. "In that case," he said, "consider this a formal request."

"*But—*" Madred began.

Again Anduar's hand imposed silence. "Madred, you are witness—"

Whatever else Anduar might have said remained unknown because at that moment they were interrupted by a shout from the far end of the empty Audience Chamber. Several figures burst through the double doors and came running towards them. Nagaro saw Nevien among them, as well as Taru and Pavo. Vell was in the lead and the young Leithian skidded to a stop on the polished floor as he reached the three startled men standing in front of the dais.

"My Lords!" he gasped. "They're here— Lothard and Grimbold and their armies! Outside the city gate! Lothard is demanding that Elgurn come out and face him. He's challenging the king for the crown! And Devral's army has been sighted on the High Road. They'll be here within the hour!"

"The devil, you say!" Madred looked shaken. "They'll be at each other's throats!"

Even Anduar seemed to have lost his coolness. "*Blast!*" he muttered as he cast his glance around the Audience Chamber. "Where is that Sergeant-at-Arms? And where is Elgurn? How long can it take to arrest a man?"

Chapter 25

Dreigen At Bay

Nagaro climbed the main staircase, two steps at a time— until a stab of pain in his chest brought him up short at the second floor landing. He halted with his hand to his chest and stood with his head down breathing slowly, trying to dispel a wave of anxiety.

"Are ye all right, Nagaro?" Taru sounded alarmed.

Nagaro twisted about to look behind him. Taru and Pavo had halted, standing abreast two steps behind him. Both looked worried. And beyond them he could see Nevien struggling to catch up, gripping the handrail with one hand and her skirts with the other, her eyes fixed on him, her brows constricted sharply.

He forced himself to straighten. "I'm fine."

"Nagaro, I said you don't have to do this." Nevien tucked up her skirts and slipped past Taru and Pavo. "You know how Dreigen affects you. And once he understands who you *are*, he'll probably try to kill you! I can give them the news."

Nagaro moved to bar her path. "No, Nevien. It's *you* who shouldn't be here. Dreigen won't hesitate to attack you to try to hurt your father."

She lifted her chin. "I'm not going to go back down and let you face him alone!"

"I won't *be* alone. I have Taru and Pavo. Not to mention all those who are up there already—"

"I mean without *me!*"

"Hamanei mata noa!" Taru rolled his eyes. "Listen to them, Pavo! Ye'd think they were already married! I'm sure it doesn't matter who brings the news. Dreigen's probably trussed like a pig for market by now."

Pavo shrugged his massive shoulders. "This is why I have said we should all go together. It makes more safe and less argument."

Nagaro heaved a sigh. He'd initially volunteered to inform the king of Lothard's arrival, seeing that Anduar and Madred were both anxious to be where events were unfolding at the Main Gate. His offer had been accepted, and the argument had begun only after the two council members had rushed off with Vell. He had agreed to Pavo's solution, but he wasn't happy about it. He hoped Taru was right about Dreigen, but when it came to that cold and treacherous man, he found it hard to put fear aside.

Seeing that Nevien was still determined, he turned and started on up the stairs, though at a slower pace, partly because he realized that he'd been over-taxing himself and partly because a shadow of dread was beginning to settle on him.

Nevien pressed forward until she was at his side. She seemed to be unafraid, a fact that both impressed and worried him.

She put a hand on his arm. "They told me what my father did," she said. "And what you did in return. I'm proud of both of you."

He shot her a dark look. "Don't expect us to be friends."

"Oh, I won't."

He could hear voices on the floor above them now, speaking in low tones. "Everything seems calm—" he began, just as a bloodcurdling scream pierced the air. It was a man's scream— which somehow made it worse— and it was followed by shouts and the sound of running feet.

They had all jumped at the scream, and this time it was Nevien whose hand flew to her breast. "*Sweet Lady!*" she exclaimed.

Nagaro momentarily forgot his dread and plunged ahead up the last flight of steps. *Someone needed help!*

He reached the top, stepped into the open area where the third floor hallways crossed, facing the west wing— Dreigen's wing— and stopped.

Theren was coming straight at him.

The Kelorin lord was staggering and flailing about with his arms. "*Away! Away!*" he cried. "*Ai! Ai! Get them away from me!*" And then he screamed again, the same ear-piercing scream that Nagaro had heard on the stairs.

Nagaro spread his arms, trying to bar Theren from a possible fall. The stairway came up through an opening in the floor, with nothing but a waist-high railing around the other three sides of it. In Theren's state, the man might actually be able to fall over the railing. "What's wrong?" he cried. "What's happened?"

Theren was in no condition to answer. The lord came to a halt in front of Nagaro, cringing and waving his hands over his head as if warding off blows while making *hsst! hsst!* noises. Beyond the afflicted man, Nagaro saw Soren, hanging back, white-faced, as if he feared the younger lord's affliction might be contagious. There were other figures beyond Soren, but Nagaro had no attention to spare for them.

Nagaro desperately addressed Soren. "What's *happened?* Is this Dreigen's doing?"

"I... yes!" The old lord stammered. "He... he threw some dust in Theren's face—"

Theren suddenly shrieked, "*Ai! Ai! Ai! Ai! Help me!*" and spun about, flailing at the air, then struck off, running wildly down the hall that led into the south wing.

Dust... powder... Nagaro's mind made a connection. "It must be what he used to drive Gillard Marchent mad— that made him leap to his death!" *And Theren was running straight towards the doors that opened onto the third floor balcony.*

Without hesitation, Nagaro raced after the Kelorin lord, overtaking him in a dozen strides and catching hold of him from behind. Theren struggled wildly, trying to free himself and stumbled, pulling Nagaro off balance so that they both fell. Pain stabbed through Nagaro's chest as he twisted in an effort to avoid hurting either himself or the other man while still keeping his grip. Once they were both down, he managed to effectively pin the thrashing man with his body as Theren continued to scream in terror.

Twisting about to look over his shoulder, Nagaro saw his three companions standing at the top of the stairs, frozen with looks of horror on their faces. "Pavo!" he cried. "Come here! There's no danger! Help me hold him!"

"Aye, Zirda!" Pavo sprang to obey.

"Someone find something to bind him with! A belt. A curtain pull... Anything!"

A minute later Theren was being securely trussed with his own belt and the sash from Nevien's gown. Nagaro looked for Soren. The old man had approached and was standing, looking shaken, as he watched Pavo and Taru secure the younger lord.

Nagaro had to step directly in front of Soren to get his attention. "Where is Dreigen now?" he asked.

"He... he got past us!" the old man stammered. "Theren and I were trying to keep him from getting to the stairs... but he... he attacked Theren... and then he bolted for the North Tower. Odus and one of the guards went after him." He paused, his eyes on Theren who was struggling against his bonds, rolling his eyes, and screaming as if terrors were assailing him from all directions. "Wh–what will happen to him?"

"I believe it's temporary. He should come to himself in a little while. But I came to tell you that Lothard and Grimbold have arrived. Lothard is calling for a challenge to the crown. Where is Elgurn?"

"Back there." Soren waved a hand vaguely behind him. "He's been hurt—"

"*My father hurt?*" Nevien had been hovering over Theren after donating her sash, but she now swept past Nagaro and Soren, running back along the hall with an urgent rustle of skirts.

Instantly afraid for her safety, Nagaro ran after her, crying, "Nevien, be careful! Dreigen is still loose!"

She paid him no heed, running on before him. Hard on her heels, he followed her around the corner near the top of the stairs, entering Dreigen's wing— where he immediately saw Elgurn.

The king was leaning slumped against the wall just beyond the door of Dreigen's chambers. His face was ashen, his eyes squeezed shut, his mouth set in a grimace of pain. He clutched his right arm protectively against his chest. One of the palace guards hovered beside him, a young man not more than twenty, red-haired with freckles standing out sharply on his pale face. Another guard lay face down— half in, and half out of, the doorway, as if he'd fallen there while trying to flee from the Lore Master's chambers. It was the Sergeant-at-Arms.

Nevien ran to her father. "Let me see your arm!" she cried. "*Please,* Father!"

Nagaro stooped over the sergeant and felt for a pulse. There was none, though he saw no mark on the fallen man, no blood. Feeling sick at heart, he stood up and found that Soren and Taru had followed him.

"Pavo 'll mind the mad lord—" Taru began. Then his eyes were drawn to the body of the Sergeant-at-Arms. "What happened t' *him?*"

Soren wrung his hands. "He tried to hold Dreigen— there, inside the room— and the... the monster touched him! Just grabbed his shoulder, and... and... *this!* What manner of evil magic—?"

"Poison," Nagaro corrected. "Dreigen has made a study of it—"

He was interrupted by a shriek of horror from Nevien and spun to see her backing away from her father, a hand pressed to her mouth, her eyes staring fixedly.

He followed her gaze and found that Elgurn had moved. He still leaned against the wall for support, and his eyes were still closed against the pain, but the arm he'd been cradling against his body was now held out before him in plain view. The sleeve of the king's shirt hung in smoking shreds, revealing a bare forearm the skin of which was an ugly red mess, hideously blistered and oozing.

Nagaro sucked in his breath at the sight. Instinctively he moved to support Nevien, placing an encircling arm around her shoulders. "How did this happen?" he asked, addressing anyone who could answer.

"Oh Zirda!" the young guard cried. "It was some... some liquid— in a glass bottle! Dreigen threw it... an' it broke... it splashed—" He gestured vaguely with his left hand. His right hand clutched the hilt of his drawn sword as if it were his last salvation. "Sergeant told me to protect the king," he added, his voice rising to a plaintive wail. *"It's the last thing he ever said!"*

At that moment an eerie wailing howl rose on the air. It seemed to come from some distance away, and it carried a chill that made Nagaro shiver.

"What was that?" Nevien pulled away from him, staring about, wide-eyed.

"Oh, Gods..." The young guard's eyes rolled upward and his lips moved in silent prayer.

Soren pointed a trembling finger. "It came from— *there!* From the North Tower! What's that monster doing now?"

The howl came again, and this time there seemed to be an edge of rage to it.

At the sound, Elgurn came to life. His eyes snapped open, burning with a terrible intensity. *"Kale!"* he breathed, voicing the very thought that had sprung to Nagaro's mind. The king groped for his sword hilt with his left hand. "If that bastard harms my friend, I will send his soul straight to Hel! By all the Gods, I swear it!"

"No! You shouldn't try to do any more!" Nevien had shaken off her horror. "Your arm needs a healer!"

Elgurn's eyes came to focus on her. "You shouldn't be here, Daughter! Go for the healer, then. Send him up here— but *you* stay downstairs where you're out of harm's way!

"That's a good idea— Nagaro began, although he read rebellion in Nevien's eyes. Then he remembered his charge. "Elgurn, you're needed at the Main Gate. Lothard is making a challenge—"

"Lothard be damned! I haven't finished here!" Elgurn used the wall to push himself upright, then managed awkwardly to draw his sword with his left hand. He held his right arm away from his body, the hand frozen and useless. "Dreigen murdered my sergeant right before my eyes! His life is forfeit!"

From the direction of the north tower, there came a series of thumps and a crash, as of china breaking, followed by shouts and another howl.

Elgurn uttered an oath and began to move, with a remarkably steady stride, in the direction of the hall that led to the North Tower.

"My Lord!" The young guard wailed, and started after him.

"Father!" Nevien would have followed him as well.

Nagaro caught her arm. "Go for the healer, Nevien."

"I won't leave him! I won't leave *you!*"

"Keshaal!" Nagaro released her and turned to Taru who was still standing frozen beside and equally paralyzed Soren. "You go, Taru! Get Tred if you can— or the other healer, master Nildred. Get any healer you can find— just make sure he has his bag!"

Taru shook himself. "Aye, Capt'n!" He dashed away, making for the stairs.

Nagaro felt ice in his stomach. He knew he should go after Elgurn. *If only he had his sword!* There'd been no time to go back and argue for its return. He stooped over the body of the Sergeant-at-Arms only to find that the man's scabbard was empty. "What happened to his sword?" he asked frantically.

"Dreigen took it." Soren seemed to have shaken off his dismay. "I suppose we should help bring the man to justice," he added with a grimace. He drew his own weapon, clutching it with a bony hand and trying to look resolute.

Any thought of Dreigen made Nagaro's heart quail. He didn't know how much help Soren would actually be, but he had to support the old man. He wasn't sure what it meant that Dreigen had armed himself with a sword. "I hope it means he's run out of other tricks," he muttered as he squared his shoulders. "All right," he said. "Let's go."

He set off with a long stride after Elgurn and the young guard who had disappeared around the corner into the North Wing. Within a few paces he had to slow to let the aging Soren catch up. Nevien had tucked up her skirts and was close behind them.

Nagaro knew the North Tower well. Its third floor was dominated by a large sunroom with windows looking west, north, and east. Kale was housed on the floor above, in a chamber reached by a concealed stairway. This he explained between breaths to Soren as they turned into the north hall.

The king and his young protector must have already reached the sunroom, for the short north hallway was empty. They heard voices as they approached the sunroom's open door. Some were raised in anger, but the words were indistinct. There was another crashing thud, this time sounding more like furniture being upended than breaking crockery.

Nagaro halted just outside the doorway, out of view of the occupants, and gestured for Nevien to stay back. "Stay outside," he hissed. "Or stay behind us." White-faced and breathless, this time she nodded.

In the next instant, Kale's voice came to them, raised as if declaiming upon a stage so that the words were clear: "*Blood for blood, we've taken, and all the fields run red with gore!*"

A confusion of indistinct voices followed. Soren cast Nagaro a baffled look.

Nagaro remembered his earlier encounters with the madman. "Kale speaks in literary quotations," he explained. "Sometimes they almost make sense."

His heart was hammering but he forced himself to creep forward. Soren moved beside him although the old man's sword trembled visibly in his hand. In this way, they at last reached the threshold of the sunroom and got their first glimpse of the scene within.

The large room was a shambles. Two of the three small tables it contained had been overturned and the fragments of a porcelain vase lay scattered on the floor. In addition, the tapestry that normally concealed the door to the stairway leading to the upper floor had been pulled down and lay in a heap. The exposed door gaped open wide.

Part of Nagaro's mind registered these details in the instant after he crossed the threshold, but from that point on his attention was held by the tableau of the room's six occupants.

The king and Lord Odus, flanked by the two guards, were spread out in an arc with their backs to the doorway where Nagaro and Soren stood. All four held drawn swords, and all were focused on the last two men— Dreigen and Kale— who faced each other on the far side of the room, brandishing weapons. One of the room's large padded armchairs stood between them like a defensive barricade.

It was a bizarre standoff. The two could hardly have been stranger adversaries. The Lore Master, on the right, was an imposing figure with his fierce, dark, chiseled features and burning eyes. He was dressed in flowing robes, and his sleek black hair was streaked with gray. Kale, in contrast, was a ravaged scarecrow, wild-eyed, barefoot, and clad in garments that were nearly rags. His untrimmed beard was flecked with spittle, his unkempt mass of graying red curls stood out from his head in all directions.

The two men were threatening each another with weapons that were equally mismatched. Dreigen held the stolen sword extended before him menacingly with one hand, while he clutched a short-necked spherical glass flask in the other. The look in his eyes said plainly that he was prepared to use the sword, although the way he was handling it made it clear that he was not well-practiced with one.

Kale, on the other hand, had been born and bred among the nobility and had clearly studied swordsmanship at some point in his life, even though he'd never been known as a warrior. The flourishes he was making in the air with his weapon would have been quite impressive if the object hadn't been an ornate brass-handled fireplace poker. The mad swivelling of his eyes made his intent uncertain and his melodramatic utterances did little to enhance his credibility. Under other circumstances his performance would have been comical.

"*If thou be not yet a corpse,*" Kale intoned, leveling the poker at Dreigen's face. "*I'll make thee one!*"

"Be silent, mad dog!" Dreigen snarled. "I took your mind, and I can take your life!" He dodged around the armchair and made a thrust with his sword at Kale's chest— a thrust that the deranged man turned aside with a theatrical flourish of his poker.

There was a metallic clatter as the madman took a step to complete his maneuver, and Nagaro saw that Kale wore a shackle on his left ankle with a length of chain attached that ended in a heavy bolt with plaster clinging to it. Nagaro smiled in spite of his thudding heart. Kale must have forcibly freed himself. Dreigen had likely come seeking a hostage for his safety— or to deal the king another blow— and had gotten more than he'd bargained for.

Elgurn flinched visibly at the exchange between the two combatants. "Move away from him, Kale! I'll finish him for you!"

"No, My Lord," Odus protested. "You're wounded! Let us take him!"

"You're wounded yourself!"

Nagaro could see that this was true. The sleeve of Odus's shirt bore a spreading scarlet stain near his right shoulder.

"A scratch, My Lord." Odus dismissed it. "The creature caught me by surprise. He won't do it again." He gestured with his free hand for the guard beside him, and began a cautious advance. The guard, a seasoned, grim-faced Kelorin with short black hair peppered with gray inched forward beside Odus, his sword held ready.

Soren began to edge forward as if to join Odus. Nagaro moved as well, but in a different direction, circling to the left, trying to find a way to approach Kale from behind. It was safest not to look at Dreigen, lest he lose his nerve, but Kale was another matter. Kale was someone he could possibly help.

Elgurn began a more rapid advance of his own, trying to get ahead of Odus and the Kelorin guard.

Unfortunately, the three men's movements suddenly drew Dreigen's attention. The Lore Master hissed, and brandished the glass flask aloft.

"If I break this, we all die!"

The advancing men froze, stymied.

Without warning, Kale sprang forward crying, *"Kill them! Kill them! Slay them all!"* He bounded first to the seat of the chair, then launched himself at Dreigen. It happened so fast that the madman had his hands around Dreigen's throat before the Lore Master or any of the onlookers could move. The discarded poker clattered on the polished oak floor.

Dreigen emitted a strangled cry. Dropping his sword, he clawed at his attacker with his free hand. His other hand, holding the glass flask, flailed wildly.

"Kale, no!"

"Be careful!"

"If he drops that flask—"

Everyone was moving— gingerly inching forward or drawing back, while gesturing frantically at Kale.

Dreigen was struggling to loosen Kale's grip, his face beginning to turn purple. His eyes bulged alarmingly in their deep sockets, but his hand holding the flask was still raised, his grip on it so tight that the knuckles showed white.

"Kill them! Kill them!" Kale maintained his grip, dodging Dreigen's free hand and snapping at it with his teeth. He was frothing at the mouth, his gaunt face a mask of demonic rage. He seemed completely heedless of Dreigen's up-raised flask that threatened death to all of them.

Nagaro couldn't bear seeing Kale— the gentle scholar— transformed into this murderous beast, driven by single-minded viciousness. "No, Kale!" he cried. "You're not a killer!" And he strode forward, thrusting between Elgurn and the cowering younger guard to seize Kale's arms. He had no thought for Dreigen's proximity, focusing only on the red-haired Leithian who had once showed him kindness. "Kale! *Let go!* He'll be brought to justice, but not by your hand!"

The shaggy head swung around. The red-rimmed eyes locked onto Nagaro, and the grimy fingers loosed their grip as the madman turned towards him.

Dreigen slumped to his knees, gasping, still clutching the deadly flask.

Nagaro dropped his hands from Kale's arms and stepped back, instinctively moving away from Dreigen. Kale followed, his eyes still fixed on Nagaro's face. The insane fire in them had ebbed. Nagaro searched those eyes for some vestige of human reason. "Good, Kale, good," he murmured. "You're not a killer..."

Kale blinked and raised a hand as if he meant to touch Nagaro face. *"Pity the poor orphan child,"* he intoned. *"And weep, weep, Oh Edrovir!"*

Nagaro recognized the words, the same ones Kale had spoken at their last encounter. "That's right, Kale," he said eagerly. "I'm the child of Tevren and Lindra." He kept backing and the madman stalked after him, intoning more words from the same source.

"Dead is the father, dead the mother..."

"Yes, Kale."

"Lying in blood..."

"Kale, I want to help you. There's a—"

But before Nagaro could say anything more, the wild light flared again in Kale's eyes and the man lunged for his throat, shrieking, *"Kill them! Kill them! Slay them all!"*

Nagaro's natural quickness saved him. He dodged to one side, and when Kale's startled hands closed on empty air, he grabbed one of them and stepped behind the man, twisting Kale's arm behind his back. Kale gave an outraged screech and kicked backwards, knocking Nagaro's feet from under him and overbalancing himself at the same time so that they both went down. For the second time that day Nagaro found himself wrestling on the floor with one of Dreigen's mind-ravaged victims.

Kale was surprisingly strong and his madness made him murderous, but Nagaro outweighed him. Despite several sharp twinges in his chest, he managed to maneuver so that he was kneeling on Kale's back, holding the man's twisted arm in position with both hands.

Finding himself pinned, Kale's furious raging abruptly lapsed into pathetic repetitions of, "*Mercy on the poor old man,*" as he beat the floor with his free hand.

"I'm sorry, Kale," Nagaro murmured. "I really want to help you..." but his voice trailed as his attention was belatedly drawn back to what was happening in the rest of the room.

The other men had been cautiously closing in on what they assumed was a half-asphyxiated Dreigen, only to have the sagging Lore Master suddenly stagger to his feet, snarling, and turn on them with the deadly flask held up like a talisman.

"*Back! Back!*" Dreigen screamed, his voice hoarse from the choking.

And the men moved back. The semicircle of drawn swords wavered and widened, though the points of the swords remained directed at the Lore Master.

Dreigen's black eyes glittered maliciously as he swept the men's faces. Then he laughed a horrible laugh. "*Now you will die!*" he croaked, and with an exaggerated swing of his arm he tossed the flask high into the air, almost straight up, so that it tumbled— end over end— in a narrow arc that would peak just below the ceiling of the high-vaulted room.

All eyes followed it.

All except Dreigen's. The Lore Master took advantage of his enemies' horror-stricken distraction to bolt around them and make straight for the door that led out of the sunroom into the short north hallway.

Chapter 26

Elgurn's Justice

As Dreigen made his move towards the door, the stoppered flask reached the top of its arc and started down, still tumbling end over end, descending like the hammer-stroke of doom.

Again everyone moved at once. They all saw the need to both intercept the spinning flask and bar Dreigen's path. Some started one way and some the other, colliding with each other.

"Stop him!"

"Somebody catch it!"

"Don't let it break!"

"I have it!" Nevien suddenly darted forward with her skirt held in her spread hands like a basket. She slipped between the astonished Odus and Soren. Her green eyes tracked the trajectory of the falling flask as she moved, and she caught it neatly in the outstretched skirt before it could strike the floor.

There was a chorus of elated cries from the onlookers. Nevien turned towards Nagaro, beaming— even as Elgurn finally blocked the door, cutting off Dreigen's escape.

For a moment it seemed that they'd won. The Lore Master pulled up short, then reversed his course, backing away from the men's swords. His eyes darted this way and that, until they fixed on Nevien. Catching the flask had placed her in front of the line of men, rather than behind it. *And she had her back to Dreigen.*

Nagaro saw the danger. "Nevien, look out!"

But it was too late. Swift as a striking snake, Dreigen caught Nevien from behind with an arm about her throat. She let out a startled shriek that was cut short as Dreigen throttled her. At the same time, he stooped, groping for the flask the princess cradled in her skirt.

Nagaro's heart lurched. He dared not let go of Kale, but Dreigen was choking the life from his beloved! His groan was lost among the general outcry.

Nevien, however, quickly demonstrated that she wasn't in immanent danger of being strangled. Deducing what Dreigen had in mind, she shook out her skirt, sending the flask rolling across the floor in a series of trundling arcs that took it between Odus and Soren, and past Elgurn and the two guards— all of whom stared at it with a kind of horrified fascination— until it fetched up, intact, against the opposite wall of the room with a brittle *clink*.

Elgurn was the first to react. "Someone throw that thing out the window!" he commanded. "As far as you can— But be sure there's no one below!"

"Aye, Zyrda!" The older guard gingerly picked up the flask and ran to the north window. Flinging the pane open, he leaned out briefly and hurled the flask as hard as he could, waiting several seconds before reporting, "I saw a puff of smoke, My Lord. It must have broken."

"Ha!" Elgurn barked a laugh. "Well done, Zirda! And well done, Daughter!"

Dreigen hissed, "Filthy little bitch! She could have killed us!" He tightened his arm around Nevien's neck.

Nevien squeaked, and her eyes widened in panic. Her hands, now free, sprang to her throat and she clutched at the encircling arm, trying futilely to free herself.

"*Nevien!*" Nagaro let go of Kale's arm with one hand and started to rise.

Elgurn, still near the door, caught the motion and flung up a commanding hand to stop him. "You hold Kale and keep him safe!" he thundered. "Let me tend to my daughter!"

With a frustrated groan, Nagaro sank back, resuming his grip. The king was right. The last thing they needed was to have Kale running amuck again.

Elgurn shifted his grip on his sword and strode towards Dreigen, the other men parting to let him pass.

"*Release her!*"

Dreigen made no move to comply. Instead he reared his head, his black eyes burning in their deep sockets. He raised his free hand and held it poised above Nevien's shoulder. On the middle finger of the hand was a heavy ring with a polished black stone. "Come one step closer and she dies!" he rasped. "My touch is death. You've seen it!"

Elgurn faltered to a halt. The tip of his sword dipped.

But Nevien was shaking her head frantically. She managed to twist sideways in Dreigen's grip, diminishing the pressure on her windpipe. "*Bluffing...*" she gasped. "*Poison ring... one dose... spent on the sergeant!*"

Dreigen's eyes flashed. "That's not true!" he cried imperiously. "She guesses! She doesn't know—"

"Oh, yes she *does!*" The point of Elgurn's sword came up again. "She's read your notebooks, you snake! You have no fangs left!" He spoke to the other men, "Let's take him!"

They all began to move forward then, but Dreigen didn't wait for them to close. "Wretched female!" he snarled. "*Filthy little sneak!* And he flung Nevien away from him so violently that she went sprawling on the floor. Three strides took the Lore Master to the sword that lay where he'd discarded it. He snatched it up, spinning to face his adversaries with the weapon held defensively in front of him.

"*Nevien!*" It was all Nagaro could do not to let go of Kale and spring to her aid where she lay gasping on the floor.

"I'm all right!" Nevien croaked. She started to rise, and both Odus and Soren hastened to assist her.

Elgurn seemed satisfied with his daughter's word. He began to advance again on Dreigen. "This man has been my bane, and I shall deal with him," he said in voice that was pure ice. "Let no one intervene unless I fall."

"My Lord!" Odus cried in dismay. "If you fall, Edrovir has no king!"

Elgurn laughed a short, bitter laugh. "Oh, not for long, I'm sure. Anduar, the king-maker, has doubtless already chosen my successor and will contrive to see him crowned."

The king advanced even as he spoke, step by step, his sword steady in his left hand, the blade leveled at Dreigen's chest. His injured right arm he held away from his body and a little behind him, out of harms way.

Dreigen backed away from the king, still holding the stolen sword out before him. His black eyes glittered. He licked his thin lips. "Aren't you going to *arrest* me, My Lord King?" His tone was derisive, defiant.

"We already tried that." Elgurn's voice was cold and flat. "You declined once. Will you now lay down your sword?"

"Why should I?" Dreigen sneered. "So you can murder me with a rope?" He made no move to lower the sword, but moved sideways and backwards, inching towards where Nagaro held Kale prone, less than ten feet away.

Nagaro tensed at the prospect of having to move the madman, knowing he'd need to let Kale stand up to do it.

Elgurn, however, must have seen the danger. He sidestepped, swiftly interposing himself between Dreigen and his boyhood friend. "There would be a tribunal," he said levelly. "You would have justice—"

"*Your* justice?" Dreigen was finely contemptuous. "You *highborn* do whatever you please, and call it justice! But if you don't like what *I* do, you call it a crime! I expect no justice for a fatherless bastard from the likes of *you!*" Dreigen was still moving, shifting his position, his glance flicking fractionally this way and that, though it always returned to the king.

"This isn't about your birth, Dreigen." Elgurn was clearly losing patience. "You murdered my Sergeant-at-Arms in cold blood! You resisted arrest! You assaulted your king—"

"*And* you murdered Darion the Great!" Nevien added pointedly. She was on her feet and had retreated to a place near the chamber door. "*And* Berinar Sundorin. *And* Gillard Marchent. Not to mention that harmless old man who helped in the kitchen. The confessions are in your notebooks! I've read them all!"

"And poor Kale read them too, before you silenced him by driving him mad." Elgurn still refrained from striking, letting the talk run while never taking his eyes off the man. "The evidence of your crimes is overwhelming," he continued. "Under the law, I have the right to serve justice on the spot!"

"*My crimes!*" Dreigen spat the words. "Darion's death made you king! Removing Berinar evened the number of Pact Signers! And Gillard was threatening to tell what he knew about how you used that bastard boy! Gillard would have brought you down if I hadn't dealt with him. You should be grateful for my service!"

Nagaro could see the king's rising anger in the tightening of his jaw as he listened to this litany, could read danger in Elgurn's eyes.

"I never ordered any of that Dreigen!" Elgurn grated. "I never wanted it! You've always been the tool of the most ruthless elements of the Leithian Faction— or have simply served yourself! Gillard threatened you as well!"

Dreigen's lips curled into a nasty smile. "Oh, you may deny wanting those things, Elgurn," he hissed, "but you can't deny killing the Virden woman. You used her to try to control the boy, and when that failed, *you killed her with your own hands!*"

The barb was well-aimed. It struck a deep vein of guilt in Elgurn's soul and when Nagaro saw the king falter, he could not keep silent. "No!" he cried. "Maramine's death is on *your* head, Dreigen! *You* withheld the full truth about heskial. *You* told him she couldn't be saved! He killed her to end her suffering. I was there! I was that boy—"

And there he stopped, any further words frozen in his throat as Dreigen's attention snapped to a focus directly on *him*. The Lore Master's gaze blazed like a furnace, and for the first time there was recognition in the fierce black eyes. That would have been bad enough, but there was something else as well— a malice so potent that it held Nagaro transfixed like a shaft through the chest. He felt as if he couldn't breathe.

And then Dreigen spoke.

"So *you're* the puppet prince?" he snarled with scathing derision. "*Who gave you linjana?*" And even before he'd finished speaking, Dreigen sidestepped the king and made a lunge with his sword, driving straight for Nagaro's throat.

Several voices cried out.

Nevien screamed.

Fighting down his paralyzing horror, Nagaro flung himself flat on top of Kale, half expecting to feel the blade cut into his back. Instead he heard a clash of steel on steel, right above his head, and a pair of boots filled his limited field of vision. Twisting his neck where he lay, he saw that Elgurn had come to his defense.

The king had struck Dreigen's blade aside, interposing himself. *"So you did know about linjana, you bastard!"* Elgurn raged as he struck a furious blow at his nemesis. The swords rang together again as the Lore Master inexpertly parried the stroke with a two-handed swing and lunged again, this time at the king.

"My Lord!" came an anguished cry from Odus.

"Stand back! He's *mine!*" Elgurn barely evaded Dreigen's stroke and circled, shifting his left-handed grip on his sword. He was breathing hard.

So began the final conflict between these two men whose lives had been perversely intertwined, to one's advantage and the other's pain. The battle didn't last long, though it seemed longer to those who were watching, holding their breaths.

The combatants were more evenly matched than it might have appeared. Dreigen was desperate, fighting for his life moment by moment, the king severely hampered by not having the use of his right arm. Four more times their weapons came together, with a shuddering clash or a skreel of metal sliding on metal, before Elgurn found an opening and drove his sword blade home, running the Lore Master cleanly through the heart.

Dreigen went down without a word. Toppling backward as the king withdrew his blade, he came to lie, stretched on the floor, his fingers still clutching the sword hilt and his terrible eyes staring at the high-arched ceiling overhead.

Elgurn stood over his vanquished foe, his head bowed.

For a long moment no one spoke.

It was the welcome voice of Tredhold Ferth that broke the silence. "Well," the jaunty little healer said, "it looks as if we've come just in time for the mopping up. Which should we attend to first? The mad lord, or the monarch?"

Nagaro struggled into a kneeling position on top of Kale, and turned to see Tredhold standing in the doorway with his healer's bag. Beside the sandy-haired ship's doctor stood Brandle, behind them were Taru and Master Fineas, with Pavo's massive figure looming in the rear.

Elgurn answered. "If you have the linjana, give it to Kale now. I can wait."

"Do you want me to hold him?" Pavo asked. "Brandle says I am very good at sitting on mad lord."

"By all means, yes. Several of you can hold him and give Nagaro a rest. But be gentle with Kale!"

Nagaro gratefully relinquished his task to Pavo, Taru, and Brandle. "Where is Theren?" he asked as they grasped Kale and turned him over. Kale had been quiet throughout the sword battle, but now he struggled and resumed his litany of, "*Mercy on the poor old man!*"

"Two guard have take Lord Theren away," Pavo responded. "Already he is little bit better."

"Oh. That's good. I don't think there should be any recurrence if he got only one exposure to the powder. But they should still keep a careful watch on him for at least a full day."

"Don't worry, Captain," Brandle interjected. "They will."

By this time, Taru was holding Kale's arm in position and Tred was readying a bladder-thorn. Nagaro stepped back and turned away. He felt no need to watch the administration a second time.

Nevien ran to him. "Nagaro!" she cried. "I'm so glad it's finally over!"

He found himself enveloped in her arms and he gladly answered the embrace, holding her to him, savoring the warm contact of her body. "So am I," he said fervently.

She squeezed him harder. "You were so brave."

"Not as brave as you."

There was a small but significant cough.

Nagaro turned, startled, to find Elgurn regarding him severely.

The king's face darkened further when Nagaro didn't immediately drop his arms. "I don't recall having asked you to comfort my daughter on this occasion," Elgurn said gruffly.

Nevien cast her father an exasperated look and tightened her grasp. "We're going to be married, Father," she said firmly. "He asked, and I said yes. And that is that."

"Oh, is it?" Elgurn bridled, his pale blue eyes flashing.

Nagaro gently extricated himself from Nevien's arms. "I would perhaps have been more diplomatic, My Lord," he said. "And I hope you will give us your blessing. But the truth is that we intend to marry, with or without it."

Elgurn's face grew thunderous. "*Why, of all the—*" he began. But then he stopped and his frown dissolved, and he actually laughed. "What am I saying?" he cried, wiping a tear from his eye with his left hand. "And why should I say anything at all— when this is the very match I was trying to arrange ten years ago? By all means, Zirda. Take my daughter. And my blessing!"

Nagaro was not inclined to share the mirth. "A man has to come to a thing in his own time," he said stiffly.

Elgurn sobered. "Ah, yes," he said. "This I have come to understand. But it appears that you have won her heart—"

"And she has won mine!"

"Then allow me to offer both of you my congratulations." Elgurn made them a one-armed bow.

At that moment Tredhold approached them, carrying his bag, and said, "My Lord King, I'll look at your arm now, if ye will please sit down over here." He motioned toward the nearest armchair.

Elgurn grimaced and began to move in the indicated direction. Nagaro and Nevien followed.

"How is Kale?" the king asked as he took his seat, glancing at where Fineas and Brandle were kneeling beside the recumbent red-haired lord. "How did he take the linjana?"

"He slipped right into a deep sleep," Tred responded. "Not at all like Sindar. But then their afflictions were different. Master Fineas will take charge of him. He says there will likely be some loss of memory, but he can't say how much, or how long it will last."

"Ah. I see." Elgurn averted his eyes as Tred began to examine the raw flesh of his right forearm.

The healer frowned in concentration. "It appears to have been burned by some kind of vitriol," he muttered. "But the stuff has spent itself. The damage isn't progressing. Given time, it should heal, but there will be scarring..."

Elgurn didn't appear to be listening. He was looking at Nagaro. "Did you experience a loss of memory? From the linjana?"

"I... yes. When I woke out of the fever I remembered almost nothing. The spirit magic of the linjana gradually gave me back bits and pieces of my life, but it was a year before I remembered who I was and what had happened to me. By then I was a galley slave chained to a bulkhead."

The king's eyes clouded, and he winced and paled as Tredhold began to gently clean the wounded arm with a moist cloth. A basin of water had appeared from somewhere.

"*Great Gods,*" Elgurn murmured. "I am sorry!"

"It... was better so. I was terribly angry while it was happening. But by the time I was free to make my own way in the world, two and a half years had passed. I was far away, on Pakoa. Nevien was married to another man..."

Elgurn's gaze slid away. Another spasm of pain crossed his face as Tred continued to work on his arm. He appeared to make an effort to focus on Pavo and Brandle who were gently lifting Kale's insensible form, under Fineas' direction, preparing to carry the man away to a place where he could be better tended. "Is that why you didn't come after me?" the king asked after a moment, "seeking vengeance?"

Nagaro looked away as well. "That was at least part of the reason." He watched as two guards, under Lord Odus' direction, unceremoniously picked up Dreigen's corpse and started for the door, with Soren trailing behind them. *That, and I was afraid...* he thought. *Afraid of you. Afraid of Dreigen. Afraid of the laughter... the ridicule...*

Elgurn gritted his teeth as Tred began dabbing ointment onto his wound, but didn't turn his head to look at what the healer was doing. The bearers had gone out with Kale, but still the king seemed to gaze unseeing at where the man had lain.

"For a long time I hoped you were alive," he said, without looking at Nagaro's face, "...in spite of what Dreigen said. I called off the search early, that day. As long as there was no body, I could imagine that he was wrong— that somehow, I hadn't killed you. I prayed to the Gods that you were alive. And for months I kept expecting you to step out of some shadow, with a knife, or a sword. It was what I deserved. But the years went by— seven years— and when you finally came, I didn't know you. You were nothing that I expected— a brown-skinned, bearded, pirate captain from the southern isles, who wanted only to route the Mahuk warriors and make the palace secure. By that time, I'd given up hope—"

Elgurn broke off as Tred directed him to lift his arm so he could begin to bandage it. After a moment he continued, however, his thoughts still running in the same vein.

"I rehearsed a thousand times the words I would say to you if the Gods ever granted me the chance to say them. But I'd long ago given up any hope of ever speaking them to a living man— or having any chance to redeem myself. And then.. *today...* the Gods answered prayers I'd never dared to utter."

Nagaro made no answer. He was only half listening to Elgurn's confession, was only half aware of Nevien still standing at his side, her hand resting possessively on his arm. He was staring at the spot where Dreigen's corpse had lain. The guards had removed the body, and all that remained was a dark blood stain on the polished floor. He was trying to grasp the idea of a world without Dreigen in it— a world in which he would never again have to fear that he might walk into a room, or turn a corner, and see that figure gliding towards him like a malevolent shade— or meet the unnerving glance of those serpent eyes. *And it was Elgurn who had done the thing... faced the fear... brought the horrible creature down...*

"Thank you for defending me," he said, "from Dreigen... with your sword."

Elgurn seemed to shake himself out of his own reverie. "You are most welcome," he said gravely. "And thank you for taking care of Kale."

Nagaro shrugged. "I couldn't do any less."

"And for the words you spoke to Dreigen in my defense—"

"They were the truth."

"Still, it did me good to hear them from the lips of another man." Elgurn repositioned his arm as Tredhold continued bandaging. "They were what I needed at that moment so I could finish the deed that needed doing. And you will soon have an opportunity to do me another service."

Nagaro's attention came abruptly back to full focus. "What do you mean?"

Elgurn gestured at his damaged arm. "You came to tell me that I face a challenge for the crown," he said. "I could do for Driegen as I am, but I'm in no case to fight a man like Lothard. I therefore require a champion."

"Oh."

"I suppose I can rely on you?"

Nagaro felt Nevien's fingers tighten on his arm. She leaned close to his ear to whisper urgently. *"Nagaro, you don't have to. By the law, you can refuse."*

That was what she said. And he knew what she meant— knew what trouble his wound still gave him. But he also remembered what Kuran had said— that no one else had as good a chance of prevailing against Lothard Hurn. And what else could he say to the man who was still the King of Edrovir?

Nagaro swallowed. "Yes," he said. "I suppose you can."

Chapter 27

The Best-Laid Plans

From the top of the wall above the Main Gate of the city of Lankura, the assembled armies looked like toy soldiers on a tablecloth. The encampments of armed men and horses filled a rough semicircle, beginning within a few dozen yards of the Circle Road that ran along the base of the city wall and extending for a quarter of a mile across fields that in a few weeks would be sprouting wheat, oats, beans, and potatoes. From his vantage point, Nagaro could easily distinguish the different colors of the soldiers' uniforms. He could see that the four major armies occupied areas shaped like slices of pie with the points converging on the crossroads in front of him where the High Road met the Circle Road. It was the very spot where he and Kuran had spoken with Commander Korenthos earlier that day, an event that now seemed an age and a half ago.

Nagaro knew the liveries of the major players, and he saw that Korenthos had successfully enforced his plan to use the High Road to separate the opposing forces. There were a score of mounted men in the uniform of the City Guard patrolling the road, although those poor souls would clearly find themselves quite helpless if tempers on the two sides were to boil over.

The armies of Lothard and Grimbold were north of the road, with Lothard's men— the largest single force on the field— occupying the position closest to the High Road, and Grimbold's farther to Nagaro's left. On the right, Devral's army, which had arrived less than half an hour before, made an impressive wedge that thrust in along the southern margin of the High Road. And on the far right, closer to the river, was the force that Pendrik had assembled, composed of contingents wearing several distinctly-colored liveries.

Nagaro was relieved to see that Rastyl's men and the others who'd accompanied him that morning were clustered near the Circle Road beside Pendrik's motley force and well away from Lothard's. The farmers and herdsmen weren't in evidence and must have retreated or found cover. There were other smaller groups of men in contrasting colors here and there on both sides of the road, but these he couldn't identify.

Any of the city guards positioned along the top of the wall could probably have told Nagaro whatever he wished to know about the various liveries, but he hadn't troubled to ask. He hadn't come to the top of the wall to study the opposing forces. He'd come to get some air, to find a little peace, and to gather his strength for the next task that Lokundas had set before him.

He was tired, physically, mentally, and emotionally. He had ridden with Elgurn, Odus, and Soren from the palace to the Main Gate, because it had been the obvious thing to do. Nevien had ridden with them as well, having told her father in no uncertain terms that she wasn't going to sit in the palace and worry while those she cared about were facing danger.

Remembering the way her eyes had flashed as she'd spoken made Nagaro smile as he stood by the parapet. But the smile faded as he also remembered how she had looked away whenever he tried to catch her eye. He could guess what she was thinking.

When they'd dismounted at the gate, she had briefly moved close to him and reached out to squeeze his hand, finally meeting his eyes. He'd told her not to worry, reminding her that the challenge wouldn't be fought to the death. "I know," she said, giving him a bright, brittle smile. "They changed the law after Tevren was killed." But then she hadn't looked at him again until after they had entered the tower and climbed the stairs.

In a room on the second floor of one of the gate towers, Commander Korenthos had offered them bread, cold meat, and sothiril. Dealing with Dreigen and attending to Elgurn's wound had taken so long that it was, by that time, two hours past mid-day and more than six hours since Nagaro had eaten breakfast. He knew he should try to keep up his strength, but he'd been too tense to eat very much.

After the meal, Elgurn, Odus, and Soren had sat down with Anduar and Madred for a discussion of strategy, and Nagaro had excused himself. Nevien had remained, taking up her frequent role as an observer of what amounted to a Council meeting with Soren standing in for Theren, who was still recovering. She'd told him in a hurried whisper that she would be his ears, and he'd been more than happy at that moment to let her remain behind.

He'd needed to get away, to be alone, even if only for a little while.

The top of the city wall between the two gate towers was a stone-paved walkway some twenty feet long and six feet wide, with a four-foot-high parapet on either side. The nearest guards were manning the tops of the gate towers, so Nagaro had a little solitude where he stood, midway along the span, above the gate's great wooden doors. He leaned on the east parapet, gazing out over the landscape, trying not to focus on all the armed men. There were a few scattered farmhouses out there with thatched roofs above gray stone walls. There were some copses of trees, just showing bright new green. There was a low hill, beyond which the river gleamed, reflecting blue sky and the dark shadows of its banks.

A gust of wind ruffled his hair and he shivered so hard that the sword at his side rattled in its scabbard. The air wasn't nearly as cold as it had been when he'd left Loros Hall, but the wind was chill and he wished he'd worn his cloak instead of leaving it on a peg in the gate tower. He glanced at the sky. The bright blue expanse above him and to the east was feathered with pale streamers of cloud, but when he looked over his shoulder, westward into the wind, he saw a heavier, darker, cloud bank bearing down on the city.

So there might be rain later. Maybe it would interrupt the challenge bout... He caught himself and laughed, bitterly. Was he reduced to hoping for such things? With a sigh that was half a groan, he turned his back on the scene and sat down on the stone paving with his knees drawn up and his back against the parapet. He closed his eyes. "Vothra," he murmured. "Give me strength."

He felt it almost immediately— the sense of a presence— and words came to him, spoken in that familiar calm, ineffably gentle voice.

I cannot literally do that.

"I know." He spoke his answer aloud, though he knew the voice had been only in his head. He kept his eyes closed as well. It was easier to carry on a conversation with a being who wasn't physically present if he imagined it standing in front of him where the voice seemed to be coming from. Vothra could, of course, conjure an image in his mind to match the voice, but he didn't like to put the Benevolent Spirit to so much trouble. "I didn't mean to call you," he added. "But I'm glad you're here."

I am staying close to you this day.

"Thank you. And although you can't give me strength, you did help me, earlier, in the Audience Chamber. I felt it."

I placed myself between the anxiety you were feeling and your awareness of it. Much the same way that I can block your perception of pain.

"It helped. I don't think I could have done any of that without it."

You did much more than you realize, Spirit called Nagaro. I let go of you the moment you saw the need to help the one you call Sindar. You find your strength when presented with another's need.

"Oh." Nagaro experienced a moment of astonishment, to think that he'd gotten through so much of that ordeal unaided. In the next moment, however, he remembered that another ordeal lay before him. "They want me to fight Lothard."

I know.

"Is my wound truly healed? You can see... inside of me. Is there really no danger? Master Ambras said he was sure, but... there's the pain."

The pain is only pain. There is a scar inside of you that is, in a certain place, a little too wide so that it pulls sometimes, and you feel it. That is all. There is no weakness there. No danger.

"I see." He could believe it, but he wasn't sure it would help.

I do not expect you to be able to ignore the pain, but you must discount it.

"I *do* discount it. Or I've tried to...but it's hard not to react to it first, and—"

—when you react to the pain it can give the other man an opening.

"Yes." He was relieved that the Spirit understood. Vothra always understood, but again it didn't help. Understanding wasn't enough. There was nothing left but to ask the question that was in his mind, so he drew a breath and asked. "Can you help me when I go against Lothard? Can you take the pain?"

And now there was a pause, as if Vothra felt some discomfort or uncertainty in answering. And when the answer came, it wasn't what he hoped for.

I am sorry, Spirit called Nagaro. The truth is that I cannot. To block a pain, it must first be there. I must see it. The pain that troubles you comes in one instant and is gone the next. There is no time.

"Oh." He let his breath out, and hope went with it. "Is there no other way you can help me?"

There was another pause, long enough this time for Nagaro to become aware of the wind on his face and the hard, cold stone on which he was sitting. At last the Spirit spoke.

I gave the simple answer to your other question, but this requires a more complicated one. Do you know the tale of Atheran?

Nagaro nodded. "He was the leader of the people who left the Kelorin Isles long ago, in ships. He led them over the sea to the land of Arlinas that lies beyond the Goreitha Mountains. All the Kelorin folk of Edrovir are descended from those people that Atheran led."

Yes. Do you know how he was able to find his way?

Nagaro frowned. "The tales say that you— Vothra— showed him the way."

It was my earlier self. Some of the spirits that were part of it are also part of me, and some are different, and time has passed. I remember doing it, because some parts of me remember. But in another sense it was not me. The voice seemed to sigh. *Let us say that I was younger. Less experienced in doing what I do. I saw a land that was unpopulated and I led my people to it because they needed a place to go and there was no one there to be displaced. I did not stop to wonder why that land was empty. In time, I came to understand that the people who had once been there had destroyed themselves, and that the rithral stones the Kelorin folk found there were involved in that destruction. I tried to warn my people of the danger, but they saw only the power that was in the rithral stones. They did not listen to me, and many turned away from me because they did not want to hear. Since they didn't want me, I chose to let my constituent spirits disperse, and for a time I ceased to be.*

There was another sigh and a very short pause, but then the Spirit continued. *I do not know all that happened in Arlinas during the time of the cataclysm, because I was not there in my proper form to watch it. There was much grief, that I know. Much suffering. The rithral stones were cast aside. Abandoned. The Kelorin people, and the Leithians who had joined them, fled, and the land of Arlinas lies under a curse to this day. It is empty again, or nearly so. And all of this came to pass because of what I, Vothra, did—with the best of intentions—in an effort to save the people I cared for.*

The voice stopped speaking.

"But you couldn't possibly have known that all those things would happen!"

That is exactly my point, Spirit called Nagaro. The voice, already tinged with melancholy, grew sadder still. *I set out to change events without knowing what would happen, and I tell you this to explain why I have resolved not to interfere again in the world in that way. I try to help people understand themselves, and understand others. I try to help them find hope, love, happiness, or peace. I trust that, as a result, there will be more of those things in the world, and that there will be less misunderstanding, intolerance, bloodshed, and pain. I believe that most people wish it to be so. But trying to influence events is perilous, because one cannot foresee all of the consequences of even the smallest act.*

"So you're saying that because of this... you won't help me now? Yet you did it... at Osfaraad..."

Yes. I broke my rule at Osfaraad. I am not always good at keeping my resolve when I am tempted—which happens most when I care the most. After Osfaraad, I tried to keep a greater distance from you to avoid temptation even though I suspect that Roheed would have done what he did at Osfaraad regardless, and my actions likely changed nothing. Still, I kept my distance from you until the knife attack. That alarmed me because you so very nearly died, and so I have been watching you more closely again. And, yes, there are things I could do to help you, Spirit called Nagaro, but I will try not to do them. I do not know what this day may bring. The future is an unknown land into which we can only walk one step at a time. But I promise I will be watching you.

When the Spirit grew silent, Nagaro sat for a long moment with his head bowed, trying to think what he should say. He was conscious of the honor that Vothra did him by speaking so candidly, and aware of how deeply the Spirit cared for him. He was also ashamed of having begged for the Spirit's aid. Before he could find words, however, his thoughts were interrupted by a voice that was plainly not inside his head, one that spoke from some distance to his right.

"Nagaro! There you are!"

His eyes snapped open and his head came up. He turned to see Vell striding towards him along the walkway, even as he felt the presence of Vothra's spirit slip away. Hurriedly he got to his feet. "I was... trying to rest," he said as the Leithian came abreast of him.

Vell seemed to accept this explanation without a second thought. "They sent me to fetch you," he said. "The Council, I mean. I confess that for a moment I thought you might have fled. An unworthy thought, I suppose, but I wouldn't have blamed you." He smiled crookedly.

"They've told you what they want me to do?"

Vell nodded. "Stand the king's challenge for him. And I wouldn't want to be in your place— not against Lothard." He glanced out over the parapet as he turned to lead the way back to the gate tower and the stairs. "That should be *my* army over there, but there's not a chance of my uncle giving it up." He jerked his head in direction of the pie-slice of men in cream-colored tirkas and purple bandoliers that identified them as soldiers of Sobring Hold.

"Has Grimbold been informed that he's no longer the lord? That your Elders chose you instead?"

"Ha! Madred and Anduar sent out a messenger to inform him. Grimbold sent a message back saying it was a lie and a trick, and he had no intention of stepping aside for '*that stripling*'." Vell cast Nagaro an aggrieved look. "Stripling, I say! Do I look like a stripling to you?"

"Certainly not."

They had reached the tower top, where a doorway gave access to the stairs leading down.

They didn't speak as they descended to the second-floor tower room where they found Elgurn, Anduar, and Odus still sitting around the table with their heads together. Madred must have already gone, and Nevien was also not in evidence. The three lords interrupted their conversation when Vell and Nagaro entered. Odus rose and caught Vell's eye and the two of them promptly excused themselves and left together.

Elgurn beckoned with his good arm for Nagaro to join him and Anduar at the table. The king had changed his bloodied shirt and donned a richly embroidered tirka of burgundy velvet before leaving the palace. His injured arm was done up in a white cotton sling. He wore the crown of Edrovir, a simple circlet of bright yellow gold that contrasted strikingly with the pale silver of his hair. At that moment his expression was very grave and he looked every inch a king.

Anduar looked uncharacteristically tense. Though he leaned back in his chair, the fingers of his right hand were massaging his chin. and his mouth was set in a hard line as his gray eyes studied Nagaro.

Elgurn spoke as Nagaro took a seat in the chair he had indicated. "I didn't know you still had pain from the assassin's blade," he said, frowning. "You should have spoken. I'm loath to hold you to this if it would place you in peril."

Nagaro winced inwardly. *Had Nevien done more than merely listen?* He searched the king's eyes and found nothing but sincere concern. "I've been assured that the wound is fully healed," he said carefully. "The pain is only pain—"

Anduar broke in. "Still, it affects your ability to fight. You've recently lost bouts to Kuran."

Nagaro frowned. "Who told you that?"

"Kuran himself. He spoke to me at the palace before returning to the Fleet Compound to marshal a force of Fleet Warriors."

So not Nevien, but Kuran. Nagaro grimaced. "Then he will also have told you that I'm improving. In our last practice session I bested him three times out of four."

Anduar raised an eyebrow. "Are you, then, confident that you can defeat Lothard?"

"No!" Nagaro was annoyed by both the question and its tone. "I am by no means confident. But I wouldn't permit myself to be confident even if there were no pain. I haven't fought a full bout with Lothard or had a chance to observe his moves." He shifted in his seat. "The pain I have comes and goes suddenly. It distracts me. I've been trying to learn to ignore it, and I confess I would feel better about facing Lothard if I'd made more progress." He looked from one frowning face to the other. "Is there someone else?" he asked. "If you don't think I'm the best man for this, I will gladly step aside. I know how important it is."

Anduar didn't answer. Instead, the Kelorin lord removed his hand from his chin to pinch the bridge of his nose, briefly closing his eyes.

Elgurn looked uncomfortable. "We have Geldoran and Rastian from the Fleet. Kuran will bring them. Besides that, Odus is willing and so are Varsyl and Rathdar."

Nagaro felt chagrined. "So many?" he murmured. *He had thought they were counting on him.*

Elgurn heaved a sigh. "I hope they will be enough. And I wish we had more Leithians. Perhaps more will come forward when they see the need."

"You want *more?*" Nagaro was bewildered.

Anduar made a small impatient movement. "If the first champion is defeated," he explained, "the king has the right to counter-challenge by calling a second champion, and a third if the second is defeated, and so on. It was intended to test the extent of the king's support. One who ruled well would presumably find more men ready to defend him, while one who ruled badly would stand alone."

"It gives us the hope of wearing Lothard down," added Elgurn.

"Of course Lothard can answer a counter-challenge with a surrogate of his own," Anduar continued. "But he has none among his supporters who comes close to his prowess, so we can hope he'll choose to face the counter-challenges himself— especially given his arrogance. The question is where we ought to place you in the order—"

"Or whether to put you in at all." Elgurn cut in, giving Anduar a sharp glance.

Anduar spread his hands placatingly. "Of course we won't ask you to do anything you don't wish to," he said smoothly to Nagaro. "Well? What do you think?"

Nagaro stared at him. "I think it's ridiculous! If you wish to test the king's support, you should call for a convening of the Council of Lords and hold a new choosing. Who designed this absurd arrangement?"

Now there was frost in Anduar's stare. "Twenty-seven years ago, men were not ready to accept the alternative you suggest," he said coldly. "And this 'absurd arrangement' has not in fact been tested until today. After men have seen it in action, they may very well be willing to amend it. But for now, we must work with the law as it stands. May we return to the matter of the order and your place in it?"

"Yes... of course." Nagaro felt it wisest to concede the matter.

Elgurn looked as if he wanted to say something, but Anduar shook his head at him and continued. "I had originally thought to put you first, in the hope that the challenge could be resolved in a single bout— which is what would happen if you won. The king may counter-challenge if his champion loses, you see, but the challenger must simply accept defeat whenever it occurs. Since your ability to defeat Lothard is in doubt, however, I suggest leading with whichever of our men we think has the strongest chance of a lucky win. That would be Geldoran, or Rastian. If that man wins, the challenge is officially at an end. If he loses, we then throw our men at Lothard one after the other until he begins to flag, and *then* send you in against him when his weariness will balance your handicap. Does this sound reasonable?"

Nagaro shook his head. "I don't like it," he said. "Using other men to set things up so I may win. It seems dishonest— and too much like the way Reith Hurn defeated Tevren."

"Some might call it poetic justice."

"I... suppose. But I don't see the need for it. As long as Lothard's challenge is beaten back, I don't see that it matters who does it."

Anduar's mouth twitched. "In theory perhaps is doesn't. But the symbolism of Tevren's son going up against the son of Reith Hurn will not be lost on anyone. Most especially it won't be lost on Lothard Hurn."

"Well... yes... but I still don't see why—"

Anduar abruptly leaned forward, bringing his palms down on the table. "Do you really think that Lothard will accept it gracefully and walk away if he's beaten? Do you imagine that will be the end of if?

Nagaro thought of all those armed men spread out on the field beyond the city wall, remembering how many of them wore the red, white, and black livery of Hurn Hold. He felt a chill. "*So...*" he said slowly. "You're saying that if Lothard loses, there's likely to be war."

"There is also likely to be war if he wins."

And this time Nagaro thought of all those other armed men, the ones encamped on the other side of the High Road. "But... if you don't expect the challenge to avert the war—"

"Why bother with the challenge?" Anduar sat back in his chair and crossed his arms. "Because it offers us the best chance to do the one thing that *will* avert the war. It offers us the chance to remove Lothard from the play— *permanently.*"

This time Nagaro felt a knife of ice slide into his stomach.

So that was it.

"You want me to kill him," he said quietly. "But I don't understand. The law forbids it. The challenge isn't fought for blood."

Elgurn had sat silent, tense and frowning, letting Anduar have his say. Now he cleared his throat. "The prohibition against fighting for blood ends the moment either man violates the honor of keeping it," he said. "If Lothard makes a clear attempt to kill you, then you are permitted to try to kill *him*. This is the jeopardy into which Anduar proposes to place you."

Nagaro looked from one to the other of them helplessly. "But why me? Surely any of the other men could do this deed as well as I!"

Again Anduar leaned forward, his glance as sharp as a blade. "Any one of them could try, *if* Lothard makes a move to kill him," he said, placing his words as if he were laying bricks. "And Lothard *might* do that— if he felt he was losing the bout. He's a treacherous man by nature. But *you* are the one man in all of Edrovir for whom he is most likely to cross that line. You're the man he's found in his way, time and again. He sees you as a rival. He's tried to kill you once already, if I'm not mistaken. Madred has heard the testimony of a former member of the Palace Guard, a young Leithian named Groft, whose task it was to lure you into a dark street where men were waiting."

Nagaro was no longer listening. He was staring past Anduar, remembering that night... the dark, narrow street... the wind... the shadows... "Yes," he said. "I recognized the voice as Lothard's, speaking words I'd heard him say before."

Anduar's voice reached him. "And now the man he failed to kill with the assassin's knife returns to face him as the King's Champion, under the name of Alorin Loros. When Lothard looks across the point of his sword and sees you standing there, can there be any doubt that he'll try to finish the job?"

Nagaro felt his stomach knot. He could hear in his mind the voice of Lothard speaking to Kenthos outside the garden gate at Loros Hall, declaring that he would finish what his father had started. He closed his eyes.

It all made sense— Anduar's assessment, this carefully constructed plan. And though he detested Anduar's manipulations, he had done this kind of thing before. Vothra trusted him to do it— to be honor's executioner. *More than any other living man, the Spirit had once said.* And if Lothard was a man who failed the test of honor when it counted most, then he would never make a good king. He could not be permitted to take the crown— not by law, by treachery, or by force.

And if at all possible, the country must not be driven to war for the sake of one man's ambition.

Nagaro opened his eyes and fixed his gaze on Anduar. "I must face him, and I must be the first."

"My Lord!" Elgurn spoke, and his distress sounded genuine. "You need not do this! It's well known that you have suffered a grievous wound. At least let our other fighters wear him down!"

But Nagaro shook his head. "If you do it that way, it will look as if Lothard was harried and driven to it— set upon by man after man until he was tempted by desperation. He'll gain sympathy, just as Tevren did. Men will say it was unjust. No, I must face him first. If he makes no false move, then you've lost the gamble, whether I win or lose, but you would have lost it anyway. If he bests me, without treachery, the other men will still have their chance."

"And what if he kills you?" Elgurn demanded.

Nagaro sighed. He felt a weight that he couldn't un-shoulder. "In that case," he said, "Can't you execute him for murder?"

Anduar considered him with narrowed eyes. "We could try," he said carefully. "It would be lawful, if he were the first to draw blood. And there would surely be a great public outcry over your loss. Emotions *might* run high enough that the Brothers of the Blood wouldn't dare to intervene by force—"

"I won't have this!" Elgurn interrupted. "I won't have you sacrifice yourself!"

"That's not my intention."

"I still don't like placing you at risk, when you've only just absolved me of past sins."

Nagaro stiffened. "This time it's *my* choice, Elgurn! And it remains to be seen how Lokundas will turn these events."

Elgurn studied him gravely, while Anduar watched with narrowed eyes. Finally the king said, "You're determined, then?"

"I am." Nagaro spoke firmly, though he felt as if he was standing on quicksand.

The king bowed his head. "Then so be it," he said. "And may the Gods protect you." He studied the table top in silence for the space of several heartbeats. Then he sighed and pushed back his chair. Rising, he turned to Anduar. "Come, My Lord," he said. "We've been long in our deliberations, and I'm sure the enemy will not have grown more patient."

With that, he rounded the table and strode towards the stairs that led down to the street below.

Nagaro heaved a sigh of his own. He rose and followed with a more reluctant tread.

Anduar brought up the rear, his expression impossible to read.

Chapter 28

The King's Champion

When Elgurn, Anduar, and Nagaro stepped out of the tower into the area beneath the gate's broad arch they found the space immediately behind the huge wooden gate crowded with men and horses. Twenty men of the City Guard, intended to be the king's escort, awaited the order to mount. The rank on the side closest to the city street were holding back an eager throng of gawking townspeople.

Nagaro saw Odus among those waiting under the arch, as well as Vell, and Madred. And Nevien was there, beside her white mare.

Nagaro found it hard to meet her eyes. He kept his averted as he moved to where Thunder-Heels was tied to a hitching rail. He couldn't escape her, however. She was suddenly there, planting herself by his side.

"You're going to fight him, aren't you?" she said accusingly. "Even now that they know you still have pain from your wound! Did they make you think you haven't any choice?"

He reached for the bridle, studying his fingers as they unknotted the reins. "I'm sorry, Nevien. I believe it's the best chance we have to avoid a war—"

"Nagaro, you could be killed!"

He did look at her then, and was shocked by how pale she was. "How many more will die if there's a war?" he asked. "And do you think I wouldn't be involved in it? I'm a Wared lord now."

"Nagaro!" She gripped his arm and clung to it. "I... I don't want to lose you when we've only just found each other!"

"And I don't want to be lost!" He felt an ache in his throat. "I just have to do my best to make sure that doesn't happen."

A moment more she searched his face. Then she leaned close and kissed him lightly on the cheek. "See that you do that," she said and spun away, leaving him standing looking after her, heedless of the astonished eyes that stared at him or followed the princess as she returned to Snowdrift's side.

Nagaro shivered. "This is such madness," he muttered to no one in particular. "If I were king, the first thing I'd do is abolish the Challenge by Combat. Let any lord who thinks the king unfit to rule call for a new Choosing—" He broke off, suddenly aware that Vell, Madred, Soren, and Anduar were all there looking at him. He closed his mouth and gave his attention to his saddle harness.

A moment later, Elgurn gave the order to mount. Nagaro swung into the saddle, doing his best to move just as smoothly and freely as if he hadn't felt the small, sharp jab of pain in his chest. After a hurried ordering of the ranks, the two massive gates swung open. Two blasts were sounded on a trumpet and the little party issued forth. They hadn't far to ride, quickly arriving at the bare ground at the edge of the crossroads. The king and members of the Council rode in front. Nagaro was back a little when he came to a halt, between Vell and Soren and flanked by half a dozen guardsmen on each side.

The view from the ground was in some ways more impressive than from the top of the wall. Nagaro couldn't see the full extent of the forces arrayed before them from this vantage point, but he could see the sweep of the front lines. The closest warriors were no more than thirty yards away, on either side of the High Road, and were visible in every detail. He saw pennons snapping in the wind and horses pawing the ground or shifting from hoof to hoof. He saw hands on sword hilts, and expressions on faces, grim or expectant. He saw how every eye converged on the king's party, all focused on Elgurn at the front and center, astride his chestnut charger.

He could also see how poor a barrier the High Road made between the opposing armies. Its paved surface stood at this point no more than two feet above the level of the surrounding fields, and the ditches that flanked it were neither very wide nor very deep.

Scanning the assembled warriors for any that he knew, Nagaro saw that the Fleet contingent had arrived since he'd left his vantage above the gate. In royal blue, they blocked the southern limb of the Circle Road that ran between the river and the city wall, the road leading to the South Gate and the Fleet Compound. He saw Kuran there in the mounted front rank with Geldoran beside him. A bit behind them, he caught a glimpse of Pavo's shaggy head standing above the crowd of men on foot. Taru and his other friends must be there as well.

He picked out banners, clustered together, marking the positions of the companies belonging to Rastyl, Endemar, and Varsyl. Kenthos and his irregulars he supposed must be with them. A quick glance to the left showed another late arrival. A troop of men whose livery he didn't recognize blocked the north limb of the Circle Road even as the Fleet men blocked the south limb.

"Who are the men in sky-blue tirkas?" he asked Vell in a low voice.

"They're Lord Ranse's, from Heldring Hold. He's one of the lesser lords who's joined the Brothers of the Blood. There's several others here, as well— come out in support of Lothard."

"Oh." As Nagaro's eye swung back towards the center, he spotted Grimbold sitting his horse under the purple standard of Sobring Hold.

And then he saw Lothard— just to the left of the High Road and almost directly across from where Elgurn had come to a halt. At that very moment, the lord of Hurn Hold abruptly pressed his mount forward to stand clear of the vanguard of his army. There he sat, astride his impressive roan stallion, resplendent in a scarlet tirka crossed by a gold baldrick, he carried his big frame proudly erect and controlled his impatient mount with a tight rein. The afternoon sunlight flashed off of polished silver-work on the horse's bridle and struck gold in the man's blond hair. Even as Nagaro watched, however, a cloud moved across the face of the sun and its shadow swept over the scene, dimming Lothard's splendor.

Vell reached out a hand to touch Nagaro's arm. "Did you see that?" he said in an awed whisper. "That's Hrathgard's sign! And he favors you, Nagaro. You're sure to win the challenge!"

"It's only an approaching storm," Nagaro muttered under his breath. "They're common at this season."

He was answered by a gust of wind that seemed to snatch his words away.

Elgurn's trumpeter blew another blast and the king pressed his horse forward a few paces, raising his good arm. Taking no particular notice of Lothard, he addressed the crowd in a commanding voice.

"People of Edrovir! I see that you have come, in great numbers and bearing arms, to stand before the gate of your capital city. You know that I have always striven to hear all complaints, and redress all wrongs. If any man here bears a grievance, let him speak!"

For several heartbeats, there was no sound but the whistling of the wind around the gate towers overhead. Then Lothard reared his horse, drawing all eyes.

"I have a grievance, Elgurn!" he cried. "My grievance is *you!* You're a weak king! You make peace with our enemies!" His voice dripped scorn. "You let the Jinari Council tell you what to do, and bow to the Mahuk Emperor! You make Edrovir weak like you, and I say that we must put an end to this! It's time for a strong king— one who'll make Edrovir strong, and lead us to Victory! I challenge you for the crown! Either fight, or step aside!"

This speech was followed by shouts of support from some of those gathered on the northern half of the field— and scattered protests from the southern side.

Elgurn spoke out of the side of his mouth to Anduar, who sat close beside him on a black horse. "He doesn't beat about the bush, does he? Well, no more shall I." Then he addressed the crowd once more.

"I will not step aside!" he cried. "I don't apologize for making peace—peace that leads to trade by which we prosper. And treating with the Emperor has brought our citizens home, and stopped the taking of galley slaves!"

This drew cheers from the king's supporters.

"What Lothard calls strength would wipe all of that away!" Elgurn continued. "Making war with people who prefer peace isn't strength, it's folly! So, by the law, I must accept this challenge, but—" and here he gestured at the sling that cradled his right arm. "It catches me at a bad time."

"How very *convenient!*" Lothard's words were a sneer.

Odus pressed his horse forward. "Know this!" bellowed. "King Elgurn has fought a dangerous foe this day. The treacherous serpent, Dreigen— the murderer of Darion, of Berinar Sundorin, and Gillard Marchent— assaulted him and burned his flesh with vitriol! This I have witnessed with my own eyes! But Elgurn has prevailed, and Dreigen is dead. He will trouble Edrovir no more!"

The cheers that followed this announcement did not come solely from the men on the south side of the field.

Elgurn gave Lothard no chance to make a retort, but raised his own voice over the dwindling acclamations. "Since it will be some weeks before I can use my sword arm, I will choose a champion to fight in my stead!"

The shouts died to a murmur, and in the near silence there came a low rumble of thunder. Many eyes glanced at the sky. Some pointed at the mass of storm clouds that was riding the wind out of the west.

Lothard only laughed and dug his spurs into his horse's flanks so that the stallion pranced and fought the bit. "The Great God Hrathgard sends me his favor!" he cried. "Choose whatever champion you will, Elgurn. I'll make good sport of him!"

Elgurn made a show of reining his horse back into the company of his Council members and turned in the saddle to face Nagaro. He extended a hand in a supplicating gesture. "My Lord Alorin," he said deferentially. "Will you do me the honor of standing this challenge, for the security of the crown and the good of Edrovir?"

Nagaro understood that this formality was for the benefit of any who might suppose that the thing hadn't been pre-arranged. He swallowed.

"Yes," he said, forcing himself to speak loudly. "My Lord King, I will." And he pressed his heels to Thunder-Heels' flanks to urge the stallion forward into the front rank, where Anduar maneuvered his mount to one side to make room.

Just as he did so, the sky behind him lit up with a flash that cast the city wall and gate in stark relief against a backdrop of roiling cloud. Five seconds later came the dull boom and rumbling roll of thunder. Many of those around him cast their eyes heavenward, and he heard some of the Leithians exclaiming, *"Hrathgard's Sign!"*

Even Odus murmured, "By the Gods, we may yet win!"

Nagaro frowned darkly and muttered, "I wish everyone weren't so impressed with the weather."

Anduar cast him a significant look. "I'll be impressed when the lightening strikes Lothard dead," he observed dryly.

Elgurn motioned his lords to silence. He leaned close to Nagaro. "I thought to present you by the name and title you have claimed today," he said. "Is there anything you would have me say or withhold?"

Nagaro dropped his voice so that his words were for Elgurn's ears alone. "I don't wish it known that I was ever Leyel Virden. For the rest, you may say what you will."

Elgurn nodded, then faced the assembled hosts. "Let me present my champion!" he cried, indicating Nagaro with a dramatic gesture and enunciating each word with elaborate care. "Though you may not recognize him, yet he is known to you. This is Lord Nagaro Alorin Loros, son of Tevren and Lindra of Loros. He has proven his parentage this day before me and my Council, and we recognize him also as the lawfully chosen lord of the new Loros Wared!"

A stunned silence followed this pronouncement. It lasted for the space of several heartbeats and ended in the eruption of wild cheers that began in the vicinity of Rastyl's and Varsyl's banners and swept over the entire southern half of the field. The cheers were echoed from atop the city wall, which had apparently been made available to members of the general public so they could witness the spectacle unfolding below. Some of those on the wall began to chant, and the words were picked up by many in the field as well:

"Nagaro! Nagaro! Nagaro!"

"Loros! Loros!"

Elgurn attempted to shout over the chanting. "Peace, good people! Peace! There is a challenge to be fought!" He had to repeat himself twice before the clamor finally subsided.

Nagaro sat numbly through it all, humbled by the show of support. *Please...* he thought. *Don't let me disappoint these people.*

His thoughts were interrupted by an outraged howl from Lothard.

"That's your champion? They won't be cheering after I've finished with him!"

Nagaro's sideways glance surprised a satisfied smile on Anduar's face before the Kelorin lord smoothed his countenance. Nagaro knew the reason for the smile. Lothard was glaring at *him*, and the Leithian's voice had carried a hint of jealousy. *How little might it take to drive the man to murderous rage with him as its target?*

Nagaro fixed Anduar with a smoldering glance. "Exactly how long have you been hatching this plot?" he inquired.

The Kelorin lord returned him a flinty stare that grew distinctly less flinty when Nagaro unflinchingly held his gaze. "Since I first became convinced that the tales of your prowess weren't exaggerated," he conceded. "But *I* didn't bring you to this place."

Before Nagaro could respond, he was distracted by a flickering cascade of lightening in the sky to the northwest. It was followed by a roll of thunder and a flurry of wind that carried scattered raindrops. As if in answer, Lothard began railing at Elgurn.

"How dare you call him the heir of Loros!" he cried. "That *pirate upstart* told me himself that he's a farmer's bastard! This is all lies and trickery!"

Elgurn stood stone-faced. "It's neither a lie, nor a trick," he said coldly. "The evidence is overwhelming. But we'd best get on with this, Lothard, before the storm breaks. I've chosen my champion. Will you choose a man to stand as your Second?"

Lothard made a rude gesture. "It doesn't matter who your champion is, since I mean to trounce him. I choose the Lord of Sobring for my Second."

"Can you mean Lord Vell?" Elgurn feigned surprise. "We have this day recognized him as the lord of Sobring Hold, at the request of the Sobring Elders—"

"Is there no end to your tricks, Elgurn?" Lothard was raking his horse's flanks in his wrath while keeping so tight a rein that the stallion's chin was nearly on his chest, with the result that the big roan danced in harassed frustration. "I mean Grimbold Sobring, and you know it!"

Elgurn shrugged. "Very well. Grimbold Sobring it shall be. And now I must choose a Second for my champion."

At this, there came a shout from Kuran in the front rank of the Fleet Warriors. The Lord of the Fleet spurred his horse across the intervening space and drew rein in front of the king. His face was set in grim lines as he addressed Elgurn.

"My Lord, I will stand as Nagaro's Second."

Anduar cleared his throat and lowered his voice. "I intend to do that."

Kuran reined his horse around to face the Kelorin lord. "Isn't it enough that you've ignored my wishes?" he demanded, his voice tight with anger. "He is *my* heir, and it's surely my right to stand as his Second!"

"It is not a matter of *right*," Anduar responded sharply. "It is a matter of *capacity*. My arm is longer and—"

Kuran's eyes flashed. "And I'm a younger man than you and doubtless more spry! And I know that *I* won't throw him to the wolves!"

Anduar reacted as if he'd been struck. "He may be *your* adopted heir, but he's *my* blood kin! Or had you forgotten that the House of Loros was split from the House of Tyronin? By the Eyes of Vothra, Kuran, if you think—"

"*Gentlemen! Please!*" Elgurn drove his horse between the two men to intervene. "We are watched!" He looked exasperatedly from one man to the other. Both were still bristling. "Since I cannot choose between you, you shall both stand. There's no law to say there must be only one Second." He spun his mount about and addressed the crowd.

"A challenge for the crown demands the closest observation and the surest enforcement of honor," he declaimed. "Therefore, there shall be two Seconds on each side. For Lord Alorin, I choose the lords Kuran Kel and Anduar Tyronin. Let My Lord Lothard choose a second man. And to ensure the proper conduct of this bout, I name Lord Madred Furthing to be the Arbiter of any disputes."

Nagaro had sat through the altercation between Kuran and Anduar in stunned embarrassment. Anduar's heat surprised him, not to mention the claim of kinship. But he found Kuran's words unnerving. His mentor obviously doubted his readiness to face Lothard. He tore his eyes away from the two men, who were still glowering at each other, to note that Lothard was watching them all with a leering smirk on his face. The Leithian had plainly observed the dispute and was pleased by it, even if he didn't know its cause.

Nagaro shook his head and muttered, "Quarreling doesn't serve us well." He was gratified to see Anduar actually look chagrined. Kuran only shot a worried glance in his direction.

The need to name another Second caused some controversy in the ranks of Lothard's followers. Several mounted men converged on Lothard's position to vie for the honor, mainly the lesser lords and leaders of small forces including the one who must be Lord Ranse of whom Vell had spoken. When Lothard finally settled on a tall, slim youth mounted on a white horse, Madred and Odus immediately concluded that Lothard had been unable to chose among the competing lords.

"Why?" Nagaro asked. "Who is that young man?"

Madred answered. "Beinard Hurn," he said. "Lothard's younger brother."

"I didn't even know Lothard *had* a brother."

Madred shrugged. "There are twelve years between them, and he is so recently come of age that almost nothing is known of him— save that he seems to lack his brother's ambition."

"Well, at least that's something." Nagaro was trying not to think about the fact that young Beinard Hurn was going to witness whatever happened that day.

While Lothard had debated his choice, the sky had continued to darken. Racks of cloud now spread across it, flying before a gusting west wind. Flecks of rain peppered the dust of the crossroads as Lothard, Grinbold, and Beinard left the ranks of fighting men and rode out to meet Elgurn and his chosen champion.

There came another flash of lightening and an answering roll of thunder.

Nagaro touched Thunder-Heels' flanks with his boot heels. Directing the big gray with a slight pressure of the reins against the stallion's neck, he joined Elgurn, Anduar, Kuran, and Madred as they rode out to meet Lothard's party.

Elgurn reined in his mount a dozen yards from the three Leithians. "Gentlemen!" he said loudly, "prepare yourselves!" Then he glanced significantly at the sky and lowered his voice to address Nagaro. "Will the rain trouble you?"

Nagaro shook his head. "I have fought in wind and rain, and on the decks of ships that were awash with seawater. Rain is the least of my worries." A gust brought another flurry of drops. "Let's get on with it."

He swung out of the saddle, willing himself once again to perform the movement as if he weren't anticipating the pain in his chest. He was aware of others dismounting around him, and of Elgurn calling for members of the City Guard to hold back the crowds of onlookers. He was focused, however, on removing his cloak and securing it to his saddlebow. After a moment's deliberation, he removed the blue velvet tirka as well. *There was no sense in putting Tira Theseline's handiwork at risk.*

Thunder-Heels snorted softly and nuzzled his shoulder. He stroked the stallion's neck. "Take care of yourself," he murmured. "Brother of the wind."

He no longer felt the weariness that had troubled him earlier. Perhaps he was too tense for that. His mind seemed steady, though his nerves were taut as bowstrings. A hand touched his elbow and he started slightly to find Kuran at his side. The depth of the older man's apprehension was betrayed in the lines of his face.

"You think you can do this?" Kuran's eyes searched his.

"It seems that I must. And I did choose it, Kuran. I know what I have to do."

"Yes, of course." Kuran's smile was too quick and contained too little confidence. "Just fight as you did in our last bout and you'll be fine. But be wary of Lothard. He's a devil for feints, and quick as a snake. He hits harder than he has to— to unbalance you and tire you, or to strain the muscles of your sword arm. So mind your grip. And don't trust him for anything." Kuran leaned close and lowered his voice. "It wouldn't surprise me," he muttered, "if the rotter went for blood."

Seeing the worry in those dark eyes, Nagaro couldn't bring himself to admit that the idea was hardly a new one. "I'll keep that in mind," was all he said.

"Good." Kuran looked at the ground, then up again. He reached up to clap Nagaro on the shoulder. "May Vothra keep you," he said, his voice catching. "Shall I lead Thunder-Heels aside for you? The guards may have trouble with him."

Nagaro nodded, not trusting his own voice.

Thunder-Heels tossed his head at the mere notion of having Kuran take his bridle, but Nagaro spoke a few words and the big gray went quietly.

No sooner was Kuran out of earshot than Anduar stepped into his place. "You've fought both Geldoran and Rastian, haven't you," he said. "Which of them would fare better against Lothard?"

Nagaro gave the Kelorin lord a stony stare. "I don't know, because I don't know Lothard," he said flatly. "Ask me after I've fought him."

Anduar's mouth twitched. "It might be too late by then, and I didn't want to miss this opportunity."

"In other words, you're planning who will be your next pawn after I fall? Don't you ever stop scheming, Anduar?"

Anduar offered a wry flicker of a smile. "Not for more than two days together, I'm afraid. But in this case I'm only trying to plan for all possible contingencies. Can you at least give me your assessment of their strengths?"

Nagaro sighed. Anduar, he supposed, was only being Anduar. "Both are very skilled and very quick," he said. "Geldoran has more experience and is the more consistent fighter, but he's also more predictable in his moves. Rastian can be erratic, which can hurt him, but it also means he's more likely to take his opponent by surprise."

"I see. Thank you." Anduar continued to study him. "Were you aware that my grandfather and your great grandfather were the brothers Hindrath and Nevrath? It makes us cousins of a sort."

Nagaro held the other man's eyes. "I confess that I hadn't thought about it. I've only recently begun getting used to the idea of having kin of any kind."

"Mm." Anduar nodded. "I suppose it must be a bit of an adjustment." He paused, looking past Nagaro's shoulder. "They were never truly enemies, you know— those brothers. Despite the trouble that came between them and the splitting of the House of Tyronin."

"So I've always understood," Nagaro responded coldly. "But then, Hindrath didn't actually hatch the plot that almost took Nevrath's life."

"Ah." Anduar winced. "A hit, I think. But I've never wished you harm, and I wish you'd save your ire for Lothard who deserves it much more than I." He glanced again past Nagaro's shoulder. Nagaro followed the glance this time and saw that Kuran was coming back in their direction. Anduar abruptly stepped closer. "Don't take any chances with Lothard," he said, speaking fast and low. "Finish him at the first sign of treachery."

Nagaro returned Anduar's look with a cool stare. "You may drag me into your plans, Anduar," he said, "but I will do things my own way. You should know that."

The steel-gray eyes flickered, but Anduar stepped back just as Kuran arrived at Nagaro's side, and he added, as if continuing a natural conversation, "Lothard sometimes leaves himself open after a feint. It's the best time to hit him."

Nagaro had no time to make a response, for at that moment they heard Elgurn calling for them all to take their positions. The challenge for the crown was about to begin.

Chapter 29

The Honor Of Lothard Hurn

E lgurn issued his final orders from astride his horse, arranging the various participants within the cleared area at the center of the crossroads where the match was to take place.

Nagaro was directed to a place on the south side of that space, facing Lothard who stood on the north side. Lothard was eyeing him with swaggering disdain. The Leithian had discarded his cloak, but retained his scarlet tirka and gold baldrick. While their colors didn't blaze so brightly under the threatening sky, Nagaro was still conscious of how drably he was dressed by comparison, in his plain white shirt and black pants. The only color he sported was in the gold filigree that adorned the guard of his sword and the polished green stone in its pommel.

The four Seconds took their places— two on the east side and two on the west, so that they formed the corners of a square with each combatant having his own two Seconds on his right and left hand. Kuran and Grimbold were on the east, Anduar and Beinard on the west. Madred, the Arbiter, stood between Anduar and Beinard with his back to the city's East Gate. Beyond the Seconds were arrayed the guards, to east and west, a dozen on either side. Their task was to prevent interference from the spectators, though those on the east could scarcely have blocked an assault from even a tiny fraction of the gathered armies.

Once all were in place, Elgurn surveyed the participants with a grim face. The wind gusts had died down, and in the stillness one could hear all the little sounds made by the watching multitude— the jingle and creak of harness, the stamp and snort of horses, and the whispered mutter of expectant voices. Elgurn raised his good hand for attention and began to speak, pitching his voice so that it would carry to the soldiers in the front ranks and the watchers on the city wall.

"This match will be fought according to the law!" He paused, as if for effect, before continuing. "It will be won by the first man to achieve five hits. The combatants are bound to fight honorably, and, to the best of their ability, to avoid drawing blood. This is no fight to the death! If it is determined by agreement of the Seconds, or by judgement of the Arbiter, that blood was willfully drawn, this shall be deemed an act of treachery. If the wounded man then elects to continue the fight, it shall be understood that he may respond to the drawing of blood by drawing blood in kind— even to the extent of taking his opponent's life if his opponent should attempt to slay him."

There were mutters from the onlookers in response to the last point. Elgurn raised his hand for silence, waiting until the sound of the voices died away. "So the law is written!" he cried, and he bent his gaze sternly upon each of the two combatants. "And so it shall be kept! Do you both swear to conform your behavior to the law?"

Nagaro answered immediately, his voice ringing clearly in the sudden hush. "I will follow the law as written. I swear it on my honor and in Vothra's name!"

"And you, Lothard?" The king turned his attention to the Leithian lord. "Do you also swear to follow the law?"

It seemed to Nagaro that Lothard hesitated and that his expression fleetingly betrayed uncertainty. He wondered whether Lothard had been aware of all of the elements of the law. Could the man have come to this place without a full knowledge of what a challenge match entailed?

Lothard didn't hesitate for long, however. He tossed his head and declared, "I will conform myself to the law according to the will of the Gods!"

Elgurn frowned. "This is your affirmation? This is how you swear to follow the law as I described it?"

A brief look of annoyance crossed Lothard's face. Then he threw up a hand in a dismissive gesture. "Yes, yes, it's an affirmation," he snapped. "I've sworn it by the Gods!"

"Very good. I leave it to Lord Madred to mark the beginning of the bout." Elgurn turned his horse and rode back through the line of mounted guards to join Odus, Vell, Soren, and the others who watched from just outside the gate. Nagaro tried not to think about the fact that Nevien was there somewhere as well.

He couldn't help wondering whether Lothard's unconventional wording had been an effort to avoid a binding oath. If so, Elgurn had been wise to call him on it. The observers would likely have been left with the impression that Lothard had sworn as Nagaro had, regardless of the Leithian's intent.

Madred raised both hands. "Gentlemen!" he cried. "Be on your guard, and await my signal."

Nagaro's hand went to his left hip and in a smooth motion he drew forth the Sword of Shofeer. Even in the dim light of that overcast afternoon, a gleam of silver ran along the slightly curved blade. As he brought the sword into position, he dropped into a fighting crouch.

Lothard had done the same. The Leithian's sword was straight, and long. Nagaro judged it to be an inch longer than his own, and it looked heavier.

Madred raised his right hand. "Are you ready, gentlemen?"

Both men nodded.

"Then, let the bout begin!" Madred's hand came down.

It began to rain. Not the downpour that had been threatened, but a fine, soft drizzle that came without even a flicker of lightening for warning or the fanfare of thunder.

Madred threw his hands up again. "What say you, gentlemen? Will you fight this bout now, or shall we delay it until the rain has passed? Or perhaps until tomorrow, since the afternoon is already waning?"

Lothard gave a scoffing laugh. "Is my opponent afraid of getting wet?" he jeered. "What's a little rain but the blessing of Father Hrathgard? I will finish this before the water comes through my tirka!"

Nagaro smiled faintly. Overconfidence could be a weakness. If it *was* overconfidence. In any case, he had determined that he must fight this man, come what may, and the thought of waiting through a fretful night held no appeal. "I'll do as Lothard has chosen," he said.

So Madred gave the signal again, and they began to circle while the soft rain fell and the spectators held their breath. The dust of the crossroads began slowly turning into mud.

Nagaro's face was wet. He could feel the rain soaking into his hair, and his damp shirt was beginning to cling to his back and shoulders. He shivered, though the wind had died and the rain wasn't cold. Lothard was smirking at him, yet all the while the Leithian moved like a cat. He was a big man and well-muscled, an impressive figure even with his hair hanging lank and slick and the scarlet of his tirka darkening towards burgundy where the rain was soaking in.

Nagaro was waiting for his opponent to make the first attack, waiting to see how the man moved. Lothard was likely doing the same, but the Leithian apparently lacked the patience for it because he presently began to taunt Nagaro.

"So you're Lindra's brat, are you?" he sneered. "The son of that low-born bitch?"

"It appears so." Nagaro ignored the insult, trying to keep his focus on Lothard's movements rather than his words.

"Well fancy that!" Lothard leered. "*If* it's true, then my father killed your father. Did you know *that?*" Lothard attacked as he spoke the last word, coming in swift and low in an effort to get under Nagaro's guard.

Nagaro parried with a lightning-quick movement that fortunately failed to cause him pain. "Not alone, he didn't!" he retorted. "He would have been hard-pressed to—"

"*Liar!*" Lothard attacked again before Nagaro had finished speaking, diving at him and thrusting with such speed that Nagaro had to twist aside and parry at the same time.

Pain lanced sharply through his chest and caused him to falter so that, although his blade met Lothard's, he failed to block the full force of the blow and felt Lothard's sword strike his shoulder.

"A hit! A hit! First hit for Lothard!"

Grimbold's exclamation was exultant, and there were cries and groans from the spectators. Through the rain Nagaro caught a glimpse of Beinard's face, his eyes shining.

"Yes, it was a hit." Kuran's voice was tight as he acknowledged the score.

Nagaro backed and circled, trying to put distance between himself and his opponent— trying to breathe and focus his mind as he had been learning to do when fighting Kuran. But this was no practice bout. Lothard gave him no time to rest. The Leithian came at him with a storm of blows— thrusts, feints, and cuts. Nagaro managed to turn the strokes despite twinges of pain that accompanied some movements but not others, but he was fighting defensively, guarding himself against the threat of pain, and retreating step by step.

His hands were wet now, also, from the rain, and Lothard's strokes fell like hammers. He began to fear that he would lose his grip on his sword hilt. *This isn't going to work*, he thought. *I'm not ready, and he's too strong! I'm going to fail...*

Lothard made a particularly subtle feint. Nagaro saw the change of direction just in time to respond, but Lothard's move was terribly fast and he had to bring his hand up and turn his blade with lightning speed to block it. The movement sent pain lancing through him, and he flinched, then got a second jolt when steel met steel and his arm took the force of Lothard's blow. He flinched again, grimacing.

Lothard had read Nagaro's face. The Leithian uttered a barking laugh as he understood his opponent's trouble. Even as he disengaged, he struck again, flicking the flat of his blade hard against Nagaro's wrist, scoring a second hit.

It was a punishing blow despite the insulting way it had been delivered, painful though it drew no blood. Nagaro barely managed to maintain his grip on his sword as he leaped away. He was vaguely aware of voices calling the hit and a muddled roar of reaction from the crowd, but he dared not take his attention from Lothard. The man was still laughing, even as he attacked again. It was a direct thrust this time, and Nagaro blocked it easily, but their sword hilts locked and he found himself pressed backwards and down, as Lothard tried to force him to his knees. His feet were slipping in the mud and his wrist screamed agony as Lothard's face came within a foot of his.

The Leithian leered exultantly. "You feel it, don't you?" he hissed. "My knife in your ribs! Your precious princess won't save you this time. I'll finish you, and win the crown, and then she'll be mine!"

"No she *won't!*" The mere thought of Nevien being forced to endure the attentions of this swaggering brute gave new strength to Nagaro's limbs. Ignoring the pain, in his outrage, he heaved himself free. "She's going to marry *me!*" The effort caused a sharp stab in his chest, though it seemed less shocking when he was already gritting his teeth against the pain in his wrist. He twisted sideways, throwing Lothard off balance, and saw an opportunity to strike as he circled away. He brought the flat of his sword around to connect with Lothard's buttocks with a resounding *smack*. "I asked her," he cried, "and she said yes!"

"A hit, a hit! One for Nagaro!"

There were shouts and cheers, even some laughter at Lothard's expense, but it seemed to come from miles away as Lothard quickly recovered himself and leveled his sword at Nagaro.

"How dare you strike me so, *you filth!*" he roared. "And how dare you say you'll marry Nevien!"

Anduar must have heard the words from his place on the sidelines, for he called out in a voice like satin over ice. "It's true, Lothard. Elgurn gave the match his blessing."

"*What?*" Lothard's face turned bright crimson. He rounded on Nagaro. "*This is vile treachery!* I've been courting her for months! And you steal her like a thief!"

The Leithian lunged, serpent-quick, his blade leveled dead at the center of Nagaro's chest.

Several voices cried out, but Nagaro heard only one. Even as he dodged sideways, his eyes sought its source— Nevien astride her white mare, eyes wide in horror and both fists clutched to her mouth. His eyes stayed on her only long enough to burn the image into his brain before they snapped back— just a little too late to fully dodge Lothard's amended lunge. The blade struck him under his right arm, shearing through the fabric of his shirt and slicing into the flesh beneath. The blood came quickly, wicked into the wet cloth that clung to his skin.

"*A hit!*"

"*He bleeds!*"

"*Lothard has drawn blood!*"

There was a wild commotion. Nagaro staggered, reaching around with his left hand to clutch at the wound, trying to keep his sword up and ready as the pain of the sword cut seared his side.

Lothard leaped away, even as Kuran and Anduar both charged out with drawn swords to interpose themselves.

Kuran cried, "That stroke was meant to kill!"

Anduar added, "Lothard is a traitor to his oath!"

"No, no!" Grimbold protested. "An accident, clearly!"

All eyes turned to Beinard, the remaining Second. The young man looked acutely uncomfortable. "I... didn't see it clearly," he said, dropping his eyes.

Anduar turned to Madred. "My Lord, you must rule. Was this blood drawn willfully?"

Madred cast Lothard a deeply disappointed look. "I judge that it was," he said.

Lothard stood glowering. "It was an accident," he growled. "And the way he struck me was an insult!"

"That may be," Madred responded. "And an insult may justly provoke a man's anger. But anger is no excuse for oath-breaking, and a man who would rule a country should better control his temper."

"You rule against me, Madred? You betray our people?" Lothard's lip curled. "But what else can we expect! Elgurn put you on his Council, so you're his man now!"

Madred did not deign to reply. He stood erect and proud as he turned his gaze upon Nagaro. "Are you able to continue, My Lord Alorin?" he asked with exaggerated deference.

Nagaro dropped his blood-smeared hand from his side. He swung his right arm experimentally. The cut was more than a scratch. It stung sharply even when he stood still, and cruelly when he moved, but he had fought with such wounds before. In the heat of battle, such pain could be ignored because it was predictable. It increased whenever he moved.

He frowned. The wound, left untended, would eventually sap his strength. He was behind on hits, with just one to Lothard's three. And Lothard was a formidable opponent, one who would stretch his skill even under the best of circumstances. *Which meant the man was beyond the skill of either Geldoran or Rastian.* He knew he should be the best man for this match— if only he could *fight!* But, scarred and wounded as he was, he might well die at Lothard's hands— a death that could serve the need of Edrovir, but—

The image of Nevien's face rose in his mind. *Oh Vothra,* he thought. *I don't want to die today!* He frowned harder. *The pain increased whenever he moved...* An idea was taking shape in his brain. And with it came a terrible resolve. He met Madred's eyes. "Yes," he said. "I will continue."

"Very well. You may begin again on my signal." Madred motioned for Anduar and Kuran to return to their places.

Kuran shot Nagaro a quick, agonized look and went, tense and stiff-legged.

Anduar managed to catch Nagaro's eye as he turned to go, and he mouthed, *Well done. Now finish him.*

Nagaro could only stare at the Kelorin lord's retreating back with outraged incredulity. Did the man think he was pretending to have difficulty? That he'd gotten himself wounded on purpose?

He was given no time to think about it, however, because Madred immediately gave the signal to resume the match.

Nagaro dropped into his fighting stance, shifting his grip on his sword hilt. The drizzle had diminished to a fine mist. It scarcely mattered since he was already thoroughly wet, but at least he could keep a surer hold on his weapon. The pain in his wrist had subsided to a dull ache, that shouldn't trouble him much. The pain from the cut in his side was a shrill, constant note sounding in the background of his mind.

Lothard advanced, crouching like a cat ready to spring, and glaring at him with a coldly calculating hatred that was much more dangerous than the blind rage he'd displayed earlier.

"You think you won that, you stinking *pig?*" the Leithian growled when he got close enough to be heard only by Nagaro. "Because Madred sided with you? It only means that now we can *really* fight, and I can finish you!"

Nagaro circled warily to the right, forcing Lothard to keep turning to face him. "If you don't try to do me any more harm, Lothard," he said levelly, "I won't harm you."

Lothard laughed. "*You* won't harm *me?* You misbegotten whelp! You only touched me once— and that was luck!"

Nagaro swallowed. There was nothing for it but to try. He smiled his very best pirate smile. Then he attacked.

It was a low, swift lunge that made the cut on his side shriek like the tortured note of steel scraping steel, but he'd anticipated the pain, and he moved with it—

I could take this new pain. Vothra's voice spoke in his mind.

No, he thought fiercely. *Leave it. It's going to help me.* The simultaneous stabbing pain in his chest became one with the new pain, as two separate notes are part of a single chord, and he finished the lunge, scoring a hit— neat, precise, and bloodless— on Lothard's flank.

He was vaguely aware of the cries of the Seconds and cheers of the crowd. Lothard's expression registered astonished outrage, but the Leithian had the presence of mind to leap away, almost overbalancing in his effort to get out of range.

Nagaro went after him— and scored another hit before the man could recover his equilibrium. *Now they were even, three hits to three.* But he knew Lothard wouldn't let himself to be taken by surprise a third time.

Even as distracted and as ineffective as he had been at first, he had still been observing the way Lothard fought. He'd seen that Lothard used speed and strength alternately, not together. And while the man had made some very clever feints, Nagaro had seen only three basic patterns to them, each repeated more than once. Lothard, on the other hand, had seen only a sampling of Nagaro's moves. This would change, of course, the more Nagaro pressed his attacks. He would have to act quickly to make any additional use of his temporary advantage.

In fact, Lothard recovered himself quickly the second time, and immediately tried an attack of his own. It was one of his usual feints, and very fast. Nagaro expertly dodged and parried the blow.

"You *swine!* You tricked me!" Lothard snarled. "Pretending to be weak!"

"No trick, Lothard," Nagaro gasped as he aimed a thrust at the man. "But you shouldn't have cut me."

Lothard countered Nagaro's attack and launched another. There followed some furious swordplay as the two men tried without success to get past each other's guard. The swords flashed and rang as the men danced and wove around each other. Relieved of his handicap, Nagaro was, at least for the moment, fighting at the top of his form. He was wholly absorbed in the task now, oblivious to the world, the watchers, the weather. His nerves were singing that familiar song of power and control, speed and motion.

Lothard, in contrast, was experiencing a dawning realization that he might have met his match— which was for him a truly novel thought. The Leithian lord had always taken his superiority for granted, whether it was social superiority, or his prowess with the blade. Now he was being forced to fight defensively and to eschew his punishing power-strokes in his efforts to deal with Nagaro's speed. Most galling of all, the freedom to draw more blood was doing him no good at all! The attacks he managed to make were blocked at every turn. *This shouldn't be happening!*

Lothard parried one of Nagaro's thrusts, feinted, and took a vicious swing aimed at Nagaro's sword arm. Nagaro deftly caught the blow on the guard of his sword, and twisted in an effort to disarm the other man. The strength of the Leithian's grip was all that saved him from having the weapon wrenched from his hand. Swearing, Lothard staggered back. He saw an opening— that somehow wasn't there when he tried to make use of it!

The impasse continued.

Nagaro was equally frustrated, if not as shocked. It was a relief to find that he was equal to Lothard in speed and skill, but he needed two more hits and he could feel himself beginning to flag. Lothard would be tiring too, of course, but Nagaro feared he would reach his own limit before he could finish his task. Grimly he recalled the words of Master Fendar. *No matter how good the other man is, you can beat him. And no matter how good you are, he can beat you.* All that was needed was for someone to make a mistake...

And then Lothard made one.

It happened just as Anduar had said. Following a failed feint, the Leithian briefly allowed a chink in his guard. Nagaro saw a little hole in space and time— and put his sword through it to land a bloodless hit on Lothard's right shoulder.

"A hit!"

"Four hits for Nagaro!"

Vaguely he heard the cries. He was breathing hard and the muscles of his sword arm were threatening to knot... *and still he needed one more hit!* He circled away from Lothard, trying to buy a little time for his aching limbs.

Lothard, of course, knew the score as well. He was just one hit away from losing his bold gamble, his long-planned power-play— and losing it to *this!* This one-time slave— this Kelorin pirate upstart! *It was insufferable!* The man was wearing him down, and he had to find a way to win, but his usual feints had failed over and over. At last, desperate, he determined to use a trick he had once devised.

It was a different kind of feint, both more devious and less honorable. Pretending to stumble in the mud and lose his balance, he pitched towards Nagaro, then caught himself at the last instant and took advantage of his low angle and momentum to make a powerful swing at Nagaro's ankles. It was a potentially crippling blow, carrying enough force to cut through boot-leather into flesh.

Since it was against Nagaro's nature to take advantage of a foe's misfortune, he refrained at first from striking the stumbling man. By the time he recognized Lothard's treachery, there was no time to block the swing with his sword. As screams and cries of dismay erupted from the onlookers, he did the only thing he could. He leaped into the air— tucking his feet up so the blade passed cleanly under him— and landing squarely with his sword ready in his hand.

The crowd gasped, then held its breath as Lothard completed his swing. The Leithian had counted on his blow connecting with something solid. When it failed to do so, he was thrown off balance. In that instant, Nagaro saw the final opportunity he needed. Driving his sword in swiftly past the Leithian's guard, he drew blood this time—letting his blade slice into Lothard's left side, making a wound that was nearly a mirror-image to his own.

The crowd erupted into wild cheers.

"*A hit! A hit!*"

"*Five for Nagaro! He wins! He wins!*"

"*Match! Match!*"

Responding to the crowd's reaction, Nagaro started to bow to the spectators.

Lothard had spun away, bleeding, momentarily stunned by his defeat, but then he gave a wild howl of rage that was lost in the din, and charged at Nagaro with his sword extended.

Nagaro's Seconds both leaped into action, but he didn't need their services. With blinding speed, he whipped his sword up to catch the other man's blade on the guard of his own. Once again he *twisted*, harder this time. And this time the Leithian's sword was torn from his grasp, falling heavily to the muddy earth. Lothard paled, finding himself weaponless with the point of Nagaro's sword leveled at his throat.

There was a slick metallic sound as Grimbold drew his sword. Beyond Lothard's shoulder, Nagaro could see the horrified face of the man's brother, Beinard. Many of the onlookers cried out, anticipating blood.

But Nagaro didn't strike. Instead, he lowered his sword, though he held it at the ready as he spoke into the expectant hush, addressing his opponent.

"The match is over, Lothard," he said. "You've lost. I suggest that you accept it with grace and go back to your Hold to rule your people as wisely as you can."

With that, he took two steps back and turned away from the furious, mortified, and shaking Lothard to face Lord Madred. As he did so, the clouds overhead parted and the light of the setting sun slanted down onto the patch of ground where he and Lothard stood. The afternoon was so far-advanced by now that the shadow of the city wall extended over the people who were gathered between the crossroads and the East Gate. Elgurn was there in that shadow, sitting astride his horse with his hood thrown back, now that the rain was gone. The pale gold band of the crown of Edrovir was visible across his brow.

Madred cast his eyes heavenward, as did many others among the spectators on both sides of the crossroads. "The Gods smile upon this outcome," he murmured, and the sentiment was echoed by other voices. Then he lowered his eyes and raised his hands to call for silence.

"People of Edrovir," he cried. "I hereby declare this match well and truly won by Nagaro Alorin Loros, fighting on behalf of Elgurn Harlind who thereby retains the Crown of—"

That was as far as he got, because he was interrupted by Nevien's scream.

"*Nagaro, look out!*"

Nagaro heard her, but he was already moving. He had been watching Anduar's face, not Madred's, and Anduar hadn't taken his eyes off of Lothard. Several other people cried out as well in the instant after Nevien's warning, but they would all have been too late to save Nagaro if he hadn't started to turn the instant he read the news of Lothard's treachery in Anduar's eyes.

When he turned, he found that Lothard must have recovered his sword and was now hurtling towards him with the blade extended, in a lunge that had been meant to impale him while his back was turned. The Leithian's face was a mask of rage.

Beinard screamed, "*Lothard, don't!*" But nothing could have stopped that juggernaut.

With the speed of thought, Nagaro stepped to the right and turned his body sideways, flattening himself, so that Lothard's sword passed harmlessly within inches of his chest. At the same time, his own sword whipped out, aimed straight at his opponent's body. The Leithian's own momentum carried him onto the point of it and only a little extra force was needed to finish running the man through.

Lothard fell heavily, sprawling face down in the mud at the center of the crossroads as Nagaro yanked his sword free and leaped clear.

For the space of several heartbeats there was no sound but the soughing of the wind around the tower battlements. Then there came a confused roar of voices— exclamations, cheers, and groans. Nagaro felt it as much as heard it, a sea of sound that beat upon him in waves as he stood in the pool of golden light, staring down at the body of his fallen foe. He bowed his head and murmured the Kelorin invocation that served both huntsman and executioner.

"Vothra guide this spirit, as I would have you guide my spirit in the hour when my time shall come."

Be assured, I will.

"That was your way, was it? It will play well, though you took a terrible chance turning your back to him."

Nagaro looked up into Anduar's steely gaze. "I was watching your face," he said wearily. "You were my eyes. And I had to give him one last chance—"

"To kill you?"

"To refrain from killing me— one last chance to act with honor. And if I truly could have had it my way, there would have been no killing."

Anduar shook his head. "You would have been looking over your shoulder as long as you both lived."

Nagaro shrugged. He stooped to wipe his sword on the dead man's tirka and straightened to sheath it. "You were also sure that he would attack me— and you were right. But I didn't do this for myself, Anduar. I did it for Edrovir. I only pray it wasn't done in vain."

Anduar grimaced. "As do I." He bent over Lothard's body. "Beinard isn't doing his duty here," he remarked. "Someone should tend to it, and it might as well be us. We can't have it said that Lothard wasn't shown proper respect in death. And it would be well if you made some overture to Beinard."

Nagaro nodded. Following Anduar's lead, he helped turn the dead man over. While the older man closed the staring eyes and wiped the mud from Lothard's face, he extricated the hilt of Lothard's sword from the dead fingers. He wiped the blade, sheathed it, and unbuckled the belt and scabbard from Lothard's waist. Then he looked about for Beinard.

His eyes found the younger scion of the House of Hurn still standing where Madred had placed him. The youth was very pale. His eyes were directed at the spot where his brother lay, but he looked dazed, as if lost in his own thoughts. Nagaro drew a long breath and left Anduar to the task of finding men to take up the corpse. Carrying Lothard's sword, he walked with a measured tread across the muddy crossroads and came to a halt in front of Beinard. The young man raised his eyes and shook himself.

Nagaro swallowed. "I'm truly sorry for this outcome, Beinard," he said. "I wish Lothard had chosen a different path." He held out the sword.

Beinard ignored the weapon. "My brother dishonored himself in front of all these people!" he cried, and he seemed to be voicing his own train of thought rather than responding to Nagaro's words. "Now he can't be buried with honor— and our Elders must condemn him! How can the House of Hurn redeem itself?"

Nagaro winced. "I truly am sorry—" he said again. The words felt horribly inadequate.

Beinard's cheeks reddened with embarrassment. "You shouldn't be!" he blurted. "He tried to kill you! I don't mean only today, either. I mean months ago. I... I think he was the assassin who—"

"I know."

The youth's eyes widened. "You *knew?* And you left him living at the end of the match?"

Nagaro shrugged. "I was fighting as the king's champion," he said. "It wasn't the time for personal revenge. But won't you at least take the sword? I expect it's an heirloom—"

"No!" Beinard abruptly squared his shoulders. "Leave it with *him!*" He flung out a hand in the direction of Lothard's corpse. "Let them bury it with him! *My* father killed *your* father with that sword, and my brother would have killed you with it if he could. He swore he would finish what our father started, and this is where it brought him! That sword has seen nothing but dishonor!"

Nagaro stood a moment in dismay before the flaming rebellion in the young man's eyes. *It was only a sword... a piece of sharpened steel.* But something told him not to voice that thought. Instead he said, "So be it. I'll lay it on his chest." Then he added, "What will you do now?"

This time the young Leithian's shoulders sagged. "Go home," he said. "I'll take the army, and his body... and... just... go home."

"Will the army follow you?"

The youth drew himself up again at that. "They'd better follow me! I am the heir of the House of Hurn!"

"You will be the new lord of the Hold?"

Uncertainty flickered in Beinard's eyes. "I don't know," he admitted. "I have two older cousins. Maybe it will be one of them. Our Elders will have to choose."

"I see." Nagaro held out his right hand. "Good luck to you then— and to your House, and to the Elders and the people of Hurn Hold. I'd have them know that I bear them no ill will."

Beinard took his hand. "Thank you," he said awkwardly. "I'll see that they know it."

Nagaro turned to walk back to where Lothard's body lay. He suddenly felt terribly tired. He had been almost numb, he realized, but now he was aware that the wound in his side was stinging viciously, he could feel blood tickling, and it seemed that his very bones ached.

With the Challenge Match over, the order imposed by Elgurn on the participants and the spectators was breaking down. Men were moving in and around the area of the crossroads, bent on various purposes. He noticed vaguely that Madred and Kuran were remonstrating with Grimbold and Lord Ranse, and he saw Vell go striding off to join the altercation with his chin out and his mustache bristling.

He found that a litter had been brought to carry away Lothard's body. Four men in the livery of Hurn Hold stood about, talking among themselves as they waited to pick it up. Anduar was just finishing composing the body as it lay on the litter, with the hands folded over the wound on the chest. The Kelorin lord straightened. "Will we have any trouble there?" He asked, gesturing with his head toward Beinard.

Nagaro passed a hand over his eyes. "Not from him. He means to take the army home, but he's not sure who the next lord will be."

He lowered himself stiffly to his knees to place the sword, and discovered that he was shaking as he gingerly lifted the dead man's hands.

"He wouldn't take the sword from you?" Anduar asked.

"He... wants it to be buried with Lothard. Because of the dishonor associated with it. It seems a waste of a good blade." Nagaro had finished his task, but he remained kneeling, gathering strength to stand.

"No, it's a good thought really. It was Reith's sword. He had it forged especially for— *Are you all right?*"

Nagaro had stood up, then put a hand to his forehead as he suddenly felt light-headed. "I'm... fine..." he said. Then he took a step sideways as the ground seemed unaccountably to have repositioned itself and the world began suddenly to go gray around the edges.

The next thing he knew, there was an arm around his chest and Anduar's voice was calling urgently, from somewhere next to his ear, for Kuran.

Kuran appeared, his worried face swimming into Nagaro's field of vision. Then there was a second arm around him, a little lower down, and he heard Kuran speaking next to his other ear.

"I'm not surprised. He's done far too much today. And that wound should be seen to."

Hands were tugging at the bloody fabric of his shirt where it was plastered against his side. There came a sharply indrawn breath and Anduar's voice said, "That looks worse than what was needed for the purpose—"

"Purpose! *What purpose?* Don't tell me that getting him wounded was part of the plan!"

At this point Nagaro managed to say, "*No,*" at the same time that Anduar said, "*Yes.*"

"The devil take you, Anduar! You and your games! Nagaro, don't try to talk. Can we get a carriage for him?

"I'd rather get him to his horse. It would look better if he left that way."

"To Hel with appearances! In his condition—"

"Nagaro?" The arm that was the higher of the two tightened a little, and Anduar's voice addressed him. "Can you ride?"

"'Course I can," he mumbled. He couldn't conceive of being unable to sit a horse. *His feet were still under him, weren't they? More or less?* The world seemed strangely distant and it had become filled with little dancing motes of light.

"Oh, very well! The horse then, but hurry. I want to get him to the Fleet Compound. That wound needs tending!"

"As the King's Champion, he should be housed at the palace—"

"*Vothra's ass, Anduar!* He's one of my officers, and I say it will be the Compound!"

Nagaro was shaking his head, trying to clear it, but the effort only made the motes dance faster. "I'm for th' Fleet—" he said muzzily. "'s closer—"

"He's right, you know."

"Oh, *very well!*"

He blinked hard, but the motes of light were still there. "An' Tred. I want Tred—"

"Here I am, ye great fool. What did ye go and let him cut ye for anyway?" The voice was Tred's, and there was the man, materializing in front of him, grinning jauntily. "And I seem to have brought your horse." Tred jerked a thumb over his shoulder.

It would not have been accurate to say that the sandy-haired healer was leading the big gray. The horse was following the man, reins hanging slack and no hand on his bridle. Thunder-Heels snorted and tossed his head at the smell of blood, but stood still in spite of it to be mounted.

Nagaro couldn't have said afterwards exactly how he got into the saddle. He remembered setting his foot in the stirrup and making the effort to raise himself. There had been pain of various kinds and a great many hands, pushing and pulling. And then he was astride, gasping, and clutching the saddle bow while his head swam. Presently he was aware of Thunder-Heels moving under him.

"Hold him! He'll fall!"

"Nonsense! That's a trained war-horse. Thunder won't drop him!"

Nagaro opened eyes that he didn't remember having closed as the familiar sound of the last voice sank in. "Landros? Is that you?"

"Aye, lad." Landros beamed at him, from where he and Tred stood, at Thunder-Heels' head. "Geldoran gave us leave to congratulate the conquering hero. And I must say ye were magnificent! Once ye really commenced to fight, I mean. Four hits in a row— clean an' clear— and against Lothard Hurn! After that first cut, he never touched ye!"

"I'm here too!" Taru's voice came from near Nagaro's right knee.

"And I am also." Pavo spoke from a similar position on the left.

His two friends grinned up at him. They were walking on either side of his horse and he realized that each of them was grasping one of his booted ankles. He frowned. "I'm all right, Taru, really."

Taru gave him a sheepish shrug. "Of course ye are," he said. "And Thunder is a good horse, just as Landros said. This is just *insurance.*"

"That is right." Pavo nodded sagely. "So you will not fall on ground if you faint again."

Nagaro was just starting to say that he hadn't fainted, when he heard the sweetest voice in the world call his name. Instantly he sat up as straight as a pikestaff and turned to see Nevien riding towards him from the place in front of the Main Gate where he had left her, an age and a half ago. She was smiling at him, her eyes alight, and he reached for the reins and drew Thunder-Heels to a halt.

"Oh Nagaro!" she cried. "You were wonderful! But when he wounded you and I saw the blood—"

"It's not as bad as it looks—" he interrupted hastily, then stopped as he realized that she couldn't see the wound because his cloak was covering it. And then he realized to his chagrin that he must have fainted at least once because he had no idea how the cloak had come to be there. Nor had he any idea when Kuran and Anduar had mounted their horses, yet both men were riding, Kuran in front of him and Anduar behind.

Nevien seemed not to have noticed his confusion. "Oh, I know," she said brightly. "Vell explained that the blood looked worse because everything was so wet. But the way you fought was astonishing! I've never seen anything like—"

Shouts abruptly broke out somewhere behind him. Startled, Nagaro turned, twisting painfully in the saddle, trying to see what was going on. "What's happening?" he asked in some alarm.

It was Anduar who answered. "Grimbold tried to run for his horse, but Vell ordered him stopped. And it looks as if two of Grimbold's own captains have apprehended him. So it seems the men of Sobring Hold have figured out who their proper lord is."

"Or perhaps those two just decided who they'd rather follow," Kuran suggested dryly.

"That is also possible—"

Anduar undoubtedly had more to say, but Nagaro realized that Nevien was speaking to him again and she instantly commanded his full attention.

"I'm so sorry that I screamed, Nagaro," she was saying. "It's just that I was terribly afraid, at the beginning, when it looked like he was beating you. Can your forgive me for doubting you?"

Nagaro stared at her in utter astonishment. "*Yes!*"

"Not that there was ever any real doubt," Landros put in quickly. " Making out that ye're in trouble is an old trick to put the enemy off his guard—"

"*Landros!*" Nagaro gaped at the old Fleet Warrior.

And just then a trumpet blared, sounding three long, strident notes.

"Now what?" Nagaro tried again to turn and look behind him. He felt Taru and Pavo tighten their grips on his ankles.

"It's my father." Nevien was looking past him. "He's going to speak. He'll have some announcements to make, and I should be at his side." She turned back to him. "When can I see you?"

Kuran spoke before Nagaro could say anything: "Tomorrow morning would be soon enough, I think. He'll be at the Fleet Compound. If you inquire with me, I'll tell you where he's housed."

"And don't ye fret, My Lady," Landros added. "There'll be nothing but the best for the man that rid us of Lothard Hurn! We'll take very good care of him."

"I'm sure that's true." Nevien beamed at Landros. Then she turned her dazzling smile on Nagaro. "Until then, My Love!" She blew him a kiss, turned her horse about, and was gone.

Kuran started forward, and Thunder-Heels began to move again.

Nagaro frowned. Perhaps it was seeing Nevien, or perhaps it was just that the fit of faintness had passed. Regardless, he was feeling quite a bit better. "Couldn't we stay?" he asked. "I want to hear what Elgurn says."

Behind him, Anduar cleared his throat. "He's going to say that he's ready to see the crown pass to another head. He'll call for restoration of the Council of Lords and request that it meet in one month's time to hold a formal Choosing."

"How do you know that?"

Anduar laughed mirthlessly. "We were only waiting for Lothard to be removed from play."

Kuran made a small choking sound. "Shouldn't you be back there, Anduar? At Elgurn's side? I wouldn't think you'd want to miss such a moment."

"Oh, no." Anduar's voice was a silken purr. "I'm exactly where I want to be."

They had left the crossroads behind, following the Circle Road, and were approaching the contingent of Fleet Warriors gathered there under Geldoran's command. As they neared the front rank, Geldoran spoke a word and the men parted to make a path for them. At the same time the men flanking the path drew their swords and raised them in salute, crying, "Hail Nagaro! Lord of Loros!"

Nagaro covered his face with his hand. "How much more of this must I put up with?" he wondered aloud.

"A lot, I'd say," Tredhold volunteered.

"Aye lad," Landros affirmed. "Ye'll not hear the end of this in a month o' new moons!"

Nagaro shot the grizzled warrior a flaming glance. "*You* made it worse, Landros! Saying I was pretending that Lothard was beating me at first. He *was* beating me! Now I'll have to set Nevien straight!"

Landros clucked his tongue. "Now, now, there's no sense in frightening the womenfolk," he said. "Besides, when a woman says she thinks ye're wonderful, ye don't argue with her. Ye bask in it!"

"But it's not true! If he hadn't cut me badly enough to really *hurt*, there's a good chance he would have killed me!"

"Is *that* what made the difference?" Kuran had apparently been listening. "I did wonder."

"The new pain covered the old, that's all. And I didn't let him cut me on purpose, either. That was the hardest fight I've ever had in my life, and I'd rather people knew it!"

Landros chuckled. "Ye can tell 'em, lad, but they'll never believe it," he said. "That's the hazard o' being so good at a thing. Ye make it look easy—"

"And what would *you* know about that, Landros Torenin?" Tred put in. "Ye old bilge-bucket!"

"Me?" Landros waved a hand airily. "Why I'm so good at what I do, that half the time folk can't tell I'm doin' anything at all!"

They rode on amid general laughter.

These are my friends, Nagaro thought, and he had never felt more blessed. *I won the challenge. And Nevien loves me. Vothra, it's good to be alive!*

Just before they rounded the first curve on the way to the Fleet Compound, he turned to look east. The rags of the storm were blowing away, fleeing into the north. The eastern sky was clear, a deep cobalt blue, as the afternoon ran towards evening. The two moons were newly risen and nearly full, with just a little bit of a ragged trailing edge to each of them. He had been too preoccupied for many days to mark their progress, but now he saw that Naru's pale disk was nearly in the center of Talebra's face, the larger, brighter moon made a nearly perfect ring around the smaller, darker one.

It was supposed to be a sign, if everyone weren't too busy listening to the king's speech to even notice. Nagaro could hear Elgurn's voice, too far away to catch the words. He didn't believe in signs, of course. It was too hard to imagine that the configuration of two remote celestial bodies determined the fate of the world —or the fate of the little land of Edrovir.

War or love? Love or war? Who will win, the warrior or the lady?

It seemed to Nagaro that Lissafel had won, this day at least, and he was glad to have been her champion. But the fate of Edrovir still lay in human hands. *Other hands now, not mine*, he told himself. He'd done his part to help avert a threatened war. He would be one of those lords, of course, who met in a month's time to choose a new king. He'd do his part again to help keep the country on a path of peace, but he would be only one voice among many. The responsibility for the fate of the country ultimately would rest with the new king, whoever that might be.

Chapter 30

Loose Threads

"Why didn't ye tell us last night that ye'd got the most krits?" Taru asked, as he reached for the honey pot.

Nagaro paused with his fork hovering over his half-eaten stack of pancakes. "It was more important to celebrate your being made captain of the *Sword of Freedom*," he said. He wished that his friends hadn't asked for more details this morning than they'd been satisfied with the night before amidst the heady news of Taru's advancement in rank.

"But doesn't it make ye the new king?" Taru inquired pointedly.

"I only got ten out of twenty-eight. That's less than half. Madred got eight. Theren got four. And Elgurn three... and it doesn't matter, anyway, because the first casting is preliminary."

Nagaro had gratefully accepted Taru's invitation to stay with him and Pavo and their families during the meeting of the newly constituted Council of Lords. As a Wared lord, he had a right to a room at the palace, but he was more comfortable with his friends. Besides, he'd wanted to see the three-story row house they were renting together on Sail Makers' Lane near Lankura's South Gate.

Nevien had taken a coach from the palace to join them for breakfast. She and Nagaro were now sitting with Taru, Hamani, Pavo, and Tenepti, around the table in a warm, cozy kitchen with simple cedar furniture and a white-curtained window through which the bright morning sunlight streamed. The six adults were finishing plates of pancakes and sausages prepared by Hamani and Tenepti. Pavo and Tenepti's little son, Chotao, had already been lifted down from his high chair to toddle about in search of two-year-old mischief.

Pavo fixed Nagaro across the table with his narrow dark eyes. "What does it mean, *pre-lim-in-ary?*" he asked.

Nagaro frowned, but before he could answer, Nevien jumped in. "They used to call the first casting the 'Heart's Choice'," she said. "People cast their krits for their friends, or for someone they're indebted to, but who hasn't any chance of winning the crown. So no one expects the first casting to actually count."

Nagaro nodded gratefully. "That's right," he said. "I cast my krit for Kuran, and he cast his for me, and we both laughed about it."

He hadn't thought much about the royal choosing during it the past month. After two days in the Fleet infirmary, he'd returned to Loros Wared to oversee the continued resettlement, the training of troops, and the completion of the Hall's fortifications. He had learned about the renting of the house and the arrival of Pavo's wife and son by messenger. There had also been a brief trip to Kel Wared to attend the wedding of Kuran and Lady Merriel, but he hadn't returned to Lankura until just the previous day. He had arrived at mid-morning, just in time for the Council of Lords' opening session.

"What took them so long then?" Taru demanded. "If they only did one casting that didn't even count?"

Nagaro grimaced. "There were speeches. They went on for hours." It had seemed that almost every lord felt the need to stand up and read or recite something for the historic occasion. There had been some discussion, as well, after the speeches and before the casting. *And after the casting there had been even more discussion...*

Pavo had absorbed Nevien's explanation with equanimity. "So today they will do real casting, and choose king?" he asked.

Nagaro swallowed a bite and reached for his mug of sothiril. "There could be two or three castings before it's settled," he said. "They want a clear majority this time— not the way it was with... *my father.*" He frowned, remembering the last discussion of the evening, and covered his unease by taking a long swallow of sothiril.

There were uncomfortable glances exchanged around the table.

Pavo looked across at Nevien. "How can they change their mind, Lady Princess?" he asked with a note of concern. "Can man who have cast krit for Nagaro now cast it for some other man?

Nevien daintily put down her fork. "What's supposed to happen," she said, "is that those who chose less popular candidates will change their choices as they see who really has a chance of winning. They'll cast their krits for whichever of the leading candidates they like best— or have the least objection to."

Pavo looked relieved. "So Nagaro will get more krit next time," he said with obvious satisfaction.

Taru grinned around a mouthful, and Hamani and Tenepti also looked pleased.

Nagaro hastily swallowed his mouthful and shook his head. "I told them not to," he said flatly.

"Ye *what?*" Taru sputtered.

Hamani looked shocked. "But, so many o' them already want ye, Nagaro!" she exclaimed.

"Do they have to do what ye ask?" Tenepti wondered, her almond eyes wide. "Can't they cast their krit for whoever they want?"

Nagaro frowned in annoyance. "Of course they can. But after they did the count, I made it very clear that I don't want the crown. So at least *some* of those who chose me should be decent enough to pick somebody else. It will help, though, if I can be the first one to cast my krit today."

"What d' ye mean, the first?" Taru had demolished his pancakes some time ago and now leaned forward across the table. "Don't they all cast them at once?"

Nagaro shook his head. "The king chooses someone to go first, and the rest follow, one at a time, around the circle, he explained." It was a feature that he'd come to realize was designed to allow some manipulation of the outcome. "I plan to change my choice to Madred," he continued. "When the others see that, those who had cast their krits for me should do the same— most of them anyway. It won't take much to get Madred's count above mine."

Pavo turned to Nevien. "Lady, do you think they will do this even if they think Nagaro is best man to be king?"

Nevien examined the tabletop. "I don't know," she said. "We'll have to wait and see."

"But some o' those that chose Elgurn or Theren can change their choices t' Nagaro, can't they?" Taru protested. "He could still get more krits."

Nagaro's brow darkened. "Yes, but I *told* them I don't want it!"

"But ye didn't tell 'em ye wouldn't *do* it, did ye?"

Nagaro set his teeth. "They can't *make* me do it. They can choose me, but I can still say no."

Taru threw up his hands. "Then why are ye so worried about the count?"

Nagaro evaded Taru's triumphant eyes. "I don't want to have to say no," he muttered. "They shouldn't put me in a position where I have to say no."

Glances were exchanged again, and for a moment the silence was awkward. Then Hamani rose and started collecting the dishes and Tenepti immediately stood up to help her. Nevien, who had been studying Nagaro's face, quickly banished her own worried expression and turned to the other two women with a smile. "Thank you for a lovely breakfast," she said. "I'm sorry we have to rush off, but Nagaro has some business at the palace before the meeting of the Lords' Council."

Nagaro managed a smile. "Yes," he said. "We should go. And it *was* an excellent breakfast."

Hamani beamed at him over a stack of dishes, then tried to look severe. "Ye shouldn't be praising another woman's cooking in front o' your bride-to-be."

Nevien made a rueful face. "He's quite safe, Hamani. I can't cook a thing!"

"Oh, goodness!" Hamani colored. "The Spirits save me, My Lady! I didn't mean to embarrass ye."

Nevien laughed. "You haven't. Princesses aren't taught to cook, that's all. When I was a girl and I wanted to try, all the cooks would ever let me do was arrange strawberries on top of the cake and that sort of thing."

Hamani was staring in horrified disbelief. "That's dreadful! Would ye like me t' teach ye? I–I mean... if it's... allowed..." She stammered her way to a halt, clearly mortified at her own forwardness.

Nevien was instantly serious. "Would you, Hamani? I'd like that very much. Only... I don't know *where...*"

Hamani looked relieved. "Could it be *here?*" she asked. "Ye could both come visit— after ye're married— and stay the night."

"That's right," Taru put in. "The spare room up under the roof where Nagaro slept last night will always be there— though it's hardly fit for a lord and lady."

"It's a *fine* room!" Nagaro defended his choice. "I slept much better there than I would have at the palace— surrounded by all those other lords talking politics. I'll surely have to come to Lankura fairly often on Wared business, and we could stay here, couldn't we, Nevien?"

"Of course. As long as we wouldn't be imposing." Nevien looked to Pavo, whose house it also was.

Pavo inclined his head to her and turned his eyes on Nagaro. "Always both of you are welcome here. This will be true no matter what happen today at Council Meeting."

Nagaro hesitated under Pavo's unwavering gaze, not liking the implication of his friend's words. He decided, however, to let it go. "Thank you, Pavo," he said. "And thank you for inviting Nevien to join us this morning." He pushed back his chair and stood up.

"It was Tenepti that have that idea." Pavo smiled at his wife.

Tenepti, standing with a stack of cups in her hands, bestowed her sunshine smile on Nevien. "It's been a pleasure wild an honor, My Lady" she said.

Nevien beamed back at her. "I've been wanting to meet both you and Hamani," she said, rising. "And it's been a pleasure and an honor for me, too. I only hope that I can persuade you both to drop the 'My Lady'."

Tenepti blushed charmingly. "Maybe that won't seem strange after ye and Nagaro are married."

Pavo escorted them to the door by way of the house's small parlor and entry hall. The coach in which Nevien had arrived was waiting outside to return to the palace. Brandle sat, apparently dozing, on a seat inside of it, but the coachman was nowhere in evidence.

Nagaro stood waiting on the steps while Nevien lingered inside, talking to Pavo. He'd slept well in the loft bedroom partly by convincing himself that the other lords would be sensible and not press the crown on a man who didn't want it. He'd kept the dinner conversation confined to harmless topics by saying there was as yet no king. But now his doubts were stirring and his stomach had begun to churn.

To distract himself, he watched the people passing in the narrow street. It was still early and there weren't many folk abroad. The buildings flanking the street were two- and three-story houses, sitting shoulder to shoulder, some with shops on the ground floor. Since this was the South Gate District, closest to the Fleet Compound, many of the houses were occupied by the families of Fleet men. Of the dozen or so people that Nagaro could see that morning, roughly half were known to him. Several raised hands or called out greetings, which he returned.

Tredhold's plump, flaxen-haired wife, Ilsafeth, emerged from the house two doors down, a broom in her hands. She swept the previous day's dust and detritus out onto the stone doorstep and then swept the doorstep clean before she noticed him. Then she stopped to wave cheerily.

"Good morning, Captain," she called. "It's good t' see ye! Tenepti said ye were staying the night. Have they chosen ye king yet?"

He tried not to let his dismay show in his face. "Ah… no one's been chosen," he said hastily. "They only did a preliminary casting, and they want a clear majority this time."

"Of course they do." Ilsafeth bobbed her head, still smiling.

Nagaro forced a smile, not having the heart to tell her that he hoped the lords would choose someone else. He was relieved when she disappeared back into her house.

Ilsafeth was no sooner gone than he caught a movement out of the tail of his eye, and turned quickly to see an unexpectedly familiar figure emerging from the baker's shop on the bottom floor of the house next door. The grizzled little Turo with a face like leather was eating a cinnamon bun, and although he was dressed in cloth garments instead of his usual leather, he was quite unmistakable.

Nagaro's frown returned. "Jato! Come here, you old rogue!" he exclaimed. "I want to talk to you."

The woodsman looked up, startled. A guilty expression flitted across his face, but then he swallowed his mouthful of bun, grinned, and sauntered over, licking his fingers. "Why, Capt'n Nagaro— or, should I say, M' Lord? Fancy meetin' ye here like this."

Nagaro's eyes narrowed. "Don't play the innocent, Jato. You've no good cause to be in this street. The nearest inn is over on Haymarket Road. Are you still spying on me for Anduar?"

For a moment it looked as if Jato might try to deny it, but then he gave an eloquent shrug. "Aye, though I'd rather ye called it, 'keeping an eye on ye.' The other sounds so unfriendly-like."

"So you only do *friendly* spying now?"

Jato looked hurt. "It's all I've ever done when it comes t' *ye*, Zirda. Lord Anduar's yer friend, whether ye know it or not."

"What has he done for me lately?" Nagaro was in no mood to be conciliatory.

"I don't know about *lately*, but there was all them rumors he was spreadin' last month— about the heir o' Loros bein' everywhere but Loros Wared."

Nagaro gaped. "*Anduar* was behind that?"

"Aye. Turns out he was, though he didn't trouble t' tell *me* 'til last week. He didn't want Lothard marchin' his army over t' Loros Hall, 'cause he knew ye had no defenses."

Nagaro's eyes blazed. "Anduar wasn't supposed to know I was *at* Loros Hall. *You* weren't supposed to tell him! I thought we had an understanding, Jato!"

The old scout paled under the searing gaze and took a step back. "I never told him a thing but what we agreed to, Zirda! I swear it by Hakura Kili! He's just too clever by half, and he can put two an' two together. But he never figured ye were the real heir o' Loros. He thought I'd just heard yer friend's jestin' with ye, and he didn't mind if folk *thought* it was true. But it fair knocked him out of his boots when it turned out it really was!"

For a moment Nagaro stood seething, but his anger ebbed in the face of Jato's offended innocence. Anduar's initial surprise in the Audience Chamber upon hearing the final revelation *had* seemed genuine. "All right," he muttered. "I believe you. I'm sorry."

"He's just trying t' keep ye *safe*, Zirda," Jato said pleadingly. "He doesn't want ye comin' t' no harm."

"*Still?*" Nagaro scowled darkly. "That might have made sense when I was at Loros Hall and Lothard was raising an army. But Lothard is dead now, and the army's disbanded. I did the task that needed doing. What more does he want of me?"

Jato blinked. "Why, t' be king, o' course!"

Nagaro nearly choked. "*Anduar wants me to be king?*"

"Aye, Zirda. Ye didn't know?"

"But he... he cast his krit for Madred! And why on earth would he want *me?*"

"Because ye're the best man for the task."

"*Anduar* thinks that?"

"Him an' everybody else."

"No! Not *everybody*—"

Jato shrugged. "Everybody *I* know, Zirda. The Turo are all behind ye, o' course, but it's not just them. It's all the common folk, really."

Nagaro might have said more, but at that moment Nevien finally stepped out of the house, her attention focused on the coach. "Brandle!" she exclaimed. "What's become of my coachman?"

Brandle hastily swung open the coach door and started to climb out. Before he could finish stepping down, however, Jato piped up.

"He's in there, M' Lady." The woodsman jerked a thumb at the baker's shop. "Buyin' bread for his family. D' ye want me t' fetch him out?"

"No, Jato." Nagaro stepped in. "Let Brandle do it. I want you to get up on the back. There's a place to stand, and a hand-hold. If you're going to follow me anyway, you might as well ride."

"Aye, Zirda!" Jato managed a fair approximation of a proper salute, then spoiled it by adding a wink and a grin. "That'll spare me poor legs, that will, Capt'n!"

***

The coach jolted over the cobblestones. The driver had been very apologetic about the delay and was apparently making up for lost time. Nagaro and Nevien sat chastely inside, across from each other. Brandle had accompanied the princess as both bodyguard and chaperon, but the big Leithian had given them a wink and mounted to the seat beside the driver instead of sitting inside. It was an unmarked coach, and Brandle was out of uniform, so their passage drew little attention.

Nagaro sat looking out the window, too unsettled to think about taking any romantic advantage of the situation. His thoughts were running in disquieting directions. Since Elgurn had given him permission to marry Nevien without bringing up the crown, he'd assumed he had nothing to fear in that regard. Clearly he'd been naive. He reached into his tirka and drew out the official krit of Loros Wared that he would be casting again in just a few hours.

He studied the bit of carved wood. He had found it at Loros Hall after a concerted search. It was such a little thing— a flattened, tapered wand about six inches long, the wider end bearing the familiar design of rising sun and twining farusia blossoms. The use of krits for choosing kings was actually an old Leithian custom. Originally men had used daggers laid in front of the man they favored, but real weapons were too easily turned to less benign purposes. So they'd substituted little wooden replicas that had become increasingly stylized. Darion had embraced the custom because it was Leithian in origin, yet embodied the second corner of Kelorin law— that leaders should be chosen by those they led.

It was considered one of Darion's more inspired moves, yet it hadn't made him popular enough to discourage some of the Leithian lords from seeking his death. And Darion was the most popular king Edrovir had ever had. Nagaro sighed as he returned the krit to the interior pocket of his tirka.

It didn't surprise him that his friends wanted him to be king. They had no idea what kingship entailed. Nor was it surprising that many Turowan folk, or the common people in general, would favor him. On top of his long-standing popularity, he had just slain Lothard and averted a civil war. That was a poor qualification for kingship in Nagaro's opinion, but it tended to impress people. And of course the word had gotten out that he and Nevien were betrothed. Nevien was very popular and it had always been assumed she would be queen one day... But *Anduar?*

He turned to look at Nevien, and surprised her eyes on him. She immediately gave him a reassuring smile, but he'd already read the worried frown that had preceded it.

"What has Anduar been doing this past month?" he asked.

"Anduar?" The frown that now wrinkled her brow was merely thoughtful, not worried. "Very little that I've noticed, though most of what Anduar does is usually invisible. Why?"

"Your father called him 'the king-maker'. And Jato just told me that he favors me for the crown."

Nevien's frown turned worried again. "It wouldn't surprise me," she said. "Even Kuran would like to see you take the crown. He won't say it to your face, because he knows how you feel. And he'll cast his krit as you cast yours, but he thinks you would be good for the country."

Nagaro shifted uncomfortably. Kuran thought too highly of him by far. To change the subject he asked, "What did Pavo want to talk about?"

This time Nevien looked uncomfortable, but she answered. "He wanted to know whether you would really refuse the crown if the other lords chose you."

"What did you tell him?"

"That I thought you would."

"Did he accept that?"

Nevien sighed. "He said it wouldn't matter— that Sheptuum would find a way. He seems to think of your life as a story that has to have the right ending."

Nagaro sighed. "Pavo can be very stubborn about some things, and that is one of them. But he'll get used to it in time, I'm sure."

They rode on in silence, Nagaro's thoughts running in dark spirals. Staring out of the window again, he saw that the coach was moving up Market Street. He looked back at Nevien and caught her watching him again. She gave him another quick smile.

She was supposed to be queen, he thought. All of her life, she had been preparing to stand beside the man who was king and help him rule wisely. But it hadn't turned out that way. *Nevien's life had turned into a nightmare ten years ago...*

He spoke his next thought aloud. "I was wondering... on the day your father came to Averwin with his proposition, what would have happened if I'd said, 'Let me come to Lankura and see what I think of this princess'?"

Nevien stirred. "I've thought about that too," she said. "Father and I talked about it recently. He's convinced, now, that it would have turned out badly— although he wanted it at the time. People would have guessed who you were, he says. Some of them did, you know— until they *saw* you—" She stopped, reading the pain in his face. She tried again. "Some member of the Leithian Faction would have decided you were a threat and had you killed— poisoned, probably. Dreigen was right there, and he was their tool."

"What if your father had just accepted my answer when I said no?"

"He thinks that would have ended the same way, but then he always thought so. It was one of the things he and Maramine disagreed about."

Nagaro frowned. "Your father and Maramine talked about me?"

"Several times."

Nagaro's frown deepened and he leaned forward in his seat. "How long did your father know who I was?"

Nevien hesitated under his burning gaze. "Are you sure you want to talk about this right now?"

"Yes! Vothra knows I'm not *that* fragile."

Nevien drew a breath. "He told me he'd guessed by the time you were six years old."

Nagaro winced. *Elgurn had known for more than ten years before their fateful encounter.*

Nevien continued. "A lot of people were looking for Tevren's heir in those early years," she said. "My father wanted to know, as much as anyone. Like Rastyl, he was suspicious of any male Kelorin child of the right age, and they both discovered your existence within a matter of months. When it turned out that Maramine had been with child when she came to Averwin, it put them both off the scent. But my father found out— quite by chance— about the connection between Lindra and Maramine. That led him to find and question the midwife who delivered Maramine's stillborn child. After *that* he made several secret visits to Averwin, just to watch you. But he didn't confront Maramine until you were almost twelve. They both agreed at that time that it was best to leave you where you were until you turned eighteen and could be told of your heritage."

Nagaro groaned. "Except that *I* decided, when I turned *seventeen*, that I wanted to go to Lankura to join the Fleet or the City Guard!"

Nevien nodded. "Yes. That was when things got... *complicated*. Maramine insisted on keeping her promise to Tevren, and my father respected that, so that meant you couldn't be told. *She* thought you'd be safe as an ordinary recruit in the Fleet or the Guard— that your own ignorance would keep you safe. But my father believed your talent for swordsmanship would draw immediate attention. He thought you'd need protection— *his* protection, of course. So he formed his original plan— which coincidentally *also* involved wedding his daughter to the entire legacy of Loros." Nevien made a wry face.

"Only I said no." Nagaro studied his hands.

Nevien nodded. "My father thought it was the wrong answer, but it pleased Maramine because she was determined that the choice should be yours..." Nevien's voice trailed.

Nagaro closed his eyes. The movement of the coach still jostled him, but the beating of the blood in his ears drowned out the creak and clatter that went with it.

"So *I* caused it all—"

"*No, Nagaro!*" Her voice broke through the pounding in his ears. "You were *seventeen*, and you had no idea what was at stake! Maramine and my father both made choices that shaped what happened. Tevren's original choice played a part too. And then Dreigen stuck his hand in— *and* Bron Sobring. My father believed that Bron was loyal to the crown, by the way. Bron hadn't told him how much he hated Darion for killing his father— a hatred he took out on you. He repented later and confessed everything to my father as he lay dying on the battlefield. My father forgave him for the sake of his soul. Gillard Marchent was Bron's pick for a co-conspirator. My father didn't vet him well enough."

Nagaro leaned heavily against the seat cushion and bowed his head. She was right about the blame, of course. It wasn't simple. But what if none of them had been forced to make those choices? What if his parents had lived as king and queen and hadn't needed to send him away? *He would have grown up as a prince, possibly expecting to be king...* He raised his eyes and studied the worried face of the woman who had suffered in the place that would have been his. *Suffered with such grace.*

"Nevien, why aren't you disappointed in me?"

She stared at him in dismay. "How can you ask that? How could I be?"

He swallowed. "I've always admired the way you faced whatever your father and the Council demanded of you— even if I thought they were wrong. If you believed a thing was for the good of the country, you did it, no matter how hard it was."

"Well, I *tried* anyway—"

"That's right!" His words came out sounding harsh. "You always at least *tried*. But *I* don't even intend to try, because I—"

"*Don't, Nagaro!*" Her eyes welled with tears. "Haven't you done enough already? There are hundreds of men that were slaves who are free because of you! The Emperor of the Mahuk Baar has ordered his warlords to stop taking our gold and our people, because of you! You've put yourself at risk to turn aside the threat of war— twice! No one has any right to ask for more!"

Nagaro dropped his eyes. "It's not as if I *couldn't*," he said. "I just don't want to—"

"But I understand that too!" Nevien spoke fiercely. "After all you've been through, after what was done to you, it's hard for you to be constantly in the public eye. And the story that you were Leyel Virden will come out. It's already being whispered. There were just too many people in that Audience Chamber—"

Nevien stopped as she saw him flinch.

This was news that Nagaro hadn't heard— unwelcome news. He tried to rearrange his expression into more neutral lines, but it was already too late.

"You *see?*" she said. "People don't realize how hard it is for you. We haven't any right to ask you to be king when you have that to deal with."

"Would you ask it of me otherwise? Do *you* think I should be king?"

She looked reproachful. "I promised I wouldn't push you."

"Well I wish you hadn't, if it means you won't answer my question! I'll have to deal with the rumors and tales whether I'm king or not, so please just tell me: *Do you think I'd be a better king than Madred?*"

For a long moment Nevien eyed him warily, but then she said, "Yes, Nagaro, I do."

He managed not to wince. "Why?"

"Because you would try to do what's best for Edrovir— for *all* its people, Kelorin or Leithian or Turowan. Highborn or low— without showing favor to anyone."

"And Madred wouldn't? I've heard it said— over and over— how fair he is, and how honorable. Most of the other lords seem to respect him."

Nevien sighed. "To give him credit, Madred *is* a true man of honor," she said. "But he believes the 'noble' class is born to rule and the common folk to serve. The other lords respect him because they see that he respects *them*— but he does so because they're highborn. He would try to let the Kelorin and Leithian lords keep their own traditions in their own lands, and if there was a conflict between them, I don't know what he'd do. I don't have faith that he'd do what was best for all of the people."

Nagaro sat for a moment after she ceased speaking. She had assessed him accurately, he knew, and quite possibly Madred as well. But would he really make a better king? He thought of Madred's recent performance in the Audience Chamber, or as the Arbiter of the King's Challenge— both of which had impressed him. "Madred would surely listen to reasonable arguments, wouldn't he?" he said at last. "He could learn to take a broader view couldn't he?"

"Would Madred take instruction?" Nevien looked thoughtful. "Well, on some things perhaps... He's not stupid, after all—just complacent, and old-fashioned. He's a traditional Leithian at the core."

The coach had slowed, and now it lurched to a halt. A glance out the window revealed that they had arrived in the palace's stable yard. Nagaro hadn't even noticed when they'd passed through the City Gate.

Nevien's last words conjured the scene at the border of Sobring Hold, where Madred's stubborn traditionalism had caused a painful rift with Brandle, his own son. The memory gave Nagaro pause, but there were by now only two hours before he needed to be at the building on Broad Street where the Council of Lords would meet, so he got quickly out of the coach when Brandle opened the door, and turned to help Nevien down the little step. She instructed the coachman to wait, explaining that Nagaro would need transportation to Broad Street when his business at the palace was done.

By the time Nagaro thought to look, he discovered that Jato had made himself scarce. Probably the man had gone to make a report to Anduar. *Well, there was no help for that.* Nagaro shrugged and started towards the palace's side door with Nevien on his arm. Brandle came discreetly several steps behind them, dutifully silent and stone-faced.

"I'll leave you here then," Nevien said as they entered the little hall that contained the bottom of the back stairs. Brandle took the cue and slipped past them to precede her up the steps.

"How will you spend the rest of the morning?" Nagaro asked, pausing as she disengaged her hand from his arm.

"I'll try to work on the wedding plans," she said. "It would help if I knew where it will be and how many people will be present."

"That's easy— Loros Hall, and as few as possible."

Nevien hesitated. "Father says it should be here at the palace, with all the lords in attendance," she said carefully. "And as long as he's still king and I'm still the princess, I'm afraid he has a point."

Nagaro felt his anxiety begin to rise. "I was thinking of the dining room at Loros Hall. The Great Hall here is so *very* big."

"I thought perhaps somewhere in the garden," she ventured. "It's less—"

"*No!*" Ice slid into Nagaro's stomach at the mere thought.

She reached for his hand. "Not the same spot," she said quickly. "There are lots of other spots—"

But he turned away, eluding her grasp. "No!" he said again. "No gardens. It has to be *different* this time— as different as possible." *No matter how hard he tried, he couldn't forget that other wedding...*

"All right, my love," Nevien said quickly. "No gardens. And please don't worry. I'll work something out with Father."

And then she was in front of him and reaching up to kiss him. He folded her into his arms and clung to her desperately as their lips met. And after a little while, it was all right.

She drew away from him and smiled. "It doesn't matter a bit to me what happens in the Council Hall," she said. "All I need to be happy is to spend my life with you. It doesn't matter whether I'm your wife, your lady, or your queen."

***

As he moved through the halls of the palace with his ears still full of Nevien's parting words, he had to remind himself of the importance of finding Elgurn. He needed to ask to be the first to cast his krit.

But Elgurn was not in his office, which adjoined the Audience Chamber. The guard at the door saluted him, called him 'My Lord,' and respectfully suggested he seek the king in his chamber on the third floor. As Nagaro made for the main stair, unescorted and with his sword at his hip, he reflected on what a difference a month had made.

Halfway to the stairs, he met Vell coming the other way. The new Lord of Sobring Hold was dressed to look the part. He wore purple britches and a white satin tirka with scarlet embroidery. He looked a bit stiff in it, but Nagaro was disinclined to comment. *He*, after all, was wearing the same deep blue tirka with the gold embroidery that Tira Theseline had made for him. It was the only thing he owned that was remotely suitable to wear for the royal choosing.

Vell seemed very relieved to see him. "There you are, Nagaro! There's something I need to tell you."

"Oh?" Nagaro was nonplused. "What is it?"

"I wish to assure you that you need not worry any more about Grimbold."

Nagaro blinked. "I haven't thought about the man even once in the last month."

"Oh. Ah, that's good." Vell's relief increased visibly. "In that case, I trust I may inform the Elders that you don't intend to press any charge against him. Though we understand that you would be entirely within your rights to do so," he added hastily. "For imprisonment on false charges."

And now Nagaro was frowning. "Well, I'm glad they realize that's what it was! Has he been punished in any way?"

"He is barred from holding any position of power, and is confined to his country estate for the rest of his days."

"Confined?" Nagaro's frown evaporated. "For *life?* That's a bit drastic, don't you think?"

Vell gave him a wry look. "If you saw the estate, you might not think so. It has a private forest for hunting. He'll be able to shoot all the deer and partridges he likes. And get drunk every night. As far as my Uncle Grimbold is concerned, that means there's no reason to ever leave the place."

"I *see.*" Nagaro's brow darkened again.

Vell looked apologetic. "The Elders decided his actions were... ah... '*reprehensible, and highly inappropriate*'." Vell's brow furrowed as he quoted from memory. "But that they were '*undertaken out of concern for the interests of Sobring Hold, rather than for personal gain.*'"

"Do you think that's true?"

"I'd say— more or less. The Elders would be grateful if you would say that you're satisfied. Formal charges would be... well... an embarrassment to the Hold."

"I see." Nagaro sighed. "Well, if your Elders disapprove of what he did, and he can't cause any more trouble, I suppose I'm satisfied." He paused as a thought occurred to him. "But what about Sindar and Simion? Are *they* satisfied?"

Vell looked blank. "They're commoners—" He winced as he saw the storm clouds re-gathering.

"*So was I*— for all anyone knew at the time! They were both held captive longer than I was. Sindar must have been held for months! And he was drugged! They both were!"

Vell nervously fingered his mustache. "But they're *still* commoners. I suppose their Wared lords might speak for them, but what do you want *me* to do about it?"

"What do I want? Only a little justice— some form of recompense for these men! I would think that your Elders would *want* to do anything they could to set things right— since they admit that what Grimbold did was wrong!"

"Ah. Some money, you mean." Vell looked both relieved and resigned. Then his expression became worried. "But I've no idea *how much*."

Nagaro gave him an exasperated look, but then took pity. "Try to put yourself in each man's place. Consider his circumstances and what he suffered. Then ask yourself what amount of money would make you feel better about the whole thing."

"Mmm." Vell's brow puckered in thought. "That sounds fair enough. I guess I can try to do that. Thanks." He stuck out his hand.

Nagaro took it.

"I'll not keep you any longer then," Vell added hurriedly. "Must be going. There's a meeting and I don't want to be late—"

"There's a meeting? Now? *Before* the Council meets? Have I missed something?"

"Ah... no." Vell looked embarrassed. "This meeting is for... ah... Leithians. No need to concern yourself." And with that, the young man made a rather hurried exit.

Nagaro stared after Vell's departing figure, trying to make a decision. He needed to find Elgurn, but he now realized that he also needed to talk to Sindar about the idea of recompense before anyone from Sobring Hold could approach him. Sindar had a history of proudly and stubbornly rejecting aid. Nagaro had intended to look in on the former slave in any case. He knew that Sindar was still housed in the palace. He even knew where.

After a moment's indecision, he decided that finding Elgurn could wait just a little longer. He should talk to Sindar now while he was thinking of it.

As he approached the open door of Sindar's room, he nearly collided with two women coming out of it. The older one appeared to be a servant, but the younger one, dressed in a gown of pale green taffeta, he instantly recognized.

"Why, good morning Lissel," he said. "I'm glad to see you here."

"Oh, Tor Nagaro. Good Morning!" She beamed at him, blushing a little. "And thank you so much for everything you've done for Sindar."

"Oh, ah, you're welcome, of course. I wanted to speak to him. Can he have visitors?"

"Oh yes," she said. "He has been up and about for a week, and he remembers almost everything that happened now, though he doesn't like to talk about it. He's only staying here until the Fleet's mid-summer muster."

"So he still wants to be a Fleet warrior?"

"Oh, yes. And Lord Kuran has assured him of a place. Just go right in. I'm sure he'll be delighted to see you." She nodded towards the open doorway. "We were just leaving," she added, blushing some more. She dropped him a curtsy and hurried away with the older woman in tow.

The room Nagaro entered was comfortable and modestly appointed, this being the part of the palace's first floor that was used for housing the retainers and other lower-ranking persons. It contained a bed, with a washstand, a chest of drawers, and a small table with three chairs— all plain but serviceable. The coverlet, carpet, and window curtains were all in cheerful spring colors.

Sindar was seated at the table with some books in front of him. He looked a bit thinner than Nagaro remembered, but there was color in his cheeks and an eager brightness in his eyes. He greeted Nagaro with a wide smile.

"Nagaro, Zirda! You are most good person! I am grateful to you for saving me from those very bad man!"

Nagaro inclined his head. "You're very welcome, Sindar. I'm glad I was able to help."

Sindar made a gesture for him to sit in the chair on the other side of the table, and asked without preamble, "Do you see my wonderful woman?"

Nagaro covered his amusement as he took the offered seat. "You mean Lissel?"

Sindar nodded emphatically. "Yes, yes. She is beautiful. You think so?"

"I have always thought so." Nagaro allowed himself to smile as he recalled Sindar's original uncomplimentary assessment of Lissel's charms. "I'm glad that you do too."

"Oh yes! And she is also most good person. When I am very sick, she come every day to take care of me. Just like... like..." Sindar searched for a word."

"A nurse?"

"Yes, yes! She is best woman for me. We are going to be marry!"

"You and Lissel are going to be married?" Nagaro couldn't contain his delight.

Sindar nodded vigorously. "I *asked* her," he said, struggling to get the past tense right. "And she *said* yes. Then she *writed*— no, she *wrote* letter— and *sent* to her father." He rolled his eyes and abandoned the effort. "Anyway, her father say yes, too. So we are going to be marry!"

"Congratulations! That's wonderful!"

Sindar nodded some more. "Also Lissel bring me many book!" He gestured at the one open on the table in front of him. "So I can learn more word."

"I can see that you've learned a great many more words—" Nagaro began.

Simdar face suddenly clouded. "Not all of them come from book," he confided. "I do not like to think where so many other word come from."

Nagaro instantly understood. He nodded somberly. He also had learned things, whether he wished to or not, while enslaved under heskial. They were things he couldn't seem to forget. There was a moment of shared sympathetic silence, ending when Nagaro managed to say, "I know what you mean."

Sindar looked away, suddenly embarrassed. "It is easier for me... a little," he said. "To think about bad thing that happen to me, because I know it happen to you also."

Nagaro considered this. "Yes. It's easier for me too, I think. Knowing someone else has suffered the same way. Maybe... sometimes... we might meet and talk a little? When you're ready?"

Sindar brought his gaze back to Nagaro. He nodded.

Thinking about what the other man had suffered reminded Nagaro of why he had come. He proceeded to explain what he had discussed with Vell.

"They will come to give me money for bad thing?" Sindar sounded doubtful. "I thought money is only for work."

"This money will be for justice. For balance. They can't undo what was done to you— or take the bad feeling away. All they can do is try to give you something good to balance the bad. The easiest thing to give you is money. Then you can use the money to do good things for yourself, to balance the bad things. Does that make sense?"

"Yes... I think so." Sindar nodded, first tentatively, then decisively. "And I will take money if they want to give it to me," he said, smiling broadly. "I understand now that sometime man need help. Not any more do I say 'no' when people want to give me thing. Now I say 'yes.' Now I am grateful."

***

After taking leave of Sindar, Nagaro made for the main stair with a hurried stride. His sense of urgency had returned in force. As he turned from the central hallway into the room at the bottom of the stairwell, he came up short to find it filled with young women in gowns spanning the spring spectrum.

"There you are, you wonderful man!"

A feminine vision in yellow silk accosted him, flinging arms around his neck.

"I... I beg your pardon?" he stammered when he found himself released. He could feel himself turning scarlet.

The yellow silk confection resolved itself into the Lady Alisset. "Oh, you *dear* thing!" she cried, clasping her hands and literally bouncing in her enthusiasm. "I can never possibly thank you enough for telling Uncle Maded about Nile and me! Nile would *never* have had the nerve to ask, and now he doesn't have to! Because he's gone and arranged it without being asked, and we're going to be *married!*"

Behind Alisset, Nagaro could see Delasin, looking embarrassed, as well as Kendira and Lissel with their heads together, giggling. Clarimel was smirking, and Rianine was there with dancing eyes that showed she was enjoying herself immensely.

"Lord Madred has arranged for you and Nile to be married?" Nagaro hoped he had gotten Alisset's dangling pronouns parsed correctly.

"*Yes!* And it would never have happened if it hadn't been for you!"

"But— I was just trying to explain why I didn't want to marry you myself," Nagaro protested.

"Oh, *really*, My Lord!" Rianine was gleeful. "What a thing to say!"

Alisset turned on her. "Oh, but he couldn't marry *me*, Rian! He has to marry his own true love— and now he's going to!" She turned back to Nagaro. "I'm so happy I think I could just float away!"

Rianine rolled her eyes. "Well, *that's* accurate," she observed dryly. "We've had to keep tugging her back to earth all morning."

"Well, in any case, I congratulate you and Nile," Nagaro told Alisset. "I'm sure you will be very happy together." He turned to Rianine. "But why are you here? I thought you and Tamith were going to set up housekeeping in Loros Wared."

"Oh, hadn't you heard?" Rianine smiled sweetly. "We're looking for a town house as well. I've taken the post of head chaperon, since Merriel is retiring."

"Oh... well... congratulations, then. And... ah... good day to you, Ladies." Nagaro bowed hastily and stood aside to let the bevy of beauties go past.

As he headed for the stairs, he heard their voices receding, first Rianine's, then Lissel's, and the last one might have been Clarimel.

"Didn't I tell you that would be entertaining?"

"Rian, you're quite horrible!"

"But he did turn the prettiest shade of pink!"

Nagaro sighed as he climbed the stairs. *Trust Rianine to find a way around her promise not to tease him. If the direct approach is proscribed, try the indirect.* Still, he supposed, if he could learn to survive that woman's assaults on his fragile vanity, he should be able to weather anything the rest of the world could throw at him.

He emerged onto the third floor to find several rows of baskets lined up between the entrance to the north hall and the top of the stairs. They contained an eclectic assortment of objects. One was full of books, one of scrolls, and one of oddly shaped glassware. Another contained dried, stuffed animal specimens with a glass-eyed owl staring unblinkingly at him from atop a little heap of mummified lizards.

"What's going on here, Zirda?" he inquired of a small man in a linen smock who was bent over one of the baskets, arranging its contents with gloved hands.

The man straightened and turned around, and Nagaro instantly recognized the bespectacled face. "Oh," he said. "Good morning, Master Fineas."

The little man beamed at him. "Good morning, Captain— I mean, My Lord Alorin! You have caught me in the process of cleaning out Dreigen's chambers. It's my first official assignment since the king has appointed me to be his new Lore Master."

"You're the new Lore Master?" Nagaro blinked. "That's wonderful, Fineas! Elgurn couldn't have made a better choice. But isn't what you're doing here a little... nerve-wracking— considering Dreigen's fondness for poisons?"

"Well, yes, it is," Fineas conceded. He held up his hands. "But as you see, I am wearing gloves. In fact, however, the danger is not so great as you imagine. Dreigen was very careful and quite meticulous."

"Well I suppose he wouldn't have wanted to risk poisoning *himself*. But aren't you afraid he might have... set traps?"

"As he did for Kale Fendred, you mean?" Fineas shook back his sleeve and pushed up his glasses with the back of his wrist. "That seems to have been a unique instance— not his usual practice. And I have been able to identify all of the vessels containing noxious substances and have already had them taken out and destroyed." In response to Nagaro's questioning look, he added, "The first thing I did was to read all of Dreigen's notebooks from cover to cover."

"Oh." Nagaro's stomach dropped. "Then you... know everything... that he did?"

"Oh yes."

Nagaro recoiled mentally, but Fineas continued to gaze mildly at him as if it were commonplace to have read in minute detail how the man standing in front of him had been turned into an apparently mindless idiot. Nagaro swallowed "Didn't you find that rather... harrowing?" he managed at last.

Fineas did look uncomfortable at that. "Well, yes," he conceded. "Some parts were quite horrible. It was difficult to maintain a proper scholarly detachment. It seems that Dreigen had no conception of right and wrong. He was motivated by self-interest, of course, but also— more often— by curiosity. I can at least understand the curiosity, although I thoroughly disapprove of what he did in pursuit of it. It's a pity, really, that he made such ill use of his talents, and that he died before he leaned the use of kindness. He was obviously highly intelligent."

Nagaro looked at the floor. "I'm afraid I can't feel any regret for the fact that he's gone, except in the sense that his spirit will have to bear the burden of the memory of this life every time it passes through the void. At least that spirit has gone on to another life— one that will write brighter memories to set beside these dark ones." *Vothra had assured him of this.*

He raised his eyes again to Fineas' face, and asked, "What will become of the notebooks?"

"An excellent question. The king at first wanted them destroyed, but fortunately I was able to convince him that they should be preserved for the sake of their historical significance."

Nagaro grimaced. Destroying the notebooks would have been his first impulse as well, but he saw the point. "I suppose it's important for men to be able to read Dreigen's confessions, written voluntarily by his own hand. No one will ever be able to claim he was falsely accused."

"Exactly." Fineas nodded decisively. "And I also intend to publish a modest volume describing several discoveries that Dreigen made in the area of antidotes. He had to study them as well, you see, in case he accidentally poisoned himself in the course of his experiments. For example, he was aware of the existence of linjana right from the beginning. I thought that if these useful observations were made public, at least the man's talent would not have gone entirely to waste."

"That's... a good idea, too." Nagaro was thinking of Dreigen's tortured spirit. But then abruptly he remembered his errand. "I came here looking for the king. Do you know if he's in his chamber?"

Fineas looked apologetic. "I'm very sorry, but I really don't. I've been so involved in my work. You could ask the guard—" He looked past Nagaro and his face fell. "Oh dear. I forgot. I sent the man downstairs to fetch some sacking."

"That's all right," Nagaro said quickly. "I'll just knock on Elgurn's door and see for myself."

Chapter 31

The Royal Choosing

When he reached the door of the king's chamber, there was no response to his knock.

Nagaro stood outside, worriedly chewing his lip. *If Elgurn wasn't here, and he also wasn't downstairs, where on earth was the man?* After several seconds, he knocked again, a little more loudly this time. It was somewhat presumptuous, but he needed to be certain.

He was startled when the door of what had formerly been the queen's chamber— a dozen feet to his right— opened, and a man peered out.

The man was tall, thin, and well-dressed in somber shades of brown. His graying red curls were neatly trimmed and his clean-shaven cheeks a little hollowed. His clear gray-green eyes looked questioningly out of sockets deepened by age. "May I perhaps assist you, Zirda?" he inquired.

It took the space of three heartbeats for Nagaro to recognize him. "Kale," he said at last. "Kale Fendred."

The man's face clouded. "Yes. That is my name. But should I know you, Zirda? I've been ill, they tell me, and my memory has been affected."

"I am... Nagaro... We have met, but it was years ago." Nagaro decided to leave it at that. Kale was obviously sane, but there was no telling how much the man might remember. "I was looking for Elgurn," he added. "Do you know if he's here?"

"I'm afraid he isn't." Kale appeared relieved to be asked a question he could answer. "He left about a quarter of an hour ago."

"Bishka!" He had arrived too late! Nagaro had a mental image of Elgurn going down the back stairs at the same time that he had been coming up the main staircase.

"I'm sorry"" Kale looked genuinely distressed. "He has gone about something very important. They are choosing a new king."

"Yes, I know—" *Maybe it wasn't too late... if he could catch Elgurn at the Council Hall before the meeting started...*

"You could come in and sit with me while you wait." Kale's words were both eager and tentative, threaded on a strand of hope. "There's so much that I don't remember, you see, and if you know what has been happening in the world, you might be able to help me. I'd be very glad of the company."

"I'm afraid that I really should go—" Nagaro broke off, struck by the pain in Kale's voice, the unspoken plea in the man's eyes. Here was a man trying to come to grips with a present he felt un-connected to and a past that was a gaping hole. Nagaro knew how that felt. He remembered it all too well. *Surely there would still be time to get to the Meeting Hall and find Elgurn?* "All right," he said. "But I can only stay a few minutes."

The room had changed little from the last time he had seen it. Even the subtle odor of medicinal herbs still lingered, though the healer's narrow pallet bed was gone and the heavy curtains had been drawn back to allow sunlight to pour in. The familiar furnishings, no longer half-obscured by shadows, were decorated in hues of deep rose pink, white, and gold— colors that bespoke the room's former occupant rather than its current one.

There was a brocade armchair drawn up beside the bed, and near it was a small table stacked with books and bearing a pitcher and two cups. Kale offered the armchair to Nagaro and sat on the edge of the bed. "Would you like some cold sothiril?" he asked, indicating the pitcher.

"Yes. No, please don't get up. I'll pour it." Nagaro replenished Kale's half-empty cup and filled the other one for himself, then sat down. "I see that you have a lot of books," he said by way of conversation.

"Oh, yes. Elgurn brings them." Kale frowned as he reached out to touch the nearest stack of volumes. His fingers caressed the spines. "I've been reading everything I can that has any history in it, and asking Elgurn to explain how it relates to present events. But there's so much I simply don't know."

The book second from the top was a thin volume that looked familiar, but Nagaro felt he had no time to waste on it. He took a sip of sothiril as a matter of form, then set his cup down. "Kale," he said gently. "How much do you remember?"

The man's anguished eyes leaped to Nagaro's face. His voice, when he spoke, shook with emotion. "I remember my youth quite well," he said. "I remember how Elgurn and I became friends. But when I look at him, he's much older than I remember. I remember my dear wife— but Elgurn says that she died, and he won't say how, or how long ago. And my son and daughter came here to visit me, but I hardly recognized them! I remember them as children, and now they're a young man and a young woman. Nile— my son— told me he is to be *married*. He asked for my blessing! And I knew nothing of it! They said everyone had thought I was dead. How can that be? And why will Elgurn tell me anything I want to know about the world as long as it has nothing to do with my part in it? I've always believed he was my best and truest friend, but now—"

Nagaro cut in quickly. "Some things are better not remembered."

"So Elgurn says as well! Or something like it. But how can I be content with that, when I have lost years of my life? I don't even know how many!"

Nagaro sighed. "Do you remember me at all?"

Kale looked blank. "I'm sorry, Zirda."

"Then it must be eleven years, at least." It was more complicated than that, he knew, if Kale was having to re-learn all of history. Nagaro supposed the Spirit of the White Flower must be trying to keep the man from remembering his own involvement in Edroviran politics.

Kale's face was a study in dismay. "*So long?*" he murmured.

"I'm afraid so. I can guess, a little, how this must feel, Kale. I had the memories of my entire life taken from me when I was a young man. It was a year before I got them back."

"This happened to you? And it took a year? Must I also wait a year?"

"Honestly, I don't know."

"But you know what happened to me in those years, don't you? Won't you tell me?" The grey-green eyes were eager, pleading.

Nagaro reached for his cup of sothiril to give himself time to choose his words. He took a drink and put the cup down again. "Your story and mine are intertwined," he said carefully. "But I am not the one who should tell you the full tale. That is for Elgurn to do, because his hand was in it. He was witness to it all, and I believe he will tell you when he's ready. He is your true and loyal friend. Never doubt that."

"I... I don't, but... Can't you tell me *anything* more?"

Nagaro sighed. He was remembering what Vothra had told him, all those years ago, in a similar situation. "This is what you should know," he said at last. "There was a man who did us harm— different kinds of harm to each of us. He is dead now, so he can't do any more harm to anyone. Your memories are in the keeping of the Spirit of the White Flower. It is something called spirit magic that dwells in an herb from which a medicine is made."

"Was I... given this medicine?"

"Yes. To undo the harm. It is very old magic, and it works in whatever way a person needs it to. There's a kind of wisdom in it. It takes memories, not to be cruel, but to help heal. Some of your memories will be restored, I think— I'm almost certain of it. But those from the last six or seven years— I don't know. They may be lost to you forever."

"Six or seven years... *gone?*"

He saw the horror in Kale's eyes. "Believe me," he said quickly. "With the harm that was done to you, this may be for the best. Try to trust me—

and trust the spirit in the medicine. Be patient with the spirit, with Elgurn, and with yourself."

Kale sat very still, his eyes downcast. "I think I always knew there must be something evil in what has happened to me." He looked up. "So I must wait, you say? Very well. At least there are a great many books for me to read."

"Yes. Books are good. And there is one more thing I want to tell you."

"What is it?"

"If it weren't for some of the things you did, years ago, I might not be here. I was trying to die and you kept stopping me. I wasn't always grateful then. But I am now."

"Oh dear..." Kale looked extremely uncomfortable. "I... I'm afraid I must take your word for it. But, whatever happened then... I'm glad that you didn't die. It is wrong to seek death."

Nagaro stood up and made a small bow. "I would have you remember what you just said. And I will come to see you again, but now I'm afraid I must go. That meeting— to choose a new king— I need to be there."

"Oh, are you one of the lords? Then I mustn't keep you, of course. Thank you for your words. For your kindness to an old man."

As Nagaro began to turn to leave, Kale picked up the book from the top of the nearest stack, and the one beneath it caught Nagaro's eye again. "Isn't that King Tevern's journal?" he asked in surprise, pointing at it.

Kale blinked. "Why, yes. Elgurn brought it to me. You are familiar with it?"

Nagaro hesitated. His instinct told him that he shouldn't tell Kale any more of his own story, since it was so intimately connected to Kale's history. "I've... read it."

"It's quite remarkable, really." Kale put down the first book and picked up the slim volume. "The man seems to have written nothing else to give us insight into the working of his mind. A clear-sighted man he was, too. Passionate about the things he believed, and devoted to the good of the country. His suggestions regarding the tax assessment were later enacted, I am told. He was right, even though they killed him. And now, of course, we're going to see his son, Alorin Loros, take the crown."

Nagaro had been backing by inches towards the door, but now he froze. "That surely isn't certain," he said. "He's made it very clear that he doesn't want it."

Kale set the journal down. "I know," he said earnestly. "Elgurn told me. But he also told me there's no one else who is so widely trusted or who has such broad support. It's as if his whole life has shaped him for this." Kale's eyes grew bright as he began to tick things off on his fingers. "He was reared in ignorance of his origins. He wandered the world, learning its ways, growing strong, and choosing worthy causes to support. He then came to Lankura and took up the service of Edrovir. The Kelorin Faction has tried to win him, but he remained true to the cause of peace and the good of the country. The Leithian Faction tried to buy his loyalty with a wife, but he's chosen to wed the princess instead, a high-born Leithian woman beloved by all. And Elgurn says he's a man of the very highest character. A man worthy of his noble grandsire— worthy to be the heir of Darion—"

Nagaro could feel himself turning redder by the second. *Was that what they were saying? It hadn't been like that...*

"But," he protested, "if you've read that journal, you know that Tevren didn't want his son to take the crown!"

Ah! Ah!" Kale raised a forefinger. "That's not *all* it says. Here, let me find it." He opened the journal, flipping pages. "Yes. Here it is." Kale read aloud, words that all but made Nagaro's heart stop in his chest.

"Only for the sake of peace and the good of Edrovir should he take up the crown. And then, of course, if it truly is for the good of Edrovir, I would not have him refuse."

"There! You see?" Kale looked triumphant.

Nagaro sought to explain. "I don't think... this man... is convinced that the good of Edrovir couldn't be served as well by another. There's Lord Madred—"

"No, no! Not Madred!" Kale waved the name aside. "Elgurn says a third of the Leithians think Madred betrayed them when he took a seat on the King's Council. And half of the Kelorin think his repudiation of the Brothers of the Blood is a sham!"

"But how can Elgurn know these things? And if he only *imagines*—"

Kale was shaking his head. "He's been talking to the lords all of this past month. And he's talked to them more since yesterday's casting. Hasn't he spoken to you, Zirda?"

"No... I—"

"Well, you must be the last one, then. And I've no doubt that he will." Kale's confidence was unassailable. "Then all that will remain is to convince this young Lord Alorin to see reason!"

"What? Would you force a man to do something he doesn't wish to?"

"If it's necessary." Kale didn't falter. "The man's personal wishes are immaterial in the face of the greater need. He must be made to see where his duty lies. But you must go, Zirda. You must be there to cast your krit. Only be sure to cast it for Lord Alorin. He's the best choice. Anyone can see it, even a poor old damaged thing like me."

✲✲✲

The coach swayed alarmingly as it rounded the corner onto Broad Street. Nagaro clutched the seat cushion. He had told the driver to make all speed, but he was beginning to wonder why he'd bothered. Even if Kale was wrong about the views of the other lords, his assessment was surely accurate with respect to Elgurn's thinking. Kale's poor empty mind was like a sponge. He would hardly have gotten *that* wrong.

Nagaro shook his head. Why hadn't it occurred to him that Elgurn might not let him cast the first krit? Elgurn had been talking to the lords... Why hadn't *he* thought of doing that? And what was he going to do now? Begin talking to them at this eleventh hour? Try to find out how they all truly stood?

And the words that Kale had read to him kept echoing in his head: *If it truly is for the good of Edrovir, I would not have him refuse.*

The coach shuddered to a halt.

Nagaro flung open the door and stepped out into the courtyard of the building that housed the Council Hall. The courtyard was already crowded with coaches and horses and men attending them. His own driver had barely managed to find a space. *Were all the other lords here before him?* Grimly Nagaro fixed his eyes on the high-arched doorway that led to the Hall and started walking, threading his way determinedly through the throng.

Just before he reached the doorway, he found his way barred by a group of Leithians, one of whom addressed him.

"My Lord Alorin, a moment, please. We have some questions."

"Questions?" Nagaro stared at the man. "What sort of questions?" Worry and impatience made him less polite than he might have been.

He recognized the tall, graying man who had spoken as Lord Ranse. The elderly lord was flanked by young Beinard Hurn, and a man of intermediate age whom Nagaro remembered from the day before as Hilber Dorn, the lord of Borlund. Nagaro realized that he was being confronted by representatives of the Leithian Faction. And there was no way gracefully to get around them.

Beinard Sobring had apparently taken Nagaro's response as an indication of willingness to be questioned. "Is it true that you've said your first act as king would be to amend the Right of Challenge?" the young man asked. "To replace the sword challenge with a call for a meeting of the Council of Lords and a new Choosing?"

Nagaro met Beinard's gaze and read there more curiosity than challenge. He decided to answer quickly and honestly and hope that the men would not keep him long. "Yes, I did," he replied. "But I was speaking hypothetically. I—"

"Yes, we know," Lord Ranse put in quickly. "You don't wish to be king. But we wish to know whether you still stand by that pledge today. Have you changed your mind since you spoke those words?"

"I certainly haven't. Skill with a blade is no qualification for kingship, and there has been more than enough blood spilt already over the crown."

Glances were exchanged before Ranse resumed the questioning.

"How do you stand on the right of the lords of Holds and Wareds to keep their own ways?"

This at least was easy. "I think that right should exist, so far as it doesn't conflict with the good of the country as a whole."

Again the Leithians exchanged glances. There were some raised eyebrows.

"Then you don't support the imposition of Kelorin ways on Leithian lords?"

"Not as a matter of principle, certainly. Nor the other way around, for that matter. We should be trying to define what we can call 'Edroviran ways', that work reasonably well for everyone."

"I see." Lord Ranse stiffly inclined his head. "Just one more question, My Lord: What do you think should be the membership of the King's Council?"

This wasn't something that Nagaro had thought about specifically. "Well," he said, considering. "It should include members who represent the varied interests of Edrovir's citizens. The current membership balances the differing interests of the Leithian and Kelorin people well, for example, but it lacks representation for the Turowan folk."

"The *Turowans!*" Ranse protested. "When have they ever taken an interest in politics?"

"And they have no influence," Hilbert put in. "There are only three Turowan lords out of twenty-eight!"

Nagaro's face darkened. "Turowans make up at least a quarter of the population, so they're clearly under-represented among the lords—which explains why they have no influence! And just because they haven't been demanding to have their interests served, doesn't mean they don't have any!"

"Ah, My Lord Alorin." Lord Ranse held up a hand. "Perhaps you might represent them yourself? They seem to have taken you to their hearts, as it were."

Nagaro blinked. "You're suggesting that I serve on the King's Council? I suppose I could do that."

There were glances in response to this, but Lord Ranse hastily motioned his colleagues to silence. "I am sure some satisfactory solution can be found," he said smoothly. "We thank you for your indulgence, My

Lord. And now we will leave you. We look forward to seeing you presently at today's session."

As the three men headed for the doorway into the building, Nagaro thought he heard one of them say, "*But can we trust him?*"

He stared after them, trying to understand what had just occurred. They'd been asking questions about how the country should be ruled... *no*... about how *he* would rule the country! And they hadn't asked him how he meant to cast his krit. *As if they didn't expect it to matter...* He suddenly remembered that Vell had let slip something about a meeting of Leithians that was set to precede the meeting of the Council. Vell had seemed embarrassed about it...

Oh, Vothra! And Elgurn would be of no use! Maybe he could still find Madred before the meeting began... talk to him...

He hurried after his interrogators.

He had learned the layout of the building's interior the day before. The Council Hall was on the second floor and was reached by a grand stairway that ascended to a kind of large anteroom. The anteroom, in turn, opened into the Council Hall through a large pair of double doors.

The anteroom was broad, with a pair of tall windows and a polished wood floor. Nagaro found it crowded with people. The majority of these were liveried valets and uniformed members of the City Guard, but his eyes were drawn immediately to where Ranse, Hilber, and Beinard were standing just in front of the open doors of the Council Hall, speaking to a tall Leithian, elegantly attired in matching burgundy tirka and britches. The men's conversation must have just ended, for all four now inclined their heads respectfully to one another. As Ranse, Hilber, and Beinard turned to enter the Hall, the fourth man turned to face Nagaro.

It was Madred Furthing.

"My Lord Madred!" Nagaro urgently strode forward, making a path for himself. "Please, I would speak with you."

"Ah, there you are, Lord Alorin." Madred advanced to meet him with similar alacrity, though rather more dignity. He came to a halt before Nagaro, wearing a restrained smile. "I was just assuring those gentlemen that you have always proven to be a man of your word. In fact, it turns out that Alisset exonerated you completely when I questioned her."

"Oh. Good." Nagaro smiled tightly. "And I'm glad that you have arranged for Alisset to wed Nile Fendred. It will make them both very happy, but—"

Madred didn't let him finish. "Her abiding faith in the Gods should be rewarded," he said, with every appearance of sincerity. "And Nile is now available. Also, when I— belatedly— examined the books that Simeon Rudrin had kept for me, I did indeed find a record of a purchase of heskial from a source in Borlund Hold— with a notation that it was 'for Grimbold'." Madred's expression became very grave. "Torlung will face a severe judgement. And it appears that I owe Brandle an apology regarding his choice of...*friends*. I *was* right, however, about your father's noble blood."

Nagaro frowned. This was distracting him in spite of himself. "Yes," he said, "but both my father's mother and my own mother were commoners. What you saw of me in Sobring Hold that impressed you may owe as much to Selfira's fire and Lindra's way with words as to the influence of the men of the line of Loros—"

Madred cut him off. "I'm sure we will have ample time to debate the matter at a later date, My Lord." The Leithian shifted his stance, turning slightly, he cast a quick glance in the direction of the doors leading to the Council Hall.

Nagaro followed the glance, and saw that the crowd had thinned somewhat and a number of lords were visible through the doorway, already seated at the tables in the Hall. He turned back to face Madred. "My Lord," he said quickly. "I thought that perhaps if I cast my krit for you, some of those who chose me in the first casting would be moved to do the same—"

He stopped, reading something in the Leithian lord's eyes.

Madred sighed. "I've seen enough to know that being king is not an easy task," he said. "Still, I would accept the crown as my sacred duty if the greatest number of the men in that room desired it." The Leithian turned again to glance at the doorway to the Council Hall. "As it turns out, however, they clearly wish otherwise."

This time when Nagaro followed Madred's eyes he found that Kuran and Anduar were standing together in the doorway, and he was struck by how easy the two men seemed to be with one another. He also saw the look that passed between the two Kelorin lords and Lord Madred.

"*Oh, Vothra,*" he murmured. If these three men were all acting in accord, what hope did he have? His heart began to pound.

Madred made a sweeping gesture in the direction of the doorway. "Shall we, My Lord? They're all waiting."

They were waiting...

Dazedly, Nagaro nodded. As if in a dream, he began to walk beside the Lord of Furthing Hold. He swallowed. "Will you be the first to cast your krit?"

"Yes. It's been arranged." Madred's voice was matter-of-fact.

As they neared the doorway, Madred moved ahead, and Kuran and Anduar stepped into positions at Nagaro's left and right, each one taking one of his arms.

"What's this?" Nagaro tried to disengage his arm from Anduar's grasp.

The Kelorin lord tightened his grip, and said briskly, "Kuran and I have the honor of making sure you don't run away."

"But I wouldn't—"

"Of course not."

The two lords drew him across the threshold into the Council Hall.

"Steady, lad," Kuran muttered under his breath. "This is for the good of Edrovir. And it won't hurt a bit."

Nagaro cast a sharp glance at Anduar. "Is this your doing?" he hissed.

"By no means." Anduar's response was smooth. "I have learned that where you are concerned, all I need do is let nature take its course."

Nagaro turned to face the room and all of the lords assembled in it.

The Council Hall was high-ceilinged, with wood-paneled walls and a polished oak floor. A row of high arched windows along the farther wall faced onto the building's courtyard and flooded the room with indirect light. Ten massive, carved, oak tables with sets of matching high-backed chairs dominated the room's interior. They were arranged in a broad oval with their ends spaced apart just far enough to allow a man to comfortably pass between them. The chairs were on the outside of the oval, two or three to a table, and all were occupied except for four directly in front of Nagaro— three at one table and one at the next table to his left. Twenty-four faces were turned his way.

Madred moved to seat himself in the lone chair at the left-hand table, and Nagaro found himself guided to the middle of the three chairs at the table in front of him, with Kuran on his left and Anduar on his right.

As the three of them sat down, a sound like a collective sigh ran around the room. Nagaro tried to focus on the faces, to guess what the lords were thinking, but the situation seemed unreal. His mind registered looks that were variously wary, stoic, eager, or bemused. Here and there, fingers toyed nervously with carved wooden krits.

Elgurn sat in his appointed chair in the middle of the opposite side of the circle. Nagaro realized that the king was speaking, asking whether there should be more discussion or whether to begin with a casting of the krits.

"I call for a casting." The voice, from somewhere to Nagaro's left, was Pendrik's. The Leithian sounded more serious than Nagaro had believed him capable of being.

From the other side of the circle, came Devral's gravely voice. "Aye. Let's see what the night has wrought."

Other voices echoed the sentiment. "Aye, a casting!" "Let's have a casting!"

When the voices died, Elgurn spoke again. "Since there is no call for discussion, will you all please rise."

Chairs scraped all around the oval, and clothing rustled as every man present rose to his feet. Nagaro found that somehow he was standing, though his legs felt like water.

Elgurn barely waited for the ripple of motion to cease before raising his voice again. "We will begin the casting this morning with Lord Madred Furthing."

This announcement elicited only a brief mutter of hushed voices. Nagaro wondered whether the choice had actually surprised anyone.

Madred gravely inclined his head to the king. Then, stepping between his table and Nagaro's and moving very deliberately, he laid his krit in front of Nagaro, bowing as he did so before returning to his place.

Nagaro stared down at the little wand of pale wood, carved with a sheaf of wheat and a pair of crossed spears, the crest of the House of Furthing. He failed even to notice the next lord's approach, making a startled movement when a man's hand suddenly appeared in his field of vision and laid a second krit beside the first. This one was carved with the figure of a mounted warrior. He looked up into Vell's blue eyes. The young lord of Sobring Hold gave him a sheepish grimace. "Sorry," he mumbled. "Can't fight the will of Hrathgard."

Pendrik came next, and after him came Lord Theren as the sequence of the choosing moved clockwise around the oval ring of tables. One man after another stepped into the space inside the ring and crossed it to cast his krit.

The pattern was clear. All who had previously cast their krits for Madred, or Elgurn, or Theren, were changing their choice to Nagaro. None of those who had previously made Nagaro their choice were changing theirs.

The pile of little wands grew larger. Nagaro saw Elgurn's krit fall upon it, and Odus', and Devral's— Ranse's, Hilber's, and Beinard's— Soren's and Rathdar's— Rastyl's, Varsyl's, and Endemar's. He felt his stomach twist and his throat tighten. He seemed to struggle for air.

"*Vothra!*" he gasped. "*Help me.*"

He felt a hand tighten on his right arm and there was a nudge to his left shoulder. Kuran's voice hissed in his ear. "*Easy, lad!*"

Breathe slowly, Spirit that calls itself Nagaro. The familiar voice flowed though his mind like a breath of pure air. *I am here, and I will not desert you. Do not be afraid. This is something you can do.*

Keshaal! It would never do to faint! With an effort he slowed his breaths and steadied himself. He looked around the ring of tables. The ritual of the casting was nearly complete. The last of the lords at the table to his right had just added his krit to the mound of wooden sticks. It was Anduar's turn. The Kelorin lord didn't bother to walk around the end of the table.

Without taking his left hand from Nagaro's arm, he reached across and placed the krit of the House of Tyronin with the rest.

It was Nagaro's turn. The room was very still as he fumbled inside his tirka. He should have been ready, should already have had the thing in his hand. His fingers closed on the smooth wood and he brought it out, then stood for six, seven, eight heartbeats, staring down at the pile of krits in front of him. To place his there would be to accept the burden of the crown.

Was it for the good of Edrovir? Everyone seemed to think so. And after all, it could be undone if they changed their minds. He could make a law such that all anyone had to do to challenge him was to summon the lords to the Council Hall and call for a new casting.

All these thoughts came and went in a flash, to be displaced by ones that were more compelling. Oddly, it wasn't his father's words that echoed in his mind in that moment. It was Nevien's words, spoken that morning— her words, and the thought that adding his krit to the rest would result in making her the queen she was meant to be. He saw the two of them, in the Audience Chamber, standing side by side.

If she could be happy, no matter what, as long as she was with him, couldn't he manage to do his duty if he had her by his side?

He let the krit fall. The wooden clatter that it made when it struck the pile rang from one end of the Hall to the other. Two seconds later, Kuran made his move and the krit of the House of Kel fell beside it.

The casting was complete.

The room burst into sound and motion, all of which swept over Nagaro and whirled about him unheeded. His krit was cast. The fateful deed was done. Yet he felt strangely serene. It wasn't going to be easy, he knew. Anything important and truly worth doing wasn't likely to be easy. But something told him that he was as ready to face this as he was ever going to be.

And it was time, once and for all, to stop running.

Epilogue

Nagaro Alorin Loros wedded Nevien Harlind on Midsummer's Day of the year 561 of the Kelorin Calendar, in the Audience Chamber of the palace of Lankura in the presence of all the ruling lords of Edrovir. Afterward he and his bride stood on the balcony above the entrance of the palace, overlooking the great courtyard filled with a throng of people from the city and surrounding countryside. There Nagaro received the crown of Edrovir from the hands of Elgurn Harlind and kissed his queen before the cheering multitude.

Nagaro ruled Edrovir for twenty-four years, during which time he weathered several challenges from disgruntled or ambitious lords before handing the crown to his lawfully chosen successor. He and Nevien lived out the remainder of their days as Lord and Lady of Loros Wared. Following Kuran's death, Kel Wared was re-joined to Loros to form a single Wared under the name Kel-Loros.

Nagaro's reign as king was marked by general peace and prosperity. He sought to establish uniform application of the law to all people, regardless of their race or social status, especially with respect to property ownership and inheritance and the definitions of crimes and their appropriate punishments. He established four new Wareds to govern the islands, which all chose Turowan lords, more than doubling their representation in the Council of Lords. His greatest achievement is generally considered to have been the Treaty of Pakoa that sealed the peace between Edrovir and the Emperor of the Mahuk Baar. He also negotiated the Treaty of Bones, which established a method for settling border disputes with neighboring Jinara based on the location of the graves of men's ancestors. A formal treaty with Hran eluded him, although there was relatively little trouble with the people of Hran during his reign. A correspondence with the lord of the House of Pana concerning the death of the Hranji trader Zo-Hlan Tai earned him the expressed gratitude of the man's family for the knowledge that Zo-Hlan had "died righteously."

Nevien bore Nagaro two children: a daughter, Simris; and a son, Edorin. Simris became a highly respected chronicler and historian, her most famous work being the detailed history of her father's life, on which this narrative is based. After her father's death she was chosen to govern Loros Wared, becoming the first woman in Edroviran history to serve in that role. Edorin never took up the sword nor held office of any kind. A deeply introspective man, he devoted his life to study of the Vothrin Writings and to following the Path set forth in them. He is regarded by many to have been the first *Sokoran*, or "Hand of Vothra", although others attribute that honor to his father. Nagaro's firstborn daughter, Narei, came to live with her father and stepmother at the palace in Lankura at the age of eight. Ever bold and willful, she became Edrovir's first warrior maiden and led a life of many twists and turns before stepping into the role of clan chief of Minowei's people.

Glossary of Names and Terms

Alisset (A-lihs-seht): Alisset Sobring. A high-born young Leithian woman. One of the princess's ladies. Daughter of Bron Sobring and sister of Vell.

Alorin Loros (AL-or-ihn LOR-os): Birth name of the son of Tevren and Lindra of Loros.

Ambras (AHM-brahs): Master Ambras, a Kelorin healer, personal physician to Queen Semorel.

Anduar Tyronin (AHN-doo-ar teer-O-nihn): A Kelorin lord. One of the Signers of the Pact of Lankura and a member of the King's Council. Also ruling lord of Tyronin Wared.

Animara (ah-nee-MAR-ah): A Torowan woman. Jila's sister and therefore Narei's aunt, who raised her. Called "Ani" for short.

Arlinas (AR-lihn-ahs): The "shadowed" land to the east of the Goreitha Mountains from which the Kelorin and Leithian people fled when they founded Edrovir during the cataclysm known as the "Time of Fire and Water."

Averwin (AV-er-wihn): A small country estate in Verdin Wared. Nagaro's boyhood home, now a property of the Crown called River House.

Baalkir jir-Akaan (BAHL-keer jeer-ah-KAHN): Emperor Baalkir. A powerful Mautep warlord who has become Emperor of the Mahuk Baar. Uncle of Roheed.

Beinard Hurn (BAY-nahrd HERN): A highborn Leithian youth, younger brother of Lothard Hurn.

Berinar Sundorin (BEHR-ih-nar SUHN-dor-ihn): A Kelorin lord. One of the Signers of the Pact of Lankura. Former ruling lord of Sundorin Wared. Father of Rathdar. Author of *Rule of Loros*, his mysterious death is often attributed to the hand of the master poisoner Dreigen.

bishka (BIHSH-kah): A relatively mild but expressive expletive in Hashti.

bladder-thorn: A device used to inject a liquid directly into a person's vein, made by attaching a hollow thorn from the *scapala* tree to a bladder obtained from the marsh-bladder plant.

bodjer (BAH-jer): An expletive derived from a Leithian expression that was originally much cruder. It means roughly to "do an injury to" as commonly used in the Common Speech.

Boka (BO-kah): A Turowan woman, daughter of Luka and twin sister of Omei. One of Minowei's people of the former Loros Wared and one of the "ku taihana" who hold the names of all living members of Minowei's clan in their memories. She wears a gold earring.

Borlund Hold) BOR-luhnd hold): A Leithian territory ruled by Lord Hilber Dorn, the southern-most coastal territory claimed by Edrovir. It shares an often-disputed border with Jinara.

Brandle Furthing (BRAND-l FUR-dhing): A young Leithian, lieutenant (commander) of the Princess's Guard. A "crossed man," the older son of Lord Madred Furthing. ("dh" denotes the voiced "th" sound in the word "this")

Bron Sobring (brahn SO-bring): A Leithian lord and former ruling lord of Sobring Hold. One of Leyel Virden's "keepers." Father of Vell and Alisset, he was killed in the border war.

Burdal Korinos (BUR-dahl KOR-ih-nos): An elderly Kelorin merchant of Vered Mahir. Patriarch of the Korinos family. Grandfather of Sindar.

Chitaopa (chih-TAOW-pah): A small uninhabited island off the coast of Jinara, not claimed by any nation.

Chotao (cho-TA-o): A Hashtep child. Son of Pavo Maat and Tenepti.

Chula (CHOO-lah): An elderly Turowan man, gardener at Averwin. He taught Leyel how to swimm, and plant things, and make things out of sticks and string.

Clarimel (CLAR-ih-mehl): A high-born young Leithian woman. One of the princess's ladies.

crossed: English translation of a word in the Common Speech used as a term for homosexual.

Darion (DEHR-ee-ahn): King Darion, called "Darion the Great." Ruling lord of the House of Loros and of Loros Wared. Chosen to be the first king of Edrovir. Son of Nevrath and Minowei. Father of Tevren.

daashu (DAH-shoo): Hashti for "thank you."

dedrel (DEH-drehl): A soporific drug used as a general anesthetic.

Delasin Virden (DEHL-ah-sihn VER-dehn): A high-born young Kelorin woman. One of the princess's ladies. Youngest daughter of Varsyl.

Delvin (DEHL-vihn): A Kelorin youth. A member of the Palace Guard, well known to Landros, whom Nagaro met during the second Mautep attack on Lankura.

Devral Sedras (DEHV-rahl SEHD-rahs): An aging Kelorin Lord. One of the Signers of the Pact of Lankura and a member of the King's Council. Also ruling lord of Sedras Wared.

dokan (do-KAHN): A gold coin of Edrovir. There are ten trokins to the dokan, and one hundred rins to the trokin.

Dreigen (DREHY-gehn): A man of mixed Kelorin and Jinari heritage, the king's Lore Master. He is an expert on poisons.

Duleyin (doo-Lay-ihn): Seventh month of the Edroviran calendar, equivalent to July.

Dunrel (DOON-rehl): Sixth month of the Edroviran calendar, equivalent to June.

Edro (EHD-ro): River Edro. Largest river in Edrovir, flowing roughly northeast to southwest and emptying into the sea at Lankura where its mouth forms a major port.

Edrovir (EHD-ro-veer): A country inhabited by the Kelorin, Leithians, and Turowans, stretching from the Gorietha mountains in the east to the western sea, and from the Kor Vaskol mountains in the north to its borders with Jinara and Hran in the south.

Elgurn Harlind (EHL-gurn HAR-lihnd): King Elgurn. A Leithian lord chosen by the Pact Signers to be the third king of Edrovir. Also the ruling lord of Harlind Hold.

Elyan (EHL-ee-ahn): Prince Elyan. A high-born Kelorin man, third husband of Princess Nevien. He was fatally wounded while defending Lankura during the second Mautep attack.

Endemar (EHN-deh-mar): Lord Endemar. Kelorin lord of Kildorin Wared to whose lands were added the portion of Loros Wared containing Loros Hall, ancestral seat of the House of Loros, after the slaying of King Tevren who was lord of Loros Wared.

Estevad (EHS-teh-vahd): A Kelorin man. Clerk to Kuran Kel, the Lord of the Royal Fleet of Edrovir.

Evrel (EHV-rehl: Fourth month of the Edroviran calendar, equivalent to April.

Fargil (FAR-gihl) of Galenor (GAL-eh-nor): A Kelorin youth, son of the Lord of Galenor Wared, who is believed to have been murdered because he was courting the Princess Nevien.

farusia (fah-ROO-see-ah): A plant bearing large white trumpet-shaped flower, or the flower itself.

Fendar (FIHN-dar): A Kelorin swordmaster who was Leyel Virden's instructor, now serving as Swordmaster to the Royal Fleet.

Fenerwel (FEHN-er-wehl): A village in what was once Loros Wared, not far from Loros Hall.

Ferenan Eyilas (FEHR-eh-nahn AY-ih-las): A middle-aged high-born man of mixed Kelorin and Leithian blood. One of Princess Nevien's suitors.

Fineas (FIHN-ay-ahs): Master Fineas. A young Kelorin lore master employed at one time by Lord Madred Furthing but now keeping an apothecary shop in Brass Bell Lane.

Finorel (FIHN-or-ehl): Twelfth month of the Edroviran calendar, equivalent to December.

Furthing Hold (FER-dhing hold). The territory governed by the Leithian lord Madred Furthing. ("dh" denotes the "th" sound in "this")

Galenor (GAL-eh-nor): Name of a port town and of the surrounding Wared, located on the coast to the north of the capital city of Lankura and north of Kel Wared.

Gama (GAH-ma): An old Turowan woman, Taru's grandmother. (The word *gama* means "grandmother" in the Turowan tongue.)

Geivian (GAY-vee-ahn): A young high-born Kelorin man who has a seat at the "match table" because he is courting one of the princess's ladies (Currently he is pursuing Kendira, though he was previously "matched" to Rianine).

Geldoran Finrad (GEHL-dor-ahn FIHN-rahd): A Kelorin commander in the Royal Fleet, second in command to Kuran Kel.

Genorel (GUEHN-or-ehl): First month of the Edroviran calendar, equivalent to January.

Gillard Marchent (GIHL-ard MAR-chehnt): A high-born Leithian man, second husband of Princess Nevien who went mad and jumped from a balcony. Also called "Gill". One of Leyel Virden's "keepers."

Gilrin (GIHL-rihn): A Kelorin youth, a follower of Kenthos. A descendant of the people of Loros Wared. The doorman at Loros Hall.

Grimbold Sobring (GRIHM-bold SO-brihng): A Leithian lord. Brother, and successor of, Bron Sobring as ruling lord of Sobring Hold. Uncle of Vell and Alisset. A member of the Leithian Faction and one of the Brothers of the Blood.

Groft (grawft) : A young Leithian man, a member of the Palace Guard. Though not at the "match" table, he has been pursuing Kendira.

Grovern (GRO-vurn): A highborn Leithian man, husband of Merriel. He died of the plague.

Hakura Kili (hah-KOOR-ah KEE-lee): Guiding Spirit of the Turo, who tend to swear by Hakura Kili and all the Spirits. The exclamation "Hakura!" expresses awe or excitement.

hamanei mata noa (hah-MAH-nay MAH-tah NO-ah): A Turowan exclamation, literally meaning 'Spirits protect us.' Also shortened to just "Hamanei!" It expresses alarm.

Hamani (hah-MAH-nee): A young Turowan woman who lives across the road from Taru's grandmother in Wotana. Her name means "spirit". Older sister of Jitali.

Harmoth (HAR-mahth): Southern-most major port city in Edrovir.

Hashtep (HAHSH-tehp): The common folk of the Mahuk Baar. Also the general word for their race, which includes the Mautep or warlord class.

Hashti (HAHSH-tee): Language of the people of the Mahuk Baar (both Hashtep and Mautep).

Hel (hehl): In Leithian belief, a place of punishment for the spirits of those who have transgressed in life.

heskial (hehs-kee-AHL): A Jinari drug that enslaves the will while sparing conscious awareness. Obtained by distillation from the heskia vine, it derives its power from "spirit magic."

Hilber Dorn (HIHL-ber dorn): A Leithian man, ruling Lord of Borlund Hold.

Hranji (HRAHN-jee): An inhabitant of Hran. Also used as the plural, or to denote the people of Hran.

Hrathgard (HRAHTH-gard): Patriarchal god of the Leithians, King of the Heavens and Lord of the Wind. He is the patron of kings and rulers.

Hurn Hold (hern hold): The territory governed by the Leithian lord Lothard Hurn.

Idrin (IHD-rihn): Seven-day-long thirteenth month of the Edroviran calendar, surrounding the winter solstice and marking the 'turning of the year'. Commonly considered an unlucky time.

Ilsafeth (IHL-sah-fehth): A Leithian woman, wife of the Fleet healer Tredhold Ferth.

Indrid (IHN-drihd): A highborn Leithian woman. Kuran's wife who died of the plague, along with their young son.

Irvenen Wared (ir-VEHN-ehn WAH-rehd): The territory governed by Lord Rastyl Korven, lying in the extreme north of Edrovir.

Jato (JAH-toe): An old Turowan woodsman. One of Lord Anduar's scouts.

Jinara (jih-NAH-rah): A coastal country lying between Edrovir and the Mahuk Baar, involved in a long-running border dispute with Edrovir.

Jinari (jih-NAH-ree): Edrovirin name for the inhabitants of Jinara. Also their language and an adjective meaning "pertaining to Jinara".

Jitali (jee-TAH-lee): A young Turowan woman living in Wotana. Younger, prettier sister of Hamani. A romantic interest of Taru.

Kale Fendred (kayl FEHN-drehd): A Leithian, boyhood friend of King Elgurn. One of Leyel Virden's "keepers" who is now insane.

Kel Tierna (kel tee-EHR-nah): Port city on the southern coast of Edrovir, south of Lankura and north of Harmoth.

Kel Wared (kehl WAH-rehd): Territory governed by Lord Kuran Kel, it was part of the former Loros Wared, granted to Kuran by the Crown. (The Kelorin word "kel" means "mountain,")

Kelorin (KEL-or-in): A fair-skinned, dark-haired people originally from the isles of Kelor in the far western sea. Also their language, or an adjective meaning "pertaining to Kelor or the Kelorin people".

Kendira (kehn-DEER-ah): A young Kelorin woman. One of the princess's ladies. Nagaro had been paired with her at the match table, but they had a falling out.

Kenthos (KEHN-thos): Kenthos of Irvenen. A young Kelorin blacksmith who was for a time falsely believed by some members of the Kelorin Faction to be the long lost heir of King Darion, through his son Tevren Loros.

keshaal (keh-SHAHL): An expletive in Hashti, fairly strong.

Kildoran Wared (kihl-DOR-ahn WAH-rehd): A Kelorin Wared on the north bank of the lower reaches of the River Edro to which was added a portion of the old Loros Wared. Territory governed by Lord Endemar.

krit (kriht): A word of Leithian origin for a carved stick used to cast a vote for a leader. The carving identified the owner, who would place (cast) the krit on the table in front of the person he is choosing to indicate his vote.

Kroneg (KRON-ehg): Leithian god of war. Arbiter of the outcome of armed conflict and ruler of the dark moon, Naru.

Ku Taihana (koo tahy-HAH-na): "The Keepers" in Turowan. Turowan women who keep an unwritten accounting of Turowan family lines in their memories.

kuma (KOO-mah): Kuma stain or ointment. The ointment stains the skin brown and is made from the nuts of the kuma plant. Used by fair-skinned seamen to prevent sunburn.

Kuran Kel (KOOR-ahn kehl): Lord of the Royal Fleet of Edrovir. A man of mixed Kelorin and Turowan blood, from a merchant family but elevated by King Elgurn to the status of Lord of the House of Kel. Also ruling lord of Kel Wared, a territory the king created for him from part of the former Loros Wared.

Landros Torenin (LAN-dros tor-EHN- ihn): An older Kelorin sea warrior, former officer of the Royal Fleet of Edrovir, then a slave and one of Nagaro's followers who rejoined the Fleet. Captain of the *Sea Eagle*.

Lanei (LAH-nay): A young Turowan woman of Wotana, married to Gudo.

Lankura (LAHN-koor-ah): Capital city of Edrovir, located at the mouth of the River Edro.

Leithians (LAY-thee-ens): Fair-skinned, light-haired people originally from a land called Leith. "Leithian" denotes either a single individual or is used as an adjective meaning "pertaining to Leithians."

Leyel Virden (LEHY-ehl VER-dehn) Name given to Nagaro by the Lady Maramine Virden, under which he was ridiculed as the "idiot prince" during his marriage to Princess Nevien.

Lindra (LIHN-drah): Queen Lindra. A Kelorin woman, wife of King Tevren. She was killed, supposedly accidentally, along with her husband by Reith Hurn.

linjana (lihn-JAH-nah): A Kelorin medicinal drug used to cure mental disorders such as addiction or madness. It is distilled from the leaves and stems of a small herb of the same name and derives its virtue from "spirit magic."

Lissafel (LIHS-ah-fehl): "The Lady," Maiden Goddess of the Leithians. Ruler of the hearts of men and women, and of the pale moon, Talebra.

Lissel (lih-SEHL): A young Kelorin woman. Youngest daughter of the merchant Gedras on Pakoa Island. She is in love with Sindar.

Lokundas (lo-KOON-dahs): The "Turner of Worlds," Kelorin personification of fate. One of the old gods of the Cloud Mountain People from before the founding of Kelor.

Loros Wared (LOR-os WAH-rehd): A formerly-existing wared, lying on the northern bank of the River Edro, near its mouth. Founded by Nevrath Loros, father of Darion and grandfather of Tevren, it was cut into pieces after Tevren's death.

Lothard Hurn (LO-thard hurn): A Leithian lord, son of one of the Signers of the Pact of Lankura (Reith Hurn) and currently ruling lord of Hurn Hold and lord of the House of Hurn.

Luka (LOO-ka): An old Turowan medicine woman known to Nagaro from his childhood at Averwin. Mother of Boka and Omei.

Madred Furthing (MAH-drehd FUR-dhing): A highly respected Leithian Lord, the ruling lord of Furthing Hold. Father of Brandle and a leader of the Leithian Faction. ("dh" denotes the "th" sound in "this")

Madrel (MAH-drehl): Third month of the Edroviran calendar, equivalent to March.

Mahuk Baar (MAH-huke BAR): A coastal country, and islands, lying beyond Jinara to the south of Edrovir. It is nhabited by the Hashtep people with their Mautep warlords and ruled by an emperor. "Mahuk" is often used for the nationality, as in "Mahuk warships" or "Mahuk waters". It is also used (ignorantly) for the people of the Mahuk Baar.

Maramine Virden (mar-ah-MEEN VER-dehn): A Kelorin lady, former mistress of the estate of Averwin, estranged from her family. Nagaro's lady guardian, she was smothered by Elgurn to end her suffering during what would have been fatal heskial withdrawal.

Mautep (MAH-oo-tehp): Ruling warrior class of the Hashtep people of the Mahuk Baar.

Medrin (MEHD-rihn): Fifth month of the Edroviran calendar, equivalent to May.

Merriel (MEHR-ee-ehl): Lady Merriel. A high-born Leithian woman, one of Queen Semorel's ladies and chaperon to Princess Nevien and her ladies.

Minowei (mih-NO-way): Princess Minowei. A Turowan chief's daughter who married Nevrath, founding the House of Loros. Mother of Darion.

Mundabo (moon-DAH-bo): A Turowan man. A former follower of Kenthos and a descendent of inhabitants of the old Loros Wared. The Steward at Loros Hall.

Murlak (MER-lahk): A red-haired Leithian, member of the Princess's Guard, transferred to the City Guard.

Nagaro (nah-GAR-o): Captain Nagaro, also known as Nagaro the Pirate, and Kiraam Shaku-Tal (Hashti for "Thief of Slaves").

Narei (NAR-ay): Daughter of Nagaro and Jila.

Naru (NAR-oo): The dark moon, smaller of the world's two moons. It travels slightly faster than the bright moon, Talebra, overtaking her at times in what the Leithians consider a portentous conjunction.

Nevien Harlind (NEHV-ee-ehn HAR-lihnd): Princess Nevien, daughter of King Elgurn and Queen Semorel.

Nevrath (NEV-rahth): A Kelorin man who left the House of Tyronin and founded the House of Loros after a falling-out with his brother Hindrath. Nevrath married the Turowan princess Minowei. Darion was their first-born son.

Nildred (NIHL-dred) Master Nildred, a Leithian healer hired by Minister Torlung.

Nile Fendred (nile FEHN-drehd): A young high-born Leithian, in love with Alisset but courting Princess Nevien. Son of Kale Fendred.

Nondorin (NOAN-dor-ihn): Eleventh month of the Edroviran calendar, equivalent to November.

Odus Morbern (O-duhs MOR-burn): A Leithian lord. One of the Signers of the Pact of Lankura and a member of the King's Council. Ruling lord of Morbern Hold.

Olomi (o-LO-mee): A Turowan woman, Taru's mother. She and Taru's father (Jomo) were both killed by Mautep sea raiders when Taru and Nagaro were taken as slaves.

Omei (O-may): Tira Omei. A Turowan woman, one of Minowei's people who lived in the former Loros Wared and one of the "ku taihana" who hold the names of all living members of Minowei's clan in their memories. Daughter of Luka. She looked after Nagaro's daughter Narei during the latter's abduction.

opa (O-pah): A potent drug used to relieve pain, noted for giving vivid "opa dreams."

Osfaraad (ose-far-AHD): An island belonging to the Mahuk Baar, near the northern border of Mahuk waters, where Nagaro's ships had put freed Hashtep slaves ashore. Site of Nagaro's surrender to Emperor Baalkir that led to the torture of three Edroviran Fleet officers, one of whom betrayed the Fleet's mission to the Emperor.

Oskampo (os-KAHM-po): A table game played with pictured cards and small wooden counters.

Oteyin (oh-TAY-ihn): Eighth month of the Edroviran calendar, equivalent to August.

Pakoa (pah-KO-ah): An island off the southern coast of Edrovir where Nagaro made his home during his pirate period. Southern-most inhabited isle of the Lomoas. Pakoa Town, on Pakoa Harbor, is its only significant town.

Papano (pah-PAH-no): Tor Papano, A Turowan shoemaker with a shop in Tanner's Row.

Pavo Maat (PAH-vo MAHT): A Hashtep fisherman's son and former slave. Follower and close friend of Nagaro who also joined the Royal Fleet. Not tortured by the Emperor at Osfaraad, he was falsely convicted of treason and rescued by Nagaro and Taru, resulting in their temporary exile. They were all later reinstated.

Pedran (PEHD-rahn): A Kelorin man, a tracker working for Lord Anduar, mercilessly slain by Lothard Hurn and his men.

Pendrik Glenmark (PEHN-drihk glehn-MARK): A Leithian lord, one of the Signers of the Pack of Lankura and a member of the King's Council. Also ruling lord of Glenmark Hold.

Rastian Korven (rahs-tee-AHN KOR-vehn): A young Kelorin officer in the Royal Fleet of Edrovir. Son of Lord Rastyl Korven.

Rastyl Korven (rahs-TEEL KOR-vehn): A Kelorin man with unusually pale gray eyes. Ruling lord of Irvenen Wared and close friend of King Tevren. Father of Rastian.

Rathdar Sundorin (RAHTH-dar SUN-dor-ihn): A Kelorin man, son of the deceased Pact Signer Berinar Sundorin. Current ruling lord of the Sundorin Wared. One of the leaders of the Kelorin faction.

Reith Hurn (rayth hurn): A Leithian lord, previous ruling lord of Hurn Hold. Father of Lothard. A Signer of the Pact of Lankura and former member of the King's Council, he was killed in the border war with Jinara.

Rianine (REE-ah-neen): A young Kelorin woman, called Rian for short. One of Princess Nevien's ladies and her frequent confidant.

rin (rihn): A small copper coin, the base unit of Edroviran currency. There are one hundred rins in one trokin and one thousand rins in one dokan.

Roheed jir-Akaan (ro-HEED jeer-ah-KAHN): A young Mautep officer, Emperor Baalkir's nephew. He speaks some Droviri, having been raised by the Kelorin slave woman Emril. The apparent death of Emril's infant son, Sindar, formed the basis of a "blood debt" requiring Roheed to save the life of someone who was orphaned.

Sedrin (SEHD-rihn): Ninth month of the Edroviran calendar, equivalent to September.

Selfira (Sehl-FEER-ah): A Kelorin woman, wife of Darion and mother of Tevren Loros.

Semorel (SEHM-or-ehl): Queen Semorel. A Kelorin woman, wife of King Elgurn and therefore queen of Edrovir.

Seralind (sehr-ah-LIHND): Name for the place of reward after death in Leithian religious belief. Equivalent to paradise or heaven.

Sheptuum (shehp-TOOM): God of the Hashtep people, including the Mautep class.

Shofeer (sho-FEER): Name of a Mautep house, the origin of Nagaro's sword.

Simion Rudrin (SIHM-ee-ahn ROOD-rihn): A young Kelorin crossed man, Brandle Furthing's lover. Former Fleet warrior and galley slave who escaped in the slave mutiny led by Nagaro.

Sindar (SIHN-dahr): A young Kelorin man held captive from infancy in the Mahuk Baar who escaped and has been under Nagaro's guidance. Grandson of of Burdal Korinos.

shapas (SHAH-pahs): A Kelorin style women's riding garment consisting of long pantaloons extending all the way to the ankles, worn with an upper garment called a shilka.

shilka (SHIHL-ka): A Kelorin style women's riding garment consisting of a close-fitting bodice, belted at the waist and falling just below the knee. The garment flares below the waist almost like a skirt but is divided, front and back, to allow the wearer to mount a horse and sit astride. Typically worn over shapas.

Sobring Hold (SO-bring hold): The territory governed by the Leithian Lord Grimbold Sobring.

Solbrid (SOL-brihd): The Leithian Mother Goddess. Ruler of Earth and giver of life.

Soren Tuveilas (SOR-ehn too-VAY-lahs): An elder Kelorin man, lord of Tuveilas Wared. Oldest lord of the Kelorin faction.

sothiril (SO-thur-ihl): Kelorin tea-like drink made by steeping the dried berries of the plant of the same name.

Takelei (Tah-KAY-lay): An aged Turowan man, brother of Luka and uncle of Boka and Omei.

Talebra (tah-LEHY-brah): The bright moon, larger of the world's two moons.

Tamith (TAM-ihth): A young Kelorin woman, descended from parents who had dwelt in Loros Wared and beloved of the Lady Rianine.

Taru Nareyo (TAR-roo nar-AY-o): A Turowan fisherman's son. Nagaro's first friend from Wotana Bay who was enslaved with him by the Mautep sea raiders, freed in the slave mutiny. Nagaro's first mate, he joined the Fleet but went into exile with Nagaro.

Tenepti (tehn-EHP-tee): A young Hashtep woman of Pakoa. Wife of Pavo Maat.

Tenorin (TEHN-or-ihn): River Tenorin. One of the lesser tributaries of the River Edro, it flows past Averwin. Called the Yuna River by Turowan folk.

Tevren Loros (TEHV-rehn LOR-os): King Tevren. The young second king of Edrovir, killed by Reith Hurn in an event that sparked a civil war. Son of Darion the Great, he was mostly Kelorin but carried some Turowan blood through his grandmother, Minowei.

Tevus Morbern (TEHV-us MOR-burn): A highborn Leithian man, onetime Lord of Morbern Hold and claimed to be the father of Odus Morbern.

Therin Oranil (Thehr-ihn OR-ahn-ihl): A Kelorin man, lord of Oranil Wared and one of the Kelorin faction.

Theseline (THES-el-een): Tira Theseline. An older Kelorin woman. An inhabitant of the old Loros Wared, dwelling at Loros Hall.

Tira (TEER-rah): Respectful from of address for a woman, roughly equivalent to "Mrs.", but with no implied marital status. Always used before a given name.

tirka (TUR-kah): A men's short-sleeved upper outer garment, opening down the front and cut long enough to cover the hips. Generally worn over a long-sleeved shirt and usually belted.

Todrin (TOE-drihn): Tenth month of the Edroviran calendar, equivalent to October.

Tor (tor): Respectful form of address for a man, roughly equivalent to "Mr." Always used before a given name.

Torlung (TOR-luhng): Minister Torlung. A Leithian of the House of Furthing, Chief Minister to Lord Madred.

Tredhold Ferth (TRED-hold furth): A Leithian healer, called Tred for short. A former Fleet warrior and ship's doctor who was held as a galley slave and freed in the slave mutiny led by Nagaro. One of Nagaro's followers who rejoined the Fleet. Ship's doctor on the *Sword of Freedom*.

trokin (TRO-kihn): A silver coin worth one hundred rins. There are ten trokins to the dokan.

Turo (TOOR-o): The Turo. Turowan name for their people, also use to refer to a Turowan man.

Turowa (toor-O-wah): Word for a woman of the Turowan people. The female equivalent Turo.

Turowans (toor-O-ahns): A brown-skinned, dark-haired people native to the coastal region and islands of Edrovir. Called by themselves "the Turo". The word "Turowan" can refer to a single male individual and is also used as an adjective to describe anything relating to the Turo.

Varsyl Virden (vahr-SEEL VIR-dehn): A Kelorin man, brother of Maramine, who slew her love, Beloras, in a sword challenge. He is now ruling lord of Virden Wared.

Vedorel (VEHD-or-ehl): Second month of the Edroviran calendar, equivalent to February.

Vell Sobring (vehl SO-bring): A young Leithian officer in the Royal Fleet of Edrovir. Son of Bron Sobring. Nephew of Grimbold Sobring who is currently the lord of Sobring Hold since Bron's death in the border war. One of three officers tortured at Osfaraad.

Venerev (VEHN-er-ehv): A Kelorin man, a follower of Kenthos.

Vered Mahir (VEHR-ehd mah-HEER): A city on the upper reaches of the River Edro above a large waterfall. Also the "bitter place" where the brothers Nevrath and Hindrath quarreled, leading to the founding of the House of Loros by splitting it from the House of Tyronin.

Vothra (VO-thrah): The Benevolent Spirit of the Kelorin, an entity composed of the combined spirits of many individuals all of whom have lived multiple lives. Vothra's wisdom, collectively referred to as "the Path" is recorded in the Vothrin Writings. Vothra has an unusually strong connection to Nagaro's spirit.

Wared (WAH-rehd): Kelorin word for the territory governed by a lord. Equivalent to a Leithian "Hold".

Worling (WOR-lihng): Commander Worling, a Leithian man. Commander of the Palace Guard.

Wotana (wo-TAH-nah): A small town on the bay of the same name, located on the Edroviran coast about twenty miles north of Lankura. Taru's home town.

Zirda (ZUR-dah): A respectful masculine form of address, roughly equivalent to "Sir" in modern casual usage.

Zirdyn (zur-DEEN): A respectful feminine form of address, roughly equivalent to "Madame" in modern casual usage.

Zomora (zo-MOR-ah): Tira Zomora. Pakoa's Turowan medicine woman, and an unofficial power on that island and throughout the southern Lomoas.

Acknowledgements

As I close the cover on this final volume of The Nagaro Chronicle, I look back ingratitude to my fans, as always, who gave me hope that I was on the right track, and especially to my first reader, Kristie McCue. I must also thank those who gave me input on the final manuscript including my test readers for the final version, Suzanne Coulter, Paul Wilde, Louise Wilde, and Gerald Wuenschell. As with other works in this series, the members of ScHoFan, a critique group under the auspices of the Greater Los Angeles Writers Society(GLAWS), gave me feedback on versions of the early chapters. In alphabetical order, they are Carol Ann Alves, Ken Hughes, Scott Kilburn, Carmen Mendivil, Robin Reed, and Taguhi Tavitian.

I continue to be grateful for the support of my husband and the other members of my family, who have gotten used to this over the years. I'm also grateful for the continuing support and encouragement of my dear friends, Suzanne Coulter and Anne Bannon. Anne's technical expertise continues to shore up the infrastructure of every aspect of my writing.

About the Author

Carol Louise Wilde is the author of the fantasy adventure series the *Nagaro Chronicle*. She long led a double life: biology research scientist by day, and by night, chief archivist for the nation of Edrovir and its neighboring states. The *Nagaro Chronicle* covers but one brief period in the long and eventful history of this world and its inhabitants. Ms. Wilde lives in Southern California with her husband of forty years. They have two sons to carry on the tradition.

About the story...

One of Princess Nevien's suitors has been murdered, just after being chosen by King Elgurn to wed his daughter. Another suitor, Lothard Hurn, is the most likely culprit, but this can not be proven. The king and the members of his council would dearly love to remove Lothard from play – permanently. But how to do it?

The plan they devise hinges upon Nagaro – Lord Kuran's recently adopted heir – by pitting the two consumate swordsmen, Nagaro and Lothard, against each other. Nevien, fearful that the trap being laid could prove fatal to Nagaro rather than Lothard, seeks to warn him, even as Kuran tries to prevent his new heir from following his heart into danger. With the Leithian and Keloran factions still at odds, and Lothard increasingly impatient to achieve his royal ambitions, the fate of the Kingdom of Edrovir hangs in the balance.